DARK
HEARTS
OF
CHICAGO

Books by William Horwood

Novels:

The Duncton Chronicles
Duncton Wood
Duncton Quest
Duncton Found

The Book of Silence
Duncton Tales
Duncton Rising
Duncton Stone

The Wolves of Time
Journeys to the Heartland
Seekers at the Wulfrock

Tales of the Willows
The Willows in Winter
Toad Triumphant
The Willows and Beyond
The Willows at Christmas

Other novels:
The Stonor Eagles
Callanish
Skallagrigg

Memoir:

The Boy with No Shoes

Books by Helen Rappaport

No Place for Ladies: The Untold Story of Women in the Crimean War
Queen Victoria: A Biographical Companion
Encyclopedia of Women Social Reformers
Joseph Stalin: A Biographical Companion

DARK
HEARTS
OF
CHICAGO

WILLIAM HORWOOD
AND
HELEN RAPPAPORT

HUTCHINSON
LONDON

Published by Hutchinson 2007

2 4 6 8 10 9 7 5 3 1

Copyright © William Horwood & Helen Rappaport 2007

William Horwood and Helen Rappaport have asserted their right
under the Copyright, Designs and Patents Act 1988 to be identified
as the authors of this work

First published in Great Britain in 2007 by
Hutchinson
Random House, 20 Vauxhall Bridge Road,
London SW1V 2SA

www.randomhouse.co.uk

Addresses for companies within The Random House Group Limited
can be found at: www.randomhouse.co.uk/offices.htm

The Random House Group Limited Reg. No. 954009

A CIP catalogue record for this book
is available from the British Library

ISBN 9780091796532 (Hardback)
ISBN 9780091796587 (Trade paperback)

The Random House Group Limited makes every effort to ensure that the
papers used in its books are made from trees that have been legally sourced
from well-managed and credibly certified forests. Our paper procurement
policy can be found at: www.randomhouse.co.uk/paper.htm

Typeset by Palimpsest Book Production Limited,
Grangemouth, Stirlingshire

Printed and bound in Great Britain by
Mackays of Chatham plc, Chatham, Kent

DAY ONE

Thursday October 19, 1893

1

Bubbly Creek

There are good times and bad times to dump a body in Bubbly Creek, as locals call the South Fork of the Chicago River.

Winter's not much good, because the Creek freezes over, so the evidence of your crime stays right where it falls. Summer's no better because the flow slows right up, the place smells bad and you don't want to go anywhere near it. If you do you'll soon work out why it's called Bubbly – the water's so polluted with bones and offal from the Union Stock Yard that it's busy fermenting with the rottenness beneath the surface.

Spring and fall are best because that is when it flows, especially after rain, and that ensures the evidence of your crime drifts slowly away, out of sight and out of mind.

You hope.

One misty morning in October 1893, a body came to rest at Benson Street, opposite Mr Armour's glue factory and a couple of hundred yards from where the Creek comes to an end as it flows into the Chicago River proper. It lay there awhile, two dogs scampering around and sniffing at it, a rat attempting to chew at it and giving up, three hens eyeing it warily while soot descended gently on it from the furnaces of the Illinois Steel Company on the far side of the Creek.

An immigrant heading for the Union Stock Yard in search of a day's hire noticed it at six, shook his head wearily and walked on by. Finding work was more important.

An hour later, two women, gossiping on their stoops, caught sight of the body lying down at the Creek's edge and, tut-tutting, didn't take long to work out from the clothes it wore what its occupation in life had been.

Finally, a barefoot boy, clambering over the mud looking for something to salvage among the washed-up detritus along the shoreline, touched its bare back with his foot and then its face.

Then he peered a bit closer, holding his breath; and closer still, looking for any valuables, when suddenly it half opened an eye and let out a watery moan.

'Jesus, it's alive!' he screamed, toppling back into the mud.

Men came running over and pulled the body up onto the street but the women took over after that, shooing the men and boys away. The girls could stay if they liked, but at a distance.

She was female and wearing a torn and filthy dress that was thick with slime. The stocking on one leg was torn and round her ankle. The other leg was bare. Her dark hair was a mess made slimy with mud.

You didn't need to be a doctor to tell she was nearer dead than alive, and you needn't have lived by the Creek for long to guess that she'd been right in it, and the water had got into her, in which case she'd be sure to fall sick and die later if not right away.

Some buckets of cold water washed the mud and slime from her and brought her to. She had injuries here, there and everywhere and the blood was still flowing. Her right eye was swollen. The nails of her hands were torn. The gibberish she spoke was a madwoman's talk.

There was nothing about her that made any sense at all: not who she was, or why she was there, or why she was still alive.

They covered her up with a piece of old sacking but left her lying there out on the street – no one wanted a living corpse like that in their home, which stank of filth and probably carried disease. A boy was sent to find a patrolman on 31st Street, who took one look at the woman and went and telegraphed Harrison Street Police Station for the wagon.

At around eight-fifteen, a square, high-sided black wagon on four sturdy wheels arrived. It looked like a paddy wagon but everyone knew it was worse than that. A few mothers pushed their kids indoors, telling them it was unlucky to see the wagon standing there.

A uniformed man climbed out of the vehicle while the driver, the boss, got down and looked the woman over. Most people knew him in those parts. He was Padraic 'Donko' O'Banion and driving this vehicle was his day job. At nights he worked in a brothel on the Levee.

'She's twenty or so,' said Donko, adding, 'and she's been beat real bad.'

'Been for a swim,' said the other laconically.

'Client tried to kill her more likely,' said Donko.

They carried on looking her up and down as one of the women threw another bucket of water over her. It was not hard to guess what the two men were thinking. Once the filth was off her, the body was good.

The driver prodded her with his foot; she turned her battered head and peered at him.

That put him off.

'Can she walk?'

It didn't seem like she wanted to.

'Throw her in the wagon just as she is,' he said.

So his companion did what he was told, leaving the woman where she fell, motionless on the wagon floor. Donko climbed back into his seat and seemed surprised when the other man bolted the car doors on the outside and chose to sit up alongside him instead of getting in with the girl.

In his younger days Donko himself would have had her there and then.

'She stinks,' was all his companion needed to say by way of explanation for his distaste.

'I've had worse,' said Donko ironically, 'and enjoyed 'em.'

He backed the wagon expertly round and then headed up to 31st and Throop Street for the run downtown. Folk looked away and got on with their business, but the boy who found the woman who had been a body stood there staring at the wagon and at the scratched and faded lettering on it.

5

He couldn't read but he knew what it said: *Cook County Insane Asylum.*

'Is that where they are taking her?' said the man who had first seen the woman earlier that morning, now returning the way he had come. He was new round here. He had the shaggy beard, the clothes and the accent of an immigrant from Eastern Europe. Now his eyes carried the despair of someone who had failed to get the day's work he so desperately needed.

'Not straight away. First they have to take her to the detention hospital and then, if it's a suicide attempt – and more'n likely it is – to the insane court,' said one of the women.

'Yeah, and then she'll go to Dunning,' added the boy, spitting tobacco juice right on the sidewalk where she had been laid, 'so she ain't *never* coming back.'

They stood in silence staring after the black wagon for a minute or so. Everyone round here knew what consignment to the insane asylum out at Dunning meant.

Then the man went one way and the boy another. Where the anonymous woman had washed up at the edge of the Creek, nothing remained but a stain of red blood turning brown in the mud.

2

The Baker

Anna Jelena Zemeckis, only child of Janis Zemeckis, a Latvian baker on New York's Lower East Side, went missing in Chicago some time between one thirty-five and three o'clock on the afternoon of September 7, 1893.

That was between the time she left Mrs Clark's Lunch Room at 145 Wabash Avenue and the time she was due to meet a friend at the World's Columbian Exposition at Jackson Park seven miles away on the city's South Side. A date she did not keep.

Anna was a modest girl, just twenty-one. She was gregarious, attractive and intelligent. Until only four months before she had been her father's mainstay in his small but well-respected and profitable bakery, responsible for keeping the accounts, as well as having a part-time job in the Aguilar Free Library on East 5th Street.

Anna's departure for Chicago came as a surprise; nobody in their little circle would have believed it possible that so loving and protective a father could let his daughter go to that monstrous city, of all places. Anna herself had often voiced her dislike of big city life and her desire to go and spend time on her aunt Inga's farm up beyond Winnipeg on Lac du Bonnet in Canada. But this Zemeckis had refused; the hardship of rural life endured by his dead wife's family in Latvia, and now in Canada, was what he had wanted to leave behind when he emigrated. He had repeatedly refused his sister-in-law's request to send Anna to stay with them. For he was a man mindful of the future, of business and enterprise and what the World's Fair might offer for modernizing his own modest but growing business. Anna must go as his representative.

So it was that on Anna's twenty-first birthday in April 1893, Janis Zemeckis made an announcement to their Lutheran friends at church.

'I am sending Anna to Chicago,' he declared, with a look of pride and pleasure on his face. 'My brother-in-law Hendriks has written confirming that she can stay as long as she likes with him and his family and see everything there is at this great Fair. She will have time to discover new things and learn all she can, as well as working part-time for the Chicago Public Library, which has been arranged for her.

'Someone from every family in America should go to this great event and, as I cannot be spared from our business, Anna must go in my place!'

Anna was as astonished as she was overjoyed. She burst into tears and she and Janis held each other tight. Janis was a hard worker and a good man, but it was rare for him to make displays of affection and generosity in front of others.

Anna's uncle, Hendriks Markulis, was her mother's brother. While her aunt, Inga, had married into good stolid farming stock and gone to Canada, Hendriks had been more ambitious and found a wife from an enterprising German family on Chicago's North Side, with whom he now ran their hardware store. He and his wife had visited the Zemeckises twice in New York and were good, prosperous people. Liesel Markulis was active in the woman's temperance movement and Janis was certain they would offer Anna a home from home and ensure that she would be chaperoned at all times.

'It's not a holiday,' warned Janis later, 'but *work*. This great exposition will have much that is new which we should know about, many technical and educational things. You will go; I can manage without you for two or three months. Your job at the library in Chicago will pay your way and you must help Hendriks in his store, but most of all you will learn, learn, learn.'

If Anna wept as she hugged her father, it was for joy; if he smiled with pride it was because, after holding on to her so protectively for so long – too long perhaps – he felt he was doing the right thing in letting her go.

So it was that Anna Zemeckis, after being accompanied across to Jersey City on the ferry by her father, set off on the Columbian Express for Chicago one day in early May, preceded by a thousand instructions from Janis Zemeckis to the Markulises about when and where they were to meet her when she arrived at the Union Depot on Canal Street, twenty-six hours after leaving the East Coast.

All of which went perfectly, as did Anna's stay with the Markulises during the seventeen weeks that followed until, on September 8, Janis received a stark, heart-stopping telegraph from his brother-in-law:

'*Anna went missing yesterday. Have you heard from her?*'

Two days after that, September 10, Janis Zemeckis closed the doors of his bakery and took the first train to Chicago on which he had been able to get a seat. What he found when he got there and in the grim weeks that followed gave him every reason to believe she must be dead.

On arrival he began searching the city for Anna. He placed advertisements in the papers, he talked to the police who advised him to visit the morgue; he did so, daily, and saw terrible things there, but he did not find his daughter. He called on City Hall officials who advised him to check out the patients at the city hospitals. He did that too, and saw yet more terrible things, but he never found Anna.

He took the new Elevated Railroad from Congress Street to the site of the World's Fair at Jackson Park, his desperate eyes searching the crowds wherever he went. He never found her. Everywhere he went, he talked to people, and then more people, showing them Anna's picture. But all they could tell him was that people go missing in big cities; it happens every day, to young women especially. Some disappear because they want to, some because they need to, some are abducted against their will, taken by men. It was terrible, truly terrible. But Janis Zemeckis refused to believe any of this of his Anna.

Nevertheless, he walked the red-light districts around the Levee asking questions. He got threatened every time, mugged twice and hospitalized once.

And then two weeks later, on September 26, running out of funds, he reluctantly went back to New York.

He returned a week later, his business left in temporary hands. But when problems arose he was obliged to return once more to New York. He knew his business was beginning to die. He knew ten years of savings would run out. But he also knew that without Anna he had nothing, nothing at all.

The search came to its final and perhaps inevitable end in the second week of October with a telegraph from a Mr Freeman of the Cook County Hospital Morgue. It was the kind of message every parent dreads and none ever wants to receive.

A body had been brought in that appeared to match the physical description Zemeckis had left of his daughter. Could he arrange to put through a telephone call and help with the identification?

He did so.

Mr Freeman was kindly and diplomatic but the job had to be done. Was there anyone in Chicago who had known his daughter and might be willing to identify her?

Zemeckis named the Markulises.

Meanwhile . . . did Anna have any distinguishing features?

Zemeckis could barely speak. His hand trembled as he held the telephone, which crackled and hummed at his ear. He could hardly bring himself to murmur into the mouthpiece.

'How did she die?' he asked.

'A streetcar accident. Now—'

'She has . . . she always wore a crucifix, but no other jewelry . . . I wouldn't allow it.'

'Mr Zemeckis, I know this is hard. But could you describe the crucifix?'

'It was special to her. Nothing much. Gray metal, not real silver. It was her mother's and she . . .' Zemeckis broke down.

'Sir, I need a better description. Its size, any particular decoration . . . ?'

Zemeckis did his best.

The silence that followed was the longest he had ever endured.

Then Mr Freeman came back on the line: 'I'm sorry, sir, but what

you've described is pretty much the same as the crucifix this girl
was wearing. But . . . we'd better wait for Mrs Markulis to come.
Maybe—'

'If she's wearing that crucifix, it's Anna,' said Zemeckis, his voice
thin and bleak. 'I've never seen another one like it.'

They arranged for another call that evening.

When the connection came through it was Liesel Markulis. She was
weeping.

'It's Anna, Janis, I'm sure of it,' she said, and that was all she needed
to say.

Janis Zemeckis travelled to Chicago a final, desolate time on October
14, exhausted and heartbroken.

Liesel Markulis accompanied him to the potter's field outside the
city where Anna had had to be temporarily buried. Her remains would
be taken back to New York after due process. They put a few flowers
on the grave marked with a temporary wooden cross and a number,
and said a prayer.

They were not the only ones in that grim place, and others arrived
as they left, searching for Chicago's lost, forgotten and unidentified
dead.

They went next to the morgue and met Mr Freeman. The first thing
they were shown was the dress the body had been wearing. Any lingering
doubts Zemeckis might have had evaporated. Though it was torn and
bloodstained he recognized it at once, just as Mrs Markulis had done.
It had been made by Anna herself.

Holding it in his hands, Zemeckis wept. But when he was shown
the crucifix he fell silent, head slumped. It had been bought as a gift
for Anna's Catholic mother during a religious pilgrimage in Latvia
when she was a girl; Janis had handed it down to Anna on her mother's
death.

No further confirmation was needed for Janis Zemeckis, but when
the morgue asked that he formally identify his daughter from photographs of the corpse, he numbly agreed, words failing him.

He said nothing then, or for hours afterwards. Nor did he discuss
with his sister-in-law the obvious question – what Anna might have
been doing during the five weeks between her disappearance from
their home and her tragic death on Michigan Avenue. He retreated

into silence and asked for only one thing more – that Anna's body be exhumed so she might have a proper burial back home in New York.

This was arranged for two weeks' time. Janis Zemeckis finally returned home on October 17, his search over. He felt and looked a broken man. Anna was never coming back and he knew that he had failed her. Almost overnight it seemed he had lost his reason for living.

For two days he did not sleep. Nor did he open up his shop. He felt he never would again. What made it all the worse for him was the fact that it now seemed certain that Anna's disappearance had been of her own volition. It was bad enough that she had left the Markulis household without an explanation, but to make no attempt to contact him was both selfish and cruel.

Very soon, however, his inward grief gave way to outward anger – at Anna and at Chicago, a city which had failed to protect her. His anger deepened and for a few hours he was incoherent with rage.

Then it gave way to a different emotion: pity, forgiveness of a kind, and a desire to warn other parents of the perils of allowing their daughters to venture forth to distant cities.

On October 19, having had a notice placed in the Chicago newspapers announcing Anna's death, Janis found himself in the Aguilar Free Library at 206 East 5th Street, sitting, staring sightlessly at that day's copy of the New York *World*, doing nothing. He could not remember how he had got there and he saw he was not the only one. Cities have many casualties.

Unable to suffer his loss and pain, anger and shame any longer, and hoping to forget it for a little while through activity, he impulsively wrote a letter and put it in the mailbox.

The letter was addressed to the proprietor of the New York *World*, Mr Joseph Pulitzer, the greatest newspaper man of the age.

What Janis Zemeckis sent was rather more than a letter. It was a prayer, an agonized cry to other parents and it was a warning. Don't let your daughters out of your sight. But if you must, *never* let them go to Chicago.

Naturally he had no hope his letter would ever be read or taken notice of. This was America and, angry and disillusioned as he had now become, he thought he knew what that meant: no one would help, no one would listen, no one would offer comfort.

But Janis Zemeckis was wrong.

Someone did listen and someone did act.

DAY TWO

Friday October 20, 1893

3

Night Terror

Cook County Insane Asylum – or Dunning, as Chicagoans called it, after the farmer who had owned the land on which it was built after the Civil War – lay across the prairie, eleven miles northwest of the city centre.

It was a vast, forbidding establishment, newly rebuilt in Gothic style, complete with a nicely turreted gatehouse to make it look solid and respectable.

Close to, it was anything but. Not that it mattered if you were an inmate; once in you didn't need to come out again, because Dunning was entirely self sufficient and had everything, from its own bakery to a separate burial ground.

It was originally built in the spirit of public philanthropy to house the poor on one side and the mad on the other. Over the years they got all mixed up. The poor got to look after the mad, and when the poor fell sick it sometimes went the other way about.

Nobody outside cared much, provided the inmates of Dunning stayed out of sight of decent folk and didn't cost too much. With time, the upright citizens of Chicago, in the drive for economic growth, had lost their generosity of spirit. Christian charity and compassion had been replaced by meanness of spirit and contempt.

These days they felt it only right that the undeserving folk at

Dunning were kept uncomfortable. Many were immigrants anyway, driven mad by poverty, dashed hopes and failed expectations. They should have known better than to come to America if they weren't up to it.

So they stopped giving the inmates hot water to wash in; they kept the heating spasmodic and inadequate, and oftentimes the food was inedible, no better than pigswill, made up of ingredients already condemned by city inspectors. The regime that ran the place – a few key attendants backed up by complacent governors, physicians and alienists – was ignorant, repressive and often cruel.

No wonder that kids in Chicago who didn't do what their parents told them were warned, 'Be careful, or you're going to Dunning.'

It gave them nightmares; nightmares that reminded them of the virtues of obedience and the fact that those who do wrong on this earth may find themselves in hell sooner than they think.

The same night that Janis Zemeckis's letter was wending its hopeful way, courtesy of the US postal service, to Mr Joseph Pulitzer of the New York *World*, someone who was neither a lunatic nor a pauper was tossing and turning in his bed at the Dunning Insane Asylum in the grip of a night terror.

His name was Dr Morgan Eels. A few hours previously, the commissioners of the Cook County Board, after a month's trial period, had ratified his appointment as successor to Dr Benjamin Brown, superintendent of the Dunning Institutions, who was to be retired early as from October 31 – eleven days' time.

One might think that this would be cause for celebration rather than nightmare for Dr Eels. But all his life, Eels had been subject to irrational fears and fancies of the most extreme kind. And they revolved around two scenarios: the first that he was confined in an enclosed space that was closing in on him; the second that he was being castrated without the benefit of ether.

Fortunately for him, these two very different horrors had never come together in one appalling whole.

Tonight he was in the grip of the castration fear and it would not go away.

Its cause was easy enough for the most amateur of alienists to have worked out. First, on this same day of Dr Eels's promotion to a position of absolute power over some eight hundred lunatics and fifteen hundred paupers he had completed his list of the twenty men on whom it was his intention to perform a new medical procedure in his continuing search for a surgical cure for lunacy and idiocy. In a day or two more he would also have completed a similar list of women.

But for now, no doubt, it was the fate of the men that was preying on his mind.

Second, in three days' time he had to give the most important lecture of his life to a select and critical audience, one on which the future funding of Dunning and therefore of his own career would depend. Eels was a good, sometimes inspired, speaker, but like many people he suffered from stage fright.

So it was that he awoke suddenly in a sweat and went straight to the window for some fresh air. He opened it wider and heard the usual distant screams, shouts, moans and grunts of the patients, which the prairie wind carried into his room, from among the gaunt buildings. He sought in vain for a sight of stars or moon. These might have been a comfort.

He stood awhile in his nightshirt, cooling down in the breeze. He tried to think with pleasure of his promotion and how it vindicated the valuable research work he was now embarking upon.

One of those opposed to Dr Eels's appointment had been the present medical superintendent, Dr Benjamin Brown, one of the old school, in Eels's opinion, who thought too much about moral education and too little about modern medical solutions. Then there were the medical men in New York who had always stood in the way of his advancement and no doubt saw his defection to Chicago as an admission of failure.

Eels smiled thinly and tried to imagine how his enemies would react when they learnt that he was about to become one of the youngest, if not *the* youngest superintendent of a major insane asylum in the United States of America.

He tried, but it was impossible. His pleasure in things was always blighted by the fear that something would go wrong, that what was his would be snatched away from him at the eleventh hour and what he had earned by dint of hard work and natural brilliance as physician and surgeon would be stolen from him.

19

'Not this time,' he muttered resolutely, beginning to shiver with cold.

The hospital clock struck midnight and he turned back to his bed, climbed in, and laid his head on the pillow, determined to sleep.

He visualized his first meeting as superintendent with the Board of Managers and smiled triumphantly in the dark. But his pleasure was short-lived; the image faded at thoughts of the impending, all-important fund-raising address he had to give.

It *had* to go well.

He frowned and turned on his side and fell into fretful sleep. Within moments he was once more turning violently one way and then another before the terror took him and he did what he always did.

He curled unconsciously into a fetal position and cupped his testicles in the fingers of his right hand in a vain attempt to protect them from the demons of his mind.

DAY THREE

Saturday October 21, 1893

4

Emily Strauss

The notice outside the gated entrance to 'Chatwold', the private residence of Mr Joseph Pulitzer, read as follows: *In justice to his work and peace of mind, Mr Pulitzer is compelled to deny absolutely all personal interviews. No permission will be granted to visitors desiring to enter this property without prior permission.*

Out-of-work journalist, Emily Strauss, aged twenty-two and down to her last few dollars, read the notice without expression. She was aware that a few yards away the gatekeeper in his box was watching her with interest.

She was unsurprised by the notice and kept calm. Having spent a good part of her rapidly dwindling funds and many weary hours changing trains between Manhattan and Ellsworth before hiring a hack to cover the last eleven miles to Bar Harbor, she was not going to blow it by looking anything but supremely confident.

She paid off the hack, turned back to the gate and, doing her best to look disappointed that the gateman had not jumped to and opened it, she rang the bell.

It was only then that her heart began to thump at the enormity of the stunt she was about to try and pull and the realization that if it went wrong then likely as not no newspaper in the world would ever employ her again.

*   *   *

Emily Strauss had spent the last six fruitless days learning the ways of
New York journalism fast. It was harder, meaner and a deal more
ruthless than anything she had ever experienced on the Pittsburgh
Daily Echo in her past twelve unhappy months as a cub reporter – a
job from which she had been fired a month before. New York promised much more – or had seemed to, until she started tramping Newspaper Row in search of a reporter's job and had received nothing but
a score of rejections.

October in the city had proved unexpectedly warm and had left
her hot and perspiring. But now the weather out here by the ocean
was changing fast; a chill wind was blowing from the northwest and
she was shivering in the gored skirt, white tailored shirtwaist and thin
jacket she had donned in the hope of charming the great Mr Pulitzer.

His was the one name that everyone feared – and everyone revered.
He was also the one man no one ever seemed to get to meet, since
he was in ill health, almost blind and lived in seclusion in Maine when
he wasn't gallivanting off in his private yacht to the south of France.
That didn't stop him running his newspapers, it just made him harder
to meet.

'Don't even try,' she had been warned again and again.

Which made Emily Strauss want to try all the harder.

But she knew she had to understand the personality of her mark
if she was to be successful.

Two days previously she had stopped knocking on doors. She had
sat down on a bench in City Hall Park, which fronted most of the
newspaper offices she had tried so hard to get into, and had a think
about Mr Pulitzer. She had read a few articles about him; she had
met people who claimed to know him or know about him and who
worked for him.

She came to some conclusions, asked herself a question and decided
on a course of action.

The conclusions were that Mr Pulitzer liked women, liked people
who showed spunk and, being a gentleman, probably would not want
to say no to a lady, providing that lady could get near enough for him
to say yes.

The question was: what would Mr Pulitzer himself have done in
her situation?

To which the answer brought her pretty quickly to her decision: beard the lion in his den. That's what he would have done when he was still trying to make it himself as a news reporter. It's precisely what he *did* do. And she had decided to do the same.

Now here she was out at Bar Harbor, her heart thumping and the gatekeeper showing no sign of moving.

Emily Strauss decided that the time had come for her to make sure he did so.

She stuffed her valise through the bars of the gate, hoisted up her skirt and began climbing the gate.

The gateman got off his butt fast.

5

Far Side

'*Jane!*' yelled Riley, the senior attendant of the female wards at Cook County Insane Asylum, grabbing the arm of the woman from Bubbly Creek, 'Jane, you're goin' to the doctor. Put this shift on and come with me.'

'Jane', as they called any woman whose name was unknown, or to whom a better one than 'Jane Doe' had not yet been given, jumped to. She had only just got back from her daily exercise round the central main block of the vast Dunning grounds. It had been the first time she had been out and she had only just made it, feeling sick all the way from her time in the creek.

At least it gave her some fresh air and the chance to see the lie of the land in this godforsaken place.

Now she found herself being dragged back out of the ward, but she did not resist. The woman they called Riley gave no second chances.

She was in charge of what they called 'Far Side', the grimmest, oldest and most rundown part of Dunning. The part that visitors, even governors, never got to see. It was stone built, damp, broken windowed and freezing cold most of the time.

It had big wards and small wards, iron doors and wooden ones, nicely studded with metal rivets. It had a first-floor reception that conveyed a congenial enough atmosphere, but for the rest – upstairs and down – it was medieval in feel, condition and appearance, and in the basement there were cells so far back, so thick walled, so secluded and lost in a maze of corridors and walkways that the most agonized groan or loudest scream would never have been heard.

As for the pitiable cries of the abandoned mad and the pauper sick, upstairs or down, they were lost in the drip-drip-drip of the fetid drains and the creaking of hinges and boards and spy-holes that few knew were even there.

This was Riley's domain, as it had been her father's before her, and his father's before that.

Far Side was imbued with the vile odor of an evil family whose pleasure was control and whose middle name was callousness.

Maureen Riley was tall, like her father, a shade under six feet. Her arms were a man's, her hands too. And her face was a granite block with pig eyes.

Her upper lip was stubbly with hair.

Her teeth were stained with tobacco.

Her breath stank of liquor.

She knew how to put fear into the most difficult of inmates, and to control them physically and mentally. As far as the women inmates were concerned, and on occasion the men, Maureen Riley was the official reception committee.

When the woman from Bubbly Creek had arrived two days before, Riley had grabbed her by the hair and arm by way of welcome and, on the principle that all new inmates were potential troublemakers, crashed her into the stone upright of the door into the building and then dragged her up some steps, two at a time, before hauling her bodily through a ward of eighty women, who stared and laughed and dribbled and spat.

They watched the woman's humiliation with the smug looks of those who know that they are not about to be punished but who know what lies in store for the one who is. Riley reached an isolation room, opened the door and threw the woman in. She left her there a few hours.

It was a procedure that had a marvelous subduing effect on everybody, lunatic, pauper, hysteric and wanton alike. They all emerged from the experience quieter than when they began it.

In her own way, Maureen Riley was as skilled as any alienist and as clever as any surgeon, and the results she got were cheaper and far more dependable.

'Jane' was freed from isolation in the evening, and given a crib in a ward so big she couldn't see its other end in the gloom. On one side was a damp wall and on the other side a frightened, half-demented young woman in the next crib who whispered that her name was Mary.

The woman from Bubbly Creek stared in horror at Mary's fingers on the sheet. She was only in her early twenties, but they were twisted and contorted with worry, like those of an old woman, and they twined and intertwined endlessly, like thick worms that could not sleep.

'They killed my sister, you know. *She* did it . . . Riley did it . . . Killed my poor Ida . . . Don't you trust any of them and don't let them go taking you to that new Dr Eels either,' Mary continued in a whisper. 'Heard he sticks and cuts and he pulls your brains out. He does, he does. Don't let him . . .'

For 'Jane' this was just the beginning that first night.

Stick-stick, cut-cut, snip-snip, Mary muttered all night long. No wonder no one slept deep sleep in that ward.

But in the morning Mary seemed better, her eyes clearer and more intelligent. She wasn't demented – just scared. Her ever-twining fingers were the expression of that fear, but for a little time at dawn her eyes, suddenly gentle, were the one reminder of what she had once been. They were almost beautiful.

The wake-up call was the rap of a nightstick on the metal bars of the window; the women got up fast for fear of being beaten.

Breakfast was no more than grits, stale bread and bad coffee.

For some reason, Riley seemed to have taken against 'Jane'. There was a look in her eyes that came close, she declared, to insubordination. So she hit her a few times and that morning made her do jobs like cleaning up the vomit and emptying the slops and de-lousing the bolsters, just to show her who was boss.

'Jane' didn't complain. Her memory was coming back to her and, even if the events leading up to her falling in the Creek were vague and confused, she knew enough to realize that she had to get out of

Dunning whatever it took. If that meant being docile, docile was what she'd be.

Now the doctor wanted to see her, she was told. As Riley led her away from Far Side, she took advantage of a second opportunity to work out the hospital's layout, not easy in such a huge establishment. But she caught a glimpse of the prairie, and from that and what the women had said she had an idea which way Chicago lay. She made a mental note too of the fact that somewhere near, though out of sight, she heard the chuff-chuff and whistle of a locomotive and the shouts of men.

Then Riley slammed open a door right in front of her and she was inside what they called 'Main Building' and being told to climb a flight of stairs. She did so obediently, aware of Riley's wheezing, aware of the smell of antiseptic, polish and urine all at one go. Better than the malodorous air of Far Side.

'Sit there!'

The seat was cold and her shift provided no warmth, but she knew not to complain. The other women there, inmates and orderlies alike, all knew passivity was best when Riley was around.

'Next!'

She heard a male voice as a door opened.

'In you go,' said Riley, dragging her upright and pushing the woman from Bubbly Creek straight into the doctor's examination room. The woman stumbled, then righted herself. The moment she looked up and saw the doctor standing there in the middle of the room with his cruel mouth and steel spectacles, whose lenses seemed like two mirrors, a shiver went through her.

'I'm Dr Eels,' he said, 'and I'm going to make you better.'

His voice had the edge of oiled steel to it, his brief smile was like a momentary break in bleak midwinter.

Make me better?

Stick-stick, cut-cut, snip-snip, Mary's voice came back to her.

She stared at him and felt fear. Never in her life had the promise of something good seemed so like something bad and she visibly shuddered, fearing, as an animal does, that she had met her executioner.

6

Pulitzer

'Mr Pulitzer, sir, you have a visitor. A very insistent one. And she's female.'

It was just after twelve and Joseph Pulitzer was taking a break, in anticipation of his lunch and afternoon nap.

Seated in a vast wicker chair in his conservatory, a glass of water before him, neat piles of books and papers on a table nearby, he turned towards his secretary. His left eye was dull and half closed, his right was bright blue and seemed to see, though in fact it did not.

'What does she want, Mr Butes?' he said.

Arthur Butes was one of Pulitzer's four male secretaries. He was English, discreet and well spoken, with just that combination of learning, quickness and subservience that the great man liked. He hesitated briefly and then said, 'Well, she hasn't much English, but as I understand it she insists she is a relative of the distant sort . . . the daughter of Mrs Pulitzer's niece . . .'

'Let Mrs Pulitzer see her then,' his employer said, turning away.

Butes was unruffled. 'She has specifically requested to see *you* sir,' he continued with calm assurance. 'Indeed, she refuses to budge without doing so.'

The afternoon was a bright one after several days of rain and, though it was cold outside, the sun made the conservatory pleasantly warm. Joseph Pulitzer sat thinking awhile, the light emphasizing the striking contrast between his thick brown hair and the red of his beard.

'Chatwold', his rented home at Bar Harbor, had fine views over the sea where his yacht, *Liberty*, was anchored. Joseph Pulitzer could see neither, but close-up things were easier. The touch and aroma of his plants pleased him and the fresh sea breeze at open doors and windows helped if his throat and lungs were troubling him, which they often were.

He liked nothing worse than idleness. His great wealth had brought him no contentment, no peace: he was as he looked – restless, hungry to be doing, always imminently bored, permanently dissatisfied.

Butes had judged his employer's mood right that afternoon, but it was no surprise that before proceeding any further Mr Pulitzer wanted some hard facts.

'So, Mr Butes, what exactly does her card say?'

'It says she's a Fraulein . . . Eva Berger, of . . .'

'Repeat that, Mr Butes. You're mumbling.'

'*Berger*, sir. Of Mulheim.'

'Address?'

'Ponitz Strasse, number ten.'

Pulitzer frowned.

'I don't believe it,' he said matter of factly.

'I'm inclined to agree, sir. She says she's just arrived from Europe, but she doesn't look like she has to me.'

'What's she look like?'

'Tall, fair-haired, handsome I would say. Perhaps twenty-two or three.'

'Intelligent?'

'Possibly. Bold certainly. She's not the kind of lady who will go *easily* sir.'

'But she speaks real German?'

'Well, I'm no judge of the German tongue, Mr Pulitzer, but it strikes me there's a certain oddity about her accent . . .'

'You'd better show her in then. But if she looks as if she's going to cause trouble, remove her immediately!'

A minute later, Butes came back through the door with Emily.

Joseph Pulitzer stood up to offer her his right hand, and then, after a brief exchange in English, they both sat down.

Emily eyed him nervously, wondering how long she would be able
to keep the game up. Joseph Pulitzer was altogether more intimidating
than she had expected: he was taller, his presence was powerful, his
supposedly blind gaze was – or seemed – penetrating and his face bris-
tled with intelligence.

She decided to let him take the lead.

'Von *Mulheim?*' he said, his emphasis conveying general skepticism
about her story.

Since he spoke in German she replied in it. It was, she guessed,
about her only trump card. The rest were all poor ones rubbed up to
look good.

'Ja, Herr Pulitzer, ich—'

'Von Ponitz Strasse, im nord der stadt?'

'Jahrwohl, ich bin . . .'

She stopped, taken unawares at her own sudden inability to keep
the pretence going. Not that she couldn't speak fluent German; no,
her father had insisted she always speak it at home. It was just that
now she had finally made it into the great Joseph Pulitzer's presence,
her nerve was failing her. Her stunt felt cheap and tawdry. There was
nothing for it but to come clean and hope he was indeed the man his
own newspapers said he was, that he would listen to what she had to
say, weigh it on its merits and give her the assignment she craved.

Pulitzer immediately picked up on her hesitation.

'Let's talk English, Miss Berger. Only that isn't your real name, is
it? And you're no relative of my wife's, newly arrived from Germany
either, are you? Your German's good but it has an American twang.
Even Mr Butes here, and he's English, picked that up. How long have
you lived in America?'

'I was born here sir,' she admitted after a pause, looking at the floor,
'in Pittsburgh. My father was a steelworker.'

'Was?'

'Died last year.'

'In the Homestead Strike?'

'Yes, sir.'

She studied his face but, expressive though it was, it looked inscrutable
now.

After a pause he said, 'I reckon I'm a pretty good judge of character.'

'I expect you must be, Mr Pulitzer.'

'And I would say, on the strength of this brief acquaintance, which is not going to last much longer, that you're a willing liar when you need to be, as stubborn as a mule, and you don't give up on anything, which must be trying for those who know you. Am I right?'

'Pretty much sir. But from the descriptions I've read of you in your own newspapers, sounds to me as though you've just described yourself.'

He looked surprised at her audacity rather than amused, eyeing her in that strange, disconnected way of his, and reached out unerringly for his glass of water, from which he slowly took a sip or two.

She waited, judging he was a man who liked to set the pace. She would have liked to put on her most charming of expressions for his benefit, but knew it would have no effect.

'So why are you *really* here?' said Pulitzer, beginning to sound bored.

'I wrote to you, I—'

'Lots of folk write to me, *lots*.'

'I telegraphed—'

'Folk do that too. Lots of them.'

'I visited the offices of the *World* and—'

'How far did you get?'

'Not very.'

Pulitzer nodded and smiled.

Emily paused and decided to take a different, more direct, tack. Her time was running out and she'd better get to the point fast.

'I just wanted a tryout,' she said simply.

Pulitzer let out a groan and turned toward Butes.

'If she's what I'm beginning to fear she is, Mr Butes – a cub reporter from out of town – you're going to get fired.'

He turned back to Emily.

'Well?'

'I *am* from out of town but I'm no cub. I've done twelve months on the Pittsburgh *Echo* and I've just finished a stint in Chicago, working women's angles at the World's Fair. I resigned. Mr Coombs wouldn't give me a raise or a byline.'

It was her turn to pause. Then she added, a smile in her voice, 'I reckon that all adds up to Mr Butes here maybe having his pay cut but keeping his job.'

Pulitzer laughed aloud. Then he leaned forward and his expression turned mean.

'You know that one word from me can ruin your journalistic career forever?'

'I do. But I also know that one word from you can give it the kind of leg-up no one else can,' Emily replied coolly. 'I thought it a risk worth taking and that if you heard me out you might agree!'

Pulitzer settled back in his chair, scowling.

Emily's heart thumped. She knew she was about to be either given her chance or thrown out but she couldn't guess which.

'You better make it good,' he said with a scowl.

Emily took a deep breath. This, she knew, was it. Yet she hesitated. She had travelled a long way in her short life for this moment and, now it was here, she still wasn't sure she knew the right way to pitch ideas to a man as highly critical as Joseph Pulitzer.

One thing she did know though was that her time in Chicago had convinced her that it was people themselves she wanted to write about; people and the everyday human dramas of their lives. She had put such thoughts a hundred different ways to a dozen different, hard-boiled editors – all men – more in the last few dispiriting days than ever before. They had all ended up saying the same thing, some politely, most less so: 'There's nothing new in this. It's been done before. You've got to shake the competition and give us sensation. We don't believe in women in journalism anyway, so if you want to get on, go away and come back with something better – a whole lot better.'

Composing herself, she launched into what she knew would be her one and only chance.

'Did you know—?' she began.

'I know lots of things,' Pulitzer growled, making it hard for her.

'I mean to say—'

'She must mean something!' Pulitzer called over his shoulder sarcastically in the direction of Butes.

'When I was in Chicago—' Emily tried yet again, but that didn't work either.

'I don't want a travelogue,' Pulitzer interrupted, 'I want a *story*. But that's only the first of it. I want people who can quickly and accurately ascertain the facts that warrant the story. I want a story that the readers of the *World* can understand but which also makes 'em think. I want it to grab readers by the throat and make 'em read so hard and fast that they're disappointed when they come to the end. I want 'em ending up wanting more and finding there isn't any, not today anyway, so they're going to have to buy tomorrow's paper in hopes there will be.

'Now, Miss Strauss, all of that takes brains and guts and skill and courage – and something else besides. You know what that is? Heart. It takes heart. And that's hard to find these days or any day. So what story have you got then? Eh?'

His voice had grown steadily louder as he spoke and he finished with a kind of triumphant shout, like a man who is certain there is no ready answer to what he has just said. And now he stood looming over her, his great hooked nose making him seem like an eagle about to strike.

There was, however, something Joseph Pulitzer did not know, something which until that moment Emily had not really known herself – and it was this: her father, who had died for his beliefs in Pittsburgh during the bloodiest industrial strike in American history, was a man after Pulitzer's own heart. Otto Strauss had often put the fear of God in her as a child. But as she had grown up she had learnt that it's no good feeling afraid in the face of aggression. The best thing is to breathe deeply, stay cool and steady, and just keep plugging away for the thing you want.

Emily Strauss was not going to be scared off that easily.

'Seeing as you're standing, Mr Pulitzer, I hope you'll not take offence if I stand too,' she said.

She stood up and eyeballed him.

'Not long back I remember reading what you said about the kind of stories you wanted on the *World*. You said you wanted a story that's original, distinctive, dramatic, romantic, thrilling, unique. That as far as social issues are concerned you wanted to talk to a nation, not a select committee. Well, I can offer you all that. I can offer you the human angle, the *woman*'s angle. Trouble is most of your reporters are men and all the top people hiring them are men. So who do they think like? Men of course. But how many of the *World*'s readers are women? A lot I should say. A *whole* lot!'

She had expected to be interrupted by now, but Joseph Pulitzer was pacing about among the hothouse plants, glowering. She could tell, however, that she had his full attention and he was listening hard.

'Every day of the week there's stories in the *World* and every other paper I read that I reckon I could investigate better than your men do, and write up better too, not because I think I'm better than male reporters but because I think and feel like a *woman* and that means I've got a different angle. And your female readers – and maybe some of the men – will surely appreciate that.'

She fell silent, breathing heavily.

'You just want your chance, eh?' muttered Pulitzer.

'A *fair* chance, yes. That's about it. You want people who can write with heart? Well then, give *me* a chance and I'll do so!'

'Butes!' barked Pulitzer, having suddenly lost track of his bearings. His secretary guided him back to his seat.

'Where's the latest post from readers?'

'Right here, sir.'

'Give it to the lady.'

Butes handed Emily a pile of twenty or so letters from the table nearby.

'I like to stay in touch with what my readers have to say and they like to stay in touch with me,' growled Pulitzer. 'Here's the latest batch. I'm going to take a little walk around my garden for about a quarter of an hour or so. That's the time you've got to go through these letters and come up with something worth writing. Let's see if you're as good as you think you are.'

As he got up and headed for the door into the garden on Butes's arm, Pulitzer called back at her:

'A quarter of an hour. After that I expect you to leave.'

'Thank you, sir,' she responded demurely.

'By the way,' he added, 'you never told me your real name.'

'Emily Strauss,' she said with a disarming smile. Trouble was, he couldn't see it.

7

Eels

Dr Morgan Eels, the insane asylum's newly appointed deputy medical superintendent, stared at his latest patient.

From her physiognomy, on which subject he had made himself a diagnostic expert, he was certain she was of low immigrant stock. Probably Bohemian or something like it.

'What's her name?'

Eels addressed this to Riley and his voice was sharp and unpleasant, its affected accent more English than American.

Riley explained that no one knew her name, including even the patient.

'Forgot 'erself,' said Riley, 'or won't say. The court sent her over without one. Hoped you'd find it out, I expect.'

Still not moving, Eels examined the woman for a full minute more from where he stood.

'Where did they find her?'

'She was the one they fished out of Bubbly Creek two days ago.'

Eels eyed his patient some more.

'Turn round,' he commanded her.

'Jane' seemed slow to move, so Riley gave her a shove.

'By herself, if you please,' said Eels sternly.

His examinations had method and purpose. He liked to see how patients responded to his instructions.

'Turn round again,' he said finally.

The woman did so, aware of the doctor and the orderly staring and of Riley looming behind her. She had been uneasy from the first but she felt even more so now. She tried to pull the ill-fitting shift closer to her.

Eels was of medium height and thin, with eyes so dark and expressionless behind his spectacles that it was hard to tell where the pupils ended and the rest began. They had a nasty glitter to them.

He stood unnervingly still in the middle of the room, from where he stared at his latest patient.

His mouth was a scissor-snip in pinched pale skin, his face clean shaven, his nose pointed. His thin, dark, neatly trimmed hair was lightly greased with a lotion that gave out the scent of lemons.

Eels wore a jacket, waistcoat and pants in the style of an East Coast medical consultant. His shoes were all polished and squeaky. He wasn't more than twenty-nine or thirty, but he looked like a man for whom the financial rewards of a successful medical career were already coming his way.

A man in a white jacket stood behind him to his right. His thickset shoulders and wary, ready-for-anything expression suggested he was an asylum orderly rather than a male nurse. Maybe some patients were inclined to violence; maybe all patients needed a degree of intimidation.

In fact this was Mr Mould, Eels's long-term assistant and technician who helped him with his laboratory work.

Neither man wanted to be working on a Saturday but it was the only way to clear the backlog. Dr Eels was on the hunt for patients suitable for his investigative research and he was under pressure to get on with it fast.

Eels conducted his visual examination of the woman quickly but methodically, walking right round her and then halfway round again. He was well aware that his method was unusual – a patient such as this might normally be sitting or lying – but his approach was born of experience and had, it seemed to him, a certain logic.

He had noted with interest the woman's failure to object to the examination, attributing this acquiescence to her having reached the abject phase of nervous hysteria. The unconscious wantonness of women in such a state was a matter of common record – findings confirmed by his own observations at his former post at Danbury. Many of the lower kind were deliberately immodest; most more so than this woman. But in the end the behaviour was the same, the rest being simply a matter of degree.

He could see that she presented no difficulty and ordered his assistant out of the room for the more intimate part of the examination.

'But stay close by, Mr Mould. I will need you for the photographic work,' he murmured.

He kept the woman standing while he completed his preliminary notes and then ordered her to sit on a couch covered in shiny black oilcloth.

'Remove your shift.'

When she did not do so, pretending not to understand perhaps, he nodded at Riley, who did it for her. The woman made no move to stop her.

He examined her face, head, eyes, nostrils, mouth, teeth, her ears and her scalp. That done, he laid her back on the couch and examined her some more, beginning at her head and ending at her feet, including everything on the way, front and back.

He continued to jot things down in boxes on the printed sheet on his clipboard. The document was of his own design, for Dr Eels prided himself on his methodical approach to diagnosing mental illness. He believed it had distinct physical origins and he had dedicated his life and his scientific research to pinpointing them. He then took some large callipers and measured the dimensions of her face and head, her pelvis and her back.

She might just as well have been a cadaver from the matter-of-fact way he did it.

'You're being mighty thorough, Dr Eels,' observed Riley.

'I like to be,' he said coldly, adding, 'and this one will be a good subject for our experimental investigation.'

Eels turned back to his patient. 'Do you remember anything?'

She shook her head.

He stared at her and she at him, a shade too boldly. What was it, Dr Eels pondered, hysteria or intelligence? Or both? He was sure she remembered something.

He turned away and wrote up his notes.

'Stand her over there,' he said finally.

He nodded towards one of the walls of the room along which a pale green sheet had been hung. Riley knew the routine. When the woman went to put her shift back on she stopped her.

'Not yet,' she said.

Eels pulled back a screen opposite revealing a camera on a tripod.

That was when the woman spoke her first words.

'Please, no,' she said, covering her modesty with her hands.

'Mr Mould!' called out Dr Eels. His orderly appeared at once. The woman fell silent, eyes wide.

'Please stand still,' said Dr Eels, as he lined up the camera and checked the magnesium powder in the flash pan. As he took her photograph, the flash made Anna screw up her eyes, which now registered extreme distress.

'*Please, no,*' she said again, raising her hands to her eyes.

'An interesting reaction,' mused Eels to his orderly. 'Patients rarely object to being photographed and never to the flash. Fear, yes. Objection, no.'

He nodded at the orderly. 'Turn her to the right,' he said, ignoring the woman's protest. The second flash distressed her still more but this time she said nothing. She let them take the final two photographs, of her left side and a rear view, without further protest.

'Good,' said Eels finally. 'Now put your shift back on. Take her back to her ward, Riley. I will not need her again today.'

As he said this he was watching the woman closely.

He saw her relax, he saw her breathe more easily.

He watched as she headed with Riley for the door.

'Stop!' he called out at the last moment.

'*Do you remember your name?*' he said, as the woman turned, his voice sharp and commanding once more. He took up his clipboard and silver propelling pencil. 'Eh?'

He looked hard as if he could read her thoughts.

'I . . .'

Even had she been able to remember it, she knew she must not say it. 'I . . .'

But she did not know why.

'Well?' he said softly, the silver pencil glinting in his hand, the lens of his spectacles flashing too.

'I . . . can't remember.'

'Oh, but I think you do,' said Dr Eels coming closer.

I don't know it, mustn't say it, I mustn't, I . . .

'Well?' he purred.

She could smell lemons and wondered why.

His eyes were silvery pits.

It was then she finally remembered her name.

Anna Zemeckis, the baker's daughter screamed inside herself in relief and terror, *but I mustn't say it.*

Why? This doctor wanted to make her better.

I mustn't say it. ANNA ZEMECKIS!

She thought she was going to burst.

'I can't remember my name,' she said, flushing at the lie.

'I think you can and that you will,' said Eels, studying her. He was frowning.

'Eh?'

'I don't know my name,' said Anna Zemeckis.

And I don't know why I mustn't say it.

It was that that made her want to scream.

'Take her away, Mrs Riley,' said Eels with a look of distaste. 'We will continue tomorrow.' He would get her name out of her if he had to cut it out with his scalpel.

Eels took a patient's failure to yield to his demands personally. He also read it as a sign of their willful madness which made their cure so difficult and their need for a cure so important.

Anna was so upset that on her way out she bumped into the next patient coming in.

It was Mary, the woman who slept in the crib next to hers in the night ward.

Her fingers were locked together in the same, terrible, never-ending embrace; her eyes were terrified.

41

'I don't want to,' she said as she passed Anna by, 'I don't.'

Before Anna could respond she felt Riley's grip once more and was dragged off back to Far Side.

Dr Eels looked up at the new arrival in surprise.

'Aah!' he said, taking out his pocket watch. 'You're in the wrong place. We can't carry out the procedure here.'

He told the orderly to take Mary downstairs where his assistant Mr Mould would ready her for surgery.

'I don't want . . .' whispered Mary hopelessly.

'You want to get better,' whispered Eels confidingly, 'don't you?'

'I don't know . . .'

'Take Nevitt away!' said Eels sharply. But the smile on his face was benign, magisterial, professional.

'You'll feel better in no time,' he said.

He took out his propelling pencil and twisted it slightly to get a fresh bit of lead. Then he surveyed the clipboard of forms and lists on his desk, pulled out one from the bottom and clipped it to the top. In a box in the top left-hand corner a number had been written earlier by someone else: 18.

'Two more needed after this one,' said Eels softly, his thin lips puckering into a tuneless whistle, his mind returning for a moment to his previous patient.

Trouble was, he still did not have the name of the woman from Bubbly Creek, and Eels was meticulous about keeping records, especially for important experiments of the kind he had now decided she should be part of. He did not like gaps and he did not take kindly to being bested.

'I *will* have her name,' he whispered as he put the clipboard back in place on his desk. He now turned his attention to another file and another matter entirely, pulling towards him the notes for the lecture that he was to give before an invited audience at Dunning in two days' time.

He had given it various titles over the previous weeks, each of which had been successively scratched out on the file cover. Now he dipped his pen in the silver inkwell on his desk and wrote: *Lecture before an Invited Audience at Cook County Insane Asylum October 23, 1893.*

42

Then: *Given by Dr Morgan Eels MD, Deputy Medical Superintendent of Cook County Insane Asylum and former Medical Superintendent of the Insane Asylum and Home for the Feeble-Minded in Danbury, Western Connecticut.*

Then, quite unexpectedly, the title came to him: *The Imbecile and the Chronically Insane – Care, Cure and Remedy.*

'Yes,' breathed Eels with evident satisfaction, 'yes . . .'

He glanced at his watch and got up.

He went to the sink at the back of the room and washed his hands carefully.

Then he took off his jacket and hung it up and donned a white robe.

He took a bottle of lemon balm oil from his cabinet, sprinkled a little on his hands and dabbed it on his pale face. Dr Eels liked to feel antiseptically clean and sweet smelling before he cut into patients' brains.

8

Assignment

It was the very first letter Emily read that had spoken to her, though she skimmed the others through, just to be sure, before coming right back to that one.

Now she had no doubts. The moment she saw the black ink and the tight, anguished letters of its handwriting, she knew its heart and its soul and guessed at its private agony. If Joseph Pulitzer did not say she could chase this story she would do it anyway.

'Well?' he said, returning fifteen minutes and a few seconds later.

She held up the letter, forgetting he could not see.

'This is the one,' she said.

'Read it to me.'

She did so.

It was short and stark and sad.

It was from a Mr Janis Zemeckis, a Latvian baker on the Lower East Side. He'd been in America ten years. His only daughter had disappeared in Chicago six weeks previously and had only now turned up again – apparently killed in a horsecar accident. He had written begging Mr Pulitzer to warn his readers not to make the mistake he had made of letting his child go off to the World's Fair in that terrible place, a city that was no better than the wild frontier, where bad things happened. He had made that mistake and now his daughter was never

coming back, not ever. But others could be warned and so saved from
the anguish he was now going through.

'What's the story, Miss Strauss?'

'The dangers of the big city for single women. I know it's true
because women in Chicago have been going missing during the Fair.
I filed a story on it myself a couple of months back which the *Echo*
never used.'

'I am not surprised. Women in cities have been vulnerable since
time immemorial. That's what *happens* to them. It's an old story.'

'But it hasn't been done through the eyes of those left behind, not
through Mr Zemeckis's eyes. Not through the eyes of others like him
who've lost their loved ones. There's been a cover up about this in
Chicago. Mayor Harrison doesn't want bad news ruining things for
the World's Fair. Crime's gone up since long before it kicked off in
May but you wouldn't know it from what you read in the papers.
Dozens of women – men too – have disappeared in the last year or
so, but the police don't have the manpower or the time to investigate.
All the papers want to print is how big and great and modern Chicago
is and how revolutionary all that stuff is that they have on display at
Jackson Park. Well, I may not be a Chicagoan but I've walked its
streets, especially some that visitors don't get to see, and I can tell you
it's not all pretty and modern and going places by any means.'

'But it's all been done before,' repeated Pulitzer, with rather less
conviction now. 'You can warn all you like, but girls are still going to
head off to the city, and predators of all kinds – good and bad, wicked
and worse – will still be there waiting for them.'

'Yes, and they're mainly men! No wonder your editors don't run
stories like this. They're men too!'

'All in all, you don't have a very cheerful view of the male of the
species, do you Miss Strauss?'

'I have a more cheerful view of the female, Mr Pulitzer. Otherwise
I wouldn't be standing here right now asking you to send me to Chicago.
Let me chase this story and come up with something that the gripman
on a New York streetcar and his wife want to read because they both
understand it and it grabs their hearts. Let me get to the truth of this
girl's story and others like it and you'll have a story that's worth
printing. Send me to Chicago.'

Pulitzer said nothing, he was thinking.

'The Fair ends when precisely?' he finally asked.

'Thirtieth of this month,' said Emily. 'Nine days' time.'

He thought some more; Emily held her breath.

'That should give you time enough to investigate Mr Zemeckis's story for the *World* and turn it into something worth reading on the thirtieth.'

Emily's eyes widened, but she kept her nerve.

'I'll need an advance,' she said boldly. 'I'm out of funds.'

'Our men get paid after the event, by the space they fill.'

'But I still need money to do the story,' Emily said firmly.

'Then I'll put you on our standard tryout rate – fifteen dollars a week, plus expenses. And be sure you account for everything.'

There was a very long pause indeed, as Emily weighed up what to her was a disappointing offer. But before she could protest, Pulitzer added, 'That's the deal, Miss Strauss. Mr Butes will telegraph our city editor, Charles Hadham, to discuss your assignment. Warn him a gate-climber's on her way, Arthur. Tell him to make time to see her in the office tomorrow.'

He stood up and stretched out his hand.

'You've not asked for my press clippings,' said Emily.

'Don't need to. It's you I'm hiring, not bits of paper. I've got a team of editors on the *World* who are paid to lick reporters' copy into shape. You want to meet some men who *really* make life hard for women? You just wait and see their blue pencils go to work on your copy when you file it!'

He was suddenly relaxed.

'You will find Mr Hadham helpful in every way. Mr Butes here will alert him to this conversation. I wish you luck. You ought to do the same for Mr Butes, seeing as you've forced me to consider his future! Meantime, he can ensure that the kitchen provides you with some-thing to eat and drink before my carriage gets you safely back across the causeway to Ellsworth ahead of the tide coming in.'

'Thank you Mr Butes!' Emily said after they had left Joseph Pulitzer's sanctum, 'I'm sorry about the—'

'Imminent firing? It happens once a week at least. Be warned! It'll happen to you one of these days if you get a job on the *World*. Meanwhile, I will make sure that Mr Hadham sees you tomorrow. He's a good, fair man. I'll tell him to expect you around two-thirty. Don't waste his time. You won't get a second chance. And one more thing, Miss Strauss.'

She looked enquiringly at him.

'Trust no one. *No one*. That's the only way you'll survive working for the *World*. No one.'

'What do I have to do to get a permanent job there?'

'You really want that, don't you?'

She nodded.

Alfred Butes looked at her and then at the letter from Janis Zemeckis that she still clutched tightly in her hand.

'You must find out what happened to the girl, Miss Strauss. That's the only way. *Find out what happened, get your story in by the deadline – and tell it to the world!*'

DAY FOUR

Sunday October 22, 1893

9

Audit

The national convention of any well-run organization, whatever the delegates may think, is no place for serious decision making, because democracy and public debate have a nasty way of upstaging those who like to run the show.

The politically astute and influential members of the Audit Committee of the Old America Association were well aware of this. As they were the OAA's policy and financial power base, they generally met a few days or so ahead of the association's two-day convention. They did so in private chambers, well away from where the main events would be taking place.

Because the OAA's 1893 Convention was slated to be such a special one, it being that organization's twenty-fifth anniversary and also being the year of the World's Fair, it had long since been decided to hold it in Chicago's newest and finest theater, the Auditorium on the corner of Michigan Avenue and Congress Street, on October 27 and 28, two days before the Fair's end.

The place chosen for the all-important meeting of the Audit Committee was a prestigious one: the twelfth floor of Chicago's vast new twenty-two-story Masonic Temple, boasted to be the tallest building in the world and a major tourist attraction during the World's Fair for its roof garden, shopping galleries and 2,000-seat basement restaurant. This gave time for any contentious matters to be debated and decided behind strictly closed doors and for any orders, secret and otherwise, consequent on those decisions, to be carried through efficiently and effectively.

It had been decided, too, to convene the Audit Committee especially early, there being a great many sensitive matters to discuss, some of them difficult and a few seemingly impossible to resolve. One in particular would need a few more days if it was to be satisfactorily resolved before the main convention. This was the important question of who it was should succeed Jenkin Lloyd Rhys, the New York civil engineer and inspiration behind the founding of the Old America Association. But that decision was closely linked to another equally contentious one: what should the OAA's stance be on the immigration 'problem', as it was now perceived.

The OAA, like the Audit Committee, was pretty well divided down the middle between the Rhys faction, which favoured a laissez-faire approach to immigration and the faction led by Paul Hartz, the OAA's executive vice president, and his son-in-law Gunther Darke, both of whom favored a tougher stance on immigration from Eastern Europe.

It had long been foreseen that these would not be easy decisions, and for this reason the Audit Committee was convened for its final business of the year on Sunday October 22, six days before the bigger convention. The idea was, so far as the affable and charismatic Rhys was concerned, that this would give plenty of time for whatever horse trading needed to take place to be over and done with and for his allies, of whom there were many, to work their usual strong-arm and velvet-glove magic and make the election of his successor an exercise in the rubber stamp.

That was the theory, and Hartz who, though fifteen years younger than Rhys, was one of his most trusted colleagues and himself a co-founder of the OAA, went along with it. As an adopted Chicagoan – he was born in New York but now controlled a majority stockholding in Darke Hartz & Company, one of the city's largest meatpackers – he knew very well that the last days of the Fair were likely to be filled with unprecedented revelry and partying, not suited to serious committee meetings.

Best, he agreed, to get the serious issues sorted and agreed well ahead of the convention so that when it came to it everybody could relax and enjoy themselves.

But as the clock in the boardroom where the Audit Committee was having its meeting chimed ten o'clock, there was only one problem: the supremely time-conscious Jenkin Lloyd Rhys had not arrived.

He should have come for an earlier meeting with the three most senior officers at nine that morning; when he did not show, word was sent to his hotel. Perhaps, having arrived in Chicago only the evening before, he had overslept, though that seemed unlikely. Perhaps he was ill.

The message that came back, confirmed by Paul Hartz personally by telephone a short while later, was that Mr Rhys had checked in the night before and, after dining with some friends, had gone out alone for a walk from which he had not returned. There was no indication of any kind of struggle in the room, but when the hotel manager spoke to Hartz, he suggested that it might be better if someone from the OAA came over before the police were called.

'Leave things as they are,' said Hartz firmly. 'There is no need yet to inform the police. I shall come personally to investigate later this morning after our meeting is concluded.'

It might well be that there were personal and business papers and effects in Rhys's suite which it would be better if the prying eyes of the police did not see.

'Gentlemen,' began Hartz shortly after ten o'clock, 'as Mr Rhys cannot be with us at present, I shall take the chair this morning.'

This was the first that the senior members of the OAA had heard of Rhys's disappearance and several of them saw at once that with the coming election of a new president this might well change things – weakening the position of the president's allies while strengthening that of Hartz and his anti-immigration faction. They surmised that this was an unexpected bonus which Hartz could not have foreseen but one which, if he was clever, he could make use of.

A short time later, after Hartz had briskly moved the committee through the previous meeting's minutes and matters arising, they moved on to finance, his own area of interest.

'I think I may say, gentlemen,' he began with a confidence made

53

somber by the peculiar circumstances in which he had had to assume the chair, 'that never before in the history of our organization have we been in as strong a position as we are today . . . I know Mr Rhys himself would be the first to point this out, were he able to be here . . .'

Some of the committee members nodded appreciatively at this acknowledgement of their absent friend and mentor.

Others did not bother.

Paul Hartz allowed himself a brief, inward smile and then turned his attention back to the more important business of the meeting. It seemed to him that things were going better than he could have hoped.

'Now,' he said, 'let us turn to the matter of Mr Rhys's successor. Had Mr Rhys been here then I am sure we could have resolved this issue. We all know who his nominee is . . .'

Hartz turned to Chester W. Allen, the OAA's long-term honorary secretary and Rhys's closest friend and ally and smiled warmly. The two men loathed each other.

'. . . but I think Mr Allen would agree with me that we should defer the matter of succession until Mr Rhys has joined the meeting . . .'

Chester Allen, a Manhattan lawyer of some eminence but also considerable dullness was forced to agree. This was not the outcome of the meeting he would have wished for and his growing sense of unease at Rhys's absence mounted.

Where the hell was he?

Nothing more was said, but the smirks of the anti-immigration, pro-Hartz faction, who now had the upper hand, were unmistakable.

The only question in everyone's minds now was whether a Hartz nominee was suddenly about to enter the frame, and if so, who was he going to be?

'Let us move on, gentlemen,' said Paul Hartz warmly.

He had not made his millions by being warm. He had done it by careful planning, riding his luck and getting the timing right.

The moment was not yet.

Despite the smiles and the pervading air of courtesy, the private boardroom in the Masonic Temple that morning crackled with an undercurrent of duplicitous tension.

10

Zemeckis

At noon Emily Strauss called on Mr Janis Zemeckis. She did this ahead of visiting the *World*'s offices on Park Row in Lower Manhattan in the afternoon, feeling she needed to show she had already begun work on the story.

The Zemeckis bakery was located in the Lower East Side, just off Mulberry Street. But when she got there, it was closed, the shop door locked and the business for sale.

A side door led to apartments above, while three steps down from street level there was a window which gave access and light to a basement where she guessed the baking was done.

Emily found a tenant at home on the top floor, a Czech widow, a cigar maker from whose rooms there came a strong smell of tobacco. Mrs Kopecky did not hesitate to offer her own version of events.

Yes, Zemeckis owned the building but was in debt to the bank for it. His daughter was dead, or gone. Now the man himself was as good as dead too, his business for sale. But what business? *He* was the business. Good bread, healthy bread, the best she knew. But where was Janis Zemeckis now? He spent his days wandering the streets, sitting in parks, reading newspapers, filling in time, trying to forget the unforgettable.

His money, and he had some once, was surely all gone by now.

America was killing him just like it had killed so many immigrants before him. Knock on any door in any tenement and there were people dying in body, mind and spirit, especially Bohemians and Eastern Europeans like them. Zemeckis? He was just another one, no more than a passing shadow on the sidewalk.

His daughter Anna Jelena? Such a good girl. A good, strong Latvian girl who was quiet and modest, studied English properly, and could read and write so well she had got herself a job as a librarian.

'Where will I find him?' Emily asked. Talking was one thing, getting real information another.

'What do you want with him?' asked Mrs Kopecky, pursing her lips and suddenly suspicious, as she retied her black scarf tight about her head.

'I want to help him. Where is he?'

'You want to buy bread? You'll not find any as good as Zemeckis's, except maybe in Riga!'

'I just want to talk to him.'

'Go to the library where Anna used to work. You'll find him there. Even on a Sunday. He often just goes there and sits on the bench outside. You'll know him when you see him. You'll know. So pale, such sadness in his eyes. You'll *know*.'

Emily went to the Aguilar Free Library on East 5th Street, but it was closed. She looked around for Jan Zemeckis in the nearby streets but he was not there either, so she decided to wait.

'A shadow on the sidewalk,' was how Mrs Kopecky had described him, and she was right, that's what he looked like when she finally spotted him. A pale man, hunched and shrunken rather than small, seeming unable to make up his mind how to cross the busy street as horse cars, trams, drays, and carts rushed on by in either direction. She had never seen such sadness in a face, such despair. She noticed how he searched the faces of the passing crowd – still hopelessly seeking his daughter.

His eyes were shadowed, his mouth thin, and each cheek was etched with a vertical line from a lifetime of early rising and hard physical work in sunless basements.

For a moment Emily felt that she should not intrude upon his grief. She could offer no hope to such a man.

Then she heard herself say, 'Mr Zemeckis? Mr *Janis* Zemeckis?'

He looked at her uncomprehendingly.

Then, finally, with hesitation, he replied, 'Yes, I am Zemeckis.'

Hope began to dawn in his eyes, much as Emily had feared.

'You wrote to Mr Joseph Pulitzer, I . . .'

His mouth dropped open. More hope.

She shook her head and immediately said, 'I'm so very sorry about your daughter. There's nothing I can do or say to bring her back . . . but Mr Pulitzer thinks that other parents might be warned if I were to tell your story . . .'

His eyes receded into despair again.

'Yes, she is dead,' he said matter-of-factly. 'But right now I am not sure I am able to talk about it . . .'

'Mr Pulitzer thought that maybe your story would . . .'

He nodded his head.

'In my letter I said to him, "Mr Pulitzer, I lost my Anna but that is not why I write. I looked for her in Chicago, everywhere, and nobody wanted to know or to help. If America does not care to look after its young people, what *does* it care for? My Anna, my child, was taken and nobody can tell me why. When I finally found her it was too late and she was dead. Maybe if people had been more helpful I would have found her alive." These things I said.'

'I read your letter, Mr Zemeckis. Mr Pulitzer wanted me to talk to you and then go and find out about the kind of dangers young women face in the city.'

'What is your name?'

'I'm sorry. Emily Strauss.'

He reached out a hand formally and shook hers.

'Mr Janis Zemeckis,' he said unnecessarily. He looked hard at her with intelligent eyes and said, 'You are a reporter?'

'Yes.'

'Miss Strauss, it is not just young women. Men also. Children too. The city is full of predators and people disappear. Hundreds of them. Can you imagine? And no one cares.'

'I'd like you to tell me your story, I . . .'

'Mr Pulitzer sent a girl to find out what happened to my daughter!' he interrupted with a bleak laugh.

'Something like that Mr Zemeckis. I believe it is important to tell
your story. I can find out how many girls disappear, maybe, and how
much of a problem it is. If people in Chicago pretend it does not
happen, then that is a scandal and it needs to be reported.'

He stared into her eyes, hesitating.

'Maybe if you let me tell them about Anna,' she prompted, 'then
what I write will help find others, maybe stop more people disappearing . . .'

'I will tell you. I take you to our home and you will see for yourself she is a good, well-brought-up girl. She did not run away. Someone
took her. She is a good girl. I will show you . . .'

He pulled a small photograph from his jacket pocket and proffered
it to Emily.

It showed a girl like a hundred thousand others – dark, thick curly
hair pinned up under a modest little hat; a good young figure in a
pretty day dress with lace insets and wearing a distinctive crucifix –
the one whose discovery in the morgue had confirmed for Mr Zemeckis
that his daughter was dead.

She was by no means a beauty, her face being solid and rather plain,
but she had the same intelligence in her eyes as her father and something
he did not have any longer, a belief in life, a joy in living. A good
daughter and, had she had the chance, a good wife and mother in
her own turn.

Back at Mulberry Street, the shop, as well as the bakery below, were
clean, tidy but almost bare.

'The better to sell it,' he explained.

'You don't want to make bread any more?'

He shook his head firmly.

'An unhappy baker bakes poor bread. I came to America to forget
that I had lost my wife and my son. Now America has stolen my
daughter and my livelihood. Where do I go now? I don't know. I show
you Anna's room . . .'

They had lived together in the apartment above the shop which
was modest but comfortable.

Zemeckis made Emily coffee and offered her some gingerbread.

'The last I made.'

He needed little prompting to talk. He told her about Anna and why he had sent her to Chicago.

At one point he paused and said quietly, 'If I had known what a wicked, sinful city Chicago was – if I had seen with my own eyes those prostitutes in the streets, and the men whose eyes were so hungry for young women – I would never have sent her. Never, never, never. By the time I did, it was, of course, too late . . .'

'But you had dreams for her and yourself, didn't you?'

'Yes, I had dreams before the nightmare that is now.'

He smiled and then told her of those simple hopes and dreams, and Anna's too.

'She wanted the love of a man, a good man, like all women. One to make her proud, to give her children, to look after, to share life with. She knew what her mother had been to me; she wanted the same for herself and knew it would give me happiness if she found it. But I know she would not encourage the wrong kind of man and that she would tell me or her aunt and uncle in Chicago.'

'Did she have admirers?'

'Some. I did not like them. Young, no-good men. She was too young.'

Emily smiled slightly. She had had the same conflict with her own father, but he had been less strict.

'Did she have a special beau?'

'Of course not.'

'Did she have a job to go to in Chicago?'

'I told her she had no need to work, but Anna did not want to be idle. The library here where she worked arranged for a tryout for her at the Chicago Public Library. But as this was only part-time, she also took on some work in the Administration Building at the World's Fair, arranged by my sister-in-law.'

'Did she write home?'

'Yes, regularly. I show you. I show you her letters . . .'

He disappeared into another room and came back with a bundle of letters written in a neat, round, girl's hand.

'She writes this first sentence in Latvian so I translate for you. "Dear Papa," this is the first she wrote, "I tell you first about the journey to this great city by train after you waved goodbye and I waved back.

59

Do you remember? I was crying a little but I was also excited . . ."
And now she continues in English because I told her, "We are Americans
now, this is our language and you must use it."'

Janis Zemeckis's eyes suddenly filled up and he bent his head and
he let out a terrible cry. But he shook his head when Emily reached
out a hand to comfort him.

'She was my *daughter*,' he said, 'my *life*.'

He reached into his breast pocket and produced a crucifix on a
chain. It was of gray metal and quite bulky and distinctive.

'Mr Freeman returned it to me on my last visit, once they had
completed the formalities. I keep it with me now, always. I cannot
forget her. She left me but she cannot leave my heart.'

If there was a moment when Emily Strauss decided that this was
a story she must follow to its very end, that was it. She was not looking
anymore for a story about someone called Anna Zemeckis – she was
going to find out the truth about this man's child, his daughter, his
everything. She was going to find out what had happened to a woman
upon whom, it seemed, America had turned its back, until it was too
late and she had turned up dead.

'Please,' said Emily, her own voice shaking, 'read her letters to me.
I need to get to know her.'

Two hours later, Emily felt she knew the young woman who had been
Anna through and through, even though the letters seemed to contain
little that was unusual and gave no indication at all of any men or
women whom Anna might have known and of whom, naturally, her
father would now have been suspicious.

She had got all the background she needed on Zemeckis's search –
where he had been in Chicago and who he had seen or tried to see.
She could not immediately think of anywhere she would have gone
herself which he had not already tried. She asked if she could borrow
Anna's letters to read at her leisure in case there were any clues in
them they had missed. And then Janis handed her the precious photograph as well.

'Really, I can't take that Mr Zemeckis . . .'

'It might help,' he said, closing her fingers over it with his own, 'so
please, take it. Give it back when you know the truth.' It was as though

60

in the act of giving the photograph to her he passed over to Emily the responsibility for finding out what had happened to his daughter during those lost weeks and it made it easier for himself to live with his loss.

'But do not lose these things Miss Strauss! They are all I have left of her . . . do not lose them!'

11

Chilled

In the pitch darkness of an isolated warehouse somewhere on Chicago's South Side, Jenkin Lloyd Rhys, president of the Old America Association, was suffering the first stages of hypothermia.

His wrists were trussed tightly behind him with twine, which was looped up around his neck and down to his ankles in such a way that when he moved his arms he began garrotting himself.

To ease the pressure he had slumped sideways to the floor, his back and hands resting against a freezing brick wall.

It was not so cold that he was likely to freeze to death, but his legs were shaking uncontrollably and his teeth chattered so much that his denture had come loose and was halfway out of his mouth.

He had no idea where he was or what had happened to him. He remembered leaving his hotel at around seven the evening before to take a stroll over to the lakefront before retiring for the night. As usual his wife had not come to Chicago with him as she did not like long rail journeys or strange hotel beds.

The weather was fine and the sidewalks crowded but somewhere on Adams, just as he came within sight of the Art Institute on the other side of Michigan Avenue, a man passed him, blocked his path and halted, causing Rhys to stop as well. The man was not especially tall but he was most certainly broad. He turned, apparently in apology, and the next thing Rhys knew was that his right arm was being gripped painfully tight and before he could even shout he was pushed down an alley near a saloon and . . . and that was the last he remembered.

He had woken up in the dark trussed like a goose and with no idea where he was and nothing for company but the sound of a railroad and the coming and going of locomotives and box cars. He called out a few times but doubted if anyone could hear or would ever hear.

He lay shivering for a while before remembering that he knew enough about the cold and what it did to a man to know that he better start moving. Which was not easy with that cord round his neck.

Yet somehow or other he succeeded in turning on his front and then, getting into a kneeling position, he was able to use the wall as a prop to push himself up, hopping against it because his ankles were bound together.

All this in pitch darkness with just the sound of the trains and a chill, sweet smell in the air.

Unable to feel his way in the dark with his hands, he decided to stay with the wall and edge his way along it. It was perishing cold and streaming with condensation, and his breaths came out in staccato grunts of pain and discomfort as he staggered along, probing his way on the floor ahead with his feet and then with his shoulder on the wall.

Reaching a corner of some kind he turned it and finally saw light, dim and distant, no more than a crack. He staggered towards it and was doing well until, missing his footing, he fell sideways into what felt like cold flesh from which, instinctively, he turned, bumped into more as with a sudden, unexpected shocking thump something, someone, crashed into his back and he fell to the floor, gasping for air from the ligature round his neck.

Only when he had lain there for a time and smelt the sickly sweet odour of the slippery moist floor did he realize he was in a cold store of some kind among the hanging carcasses of meat.

Once more he struggled to stand upright, but he was colder now and weaker, and frightened. As for his hands, the twine was so tight they had lost all feeling, but for the thump-thump-thump of a protesting pulse somewhere in his left arm.

He finally got up again and headed on towards the light until, turning yet another corner, he saw it was a door of some kind.

Risking losing his balance again by breaking from the support of the wall, he turned finally toward the door, hoping to kick it to attract attention and to shout if he had any voice left in him at all.

'Help!'

It came out as no more than a croak.

'Help!'

He reached the door, went to kick it, but it flew suddenly open, blinding him with daylight and the brief vision of a man whose breadth filled the doorway, the same man he had met the evening before.

Jenkin Lloyd Rhys was the son of Welsh immigrants who had come to the USA when he was eight. He had risen from humble beginnings in a mining community east of Pittsburgh to pre-eminence as a city engineer in New York. As with a lot of self-made men, fear did not come easily and he knew the power of reasonable words.

He demanded to know where he was and why.

The man said little. Just a place and a date. And all of a sudden everything became clear to Rhys.

'But the enquiry cleared me,' he began, 'and it cleared my people too. Why, we . . .'

He could not see the man's face or eyes, just his silhouetted bulk. It moved forward and blocked out the light behind and in that moment he was able to see the eyes of his abductor. They were colder by far than the cold store where he was being confined.

He felt himself suddenly picked up bodily and put over the man's shoulder like a side of beef. For a moment he thought he was being carried back into the darkest depths of the place from which it had taken him so long to find the way out.

He tried to shout but only a frightened whisper came out of his mouth.

Then the man grunted, turned right round, and portered him out of the warehouse as if he were no more than a sack of feathers, across some rail tracks before heaving him straight through the open doors of what he recognized at once as a refrigerated box car.

He tumbled helpless on the floor, his face and knees grinding across its rough surface. He tried to turn, perhaps to kick with his feet as some form of defence.

The ligature cut into his neck painfully, forcing him to gasp for breath.

He opened his eyes and saw that the man had got in the carriage with him. He bent down and pulled out a knife and put it to Rhys's throat.

He cut the ligature and for a short while Rhys breathed freely again.

It did not last long, for the man suddenly and effortlessly hoisted him up and carried him to the darkest end of the wagon, past hanging sides of beef, and finally heaved him upwards and placed his right armpit onto the upturned spike of an empty meat hook suspended from the ceiling.

'N . . . n . . . noo . . .'

Rhys felt a pain so terrible in his shoulder that he briefly lost consciousness.

When he came round he felt two great hands grabbing at his ankles and then a brief tug down drove the hook through sinew and flesh and straight into bone and Rhys knew a pain and fear beyond anything he had ever imagined.

He blacked out again, only to be brought back to his world of pain by the crash of the wagon doors being slammed shut and the knowledge, as his shocked eyes stared past his suspended feet to the floor below, that the wagon and the train of which it was part, were beginning to move.

Jenkin Lloyd Rhys, who sincerely believed he had never hurt anyone in his life, thought of those brief words the man had said to him and one word in particular. *Johnstown*. It was the name of a town in Pennsylvania.

'*Oh dear God*,' he sobbed, as he hung there in the lonely dark and the wagon began moving off with a creak and a groan.

12

In the Ward

Anna Zemeckis crouched down in a state of fear on the floor of the ward on Far Side. It was a long, damp, louse-infested room inhabited by eighty women in every stage of lunacy. They terrified her.

She had just learnt the hard way not to make eye contact with anyone. To do so was to invite trouble. Someone she had glanced at had hit her hard in the belly without further provocation and that had made her nauseous. It was a random act of violence of a kind she guessed would be the first of many if she did not find a way of getting out.

Some of the inmates were strong and vicious and lashed out if she went anywhere near; others looked weak but grew suddenly angry for no apparent reason, scratching and gouging others at random until one of the stronger ones beat them onto the floor.

Night wasn't so bad, because then the women were confined to their cribs with an orderly watching over them. But in the day they herded everybody into the day ward, which was no more than a vast wide corridor with locked doors either end and three chairs for eighty women. The chairs were taken by women who might have been orderlies or trusties – either way Anna did not like the look of them.

When the food came the women practically fought for it and when they had a share they hunched in corners guarding it as they gobbled it down or, their first hunger satisfied, secretly eking it out, salivating, sometimes playing with it.

Root vegetables became dough, the thick brown bread became mush, beans turned to paste, all of it squeezed between fingers, plastered onto mouths, spat out on the floor, trodden in and scooped up by someone else. Filthy food became an insane comfort in an insane place.

The first thing Anna learnt was to look where she put her feet. When fatigue had first forced her to squat down too, she chose the least filthy spot she could find. Some of the women were so demented that they did not bother to make the short journey to the water closets at one end of the ward and messed themselves where they squatted or sat.

A woman came at her suddenly, giggling. An old hag of a woman with only two teeth, her mouth opening wide into a wet gummy void when she silently laughed, which she now did. This woman tried to touch Anna, first her breasts and then her privates, cackling about friendship as she did so.

Then she began to touch herself obscenely and Anna had to look away. It was a terrible thought that this lunatic woman was the only one who tried to make contact with her.

Anna pushed her away again and again until, when she came once too often, and Anna saw others were watching and waiting to see what she would do, an instinct to survive took over and she hit the old lady hard.

After that no one touched Anna much or came near. She found herself crying for the terrible thing she had been forced to do. She couldn't ever remember hitting anyone in all her life and she guessed that something good in her was already beginning to die.

So she crouched down low now and looked at no one, praying that no one would notice her.

I've got to get out, she told herself.

It didn't help that she ached through and through – outside from the blow she had received, and inside because the swill they called food had made her sick.

Later, when she had recovered a little, she hauled herself to her feet and pushed her way to a barred window whose glass was all gone.

She stared out. She wanted to get a better sense of Dunning's layout. Her head was beginning to clear and she knew she would have to know something about the place if she was to get away from it

The window overlooked what she guessed was Main Building, the one in which the doctor had seen her. A thick black cloud of smoke billowed from the boiler house she had seen from the yard to the north of Far Side, right across from Main Building. She could just make out the chimney she had seen the day before.

Off to her right, beyond a complex of buildings, the grounds opened out in the far distance to parkland and trees and then open prairie. But before that were piles of coal and sacks of grain and other provisions along a railway track which men were portering into storage.

Nearer, at the far corner of Main Building, were the garbage cans and rubbish which Anna guessed were the source of the odor on the wind. She noted that the building had a basement. There were steps down to it here and there and along its length were the rounded arches of half-windows, murky, broken, filthy with soot.

Above all of this, incongruously, was the wide blue prairie sky whose drifts of white cloud made it seem brighter still. Anna leant her head against the bars and was about to cry for fear and loneliness when suddenly she heard a cheep-cheep overhead and a flock of plover shot into view, angled towards Main Building, and flew right over it, their wing beats a marvel of speed and synchronicity before they disappeared beyond the roofs and turrets of Dunning, as free in their own world as she was captive in hers.

Got to get out, thought Anna again, turning round with a look so determined and fierce that it was the other women who looked away from her now.

Finally she slumped back onto her haunches, glowering.

Her expression might be blank, but her mind was feverishly active. She was going to find a way out because she *had* to. There was something she had to do, outside in the real world, but . . . she frowned, clenching her fists, willing herself to recover more of her memory.

When she had first remembered her name during Dr Eels's examination of her the day before, it felt like she had regained her soul. But the relief had been short-lived.

Since then other memories had bombarded her but they were all

jumbled. All they seemed to be were moments too brief and disconnected to make much sense, but which nevertheless were unpleasant and
terrifying flashes of recall. The chief of these was that she was running
from someone, but she did not know who. But there was something that
troubled her even more: the feeling that whatever she was running from
was caused by the need to protect something, but she had no idea what.

A woman came and crouched down next to her and for the first
time that grim morning Anna dared to smile. It was the woman who
had the crib next to hers at night and she was all right.

She's all right, Anna told herself as the woman's shoulder touched
her own.

Anna closed her eyes and, feeling the touch of another human
being, a tear coursed down her cheek.

She could remember she had been running, running, running before
she fell into Bubbly Creek. She had seen something so shocking, so
frightening, that just to have seen it was a sin for which she could
never be forgiven and for which she would be better off dead. But it
still didn't make any sense. There had been hogs, and knives and men
in white . . . butchers, killing and blood.

That's when she ran and ran, but it was hard because she was
carrying something she had to protect.

'I can't remember what it was,' she whispered to the woman next
to her. 'But I've got to get out of here.'

The woman stared at her and put an arm around her, seeming
unable to say anything, but her eyes spoke loud and clear. 'Why?' she
said finally.

And a slow tear came from one of Anna's eyes.

'I've done something terrible,' she whispered.

What? her new friend seemed to say.

'I don't know,' said Anna and it was the not knowing that was her
agony. *'I can't remember.'*

At that moment, there was a sudden hush right through the ward,
as if the women there had heard what Anna had said.

But it was something else.

Maureen Riley had walked in and she looked mean.

'Where's that Bubbly Creek bitch?' she snarled, looking up and
down the ward.

There was a sharp intake of breath from Anna's new friend.

'Don't tell 'em a thing,' she whispered urgently, 'and don't sign nothing 'cos then they can't *do* nothin'.'

Anna stood up.

Her legs were shaking and her breath coming out in staccato bursts.

'You're wanted,' said Riley, '*now!*'

A few minutes later Anna found herself back in Main Building, sitting once more in the corridor outside Dr Eels's examination room. Two other women were there as well, one old and raving, the other silent and middle-aged. They made no eye contact with her at all.

Riley stopped to speak to an orderly standing nearby.

Anna's instinct was to run. She peeked out of a nearby window and then stood up to have a better look. She could see Dunning's gatehouse and what looked like the railway line, which ran away out of sight to the area where she had seen the piles of coal. The gatehouse itself was guarded by a man in uniform.

Men in pale jackets and dark pants, inmates she guessed, were working out front raking gravel. There was a line of leafless trees. It looked as if it was going to rain.

'Sit down!' called out Riley.

Anna did as she was told.

13

The *World*

Arriving in the foyer of the *World* offices on Park Row, Emily was struck by how busy with visitors, errand boys and newspaper men it was for a Sabbath. But that's what she wanted – an exciting life that had new things round every corner.

The name Charles Hadham carried Emily straight past the uniformed concierges at the main entrance. Then it was up in the elevator to the eleventh floor, led by a copy boy right through the hum and bustle of the editorial offices, of which there seemed a confusing number, to the inner sanctum of the city room. It was a vast, cavernous place, ablaze with lights even on this bright sunny Sunday, with row upon row of flat and rolltop desks crammed together in every available inch of space, most of them occupied by newsmen in rolled-up shirt-sleeves. And everywhere the constant din of typewriters and the click of telegraph machines. Over in the far corner near the door were a group of desks on a raised platform – the 'throne' of city editor Charles Hadham, a big, restless man who looked as though he might have been a quarterback in his college days. He sat smoking a pipe at a large untidy desk, surrounded by papers, files, two telephones, people and more people, most of them men.

Someone whispered in his ear that the 'girl reporter' was there and he looked up and waved her over.

71

'Haven't much time,' he said. 'JP said you'd make an appearance. Warned me in fact.'

He gave Emily a rueful grin, quickly dealt with a couple of things and then turned to her, somehow managing to make her feel she had his full attention.

She told him about the Zemeckis letter, what she had done already and what her plans were. He nodded now and then, asked a few questions, and then scribbled a note and handed it to her.

'Here's an order on the cashier for your expenses. Have you booked a hotel . . . ? Mack!' he called out, turning to a man of fifty or so in shirt sleeves, 'this lady is Miss Strauss and she's going to Chicago on a tryout for Mr Pulitzer, so you better be kind to her when she files her copy.'

Mack nodded, shook Emily's hand, but did not smile.

'God help you,' he said.

'Mack's one of our story editors and more than likely any story you file will cross his desk. He's Scottish and can only cope with very short sentences and no long words.'

Mack shrugged, looking as if he had heard it all before.

'So, *have* you a hotel? I guess you'll need one, the Fair being on.'

Emily nodded, eager to show she knew the ropes.

'Yes, at the Annex to the Auditorium Hotel. It's near—'

'I know where it is. Opposite the lake on Michigan Avenue. You were lucky to find a room, but it will cost with the Fair being on.'

'I should say! There wasn't a room to be had in the whole of Chicago, but I know the management. I've stayed there before and did them a favor or two. When I explained the urgency, they offered me one of the maid's rooms in the attic – it was that or nothing.'

He nodded approvingly.

'Listen Miss Strauss, don't set your hopes too high. Like as not you won't get a story. If you do it probably won't get used. If it does you won't get a job anyway. Nobody does first time. There's a shortage of them for men round here, let alone women. As for JP . . .'

'He changes his mind about people,' said Emily matter-of-factly.

'It has been known.'

'Then I'd better do well, hadn't I, Mr Hadham?'

'I guess you'd better!' he replied with a smile.

People came and went, putting sheets of copy on Hadham's desk, picking up others, speaking the whole time across the conversation they were having. He nodded here and said a word there, but somehow continued to engage with Emily.

'But you never know. You might find something. Might even be worth printing. If you do get something, file it via Mack not me. If it's any good he'll make sure I see it. If we use it you'll get space rates. You know what that means?'

'I get paid by the inch not the strength of the idea. Thanks. Just like the *Echo*.'

'Humph! If the idea's really good Mr Pulitzer might give you a bonus.'

'And I get a byline?'

He pursed his lips.

'Emily Strauss will do,' she said resolutely.

'Most women reporters use a pseudonym. Something poetic or alliterative, like Lucy Locket or Bessie Bramble.'

'I like my *own* name, Mr Hadham.'

'Well maybe, just maybe – if it's *really* good and we use it you may get a byline, but no promises,' he said mock-wearily. 'Now listen. You know Chicago already so you know it's a tough city. You're going there to find out if there's a cover-up over women disappearing. You're *not* trying to find anyone specific or solve a crime, least of all how this girl got herself mislaid months ago.'

'Less than two. She turned up dead last week.'

'Makes no difference . . . You're not there to find out how this particular girl ended up in the morgue or you might easily do the same yourself. Chicago's a dangerous city and corrupt as they come. You do *nothing* stupid. Just find out why they don't help people find their relatives; or if they *do* help people, why they're slow about it; or if they're *not* slow, why they're not faster. The Fair ends on the thirtieth of this month: that gives you a week by the time you get there. Our star reporter will be filing something in the *Sunday World* for the Fair's end on the twenty-ninth, but we'll still have the last day to cover on the thirtieth. That's your chance. But be sure to file your story by the night of the twenty-ninth. We don't *like* Chicago in this office. It stole the World's Fair from under New York's nose. Get us a good story, just to

73

tarnish things for a bit for Chicago, get us some dirt. Just try to make sure it's half-truthful dirt and something we can use ... '

He stopped, raised a hand and signaled someone over.

The man was in his mid-twenties, dark-haired and personable. He had a wide grin and white teeth.

'Benjamin B. Latham,' he said, shaking Emily's hand.

'Emily Strauss.'

They eyed each other and liked what they saw.

'Miss Strauss is going to Chicago for a tryout, courtesy Mr Pulitzer,' said Hadham. 'The disappearing women cover-up.'

'Didn't know there was one.'

'There's one now and Miss Strauss is going to nail it or you won't be seeing her again.'

'So maybe she'll disappear too? Sad; and possibly unpleasant,' he added coolly, in a nice, clean-cut New England accent.

Emily smiled.

His grin widened.

'One of our readers lost his daughter there,' Emily explained. 'Claims there's been a lot of disappearances during the Fair and Chicago City Hall's been covering them up.'

'Course it would. Bad publicity. Doesn't want visitors to stop coming. But proving it could be difficult.'

'We'll see,' said Emily.

'And *you're* going to help her,' said Hadham to Ben Latham before turning back to Emily.

'This gentleman is an illustrator,' he explained.

'News illustrator *and* photographer,' said Ben, handing her a card.

'Yes, well,' said Hadham doubtfully, 'be that as it may ... I'm sending Mr Latham out to Chicago in a few days' time, after he's done a couple of things here, to cover the closing ceremony of the Fair. He can help illustrate your story too if you find something worthwhile. Meantime he can check things out for you this end if you need it. By telegraph. Be sure to check in with him daily, Miss Strauss.'

'My pleasure,' said Ben cheerfully.

'And you can start by showing her where to get her money.'

Ben raised his eyebrows and looked impressed.

'She gets money *before* she files?'

74

'She does.'

Charles Hadham suddenly looked tired, or maybe he was just bored. Emily knew it was time to go. But he had some final advice. 'Don't antagonize anybody, Miss Strauss. Stay sweet and keep them sweet. Don't go anywhere unsafe. Do *not* try to risk your life trying to find out why this girl ran away or was abducted, or whatever the hell happened to her, because it will be something that's not safe to know. We've got male reporters who do those kinds of stories. *Understand?'*

Emily nodded. She took a final look around the office and its staff, and as she did so she felt its buzz and with it a palpable excitement. She wanted to come back. More than anything she wanted to work here. A desk on the eleventh floor of the *World* building would be a dream come true.

'Follow me,' said Ben Latham, 'and I'll introduce you to the meanest man you'll ever meet – our cashier. I want to watch him suffer the pain of giving a woman money.'

Emily got her money without difficulty or pain, much to Ben's surprise.

'I have a nice smile,' she explained.

'I doubt it was the smile that impressed JP though,' said Ben. 'It was that stunt you pulled over at Bar Harbor.'

Emily flushed.

'You know about that?'

'Whole office knows about it.'

Emily grinned, liking the admiration in his voice.

'You really want a job on the *World*, don't you?' he said after a pause.

'I do,' said Emily, 'and I intend to get one.'

'It's not a nice place,' said Ben matter-of-factly. 'The work's exhausting, badly paid and often unpleasant. The *World* eats people alive. As for the folk here, they're all tough as hell and most of them are men and most of *them* think women are good for only one thing.'

'And you, Mr Latham, what do you think women are good for?'

'Lots of things,' he said easily, without any suggestiveness at all. 'I guess I take women as I take people – as I find them. If they play fair by me I play fair by them. If they don't . . . well then, I make sure they count for nothing in my life, professionally and personally. That's about the size of it.'

He spoke slowly and clearly. His voice had about it the feel of solid gold.

'And another thing, if we're going to be working together you can drop the formality: call me Ben.'

Emily looked at him appraisingly.

'Tell me, Ben: if working on a newspaper's so bad, for men as well as women, what are *you* doing here?'

'Me? I worked at Eastman Kodak over in Rochester before this, learning the business of photography. But I don't want a life working in a laboratory or on the road in sales. Cameras are for taking pictures, and the more interesting they are and the more difficult the pictures are to get, the more I like it.'

'But I thought Mr Hadham said you were an illustrator?'

'Sure, by training. It's how I got my job on the *World*. I carry my sketchbook with me everywhere,' he added, patting his jacket pocket, 'but I reckon photography is the coming thing for newspapers – and there's another thing . . .'

He hesitated and stopped talking.

'What?' said Emily.

'You get to meet pretty girls,' he said shamelessly. 'Girls'll do a lot to have their picture taken.'

'I'm not that kind of girl, Mr Latham, and right until you said that I took you for a clean-living, nice kind of gentleman but now . . .'

He grinned, boyishly.

'I am really,' he said. 'That was just talk. And you?'

'Me?' she said. 'I guess I'm all talk too. But I want to give this my best shot, just like you do.'

Her face went more serious.

'What do I have to do to get to work for Mr Hadham in the city room?' she said impulsively.

'That's easy. Ignore what he said and find out what happened to the girl, why she ran away,' he said, echoing the words of Arthur Butes.

Then he got serious too.

'But if I were you I wouldn't even try. Staying alive is more important than getting a job on the *World*. Chicago's not a safe place for lone girl reporters.'

He paused and a moment's worry crossed his face.

'But whatever else you do, don't forget that deadline. *Whatever you do*, the story's stone-cold dead if you don't get it in for the October 30th edition when the Fair ends. No story from Chicago, however good, will take the gloss off the closing ceremony for the Fair once it's over and done with. So whatever you file, it'd better be on time. But if Hadham doesn't change his mind, I'll be in Chicago with you by then so—'

'Whether you're there or not, I'll file in time,' said Emily cutting him short.

He grinned good-naturedly once more and then impulsively stretched out his hand and shook hers.

'Welcome to the *World*,' he said.

14

Cadavers

'Dr Eels! I'm sorry . . . the women are waiting.'

'They can wait a bit longer,' Morgan Eels replied coldly, without looking up from the cadaver before him. It was – or had been – a man, thin as a rail, about fifty. Its face was waxy, gray and gaunt, its scalp shaved.

'How many women are left to examine now?' he asked without looking up.

'Four, sir,' said the orderly who had just arrived.

'Who are they?' murmured Eels to Mould, his assistant standing next to him.

'There's the Nevitt woman on whom you'll be doing a new procedure tomorrow. Then there's the Bubbly Creek woman and two more, all suitable for the clinical trial this coming Friday.'

'Excellent,' said Eels as he sighed and straightened up. He arched his back into a stretch. He and Mould were both gowned up in white, from head to toe, but Eels wore nothing on his head.

Behind them, on a trolley, was another cadaver. It was female, and it too had a scalp that had been shaved, this time only partially: the top right side had been partially cut and folded back with the skull, exposing the brain, into which an instrument had been stuck, up to its thin steel handle.

The area they were working in was little more than a corridor converted into a pathological laboratory. Its walls were peeling, its high ceiling cobwebbed, its single window filthy. There were two gas lights and an electric light that flickered on and off.

'I'm sorry Dr Eels, it's Riley', said the orderly, interrupting again. 'She doesn't like being kept waiting.'

Eels let out a grunt of exasperation and frowned.

'So I've noticed. The tail most certainly wags the dog in this establishment! *That* will have to change.'

He straightened up again.

'Inform her I shall be there to examine the patients at quarter past the hour. Have the papers ready.'

'Yes, Dr Eels.'

Eels walked round to the cadaver's head and examined its right temple.

'Getting these cadavers ready for tomorrow's presentation won't take long I think. Swing it round a little more, please. It's important we get everything just right. There'll be important people in the audience, members of the Old America Association, and Mr Hartz and I are confident that if we pitch things right then we'll raise a lot of money and support.'

Another orderly by the trolley stepped forward, applied pressure to the side of the slab and reorientated it.

'Hold it still.'

Mould stepped forward. He placed his hands on the dead man's head.

'More to the right,' breathed Eels, positioning the drill and then widening his legs to brace himself.

'Yes, that will do.'

He handed the drill to Mould who gave him a mallet and a thin chisel in its place.

Eels applied the chisel at right angles near to the cadaver's temple, at an intersection of two lines drawn on the scalp with the blue-purple dye of gentian violet, and readied the mallet.

'Now . . . we make an impression . . . so!'

He tapped the chisel through the skin and dura to the bone.

'And . . . *so!*'

He tapped again, hard. There was a slight, muffled, *thunk!* as the

chisel sank in. He pulled it out at once and gave it and the mallet to
the orderly.

'That will stop the drill from wandering,' he said to no one in particular. Then, to Mould he growled, 'Hold still if you please.'

Mould steadied himself.

Eels took up the drill once more, repositioned his feet, and set the
bit to the incision made with the chisel, pushing firmly into the skin
and on to the bone. He began to drive the bit into the skull.

Twenty-five minutes later, having removed his white robe and put his
collar and cravat back on, Morgan Eels had transformed himself from
surgeon back to alienist and returned to his examination room on the
floor above the laboratory.

He had three women to see and he did so briskly. Surgery, even
exploratory dissection of a cadaver, always put him into a good, assertive
mood and eager to get on.

The first two women were straightforward. One was an imbecile
who had been at Dunning for many years and, so far as anyone knew,
had no relatives or other parties interested in her well-being. Riley
confirmed her identity, which both knew anyway, and Eels signed the
necessary papers and prepared the record.

He thought about the second. She was a younger woman of twenty,
a tiresome hysteric, inclined to a whole range of nervous symptoms
including crying spells, indecisiveness, suspiciousness, meticulosity of
a particularly irritating sort (she was inclined in her more lucid phases
to tidy up other people's clothes and shoes), negativism, obsessive talking
and restlessness. He had never known a patient whose fingers twined
and intertwined so much as she talked. This was Mary Nevitt, whom
he had seen two days before.

She would undoubtedly benefit from the procedures he proposed
to carry out on her, as would society from her cure. But Mary did not
want to agree to anything and was a most reluctant patient.

Fortunately for Dr Eels, Mary had no known next of kin, they
having long-since abandoned her. In their absence, Mary was prevailed
upon to sign the forms herself. But she didn't trust Eels and his smooth
words, despite all his assurances that tomorrow's procedure 'will most
probably benefit you considerably.'

'What will you do, doctor? Will you pull my brains out?' she had asked, her fingers uncontrollably grabbing at and rucking up her shift.

'Nothing of the sort,' said Eels with a smile. 'It is a very simple and safe procedure, Miss Nevitt, and you will hardly feel a thing.'

'They said . . . I mean . . . What exactly will you do?'

'The procedure is quite straightforward. It will get very quickly to the seat of your problem and has every chance of curing it once and for all. If you wish me to explain it in layman's language then . . .'

Eels sighed at this point, looked at his pocket watch and managed to seem irritated.

'I don't want you to cut my brain,' muttered Mary, her hands writhing more than ever.

'The only outward sign that we have operated on you will be a loss of hair because we will have to shave a small area of your scalp. But it will grow back, it really will! Now.'

He stood up and nodded at Riley.

'Tomorrow, Miss Nevitt, tomorrow . . . And now Mrs Riley will see you safely back to your ward.'

Mary Nevitt shrunk back as Riley grabbed her arm and marched her out of the room

Eels gazed after her, bored but strangely reassured. He believed he was beginning to build trust with these patients, even though they tried his patience when they asked questions whose answers they could not possibly understand. No matter: once he had perfected his general and universal surgical cure for certain types of insanity, his name would be made, and that of Cook County Insane Asylum too.

'Next!' rapped out Eels as he sat back down in his chair.

15

Questions

'The question is . . . ?' the man murmured to himself, not finishing the sentence.

He was stolid, thickset, and heavily mustachioed and he looked no different from a dozen other prosperous market traders who frequented Sol Bann's saloon at the northwest corner of State and Randolph.

He had spent most of the day contemplating what looked like paper-work: an order book, maybe; a money account perhaps. Occasionally he wrote something in it, but never much.

He had a drink in front of him – his fifth that day – and a plate of food from the free lunch counter, and sat by the window looking out, ignoring everyone inside.

But one person in the saloon was not ignoring him and that was the proprietor, Sol Bann himself. He had an extra five dollars in his pocket and clear instructions to 'leave me be' and that's precisely what he'd been doing since just after nine that morning when the man had first arrived.

Sol, who survived by being a good judge of character could not work this one out at all, except he didn't look like a Chicago man. Maybe he was a Milwaukee fruit-man off a freight ship who had done his business early in South Water Street Market and was whiling away the hours waiting for his passage home.

Sol could have suggested better things to do, starting with the nice little whorehouse at the back of his place.

... And another five when I leave if you make sure no one disturbs me, the man had said, and Sol was not going to say no to that. *Just keep my glass filled – with water. And send over a plate of food every so often.*

Sol didn't argue with that either. He wiped a glass and shook his head. No, he wasn't from Milwaukee, looked too damned intelligent.

Whatever the man's game, and it looked suspicious, five dollars for water is five dollars for nothing and the food was free anyway.

All he had done all day apart from pretending to note things down in his little book was to stare out of the window at the Masonic Temple, but then that was nothing new. *Everybody* stared at the tallest building in Chicago. But all *day?*

Sol did not like mysteries, but all he could do was sigh, serve another customer and keep on wondering.

'The question is,' murmured the man again, looking at his list and shaking his head, 'have I missed him?'

But he was certain he hadn't.

From this vantage point the man had a perfect view of the main entrance into the Masonic Temple. There wasn't a person going in or coming out he didn't see.

His list, which had been prepared the night before, had fourteen names on it. Eleven had two ticks against them, each tick having a time set against it – when they went in and when they went out.

Two had one tick against them, both earlier that day, and they hadn't yet come out.

The man glanced at his pocket watch and carried on watching.

One name had no tick at all and that had troubled him for hours.

Then, suddenly, he was on the alert.

The two men on his list who had not yet emerged were finally coming back out. He watched carefully, scanning the people around them to see if the man who had not showed at all was with them. But no. They got into two separate cabs and went on their way.

The man added a tick against the name of Paul Hartz, vice president of the Old America Association, and the time: four-fourteen.

Then he did the same against the man who had emerged with him.

He sat for a moment more, contemplating the name at the top of the list, the one without any ticks at all.

It read, *Jenkin Lloyd Rhys*.

'The question is,' the man asked himself, his eyes now serious, 'where the hell has he disappeared to?'

He glanced around the saloon and caught the bartender's eye. Sol came over and took a second five dollars.

'So tell me,' said Sol affably, 'what's your game?'

It was said with the practiced ease of a man who had been among working men all his life and knew which would take offense and which wouldn't. This one would not.

'Fruit,' said the man standing up, 'I'm a fruit-man from Milwaukee. Didn't I say? I gotta boat to catch. Nice doin' business.'

'What kind of fruit?' said Sol with a grin, standing to one side. The man was bigger than he had realized earlier and looked like the kind of fellow you'd be a fool to cross. Still, he didn't look put out by the question. Maybe he'd come by and do business again. Sol liked to build an understanding with his customers.

'What kind? The watery kind,' said the man.

'See ya!' said Sol.

'Maybe,' said the man with a nod and a smile before he walked outside and disappeared into the crowd, southward along the sidewalk on State.

16

Caught Out

A few minutes later and eleven miles away, the woman from Bubbly Creek entered the doctor's examination room, Riley's lumbering presence just behind her.

One glance told Eels the woman had deteriorated since yesterday and might well be reaching a critical point. She presented symptoms of extreme nervousness, exhaustion and obvious emotional instability.

He judged that for her the procedure was a matter of urgency.

The matter should have been straightforward. She was clearly hysterical, plainly she needed treatment and had expressed the desire for it, but . . .

Instinct told Eels this woman would not be easy. She had, he guessed, the peasant intelligence that he had often found in Eastern Europeans. Being uneducated and generally lax in their habits, this unfortunately expressed itself in stubbornness and an unwillingness to accept authority.

A great deal of time was being lost in Chicago, as in New York, in pandering to wantons such as these, and today Dr Eels had no patience for it.

'Do you know your name?'

She hesitated, and immediately he knew she did, just as he had suspected she had the day before. That annoyed him. *He had no time for this.*

He eyed her coldly.

Since the woman had come to Dunning as a ward of Cook County Insane Court, and no relatives were known, Eels did not need her full and proper name for his purposes. 'Jane Doe' would do.

Nor did he need any signature to proceed with her treatment, apart from his own as medical superintendent in waiting. But . . . it rankled that she was deliberately withholding her surname when he was sure she knew it.

He relaxed, suddenly beginning to enjoy himself. He eyed the forms on his desk but did not touch them. He didn't need her name, but . . . it would be satisfying to see if he could trick it out of her.

He smiled: 'This need not take long. A few more questions so that these forms are complete. I'll explain what we are going to do.' He leaned forward reassuringly and added, 'That's all that's needed.'

'What is wrong with me, doctor?'

She made herself sound meek and pathetic, but her head was full of thoughts of escape.

Eels shrugged dismissively.

'It has many names but I think the one you will best understand is hysteria. It is common enough in one of your sex and age who may have suffered trauma of some kind. It is curable. I would be grateful if you could try to answer the following questions as fast as possible. There are no correct answers; rather it will help me to ascertain your level of intelligence, for that is a factor too.'

He paused.

She stared at him uneasily. She felt frail and sick. Yesterday he had seemed merely unpleasant. Now he seemed positively evil, his smile reptilian.

'First, colors. Respond as quickly as possible. Simply give the color that comes into your head.'

She nodded, puzzled.

'*Tree* . . . ?'

'Green.'

'*Sky* . . . ?'

'Blue.'
'*Snake* . . . ?'
'Black.'
'*Yolk* . . . ?'
'Yellow.'
'Excellent. Now let's try city and state names.'
'*New* . . . ?'
'York.'
'*New* . . . ?'
'Jersey.'
'*West* . . . ?'
'Virginia.'
'*North* . . . ?'
'America.'
'*Great* . . . ?'
'Britain.'

The pace was getting faster and their eyes locked onto each other, with Eels leaning forward assertively as he fired words at her. Anna was suddenly enjoying the harmless game, taking pleasure in using her mind, forgetting her dislike of him in the rush and challenge of the words.

Sweat showed on his pale yellow brow.

The sky outside changed from blue to gray and rain beat suddenly, angrily, against the windows behind him.

'Or just words that go together,' he said suddenly.

'*Table* . . . ?'

'Leg.'

'*Pork* . . . ?'

'Pie.'

'*You are?*'

'Anna.'

She gasped at the fact she had said it.

Eels relaxed and smiled again.

'Well, done, Anna,' he said. 'You see there really is nothing to be afraid of!'

I must not say my surname, I must not . . .

She had the uneasy feeling that he knew something she didn't, something important.

'*President* . . . ?'

'Lincoln.'

'*Doctor* . . . ?'

'Eels.'

He smiled and she smiled too. His shining spectacles were pools of light in which she was drowning.

'Now, Anna, just repeat the number that follows the one I say. 'One . . . ?'

'*Two.*'

'Forty-two.'

'*Forty-three.*'

'One hundred.'

'*. . . and one.*'

'Excellent. Now let us do it for speed. Beginning simply, with numbers. One . . .'

'*Two!*'

'Three.'

'*Four!*'

'Five.'

'*Six!*'

He smiled and nodded approvingly, glad to see her relax. He was almost there.

'Seven.'

'*Eight!*'

'Nine.'

'*Ten!*'

'Anna!'

'*Zemeckis.*'

It came out before she could stop herself and she stared at him in horror.

Eels smiled with pleasure and looked smug. It was really no more than a party trick.

'I didn't mean . . .' she began. 'I didn't want . . .'

'That is perfectly normal, perfectly. I am here to help you, to find a cure. You are not well, Miss Zemeckis, not well at all and—'

'I don't *feel* well, doctor. I feel sick. The food's dreadful and . . . and . . .'

His glasses shone brightly, dazzling her, and the rain on the window now shone with the sun that had come out again.

Dr Eels reached smoothly for the form he wanted her to sign. He had her now, it was just a question of timing.

'You will need to sign . . .' he began quietly.

He watched her intently, a snake watching its prey. She tensed up and immediately he went in for the kill.

'You know, do you not, that you are with child?'

Her eyes widened and her mouth dropped open.

'Pardon me?'

'You are *pregnant*, Miss Zemeckis. My examination yesterday confirmed that your constant nausea is a common symptom.'

He was right, she had not known. Or if she had it was part of her memory loss, possibly its cause.

'I . . .'

The room whirled in Anna's head and the lights seemed to whirl as well. She began hyperventilating.

'I can help you – with the baby, and with your mental distress,' said Eels, pushing the form forward to the front of his desk and reaching for a steel pen which he dipped into ink.

'You can write your signature? Yes . . . yes? Just sign, and then I will be able to help you.'

She took up the pen in a daze of shock and bewilderment.

'You . . . I . . . you can help?' she whispered.

'Of course,' he said reassuringly.

Maybe it was the thin, mean mouth; maybe the unpleasant way his spectacles caught the light.

Maybe it was animal instinct.

Anna put down the pen abruptly.

'No. I won't,' she shouted. For now she understood. It was the child in her womb that she had been trying protect without realizing it. It was the child that had sent her running from the men that night into the blackness and oblivion of Bubbly Creek; the child that, in the end, was giving her the will to survive.

Eels visibly contained his anger.

He pulled the form back, attached it with the others on his clipboard and put it neatly to one side.

'Of course,' he breathed, his eyes cold again, 'we don't actually *need* your signature, Miss Zemeckis. But I prefer my patients to be compliant – it helps their recovery, you see. I shall recommend the treatment anyway . . .'

He turned away.

'What will you do to me?'

He stared at her.

'There will be some small discomfort but . . .'

She stared at him, still in shock but beginning to make sense at last of the physical and mental confusion she had been suffering.

I am with child and that is why I . . .

'I do not want to lose my baby,' she said simply.

'Aah,' he shrugged. 'But if I am to make you well again, Miss Zemeckis, then we must deal with this matter before your surgical procedure next week.'

'No! I do not want that,' said Anna, her voice rising as she stood up.

'There is nothing to be afraid of, Miss Zemeckis,' he said, also standing up. 'I promise you, all will be well. Mrs Riley, take Miss Zemeckis back to the ward. And be sure to take good care of her until Thursday . . .'

'I don't want you to . . .'

Riley had Anna in an iron grip.

'See she is close-watched,' snapped Eels as Anna continued to protest.

'They don't escape from *my* wards, Dr Eels,' said Riley as she manhandled Anna out of the room.

'I don't want . . .' shouted Anna, hysterical now.

'Take her away,' snarled Eels.

In the corridor outside, Riley swung Anna round and slapped her face, hard. Then she shoved her harder still against the wall.

'You wanna fight?' she said, her fist rising.

Anna stared at her, breathing heavily, sobs breaking in her throat.

Earlier that day she had hit an old lady and been appalled that she had done so.

Now she felt a worse emotion still.

Staring at Riley with her filthy teeth and raised fist, her cropped hair and man-arms, Anna felt hatred and an absolute certainty. If she had to, if it was what she must do to save the life of the child inside her, she would kill this woman and anyone else who got in her way, *kill* them.

Anna bent her head and wept to think such evil thoughts. But she knew the tears would not wash away her sense of purpose.

She let Riley lead her away without a further struggle: along the wide corridor that overlooked the gatehouse, down a series of stairs to the back of the building, out through a side door to the wide open space between Main Building and Far Side.

By the time she was back in the day ward, the women were being sent to their cribs for the night even though it was not yet six. It was just one of the many ways Dunning's staff under Riley's regime had learnt to cheat the system: get the patients into bed early and fewer staff were needed, meaning half could slide off home early before the night staff came on duty, but still get paid for the hours they were meant to be there.

When she reached her own crib, Anna saw that Mary was already in her own and fast asleep.

Anna touched her shoulder but she did not wake up.

But deep in the night she was woken by something that might have been a scream.

It could have been any one of the dozens of women in the ward. She looked across at Mary and saw, in the gloom of the night, that she was on her back, her hands with their twisted fingers by her side, her eyes wide open.

Anna stared and realized immediately that something was different. The fingers were still now, utterly still, as if the life had fled from them.

'Mary?' she whispered, moving quietly to her side and placing a hand on her arm.

'Are you all right?' whispered Anna.

She leaned near to look into Mary's eyes, which had always been so frightened yet sometimes so gentle.

'*Snip-snip, cut-cut,*' Mary muttered, and then in a voice that was almost a whisper, '*don't . . . let him. Don't let him cut your brain.*'

It took a while in the dim light to see the expression on Mary's face, but when she finally did it hit Anna with the force of a violent blow.

The only thing in those beautiful eyes now was anger, and unutterable hatred.

Anna crept back into her crib and lay wide awake. She knew what she was, she knew it now.

She was a cornered animal with young to protect, and she had never felt so powerfully alive. Her mind might be confused, her memory a ragbag of flashing lights, of Bubbly Creek, of men, of all sorts of things she did not want to think about. But she was very, very clear about one thing – getting out.

What day is it? she asked herself.

Sunday. *When must I see the doctor again?*

Soon. Too soon.

'We have to get away from here,' Anna Zemeckis said aloud, and this time she was speaking to her unborn child.

DAY FIVE

Monday October 23, 1893

17

On the Train

The following morning, Monday October 23, Emily Strauss boarded the Exposition Express at Jersey City for the twenty-six-hour journey to Chicago.

The first time she had made the journey, back in September for the *Echo*, she had been overexcited, overdressed and had taken far too much luggage. But for a natural ability to fall asleep when she felt like it, she would have arrived totally exhausted and taken days to recover.

This time she traveled light, dressed sensibly and kept calm. She also invested some of her funds in a comfortable sleeping berth to which she could retire when the public compartment became too crowded, hot and noisy, packed as it was with travelers eager to take a final opportunity of visiting the World's Fair before it closed the following week.

But for the time being Emily was enjoying herself. A Bavarian with an accordion was entertaining his family and everyone else with songs Emily herself had known from childhood; while two delightful rotund middle-aged sisters of Italian origin regularly produced little cakes and delicacies from a hamper which they distributed to all and sundry.

The spirit was festive, and everyone mixed in with everyone else along the corridors, except for a group of Lutherans in one compartment who, not liking the sight of wine and beer flowing quite so freely, pretended to be asleep.

They stopped at only major stations on the way north and west, but even so there were constant delays which added to the general sense of excitement, expectation and the party atmosphere.

A whole cross-section of Americans seemed to be on the train, from children to the old, traveling salesmen to families on vacation, from matrons to mashers, from newlyweds on honeymoon to single men and women, whose eyes were on each other as much as the passing landscape.

After the initial excitement of departure, Emily went through Anna Zemeckis's somewhat girlish letters to her father, her own notes, and some clippings which, as an afterthought, Ben Latham had sent to her from the *World*.

She had decided that she would initially cover the same ground as Janis Zemeckis had done, pretending, if need be, that Anna was her sister. But time being short she wanted to arrive up and running, so before she left that morning she had sent three telegraphs to contacts she had made during her previous stay.

The first and most important was to Fay Bancroft in the Woman's Building at the World's Fair, whom she knew to be one of the most respected organizers working under the redoubtable Mrs Potter Palmer, doyenne not only of the Fair but of Chicago society as a whole.

Fay had become a close and valued ally to Emily on her previous trip, and it was only to her that Emily gave any intimation that she was coming back to work on a new story for a more important paper. She did not say what the story was, but asked Fay to get her an introduction to one or two people who might have better contacts than she had been able to establish.

Fay had telegraphed straight back telling Emily to come to the Fair the day she arrived so they could talk over lunch.

The other telegraphs were sent to Mrs Markulis, Anna's aunt, and to Julia Lathrop, a contact at Hull House, the settlement house on the West Side. Emily was confident that Miss Lathrop could give her some useful leads because the ladies at that institution had unparalleled access to all levels of Chicagoan society. She doubted anyone at City

Hall would admit publicly to any problem about women going missing – or any other problem come to that, since they were all so busy promoting Chicago as the greatest city in America.

She read, she chatted, she stared out of the window at the passing landscape, barely able to conceal her excitement; but when the train encountered a series of slow-downs and halts in the early afternoon, Emily retired to her berth for a rest and fell at once into the contented sleep of someone who has worked hard to get where they are going and deserves some rest before the real job begins.

She awoke suddenly to find the train at a standstill, a rainstorm raging outside.

'Where are we?' she asked a passing guard in the corridor outside.

'Bald Eagle Mountain, miss. Train always stops here, especially when it's rough outside. Should be in Altoona by nine.'

The train moved forward, jolted, swayed and then stopped again.

'Often like this in these parts,' added the guard philosophically. 'Mountains weren't made for passenger trains. Mind, what we lose on this section we generally make back after Pittsburgh.'

Emily went back to her berth and glanced at her pocket watch. It was a few minutes before six and for no reason she could think of, her mood had changed to one of deep unease.

Wind and rain suddenly lashed the carriage window so hard that for a moment she fancied it was trying to lash her too.

18

Cures and Remedies

At six that same evening, Dr Morgan Eels was pacing nervously up and down the back of the hall in which he was about to give his lecture. He had bowed to the greater experience of Paul Hartz in fund-raising and how to make this important presentation to his fellow members of the Old America Association.

'Give 'em a show,' was the advice. 'Say that the problem's reached dangerous proportions, offer a solution they can afford, make them understand that their help will bring honor to themselves and Chicago and, trust me, Eels, they'll open their pocketbooks.'

Hartz, now in his sixties but still formidable and used to having his own way in everything, liked to be on time. He told Eels to stay at the back until he was called forward and then strode down the aisle to ready the audience.

He was a master of smooth talk and salesmanship and began his introduction right on the hour.

'Ladies and gentlemen,' he began, 'honored guests, Dr Brown and fellow members of the Old America Association . . . I have had the pleasure of introducing presidents, as well as foreign dignitaries, in some of the most prestigious and impressive venues in this great city of ours; I have been privileged to give welcome to some of the great captains of industry, to military men and to extraordinary women of the arts and social welfare; but never, not once, have I felt as excited as I do this evening as I introduce to you one of the rising young men of American medicine.

'The walls of this miserable hall may be damp, the seating poor, the lighting wholly inadequate, our funds deplorably low, but this man of brilliant vision and unassailable purpose from the East Coast has cast his lot in with ours because he believes in our cause!'

The audience clapped and some peered round to the back of the hall.

'Dr Morgan Eels, late of the Danbury Asylum in Western Connecticut, which his extraordinary work has made famous, believes as we do that the menace of uncontrolled immigration has resulted in the tragedy – moral, economic and spiritual – of this tidal wave of the incurably insane; and the danger – real, terrible and so far unabated – that good American blood is being infected by something vicious, pernicious and diseased.'

The audience applauded to show their support for this idea.

'But he also believes, and has the scientific knowledge to prove it, that there are solutions. But you've come here tonight to hear what those solutions may be from a younger man, and not to be evangelized by this older one! Please, now ... give Dr Morgan Eels a warm Chicagoan welcome!'

They did, and by the time Eels had reached Paul Hartz, shaken his hand and been shown the lectern, he found himself being given a standing ovation before he had even begun.

As he opened his mouth to speak, the words that Hartz had whispered to him earlier echoed in his mind: *Give 'em a show!* His heart thumped so hard he thought his chest would burst.

He opened his mouth to speak but it was dry. He looked at his notes but they swam before his eyes. The clapping died, and for a moment or two all he could hear was a terrible silence. Then, sensing that if he could only get this right his life might change now forever, Dr Morgan Eels found himself. He looked at the audience and discovered, to his astonishment, that he felt in utter control of it.

Eels coolly helped himself to a drink as Hartz had done, pushed his notes to one side and stepped right out past the lectern.

He had no need of the careful opener he had prepared, for, with the confidence of someone who knows his material inside out, Eels knew he had the measure of his audience and what he was going to say.

He stood very still, the gaslight slanting across his pale face, his arms and hands by his side, his legs together – a strangely compelling figure.

Finally he began, in a low, somber voice, like someone who has studied the world's ills and come to his conclusions only after much thought. He did not waste time getting to the point.

'America is in grave, grave danger,' he declared. 'Weakness and vice are everywhere about us, crime is outrageously rampant and the remedial measures which this noble society has devised over the years in a spirit of philanthropy, generosity of heart and democracy have proved themselves inadequate for its protection.'

He paused and then repeated, with sudden anger, '*Utterly* inadequate.'

He barked this out so vehemently that many in the audience sat up straight.

'My friends and colleagues,' he continued, stepping even further forward, 'we have allowed the idiot, the imbecile, the epileptic, the habitual drunkard, the murderer and the harlot to run riot among us. Criminals who might be deemed incorrigible by any sensible judge are set free by those of liberal inclination to commit heinous crimes again; imbeciles, who, were they denizens of the animal kingdom would long since have been extirpated by natural selection, are allowed to be a burden on the state.'

He paused and stared, his face suffused with anger.

'A burden! To our cities and the state! To *their* own misery and at *our* great expense.'

He turned and looked behind him.

'*Curtain!*' he commanded.

At this the curtains behind Eels suddenly opened to reveal a startling scene, but one kept for the moment in semidarkness: two slabs on which were the indistinct figures of two cadavers covered in sheets, alongside which stood a nurse in uniform; and Mr Mould, in his white gown, holding another gown and mask at the ready, obviously intended for Eels.

These living figures stood unnaturally still, as Eels had commanded them to, and were a counterpoint to the two corpses, the outlines of whose heads, shoulders, chests and lower extremities beneath their coverings were lit for now only by flickering gaslight. They were the same cadavers Eels and Mould had prepared the day before.

The audience had barely adjusted its eyes to this strange tableau before the orderly threw a switch; a bright electric light, directly over one of the cadavers, illuminated it. A moment's further pause and then Mould expertly pulled away its covering.

The audience gasped.

What was revealed was the gray corpse of a man, completely naked but for some muslin placed over his genitalia and a bandage over his skull.

Eels went straight to the cadaver's far side and stood under the bright light, where he allowed himself to be robed up ritualistically by Mould, like a medieval knight being dressed in armor by his squire before a battle.

'This evening I wish to say something about cures and remedies,' continued Eels. 'The insane fall into two categories – the chronically melancholic and what I term the psychoschismatic, those whose mental state is so disrupted that they are unable to connect with reality.

'Alienists would have us believe that, because the symptoms presented by these conditions and their variants are so different, the causes are different too. So different that there is no hope of finding a single cure. It is not for me to suggest that this attitude keeps alienists in business, since I am myself a trained alienist!'

The audience appreciated this and laughed with him.

'But . . . I am also a trained surgeon and neurologist and it is in that capacity that I speak tonight.

'Neurologists such as I, who believe in real science, real facts and proper investigation, have come increasingly to the opinion that a single, physical cause lies at the root of all these mental conditions. Great honor, *international* honor, will come to the institution that succeeds in lending its name to a cure for insanity, and it is my hope, ladies and gentlemen, that before the World's Fair is over we shall announce that a program of clinical investigation has already started here at Dunning to find that cure! But we need to secure the funds to see that research through.

'Let me explain how this may be achieved, starting with this male specimen first,' continued Eels, placing his hand on the head of the cadaver and eyeing it with what seemed like contempt.

'In life this case was, regrettably, typical of many. A Bohemian, uneducated and of low intelligence, probably the product of perverted in-breeding, he arrived in this city in 1888. In a short space of time he proved himself deviant and vicious and committed various acts of robbery and violence on several upright citizens, resulting in the death of one of them.

'However, in its wisdom the court at the detention hospital declared him insane and committed him to the care of this institution, where he continued to cause such difficulty that his delusional behavior, which if resisted provoked only violence, had to be controlled by physical restraint as well as opiates.

'Some among us might think it would have been best if this man had never been allowed to immigrate into this great and too-generous land by stricter laws than we presently have. For once domiciled here, he became nothing but a danger to his fellow man and a drain on our resources.'

He paused for a moment and then added magisterially, 'In death, however, he can finally serve a useful purpose.'

With that Eels turned the cadaver's head sideways so that its half-open eyes seemed to stare at the audience.

'It has been known for several decades that there is a direct connection between the neocortex, which is that large upper and frontal part of our brain that distinguishes us from other mammals, and our behaviour and emotions. Put another way, we know that changes to certain parts of the lobes of the brain affect how we think and feel and what we do . . .

'We have learnt a great deal in recent years about the more detailed anatomy of the brain and in particular which parts affect which emotions and senses.'

With that, Eels undid the bandage around the cadaver's head and revealed what at first appeared to be no more than scratches on its shaven scalp and temple. Even so, the audience, already hushed, now grew deathly silent.

'Let us take a closer look,' began Eels, as he coolly reached towards the cadaver's temple and suddenly pulled forward an entire flap of the skin and bone to reveal a part of the gray-white of the brain underneath.

Someone in the audience, a lady, moaned slightly. Elsewhere a gentleman grunted. A few covered their eyes, or peeked through fingers, but most craned forward for a better look, and some at the back stood up.

'The procedures required to prepare the cranium in this way can be safely performed *in vitro* but it requires special skill and takes time.' With a deft movement, Eels now removed the entire top of the cadaver's cranium, revealing much more of the brain.

'Why would we wish to gain access to a living person's brain in this way? I will tell you. Because we now have an almost overwhelming body of evidence – some accidental, some the result of deliberate investigation by myself and my colleagues in this field – that shows that quite minor physical changes in the brain can radically improve the behavior of the individual concerned.

'To put it simply, it may well be that we can quite literally cut out the problem areas and render the disturbing symptoms of insanity harmless and benign. In short, a physical cure of insanity is finally possible, if only we can find out from where in this extraordinary and marvelous structure – with which, as you see, even the meanest and most vicious of individuals is endowed – the symptoms of insanity emanate.'

Eels eyed his audience.

'Ladies and gentlemen, there is no single word in the medical lexicon to describe this new branch of medical science. And so I have created one myself. I call it psychosurgery.'

He then signaled to his assistant, who handed him a tray from which Eels took what looked like a long thin needle with a ball of colored glass at its end.

'The ladies among you will recognize that this is nothing more or less than a hat pin. I use it for demonstration purposes only, to make easily visible where we believe the root of the problem – and the cure – lies.'

With that Eels slowly pierced the brain of the cadaver with a succession of hat pins, each time from a different direction, each time towards the same two locations, near its frontal area.

'A year ago, my distinguished Swiss colleague, Dr Gottlieb Burck-hardt, operated in Berlin on six insane patients, removing offending matter from their frontal lobes, roughly speaking at the points to which these needles have penetrated.

'The results were mixed, but extraordinary enough in some cases to give me confidence that further investigation of this kind of surgery may bring us close to a cure that would change the treatment of insanity for ever. In the case of Dr Burckhardt's work, and in others, patients have become calmer, more easily managed, and a credit to themselves . . .

'Now . . .'

Eels turned to the second of the cadavers – a woman, whose head Mould now uncovered.

'This case was typical of the armies of wanton women, many no better than hysterical harlots, most of a low-grade stock, who freely roam our cities day and night, spreading disease and moral corruption among our fine young men.'

He eyed the corpse, his hand resting on its lank dark hair before easing the head towards the audience.

'She was but one of the many women housed in our asylums in a state of secondary dementia who showed various degrees of mental dissolution. From the onset of puberty her mental defect, all too common in her class, displayed itself in a chronic wantonness which meant that, up to the point of her committal to this asylum, she had borne no less than six children by several different men. To most of these men she gave disease, the same she passed on to her brood, several of whom are syphilitic imbeciles, who remain locked up at our expense in various institutions in the state of Illinois.

'One of her vile offspring, now eight and roaming free, is a boy of unusual animal strength, who already displays criminal tendencies. I have no doubt that he, like the others, will have a propensity to that excessive reproduction of the species which characterizes their kind. This case, like the first, was a recent immigrant of the type and grade that comes from certain parts of Lesser Europe. Yet –' Dr Eels took another of his needles and placed its point by the woman's right nostril – 'it may well be that an operation as simple as the one I am about to perform, if conducted when this woman had been a girl, would have prevented all the tragedy implicit in what I have outlined. Note that with this procedure there is no need to trephine the skull as in the previous case, which I used for demonstration.

'If I insert the needle, so . . .'

Eels gently pushed the needle up the cadaver's nostril towards the skull and the frontal lobes of the brain. Explaining that at this point the cranium was at its thinnest, he took a small steel mallet and tapped the needle into the brain.

'It is, in theory at least, simply a matter now of manipulating the insertion instrument between the lobes and the limbic mass in such a way that it severs forever the bad connections, if I may so put it, that plagued this woman's life and those with whom she came into contact.'

Mr Mould gave him another needle which he applied through the other nostril.

'However, there are certain problems of hygiene and what I might call "access" with this particular approach and so, until we find a better way, then trephining it must be, which is a relatively slow procedure given the many hundreds of thousands of imbeciles with which the state is burdened.

'Ladies and gentlemen, we cannot prove without further investigation how effective such radical yet simple cures as these will be, but I am confident that they will be so.

'There is much else I could say, but I have been asked to limit my remarks to forty minutes, which I have done. But if there are questions . . . ?'

There were, a great many, and Eels dealt with them fluently, provoking a debate that ranged far and wide and prompted several public pledges of financial support for his program of research at Dunning from the guests.

At eight o'clock, Paul Hartz rose to conclude the meeting by inviting Eels to offer some final thoughts.

'You have educated us, Dr Eels, and entertained us, and I would like finally to ask you to enlighten us. You spoke of cures but you also mentioned "remedies". What might those be?'

'Matters of science are one thing, sir,' said Eels rather grandly, 'but matters of policy are another and not my responsibility. But if I may be permitted . . .'

The audience murmured its desire that he should continue.

'Thank you,' continued Eels. 'Then I will say this. We are agreed that poverty, disease and crime are traceable to one fundamental cause – depraved heredity. It is often not understood that much of this results from our toleration of the weak and vicious. Such base scions of humankind not only vex their own generation, but contaminate posterity through the uncontrolled proliferation of their seed until whole nations are infected.

'There is a danger – no, a strong belief based on sound demographic research – that that is what is now beginning to happen here in America.

'We should learn from nature's method for the preservation and elevation of races, namely the selection of the fittest and the rejection of the unfit . . .'

Eels grew deathly still as he spoke and his voice quieter. He stood now as he had at the beginning, his hands by his side, his feet together. But his eyes blazed behind their silver spectacles, two fierce fires burning bright.

'It is finally a matter of arithmetic. For the rejuvenation of the race we need to multiply those individuals whose dominant craving, like our own here tonight, is the altruistic sense, while eliminating those whose lives are ruled by the baser selfishness. I believe we should take steps to limit the multiplication of the organically weak and the organically vicious.

'There are two approaches. The first is a program of enforced sterilization of defective men and women, procedures which are generally simple and speedy and produce beneficial side effects including a calming of the nerves and compliance with authority.

'But the surest, the simplest, the kindest and most humane means of preventing reproduction among those whom we deem unworthy of that high privilege is a gentle, painless death. This should be administered not as a punishment but as an expression of enlightened pity for the victims – too defective by nature to find happiness in life – and as a duty toward the community and our own offspring. This I believe!'

Eels fell silent and someone shouted, 'Hear, hear!'

'Thank you, ladies and gentlemen, for your kind support. I am pleased to announce that later this week I shall initiate the first part of the program of investigation into surgical cures for insanity with the help of a new group of volunteer patients involving cerebral surgery and, in some cases, curative sterilization from which I expect speedy and excellent results!'

As Eels sat down, the audience rose as one and gave him an ovation such as he had only ever dreamed of. Over the next half-hour, Eels and Paul Hartz between them received many verbal pledges of financial support, five significant ones coming from wealthy members of the Chicago chapter of the Old America Association.

Even so, Hartz thought it wise to have a private word with Eels before leaving.

'It went very well, Dr Eels, but take a word of advice from me – avoid going into details of your program in any public forum. Among friends, as tonight, it's fine to talk frankly, but the notions of brain surgery as well as more radical remedies are just the kind of thing liberal East Coast newspapers get hot about.

'It will be gratifying if the *Tribune* and other Chicago papers mention your formal appointment when it is ratified at the end of the month, and also the support your work is getting, but keep your records and more specific ideas safely tucked away from prying eyes! Dunning's attracted an unfair share of coverage in the papers in the past and we don't want more. Talk of brain surgery will make hackles rise in the liberal press. Eh?'

Eels nodded but he was hardly listening, so carried along was he by his enthusiastic reception, which had only reinforced his unshakeable belief that he was right in what he said and in all he proposed to do. He was happy to leave the money and the politics to Hartz.

Less than two hours later, Morgan Eels was tucked up in bed and fast asleep in preparation for the day ahead. For once he did not feel the unconscious need to hold his testicles. He had no nightmares.

But sometimes the worst nightmares turn out to be the unexpected waking ones, in the real world.

19

Stonycreek

That same night, shortly after eight, a freight train pulled out of Pittsburgh and wound slowly eastward up through the steep, sheltered valleys of the Allegheny Mountains.

It had lights front and back, but nothing much in the middle except for twenty-eight wagons of assorted goods and commodities bound for markets on the East Coast, including six refrigerated box cars of dressed hog and sides of beef. In the dark and driving rain it was hard to make things out, but the refrigerated box cars had *DARKE HARTZ & COMPANY* painted in white letters on the side.

Three of these carried sides of pork, which hung on wheeled metal hooks attached to a main central rail on the ceiling. This curved round at either end of the wagon, making it easy for the heavy sides to be rolled from either end of the carriage and positioned at the doors on each side for unloading.

The carcasses of meat were each tied to metal hoops on the floor to stop them swinging freely back and forth at bends in the track, because if they swung in unison their combined weight might be sufficient to derail the car and, in the wrong conditions, possibly the whole train too.

One of these meat wagons had unexpected human freight: a man seated on the floor; and another hung up on a hook – Jenkin Lloyd Rhys.

The man on the floor was well wrapped up against the chill from
the air vents front and back that kept the ice in the wagon cool. By
his side was some food – bread, ham, cheese – and a pitcher of water,
not beer. His powerful body swayed with the movement of the train,
as did his feet. His eyes were closed, as if he was asleep, but he was
not.

Not since they had left Pittsburgh. He was listening to the run of
the train and the grind of the wheels on rails, and the wind and rain
outside. Inside, there was just the sound of the creaking, swaying sides
of meat as they strained on their hooks above and the restraints below.
That, and the weak moans of the dying man Rhys.

Twenty minutes out of Pittsburgh the train ran through the mining
town of Johnstown. It did not stop but the driver up front sounded
his whistle four times. It was enough for the man's eyes to snap open.
He struck a match and lit a lantern.

It cast enough light to show the sides of pork as they swayed back
and forth together, and Jenkin Lloyd Rhys as well. His feet were not
tied to the floor so his body swung back and forth, sometimes from
one side to the other, sometimes, when the train jolted, forward and
back, where it hit or was half crushed by the heavy sides of pork.

The man on the floor got up and picked up the lantern. Holding
on to the side of the swaying wagon with practiced ease he moved
over to have a look at Rhys, raising his lantern so he could stare into
his face.

His dry mouth hung swollen and loose now and he stared from
eyes that were nearly insane from his hours of suffering and pain.
The life of Jenkin Lloyd Rhys, which had begun inauspiciously in a
humble cottage in the South Wales mining town of Ebbw Vale, was
coming to a dreadful conclusion, made all the worse by him having
had to dwell for the past hours on the injustice of this terrible end
to his life.

He had served his adopted country well, very well. He had played
fair by all with whom he did business; he had given a helping hand
to many a young man; he had looked after his employees as he had
his own family; he was responsible for many philanthropic endeavors;
he was God-fearing, a pillar of church and community; and he was
founder, leader, and president of the Old America Association, whose

worthy aims, of preserving and promoting all that was good in the way of traditional American values, surely no reasonable man or woman could condemn.

Suddenly a double whistle sounded. The man turned from Rhys and untied two of the pork sides before expertly running them on their wheels right down the carriage so that he could get at the hook from which Rhys hung.

He put the lantern safely out of the way on the floor, pulled back the great bolts on the double door and, with two great pulls, opened the doors to right and left.

Wind and rain rushed in and the sides of meat swayed and pulled on their restraints. The man grabbed the shank of the hook Rhys was on and, with a heave, got it moving one way before swinging it round on the curve at the end and back along the wagon side to the open door.

Rhys's eyes opened wider.

Often, in the final agony, a man doesn't want to die. Extinction seems worse than any pain, even to a churchgoing man who says he believes in heaven.

Rhys's tormentor pulled out a knife and cut through the twine that had tied his hands behind his back. They swung free now but they were useless, blackened, engorged parodies of the manicured, smooth things they had been only twenty-four hours before.

Not for the first time but most definitely for the last, Rhys spoke: 'Why?' he managed to say.

'Stonycreek,' the man replied.

Rhys's eyes registered protest and he even managed to mouth a few words: 'It wasn't my fault.'

The man ignored him and pulled a knife from the leather sheath on his belt. He reached forward with his massive left hand and cupped the back of Rhys's head to hold it steady against his chest.

Rhys whimpered.

Then, as the man carved four letters, one after the other on his forehead, Rhys screamed. Blood blinded his eyes and dribbled down into the froth at the corner of his mouth.

His work done, the man let Rhys swing for a moment as he peered out into the dark, cocked his head to one side as if listening, waited a minute or so and then, apparently satisfied, turned back into the carriage. He put an arm and shoulder to Rhys's body and expertly hoisted him up and off the hook. Bloody drool came from Rhys's mouth; the sounds he uttered were those of an animal dying in fear and in pain.

The man carried him the short distance to the open door and held him there.

The train was going nice and slow as it pulled onto a great, high bridge, so narrow that it was possible to peer down and see – but better still hear – what rushed and roared through the steep ravine far below.

'Stonycreek,' said the man again. It was an accusation as much as a statement.

Maybe Rhys then understood, maybe he was too far gone to know or finally care as he felt himself propelled out over the side of the bridge into the night, arcing away in the dark, his useless hands and arms flailing helplessly at the rain as he fell into the broiling waters of the river far below and drowned in the darkness and anonymity of the night.

The train rolled on and, not long after, picked up speed for the long drop down to Altoona.

There, briefly, it made an unscheduled stop, long enough to allow a man to get out of Wagon 27 and secure the doors again.

He was now carrying a small valise and wore an overcoat and curled bowler against the inclement weather. He crossed the tracks, made his way to the main part of the station and joined the few dubious characters who hang round depots like that at this time of the night.

He showed no fear.

Someone asked him what train he was waiting for.

The man turned full on him, making the enquirer back off at once.

'Exposition Express,' he growled.

There was laughter.

'Don't stop in *Altoona*,' said someone. 'It's full of New Yorkers bent on going to the Fair.'

Eight minutes later, the train hove into view, lights ablaze, like a passenger liner out on the Atlantic at night. It slowed right down and

a guard leaned out, looking for the man who raised a hand in acknowledgement.

The watchers were amazed to see the guard take the man's valise
and then reach down a hand to help him aboard.

'Who the hell was that?' someone said.

The others shrugged as the Exposition Express disappeared on into
the night.

Up in the train the guard said respectfully, 'It's all ready for you Mr
Krol,' and showed him straight to the special berth reserved for directors
of the railroad and their friends.

'Have a good night, sir. I'll wake you for breakfast.'

Krol nodded but did not smile.

He closed the carriage door behind him, undressed to his combinations, shook his head as if to shake off the effort of his murderous
work over the past twenty-four hours and eased his huge, muscular
frame onto the bunk before covering himself with a sheet and blanket.

He laid his head on the white starched linen of the pillow and closed
his eyes.

Not long after that, the train rattled its way across the bridge that
spanned the ravine through which Stonycreek roared endlessly below,
but Dodek Krol never knew that: he was enjoying a sleep so deep it
might almost have been the sleep of the dead.

Nor did Emily Strauss know they had crossed Stonycreek either,
though if she had she would have recognized its name at once. Not
so long before it had been the scene of the worst disaster in American
history. The rest of America would have recognized it too. That night
one more name had been added to the death toll.

But as it was, Emily Strauss, five carriages along from Dodek Krol,
was as sound asleep as he was, unaware of the rattle of the train and
the rain's drumbeat on the roof.

DAY SIX

Tuesday October 24, 1893

20

Garbage

At seventeen minutes past nine the following morning, Anna Zemeckis began running for her life, and for that of her unborn baby, for the second time.

The first had sent her tumbling to near-death in Bubbly Creek. This time she had no idea where it would take her. She knew only that if she did not get out of Dunning and away from the so-called care of Dr Eels and Riley, there would be no baby and probably no Anna Zemeckis either.

The day had started badly and rapidly got worse.

Anna had no sleep at all, made anxious as she was by Dr Eels's threat the day before that he would abort her baby whether she agreed to it or not.

At a quarter past eight Riley appeared, belligerent and smelling of liquor and warned several of the women to be ready to go over to Main Building to see Dr Eels at nine o'clock sharp. Anna was one of them.

She had no doubt about what they were going to try and do to her.

She grew ever more desperate to find a way out of the ward but realized there was none. The doors were watched either end by the trusties, as well as the two orderlies who were already back on duty.

The only time she was allowed out of the building was for the daily supervised walk around the yard, from which she knew there was no hope of easy escape.

I am not going to let them harm my baby.

Cold anger and clearer thinking now began to replace her sense of desperation, as Anna realized that her only hope was to make her escape somewhere between the ward and Dr Eels's office. After that . . .

After that, I'll kill anybody who gets in my way.

Maybe Anna Zemeckis was going mad for real; or maybe she had never been quite so sane and utterly purposeful. But when Riley returned at nine o'clock she was calm. Even when she harshly grasped her arm, telling the other orderly, 'This one's seeing the doctor first . . .' and marched her off ahead of the others.

Anna knew she must act compliant. So outwardly she did nothing but whimper and look scared. She wanted to lull Riley into a false sense of security, despite the fact that the vice-like grip on her arm was becoming excruciatingly painful.

'Come on . . . !' snarled Riley, hauling her across the yard toward Main Building.

As they approached the front entrance, Anna looked down the basement steps adjacent to it and saw that the doors they led to seemed to be in use. It seemed her best chance. Once down there she thought she could hide for a while and then find a way out, maybe under cover of darkness. It was a small hope but she had to try. She knew if she failed and got caught that Eels and Riley would, between them, destroy her and her baby.

They crossed the yard to Main Building and climbed the stairs to Dr Eels's surgery. A woman was already changed into her shift and was waiting. She was the second that morning.

Eels emerged, his white gown loose, looking pleased with himself. He took the gown off.

'Ah, Zemeckis! You look better today and you will be better still before long. Yes. Now, I don't suppose you have changed your mind and decided to sign the form I showed you?'

Anna looked at him, at the nervous woman next to her who was about to be 'treated', and at Riley and another orderly talking. For a moment she nearly ran then and there, but found herself saying, 'Yes, I'm ready to now, Dr Eels.'

She said this softly, head down, the very picture of compliance.

Eels beamed. He liked to win, even against these miserable souls.

'Good, good! We have a few moments and . . . Riley! Please bring the Zemeckis girl to my office.'

They set off together, Eels ahead, Anna in the middle, Riley behind. When they reached the familiar door into Eels's examination room, he pulled out a bunch of keys, detached them from a hoop on his pants and opened the door.

'This needn't take long,' he said leaving the keys in the lock and entering.

Anna knew what she must do, but not yet, not yet. She tried to control her breathing but failed. It came out in little bursts and breathlessness.

'No need to be nervous, Miss Zemeckis, the procedures are really all very straightforward.'

They passed the great camera on its brass tripod and the examination couch and went to his desk. Eels got his familiar clipboard, found Anna's form, clipped it to the top of the pile and put it in front of her.

'Please, sit down, it'll be easier . . .'

Riley got a chair and Anna sat, her heart thumping.

I can't . . . I mustn't . . . maybe it'll be all right . . .

Doubts assailed her as Eels dipped his steel pen in the ink and passed it to her.

Maybe Riley shouldn't have breathed just then and sent the stench of her vile liquor breath across Anna's face. Maybe.

Maybe it was the fact of the child inside her. Maybe.

Whatever it was, a sudden powerful rush of rage and purpose surged through Anna Zemeckis. She turned to Riley, stared at her ungiving face and instinctively thrust the nib of the pen, ink flying, straight into her right eye.

Then, as Riley screamed and brought her hands to her face Anna rose, picked up the metal clipboard and, using it as a weapon, whacked its edge at Eels's startled face, right into his teeth.

He grunted in pain and rage.

117

Then Anna ran out of the door, slammed it shut, turned the key
in the lock and ran for her life. Behind her the muffled screams of
Riley and Eels faded as she ran down the corridor, still clutching the
clipboard like a weapon. She made for the stairs and charged down
them two steps at a time.

Nobody was about and there were no sounds yet of pursuit.

She slowed, opened the door to the yard outside, saw with relief
that no one was around and calmly went down the steps to the basement, praying that the door would open and lead somewhere that
offered other ways of escape.

Only then did she hear a distant shout and the running of feet, but
it was nowhere nearby. Then an orderly's whistle, but that was a long
way off too.

But Anna knew she had little time.

The basement door was unlocked and she slipped inside, breathing
heavily and ready to flee back out again if someone was down there.

But it was deserted. The door opened onto a large room that was
a dumping ground for boxes, tins and bales of rotting cloth which
gave off a dank odor. There was another door on its far side which
Anna cautiously approached. It was ajar and made no sound when
she opened it wider and peered out.

She found herself looking down a dark, ill-lit basement corridor,
which seemed to go the whole length of the building. The only source
of light was from rooms like the one she had just come through, and
then only if the doors were open.

She heard more shouts from above, steps running down to the basement and a door opening. She set off at once along the corridor,
moving from door to door and thinking she could escape into a room
if someone came. She went to throw away the clipboard but stopped
herself. There were papers on it with her name. Besides, it had been
a weapon once, and it might be again.

The corridor echoed with sounds – the shouts of people, the rumble
of machinery, the whine of wind in wires unseen; and muffled steps
somewhere overhead.

She ran on, passing door after door, avoiding the boxes and rubbish
piled all along the corridor, crossing over intersections with other corridors off to her left.

The light at the end of the corridor grew brighter, and she saw it came from another open door like the one she had first come in by.

When she reached it she nearly retched. The smell of rotting food was suddenly overwhelming.

'Garbage!' she told herself and she knew exactly where she was. She had seen piles of garbage at the end of Main Building, near where the freight train delivered coal. From there they took it off to Dunning's incinerator. The door opened onto steps that led up to the trash cans and garbage put out ready for removal.

Except that some of it had slipped and slithered down the steps to the basement and, no one having bothered to shift it, it was now crawling with rats.

As she hesitated, Anna saw a silhouette at the far end of the corridor. It was large and broad and looked like one of the male attendants.

She crouched down where she was and waited until the man had gone. And then she heard it: the chuff-chuff of the freight train that serviced Dunning.

Anna cautiously climbed up the steps again and peered up into the yard. She saw the coal tips off in the distance and an incongruous line of washing nearby. The garbage lay between. Near the tip was a hut and she decided to make a run for it. When she was satisfied that no one was in the immediate vicinity, she climbed the last few steps and, still clasping the clipboard, headed for the hut. As she did so her route took her beyond the end of Main Building and into the path of the oncoming freight train which steamed and roared seemingly straight at her. As she passed the line of washing she spotted some garments – a dress, a shawl, some woolen stockings – and made a grab for them, thrusting them and the clipboard with its papers into the shawl and tying the whole lot into a bundle so that it might seem she was on an errand.

Then she made a run for the hut and crept inside.

Only just in time.

The locomotive heaved to a halt, its bulk looming at the hut's little window and some shouting ensued.

Men appeared and began loading and unloading goods from box cars. Anna crouched down in a corner, the bundle on her knees.

Then silence once more. As she rose to her feet, her head collided with a kerosene lamp hanging there, which promptly dropped to the ground with a clatter.

'What was that?' someone called from a distance.

'There's a woman loose. If you see her, grab her,' came the reply.

Footsteps crunched to the door and it opened. A man of thirty or so stood there staring at Anna.

She stared back, eyes wide, with nowhere to go.

'What was it?' the orderly shouted again.

The man at the door wore the peaked cap and blue jacket of a freight-train driver. He stared at her and put a finger to his lips. He seemed amused.

'Just some tin cans blowing in the wind,' he shouted over his shoulder, winking at her.

Then he said in a low voice, 'There's a hopper second from this end full of empty flour sacks and delivery crates. Get into that and avoid the other one, it's full of coal dust. No one checks the hoppers. Climb up into it when I sound the whistle and snuck right down or they might spot you from the upper windows. Get out at the fourth stop and not before. I'll come and get you and show you where to go. We'll be gone in about five minutes and it'll take an hour or more, depending.'

She stared at him.

Her eyes were filled with gratitude and held a question: *Why?*

His only answer was to shake his head and look as if Dunning did not meet with his approval as he said with another grin, 'You're the third this month.'

Then, 'Good luck, girl, you'll need it!'

In that moment of normality and human kindness, clouds cleared in Anna's mind. She remembered that her father's name was Janis and that he was a baker who lived and worked on the Lower East Side in New York where he had raised her.

The hut door closed, the driver walked away and the next five minutes were the loneliest of Anna's life.

She felt that she would never see her father or her home again. She felt utterly alone.

Then the locomotive whistle went and she remembered why she was running and what she must do. She peered out of the hut window, saw that the coast was clear, and headed for the second hopper, which was open to the sky and much higher than she expected. She clambered up its rusty ladder, threw in her shawl and its contents, and then fell right in on top of a pile of empty flour sacks. Their dry sweet smell reminded her of her father once more and all that she had lost.

She followed instructions and snuck right down on the sacks. The train took off, stopped awhile for an inspection, someone slapped the side of the wagon she was in, there was another shout and then a whistle and the train began to move once more.

Anna stayed low, saw buildings towering above her and windows too, was rocked from one side to another as the train wound its way through the grounds of Dunning.

Then suddenly she knew it was clear of that terrible place. Maybe it was the vast blue sky she saw, maybe the tops of passing trees, maybe the prairie wind.

Whatever it was, Anna Zemeckis was out of the Cook County Insane Asylum and heading back into Chicago.

'What now?' she wondered, as she made herself comfortable on the sacks.

She realized that she had absolutely no idea.

21

Everyone's Crazy

'My! Oh *my*!' cried the passengers on the Exposition Express as they crowded at the train windows to catch their first glimpse of Chicago after their long journey. 'Now that's a sight to see!'

In the far distance, across the waters of Lake Michigan, the air being clear from recent rain and the October sun quite strong, Chicago's mighty buildings, the highest and newest of which had been built for the Fair, rose shining, white and golden, in the sky.

The train had caught up on a lot of the time it had lost in the initial stages of the journey, but even so it was still behind schedule. Now it had reached the southern edge of the lake it had only to make the turn north for the final pull into the city.

'Be there by eleven,' someone said decisively after studying his pocket watch.

'It's as well that the wind's northeasterly,' said one of the seasoned travelers, pointing at his nose and winking.

Emily knew what he meant. The noxious black smoke from the innumerable chimney stacks of the famous meatpacking district, which now came into view, hung as a dark cloud over the city.

'Some days there's no city to see for all the smoke and fog; others, the stench gets to your throat before you've even reached the outskirts. Today we're not so lucky, it's drifting north. Downtown will stink!'

Moments later the scene changed once more – and for the better. There were renewed gasps of astonishment as Jackson Park and the buildings of the Fair's White City came back into view and the sun shone on them to dazzling effect.

Yet even so, some of the passengers began to hold their noses with looks of disgust: the Fair might be impressive, but there was no escaping the fact that the money that paid for it came from industries which defiled the air as much as they did the landscape.

The train pulled into Dearborn Station, where the smell of the stock yard now permeated everything. The first time Emily had experienced it she had felt revulsion and horror. It was the smell of meat and offal, the fetid garbage dump and the open sewer.

But now she had gotten used to it and the truth was she felt only excitement. She was arriving in the fastest-growing city in America to write a story for the greatest newspaper in the country and nothing, absolutely nothing, was going to get in her way.

She checked for her valise and purse and then waited as the train came to a final halt.

'After you, miss!'

Someone opened the carriage door and someone else helped her out.

A porter offered to take her valise.

'I can carry this myself thanks!' she said, 'but I have a trunk . . .'

They went to collect it together – along with dozens of other passengers who had come to the Fair and had more baggage than sense, while the more sensible ones with only a carpet bag or valise to carry pushed past them, anxious to get away.

Emily watched the rush with a mixture of alarm and excitement, hanging on to her own things as well as her porter, whose help she would need getting her trunk to the main concourse. Tall and thin, short and fat, red-faced and pale, white and black and every hue between, the whole world seemed to be descending on Chicago.

'Sorry, miss!' said one man half stepping on her toe.

'Mama!' shouted a child, rushing rudely past her.

'That's mine!' Emily called out when her trunk emerged from the baggage wagon, which meant that she did not see the man who also got down from a private carriage at the back of the train and walked out onto the concourse past her. He was not much taller than her but thickset, powerful and so intimidating that other passengers instinctively got out of his way, including Emily's porter.

'Have a good day, sir!' the guard called after him, but he was already lost in the crowd.

Finally a porter had her trunk. But getting much further proved easier said than done. The moment she left the platform and began crossing the main concourse of Dearborn Station, now crammed with visitors to the World's Fair, she felt she was fighting for her life.

'What a crowd!' she exclaimed, astonished as she took in the bustle of the city beyond.

'Hold on tight to your things,' warned her porter, '*very* tight!'

Only when they emerged through the depot's great red-brick entrance, blinking into the sunshine, did she feel able to breathe again. It was already half-past eleven and she knew she had barely enough time to get her baggage to her hotel on Michigan Avenue and then take the new Elevated out of town for her luncheon appointment in Jackson Park at twelve-fifteen.

Her porter had disappeared with her trunk in search of a cab, though she had told him not to. She felt so excited to be back that, for the moment, she closed her eyes to breathe in the atmosphere of a Chicago that seemed transformed since she was last here the month before.

At that time she had left feeling a failure: her ambitions thwarted by her newspaper, without hope of a job, no longer convinced that she had what it took to make it in the tough, uncompromising male world of journalism.

Now everything had changed.

She had met Mr Pulitzer and talked her way into an assignment, if not an actual job, on the *World*. And she had a story to work on in which she believed.

'Hey! Bring my trunk back!' Emily snapped sharply as the porter reappeared having got a cab, 'I'm being met.'

The porter shrugged, rudely dumped her trunk and stretched out a hand. She gave him a couple of dimes and, muttering, he went on his way.

A rough young man – hardly more than a boy – immediately made a play at grabbing the trunk as he spoke the name of a boarding house that was 'just a block or two away'.

Ten, more like, she told herself, hauling her trunk closer on one side and her valise on the other.

'Madam, may I be of assistance?' said a smooth-looking gentleman in an expensive silk hat, check suit and patent leather shoes.

'No you may not,' said Emily, who knew a masher when she saw one.

He went on his way at once, eyes already in search of easier prey.

Emily looked for a quiet spot where she could wait without being harassed.

'Some hope,' she thought, fending off another hotel tout.

In comparison with many of those who had just arrived on her train, she was traveling light. She would have preferred not to be encumbered with a trunk at all, but she knew that to get the kind of interviews she wanted, and to meet the kind of people who might help, she would need several changes of dress.

Spotting a space against the wall near the entrance, Emily hauled her baggage over to it. The noise and confusion did not abate.

From every direction came the constant cries of porters and cabmen, of passengers trying to keep control of their baggage, of the hawkers, pedlars and hustlers of the kind no city ordinance can ever stop from besieging the one place where such predators can guarantee finding the weak, the confused, the vulnerable and the plain stupid: rail depots.

On top of it all were the raucous shouts of young newsboys carrying their papers over their arms like billboards, offering every sensational kind of story under the sun.

'*People crowd the Fair in their thousands. Midway jammed!*' yelled out one scruffy boy, elbowing another out of the way and shoving a copy in Emily's face:

'*Inter-Ocean,* miss?'

Emily shook her head and smiled, only to have a *Tribune* boy shout in her ear:

'*Martin Foy executed in New York. Most successful electrocution since the law went into effect!*'

She hesitated, but turned away. Then she heard another shout in Italian and a fourth in German.

'Grausige Entdeckung einer Leiche an der West Side!'

This last one, with its talk of a gruesome body being found, caught Emily's attention because it was in German. The boy was selling the *Chicagoer Arbeiter-Zeitung*, one of several German-language newspapers in the city.

Much to his delight she stopped and bought a copy and was about to skim through it when she finally spotted the person she was looking for, just as he saw her and hurried over.

'Miss Strauss? Miss *Emily* Strauss? For the Auditorium Hotel?'

He was seventeen or so, tough-looking, tall but still gawky. His hands and feet were large, as if his body still had to grow into them, and his gaze was quick, eager and intelligent. He wore a tight jacket with 'Auditorium Hotel' embroidered on its lapel.

'They sent me to collect you. Said if you had more'n one trunk to take a cab.'

'I've just this one,' said Emily, stuffing the newspaper into her valise. He eyed the trunk.

'That ain't much for a lady,' he said with a grin.

He took her valise and then, before she could stop him, he heaved the trunk onto his shoulder as if it was no more than a bale of straw.

'Said if there was just one trunk to walk. It's quicker. You go in front, Miss Strauss, where I can keep you in sight. Don't want to lose you before we get there and you don't want to lose your things either, especially your valise. Hey, mister, leave off!'

The young man, whom Emily guessed was one of the hotel's bellhops, stuck out his boot and stepped on the foot of a man twice his size who looked as if he was about to hustle her.

'I've got to get to Jackson Park for lunch,' said Emily anxiously over her shoulder.

'Should've said before,' shouted the young man above the din of people and traffic. 'Make a left when we get to Wabash and stop.'

The crowds were thick and came in waves, like water in a rapid. Emily battled on, until she was brought to a halt by a tramp as they turned into Wabash. He was as bearded as Methuselah and carrying a placard which read, *EVERYONE'S CRAZY BUT ME!*

She tried to get out of his way but, whichever way she stepped, he mirrored her move.

'Please!' said Emily, sidestepping yet again and looking round for her escort. He was behind her in the crowd.

'I'm not crazy and I've got the papers right here to prove it, ma'am, and you better sign up to 'em or that impostor Mayor Carter Harrison and his crew in City Hall'll have every last dime you got for the tunnels they want to build right under your feet. Don't believe me?'

'I—'

'I got the papers to prove that too. Right here! Somewhere any rate. I . . .'

He stopped sidestepping and dug into the capacious pockets of the army greatcoat he had on and hauled out a sheaf of papers. Then more from another pocket. They had an official look about them and, to her surprise, Emily read the words 'City Hall' on one and 'Electoral Office' on another.

'Agree with 'im!' she heard her escort whisper in her ear as he caught up with her. 'He ain't bad, he's Mr Crazy.'

'I heard that,' said Mr Crazy, pulling himself up to his full height and waving his papers about, 'and you'd better agree with me, lady, because I ain't wrong and never have been. You know what's going on in them tunnels? Vegetable peelings and ashes and dust. Mayor Harrison can't last much longer on foundations made of holes. I got the proof of that too!'

He dug inside his coat and pulled out a scrap of paper which he unfolded.

'Wanna look?'

Emily could see he meant no harm. She could also see he was not going to get out of the way.

'I agree with you!' she said, adding, after a moment, 'sir!'

Mr Crazy looked pleased and beamed down at her.

He did indeed look like a benign prophet.

'I got the proof but I won't burden such a pretty lady with it right now! But *I* ain't the crazy one! Here, have this, it's the only free thing you'll ever get in Chicago!'

He thrust a wooden object into her hand, moved to one side and courteously waved her past.

They hurried away as quickly as they could.

'Don't worry about him, Miss Strauss, everyone knows Mr Crazy means no harm. It's just his way of keeping going. You can stop round that corner.'

She pushed her way out of the crowd to a quieter part of the sidewalk and found herself under the shining iron girders of the brand new Elevated on Wabash. She turned back as the boy barged his way through to join her. A train roared past directly overhead and its brakes began to squeal.

He nodded south down Wabash to some steps that led up to an overhead station where the train had just stopped.

'Best take the Elevated for Jackson from there. But if you come back after dark don't go getting *off* there, carry on up to the stop at Congress and Wabash and walk from there. It's longer but safer.' He pointed the other way.

'And you'll take my baggage straight to the hotel?'

'Straight as an arrow, ma'am.'

'What's your name?'

'Johnny Leppard.'

He put the trunk on the ground, the valise on top of it, pulled himself up to his full height, which was now, she realized, a good three inches taller than herself. He reached out a hand and said, 'John H. Leppard. The H is for Hudson, seeing as I was born near that great river.'

Then he added unexpectedly, 'I don't always want to work for a hotel.'

He had a dreamy look in his eyes.

'Who *do* you want to work for then?'

'Nobody. I want to own one.'

'One what?'

'A hotel, ma'am. One as big as the Auditorium. That's my aim in life. This position is just to help get me there!'

His determination and the grin that accompanied it were infectious. Emily grinned back, recognizing a kindred spirit. She could see that nothing was going to stop Johnny Leppard from reaching his goal, just as nothing would stop her reaching hers. Meeting him felt like a good omen.

'I better get going,' said Emily.

'Remember, miss, take the Elevated back to Congress if the light is even half gone by the time you leave Jackson. The streets round lower Wabash aren't for ladies after dark. They don't call it Hell's Half Acre for nothing.'

'No safer for boys either,' said Emily.

'I can look after myself!' he said with a frown, heaving the trunk back on his shoulder. 'Shall I tell 'em to expect you for dinner? Best to keep a table by. Hotel's full.'

She nodded.

'Make it for half-past seven. I reckon I'll leave the Fair by six.'

He nodded, turned, swayed under the weight of the trunk, regained his balance and was lost in the crowds on Wabash as he turned right for her hotel on Michigan.

Only then did Emily look to see what Mr Crazy had given her. It was a perfectly crafted wooden pipe, correct in every particular, with a folded scrap of paper in the bowl where the tobacco went. She took it out and opened it.

Everyone's crazy but me, it read.

The words were written in black ink, in the most beautiful copperplate Emily had ever seen.

22

Something Missing

Dr Eels's injuries were superficial. He had a cut lip and a cracked incisor.

Riley, however, was a different matter.

The human eye is more resilient than it looks, being surrounded by the sclera – the white of the eye – which is tough connective tissue designed to protect the delicate inner parts that make sight possible.

The nib of a pen can easily rupture the sclera and cause blindness or impair the vision, especially if it is loaded with ink. But to do that the point must be thrust straight into it. If it comes at an angle there's a good chance that the sclera will do its job and divert the intruding object upwards and to the rear of the eye socket, where it will come into contact with the bony orbit which holds the eye.

Unpleasant, possibly dangerous, but not necessarily sight-threatening.

However, Anna Zemeckis had thrust the steel pen in hard, very hard. It had been diverted all right, sliding over the sclera, and then, because she used the heel of her hand, it hit the right orbit hard and had crunched on through into the frontal lobe of Riley's brain.

Now, over two hours later, the much-feared orderly was lying on the examination couch in the doctor's surgery, helpless as a child, the pen still sticking into her eye.

Eels, his lip stitched and plastered and made ugly yellow with iodine, stood on one side of the slab.

Mould stood on the other, awaiting his master's verdict. It had been Mould who had attended to the doctor's superficial facial injuries and persuaded him to lie down for a while, during which period Mould had got Riley onto the table. He had listened to her strange ramblings, made notes as Eels had trained him to do, and been very puzzled by what he had heard.

Finally he sedated Riley – very lightly, enough to ease the pain but not so she would lose consciousness – and had gone to get the doctor up again.

'Something's strange about her,' he said with barely concealed excitement.

'Strange?'

'See for yourself, sir,' he said.

Eels had done just that. He examined the angle of the steel pen in Riley's eye but did not touch it. He asked her a few questions and listened to the semicoherent answers.

'Do you know your name?'

'Erum I . . . name?'

'Yes.'

'Dr Eels.'

'Do you know where you are?'

'Opital . . . I mean oppit . . . I mean . . .'

There was something else, something that interested Dr Eels very much indeed and sent his pulse racing, even if his mouth did hurt.

Her voice was soft, almost gentle.

That was something Riley's voice had *never* been.

Eels studied her, and the pen, and then turned to Mould.

Finally he gave his verdict – diagnosis was too strong a word – and it was in the form of two words uttered flatly but which failed completely to mask his considerable excitement.

'Interesting,' he said, 'very.'

Mould agreed.

It was.

'Have you that other pen and the surgical rule?' asked Eels.

Mould handed them over and Eels began measuring. The pen was identical to the one in Riley's eye. What he needed to know was just how far the offending weapon had penetrated.

'Five to six centimeters,' he murmured finally.

He squatted down to bring his eyes level with Riley's head.

'She's an ugly brute,' he said.

Then, raising his voice, Eels added, 'Aren't you Riley?'

Riley giggled like the woman she wasn't and never had been.

'It's hot,' she murmured with, of all things, a smile.

Whatever Riley was now, she was no longer the person she had once been.

Eels studied the angle of the pen. 'It's entered the right frontal lobe ...'

He pulled back and made a guess, for there was no other way.

'. . . at about level with the limbus, having caused a lesion, or several lesions possibly – no, probably. I know because I saw Riley herself push the pen back and forth in her attempt to get it out. That was before she passed out.'

'And what she says ...' Mould said in a low voice, 'the way she speaks, sir?'

'Highly interesting, I think,' said Eels. 'But more than that ... the eye appears completely undamaged but for some peripheral bruising and, of course, the area of the orbit is sterile and therefore ...'

'Therefore this is a far better route in than via the nostril, sir?'

It all seemed so simple, so logical.

'I would never have thought of it,' said Eels in a moment of wonder and rare candor. 'We access the brain by way of the orbits of the eye. Perhaps, if we angle the instrument right, we need only make one entry to cause lesions sufficient to deal with both lobes.'

They stared at the grotesque sight of Riley and the pen in her eye, both literally breathless with excitement at their momentous discovery. In the whole of America right now it was unlikely that anyone else knew better than Eels and his assistant Mould precisely what this signified.

They had found a practical method of quickly and efficiently pacifying the troublesome mental patient – for good. This was the 'cure' Eels had been seeking and it promised to revolutionize the treatment of the mentally ill – worldwide.

Eventually Eels said quietly, trying to sound calm, 'I'm going to remove it.'

They both knew the danger of rupturing the vessels and nerves of the eye as the nib was withdrawn and so Eels proceeded with extreme caution, surprised in the end that the bleeding was minimal and confirming that the sclera was only scratched.

'We'll just have to see how she responds when she wakes up,' said Eels.

Then, after a pause, he gave a hard, greedy look at Mould: 'Not a word of this to anyone.'

'Certainly not, doctor.'

It was not until after he had de-gowned and returned to his examination room where it had all happened that the shock finally had set in.

Eels sat at his desk and his hands began to shake.

'I'd better lie down again for a bit,' he told himself.

But he never did.

Because it was then that something suddenly came to him, something that set his heart thumping in alarm.

He got up and looked around the room.

Under the desk.

Then in the desk drawers and on the couch and under it.

Then by the camera and its tripod and then right out of the door and along the corridor outside.

Then back down to find Mould and the orderly who had come to rescue them.

'Did you see my clipboard?' he asked, with increasing urgency. 'You *must* have seen it. She had no reason to take it. Has she been found yet?'

'She will be, Dr Eels,' said the orderly, 'they always are. More than likely she'll give herself up.'

'But I need the papers on that clipboard. I *need* them. They must not fall into anyone else's hands.'

'We'll find 'em, sir,' they said.

'You'd better,' said Eels.

He began to sweat at the thought of Paul Hartz of Darke Hartz & Company and how he would react to what had happened.

Hartz was not a man who gave people a second chance. Not ever. *Keep your records safely tucked away from prying eyes*, that's what he had told Eels only the night before.

It hadn't been a warning, it had been a command.

Eels obsessively searched his examination room yet again and then the corridor outside. He went to find Mould and grabbed his lapel.

'Those papers *must* be found,' he shouted. 'If they get into the public domain they could ruin everything. People won't understand our valuable research program here. We must find that woman and when we do . . .'

'When we do . . .' agreed Mould.

He had no need to say what they would do to Anna Zemeckis when she was once more back in their care.

They stared at each other.

Mould's eyes had an evil glint to them. But his master, Dr Morgan Eels, now looked as he sounded – like a man gone mad.

23

White City

Emily boarded the Elevated for the World's Fair at Wabash and Congress. En route to Jackson Park she settled back into a seat in the crowded compartment. It had been given up to her by a sharply dressed gentleman who stood, raising his spotless hat with a charming but predatory smirk.

She knew his game. Mashers like him – smart, confident, well-groomed men who knew how to charm young, inexperienced, out-of-town female visitors to the Fair – were two a dime on that route. An offer of a seat was a well known ploy.

As she had no wish to stand in the jostling crowd and reckoned he deserved everything he got, she accepted the offer with an equally charming smile and proceeded to ignore him. Two stations on, his conversational gambits failing, he shrugged, got out of the carriage and climbed aboard the next one to try his luck again.

As they pulled out of the station at 26th, Emily got a closer view of the thick pall of acrid smoke that hung over the Union Stock Yard a few hundred yards to the west. Like other female passengers she instinctively put a handkerchief to her nose and turned towards the clearer air over Lake Michigan.

The tall downtown buildings were behind them now, the South Side approaching Jackson consisting more of low tenements, factories,

empty lots with a few hastily built hotels and the like for the Fair. The
sun was bright and the lake shone, the smoke from steamers rising in
the still air, their passage marked by wakes which fanned out for miles
across the calm waters.

Emily pulled out a man's pocket watch from her bag, gratified to
see she was now in good time. It had been her father's, given her the
day before he died of complications arising from injuries received at
the hands of Pinkerton thugs during the Homestead Strike in Pittsburgh
a year before.

'You get out of Pittsburgh,' he had said, 'you make a life for yourself.
You can do anything Emily, *anything* you set your mind to if you want
it enough. But remember that it is truth and justice you're fighting for,
not just for yourself.'

'Truth and justice,' she whispered, pulling back from her reverie as
the Elevated lurched left and braked sharply at the depot on 40th.
Minutes later it reached Washington Park, a few stops short of the
Fair itself.

Most passengers climbed off at this point so they could walk the
Midway Plaisance. Emily joined them on this exciting mile-long westward extension of the Fair, a showground for a host of overseas and
private exhibits. There were North African bazaars, Irish villages,
German Bierkellers, Egyptian donkeys, a spoof volcano that erupted
every hour – and just about every huckster, con artist, escapologist,
trickster, quack and fraud in America worthy of the name. All of them
working the fair-going crowds for everything they could get, and
charging from two dollars to go up in a balloon to just ten cents for
a trip on the sliding railway.

The fact was, as Emily had discovered during her previous visit to
Chicago, the Plaisance was more fun, more entertaining and sometimes a good deal more educational than the official buildings, programs
and worthy exhibits which lay beyond the Fair's formal entrance in
Jackson Park. The rest of the world had worked that one out too.

But now Emily headed through the crowds determined not to be
drawn into any of the dozens of attractions along the way. Even so
her eyes were inevitably drawn to the most astonishing of the Midway
Plaisance's spectacles – the gigantic, 260-foot wheel erected halfway
along it by George W. Ferris, engineer and bridge builder.

She reached the main entrance to the Fair itself a few minutes before she was due to meet Fay Bancroft.

'Can I help you, ma'am?'

It was a Columbian Guard in his blue jacket, gray pants and cocked hat, one of the special, 2,000-strong force hired especially to police the Fair and outside the control of the notoriously corrupt Chicago City Police. Their presence explained why Jackson Park itself had remained virtually crime-free at a time when rates for every kind of crime had rocketed everywhere else in the city.

'Thank you, officer, but I know the way.'

He saluted Emily and passed on by. Moments later, and dead on time, she was climbing the steps into the entrance hall of the Woman's Building. Finding a seat, Emily arranged herself as elegantly as she could, though she couldn't help noticing she was surrounded by ladies who were far more effortlessly elegant than she was.

'My dear, I've kept you waiting!' Fay Bancroft's familiar, well-modulated voice called out.

She was one of those women who, having sighted her quarry, heads directly towards it with a winning smile, while her eyes dart and glance about to left and right and straight over the head of the person she is about to greet, lest she miss something in the social scene around her.

They exchanged the lightest of kisses on either cheek, Fay pulling Emily close to and not letting go.

'That woman,' she whispered conspiratorially, 'the one in pink directly behind me whose hair is . . . strange . . . is the Honourable Mrs Fitch-Lewis, over from London. You know who she is, or is said to be?'

Emily shook her head.

Fay leaned closer and whispered in Emily's ear.

'His *mistress*!?' said Emily, eyes widening.

She was still young enough to be shocked by such information.

'Ssh!' said Fay. 'Walls have ears, especially in *this* building!'

'Are you sure?'

'Dreadfully sure,' said Fay, with a satisfied smile.

No one Emily had ever met liked gossip more than Fay Bancroft. Since this particular bit of gossip concerned a leading Republican politician, Emily had to admit she found it fascinating too.

'We'll take luncheon in the East Indian Tea House on the third floor; the Roof Garden Café has become rather too crowded for my tastes, since word got round about how competitive its prices are. It's become a victim of its own success! But the tea house is really very civilized and the gentlemen are not allowed to spit, which is a mercy. We can talk properly there.'

Fay took Emily's arm and led her to the wide stairs.

'There *is* an elevator but I prefer to walk.'

Not for the exercise, Emily suspected, more for whom and what might be seen on the way.

'It's even busier than last time I was here,' remarked Emily.

'End of the Fair, my dear, and absolutely *everybody* is coming to town. Those who have not visited the Fair till now feel obliged not to miss it; those who have been already know they must do so one last time before it ends.

'Now, my dear,' continued Fay with an enquiring look, after they had settled down and ordered, 'what is it exactly that you want to talk to me about?'

The two women had not known each other long but from the first they had discovered an easy intimacy. Fay had spotted the young reporter at a tedious function in the Manufactures and Liberal Arts Hall early on in Emily's first trip to Chicago, guessed what she was and, having a penchant for nurturing rising stars, invited her to a tea party. She had been flattered when Emily had offered to write something about her role on the Educational Sub-Committee of the 117-member Board of Lady Managers of the Woman's Building, and when that piece was published in the *Echo*, had taken Emily out to lunch downtown.

Emily quickly brought Fay up to date, telling her about the stunt she had pulled to meet Mr Pulitzer.

'I am quite appalled!' exclaimed Fay with delight. 'And what was the great man like? Did you meet his sainted wife? One hears so little of her that I sometimes wish one heard something bad!'

Their food came and both were hungry, enjoying the excellent cuisine and gossiping away like old friends.

Only when their main course was done did Emily get to business.

She produced the photograph of Anna Zemeckis and a copy of the letter written by Janis to Pulitzer.

To Fay's credit she gave it her full attention, and as she did so Emily looked at her with admiration – her day dress of colored silk so smart, her coiffure so elegantly topped by a little hat and delicate feathers from some exotic bird, her face powdered to perfection, her general appearance not-quite-vain yet most certainly consciously well-to-do.

'And no one knows where she went during those five weeks?' said Fay finally and somberly.

Emily shook her head.

'I spoke to Mr Zemeckis at length. He visited Chicago three times in all and went to every police department, every hospital, every morgue, but he didn't find her. Not until it was too late, that is, and she turned up on a slab in the morgue. She was killed in a traffic accident.'

'My dear!' said Fay softly, affecting a shudder.

'The question is, where was she and what was she doing between the time she disappeared from her relatives' home and when she was killed in the accident? I've heard that others have gone missing, other women I mean. During the Fair, quite a few.'

'Have you?' said Fay cautiously, her voice dropping.

'Most are never heard of again.'

'Aren't they?' murmured Fay.

'Mr Pulitzer said that was what happened in cities and there's nothing new in it,' continued Emily. 'I heard that more have gone missing in Chicago during the Fair than might be expected.'

Fay stayed silent.

So did Emily.

'Girls like that . . .' began Fay dismissively.

'She came from a good family,' Emily interjected at once, sensing Fay's hesitation. 'Mr Zemeckis raised her right. Didn't let her out of his sight until she came to Chicago this spring.'

'Well then, maybe a girl like that—'

'Like what, Fay? Like *me*? I'm the same, my father was no better than Mr Zemeckis. Working men trying to do right by their daughters. You can't call us all "girls like that" and sweep us under the carpet and forget about us.'

Fay reached out a hand and put it on Emily's.

'Is that why you're so interested in this girl? Something about her
that could have been you?'

Emily nodded.

'And you think she was a good girl?'

'I know it,' said Emily. 'I've seen her home. I've seen her father. I've
talked to her neighbors. I've read her letters. She was a girl who deserved
to get the best out of life. But someone, probably a man or men, have
taken that from her and now . . .'

Emily sat back and took in the elegant dining room in which she
found herself.

'I thought the Woman's Building was all about showing the world
that ability is not a matter of sex. I thought that great big picture at
the end of the main hall . . .'

'Mary Cassatt's mural?' said Fay, glancing at the table next to them
to see if its occupants had noticed Emily's rising voice.

'Yes, the one showing *Girls Pursuing Fame* if I remember right and
Young Women Plucking the Fruits of Knowledge or Science – those ones. All
finished off with a nice pretty picture of some women painting, making
music and dancing. Well, Anna Zemeckis won't be doing any of that,
not ever again, and nobody seems to care except for her father, and
Mr Pulitzer and me.'

She fell silent again, aware of the glances she was getting. 'Sorry,
didn't mean to draw attention to myself. But . . .'

Fay smiled.

'When I said, "that kind of girl", I didn't mean quite what you
thought. I know your background Emily, because you've told me. I
can guess where this Anna girl came from. You know why?'

Fay leant closer.

'Take any American woman and you know what you find not very
far beneath the surface? Someone – a mother, a daughter, maybe a
grandparent – someone in the family who came off a boat with hardly
a dime in their pocket.'

Fay squeezed her hand and smiled.

She stared into Emily's eyes and Emily stared back, suddenly amazed.

'But I thought your family had been here for generations . . .'

Fay put a finger to her lips. 'I *prefer* you to think that, and everyone
else too, so keep it to yourself. My little weakness, I guess. But I want

you to know that I *don't* judge a girl by the job she does, because oftentimes it's the only job she can get or she can do. I judge people by
what they make of their opportunities. You're right about women in
Chicago and the Fair and them disappearing more than they ought.
It's common knowledge. Chicago's still a frontier town, for all it wants
the world to think differently. It's also a dangerous place. We all know
that but we don't advertise the fact. If we had we wouldn't have had
the World's Fair here, and if we did now then people would stay away.'

'That doesn't help Anna Zemeckis,' said Emily.

'No it doesn't,' conceded Fay.

She sat thinking and Emily let her.

Finally Fay sighed and said, 'Emily, I'm going to try and help you
find out what happened to her. Give me a day or two. I'll make some
enquiries. Meanwhile . . . have you a notebook?'

Emily produced one and handed Fay a pencil.

'. . . You'll get help from the women at Hull House. You know
it . . . ?'

Emily nodded. 'Yes, I've already contacted Miss Lathrop.'

She had visited the famous settlement house at Halsted Street on
the Near West Side before; it was where she had asked for and
obtained the obligatory interview with its indefatigable founder Jane
Addams.

'Many girls in trouble turn to Hull House. I'm sure Julia will help
you. She is a good friend of mine. She does much good among the
single working girls of the West Side, for whom there is so little provi-
sion and who are naturally vulnerable. I will send her a note to say
you are a friend. As for these others . . .'

Fay jotted a few more names in Emily's notebook, explaining how
each person might be useful.

'Now,' she said suddenly, glancing at the clock, 'there's a meeting I
need to attend at two, so I must go. But at four there's a reception
over at the Illinois State Building which a number of the people on
this list will be attending. I think you'll find it useful, so perhaps you'll
be my guest for that? Say a few minutes before four o'clock in the
main hall here? Meanwhile—'

'Meanwhile,' said Emily, 'I need to go and have my credentials
updated and get my reporter's pass at the Administration Building.'

'It's down by the Basin. There are ladies' waiting rooms there if you want to rest or freshen up later.'

Emily's thanks were profuse, but Fay brushed them aside. Anna's story seemed to have touched her, perhaps sparking memories of something deep in her own background about which she did not wish to speak and into which Emily would not dream of prying.

'Till later, then, my dear,' Fay said with another brief embrace.

24

To Canal Street

Anna Zemeckis stayed low in the open hopper as it dragged out of the northwestern suburbs of Chicago towards the city center. It traveled slowly and gave her time to think.

She remembered the driver's warning to stay out of sight until the fourth stop and did not even risk so much as peeking over the wagon edge to see where she was.

At the first stop the train jolted back and forth a while and she guessed from that and the sounds she heard that more box cars were being coupled on to the locomotive.

At the next stop there was the sound of loading and unloading and Anna shrunk lower still into the bottom of the hopper that was her haven. No one came near it, thankfully. But hunger was now beginning to gnaw at her and she had nothing to drink and was getting parched.

The third stop brought the hopper right next to a massive grain elevator which cast Anna into shadow and made her cold. She guessed she must have reached somewhere along the Chicago River and the dull sound of a ship's horn confirmed it.

Her memory was getting clearer all the time, like a puzzle whose pieces kept appearing from nowhere without warning to fill in the picture of her life. But she seemed to see it at a distance, without emotion, as if the woman in the picture was not herself.

She now knew her name, that she was with child, that she came from New York and that her father's name was Janis and that he was strict and she was scared of him. She remembered that well enough. Of one thing she was also sure: he would never accept the sin and the shame of what she had done. There was no going back.

She knew also that whatever had happened to her before she fell into Bubbly Creek was still too shocking for her to remember – or, more like, to want to remember. But she knew she must try because maybe that would help her remember who the father of her child was.

The train started forward again and then stopped almost at once, another car being uncoupled. It was enough to jolt Anna back to the present. She had better get ready to climb out of the hopper because the next stop was the fourth. The train began to move and the grain elevator receded behind her, revealing the sun once more. She used the remaining time to tidy herself up a bit. Her dress was torn and stained from her escape. She took from her bundle the one she had stolen and, keeping low so as not to show herself over the side of the open hopper, she undressed quickly and tried it on. It was plain and a little large, but at least it was clean, as were the stockings and the shawl which she wrapped around herself.

Then she noticed the clipboard she had hit Dr Eels with. She was about to discard it, but decided to take a closer look at it for the first time.

On the top was some kind of list of names with something about 'experimental procedures' and Cook County Insane Asylum on it; underneath were several forms. All the names – twenty of them – were women's. And there, near the end, was her own – *Anna Zemeckis, age about 21* . . . She didn't stop to read any more. Rolling the list up tight together with the form with her name on it, she stuffed the papers down her bodice.

She pulled on the woolen stockings and felt less exposed after that. Her shoes were sturdy but grubby. She managed to get them clean with a piece of sacking.

That left her hair, which she guessed looked as messy as it felt, which was tangled and lank.

She tore off a part of the hem of the dress she had discarded and used it to tie back her hair.

But her hands and nails were filthy and her mouth felt rough; and still the sense of being sick was never far away.

I need water.

As she went, she was about to discard the clipboard and its remaining documents among the crates and sacks, when suddenly she had an inrush of new memory. She had seen official-looking papers like this before, but where?

She could remember the sense of the building, big and airy, but the people there . . .

Ssh!

She remembered someone making that sound with a finger to their lips when someone talked too loud.

No talking!

Yes, she had worked in a library. In a city somewhere. Was it Chicago? Or New York? Or was it both?

She finally shook her head, unable yet to open the door onto that particular part of her memory. A library!

Twenty minutes later, the train finally made its fourth stop. Anna peeked over the edge of the wagon and saw the Chicago River stretching away between two high factory buildings. There was a ship, some barges and some cranes, and beyond them three bridges, one after the other.

Footsteps crunched along the track and she hid back down again.

'You can come down, it's safe!'

It was the driver.

She clambered back down the hopper ladder and on to the track.

'You know where you are?'

She shook her head.

'That's the North Side industrial area. You don't want to go that way. Not nice. You go *that* way.'

He pointed to a wooden fence on the far side of the tracks.

'Climb through that gap in the fence over there and you can make your way across the empty lots to Canal Street. What are you going to do?'

'I don't know.'

He stared at her.

'I'm parched,' she said.

He was thinking.

'Well, you look a whole lot better than when you got in.'

'Took a dress from the washing line at Dunning.'

'You're no fool. Here, I've got water . . .'

He led her across a couple of rail tracks to a far corner of the sidings and a ramshackle rail hut.

'My refuge on bad days. Quiet and peaceful compared to the rackety place I room at,' he explained.

His fished about under the wooden structure, found a key and opened up the padlocked door.

'Here . . .'

As they entered he produced a tin pail of water.

'It's alright, it's clean, have some,' he said.

She drank.

He found something wrapped in paper.

'Sausage,' he said. 'You might need it.'

'You needn't,' she said, taking it gratefully.

He said nothing, but pondered for a while.

'Best bet is to get yourself beyond the reach of Cook County and across the state border into Minnesota. You can get a direct train to St Paul or Minneapolis. That'll get you out of trouble.'

'Oh, but I need to get further than that,' responded Anna. 'To Canada.' The conviction with which she said it was a surprise to her, a sudden moment of revelation. For now she remembered. 'Yes . . . my aunt, she lives there . . . on a farm, north out of Winnipeg, on Lac du Bonnet.'

'Then you'll be heading in the right direction. You can get a train straight to Winnipeg from St Paul.'

'First I need to rest and get enough money together for the fare,' said Anna, her voice dropping. 'I'll lie low, find a place to work for a week or two, and then head off,' she said. 'I've worked before, you know.'

'Doing what?'

'In a library I think . . . No, I'm sure of it. Things are coming back into my head all the time.'

'You got beaten up by the look of things.'

He nodded towards her bruised face.

Then he added, 'The girls always get beaten up in the detention hospital; and worse. Then they get sent to Dunning.'

'My beating happened before that,' said Anna, suddenly sure it had. 'It happened before I ended up in Bubbly Creek.'

He looked sympathetic.

Then: 'Not being sure what work you can do won't get you far in Chicago. Can you sew?'

'Of course.'

He nodded towards Canal Street.

'Go on past the Union Depot and down to Jackson. There's sweat work down there for anyone can use a needle and not many questions asked. But lie low. Dunning doesn't like losing patients and they'll put the police on it.'

Anna's heart missed a beat, and then some more.

'I hurt someone getting away,' she blurted out.

'Then they *will* be after you, girl. Just lie low a few days, get some money together and then get the train out to St Paul. The Fair's on and the police have their work cut out. They won't hunt you for long. Better things to do.'

He stared at her.

'Got any money?'

She shook her head and said, 'I don't want, I . . .'

He took a handful of coins from his pocket and pressed them into her hand.

'You take 'em.'

'Why are you helping me . . . ?' she stuttered. She was suddenly close to tears.

He looked at her for a few moments and stepped close.

'I'll tell you. When I came to America ten years back I was just twenty. I came with my clothes on my back and a bit of savings. I thought everybody meant well. But they don't. My savings got took by someone on my first day and the clothes wore out pretty quick. I was pretty well down like you are now. But one day somebody gave me a kind look and a helping hand. I made good but never forgot. Ever since then I've done the same for others when I can.'

'I'll pay you back.'

'You just get yourself well and help someone else when you're able. That'll be payment enough.'

'I *want* to pay you back. What's your name, sir? Where will I find you?'

'You'll find me at the end of this train,' he growled, 'or in jail for helping the likes of you. Now, off you go and I don't ever want to see you again!'

'My name's Anna,' she said impulsively.

'You take care, Anna. And don't you trust anyone. Not in a city like Chicago. Now . . . go!'

She went but when she was on the far side of the track he shouted after her, 'It's Tom. Tomas Steffens!'

She turned back and waved at him.

'I'll name my baby after you,' she called back.

He stood there watching her, right until she had slipped through the fence and was gone.

He wasn't a praying man but he said a prayer just the same, and it wasn't just for her.

25

The Illinois Crowd

The White City, which was what everybody called Jackson Park for the duration of the Fair, presented Emily with an astonishing spectacle: dozens of white-painted classical buildings, a superb Lake Front, neat pedestrian walkways and artificial lakes spread out across six hundred acres of parkland.

But she felt more and more tired.

The excitement of the past days, the journey, the rush to get out here in time for her lunch appointment, and finally Fay Bancroft herself. It was enough to exhaust anyone. She walked past the Illinois Building, the grandest of the state buildings, which looked as if it had been transported from Washington itself, then round the north Pond toward the Lake Front.

The atmosphere was calmer than the Midway Plaisance, but it was hardly less busy. Having sorted out her reporter's credentials in the Administration Building, she rented a chair and sat shoreside in the warm autumnal sun, watching the steamers coming and going on Lake Michigan as they ferried visitors by their thousands to and from the Fair.

She closed her eyes and drifted, only the sound of lowing cattle and squealing hogs from the nearby stock pavilion causing her to start and wake, before she drifted off once more. No one bothered her except another Columbian guardsman doing his job.

'You all right, ma'am?'

Emily opened her eyes, shaded them against the sun, and smiled. 'Just tired, I guess.'

'You're not the first and most certainly won't be the last. There's a ladies-only cafeteria over by the Electricity Building alongside the Basin if you . . . ?'

'I'm fine. I'll be going shortly.'

'Have a pleasant day.'

She closed her eyes again, feeling comfortable, safe and protected. She tried to turn her thoughts to Anna Zemeckis, but found she couldn't, drifting off again to the sound of the crunching feet of promenaders, their chatter and their laughter; to the hoots of the steamers and the calls, in Italian, of the gondoliers in the Basin, specially imported for the occasion.

The reception later that afternoon was busy and loud. Fay was as good as her word and introduced Emily to a cross-section of Chicagoans, to most of whom Emily gave her card and received theirs in return, though she was sure with her good memory for a face and a name that she would remember most of them.

She was allowed a few brief words with the high-ups, including the famous Mrs Potter Palmer, the life-force behind the Woman's Building, who gave her a winning smile, and Philip Armour, king of the meatpackers, who smiled politely but seemed anxious to move on. Finally, feeling like one of a dozen bees around a honey pot, she shook the hand of the mayor himself, the bearded and affable Carter Henry Harrison III. It was a chance she did not want to miss, though she would have preferred to meet him later on in her investigation.

'Good afternoon, sir. Emily Strauss of the New York *World* . . .'

One of Harrison's aides immediately closed in.

Emily ignored him. 'Any chance of a few words for the *World*?'

'Plenty,' said Harrison, 'but right now . . .'

He was smiling as he moved away.

'. . . About women visitors disappearing during the Fair.'

The moment she said it, Emily knew it was too much, too soon. Harrison showed no alarm or irritation but his aide swiftly stepped in.

'Another time, Miss . . . ?'

'Strauss.'

'Another time, lady.'

But Harrison turned back.

His smile was genuine. He had not been elected mayor five times for nothing.

'Sure there's been women going missing, Miss Strauss, and men too. But Chicago's got no monopoly on disappearances. In fact, it's about the one thing we *don't* have a monopoly on!'

There was general laughter and it was good natured.

'People go missing all over. Even in New York, as your boss Mr Pulitzer knows. As for Chicago, we do what we can for those that go missing in our jurisdiction, and with a fair amount of success. But . . .'

Someone tugged Harrison's sleeve. Emily had had her two minutes' worth.

'Maybe I can call on you at City Hall, Mr Mayor?'

'You do that. My office and my home are always open to genuine enquirers. You won't find me hard to find. But right now . . .'

He shrugged mock-helplessly, reached out a hand and shook hers again.

'Gotta go.'

He went, his entourage with him, and Emily was left feeling he was a good man who had given her more time than most.

'Did he really mean that?' she said to someone standing next to her, 'about his door always being open?'

'That's *exactly* what he meant. Everybody knows where the mayor lives on South Ashland Avenue. I reckon it's the secret of his success; he makes people feel he's accessible.'

Emily watched after him. 'I just might take Mr Harrison up on his offer . . . ,' she said to herself.

Meanwhile the Illinois crowd swelled about her and she continued on her round of shaking the hands of the great and good of Chicago. These were mainly businessmen, their enterprises ranging from real estate and finance to steel, groceries and pharmaceuticals. There were women too: some no more than pretty things on their husbands' arms, others more formidable, like Hannah Horner, the German-born wife of Henry Horner the grocery magnate of South Water Street. In no time at all, Emily had out of her the story of how on Henry's

151

premature death in the late seventies, Mrs Horner took over the business and grew it yet more.

'That's enough about me!' declared Mrs Horner adding, 'Time for you to meet the Illinois crowd!' as she introduced Emily to a group of women whose hands she shook and names noted: Harriet Isham, Katharine Field, Mrs Frederic Eames, Mrs Christiane Darke, Mrs John Jacob Glessner and several others, any one of whom might be useful in the days to come.

They were mostly friendly and freely exchanged their cards with hers. Emily was wary of explaining her mission, but suggested that she would be interested in talking to 'women of influence' as she flatteringly put it, since they had made such a mark at the Fair.

A while later Fay reappeared.

'That photograph of your girl,' she said, 'there's a place you might usefully display it and I have obtained permission for you to do so . . .'

Emily followed her to a noticeboard at one end of the Great Hall in which the reception was being held. It was filled with advertisements of various kinds. In one section, titled 'Looking for . . . !' there were dozens of cards, slips of paper with names written on them and a few images in the form of *cartes de visite* of visitors to the Fair, all for people who were looking to contact each other.

Emily pinned up the spare copy of the photograph of Anna Zemeckis she had had made before leaving New York, and scribbled her name as well as her own and her contact details, asking for any information anyone might have about her and the weeks when she went missing.

After that, Emily moved from one group to another, sometimes introducing herself as a journalist and other times not, for she knew there were some who shut up tight as a clam when they met anyone of her profession.

Then, as the numbers in the hall suddenly thinned and she saw the sun was dropping low on the horizon outside, Emily realized she had stayed later than she intended. Chicago was not a good place for a single woman to be out after nightfall. She decided to head off back downtown for her hotel supper and an early night.

The tiredness had not left her. If anything it was worse now. Suddenly the enormity of what she was trying to do overwhelmed her, and with it the seeming absurdity of thinking she could track down the story of the missing final weeks in the life of a solitary girl in so great and busy a city as this, where one person was no more than a grain of sand on the Lakeshore.

Meanwhile, elsewhere in the hall of the Illinois State Building, a woman with dark hair and pale features, modestly but well dressed, disengaged herself from a group with whom she seemed to have nothing in common and looked about rather helplessly as a woman does who is naturally shy and has lost her escort. Then, lacking anything better to do and so as not to be too conspicuous, she wandered over to the noticeboards at the end of the hall.

She read the messages under 'Looking For . . .' her eyes tired, her skin pale, her manner diffident.

Someone called out a greeting and she half turned and nodded her head, not engaging.

She looked around again for her escort and, still not seeing him, turned back to the board. She stared a long time at the faces there and at that of Anna Zemeckis. She read the note that Emily had left. Then she read some others, as if in each of their little stories she was searching for a door that would open and take her to a place that was better than the one she was in.

She turned back to the crowd and, seeming to see the man she was looking for, moved off, head down, still not engaging, through the crowd.

Which was why Mrs Christiane Darke did not notice the man who, from the shadows of a nearby colonnade, had been watching her, just as he had spent the afternoon watching others. But her especially.

Middle-aged, mustachioed, his face tough and resolute, his eyes intelligent and questing, his form muscular, his jacket of thick tweed, his boots a little scuffed and grubby, he emerged into the light coolly, contriving to seem more a shadow than a real man.

He spent his days watching people, and noting what he saw and sometimes what he didn't.

He was the same man who had spent an enlightening morning in Sol Bann's saloon at State and Randolph, taking careful note of who had attended the meeting of the Audit Committee of the Old America

Association in the Masonic Temple. Now here he was in the Illinois State Building of the White City at a reception to which no one had invited him.

He went to the noticeboard and examined it as Christiane Darke had done, only faster and more systematically. Then seeing the picture of Anna and Emily's note, he quickly and calmly removed them both and placed them carefully in an inside pocket.

If anyone noticed what he did they made no attempt to stop him. He did not look the kind of man one should challenge.

Then he turned away, checked on Christiane Darke's whereabouts and vanished into the gathering gloom outside.

As for Emily, her hopes for an early return downtown were dashed. The end-of-day queues at the terminus for the Elevated seemed a mile long and the trains were running slow.

26

Sweatshops

Anna Zemeckis's day had been the hardest of her life.

She had felt sick throughout, partly from her pregnancy but also from the worry of having neither a job nor a bed for the night. She was cold and tired and hungry.

She had done what Tomas Steffens the engine driver had advised and had set off to find a sewing job. But that hadn't proved easy. Now it was getting late.

She had started in Canal Street, which ran north–south on the west side of the Chicago River and Chicago's downtown area. It was a street of busy intersections with elevated trains crossing over at either end and the Union Depot right in the middle.

Anna hurried southward through its clamor of wagons and carts, busy warehousemen and shouting porters, keeping her eyes to the sidewalk and her shawl tightly wrapped round her.

She felt safe in the anonymity of its crowds but these thinned after she had passed the depot and continued on towards Van Buren Street and the garment quarter. She knew she needed to find employment if she was to pay for the board and lodging she must find.

She stopped and huddled in a doorway to count the money Tomas Steffens had pressed into her hand: a dollar and fifteen cents. It was more than generous and her gratitude was equaled by her determination that she would somehow find a way of paying it back.

She hurried on.

At Jackson she saw a man coming over the bridge carrying a bundle of half-sewn black cloaks on his shoulder, tied together with twine, and impulsively turned in the direction from which he had come.

It took her straight into South Market Street; in whichever direction she looked she saw evidence of the garment trade – tailoring establishments, a cravat factory, wagons with bales of cloth and some men outside a doorway with rails of dresses and some boxes of newly made men's pants.

She was just debating whether or not to approach them for a job when she saw a notice in a window on the far side of the street. The establishment was called Taylor Kirk & Co., and the notice read *HANDS WANTED FOR FINE HATS*.

When she got closer she saw that someone had added the word *Experienced* at the top and *Use the Back* at the end.

Plain sewing she was sure she could do, but 'Fine Hats' she was less sure of. She passed on by in the hope that if one place wanted hands, another surely would.

She was not wrong. A block further on she saw a huge hoarding on top of a seven-floor factory which read *INTERNATIONAL TAILORING COMPANY*.

The door at the side of the premises also advertised for hands, this time for 'finishers'. Anna went on in.

The dingy interior still hummed and vibrated with the sound of machinery, the working day in this part of Chicago not ending until seven. There was no light but what came through the door.

A boy stood by a lift which was open and piled high with garments.

'You gotta use the stairs,' he said.

'Who do I ask for?'

'Depends.'

'For work.'

'Just ask,' he said. 'Third floor.'

He spat tobacco juice on the floor at her feet.

The wooden stairs were steep and uneven and the noise got worse with each one until, arriving at the third floor, Anna could no longer hear the sound of her own breathing.

She looked in on a room filled with rows and rows of sewing machines at which men and women stood, though most had a chair. There seemed no time to sit down.

This was not the kind of sewing she was used to.

She caught someone's eye, shouted above the noise what she wanted and they pointed further into the vast room towards a door into a glass cubicle.

Since knocking on it seemed pointless, she pushed it open and peered inside. One of several men detached himself and came to her.

'Wait there!' he shouted. 'She's busy.'

Anna sat on the chair he pointed at.

Eventually a woman appeared.

'You experienced?'

'Not very but I can learn.'

The conversation was a shouted one.

'There's no one to learn you. Show me your hands.'

Anna held them out, conscious of her stubby, dirty nails.

'Yer'll not last long here. Too soft. Try two blocks on. There's always smaller firms wanting.'

Outside in the street, Anna realized she had wasted a couple of hours already. Worse still, her ears were buzzing painfully from the sound of the machines and her head was spinning. It took a while longer of wearily trudging up and down before she saw what she was looking for: *Sewers wanted.*

This time there was a man on the door at the back.

She explained what she wanted.

'Second floor,' he said. 'Stairs only.'

Anna began to climb the steep stairs, her heart sinking. She could already hear the hum of machinery and noticed the dust in the air.

She carried on climbing until she reached another room full of machines and pale people whose silence suggested that talking was forbidden.

'The gentleman who attends to the work is not here just at the present,' snapped an elderly male clerk. 'Take a seat and wait.'

Anna did what she was told, glad initially of the rest, but she soon

became restless and anxious. It was getting late and she still had
no job.

Eventually a young man, well dressed and full of himself, appeared.

'What can you do?'

'Sew.'

'We don't want any,' he said, turning abruptly away.

'Says outside you do,' said Anna. 'What *do* you want?'

He turned belligerently and stared at her for a moment.

'Not you,' he said, 'so you can leave.'

'But—'

'Now,' he snarled.

Anna turned to leave.

A girl she passed who had been watching her and heard the conver-
sation whispered, 'If you can hand-sew, Brennan's is worth a try.
Always looking for hand-finishers. Pays well if you can get in. It's on
Clark Street. Can't miss it – Brennan's Tailoring Emporium.'

Anna set off once more.

Brennan's had a shop at the front and a workplace at the back and
their products were plain to see as Anna made her way through the
gloomy stock rooms: ladies' cloaks, men's jackets and pants, and
Brennan's specialty – cravats, slip-ties, dude ties, flat scarves, four-in-
hands and bow-knots in colorful profusion.

The forewoman, Mrs Donal, was a formidable Irish lady. She said
at once she was reluctant to take Anna on, explaining that pressure
of work was so great that there was no time to teach green hands.

'But I'm dextrous and trained,' said Anna, responding to a grin and
a wink from one of the girls nearby. 'I'm experienced with cloaks and
coats.'

'Then why not get work in one of those trades? They pay better
than us.'

'You could try me for a week,' said Anna.

'Try you for a year and you'll not learn it if you don't know it
already.'

Anna sat there hopefully.

'I'll let you have a cravat and see what you can do,' said Mrs Donal.
'What's your name?'

Anna froze momentarily, remembering she must not betray her true identity, 'It's Jelena . . . Jelena Markulis.' Her mother's name had been the only one to come to her in that desperate moment.

It was a beginning and Anna set to, secretly watching another woman working on a scarf to see what she did.

The workshop was breezy and roomy and the hands had chairs and were allowed to talk: men one end, women the other. Mrs Donal ambled over an hour later and looked over Anna's work.

'Passable, I suppose.'

'What will I get paid?'

Mrs Donal snorted and walked off.

'That's a sample,' explained one of the other women. 'Don't pay you for samples. That's her privilege. She'd have told you to leave if she didn't like it. Finish it and ask for some more . . .'

Mrs Donal accepted the sample and gave Anna more cravats to do.

'Forty-five cents a dozen,' she said, 'and it's eight o'clock sharp in the morning or you're fined.'

Anna accepted the terms, grateful for what she had got.

The women wanted to know all about her. She made up a story about having been let down by a relative on the Near West Side.

'Bohemian?' they asked.

'No, he was German,' said Anna and a face she had not remembered until then came into her mind's eye.

'Didn't like him,' she said, as a new memory, of her Uncle Hendriks Markulis, came back to her.

'You German, then? We're mainly Irish here.'

Anna shook her head but said no more. But eventually, unable to contain her curiosity, the friendliest of the women leaned over and asked, 'Where are you staying then?'

Anna explained that she had yet to find accommodation.

The woman nodded, having guessed Anna's situation right.

'Try the Mission of Hope,' she said. 'You Catholic?'

Anna shook her head, 'No, Lutheran.' But something made her reach instinctively for her neck.

She remembered she had had a crucifix once. Her mother's crucifix, the one she never took off.

She felt a pang of loss and sadness.

'I had a crucifix,' she said suddenly. 'But it's gone . . . and I can't remember where I lost it.'

'They'll give you one free at the Mission,' said her new friend. 'It's on Monroe and South Jefferson. Mrs Donal'll give you a letter. They only take girls in employment.'

27

Conflicted

Cook County Insane Asylum was in total lockdown as the search for Anna Zemeckis and the missing documents continued into the evening. The weather had turned dull and gloomy and it was getting dark outside.

The patients had all been secured in their wards while some members of staff, many of them kept back at the end of their shifts, systematically searched the site.

This provoked a good deal of grumbling in the ranks. Under Maureen Riley's regime, staff frequently sneaked off early once the patients were locked into their wards for the night, leaving the institution understaffed. Which was fine, until there was an emergency. Right now there simply weren't enough people available to conduct a swift search across the huge Dunning site.

Every ward, basement, attic and outhouse in the vast and sprawling institution had to be checked, as well as the extensive grounds.

Impatient with the slowness of the search for Anna Zemeckis, Dr Eels, his mouth still throbbing from the blow she had given him, had taken command – a role that Riley herself would have assumed were she not now lying partially sedated in one of the secluded wards on Far Side. Eels had expressly forbidden anyone from seeing her but himself, Mould and a specially selected nurse.

It helped that Nurse Lutyens, a former senior matron under Dr Eels whom he had brought with him from the Danbury Asylum to assist in purely medical matters, disliked Riley intensely, a fact of which Eels was well aware. She could be relied on to keep Riley's numerous friends and allies well away.

The doctor was in a very curious and conflicted state of mind. On the one hand he felt mounting panic about the loss of his papers. He knew that if details of his work reached the newspapers it would go against him, especially as his mentor and supporter, Paul Hartz, had warned him about this very thing only the evening before. Eels feared for his promotion, perhaps even his job.

Yet, at the same time, as he waited anxiously for positive news from his staff, he was in a curious state of euphoria. He paced about his office restlessly, unable to settle to anything. He felt the growing excitement of a scientist who believes himself to be on the threshold of a discovery that might prove to be one of the most significant breakthroughs of the century in his field.

For, if he was right, then what had happened to Riley offered a practical, effective and above all simple solution to the problem of insanity.

'It is so elegant!' he kept telling himself in wonderment. 'Like all truly great ideas it is finally *so* simple!'

He sat down at his desk, drew three profiles of a skull: side, front and from above. Then he drew a line on each in turn, representing the implement he intended to use.

'We shall administer what Burckhardt has called a topectomy,' he murmured to himself, 'by accessing the lobes of the brain transorbitally . . .'

As if to visualize the procedure even better, Dr Eels placed his index finger in the recess between his right eyeball and the brow above it and pushed gently in until it hurt.

'The area is sterile,' he muttered, 'the procedure reaches the skull at its weakest point, at the very place we need to be and yet without any need to trephane.'

He withdrew his finger and blinked as his eye watered.

'Best of all, it is a very fast procedure that leaves no scars!'

He stood up again, went to the window and looked out. He saw the bobbing of storm lanterns in the dark across the grounds.

'Come on, come *on!*' he muttered. 'She must be somewhere!'

He turned into the room, eying the framed certificate from Johns Hopkins Medical School that acknowledged his status as a qualified physician, which now hung on the wall near his desk. His eyes lit up as he visioned those additional honors that would surely come his way as a result of his discovery of a procedure that would establish him as the father, the fountainhead perhaps, of the new discipline of psychosurgery.

'Yes,' he whispered, '*yes* . . .'

Then he frowned, went over to open his door and looked up and down the corridor. He stood there listening, in the hope that someone was finally coming to say that the woman and his clipboard had been found. He wanted to get *on.*

He was now desperate to get back to Riley and conduct specific observations. It was vital that the course of her recovery and the symptoms she presented were closely followed and charted. He had deputed that role to Mould and Nurse Lutyens, but he wanted to be back doing it himself.

Then he heard someone hurrying up the stairs and went to meet them, his hopes rising.

Eels had let it be known that the person who found either patient or documents – and preferably both – would be generously rewarded. But he had also made very clear that he expected not a single word of what had happened to go beyond the walls of Dunning.

'I'm sorry, Dr Eels,' began the hapless orderly, 'but we've found nothing yet.'

'Nothing?'

The orderly shook his head and described the places that had been searched.

'We're sweeping through the grounds again right now.'

The Dunning clock struck half-past six.

'Keep trying; she must be somewhere. Unless she got clean away.'

'Yes, sir.'

'No sign of my clipboard? It's metal, it's . . .'

The orderly again shook his head.

'People are asking how Riley is, sir?'

'She's making as good a recovery as can be expected,' responded Eels smoothly, 'but she needs to stay quiet for a time. Meanwhile, don't let up on the search.'

Eels turned back into his room, frowning.

He knew that what had happened could not be kept a secret much longer. Sooner or later, he would have to do the one thing he dreaded: inform Paul Hartz now before he heard it from someone else.

Eels guessed who that would be: Dr Benjamin Brown, the medical superintendent whom he was replacing in seven days' time. Fortunately Brown was old, tired and a prevaricator, and unlikely to do what Eels himself would most certainly have done were the situation reversed: go straight to Hartz now and pin the blame on someone else.

As it was, Eels had persuaded Brown to keep things quiet for the time being, partly on the promise that the patient would be found – he had not mentioned the documents – but also because what had happened might reflect badly on Brown, who wanted no shadows falling across his final days at Dunning.

Eels had already made up his mind that if anyone went to see Hartz tomorrow it would be himself; and if anyone took the rap it would be Riley, who could not answer back and would now probably never be able to if Eels was right in his diagnosis of the fortuitously selective trauma her brain had suffered.

As for Dr Brown . . .

Eels frowned again and his eyes narrowed.

His tongue flicked over his thin lips.

Eels was thinking. Hard.

He crossed his room and picked up the skull he kept in his cabinet, along with other mementoes of his medical career. It was a prized possession, given to him by the professor of neuropathology at King's College, London, during his study tour of Europe three years previously.

He picked up the skull in one hand and a silver paper knife used for opening envelopes in the other and passed its sharp point through to the back of the skull's right orbit.

His eyes narrowed as he raised the skull level with them and studied the precise point at which the knife point touched bone. Then he applied pressure to it. The bone gave with a sound no sharper than a cracker breaking and the knife passed through into the lobal cavity behind.

'Yes!' murmured Eels as fragments of dry bone fell on the table top. He was going to see to it that Brown and Riley together took the rap, not him.

28

Dead Man's Alley

The going-home queues for the Elevated at Jackson Park were so long that it had nearly gone seven in the evening before Emily finally found a seat and was on her way back downtown.

No sooner had she done so than she fell asleep. Others did the same. A day at the World's Fair brought on tiredness quicker than any sleeping draught.

The trouble was that, when she woke, which she did with a start, the carriage was emptying of its last passengers and a guard was prodding her.

'Train stops here. Got to get off.'

'Where are we? I need to get to Congress.'

'So do other folk. You'll have to walk like them.'

'Where are we?'

'Twelfth. Stay on Wabash and you'll be all right. It ain't that far. Now . . .'

The guard helped her off.

Maybe Emily was still half-asleep, maybe she was just confused; or maybe, Chicago, having given her a warm welcome and an easy afternoon, wanted to remind her of its darker side.

Within half a block she knew she was lost, the steps down from the Elevated confusing her into thinking she was going north, which she needed to do for a couple of blocks to find her hotel, when in fact she had turned west . . . or maybe . . . or possibly . . .

She couldn't make sense of where she was at all, and the more she looked around the more she did not like what she saw.

The better-dressed ladies she was used to seeing downtown had all disappeared, to be replaced by looser-looking women with garish dresses with bodices set too low and hems set too high. They stood in groups; they stared at passing men.

The men were worse still: some were well dressed but furtive, some looked like young clerks out for an evening's fun; others hung back in the shadows, bowlers at an angle over their eyes, keeping a predatory eye on the passersby.

Emily dug into her purse for the Rand McNally map of the city she had brought with her, but knew it was a mistake the moment she unfolded it and held it under the nearest light, which came from a saloon window.

Men already lurking on the sidewalk took the map as excuse to stop.

'Can I help you, ma'am . . . ?'

'No,' said Emily firmly, hurriedly putting the map away and walking on.

She stopped by a stall that sold newspapers, or so it seemed, to give herself time to think.

'They come by the half-dozen, ma'am,' grinned the stallholder.

She looked more closely. The 'papers' were a cover for something else: postcards with pictures of women in every stage of undress.

A big, rough-looking man with a curly bowler loomed over her, his smile as reassuring as a streetcar with a wheel missing.

'No, I . . .' she hurried on, realizing it was best to keep moving. She had to find a more private place to study her map.

Annoyed with herself for her stupidity she scanned the confusing scene with its lights and people, piano music and chop-house smells, for some way out. She had the alarming sensation that she was being observed, maybe already being followed and with no one, absolutely no one on the sidewalk she could trust to help her.

'Miss . . .'

Another man leered in her face.

167

If she could only see the Elevated again she could orientate herself.
If only she could see a street name . . .

'Hello, miss!"

The world seemed full of leering, grasping men, endless saloons
from which they tumbled, and then there were the women too, staring,
rouged so red they looked like Christmas lights, skirts hoisted so high
Emily could see the ribbons of their stocking tops and their bodices
unhooked far enough to show their bosoms.

She crossed the road, hoping she was heading north, knowing the
hotel could not be more than a block or two away. On the sidewalk
on the far side she spotted another road which she only realized was
a filthy dark alley when she had turned right into it.

She saw its name too late: Dead Man's Alley.

Turning back immediately she found herself face-to-face with three
or four men grinning unpleasantly at her.

'Lookin' fer someone, lady?' growled one of them.

Emily was terrified.

'Or somethin'?'

Her heartbeat was thunder in her chest.

She wanted to run, but not up the alley behind her. She wanted to
hit out, but blows against men like this would get her nowhere. She
wanted to scream and tried to, but all that came out was a croak.

'You're coming with us,' said another of the men as they crowded
her back into the darkness, '*with us.*'

But suddenly another man, bigger than the rest, and better dressed,
loomed out of the dark and faced the men down.

'Leave her be.'

He carried a cane which he only had to raise slightly before they
retreated back into the seething crowd.

'Thank you, sir. I was trying to get to the Auditorium Annex.'

He smiled but she couldn't see more than his teeth in the dark.

'That's not far. Come from the Fair? The Elevated stop short?'

'Yes,' she said, glad he understood. 'At 12th. I just want to get to
my hotel.'

'It's just a block from here, ma'am,' he said, taking his hat off and
offering an arm.

'Which way?' she said nervously.

'I'll show you. Down here's the quickest. Be there in less than three minutes. I'll show you.'

His voice was like the purr of a big tom cat.

'Where?' said Emily faintly as he led her back into the alley, the way she had not wanted to go. 'I don't think . . .'

Ten paces on he took her hand off his arm and held it in his hand, his grip like steel.

'Let me go,' she said.

'Don't think so, lady,' he said, forcing her forward almost off her feet.

Again she tried to scream, but failed. She looked desperately back towards the light of the street and saw the figures of men watching.

Emily Strauss, cub reporter, who thought at twenty-two that she knew the ways of the world, had fallen for the oldest trick in the book. Accepting help from a welcome stranger because a group of men are threatening, not realizing he's their boss.

She tried to call for help.

His hand tightened on her arm still more and her cry turned into one of pain as the shadows closed in about her.

29

Mission of Hope

Over on the Near West Side, two hundred yards down Jefferson at the corner of Monroe, stood the dour-looking Catholic mission that was about to become Anna's unlikely new home.

It was built of yellow brick in a dreary, straitlaced way with a formidable, solid oak door in heavy gothic style, its hinges massive, its lock huge and with a mean metal grille blanked off with a wooden slat which could only be slid open from the inside.

There was a range of plain rectangular windows covered in black metal bars facing the street – to stop intruders, presumably, but Anna wondered irreverently if it was also to stop the holy sisters getting out and having a good time downtown.

The place did not exactly inspire feelings of warmth, and none at all of hope, even though an extension of the building had 'Mission of Hope' painted on it in big black letters.

Anna approached the door and, before deciding whether to raise the knocker or pull the metal bellpull, read the two notices displayed.

Charity handouts only on Saturdays 5.00–7.00 PM said one of them, whilst a second announced, *Working girls only need apply.*

Anna decided to ring the bell, which clanged loudly.

Almost at once the wooden slat slammed open and two cold grey eyes stared at her from behind a metal grille.

'You should use the door-knocker after seven-thirty,' the owner of the eyes said in a thin, harsh voice.

The slat slammed shut again.

Anna looked over the door once more and saw a third notice which announced the times when applicants might ring or knock for refuge.

Unsure what to do, Anna knocked.

The slat opened again and the same eyes stared at her.

'Yes?'

Anna explained why she had come and that Mrs Donal had recommended the Mission to her.

'You're not with child, I hope?'

Anna's heart missed several beats. 'No,' she lied, 'I am not.'

The slat was shut again, bolts were drawn and the door was opened. Anna found herself staring down at a diminutive, rotund nun with gray eyes and a thin, wet mouth.

'Follow me.'

Of the next half-hour Anna remembered little.

She was tired and just wanted to sleep.

She signed some forms; she met three sisters, including the one who opened the door, who was Sister Agnes. The others were the superior, Sister Ursula, old, crabbed and stooped; and Sister Dolores, younger, bad-tempered-looking and bossy.

Who did what, Anna had no idea. She knew only that Sister Dolores demanded fifty cents from her 'against breakages' and put it in a cash box that seemed to Anna to be overflowing with money, and that Sister Agnes ran through the Rules with a capital R, the breaking of any one of which meant immediate expulsion from the Mission and the forfeit of all monies received.

Anna was too tired to take it in or even to care.

Sister Ursula sat behind a desk in the Mission office, staring through pale eyes and spectacles but saying nothing.

'Must you have the fifty cents now?' Anna managed to say.

'Yes,' said Sister Ursula, reaching out for it.

Anna's pitiful supply of money given her by Tomas Steffens was suddenly halved.

Sister Agnes took her to a dormitory and showed her the cot that was to be hers. There were no other women in there at all, presumably because they were all having supper. Anna could smell the sickly aroma of overcooked vegetables and overstewed meat. It made her stomach turn.

Finally, left alone, she lay down on the cot and closed her eyes.

'Boots *off!*' a voice shouted in her ear.

It was Sister Dolores, the younger one, appearing out of nowhere. 'The Rules are *very* clear on *that* point,' she said.

Anna took them off and lay down again.

She closed her eyes and drifted into worried half-sleep, images of the long day dancing before her, the noise of the crowds in Canal Street now soft, now loud, and then blending in with the clatter of the machinery at Brennan's, before that too melded into something else: the arrival of women in the dormitory, their boots resounding on the wooden floor, their voices subdued.

No one paid her the slightest attention and she stayed where she was, glad finally to lie down and rest her feet. At least she had a bed, of sorts, for now. And work.

The other women there were as exhausted as she was. There wasn't much said. So Anna just lay there, exhausted.

She put her hand on her stomach and wondered about so many things as sleep tried to overtake her.

But she kept her eyes open. She wanted to remember.

Then, for the first time during that long and terrible day, Anna Zemeckis allowed herself to shed a single tear for the crucifix she suddenly missed so much. The one a long, long time ago her father had given her when her mother died, which was the first thing she could remember; and she experienced again the grief she had first felt at the loss of her mother and how her long journey to America with her father had begun.

Janis Zemeckis.

He was always so strict. He would never forgive her now. *Never.*

Anna reached for where the crucifix had been and longed for her mother's touch. Then, turning, she hid her face in the bolster on her bed, her mouth open to its hardness, her hot tears flowing, her sobs as silent as she could make them.

She was not the only one weeping in the dormitory that night.

Along its walls hung poorly reproduced religious images. There were the Virgin Mary and Mary Magdalene and, in a far corner, a picture of Jesus at a door, holding a lantern, representing the Light of the World.

But strangely, in the gathering gloom, out of all these images, it was Jesus' crown of thorns that showed up best.

30

Run!

The alley was dark, dank and stank of water closets and filth, of cheroots and beer. And there were noises too: fits of raucous laughter, of rowdy men carousing in nearby saloons and, somewhere, closer-to, a drunken woman's voice warbling Mr Harris's 'After the Ball Is Over' to an out-of-tune piano.

The grip on Emily's arm was powerful and her helplessness was made worse by the fact that the man had hooked his left arm around her shoulder, pulling her tightly into his side.

'You try screaming again, lady, and I'll stick you,' he said savagely. Her left leg collided with a trash can which went flying.

Even if she had tried, which she didn't, Emily could not have screamed. Her mouth was dry, her throat knotted up with fear.

She tried to turn away and saw, in a half-open door, a man standing against a woman. His pants were half off, her hand was at his privates, his hand was up her skirt and her thighs above her stockings all bare.

The prostitute stared at Emily indifferently and went about her business.

From the direction in which she had come, she could hear the normal sounds of people in the street and the clip-clop of hacks passing by.

Meanwhile the drunken revelry and music-making in the dens and panel houses, through the blinds of which she could see people lurching about, got louder and louder as the man dragged her further down the alley. Ahead, though it seemed a mile away, the alley opened out into a bigger street. There too Emily could see what looked like normal life moving back and forth. But somehow it didn't seem real.

'Where are you taking . . . ?'

The man hit her on the side of her head and it hurt.

Ahead she saw an open door, against the side of which a girl wearing next to nothing was leaning, drunkenly mouthing the words of the song Emily had just heard to the sound of a piano from within.

There was laughter from inside the house and a man shouted, 'Hey Nellie, you get back in here!'

The noises of the night were beginning to echo around inside Emily's head and her arm felt as if it was about to break. She knew that whatever happened she must not let the man take her into that house.

She knew as certainly as night followed day that if he got her in there she wouldn't be coming out again.

'Hey! Mister!' someone shouted.

Emily's abductor stopped in his tracks and looked back the way they had come.

A lump of sawn wood came out of the darkness at him; the kind of wood carpenters use to make frame buildings – squared off, planed and heavy.

It smashed straight into the groin of the man holding Emily.

Gripping the end of the wood were two hands. As they emerged into the light Emily could see that they were attached to two strong arms and those arms to a body that was wiry and strong.

Emily was suddenly free, as the man screamed in pain and his hands went instinctively to his privates. She found herself falling forward. Another hand reached up and grabbed her. It was Johnny Leppard, the young bellhop from her hotel and he looked like a demon out of hell.

'Run!' he shouted, '*Run!*'

Ten minutes later, they slowed.

Johnny took her arm gently and helped her on.

175

'Come on, miss, it ain't far now.'

'How did you know where to find me?' said Emily.

'Heard the Elevated was stopped at 12th and went down to meet you. Other guests have had trouble when that happens so I thought . . .'

Emily felt tears coming.

She was beginning to shake.

'But I guess I must have missed you in the crowd. Man on the train said a woman like you was last off. I looked around and I guessed if you went up Wabash you'd be okay so I tried west along 12th and . . .'

Emily began to cry uncontrollably.

'It's all right, miss,' said Johnny, his hand comfortingly firm on her arm, 'you're safe now.'

But it wasn't fear that made her cry.

'C'mon,' he said, 'your luggage is in your room. I'll show you the way.'

'I'll get some supper sent up,' said Johnny when they arrived at Emily's door. 'Don't expect you'll want to come to the public restaurant now.'

'No,' she said, then, 'it's Johnny Leppard, isn't it?'

'You got a good memory, miss.'

She stared at him. He looked so young but he seemed far more than a man.

He grinned again.

'I never forget a name and a face,' she said, 'and I'll never forget yours. Thank you.'

'We can't go losing our guests, Miss Strauss, or we'd have no trade. Your supper's on the way!'

Then he was gone with a grin and an engaging swagger.

Still feeling shaky, Emily closed the door and crossed to her bedroom window. Michigan Avenue and Lake Park beyond were all lit up and still thronging with people and vehicles.

But even here, in the shadows, men still loitered, and women too.

Emily breathed deeply, cursing herself for being such a fool. She would not make the same mistake again.

Her home city of Pittsburgh had been rough and tough.

New York was worse.

But Chicago? It was something else.

She picked up the paper she had bought that morning at the depot, the *Chicagoer Arbeiter-Zeitung*, and skimmed through it, hoping to find something pleasant to lighten her mood, but it was full of obituaries, accidents, lost children and homicides.

Then she remembered the headline about the Meister killing that had caught her attention earlier. It told a nasty little story about the body of a man found dumped on 15th and Halsted. The horror lay in the fact that he had been eviscerated and none of his internal organs were to be found.

Someone in the Harrison Street Police Station had told the reporter that, 'It wasn't the first of this kind. It looks like the Meisters. They do it to their own, as a punishment, and to intimidate others.'

She put the paper down.

She frowned, gritted her teeth and looked at her hands.

They were steadier now.

She breathed some more.

Finally she said out loud, as though the whole city were listening: 'You know what? Chicago's not going to beat Emily Strauss.'

DAY SEVEN

Wednesday October 25, 1893

31

Deadhouse

At eight the next morning Emily took a streetcar from Harrison and Wabash for Cook County Hospital. It was a twenty-five-minute trip over the river to the West Side, against the run of traffic for that time of day.

The tall, red-brick buildings of the hospital with their colonnades, mansard roofs and lofty central tower were less than twenty years old. But it seemed to Emily that their ornate gothic style, pale sandstone facings and oppressive ornament already looked out of date in a city that was advancing so rapidly towards the twentieth century.

The morgue, or deadhouse as Chicagoans called it, was a different matter. It lay through the main building on the east side of the huge site in an extension hurriedly added to accommodate a need that reflected the city's exponential growth.

Like the rest of the purely medical facilities, Emily knew this part of the hospital was under the control of a brilliant Danish pathologist, Dr Christian Fenger, who was said to have bought his way into his senior position, but who was bringing to the medical side of things what the administrators were not able to bring to theirs: order, efficiency and good practice.

The deadhouse had a solid oak door and a hall that smelt fresh, looked clean and at that time of morning was still nearly empty. There was a reception desk with a male attendant but he was busy talking.

Emily gave up waiting and walked on.

She found herself in an inner hall that smelt of antiseptic, chemicals and coffee. There were some seats, a high skylight with cracked glass, a broken pulley, and a hatchway with an electric bellpush above which an embossed brass plaque read, 'Ring for Attention'.

Emily pushed and, somewhere beyond, a bell sounded.

No one came.

It was just eight twenty-five in the morning and she guessed the place wasn't quite open yet.

It gave her time to look around. Along the entire wall of an adjacent corridor, she saw a series of noticeboards that carried dozens of images of the faces of the dead, some face-on, some in profile. Most were head shots but a few were full body, minimally covered.

A number were quite disturbing, the features distorted in death or maybe by the manner of death.

'Some of them don't look too good, do they?'

Emily turned to find herself facing a man of fifty or so. His beard was trim, his eyes bright and humorous, his clothes good quality.

'I've seen worse,' she said.

She had already worked out that she was going to get nowhere in the deadhouse if she played the weak woman.

They both looked at one particular image. The face was puffed, the lips bulbous, the eyes half open but white, the chest so swollen it strained the buttons of its shirt. The shirt said it was a man but it was hard to tell.

'A drowning, I guess,' said the man. 'Chicago River. We often get them. They are the ones relatives never recognize. You live with someone for years and you'd think you'd know them in death. Often you don't.'

Emily thought back to when her father died and how, all of a sudden, he hadn't looked like her father any more.

She stretched out a hand: 'Emily Strauss, New York *World*, working up a piece on a woman who disappeared and then ended up here, dead in a road accident. The daughter of one of our readers.' She dug in her purse and found her card.

'Are you Dr Fenger by any chance?' Emily went on. 'Sorry but I've never . . .'

'I'm honored you think so,' he said, shaking his head, 'but I'm not. Don't even work in pathology. You need Mr Freeman and if you're going to get to see him you'd better make it fast because come nine the relatives and police and God knows who start turning up . . . better follow me.'

Entering through a door marked *No Admittance Except on Official Business*, Emily followed the man down a short corridor and straight into one end of an enormous, brightly lit autopsy room with tables, sinks, a tiled floor and walls, where a man sat at one end drinking coffee out of a tin mug and reading a newspaper.

Through another open door Emily spied a man in a uniform standing by a table on which lay an uncovered corpse. It was gray-colored, the body of a man. Fortunately the head was turned away. But the body cavity was open, and, even to Emily's inexpert eye it looked empty of organs. Another man, short and gray-haired, was sketching it. A third, the pathologist probably, was at a sink washing his hands.

Emily suppressed a lurch of nausea, then remembered the newspaper story she had glanced at the night before.

'Sir, may I ask you, is that the man found yesterday in Halsted Street?'

'The Meister killing? Yes, they do it to scare people.'

'Who are they?'

'Butchers,' he said shortly.

She was unsure if he was being pejorative or was simply describing their line of work.

'If you're all done with the autopsy, Mr Freeman, there's a young lady here to see you. She's a reporter. I'll leave her to you.'

Freeman put down his mug and stood up, making a feeble attempt to straighten his cravat.

'Good morning, ma'am . . .'

Emily introduced herself and explained her mission. Freeman was willing enough to help, if he could.

He listened quietly as Emily told him what she knew about Anna

Zemeckis's disappearance and her father's attempts to find out what had happened to her.

'He said he came here,' she said.

Light dawned on Freeman's face.

'A little Latvian man from New York.'

'That's the one,' said Emily.

Freeman jumped up, disappeared for a couple of minutes and came back with a file and sat down again.

'It's a terrible thing, Miss Strauss, to happen to a young girl like that. I have a daughter myself and can't begin to imagine how he feels. This city's a hard place.'

He opened the file and glanced through the autopsy report on the girl's body.

A bell rang, the same one Emily had rung earlier. Then again.

'Day's beginning,' said Freeman matter-of-factly.

Another man in a white coat appeared.

'See to it,' said Freeman, 'I'm busy.'

He led Emily to an office off the autopsy room. Its walls were lined with shelves holding large, thick ledgers. He pulled one down.

'Cases like hers where cause of death is known and properly witnessed only need a brief autopsy report. She died as a result of cranial and chest trauma sustained under the wheels of a streetcar.'

'May I see the report?'

Freeman passed it to Emily. The report was no more than a hastily written page recording answers to standard questions on the body of the deceased. It confirmed all Freeman had said, but, nevertheless, Emily read it through twice.

'What does "Other indications irrelevant" mean?' she asked, pointing to a final line before the report was signed off.

Freeman hesitated. He took back the ledger, read the line again and looked at her.

'You're a journalist, not a relative?'

'That's right.'

'You must not publish what I am about to say. Some things are very hurtful to the next of kin. We find things out which it is better they do not know.'

'Like?' said Emily.

'This Zemeckis girl. She wasn't a virgin. But this has no relevance to the cause of death, so we make no special deal of it. Mr Zemeckis did not need to know this unless it was relevant or he had asked specifically.'

Emily was frowning. There was absolutely nothing in Anna's history that remotely suggested this. Everything she had heard suggested the opposite – that Anna was a good and virtuous Lutheran girl.

'Mr Freeman, there are photographs of dead people on the wall out there.'

Freeman nodded.

'Helps identify the unidentified corpses,' he said. 'We put them in a discreet place because many relatives find them distressing. Those who want can look. We often put a name to the John and Jane Does that way.'

'You take photographs of all the deceased?'

'Most, but not all. We can't store the unidentified bodies for more than a few days, especially in the summer months, so we need to keep a record in case relatives turn up later.'

'So what happened to Anna's body?'

'She was buried in the potter's field out west of the city. It's the usual procedure. After the father came and confirmed it was his daughter, he claimed the effects and put in an application to have the body exhumed so she can be taken back to New York for burial. But that won't be for a couple more weeks.'

'Did you take any photographs of Anna Zemeckis before she was buried?'

Freeman nodded. 'I guess so.'

He looked at the file.

'A couple,' he said.

'Did Mr Zemeckis see them?'

'Sure he looked, but he found it traumatic. Hers was not a pretty death. The streetcar had mangled her body terribly. But his relative came too and confirmed the identification . . .'

'Mrs Markulis.'

'Yes. They went on the crucifix and the dress she was wearing.'

'May *I* see the photographs?'

'I guess so. But—'

'It's all right, Mr Freeman. I know what to expect.'

She didn't. And it was a shock.

The two photographs Freeman produced from a file and laid on the table in front of her were grotesque. One was of the face, split virtually in two, the flesh peeled back, only one eye visible. The mouth gaped open and ugly. The black hair was matted with blood. It looked like no man's daughter. It was monstrous.

The other was of the upper torso. The right breast and rib cage were horribly crushed. The shoulder looked as if it had been nearly wrenched from the body. The crucifix, which Emily recognized at once, lay just above the left breast and with the chain intact. It looked incongruous on such a mangled corpse. No doubt such a photograph would have been enough to rock any man's faith, let alone that of the God-fearing Janis Zemeckis.

Emily didn't need to look for long at the images. She could see why they would have disturbed Mr Zemeckis but . . .

But . . .

Freeman took them back.

But . . .

'What is it, Miss Strauss?'

'Can I take a second look at the head?'

She did so, this time more dispassionately. In among the horror of distortion and disfigurement something very ordinary indeed had caught her eye and it was untouched by the accident.

'Did you make a note of all discriminating marks and scars on the body?'

'Yes, we always do.'

'Do you have a magnifying glass?'

'Yes, but . . .' Freeman protested as he rummaged in a drawer and handed her one. 'Why, have you noticed something?'

'Yes,' whispered Emily, as she hunched intently over the photograph, 'she has pierced ears.'

Freeman looked at his report and said, 'Correct. She did have. Most women do these days.'

'That's right, *most* do, but *not* Anna Zemeckis,' Emily said.

'Pardon me?'

She studied the photograph again. Finally she looked up and said, with absolute conviction, 'I don't think this is Anna Zemeckis. Her father told me quite clearly that he refused to allow her to wear any jewelry apart from the crucifix, and that only because it had belonged to her dead mother. So unless she's had her ears pierced since she came to Chicago, this isn't her.'

Freeman picked up the picture of the dead girl and examined it himself.

'We have to be sure these marks on the ears did not occur as a result of the accident. Is there any way you can check out what you've just said?'

'Sure,' Emily replied. 'Her aunt, Mrs Markulis, who came here to identify the body. I'll ask her. But, having met the father, I'm telling you now there's no way this girl would have gone against his wishes.'

Alan Freeman thought for a moment, and then said softly, 'If this is not Miss Zemeckis, then who is it?'

'. . . and why was she wearing Anna Zemeckis's crucifix and dress?' said Emily.

They sat in silence without any answers.

'I'll have to give it some thought, Miss Strauss. If I come up with any more I'll let you know.'

He escorted Emily out to the front entrance.

'You know,' he said as Emily turned to leave, 'there's really not a lot of difference between our two professions – mortician and journalist – in the way we have to find answers to difficult questions. Is there?'

'I suppose not,' conceded Emily, inwardly glad, however, as she walked out on to the street, that her own questions generally related to the living and not to the dead.

32

Brennan's

Anna Zemeckis made sure she was on time for her first full day's work at Brennan's Tailoring Emporium. But the moment she sat down at her worktable in the second-floor back room she sensed a change in atmosphere. The women, who had been talkative before, now worked in silence, heads down. The few boys there scurried about looking over their shoulders. The men, who worked separately from the women at the far end of the great room, seemed uneasy and talked only in low voices, so far as anything could be heard above the clacking of machines.

As for Mrs Donal, who had hired Anna, she now looked jittery, her sharp, thin face very pale.

Anna soon discovered why.

It seemed that she had been lucky to come looking for a job on a Tuesday because that was the one day of the week when Mr Brennan Jr, who was in charge of the Clark Street outlet, attended to matters in his father's more classy store over on State.

Now he was back he seemed to have something to prove and Anna could see why everybody was subdued. He was tall, thin, with a long neck and prominent Adam's apple above his tight white collar. He seemed incapable of saying anything pleasant to anybody and reduced a woman twice his age to tears just after Anna's arrival because she was two minutes late. She hadn't been able to cross the bridge at Van Buren, it being raised for the passage of a ship.

'Should've thought of that and come the other way round! Fined half a day!'

'But . . .'

'You answering back? *Eh?!*'

He stood over her, his pale brown eyes furious, his mouth tight with anger.

'You carry on and it'll be money at day end, if there's any due. Eh?'

Money at day end, Anna guessed, meant being fired.

The woman wept and kept her eyes low.

Someone whispered in disgust, '*Half a day!*'

Anna settled down to her work, hoping Mr Brennan would take no notice of her.

So he did, until nearly twelve.

Then, 'Who's this, eh? *Eh!?*'

Anna looked up to find him towering over her.

'Mrs Donal said—'

'I know what she said, girl. Don't need to be told that. She said you could work. I don't like that, not at all. Eh? Where are you from?'

Anna hesitated, knowing it mattered. This was an Irish place and she guessed others weren't as welcome.

'Europe,' she said noncommittally but very quietly. Louder and it would have been seen as insolent.

She judged him right. The answer was passed over as he impatiently grabbed the item she was working on to examine it. He grabbed so hard and fast that the needle went straight into her finger and some stitches ripped as he pulled the garment, and the needle, free.

Her eyes watered with pain but she said nothing.

He peered at Anna's work, eyes ogling and then squinting.

'It'll do,' he said finally, 'but I keep a close watch on girls I don't hire myself and don't you forget it. And don't stare. Get on with the work. I *said* get on!'

Anna got on.

Only when Brennan got diverted with queries from the shop, or with the models who came up to his office to try on cloaks and other things, did the women dare talk. Then only in furtive whispers.

'We get thirty minutes' break at half-past twelve,' she was told. 'There's water to drink but you need a cup of your own. You can share mine. You eat in there if you've got anything *to* eat. Only place to get clear of him.'

Anna had nothing but a slice of bread she had secreted away that morning at the Mission of Hope. Not that she wasn't hungry, she was. But she preferred to save something for lunchtime.

She still felt sick but that didn't matter so much now; her mind had moved on to other things.

Dunning seemed a world away. She could remember dashing down a dark corridor, and before that the doctor, and before that hitting Riley in the face with the pen and the liquor smell of her.

Then she had run through some washing, stolen a dress, got on the train and then made her way up and down Clark Street until she found a job.

She could remember all that as clear as day and it was a comfort. Now, sitting at her bench sewing, she started to remember a lot more, making sense of the jumble of other images and memories she had of her life before Dunning.

Images of her father kept recurring and they weren't all bad. There had been happy times: him holding her close on a great big ship; him standing one morning in his bakery, laughing, his face covered with flour; his hand in hers when she went to school.

No, it wasn't all bad. But it was the memory of her mother that upset her because she knew she needed her and she wasn't there and never would be. And she couldn't ever go back to her father and tell him. He would not forgive her.

Thinking of her mother, Anna's head drooped low over her sewing as she struggled not to cry.

A hand touched her arm. It was the woman who had lost half a day's money. She gave her a smile and a look that said, 'I wish I could help . . .' It was a mother's look, her head a little to one side.

'I'm Jelena,' whispered Anna.

'I'm Eileen, I . . . ssh! He's coming this way. He's in a specially bad mood today.'

'Why?'

'City Hall inspector. There's one coming this afternoon.'

'Is that bad?'

'Ought to be but they never do anything. And it's good for us.'

'Why?'

'Brennan'll pick on some of the girls to take a "break" for a couple of hours, to make the place look less crowded. He gives us a dime for the privilege.'

'Why?'

'Keep our mouths shut.'

'Ten cents!' said Anna. It seemed a fortune. If she could have done her sewing with her fingers crossed that she might be chosen she would have done so.

Anna's face brightened. She had made a friend. When it came to the break, she and Eileen sat side by side, backs to the wall in the water closets with another couple of the women, not saying much.

But Anna wanted to talk. She wanted to let words lead her where her mind without them dared not go.

'Not here. After work,' said Eileen.

'By the river,' said Anna, 'we could go there.'

'It stinks,' was Eileen's honest response.

But Anna's heart thumped. She remembered the river . . . and the water . . . She knew she needed to see it, to smell it, maybe even touch it. If only to help her remember.

'No worse than this closet,' she said.

'Okay,' said Eileen, 'after work.'

She needed a friend too.

33

Riley's Men

Dr Morgan Eels had a bad night and a worse morning. All he really wanted to do was keep on monitoring Riley's progress so he could work out exactly what had happened to her. A steel pen thrust accidentally into the eye of a hospital attendant in his own surgery might look like criminal negligence to most people, but to Dr Eels it seemed nothing less than a passport to a glittering future international career. He wanted to seize the moment.

Instead, he had the more immediately pressing problem of Anna Zemeckis to deal with. No trace of her had been found, nor of the important papers she had taken inadvertently. Eels had come to the conclusion that she had escaped the grounds and therefore constituted a real threat to his future.

But, after a little thought, he had realized that she also offered an opportunity. If he could put the blame for her escape squarely on the shoulders of Riley and Dr Benjamin Brown, then he might yet turn the situation in his favor. It was just a matter of getting to Paul Hartz before anyone else did.

Eels had the bright idea of summoning Donko O'Banion, driver of the Dunning paddy wagon, and getting him to deliver an urgent message to Darke Hartz & Company's offices saying he would like to see Mr Hartz if possible first thing the following morning.

To his surprise and gratification Hartz's personal secretary had called him at nine. Mr Hartz would be glad to see him that afternoon at two o'clock sharp.

Unfortunately, Donko reappeared just as Eels was leaving, saying he wanted to see Riley. Attempting to cut him short, Eels said it was best for the patient not to be disturbed at present.

Donko mumbled something about having the 'right' to see her.

When Eels briskly asked why, he was surprised at the response: 'She's my sister, Dr Eels.'

Eels looked at the huge frame of Donko and his piggy eyes and he could indeed see a physical similarity between the two.

'Well then,' he began . . .

'And her husband wants to see her too. He's waiting outside.'

'She's *married*?' gasped Eels. This seemed impossible.

It got worse.

The man waiting outside turned out to be a uniformed officer from Harrison Street Police Station. He too was large and lumbering.

'James Flaherty Riley,' he announced. 'Where's my wife? I want to see her.'

Eels knew he could do nothing but kowtow to Officer Riley's wishes. But he worried about how the two men would react to the sight of a much-changed woman.

'You must be careful not to disturb her,' he had said as he escorted the two men to Far Side.

The problem was not so much 'disturbing' Riley as the fact that nothing *could* disturb her. They went over to Far Side and found her sitting up in a chair, glassy-eyed and immobile.

'Apart from the bruising around her eye she's, er, physically well . . . there's nothing actually physically wrong with her but . . .'

Donko waved a fat hand in front of Riley's eyes. She did not respond. She remained slumped in the chair, her legs stretched out before her, her huge arms hanging down to the floor, her hands limp, her mouth half open.

But she did seem aware there was someone there. For a moment there was the glimmer of a childish grin when she saw the two men. Then she lost interest and looked away to the middle distance.

'She ain't Riley anymore,' pronounced James Riley.

Eels said that he expected 'some' improvement and that Riley was fully functional. She was, for example, continent.

Nurse Lutyens confirmed however that at present they were having to feed her as her arms had become temporarily useless. She talked less now than she had the day before. Words seemed to be deserting her, but no doubt they would come back.

'Who did this to her?' said Riley.

Eels told them, reminding Donko that it was he who had taken Anna Zemeckis to the detention hospital and, after she had been processed and committed, conveyed her to Dunning.

Donko squinted and then frowned, which was his way of remembering things.

Light dawned.

'The ugly bitch out of the creek? The one I picked up in Benson Street who smelt like shit. That one?'

Eels conceded that it probably was. He now saw an opportunity to mobilize their help on his behalf, and through them, that of the police.

'I have a photograph of her,' he said, 'as I have of all new patients. Perhaps . . . ?'

'You bet,' said James Riley.

It didn't take much to divert Riley and Donko's anger onto Anna Zemeckis.

'You got another one of these?' asked Riley, pointing at the photograph.

Eels looked helpful.

'My assistant Mr Mould can make copies, I am sure. How many do you want?'

Officer Riley smiled grimly.

'You give me enough of them and half a day and there won't be a patrolman downtown who isn't looking for this girl.'

'Nor anyone in our whole community,' added Donko.

By 'community' Donko meant the Irish – and that was a very considerable number of Chicagoans indeed, incorporating as it did most of the Near West Side and a good few suburbs beyond.

'She won't last twenty-four hours without being caught,' said Donko.

'And she won't *want* to last twenty-four hours beyond that!' said Riley unpleasantly. 'Not alive, at any rate.'

'She'll wish she was back in Dunning,' growled Donko.

'Which is precisely where I want her,' said Eels smoothly, pleased with the way things had gone.

34

Home Sweet Home

The Markulis hardware store was a slow, two-horsecar journey from Cook County Hospital up to the North Side. Tired of sitting, Emily got off early and walked the last three blocks, glad to catch a glimpse of the clear sky above Lake Michigan at the far eastern end of North Street.

Anna's uncle and aunt lived above their store on the corner of North and Larabee Street and, at first sight, it looked an impressive establishment. The substantial building had been erected in the late 1870s by Mrs Markulis's father, a German, who had astutely acquired the lot after the Great Fire of 1871. Taking full advantage of its corner location, the building had an octagonal turret set off by wings on both sides.

Closer to, Emily could see that the entire establishment was already run-down, its once-bright fabric grimy from the soot and smoke that wafted across from factories on the south side of North Street. The front windows, which had not been cleaned in a while, were cluttered with goods, and there was a haphazard street display of brooms and brushes too, which abutted the sidewalk. There was an air of care-lessness about everything, as if the store had seen better days.

The half-moon step up into the store was dirty with dust and litter. The interior of the shop was as dingy as its windows and the male assistant who greeted her was not exactly solicitous. Mr Markulis 'never being here at this hour', Mrs Markulis was fetched from upstairs. She greeted Emily somberly, in acknowledgement of the unfortunate circumstances of her visit.

'Please, Miss Strauss,' she said rather formally, 'come upstairs to the parlor and we can talk.'

She was a pale, wispy woman in a tight-corseted, rather old-fashioned black silk dress. She wore a simple silver brooch at her throat and a thin gold wedding ring.

Her manner seemed rather strained; her eyes were more hunted than warm, and her handshake too quick, as if she did not like physical contact.

'Please,' she said again, indicating some stairs behind the counter.

The front parlor into which Emily was shown was as cluttered with polished wooden furniture, drapes and a piano as the shop below was stuffed with goods. There was a fire that struggled to keep ablaze. On a table covered somewhat incongruously with an expensive lace cloth were two exquisite coffee cups of the finest porcelain, a matching jug for cream, and a plate of homemade *küchen*.

'Please, your cloak and hat,' said Mrs Markulis, taking them herself, though there was a maid of some kind hovering, a slip of a girl who looked as uneasy as Mrs Markulis herself.

'This is very welcome,' said Emily, eying the cakes.

'I did not know . . . I was not sure . . . I mean lunch . . .'

Mrs Markulis made these social noises with little conviction. She seemed a woman to whom keeping up appearances mattered, but the strain of doing so in straitened circumstances was beginning to tell.

'Please, sit,' she said eventually.

Emily admired the porcelain.

'My father's,' said Mrs Markulis.

'And that is him?' asked Emily, looking at an oak-framed daguerreotype of a gentleman on the mantel.

'Yes, yes,' said Mrs Markulis, and then more warmly, 'and that is my mother.'

A second, smaller, framed picture of someone who looked like a younger version of Mrs Markulis herself, her hair in ringlets and old-fashioned ribbons, stood on the piano, with some other small portraits, presumably family ones.

On the wall behind the piano was a matching pair of oil paintings from the turn of the century.

'My great grandparents,' said Mrs Markulis. 'From Hanover.'

'Ah!' said Emily, 'May I?'

She got up to have a closer look.

She had heard something of the family history from Janis Zemeckis and knew that his wife's brother Hendriks, who had been a book-keeper for a timber firm in Riga, had emigrated to America in 1870 to help run his firm's office on the Chicago River. Hit by the panic of 1873, he had moved into hardware and in no time met and married Liesel Hoffmeyer, the only child of a successful hardware merchant on the North Side. Hoffmeyer senior died unexpectedly in 1878, leaving Hendriks Markulis in effective control of a thriving business.

But his and Liesel's two children had both died at birth, after which Hendriks had tried to persuade his sister and her husband Janis Zemeckis to leave Riga along with their daughter and join them in Chicago, even offering to cover the costs of travel. He was homesick and wanted some more Latvians nearby. He said there were plenty of opportunities for bakers in Chicago.

But Janis Zemeckis was cautious and finally only made the journey to the New World after his wife died in 1882, refusing his brother-in-law's offer of financial help. He had also decided against the option that Anna would have preferred, of moving to the Canadian state of Manitoba to be near his wife's sister, Anna's Aunt Inga.

After considering his options carefully, he decided New York's Lower East Side, with a strong Lutheran community, offered better opportunities than a remote farm in Canada or the additional strain of traveling out to the Mid-West.

Now, comparing Zemeckis's well-ordered bakery in New York and this untidy, rundown establishment in Chicago, Emily guessed that, so far as the Markulises were concerned, there had been a temperamental difference between the two men as well as a religious one.

Emily knew that though Janis was an advocate of temperance it was not something he especially advertised in his Lower East Side home.

But in the Markulis household it was different. It was difficult to avoid the fact that Mrs Markulis was an active member of the Woman's

Christian Temperance Union, starting with the little white ribbon she wore above her thin bosom as a sign she had taken the pledge.

Hanging on the wall, not far from the picture of the late Mr Hoffmeyer, was a framed sampler in the shape of a cross. The frame itself was painted in shiny and forbidding black shellac and the beautifully cross-stitched words read: 'For God and Home and Native Land' in English, but rendered in High German gothic-style script.

'I made it myself,' said Mrs Markulis, adding with a touch of self satisfaction, 'and the frame.'

'Really!' exclaimed Emily, aware that some appreciative surprise was needed.

The girl brought in a pot of coffee.

'I made it at the settlement house on Halsted Street,' said Liesel Markulis proudly, 'at my handicrafts class! One must keep occupied. But . . . please, Miss Strauss, do sit down!'

Emily sat down again and accepted the coffee offered her. The truth was she had half hoped for some schnapps or other light spirit, of the kind many German hausfraus offered their daytime guests and which it had been her own father's habit to provide his friends. There was a glazed glass cabinet full of cut glasses that would have served that purpose well, but coffee it was.

'Aah . . . they are beautiful things,' said her hostess, seeing Emily eye the glasses, 'and my father liked a drink but . . . well, now we are a temperance house and of course Anna was brought up that way too by Janis.'

'I guess Mr Zemeckis was rather strict in general?' Emily suggested.

'He is a good man, God-fearing. I know that.'

'But strict?' murmured Emily, following her instinct, for she felt that in some way this had been an issue – for Emily and maybe for Mrs Markulis too.

'Too strict, I think. Most certainly liquor was to be discouraged at all costs. But a social life . . . a growing girl needs that. How else is she to meet the right young man?'

Emily paused; she had at last, unwittingly, been given an opening to the one thing she most needed to find out about.

'Tell me, Mrs Markulis . . . did Anna have a beau?'

The response was unequivocal. 'She had no male friends in particular that I knew of. Any friendships she had with young men were of the harmless kind, like her colleague John at the library.'

'Oh yes, the library. Mr Zemeckis mentioned it,' replied Emily. 'You arranged that for her, did you not?'

'Yes, through my good friend Mrs Jane McIlvanie who is wife of the deputy librarian of the Chicago Public Library and a colleague of mine at WCTU.'

'So ... how close was Anna to this John?' Emily probed further. 'What did you know about him?'

Liesel Markulis seemed more than happy to fill Emily in about John Olsen English, about whom Anna had, apparently, talked often and openly. He was one of the more senior librarians but their work brought them only into passing contact. They were opposites. She was gregarious and relaxed; he solitary and almost terminally shy. But despite the differences they had struck up a firm friendship.

Anna had soon learnt John's unhappy history from her workmates and from Mrs Markulis, for it was common knowledge in WCTU that John lived with and looked after his invalid, widowed mother on the Near North Side. She made his life utter misery. His father had been killed fighting for the Unionists at Chattanooga in 1863 when John was two years old. After which Mrs English had lived with her mother-in-law, the widow of a small-time realtor on Chicago's Near West Side.

When she died, Mrs English inherited the house and an income. From that day on, she lived a life of modest and self-centered indulgence with a succession of maids, a son to do as he was told, and long-suffering friends and acquaintances from the congregation of the nearby St Patrick's Roman Catholic Church on West Adams Street to listen to her endless complaints.

After John had left college, his mother had found him a librarian's job in Chicago so he could remain at her constant beck and call.

His occasional attempts to break free, enjoy some independence and maybe even find a bride were ridiculed and promptly suppressed by his domineering mother.

It was something about which Mrs Markulis and Mrs McIlvanie frequently gossiped, for the latter's husband had found Mrs English's tentacles reached as far as the library itself, in the never-ending demands she made on her son.

'So,' ventured Emily finally, 'even if Anna and John had had romantic inclinations, Mrs English would have put a stop to it.'

'Undoubtedly. Besides, Anna's a Lutheran, and he's a Catholic.'

'Tell me, Mrs Markulis. Did Anna really *want* to come to Chicago? Or did she do so because her father wanted it?'

'Anna was happy to come here under our care but she was always honest enough to say that her real dream was to live with her Aunt Inga, that's my husband's sister, in Canada. I think perhaps . . .'

'Yes, Mrs Markulis?'

'Perhaps Anna and John might have been very well suited. For he too had dreamed of being a farmer, like the Olsens, his forebears on his mother's Swedish side of the family. I think Anna agreed to come to Chicago in the hope that it would be a first step to earning her father's permission to go north to Canada. But she would never have gone without his approval.'

'Is there any chance she would have gone there without his permission? I'm thinking . . .'

'I know what you're thinking, Miss Strauss. Frankly, when she first disappeared the same thought occurred to me: that she had run away to her Aunt Inga, perhaps because she was unhappy here.'

'*Was* she unhappy?'

Mrs Markulis hesitated, then said, 'I don't think so.'

Emily did not for one moment believe her. Anna had been unhappy; the question was why.

Mrs Markulis continued quickly, 'Regrettably none of that matters now. When I saw . . . when . . .'

Emotion overtook her.

Emily poured her a coffee.

'On that dreadful day when I saw Anna in the morgue—'

'You're sure, are you? Sure it was her?'

Liesel Markulis's face registered unexpected shock and surprise at the question. On this score, at least, Emily knew she was telling the truth.

She would have liked to have told Mrs Markulis then and there that there was evidence that the body was not Anna's, that she might still be alive, but Alan Freeman at the City Morgue had told her not to. It was better to hold her fire until she was certain of the fact.

'Of course I'm sure. The dress, she made it herself, here in Chicago. I helped her. And the crucifix . . . she never ever took off her mother's crucifix.'

Emily slowly took a sip of her coffee and then, her voice soft, low and confiding, turned to Liesel Markulis.

'There must be more you can tell me about Anna, Mrs Markulis. Please, what else do you remember . . . ?'

35

Portraits

At five to two precisely, Dr Morgan Eels was sitting waiting in the main foyer of Stock House, the administrative building of Darke Hartz & Company in downtown Chicago. New, opulent, and glossy, it rose up on the north side of Washington between La Salle and 5th, opposite the site of the half-completed Chicago Stock Exchange: a testament to the extraordinary success of the company over the last twenty years.

Eels was feeling nervous. Like a lot of physicians who spend too long in the reassuring confines of the charitable public institutions they run, he was uneasy in the world of big business, and especially with men like Paul Hartz whose offices were designed to impress and sometimes to intimidate.

The lobby was at ground level. It was spacious and airy with brass doors and elevators, stylish colored-glass windows, indoor palms and plant displays, its bright lights and mirrors dazzling the unwary.

As if that was not quite enough, it also gloried in a huge barometer, an international clock that chimed the quarters and a wind dial that moved mysteriously to register shifts in wind direction once in a while right there above the polished chairs and tables.

The Darke Hartz building exuded a sense of commercial power and drive, imparted by the hundreds, perhaps thousands of clerks and secretaries, managers and directors, suppliers' representatives and visitors who hurried back and forth across the marbled floors and up and down in elevators.

A neatly arranged set of newspapers, journals and commodity reports – local, national and international – lay on the table near where Eels was told to wait, but he looked at none of them.

He was thinking about what he was going to say to Paul Hartz, whose gilt-framed portrait in oils stared down at him from the right-hand side of the main staircase to the offices above. Hartz was depicted at a desk with leather-bound books, pens and inkwell in front of him, with a spectacular view of some trees and a lake behind. He wore a dark suit and cravat and looked as fine a man of business as ever was. Hartz was now more than sixty, but the artist had presented him as still young enough to be eternally on his way to the top.

The clock chimed the hour and Eels tapped his fingers impatiently on the table. He felt his heart-rate rise. He mopped his brow, unsure of the reception he would get. If he could only find the right form of words . . .

'Dr Eels? *Doctor Morgan Eels?*'

Eels started in his seat. It was a male clerk.

'Mr Hartz sent to say that he's sorry he's kept you waiting but he won't be many more minutes. I'll come and get you myself.'

Eels relaxed again as the clerk retreated out of sight. He found himself now looking at the portrait on the left-hand side of the stairs.

The companion piece of the famous partnership depicted Hans Darke, who had started life as a butcher with a single horse and cart in Richmond, Virginia. He had built up his business from there, diversifying into cattle breeding and setting up a stud in the Mid-West, where he made his name as a breeder who knew his product second to none and his markets too. Moving to Chicago, he had added meat-packing to his growing operation, following Philip Armour's lead in the efficient slaughter and dressing of cattle and hogs and Gustavus Swift's in the use of refrigerated box cars.

But it was only after he had been astute enough to team up with Paul Hartz that he had accumulated enough capital to become one of the big five meatpackers in the USA. In the end, what Hans Darke didn't know about meat wasn't worth knowing and no man's judgment was more eagerly sought nor more readily accepted than his.

But he was notoriously taciturn and curmudgeonly and he looked it: his dour, thickset face and stocky form did more than hint at Teutonic origins. The portrait spoke too of his roots as a cattle breeder, standing as he was in front of a pen full of longhorn steers, his two sons Gunther and Wolfgang in the background. So ingrained in Hans Darke was the German ethic for hard work that it was said he drove his people like an army at war on limited rations, and his two sons Gunther and Wolfgang hardest of all. In recent years, Wolfgang had taken increasing charge of the Darke Hartz killing floors in the stock yard, and all other matters to do with butchery, whilst the older and more urbane Gunther had moved onto the distribution side of the meatpacking operation, building up the Darke Hartz freight network that transported their meat to the rest of America. He had been given his head to run this efficient operation from the premises of a subsidiary, R. F. Whetton, also in the stock yard, but allowing him to stay clear of Wolfgang, which suited them both.

The fact was – and it was well known throughout the industry – that the two Darke brothers loathed each other. But no one was quite sure why.

This was perhaps why Hans Darke had moved north to a house he had built on the lakeside; as far away as possible from Paul Hartz, who remained in his mansion on Prairie Avenue, near the Union Stock Yard.

The two business partners were oil and water, fire and ice, chalk and cheese. They rarely communicated with each other or spent more than five minutes in the same room, except at essential boardroom meetings and the annual stockholders' convention.

But, despite all that, they ran one of the most successful businesses in Chicago.

Eels looked back across the stairwell to the more appealing picture of the urbane Paul Hartz. No sons there, just the daughter – Christiane – Gunther's wife. Paul Hartz was a firm believer in keeping money and business in the family and, even though there was as yet no heir on his side, the fact that Gunther was his son-in-law now and disliked his father and brother so much gave Paul the balance of power.

The clock chimed the quarter-hour and the clerk reappeared.

205

'Mr Hartz is ready for you now. Follow me.'

They took the stairs, the director's floor being the first flight up.

Eels looked very insignificant as he passed the two great men on the walls on either side of him.

Weevils are small too, yet, given time and opportunity, they can bring the strongest and tallest of houses crashing to the ground.

Paul Hartz was in an expansive mood and greeted Eels warmly, though he didn't get up.

He sat in a large and open office with two clerks at stand-up desks at the far end and an oval boardroom table in the middle of which a group of men sat talking informally.

There was a bottle and some glasses on the table, and the air was heavy with the aroma of expensive cigars. It looked as though a meeting of some kind had just broken up.

Hartz, it appeared, was the one who had a liking for portraiture, for he had no less than three presidents of the United States, in oils, looming on the brocaded walls behind him: James A. Garfield, Chester A. Arthur and the recent former president, Benjamin Harrison – all staunch Republicans like Hartz himself.

In addition there was a framed engraving from the *Illustrated Newspaper* of October 1881 of former Vice-President Chester Arthur taking the oath of office following Garfield's untimely assassination. Among those depicted in Arthur's entourage was a discreet-looking and decidedly younger Paul Hartz, at that time Arthur's friend and financial adviser.

Eels knew that Paul Hartz had been offered but had never accepted government office under Arthur – he preferred to remain an independent businessman, wielding his considerable power from behind the scenes. Significantly, Darke Hartz & Company's move into the big league of meatpackers had taken place during the years of Arthur's presidency, the president's patronage proving extremely profitable to both men.

As Eels advanced across this imposing chamber, the men already gathered there nodded friendly greetings in his direction, waiting for Hartz to make the introductions, which he did not do at once. Instead he signaled Eels over to his desk and invited him to take a chair adjacent to his own so that the two men could talk confidentially.

This invitation into the inner circle of Darke Hartz & Company bolstered Morgan Eels's confidence. He abandoned his carefully rehearsed words and decided to come straight out with it. He told him of Anna Zemeckis's escape and the lost documents, putting himself at Hartz's mercy without attempting to attribute blame.

Hartz listened without expression.

When Eels had finished he said, 'I was already aware of all this. Brown called me last night. If you had said differently you would have been on the train back East, Eels. But . . . we all make mistakes and I respect a man who freely admits his.'

Hartz's eyes grew hard.

'But you're only allowed one mistake, Eels. No more. Eh? I shall order my own people to deal with it. But if they do not find the girl and take her back to Dunning in the next forty-eight hours, then your job is on the line. Understand?'

Eels nodded. He felt both gratitude and fear.

'Yes, Mr Hartz,' he said. 'I hesitate to say this but in my own self-defense . . . when I formally assume my full responsibilities at the insane asylum at the end of the month, there will be certain reforms of Dr Brown's regime that will be necessary. Security will become paramount, to protect the public from any dangerous patients who might get loose.'

Hartz nodded his head absently.

'Meanwhile, I have seen to it that the police have initiated a search for the girl,' said Eels.

He smiled ingratiatingly, feeling that these few words had shifted the blame for the escape onto Dr Brown's inefficient regime, while establishing that he, by contrast, was a man of action.

Eels was so pleased with himself that he failed to read the sudden shadowing in Hartz's eyes.

'The *police?*' repeated Hartz with chilly emphasis.

Eels explained about Riley's brother and police officer husband and how he had given them copies of the photograph he had taken of Anna on her admission to Dunning. He said nothing about steel pens in eyes or scientific breakthroughs but already he was talking too much, giving Hartz too much detail. Dr Eels had not yet learnt that it is best to let a man like Paul Hartz dictate the pace.

'A photograph?' said Hartz.

Eels produced the image he had taken of Anna Zemeckis.

Hartz barely glanced at it. He liked girls but the ones he liked had class. Then he looked again, reminded of something he had long since lost touch with. Despite the bruising round her eyes the girl had an endearing look of innocence combined with pluck.

'How the hell did you lose a girl like that?' he said, seeming finally to make light of it all. But he didn't wait for Eels's reply, turning instead to the room at large. 'However, I was forgetting, you gentlemen haven't all met Dr Eels, have you? Those of you not able to attend his lecture at Dunning two nights ago missed a treat.'

A couple of men nodded their heads and murmured their agreement.

'Dr Eels has most decided views on what should be done with the feeble-minded and the insane. Eh, doctor?'

'Yes, yes I have.'

'Which are?' enquired one of the men.

Eels hesitated, remembering Hartz's warning about expressing his views too publicly.

'It's all right, Dr Eels, you're among friends. These are all Darke Hartz men and, like you, fellow members of the Old America Association. They may not agree with everything you say but they can be trusted to keep their mouths shut.'

Eels relaxed.

'It is, as you know, my professional goal and desire to find the cure for insanity,' began Eels, 'but, well . . . in some instances the only "cure" may be to put the imbecile as well as the criminally insane out of the public's way for good. The trouble is that the cost of maintaining them is high and many practitioners take the view, which I share, that such people should not be kept in idle luxury at the expense of a working population whose levels of subsistence are often lower than theirs.'

'Hear, hear!' said someone.

'I go along with that!' said someone else.

'And Mr Hartz agrees with you on this?' asked one of the younger men there.

'I believe he does,' said Eels.

'I *am* surprised,' came the instant reply.

Eels shifted uncomfortably at this unexpected challenge to Hartz and himself. Hartz scowled; Eels studied his inquisitor.

He was tall, broad shouldered, beautifully dressed and every inch the coming man. He stood up, smiling coolly, the one person in the room who, so it seemed, was not overawed by Paul Hartz.

Approaching Paul Hartz's desk, he reached out a hand and offered it to Eels.

'Gunther Darke,' he said, 'I disagree with Mr Hartz on almost everything.'

'You shouldn't mind him,' said Hartz coldly. 'He likes to play the role of devil's advocate.'

'The logical conclusion you appear to be suggesting, Dr Eels,' continued Gunther Darke, unperturbed, 'would seem to be the clinical elimination of the insane.'

'I think there is a strong case for that in certain circumstances,' said Eels.

'Such as?'

'Where an inmate of my establishment, after due process through the insane court, is adjudged to be not only insane but beyond cure.'

'Then what?'

'Then if the nuisance they cause society and the cost of their maintenance is such as to be prohibitive, I think elimination is a reasonable and justifiable course.'

To Eels's relief, from the looks on their faces the rest of Hartz's colleagues seemed to agree with him.

'And by what method would you eliminate these costly incurables?' asked Gunther Darke.

'It wouldn't be my decision, Mr Darke, but the court's,' said Eels. 'But I think most physicians who have studied the subject would agree that, given the large numbers likely to be involved in such a cull of the socially worthless, then in carbonic acid gas we have an agent which would efficiently and humanely do the job.'

Paul Hartz stood up.

'There speaks the true man of science, gentlemen! Truthful and objective but politically impractical – for now. Those who agree with us on this issue, as on the general need to protect native Americans from the incursions of the lower class of immigrant, will need to fight a strong and persuasive battle. I regret – because he is and was my friend – that the founder of the OAA, Jenkin Lloyd Rhys, did not have the stomach for that fight. Now that he is not with us – and we hope he is physically well even if, as I suspect, he has suffered some kind of mental breakdown – we will have to put forward our own candidate against the one he nominated.'

'You should stand yourself, sir!' someone cried enthusiastically.

Hartz raised a hand modestly and then, to Eels's horror, laid it to rest on his shoulder, causing consternation among several of those present.

Hartz laughed.

'Don't worry, gentlemen; it is not my intention to nominate Dr Eels for the position of president of the OAA! We need him for more important work!'

Eels gulped and looked pale, which made everyone laugh even more.

'I shall name my man in good time,' continued Hartz smoothly. 'Now, I have to go to the Grand Pacific where Rhys was staying and sort a few things out . . .'

The informal gathering broke up and Eels, confident that he had handled a difficult situation well, and somewhat puffed up with the sense that he was making a mark among men who mattered, took advantage of the dry weather and an off-lake breeze that had cleared the cavernous city streets of smoke and smog and sauntered down to Adams Street Bridge and over to Union Station for his train back to Dunning.

It was only when the journey was almost over that he remembered that he had left the photograph of Anna Zemeckis on Paul Hartz's desk.

36

Secrets

'What more can I tell you about Anna?' asked Liesel Markulis, echoing Emily's words slowly.

It was, self-evidently, the kind of probing she had dreaded. The shock of Anna's disappearance and death was written all over her face. That, and for some reason a sense of shame, as though it had been in some way her fault.

This woman, Emily realized without the need to say more, had been given the sacred charge of looking after someone else's child and it had all gone terribly wrong.

'This is so difficult,' Liesel began. 'Since . . . since then . . . I have talked to no one except Janis when he was here, but he . . . he said little because he was so upset, you know . . . and my husband, he says nothing and I . . .'

'But what was Anna really *like?*' asked Emily, hoping to divert Liesel Markulis from a torrent of words that looked as if they were heading for tears again.

It worked.

She pulled herself together, sat up straight and looked Emily in the eye. 'She was a good girl, a happy young woman, so excited to be here in Chicago at the time of the World's Fair. She was clever and adaptable and she enjoyed working in the library. Her part-time job there had left her with enough free time to see the Fair. And then there was my work with the Woman's Christian Temperance Union . . . she took a great interest in that too.'

'She was already a member?'

'No, I persuaded her to join. She came to the meetings quite regularly. She met other women there and also through her work at the Administration Building on the South Side where she later started doing a day's voluntary work a week.'

'Anyone in particular? Did she have any special friends?'

Liesel Markulis's face darkened.

'She was rather close about such things. We had words about it. I explained that, for her own safety, we needed to know who her friends were.'

Emily smiled and said, 'But she didn't want to tell you?'

'It's a serious matter, Miss Strauss. We were responsible for her . . .'

'I'm afraid I was the same with my father, Mrs Markulis. Young girls like to have their secrets.'

'Humph! I wouldn't know, I have no children of my own. I only know . . .'

Not for the first time Liesel Markulis let her mask slip and it revealed an unexpected bitterness.

'So, did you ever meet any of these friends?'

'Eventually. At the Administration Building Anna worked under the supervision of a woman called Marion Stoiber, who, we were wrongly informed, was married. She was not. I cannot say I liked her. Rather vulgar, rather too knowing. Anna fell under her spell. They used to meet for lunch occasionally on a Saturday, at Mrs Clark's Lunch Room on Wabash.'

'Marion Stoiber,' repeated Emily. 'Sounds Polish.'

Mrs Markulis nodded.

'As a matter of fact, despite my initial misgivings about her, since Anna's disappearance Marion Stoiber has been most kind and supportive and she even comes to WCTU meetings. There's hope for everybody, I think.'

'And she admitted she wasn't married, but separated?'

'Eventually, yes. She said it was unfortunate. Her husband had been incapable of holding down a job, got into debt and had deserted her. She preferred to say no more than that. I felt sorry for her, Miss Strauss . . . But, as for Mr Markulis . . . well, he said she was a fraud.'

'I'd very much like to meet her,' said Emily.

'She will, I hope, be at our annual WCTU convention tomorrow. Would you like to come? I'll introduce you.'

Emily agreed she would attend.

While Mrs Markulis was talking, Emily noticed a shadow at the door at the far end of the room. It was the girl, listening.

After hearing Mrs Markulis's side of the story, and seeing this untidy, unloved house with a shop assistant who was disengaged and a fearful maid who stood eavesdropping on her mistress, Emily wondered what Anna had made of it all. She had not mentioned it in her letters to her father. But then, had he known, he would have ordered her straight home.

'Mrs Markulis,' continued Emily after a pause, 'do you think perhaps Anna hid things from you – that she had secrets she did not want you to know about?'

Mrs Markulis's eyes widened in horror at the suggestion. She shook her head.

'No. I think no. Her father was so strict and we were under very clear instructions about where Anna could go and what she could do and whom she could meet. We even had to persuade him to allow her to join the Turners.'

'Gymnastics?'

Emily was surprised. That was an activity usually taken up only by boys and men.

Liesel Markulis smiled.

'As I explained to Anna's father, the Nord Chicago Turnverein is progressive and prides itself on promoting healthy living for all, boys and girls, men and women – and we at WCTU support it in doing that.'

'But I thought most of the Turnvereins were little more than German drinking clubs. They are in Pittsburgh. My father was a member of one!'

'Most are, I believe. But the NCT is a temperance club and its members consume no liquor. Maybe that's why they have produced the most successful team in Illinois.'

'And Anna was a member?'

'Yes. She enjoyed the activities very much – and the social contact, I think.'

Janis Zemeckis had mentioned none of this. Maybe Anna and Mrs Markulis had thought it best not to tell him.

'I guess the boys and girls socialized occasionally?' said Emily.

'I guess they did, but Anna wasn't interested in any of them. She only ever mentioned John, the young man from the library.'

'So she had no other admirers you knew of?'

'She was really very innocent in that respect. Rather afraid of men, which is no bad thing. But she was an attractive, well-made girl. People – men – naturally liked her.'

'But no special ones?' insisted Emily.

Liesel Markulis frowned and poured more coffee rather clumsily, rattling the cups.

'I think I would have known . . . I really do. She did make a nice new friend she met at WCTU, though. Mila Blazek. I'm sure she will be there tomorrow and I will introduce you.'

Mrs Markulis paused and was thoughtful for a moment. 'You know, after Anna's first few weeks here I got used to having her as a companion. I enjoyed it very much. I . . .'

It was plain enough what she meant. Having lost two babies at birth and without other family and with a husband she had so far not mentioned at all, Liesel Markulis was a lonely woman.

'And Mr Markulis . . . ?'

'What of him?' said Mrs Markulis.

'Did he and Anna get on?'

'Of course. He is her uncle. But you can ask him yourself – here's his carriage arriving now.'

Hendriks Markulis came up the stairs heavily from the store below, no taller than Emily but plump, beaming, red-faced and cheerful. He looked older than his fifty years.

'It is awful, no?' he said, after Emily offered her condolences about what had happened. 'A matter of deep sadness. Poor Zemeckis. I do not believe he will ever recover. I know I could not!'

He did not stay to be questioned, gulping down the two cups of the fresh coffee the maid hurriedly provided but so restless that he refused to sit down.

'Must work! Things to do downstairs. Please excuse, Miss Streitz.'

'Strauss.'

'Yes. Miss Strauss. Yes.'

He disappeared noisily downstairs

'May I see Anna's room?' asked Emily.

There was nothing much to see and nothing personal left in it, or so it seemed. There was a homely German picture on the wall of the kind Emily knew well, and a souvenir calendar from the Fair, adorned by a picture of the Woman's Building, the same building Emily had been in the day before.

'What happened to Anna's things?'

'Zemeckis asked me to pack them, which I did. But I found nothing that would give any clue as to why she disappeared.'

They stood in the room staring at nothing in particular.

It was as if Anna had never been there.

But then Emily noticed something. 'Look,' she said, moving to the opposite wall, 'she's circled some of the dates on the calendar.'

'Yes, I made some engagements for her,' responded Mrs Markulis. 'I circled them to remind her. And she marked others herself.'

'Seems to be Wednesdays and Thursdays,' said Emily.

'Yes, the Turnverein every Wednesday evening and WCTU meetings on Thursdays.'

'And a few others too.' Emily looked more closely, 'On Saturdays, mainly.'

'Yes, these were her lunches with Miss Stoiber. In fact, she had lunch with her the day she disappeared. See, here, September 7th.' Mrs Markulis pointed to the calendar.

'And there's another one here, a Friday in June and it has something written by it . . . "lecture" . . . A lecture about what?'

'What date did you say?' asked Mrs Markulis, looking suddenly flustered.

'June 16th. Can you remember exactly what she did that day?'

Mrs Markulis hesitated. 'June . . . yes . . . I think that is the day she attended a lecture on the Chicago meat trade and did the tour of the Union Stock Yard.'

'Did she tell you about it afterwards?'

'I can't remember her saying very much. But I think she did not like it . . . the killing floors I mean . . . the blood. She seemed upset when she got back . . . But . . . tomorrow . . . you must come along to the WCTU Convention.'

Mrs Markulis took an invitation from the mantelpiece. 'Please! Take it, I can arrange another seat for myself.'

Emily knew she was being steered away from the subject and that she would not get any further with Mrs Markulis today.

'It's being held in the Woman's Temple on the corner of La Salle and Monroe Streets starting at eleven, in the Willard Hall. It should be most enjoyable. Members of the Turnverein will be giving a demonstration. Everybody will be there.'

'I'm not a member.'

'Then you'll have an opportunity to join!'

As Mrs Markulis showed her out, Emily paused in the store below, where Mr Markulis was busying himself, packing and unpacking boxes with the help of his assistant. Both seemed in a bad temper with each other and were getting in a muddle.

'Please excuse me for a moment,' said Mrs Markulis.

As Emily looked about, she spotted the girl she had seen listening upstairs, who was still hovering in the background.

'What's your name?'

'Lottie.'

'Did you know Miss Zemeckis?' she asked.

'Yes . . . she cried . . . At night. I heard her . . . I have the little room next to hers. Maybe she was homesick, like me.'

Lottie seemed about to say something more but just then she started at Mr Markulis's voice raised in anger and ran back upstairs.

Emily decided the time had come to leave. She said her goodbyes and went by a side door out onto Larrabee Street. Finding herself among the trash cans, she paused to take in what she had discovered.

An unhappy woman, a distracted man, a fearful maid; and a business in decline.

Then she noticed something poking out of one of the cans. It was the bottom of a clear-glass bottle with an 'I' stamped inside a diamond and a G.

The Illinois Glass Company, and a year as well: 1887.

She didn't need to read the label to tell what had been in it. It was a newly finished bottle of cheap whiskey.

There was movement at a window in the house above her head.

Emily and the maid stared at each other for a moment, a moment of collusion.

Someone in the house was a drinker. It wasn't the maid and it wasn't Mrs Markulis.

It was Hendriks Markulis and Emily guessed that it wasn't just whiskey he was drinking: it was the profits as well.

37

Best of Friends

The City Hall inspector responsible for Chicago's garment trade thoughtfully sent a boy ahead of him to warn Mr Brennan Jr that Brennan's Tailoring Emporium was his next port of call and he would be arriving at twenty minutes to four.

Mr Brennan went into a well-practiced routine.

He ordered that a fresh pot of coffee be brewed and took out the bottle of the best Irish malt whiskey he kept in the left-hand drawer of his desk, and placed it at the ready, with two clean glasses.

He dug into the cash box and took out a generous quantity of dollar bills which he put in an envelope and placed carefully next to the bottle of liquor.

He then removed a little brown envelope from the cash box and checked its contents. It was filled with dimes.

The sight of the boy, followed by Mr Brennan, emerging from his poky office at the far end of the shop floor, sent a thrill of excitement and expectation among his female workforce. The men dourly continued their work at the machines and steam presses. But the women had, for the sake of appearances and the inspector's report, to be temporarily culled. This was done by tipping them a dime each and telling them to make themselves scarce for a while.

Brennan knew their hopes ran high and he enjoyed walking slowly up and then down the tables, bestowing his coins like a potentate giving alms.

If a girl looked too eager for his largesse, however great her need, she received none. If another looked abject and pitiful and succeeded thereby in touching some still functioning heartstring in Brennan's breast, she was awarded her dime.

With Mr Brennan the best tactic was a kind of suggestive, wanton flattery that implied in some silent way that the recipient of his generosity regarded him as a king, a god, a thoroughly decent and honest man, and handsome and desirable to boot.

Eileen, who though not buxom had a certain knowing way about her and was good at it, received her dime at the first pass. Anna, who naturally was new to this strange ritual, had no idea at all what game was being played.

'Look down like a good girl but thrust out your chest like a bad one,' hissed Eileen. 'For goodness' sake undo a button.'

Anna's embarrassed attempts to unbutton her bodice completely missed the mark and she received nothing.

'He'll be back. He goes round twice.'

The second time Anna must have done something right and she managed it without Eileen's coaching. She simply looked straight at Mr Brennan and gave him a smile; her look and manner were so open and direct that his conscience seemed pricked and he gave her the last dime.

'Now,' he declared, 'you lucky girls will leave quietly by the stairs and not the elevator and you will not show your faces back here for one hour and a half. Is that understood? Enjoy this little break at our expense!'

The lucky ones trooped off, suppressing their glee with some difficulty and, it must be said, occasionally throwing taunting glances at those who had failed to charm the master.

On the way down the stairs they saw the inspector himself coming up and stood in line, pressing their backs to the wall to allow him to pass. It was all part of the regular, cynical ritual.

He was a small, rat-like man with a greasy bowler and even greasier dark jacket and pants. His shoes were scuffed and unpolished and, Anna noticed, his fingernails were filthy.

He had the smug, unappealing look of officials who have power of a minimal kind which they know how to exercise with maximal effect. The inspector was, in theory, capable of shutting a place down. But it was Chicago's way of business that he never needed to, unless he was bribed to do so by a rival firm.

He doffed his hat politely at the ladies as they allowed him to pass, giving Anna's bosom a lingering inspection followed by a leer that revealed tobacco-stained teeth.

Then he moved on up the stairs and the girls exited out into the street below.

'Why here?' asked Eileen twenty minutes later.

They had bought an apple strudel to share and were leaning now on the balustrade of Jackson Street Bridge, further up Market Street on the quiet north side.

Eileen had said it would stink, and she was right. The fetid water below was so full of filth that it flowed only slowly north before – in the smoky distance – it made a right turn for the short run to where the river discharged its contents into Lake Michigan.

'Not sure why . . .' said Anna vaguely, staring with horrified fascination at the water below, then at the great derricks and grain elevators on the west side of the bank, and the bridges, one after another, where the east–west crossroads came over the river.

There were steamers docked either side, some unloading. Launches plied their trade while barges, covered with tarpaulins, were moored along the banks.

Everywhere there was the drift of smoke, and the whole place resounded to the noise of the city, from the shouts of vendors to the rattle of streetcars and here, especially, the clunk of cranes and wood and iron tackle, as the men on the wharves below went about their work.

'I . . . can't . . . remember . . .'

'What?'

'Don't know exactly. I think I nearly drowned in the river.'

Eileen looked at the water and wrinkled her nose.

'You're in some kind of trouble, aren't you Jelena?'

Anna nodded.

'Why don't you tell me?'

Instinct told Anna not to, but she began to talk all the same, and might have said more if they had not been interrupted by the noise of crowds of pedestrians tramping back and forth on the bridge's sidewalk, and the rattling streetcars running dangerously close.

'Let's go somewhere quieter,' Eileen said.

They strolled back off the bridge and down onto the embankment, picking their way among the rubbish that littered it.

'It doesn't look very safe round here,' said Anna nervously.

Although they were only yards from where they had been before, up on the bridge in the sunshine, they had now entered a different world – shadowed, thick with soupy smoke, subterranean in feel, full of garbage and every kind of ruination.

Further along two bums sat by a smoldering fire.

They looked up in the women's direction but minded their own business.

Buildings towered up about them. Across the river the Armour grain elevators were modern cathedrals against the skyline; and further along, the Kirk Soap Factory belched out its foul-smelling fumes.

'It's okay at this time of the day,' said Eileen. 'But in summer it stinks to high heaven down here. Now, you were saying . . .'

I must not mention Dunning, Anna told herself, but she felt a desperate need to talk, as if it might help her remember. But she hardly knew Eileen. Instinct and Tomas Steffens's words told her she should not trust even her. But she just wanted someone to listen.

'You mustn't tell anyone, but I *am* in some trouble, I—'

At this point, Providence smiled once more on Anna Zemeckis.

'Ladies! Good day and good riddance I say to all but good folk such as ourselves who are honest and stick to our principles. May I join you?'

The voice was booming, the figure was male and at first sight alarming by its sheer bulk.

Anna got up from the little seat they had found and was ready to flee when Eileen, with a groan but grinning all the same, took hold of her arm.

'It's alright,' she said, 'it's Mr Crazy. He don't hurt a fly.'

221

Anna looked at him and at once relaxed. Despite his size, the man exuded bonhomie and an easy confidence with himself and the world around him.

He took a seat a yard or two away from them and produced some waxed paper and proceeded to untie the string that bound it. Once open, he laid the parcel daintily on his knees as though the paper were the best linen napkin. Anna saw that it contained some dark rye bread, sliced sausage and a couple of pickles.

'Want some?' he asked.

'No thank you,' said Anna.

'Who is he?' she whispered to Eileen. While the big man tucked in, Eileen explained.

Mr Crazy, it emerged, was not exactly a hobo, nor exactly a street vendor. And despite his strange appearance he was far from being one of Chicago's low-life.

He was, in fact, one of the city's best-known, benign eccentrics – the very same wild-looking gentleman who on the day of Emily's arrival had accosted her on the corner of Polk and Wabash and given her a pipe he himself had carved.

Nobody had been able to discover his real name, and those who had known it had long since died or moved on. So he was generally known as 'Mr Crazy'. He was a man of very strong, outspoken opinions, informing all who cared to listen that the folk in City Hall, and in particular, Carter Henry Harrison the mayor, were cheating the citizens they were meant to represent in all sorts of ways.

He was not quite the city's mascot – he was too proud, too intelligent for that; and far too strange and quirky. But he was most certainly one of its treasures. Tall, bronzed, with a long white beard and always dressed in a greatcoat that went down to his boots, (some said he looked like an old Civil War general), he was always, despite his threadbare clothes, extremely clean. He had the great booming voice of an orator, and would constantly reiterate, to those who would listen, his familiar, much-repeated mantra: 'I have the papers to prove it!' His claims seemed preposterous and were never-ending.

For the past few months his latest assertion had been that the City Fathers of Chicago intended to tunnel under the city, which would make the great new skyscrapers fall down. The year previously it had

222

been that the World's Fair would end in disaster – which very obviously it had not. For the year following he was predicting revolution in Illinois state.

Meanwhile ... nobody much minded or cared, but they liked to see Mr Crazy about and would often give him the price of a meal. They also bought the pipes he carved down at his Lakeshore den from driftwood that he foraged for among the acres of garbage that had accumulated in that noisome no-man's-land.

If there was one extraordinary thing about Mr Crazy it was this: he might live in a ramshackle hovel but he always kept himself immaculately clean. And if there was one eccentricity for which he was a legend in Chicago, it was his early morning ablutions in the lake, which he did in the nude, all the year round, informing anyone who challenged him that his beard was the only covering he needed.

The Lakeshore was Mr Crazy's domain, and from its garbage-strewn wastes he emerged daily in all weathers to do his rounds. When the City Fathers were in session he sat in the public gallery, as was his right, and listened in, sometimes challenging the proceedings. Harmless though he seemed, Mr Crazy was not someone to cross in matters of liberty, justice and the law. His knowledge of civil issues in Chicago was encyclopedic and he was usually right. He knew the law books back to front and upside down. So much so that, as the years had gone by, he had earned the unique privilege, encouraged by the more open-minded of local Democratic politicians, of actually being listened to on points of order and procedure.

But he was never ever a nuisance. He never drank. He was never rude to anyone, and if he came across someone in trouble he would take them to Harrison Street Police Station or the Pacific Garden Mission or the Cook County Hospital.

It was rumored he was rich, which surely was not the case, because he always gave away what he had, including the pipes he supposedly made to sell. Probably no one in all Chicago except the man he had designated his arch-enemy – Mayor Carter Henry Harrison himself – could have relied on more people's support than Mr Crazy, had he ever asked for it. Which naturally he never did.

*   *   *

223

Right now Mr Crazy was having his afternoon tea.

Anna noticed that he carried a placard he had obviously made himself. The lettering was beautifully rendered. It read: *SAY NO TO MAYOR HARRISON; SAY NO TO THE TUNNELS.*

Then in smaller letters it said, *Apply here for the proof.*

'See, he's crazy,' whispered Eileen. 'Whoever would go tunneling under the city? The buildings would fall down.'

'She's right, madam,' said Mr Crazy, moving back into earshot again. 'And you'd do well to remember that, though I'm old, my hearing's as good as the next man's. The tunnels will make everything fall down and then I'd be a poor man.'

'Thought you were already, Mr Crazy,' Eileen riposted.

'Poverty is relative, young lady.'

'So why do you live on the Lakeshore!'

'Because my cabin is the finest residence in all Chicago. As for my being here right now, well I might ask the same of you. Only difference is that from here I can survey my extensive real-estate interests, whereas all you can look at is dirty water.'

'You're not telling me you own the Armour Grain Elevator, Mr Crazy?'

'I'm not telling you anything.'

He came over to Anna and, before she could say no, he put a neatly made sandwich of black bread and salami on her lap along with a gherkin.

'You look hungry to me. Eat.'

'Thank you, sir,' she said.

She dared to look up and found him beaming down at her, looking just like Saint Nicholas – the Santa Claus of the old Latvian storybooks she'd loved as a child. He certainly had the red cheeks and twinkly eyes, just no sack of presents.

Then he moved off to join the other two men further along the embankment.

'You can't eat it,' said Eileen.

'Oh yes, I can,' said Anna firmly.

She was thinking not just of herself but of the child she was carrying as well.

She was thinking too that what Mr Crazy had shown was something no one else had shown her in a long while: kindness and courtesy.

So, when they returned to Brennan's an hour later, Anna felt as if she'd had a real and restorative break.

38

Child

Emily had had a tiring day, and still felt frustrated by her attempts to extract information from Mrs Markulis, yet she approached the once-elegant but now dowdy two-story mansion that was the main building of Hull House with a sense of rising excitement. There was always something going on at Hull House – a social event in progress, a new philanthropic venture being discussed, or some educational lecture about to begin.

The Hull House Settlement on Halsted was a welcoming haven and had been since Jane Addams and Ellen Gates Starr had established it four years previously, providing welfare, education, childcare for working mothers, counseling and hot dinners for the poor – mainly Italian, Jewish and Greek – of the Near West Side community that surrounded it.

Built in 1856 by Charles Hull, a wealthy businessman, his cousin who inherited it had donated the place to Addams and Starr after Hull's death. They rapidly turned it into a hive of welfare for the poor immigrants who needed it, offering community activities run by those of the middle classes, mainly women, who wished to make themselves useful to society.

Before long, those who had been helped learned to help others and the true spirit of the American settlement house movement was born.

That afternoon it was the latter.

'This way please,' Emily was told the moment she entered into the lobby of the main building and, before she knew what was happening, she found herself hurried along into a lecture room that was already half full.

She saw a notice and realized she had been mistaken for a member of the audience for a series of free lectures on 'Organic Evolution'.

Come and understand DARWINISM, it read, *Paleontology and Embryology, or What the Rocks Teach about the Beginning of Life. Lectures every Wednesday at 4.30. October 25: Spontaneous Generation.*

Emily quickly escaped in the direction of the famous Octagonal Room, which was Jane Addams's office and the nerve center of the establishment, and asked if she could see Julia Lathrop.

'I'm very sorry, I'm afraid she's not here. She's out of Chicago and—'

'Sheets! Are there any sheets!?'

The young assistant who had been talking to Emily froze.

'Well someone must know where they are!'

The speaker was small, dark and wiry, like a bull terrier in skirts.

Her eyes settled on Emily.

'Do you know?'

'Just arrived,' said Emily, 'but I guess sheets are normally upstairs and not down.'

Since no one else made a move, Emily went upstairs herself, poked her head into a couple of rooms, searched along the corridor and found a linen cupboard. It was full of sheets.

She grabbed three and came back down.

The woman who had asked for them was outside on the verandah overlooking Halsted Street, talking to a slip of a girl dressed in barely more than rags. She looked dirty, destitute and desperate.

'Good,' said the woman, grabbing the sheets. 'You'd better come with me since I'll need some help. Just follow the girl.'

They hurried after the little thing, soon turning off Halsted into a side street and off that into another. The atmosphere soon became foul. It smelt of a thousand things, all of them as rotten and bad as the waste, human and animal, that lay in festering puddles along its length.

But there was another smell too, more pervasive than the rotting filth around her. And it thrilled Emily through and through. It was something only natural-born journalists can detect and when they do it is as potent and compelling as the scent of prey to a hunter. It was the smell of a good story.

'What's your name?' asked Emily, raising her skirts and sidestepping the mire.

'Katharine Hubbard, Julia Lathrop's new assistant. And yours?'

'Emily Strauss, New York *World*. Where are we going?'

'To deliver a baby.'

The girl had come running into Hull House just moments before Emily's arrival. It seemed a friend of hers in the tenement house they shared with other families not far off was having a baby all by herself.

'She's hollering something fierce: my mother says it's disgracing the whole house she is!'

But despite this, and the presence of other women in the tenement, no one would go to the girl's aid or even summon a doctor. So her friend had come to Hull House as a last resort.

'I guess the girl's unmarried,' explained Katharine Hubbard as they hurried along, 'and more than likely they wouldn't call a doctor for fear they themselves would have to pay the fee.'

'But . . .'

'There's no but about it, Miss Strauss, we'll have to go and help her ourselves.'

'These sheets . . . ?'

'You don't imagine there'll be anything clean or hygienic where the poor creature lives, do you?'

'Er, no,' said Emily.

The maze of alleys went from bad to worse and Emily lost all sense of direction.

The muddy ground underfoot had never been paved, though it might have once been boarded. For the most part it was not even recognizable as mud, but rather foul cloying muck across which it was only possible to pass thanks to the judicious placing of a boulder, or broken barrel-side, or a few crushed tins.

The tenements on either side were no better than shanties, built so

badly, so meanly, that most leaned one way or another. All were dilapi-
dated almost beyond repair, and several had collapsed where they
stood.

Yet people lived in them, along with dogs and hogs and, Emily
guessed, every species of vermin ever spawned in an American slum.
As the three women hurried along – the girl in front calling out 'Quick,
quick!' and, 'Don't fall behind!' – they noticed plenty of people, some
in chairs on stoops sucking pipes, some carrying boxes or bottles or
goods of one kind and another, and many more – all men – at the
broken doors and windows of dives that passed for saloons. But not
a single one offered any help.

Suddenly, a narrow alley opened out into a kind of square, in the
middle of which two men, with bowlers and waistcoats over their dirty
white shirts were harnessing two horses by a heap of manure. Nearby
a huge bonfire smoldered, giving off the foul stench of scorched carpet
and gutta-percha. Beyond was a brick-built tenement, five floors high.
In they went, clambering up several flights of stairs.

The screams could be heard loud and clear coming down the stairwell, and the three women had to push past a motley collection of
men and women standing idly around.

At the third floor, they rounded the stairs towards the darkest, further-
most corner of the building, and arrived at last at a one-room apartment
no more than eight feet square and with the smallest of small windows
set high in one wall.

It was hard at first for them to make out where the mother-to-be
lay, because she had slipped between the wall and her greasy mattress
in the final stages of her labor. She now lay there in the filthiest of
shifts, which had ridden up to her breasts as, legs open and baby's
head showing, she screamed out the final moments of her lonely labor.

But what shocked Emily perhaps more than anything else was that,
when her eyes finally adjusted to the murk, she saw that the woman
giving birth seemed herself no more than a child.

Of the next quarter of an hour Emily afterwards remembered every
single detail – the lice-infested bed, now stained with all the waters
and blood of childbirth; the girl's touching gratitude that she was
finally alone no more; the way Katharine Hubbard galvanized all

around her to do what was necessary to see America's newest citizen safely into the world. But at the time it was just a haze.

Emily did what she could, marveling at her companion's composure and compassion and her seeming indifference to the all-pervading squalor.

The clean sheets they had brought were laid on the decrepit bed, the girl was eased onto them, boiling water and towel were summoned up from somewhere, and one of the curious women out on the landing by the stairs was sufficiently encouraged by the appearance of the 'Hull House women' to step forward and offer her services as makeshift midwife, for she had delivered her sister's baby back in Ireland. Once her hands were washed by Katharine, she eased the baby out when it seemed to get stuck at the last moment and delivered it safely onto the sheet. A moment or two later, using a pair of sewing scissors, the cord was cut.

'There's more,' said the woman to Katharine softly, and for a horrified moment Emily thought she meant more babies . . . But it was the placenta she was referring to.

As Emily, her help no longer needed, stood back, she was moved by the way the young girl reached out instinctively to hold her baby. It was something as ancient as time – the mystical bond between mother and newborn.

A few minutes later a doctor, whom someone it seemed had finally summoned, arrived. But there was no need for him by then. Nevertheless he demanded his fee, and it was Katharine Hubbard who paid it.

Before they left, Emily noticed Katharine slip some money under the girl's makeshift pillow when no one was looking, so that it might be found later and used, hopefully, to provide extra food for a few days when it would be most needed. But at least the girl and her baby were not alone. It turned out that she shared her pitiful lodgings with her mother, who had gone that morning to do the washing for a lady over on the North Side but no one knew exactly where.

The girl who had led them to the tenement now guided them back down the maze of alleys to Halsted. Emily stopped on the street corner and took a deep breath, shaken by the experience. Katharine gave her a pat on the back in unexpected but welcome reassurance.

'What will happen to them?' asked Emily.

Katharine Hubbard shrugged.

'We'll keep an eye on them. But . . . you've seen for yourself. The tide of poverty and suffering comes in and goes out and that is not something a thousand Jane Addamses and their Hull Houses can do much about. But . . . if we refused to respond to a poor girl in the throes of childbirth,' Katharine continued, 'it would be a disgrace to us for ever more! If Hull House does not have its roots in human kindness, it is no good at all.'

They walked back to the house and it was only when they were on its front steps that Katharine turned to Emily and said, 'Now, what is it that we can do for you?'

Emily told Katharine about Anna Zemeckis, how her father had misidentified her body in the City Morgue, how she was convinced she was still alive and in serious trouble. She also confided in Katharine Hubbard the suspicion that niggled in her mind. That Anna Zemeckis might have run away because she was with child and fearful of telling her father.

'If she's alive and in trouble there's a chance she'll find her way to one of the welfare institutions with which we have contact,' explained Katharine. 'Julia Lathrop has devoted herself to forging closer ties with such places in the belief that many strands make a stronger rope. Now, please tell me where I may contact you.'

Emily gave Katharine her card.

'The Auditorium Annex! Very grand!' she said with a smile.

'Except that I'm in the attic,' laughed Emily.

'Things can only improve!'

'For all of us, I hope,' responded Emily warmly. 'Do, please, stay in touch, Katharine!'

'I will,' said Katharine Hubbard, 'come what may!'

39

Turnverein

The headquarters of the Nord Chicago Turnverein, Chicago's largest
and most successful athletic club, were on the North Side, off Goethe
Street.

For an amateur organization whose primary concerns were charitable, its new red-brick building was very striking. Over the wide
double doors of its grand arched entrance, the letters NCTV were set
in bright green, red and yellow tiles in a High German gothic script.
Inside was one of Chicago's most well-equipped gymnasiums, paid for
by the generosity of many benefactors.

The explanation for the club's extraordinary success in competition
was simple: its ability to find great leaders. From its founding in 1863
by the late Johan Sackler, who had organized it with Prussian efficiency,
the club had realized the importance of gaining support from local
businesses – and this tradition had prevailed. Sackler himself had been
in the grain business but he had passed the baton to a meatpacker,
Mr Richard Whetton, a passionate advocate of the Turner movement.

On his death Whetton's company was bought out by Darke Hartz
& Company and these new owners had donated the Whetton japan-
ning factory on the North Side to the Turnverein, on whose lot the
new building was erected in 1889. All the club needed was a new
director.

It settled on one of the finest gymnasts and strongmen in the state of Illinois, a man as popular as he was feared. He demanded a high salary and got it. He also demanded total discipline from club members, and got that too. And he demanded loyalty, which he got in spades.

The only trouble was that in two days' time he was leaving the club, and no one knew it. Because he had a second career, a secret, more lucrative and fulfilling one. And he had decided the time had come to pursue it full time in a city bigger than Chicago.

The club's director was Mr Dodek Krol and his second career was as a hired killer. He was the man who had murdered Jenkin Lloyd Rhys less than forty-eight hours before; and for the last few minutes he had been in a very bad mood indeed.

He summoned a minion.

It was rehearsal evening at the Nord Chicago Turnverein and there was unusual excitement in the air. Unfortunately, the man running the show had not yet turned up. That was even more unusual. The rehearsal was for the 'Grand Display', which was taking place the next day at the Woman's Temple.

No one minded the delay. The whole point of being a Turner, though it was rarely stated, was to legitimize harmless if often flirtatious meetings with members of the opposite sex in a supervised environment.

On an evening like this the women came into the main gymnasium from their changing rooms, wearing white blouses elasticized at the wrists and thick serge knickerbockers to below the knee. Their garments were so full and loose that any detail of the female form – calves and thighs, buttocks and breasts, stomach and shoulders – was lost beneath a rippling ocean of blue-black fabric.

Their hair was up and on their thick-stockinged feet the women wore only low-heeled black leather pumps. A few carried long black wooden batons, their ends shaped like barbells.

The men entered from the other side of the hall dressed in the regulation belted white pants and tight white vests, mostly long-sleeved. Most looked fit and well trained, especially the older men, but a few of the younger novices looked awkward and slight.

The women stayed together, separate from the men, standing coyly against the wall near the door on their side.

The men meanwhile dispersed around the hall, some trying the ropes, a few the bars, two or three warming up with an impressive swirl of Indian clubs to impress the girls.

A podium had been set up in the center of the hall for Mr Krol but he still wasn't there. Then, one of the lesser Turnmeisters, Gerhard Sanger, came hurrying in to the sound of ironic clapping and laughter.

'Mr Krol has been unavoidably detained,' he began apologetically.

'Now, I may not be quite the man our director is, but . . .'

'You're certainly not!' cried out one of the young men, and laughter rippled round the hall.

'Never will be!' someone else suggested.

'. . . But . . . I do know the program. So please, pay attention and let's begin . . .'

Dodek Krol was upset. He had been given a commission of the kind he disliked, but which he could not refuse. He had been asked to kill a girl. To make matters worse, it seemed that the initial task of finding her had been put into the hands of the police and one of the more incompetent gangs in Chicago's Ward 1 – the Tick Tock Boys. Dodek groaned. They were less of a group of professional hard men, more a gang of ill-disciplined thugs, the strong arm of Tick Tock Sullivan, Democratic Councillor of Ward 1.

A note had been delivered from one of his clients at the Old America Association. They were a very fruitful source of business. Rhys had been on their list. They were not the kind of client to say no to.

The letter came with a photograph of a girl called Zemeckis who was on the run from Dunning. Krol had no interest in young girls, especially mad ones. He had no interest in why she was being sought. He had better things to do. And he most certainly did not want to clear up this kind of mess.

He made the requested telephone call.

'I have your message but I really—'

'We need her disposed of.'

Krol listened and the more he heard the more his instincts were against it. And Krol trusted his instincts. Chasing after a girl in Chicago was neither easy nor profitable.

'The only practical way is to put the Meisters on it . . .' he said.

'Exactly. They will listen to you, Krol.'

'Why not simply let her go?'

'I have my reasons for wanting her found and . . .'

He listened again but heard nothing persuasive.

'But there are so many girls like this one, a never-ending supply. They arrive here in America from Europe daily, in their hundreds and thousands. They surely cannot hurt you. It will be cheaper to let her go.'

His client swore.

'Put the best Meisters on it, Krol. And when you've found her let me know. If you won't take it further than that—'

'I won't.'

'. . . Then I shall have to decide what to do with her.'

There was a pause. The only sound to be heard was the tap-tap-tapping of Indian clubs from the gymnasium below.

'What the hell's that?'

'A rehearsal, for tomorrow's display. Will you be there?'

'Not if I can help it.'

The telephone clicked.

Had the gymnasium been free, Krol would have gone down and exorcized his anger by lifting weights and swinging clubs.

Instead, he put his hand under the edge of his oak desk and, with one great explosive wrench, sent it spinning across the room.

It crashed into the wall and fell to the floor, one leg breaking off.

Down below in the gymnasium of the Turnverein a hundred people stopped what they were doing and looked up at the ceiling.

They had heard thunder in the heavens and it meant their god was angry.

40

Empty Hand

There were two messages waiting for Emily when she got back to her hotel.

The first was from Ben Latham in the New York *World* office, in response to a telegraph she had sent early that morning telling him the body in the Cook County Morgue was not that of Anna Zemeckis. It asked her to call him at ten o'clock that night. She booked the call at once.

The second, from Johnny Leppard, was a handwritten note which read, 'Dear Miss Strauss, I have arranged what you need to look after yourself. In the Banquet Hall at eight o'clock tonight. Yours, J. Leppard.'

The writing was none too good but, as the bellhop was nowhere to be found, Emily had to work out for herself what this meant. She remembered saying after her bad experience in Dead Man's Alley that she needed to learn how to protect herself. It seemed he had taken her at her word, contacted some lowlife friend or other who had pugilistic skills, and had persuaded him to come to the hotel to show her how to hit someone.

'I don't think so,' Emily murmured to herself as she pushed open the doors of the Banquet Hall at eight o'clock exactly.

Her eyes widened. Awaiting her was not some huge rough from the

Levee with a knife or knuckleduster. Nor a beefy gentleman with bulbous leather gloves on his hands.

It was a girl, no more than eleven or twelve, dressed in pale patterned silks with light, straw-soled shoes on her feet and with an open blood-red fan in her right hand. When Emily first caught sight of her, she was leaping through the air.

The electric lights round one half of the great airy room, combined with three of the six great chandeliers, made her shimmer like some creature from fairyland.

The girl landed on the floor right in front of Emily, then leapt into a somersault in a great flying ark of silken color, the fan in her hand opening high above her head.

At the climax of this extraordinary flight she snapped the fan shut with a metallic bang, thrusting it forward as she let out a terrifying cry. She came down to earth with no perceptible noise. But only for a moment; then she was airborne again, kicking first one foot and then the other at the face of someone whom Emily only now noticed in the shadows of the unlit half of the room.

He was a man of slight build, dressed in a robe, his hair gray-white, his Asiatic features ageless.

He cried out, as if in great pain, fell back not once but thrice: first from the blow of the fan, then from the strike by the girl's leading foot and finally from the second. But instead of landing flat on his back as one might expect, he cartwheeled away into the darkness.

In a heartbeat, he ran straight at the girl, leaping sideways to strike her powerfully on her left thigh. Although knocked off balance, she jumped away to her right towards Emily. The man followed at once, a short stick in his hand. As the girl turned and tried to recover, he went down on one knee beside her, the stick shooting forward at her exposed neck.

The girl snapped shut the fan once more and jabbed it, or seemed to, straight into the man's groin. He fell back, the girl rose up; he rolled, the girl followed; he threw the stick high in the air above their heads where it seemed to spin and hover, before whirring back down at the girl who reached up a hand and caught it.

Then, the two mock adversaries turned to face each other and bowed very slowly.

237

The man turned towards Emily.

'Miss Strauss?' Standing calmly before her, he seemed not in the least out of breath. The girl grinned, presented the stick and fan to Emily, turned and cartwheeled away into the shadows.

'My name is Hatsumi.'

He did not offer his hand but rather put his own two together and bowed his head. 'Mr Leppard said I might be useful to you.'

'Mr Leppard has maybe overstepped the mark,' said Emily. 'Really, I—'

'He said you had some difficulty last night?'

'I did and he was very helpful, but . . .'

'He has been most helpful to me, Miss Strauss. I wish now to be helpful to him.'

'Yes, but . . .'

Emily gazed over to the girl who was now sitting cross-legged on the floor, her back to them.

'My daughter,' said Mr Hatsumi. 'We are staying in this hotel. We attend the Fair on behalf of the Japanese government. We are, you might say in America, acrobats. My wife, my other daughter and my son are also in the hotel.'

'I don't think I want to become an acrobat, sir,' said Emily.

'I don't think you would make a good one, Miss Strauss. You are too womanly. Female acrobats have the bodies of young boys.'

'You are Japanese then?' said Emily, changing the subject.

Mr Hatsumi smiled. 'I am American. I live now in San Francisco. I am a teacher.'

'What do you teach?' asked Emily.

Mr Hatsumi hesitated, appraising her. His skin glowed with health, his whole being was calm and unthreatening and yet he seemed like the most powerful man she had ever met.

'I teach people how to be alive,' he said simply.

His eyes were pools of soft black light that glistened with the electric lights.

'Well, Mr Hatsumi, I did have some difficulty – as you put it – last night,' she conceded. 'A man tried to abduct me! Johnny Leppard saved me, he . . .'

Mr Hatsumi raised his hand and she fell silent.

'I know what he did. Johnny is one of my students. I help people learn the art of winning,' he explained. 'Last night a man wanted to abduct you and you wanted to resist. You succeeded, so your intention replaced his, with help from a rather remarkable young man. I help you learn to apply such skills yourself.

'It is not the same thing as hurting or injuring your enemy. To kill is not usually the best course, unless, of course, you are in mortal danger. If that is the case then it is wise to inflict swift and harsh retaliation so that you may be free to go your way in peace.

'So far as weapons are concerned I allow my daughter only two, apart from her hands and feet, which are already lethal. I permit her to use a fan, because that is ladylike even if the blow it can inflict may be either crippling or lethal. I permit her also the stick, which is harmless until it is used in self-defense, at which point it is no different from a knife or gun.

'These things I seem to teach but really I simply help my students bring out their instinctive skills.'

'So, will you help me?' said Emily, suddenly persuaded.

'I have to be sure that you have right attitude. So first we talk. Tell me about this "attack". From the beginning.'

Emily tried to describe what happened in the alley but he stopped her at once.

'Please, before that.'

She took herself back to the moment of getting off the train.

'Please, Miss Strauss, before that . . .'

Only when she reached the moment when Johnny Leppard had warned her about not getting off at 12th Street at night because he thought it would be dangerous for her would Mr Hatsumi let her begin her story.

'Your problem began from that moment. Your nervousness made you doubt yourself. From then on you were a woman expecting to be attacked.'

'Maybe I was nervous long, long before that,' she said quietly.

Mr Hatsumi smiled and nodded his agreement.

'It is a habit women are taught to have,' he said. 'They feel nervous of physical threat and that makes them vulnerable to it. So now please . . . return to the alley last night and describe what happened.'

239

As she began talking he circled her slowly.

'Please, keep turning to face me, keep moving as I move, so . . . Please, continue to talk.'

She described how she had become disorientated in the Levee and how some men confronted her at the entrance to Dead Man's Alley. A man came to her aid; she went with him into the alley.

Mr Hatsumi nodded.

'It is natural. It is the same in many societies including my own. Women are taught to trust men who offer them protection. This man is practiced in turning that impulse into a weakness and exploiting it. What happened next?'

'He grabbed my arm—'

'You let him?'

'No, he just grabbed it so hard it hurt and—'

'What did you feel?'

'Frightened.'

'Yes. What else?'

'Helpless.'

'Yes, what else?'

'Angry that it was happening, I—'

'Angry?'

'Yes. That I was helpless and couldn't break free.'

'Did you try?'

'I couldn't. He was so strong.'

'Did you *try*?'

He stopped moving and so did Emily.

She felt very strange with this man, peaceful and strange: aware of her body. Aware of her strength. Aware of her weakness. Alive.

'Did you try to break free, Miss Strauss? It is important that you tell me exactly what happened.'

'I couldn't.'

'So you did not try?'

Emily opened her mouth to protest. But when she thought about it . . . 'No, I didn't. I thought he'd hurt me even more.'

'Aah . . .' sighed Mr Hatsumi. 'That, too, women are taught to believe: that a man grows very dangerous if he is attacked. So they think that it is always better not to resist. Yes?'

'Yes,' Emily had to agree.

'So you were more or less defeated, Miss Strauss, before you ever met this man.'

Emily said nothing. She had not thought such things before.

'Mr Hatsumi, I don't like being beaten by anyone but . . . there's no way I will ever be able to fly through the air like your daughter!'

'I agree. She has been practicing the art since she was three. What I *can* show you is right attitude. What she can demonstrate is how to use the weapons you have.'

'I don't carry a gun . . . or a stick. And I don't have a fan!'

'Ah, but you have two empty hands, Miss Strauss. Used the right way they are weapons enough in most circumstances. And you have one advantage which is far more dangerous than any gun or stick or knife or fan, Miss Strauss. It is the advantage of surprise. Men in America do not expect a woman to attack. That is their misjudgment because if you learn right attitude, if you learn resourcefulness, if you prepare yourself in the right way, you will know when to attack and how.'

'Will I?' said Emily rather faintly.

'The fact that you are prepared to attack will make it much less likely that you ever will be attacked yourself. You must learn to understand this.'

'When do I begin?'

'You already have. Someone who understands that they are weak is on the road to being strong. Someone who finds their way to the right master is already a worthy student. Someone who is circled by a cobra and never once takes her eyes off him as you have never taken them off me since you met me has the potential to be a scorpion.

'You began a long time ago, Miss Strauss. I will simply show you how to continue.'

'When?'

Mr Hatsumi smiled.

'You Americans like always to be so precise. Well then, tomorrow, here, at six.'

'Six in the morning?'

'Six-thirty then,' said Hatsumi firmly. 'You have some catching up to do.'

*   *   *

241

At ten that night, Emily made her call to Ben Latham in New York.

'You got my message about Anna Zemeckis?' she said straight off. 'It wasn't her in the morgue, Ben, I'm sure of it.'

'Should we tell Mr Zemeckis?'

'Not just yet, not till I'm sure. I need another day. When are you coming to Chicago?'

'Leaving tonight. Arriving early Friday morning . . . Have you found out anything else?'

The line crackled and hummed while Emily thought for a moment. 'A few clues and new contacts . . . but the important thing Ben . . . is I think she's still alive!' The fact of it was only just beginning to sink in. 'She's *alive*. But she's in trouble. I *have* to find her. That's the most important thing.'

'No,' said Ben immediately, 'it isn't, as Mr Pulitzer would be the first to tell you. The most important thing is filing your story by October the thirtieth when the Fair ends.'

'Yes, of course,' murmured Emily, 'but I'm going to have a damn good try at finding Anna . . . *and* bringing her home.'

DAY EIGHT

Thursday October 26, 1893

41

Novice

One of the hotel maids, on her way down to work from the room next door, knocked on Emily's door at six the next morning and getting only a grunt for an answer, opened the door, filled her water jug from one she carried and pulled open the heavy curtains.

'It's your water, miss,' she said. 'You asked for it at six.'

Never one to wake up quickly, Emily lay in bed for a moment or two, disoriented by the bare surroundings of the staff bedroom she was in.

She sat up, stared blearily at the dawn light, and wondered what she should wear. A corset and day dress did not, somehow, seem appropriate.

Her problem was solved a quarter of an hour later as she completed her ablutions. It was the maid again, this time with a pair of blue flannel bloomers and a high-necked blouse of the kind women wore for physical culture, courtesy of the Hatsumis.

She preferred the idea of Hatsumi's daughter and her silk pyjamas, but what she now had on would preserve her modesty while allowing freedom of movement. Nevertheless she felt oddly self-conscious when she opened her door and set off for the elevator. She was glad the hour was early and she could make it to the Banquet Hall without meeting anyone.

Mr Hatsumi was ready and waiting, mysteriously ageless in the dull morning light.

'Good!' was his only greeting. 'We begin!'

During the following hour Emily took up various tortuous positions as Mr Hatsumi instructed, shadowing his own movements and adopting strange postures with her arms and hands that appeared easy but proved indescribably difficult to maintain for more than a few seconds.

Occasionally, politely, Mr Hatsumi would reach forward and ease her arms into the correct positions. It felt quite natural and his touch was at once firm and reassuring.

Naturally he did not touch her legs or chest, but once or twice he applied his hands to the upper and lower parts of Emily's back, some-times to show her exactly where to relax, at other times to get her to assume a slightly different position.

After only twenty minutes Emily was breathing heavily. Another ten minutes and she felt exhausted. After nearly forty minutes, when she felt ready to give up, Mr Hatsumi, his sense of timing impeccable, brought the session to an end.

'But you didn't show me how to defend myself,' she said at the end.

'I show you how to be yourself,' said Mr Hatsumi. 'That is the true nature of personal strength. Today we make preparation for your journey into self. Defense, attack, the shadow and the sun, they will come. You have done well, Miss Strauss.'

'I'll never fly through the air like your daughter, sir!' she said ruefully.

'But you already know how to fly in your mind.'

It felt like a compliment and she took it as such.

'What happens if I'm attacked again before you've had time to teach me those other things?'

Mr Hatsumi fixed her with a stare and a half smile.

'Listen to your heart and your stomach and not to your head,' he said simply. 'Tomorrow, half-past six?'

'Yes,' agreed Emily.

She returned to her room, washed again, and put on her day dress. It was not yet seven-thirty.

The early morning exercise had tired her but she felt exhilarated and ready for anything. As she pushed her way out through the hotel swing doors and into the early morning bustle of Chicago, she pondered how she would now react, should she stumble again down some blind, dark alley and find herself face to face with a predatory male.

42

Warning

Over at Clark Street, Anna Zemeckis just made it to her worktable at Brennan's with a minute to spare. Mr Jack Brennan Jr was none-too-pleased. He was a stickler for punctuality and a minute early felt like half an hour late to him. He had even been known to fine girls half a day's wages for arriving at the last moment, on the dubious grounds that it caused others anxiety, meaning himself.

'We start at eight prompt,' he told Anna, 'and that means you need preparation time before that. I'm warning you right now, girl – next time you'll be fined.'

Anna knew enough not to argue.

'Sorry, Mr Brennan, sir,' she said meekly.

She stole a glance at Eileen, who winked. They'd get a chance to talk later.

Anna was late because she had woken up feeling sick and had decided to take a streetcar. Not knowing the stops, she had missed the right one and had had to run back along Jackson Boulevard to Clark Street to get to work.

Rushing had made her feel even worse and she was now pale and sweating, her hair half undone. But despite this bad start to the day she felt more secure than she had for days.

Dunning seemed far behind her now and if only she could stick with the work for a little longer, she would have enough money to pay for the train ride away from the jurisdiction of Illinois and the Cook County Hospital, across the border to St Paul, Minnesota. From there, Tomas Steffens the train driver had told her she could get a train to Winnipeg and travel on to her aunt's farm by Lac du Bonnet.

She had confided her condition to no one at the Mission, although the place had a camaraderie that was lacking at Brennan's, and, better still, a feeling of 'Us against Them' – 'them' being the strict Catholic sisters who ran the place. This made Anna hopeful that nobody would snitch on her if they guessed she was pregnant, for the waves of morning sickness were difficult to disguise and sooner or later someone might notice.

Her mind and her memory were now almost back to normal, except for the few days immediately preceding her arrival at the insane asylum.

She remembered her life in New York and her father; she remembered her schooling, her church, her home and her friends. She remembered coming to Chicago and the Markulises. She was nice, but he . . . well, she knew her father was wary of Hendriks. But if he had known, as she had discovered, that he was such a heavy drinker, he would never ever have sent her to stay with them.

She remembered all this but as if through a tight-shut windowpane of dirty glass – the sound muted, the details obscured. But the past aroused no great emotion in her. It was gone; over and done with.

In fact it seemed to her right now that she had no real past at all. Except she knew that she had been witness to something terrible to do, not with hogs or butchers as she had first imagined, but with the man who had fathered her child. Which was why she had to run, and keep on running.

'Jelena? Jelena! We're stopping for five minutes to oil the machines.'

Momentarily, Anna failed to recognize her unfamiliar name when Mrs Donal roused her from her reverie. Around them the sounds of the machines had suddenly died into silence and the roar and rattle of Clark Street intruded once more.

'You've worked well this morning, Jelena. This is not half bad.'

This was praise indeed coming from Mrs Donal. But what followed

was unnerving and sounded more like a question – of the kind Anna
had been dreading.

'You seem unwell.'

'I *have* been unwell, Mrs Donal. I had a cold that went straight to
my stomach.'

'Hmm. Take the air in the street for a few minutes, but be back on
time. Mr Brennan likes to keep everyone on their toes.'

'Thank you, Mrs Donal.'

Anna slipped off downstairs, Eileen with her. They sat against a
wall by the back entrance, enjoying the sun.

'Did you really have a cold?'

'Yes,' said Anna firmly, 'they always go to my stomach and make
me feel sick.'

'Hmm,' said Eileen, just as Mrs Donal had done.

'Eileen,' began Anna. She wanted to confide in her, to tell her about
her pregnancy, 'I . . .'

But something stopped her.

Don't trust anyone, Tomas Steffens had told her and he was probably
right.

'Mmm?'

'I think we better go back in.'

They took a final look up and down busy Clark Street. Anna wished
she was free, to look into its shop windows, watch the world go by,
rest at last.

'Yes, we'd better,' said Eileen.

The doorman who watched the back of the premises let them take
the freight elevator back up.

'It's not such a bad place,' Anna told herself, 'if only I can stay here
undisturbed for a couple more weeks.'

But perhaps it was as well Anna was not free to roam Clark Street.

For at that moment, at the intersection with Lake, four men stood
conferring with a fifth. They had grim, unforgiving faces and wore
curled bowler hats and had the kind of aggressive attitudes that told
passersby that they were not the kind of men to mess with. Any
Chicagoan with eyes in his head would have known them to be members
of a gang from the Levee, or maybe the Near West Side.

Most drinkers and saloon slouchers would have recognized them at once as a bunch of Tick Tock boys who looked after matters in Ward Number 1 for its nattily dressed councilor 'Tick Tock' Sullivan, man of the people and boss of boodling. Together with his sidekick 'Bookman' Baxter, Sullivan ran the Ward out of a saloon known as Wolski's Yard over on Harrison and Adams. It had been Democrat ever since Johnny Sullivan – who acquired the 'Tick Tock' sobriquet from the gold pocket watch he was given by a grateful gambler in a prize fight back in '86 – had moved in that same year. Baxter, his diminutive alter ego, added brains to brawn, and together they played every low extortionate racket known to man and beast.

Donko O'Banion and James Riley could claim a close connection with Tick Tock, as could any number of Irish folk in Ward 1 who served his interests like he did theirs when it was needed.

Right now Donko had called on Tick Tock's help to find Anna Zemeckis, who had done bad things to his sister Maureen up at Dunning. Sullivan listened attentively as he sipped his water (he ran half the city's liquor trade but didn't touch a drop himself in case his wife found out). He decided to oblige in the knowledge that he would have Donko in his pocket ever afterwards.

The men now asked a question or two of the fifth man and examined a photograph he held, before breaking up to systematically work their way down the establishments on either side of the street.

It was likely to be a long and tedious task, but they didn't look like the types who gave up. Anyway, when the word got out that the Tick Tock boys were in the neighborhood looking for someone, it would be sure to bring informers their way.

And sooner or later they would get to Brennan's.

43

R.H.Y.S.

The body of Jenkin Lloyd Rhys fetched up in a tangle of barbed wire and timber some time during the night of the 25th beneath the railway viaduct just south of Johnstown, Pennsylvania – two days after Dodek Krol had pitched it out of a refrigerated Darke Hartz box car a few miles upstream.

It was spotted at nine forty-six the following morning and the sheriff was called.

Rivers like the Stonycreek and the Little Conemaugh, which together form the Conemaugh River along whose banks Johnstown is built, deal with bodies harshly when they are running high with October rain.

Rhys's head was stove in, an ear was nearly torn off, the torso and legs were swollen and the flesh all blanched. All the body had left in the way of covering was one woolen stocking, a pair of drawers and an expensive shirt whose pearl buttons had mostly popped free.

Yet for all that, Johnstown's sheriff had no trouble identifying the corpse. That was because four letters were carved nice and neat in its forehead and the name they spelt was RHYS. Clearly the killer had wanted his victim to be identified and in Johnstown the name Rhys was very well known indeed.

Four and a half years previously, Johnstown had been the scene of

America's worst natural disaster. A heavy storm traveling east from
the states of Kansas and Nebraska had hit the Allegheny Mountains
on May 30, 1889, bringing with it a torrential downpour on a scale
never before seen, and this in an area already notorious for heavy rain-
fall. In the following twenty-four hours, ten inches of rain had fallen.
The little creeks in the mountains above the town had gone into spate
and began ripping up trees and rocks. By the 31st the Conemaugh
River was bursting its banks and beginning to flood the town, which
was hemmed in on either side by its deep valley site.

Meanwhile, fourteen miles upstream the Conemaugh Lake, held
back by a cheaply built, seventy-two-foot-high dam, had filled to
capacity. Nobody worried too much, least of all the moneyed members
of the elite South Fork Fishing and Hunting Club who owned the lake
and had responsibility for maintaining the dam. Many of them lived
in their big, safe houses fifty-five miles away in Pittsburgh, overseeing
their steel, coal and railway enterprises. The members included some
of America's wealthiest: Andrew Carnegie, Philander Knox and
Henry Clay Frick.

. . . And Jenkin Lloyd Rhys too, who, unluckily for him, had been
elected three months earlier to run the club's subcommittee responsible
for site maintenance and maneuvered into the no-win task of a belated
program of dam strengthening.

But the storm beat them to it. The dam burst on the afternoon of
May 31st, propelling the lake's contents downstream in a terrifying,
death-dealing wall of water which, hemmed in by the narrow valley,
rose to sixty feet high.

Over two thousand people in Johnstown, including nearly four
hundred children, were taken by surprise. They didn't stand a chance:
if they weren't drowned, they were crushed and horribly injured. If
they escaped, something worse awaited them. They were carried
downstream to the Stone Bridge, and hurled against over thirty acres
of debris that had piled up in only a few hours.

The living soon became the living dead because, caught up among
the debris, were miles and miles of barbed wire, washed down from
the yard of a wire factory upriver, along with great logs of timber and
thick black oil.

Rescuers watched helplessly as the injured survivors, caught up in the wire and covered in oil, were overtaken by fire when the waters receded. Their agonizing screams for help were heard throughout the night and into the dawn.

The next morning only their burnt and contorted bodies were left, hanging on the wire and trapped among the timbers. The mountain of debris had become a huge funeral pyre, and it burned for three days.

Upwards of seven hundred bodies were never identified. Four square miles of Johnstown – a town that should never have been built on such a site – were completely destroyed. The shadow of death fell over its scarred and smouldering remains and the scars would run deep for years.

Yet America, in this dark hour, produced many heroes who came to Johnstown's rescue. Clara Barton, president of the American Red Cross, arrived within days and initiated an astonishing welfare operation there for nearly six months; 'Dynamite' Bill Flinn led a 900-strong team of demolition men in the dangerous work of razing the site before the task of rebuilding. Many wealthy people contributed substantial amounts in aid, among them steel and railroad man, Andrew Carnegie, who built and stocked a fine new library for the stricken township.

But the disaster also produced its fair share of villains, most of them associated with the South Fork Fishing and Hunting Club. None more so than Jenkin Lloyd Rhys who in vain protested his innocence. But a town that had lost so many of its children – and with them its future – demanded a scapegoat.

For a time it seemed that Rhys would lose everything and would even be removed from his presidency of the Old America Association. But he had friends in high places, including the powerful and influential Paul Hartz. He weathered the storm rather better than Johnstown had.

The Johnstown disaster of 1889 appeared to affect him no more. But it lived on in Rhys's nightmares until that early morning of October 26th, when his body was spotted floating by the Stone Bridge, tangled in a rusted remnant of that same barbed wire that in 1889 had caused so many deaths.

When word spread through the town that the body fished out of

the water was that of Jenkin Lloyd Rhys, there was widespread satisfaction. The town's law officers were not going to trouble themselves
unduly about how or why he had ended up dead at Johnstown. There
was a certain poetic justice in the fact that the river that had killed so
many had finally claimed him too.

The death was quickly and conveniently marked down as 'accidental',
which seemed a tall order given the letters carved in his forehead. But
maybe that was post mortem, someone suggested helpfully.

Given the state of the corpse, an early burial was called for, the
exact time depending on the response from the next of kin, Rhys's
wife, who was immediately contacted in New York.

'Get him out of here as fast as you can,' said the mayor nervously.

'Can't do anything till we get a response from the family,' said the
coroner.

'Then we'll have to put a guard on him. We don't want trouble.'

'It's kind of hard to lynch a dead man.'

'It's not so hard to throw him back in the river and let him make
his own way to Pittsburgh,' said the mayor.

Nevertheless, he bowed to protocol. Rhys's body lay in a cold locker
in the local morgue while the telegraph wires hummed between Johnstown and New York. A legal burial was in the end better than an
illegal depositing of the body back in the Conemaugh River.

A burial meant the people of Johnstown could finally dance on
Rhys's grave.

44

WCTU Ladies

By the time Emily Strauss headed off from her hotel to the Woman's Temple for the WCTU meeting, her stiff muscles and aching joints were beginning to ease. The walk did her good. She reached Monroe at La Salle, the day sunny and mild now and the traffic thick and noisy about her. The temple towered over on the northeast corner of the intersection, its facade aglow in the morning sun.

This famous new Chicago landmark, begun in 1890, was French château-style in inspiration, with its arches, bays, curves and tasteful decoration in red brick and faced stone and designed by the famous architects, Burnham and Root. Its construction had been inspired and led by Frances Willard, the formidable president of the Woman's Christian Temperance Union, who had wanted something that was powerful, yet feminine and spiritually uplifting for women – a focal point for the wider movement for religious, political and social reform that they carried out across America.

'Also,' Liesel Markulis had explained to Emily pragmatically, 'it was intended as a building that could generate great revenue for the cause.'

All Emily could see right now was that the Woman's Temple seemed to be generating great controversy. A growing crowd of men, half-heartedly held back by police officers, jostled outside its main entrance, shouting jibes at anyone entering the building.

Emily noted that most of the men were the kind of drunks and ne'er-do-wells who frequented Chicago's many saloons and bars and took the greatest pleasure in opposing supporters of the temperance movement and its calls for prohibition. Some of them were already, by mid-morning, no longer sober, but so far their jibes at those entering the Woman's Temple were of the jokey kind. 'Keep yer spirits up!' one of them shouted at a well-upholstered, prosperous matron, pulling a bottle of malt from his pocket and waving it in her face, 'Cos I'm sure as hell looking after mine.'

Emily repressed a smile but could see that the situation was rapidly degenerating.

The crowd was already spilling off the sidewalk, determined to make things awkward for the delegates as they passed under the great banner displayed over the front entrance, which read

WOMAN'S CHRISTIAN TEMPERANCE UNION
CHICAGO BRANCH
ANNUAL CONVENTION
'For God and Home and Native Land'

But, as Emily herself reached the entrance, the mood changed for the better. The mayor arrived, mounted on a white horse, looking both resplendent and jovial. He had timed his regular ride round the city to perfection. Emily had heard that Carter Henry Harrison was a past master at managing the electors: it seemed he knew a thing or two about managing mobs as well.

Once inside she found the great lobby buzzing with women. There was a reception desk and female ushers directing people to the hall on the floor above.

Most of the women wore white ribbons, the emblem of their commitment to the WCTU pledge. They were, Emily noted, well dressed and nicely hatted. But not quite all – there were some poorer sisters of the movement in evidence whose shoes were scuffed, their hairstyles plain and their hands rough. Women from most of the many different ethnic communities of the city were also in evidence, a few in their national costume.

Despite the ribald reception committee on the sidewalk outside,

257

the mood was one of good cheer and determined sisterhood.

The ticket that Liesel Markulis had given Emily was for a seat in the main lecture hall in which the event was to start at eleven. It was a vast space, with a stage at one end beneath three great stained-glass windows depicting women in heroic roles that linked them to God, Home and Native Land – everything that was good about America. There were a large number of colorful banners, bunting and flags stretched around and across the hall.

The seating had been arranged so that there was a wide, raised temporary platform in front of the stage, between it and the first row, where a special spectacle – the display by the Nord Chicago Turnverein – was to take place.

Outside the hall there were stalls touting the wares of various different local women's groups. They offered handicrafts, leaflets and badges, ribbons and other regalia of the temperance movement. Set into the walls of this elegant and well-lit space were oak-paneled alcoves in which women in small groups chatted quietly.

The chatter of the throng was loud in that high, excited way that attaches itself to crowds of sociable women intent on changing the world. Emily also noticed that there was a fair scattering of men. Many looked like ministers of religion, lawyers and members of the teaching profession, judging from their sober demeanor and clothes.

Emily was content to sit and take it all in until a voice behind her gently enquired, 'Miss Strauss?'

She turned to the young woman who greeted her.

'That's me! But how did you . . . ?'

The woman pointed across the lobby and Emily saw Liesel Markulis waving, indicating that this was one of the WCTU friends of Anna's that she had told her about.

Their greeting was brief and somber.

It was Mila Blazek, the young friend Mrs Markulis had mentioned; she was fresh-faced and seemed barely more than a girl, a first-generation Czech. It soon became clear that she was very upset about Anna's disappearance and eager to give Emily any help she could.

They pulled away from the crowd to one of the alcoves and sat down.

'The last time I saw Anna was three days before she vanished. We

were going to meet at Jackson Park on the day she disappeared,'
explained Mila, twisting her handkerchief in her lap.

'How did you get to know her?' asked Emily gently.

'We met at WCTU, and to be honest it was the social side of things
we preferred. These ladies can get a bit serious, you know?'

Emily nodded and grinned.

'I *do* know,' she said reassuringly

'You're not wearing the ribbon?' Mila expressed surprise as she indicated her own.

Emily shook her head.

'It's better for someone in my profession to remain neutral about
such things and anyway . . . my father encouraged me to drink a glass
of good German wine now and then.'

'Mine didn't,' said Mila, giggling suddenly. 'When I tried it, it made
me feel ill. That's how it was with Anna too. But I wouldn't say she
was the strict kind . . . She was fun to be with when she first got here
and very curious about everything in Chicago and at the Fair. But
later, she didn't seem so happy . . .'

'Why? What do you think happened?'

'I don't know, I can't imagine. I don't want to imagine . . . it's so
horrible. I've thought and thought about what might have happened
and if Anna ever said or did anything that might give a clue to it all.
But I can think of nothing.'

'When did you first meet her?'

'We joined WCTU together in early May when we both came here
for the World's Fair. Our host families didn't know each other but they
both live on the North Side.'

'You're Czech?'

'Yes. My aunt had a baby and I came from New York to help out.
That first evening we met, we found we had things in common,
including wanting to take the pledge, which was quite a thing for me
but not so much for Anna who comes . . . came from a much stricter
Lutheran background. We came to meetings, went to church and visited
the Fair together in our spare time. It was good to have a companion
of whom my aunt approved and I got on with the Markulises . . . well,
with Mrs Markulis.'

Emily noted the first sign of hesitation.

'And what about Mr?'

'Well, no . . . ,' said Mila.

'Liquor?' suggested Emily, voicing her suspicions.

'You know about that?'

'Did Anna say anything to Mr Markulis?'

'I don't think so. Until June, that is, when I believe she had an argument with him about his behavior. He could be "silly", you know. Annoying. I expect she was quite rude to him, but then . . .'

'What?'

'It got hot in July. She couldn't bear the heavy air; it made her dizzy. She grew fractious with everyone, including me.'

Emily fell silent. If Anna had indeed started behaving out of character by then, her hunch was right. She had become deeply troubled. Was it because she was with child?

'Got to go,' said Mila suddenly, getting up. 'I'm one of the Turner girls.'

'Yes, I gather they're giving a demonstration.'

'We call it a spectacle. We've been practicing for weeks. It'll be at around twelve. I must go and change.'

'Was Anna a Turner?'

'She was. She was very good. She would have been in this show, but . . .'

As she turned to go, she added, 'Anna was never a bad girl, you know, but she did have a mind of her own . . . '

Emily got up and joined the crowd now making its way into the hall where the female ushers were showing people to their numbered seats. Somewhere, on a balcony above, a musical ensemble was playing.

'Miss Strauss!?'

It was Liesel Markulis.

'Goodness! I thought I'd never reach you through this crush! What a wonderful turnout!'

She pointed out where Emily's seat was and explained that she herself would be sitting near the front with her local board members.

'Was Mila helpful?'

'Yes.'

'I have arranged for Miss Stoiber to come and sit next to you. Remember I mentioned her? She'll tell you what she remembers about Anna. Mila is very nice but quite young. I think you'll find that Miss Stoiber has a sensible head on her shoulders and if anyone can make sense of what has happened she can. But, excuse me, I must go . . . !'

'Mrs Markulis?'

Emily's suddenly serious tone stopped Liesel Markulis in her tracks.

'Did you notice anything different in Anna's behaviour in July?'

Emily thought she detected a glimmer of guilt in Mrs Markulis's eyes.

'I really don't know . . . Maybe she was homesick now and then, for her father, but no . . . Nothing in particular. Except she couldn't bear the heat.'

Emily nodded.

'Did Anna have her ears pierced when she came to Chicago?' she asked.

'Why no.' Mrs Markulis looked genuinely puzzled. 'Her father would not have allowed it. Why do you ask?'

'Another time,' Emily said, 'the meeting's about to begin . . .'

As Mrs Markulis moved off, an usher tugged at Emily's sleeve and she took her seat. The woman next to her introduced herself as Marion Stoiber. She was older than Mila and Anna too.

Her handshake was firm, her touch as cold as her eyes. 'We'll talk about Anna in the break for luncheon,' she said. But there was none of Mila Blazek's affection or warmth in her voice, which immediately set Emily wondering.

She opened her mouth to respond but Marion frowned, put a finger to her lips and nodded towards the stage.

Moments later a tall, elegant woman on the platform rose up, looked around like a college headmistress intent on bringing order to unruly students, took up a gavel and firmly beat it thrice on the table, bringing the good ladies of WCTU to order.

45

Mr Toulson

At about the same time that the good ladies of WCTU began settling down to the serious business of the day, a telephone rang in an obscure, out-of-the-way downtown office.

It had been established only a few months before by William Pinkerton, son of the founder of the Pinkerton Detective Agency, as a base for certain specialized covert operations, about which his regular staff needed to know nothing.

Strictly speaking, the office was not part of Pinkerton's at all; the only people who knew of its existence and used it were ex-Pinkerton men of the very highest caliber, discreetly returning from 'retirement' to undertake assignments of a very particular and dangerous kind that required their expertise.

A tough-looking, thickset individual picked up the receiver. He had taken off his jacket and sat with rolled-up sleeves and wide suspenders at a pigeonhole desk, a wastebasket to one side and a shiny brass spittoon to the other.

'Yes?'

'You have a call from New York. A Mrs Rhys.'

The man sighed.

'OK, put her on.'

There was a brief pause, a few hollow clicks, and then the distant sound of a woman, breathing heavily, the voice tremulous. 'Mr Toulson?'

'Yes.'

'He's been found . . . as you warned he might be. He . . .'

Jenkin Lloyd Rhys's wife, Ellen, began to weep.

For a tough-looking man, who had seen and occasionally had to do some horrible things in his nearly fifty years of life, Toulson's eyes were remarkably gentle.

'I'm so sorry, Mrs Rhys.'

She wept some more.

'I'm sorry,' she said eventually, 'I . . .'

'Take your time.'

The sobbing at the end of the line continued and then, eventually, Ellen Rhys said, 'He was found in Johnstown, Pennsylvania. They say it's an accidental death. He was in the river, it . . .'

'Just try to give me the facts, Mrs Rhys . . . as best you can.'

Ellen Rhys repeated what the sheriff at Johnstown had told her over the telephone. She was not to know that his version had not included everything.

'Who identified him?'

'The sheriff himself. They all know Jenkin in Johnstown . . .'

Her voice faded.

'*Accidental death?* Who's fooling who?' Toulson was incredulous.

'That's what the sheriff told me.'

'And what do you think?'

'I don't believe a word of it. JLR knew that everyone at Johnstown hated him.'

She broke down again.

Toulson consulted a tome on his desk and looked up a name.

'What else did Sheriff Bastable say?'

'He strongly advised me that in the interests of public safety my husband should be interred as soon as possible. As a precautionary measure . . .'

'You mean they fear reprisals?'

'Yes. News of the discovery of his body is all over town. In view of the situation, he wants me to telegraph permission for Jenkin to be interred in secret, given his unpopularity in Johnstown. Then, at a later date, they'll bring him back home to New York for a proper burial. But I don't know . . . What do *you* think?'

Toulson was silent at the end of the phone.

'Sheriff Bastable wanted me to call back very soon . . .'

'I'm sure he did,' said Toulson heavily.

He thought a moment more.

'Mrs Rhys, this is a very serious matter. I am most grateful for your cooperation and your courage. In time I think it may come to matter a great deal. Now, here's what I want you to do . . .'

They spoke for another five minutes or so; Toulson repeated his condolences, and then said goodbye.

He immediately picked up the phone again and gave an instruction that very few people in America, bar the president, could ever give.

'Get me Mr William Pinkerton on the line.'

The phone rang a few minutes later.

'Fifteen seventy-one?' Having set up this additional, secure office in Chicago, William Pinkerton abided strictly by its rules, addressing Toulson by number only.

'It is,' said Toulson. 'Sir, I have an urgent question. Who do we have in Pittsburgh? Needs to be someone very good.'

'They're all good.'

'I mean able to deal with troublesome sheriffs.'

'Where?'

Toulson hesitated.

'It doesn't matter. I don't need to know,' said Pinkerton. 'Give me a moment.'

There was the rustling of paper. Then a voice called out to an assistant, 'I need the register of agents.'

Half a minute later Pinkerton came back on the line.

'I have someone. He's very good.'

'Name?'

'Van Hale.'

Toulson's eyes lightened.

'I thought he was in San Francisco.'

'He moved. He's in Pittsburgh clearing up the mess left after the Homestead Strike.'

Toulson said nothing. There was nothing to say about that ignominious debacle which had left the reputation of Pinkerton seriously damaged. Toulson and Van Hale had both warned against that operation and now they were among the few senior men who had survived the shakedown that followed.

'He's perfect. Can he do it personally?'

'I'll see that he does. I'll talk to him right away.'

Toulson put the telephone down and reached for a box file. It was number ten of nineteen. They stretched right across one wall of his office. He opened it and prised free a folder, which he took out and put on his desk.

He opened the folder and pulled out some photographs, eying them with extreme distaste.

Then he reached for another box file and another folder. It also contained photographs – of women and men – just ordinary pictures that could be of any passerby in the street. Only these were of the missing, the dead and the murdered.

Impatient that he would have to wait for some time for the operator to set up his call to Pennsylvania, Toulson turned on his desk lamp, positioned it closely over the photographs and with a magnifying glass, began making comparisons between these and the other photographs.

Twenty minutes later the phone rang again.

'Fifteen seventy . . .'

'For Chrissake, Gerry,' interrupted the voice at the other end. 'Is that you?'

Toulson grinned and laughed.

'Hello Van,' he said. 'You busy?'

'Don't have to be.'

'How soon can you get over to Johnstown?'

'Within an hour.'

'Heard of Sheriff Bastable?'

'Je*sus*,' said Van Hale.

'Here's what I want you to do . . .'

When the call was over, Toulson returned to the photographs.

Moments later, he let out a long, slow sigh of satisfaction.

Leaning back in his chair, he pulled two photographs clear of the pile.

One was as lewd as photographs of its kind ever got.

The other was of Anna Zemeckis.

46

Starr Turn

Emily Strauss soon discovered that, as far as annual conventions were concerned, the WCTU ladies liked to run a tight ship, with a well-oiled procedure, punctuated with Christian songs and prayers led by a succession of obliging and acquiescent ministers of religion.

It seemed to Emily, who was raised to be distrustful of dogma and officialdom, and whose nature was too restless for organized volunteer work, that the vigorous and assertive ladies running the show had the effect of making the gentlemen present seem rather weak, as if their manliness took a poor second place to their godliness.

The program had begun with some formal speechmaking, involving self-congratulation and anti-saloon rhetoric, followed by the pleasant diversion of the Turnverein spectacle.

Marion Stoiber unstiffened a little as the intervals between speeches and activities came and went, during which, Emily noted, everybody else chattered away like shoppers along State Street on a Saturday.

'Of course, our president, Frances Willard, is not able to be here today,' explained Miss Stoiber with a pursing of the lips and a note of disapproval.

'Why not?'

'She's in England convalescing. She was taken ill after her mother's death last year. She has sent someone to address us on her behalf on the first of today's three themes.'

'Our Native Land?' said Emily.

Marion nodded.

It was not a theme or an idea Emily found easy to understand or warm to since, like so many of her friends, she still had close emotional links with her own land of origin. Her father had been more progressive than most in encouraging her to think positively about America and to accept it was their home now. But she knew many German parents in Pittsburgh who spoke their native language round the home and practiced old customs and rituals in the hope of keeping their own traditions alive.

The program indicated that Miss Willard's representative was one Amelia M. Starr.

'She's an English cousin of Ellen Starr who helped Jane Addams found Hull House over on the West Side, so I suppose that's in her favor. I believe she's just come over from England to help at Hull House for a while, bringing with her Miss Willard's latest message to the membership.'

'Which one is she on the platform?' asked Emily.

'Well, I've not seen her before but I know all the others up there by sight, so she must be the one over on the right . . . in fact she looks quite like Miss Willard herself!'

The woman she pointed out was not much to look at: of medium height with a plain, pinched face adorned by steel spectacles with hair somewhat haphazardly pulled back into a bun. She seemed like a bookish type, pale and rather lost amongst all the other committee ladies in big hats, who looked so much more colorful, better dressed and altogether more formidable than she.

Or at least most of them did.

There was a second row of ladies on the platform, behind the more important officials and main speakers, and among them Emily spotted two or three of the women she had met at the World's Fair. One in particular interested her because she looked as awkward and as nervous now as she had before in the Illinois State Building, which was unusual in one of Chicago's social leaders.

'That's Christiane Darke, isn't it? Do you know her?' she asked
Marion Stoiber.

'Not personally, she's one of our wealthier ladies I believe, both by
inheritance and marriage. She's the daughter of Paul Hartz, one of
our leading industrialists, of whom I daresay you've heard.'

Emily nodded. 'So she married into the Darke side of the business?'

'She married Gunther, one of Hans Darke's two sons. He's over
there.'

Marion Stoiber pointed to a row of seats on the right positioned
sideways on to the hall. In fact she spotted her friend Fay Bancroft
before she saw Gunther Darke, and smiled inwardly, unsurprised that
Fay had obtained one of the best seats in the hall or that she was
exchanging a few words with one of the best-looking men in it.

Gunther Darke was in his early thirties, olive-skinned and clean-
shaven but for a fine black moustache. He wore his expensive suit with
easy grace and when, after leaning forward to speak to Fay, he sat up
straight, Emily could see he was well made, and noticeably taller than
those around him.

The Turnverein entertainment, when it finally came, was a
welcome relief and in its way quite impressive. The men performed
various synchronized exercise routines and acrobatics, both singly
and together. The watching ladies, Emily included, did a poor job
of hiding their appreciation of the male body beautiful as a succession
of strong male backs, thick forearms and well-muscled thighs passed
before their eyes.

When their female counterparts followed it was the men's turn to
admire as best they could the virtues of female calisthenics, though
the sixteen performers, who wore the same style of bloomers and
blouses that Emily had donned earlier that morning, were modest to
a fault. Their routine was a collective one and was elegant rather than
athletic, but it drew rapturous applause from the largely female audience.

'That was awfully good,' said Emily effusively, hoping to draw her
new companion out, then venturing, 'how did you become acquainted
with Anna?'

Marion's faced tightened.

'We worked together in the Administration Building of the World's

269

Fair. Many of the part-time staff, like Anna, were volunteers.'

'But you were paid?'

Marion nodded.

'I'm a trained stenographer and clerical assistant. I jumped at the chance of a job at the Fair. It was a once-in-a-lifetime opportunity. Anna joined us in mid-May, a couple of weeks after she got to Chicago. You know, she came here from New York?'

Emily nodded. 'I went to see her father. He wrote to the New York *World* . . .'

She explained the assignment that had brought her to Chicago but Marion seemed unmoved.

'I doubt that I can be of much help.' Her tone was decidedly unencouraging. 'But in any case . . . not now, the speakers are about to continue.'

Emily turned back to look at the stage. The first of the three keynote speakers was approaching the lectern. But Emily's eyes were drawn to the right, towards Gunther Darke. He was talking with Fay and smiling broadly as he did so.

'He's a fine-looking man, don't you think?' whispered Emily, noticing Marion's interest.

'I suppose so,' responded Marion, her gaze wandering again, brusquely adding, 'If you have to take an interest in other women's business.'

Feeling admonished, Emily glanced at Christiane Darke up on the stage. She looked stony-faced and rather desolate.

'You wouldn't think, would you, that her husband is one of the stars of the World's Fair!' said Marion suddenly.

Did Emily detect something odd about the way Marion Stoiber said this? She thought she did.

'Why so?'

'Once a week he leads the master butchers of Darke Hartz in a demonstration of the art of dressing hogs and steer at the Agricultural Hall.' Whatever Emily had expected, it was not that.

'But you won't get a ticket to see it, Miss Strauss. It's a sellout!'

'What, men cutting up meat!?'

'You should see it and you'd know why.'

'You have, I presume?'

270

Marion Stoiber nodded.

'I got a ticket because of my work for the Fair.'

But Emily didn't have time to get Marion Stoiber to elaborate. The gavel banged on the table upfront once more and the audience fell silent.

Of the three keynote addresses that followed, it was the first, by Miss Starr, that impressed Emily the most.

After a brief and none-too-warm introduction by the lady chairman, who made a rather pointed reference to Miss Willard's absence, Miss Starr took the lectern. She was neither tall nor overly impressive, but her voice had that rare quality in a speaker, especially a female one. It commanded instant and absolute attention.

Her accent betrayed her English roots but it had none of that pretentious arrogance that East Coast ladies, conscious of their English antecedents, feel it necessary to assume. It was soft yet carried clearly right to the back of the hall; her words were well articulated but never sharp and she wasted no time on idle introductions, false modesty or extravagant praise.

'Miss Willard, your president, sends her warmest greetings to you all. She has given me no speech to read. Rather, when I spoke with her two weeks ago in London about this important event, she expressed her own heartfelt thoughts about it, and about her friends and sisters and colleagues in America and in Chicago, and expressly told me to say what I myself felt I must, in my own way and from my own heart.'

She paused for a moment, looked right round the hall and then gave a self-deprecating smile. 'But as I stand here today, only because Frances Willard herself cannot be here, it matters not who I am or what I may be. I am simply that thing which is at once sadly weak and fiercely strong; that thing that must run with the waves yet be a rock to the tide; that thing, despite its many despairs, that must forever cling onto the single faith that all in the end will be good and true.

'In other words, I am what most of you are: a woman. Before that I am what all of us are – you good men included – I am a human being. And that, my fellow sisters, is all you need to know about me.'

These few words brought the women and the men in the hall to a

271

strange stillness. Miss Starr, whether she knew it or not, had the audience in her grip.

'Five years ago, almost to the day, Miss Willard, as president of the then newly formed Chicago Women's League, invoked as her text in her address to you the words "Help me to heal the heartbreak of humanity."

'She was referring to the measureless injustice that surrounds us like an insidious atmosphere and the fathomless misery that broods over us like a malaria inviting the murmuring heart to cry out, "Had I God's power or He my love, we would have a different world from the one we see."

'Five years on, and with a few more silver threads on my head, I, like so many of you, am angry.

'Angry that the saloons we have sought to shut pump out their liquor poison to more, not fewer, of our men.

'Angry that the brewers we reason with to help are ever more unreasonable in their insatiable greed for profit that destroys the humanity in man and undermines the very soul and heart of the family.'

Someone, a woman, in the audience shouted, 'Well said!' Others cried, 'Hear! Hear!'

Amelia Starr moved to one side of the lectern to be the better seen, now speaking without reference to her notes.

'Yes, my friends, I am angry. Angry that so many of our poor sisters and their children are driven by poverty to give up the one thing they possess and with which they should be able to bargain, which is their labor; that they are forced to sell it cheap by a system that rewards the rich and to see its value eroded in conditions to which their employers would not submit their horses, their dogs and least of all their wives and daughters.

'Are you not angry at this?'

Several in the audience shouted that they were.

Someone else, a man this time, called out, 'Speak plain, sister. Make it plain!'

'I am angry that those same sisters of ours, many of whom are daily suffering the destruction of their health and the loss of their liberty, do so in garment sweatshops, in dye-houses, in match factories not ten minutes' walk from where we meet today, with no possibility of redress for the unfairness and impossibility of their situation. It should not be so! It . . . should . . . not . . . be . . . so!'

Amelia Starr paused again and returned to the lectern, leaning upon it as if she needed its support.

Then more quietly, yet still with utter clarity, reaching everyone in the packed hall, she continued, 'And yet I am angry, most of all, that your dear lady president's brother, a wonderful and kindly man, should feel the need to write to his sister ten months ago, at the time of the presidential elections, and say – and I quote from memory a letter Frances Willard read to me several times: "I was a-thinking, dear sister, that you had not the vote to bless yourself with. And so I left the Democratic Party and voted the Prohibition ticket in your name!"'

At this there was a great cheer and much clapping.

Amelia waited until the audience quietened.

'I am angry, because we who are one half of humanity – some might say the kind half, others the weaker half, yet others the more gently loving half – remain disempowered.'

Emily felt a thrill down her spine. Amelia Starr was saying things she herself felt but which, in her preoccupation with getting on with her life since her father's death, she had quite forgotten.

Miss Starr raised a hand, its fingers splayed. It seemed to Emily she looked at her directly and transfixed her where she sat.

'The coming change in which our movement is a great and glorious part, and in which we women play an essential role, has until recent years been like this open hand: a weak thing without purpose. Now, bit by bit, starting I believe with the discoveries we made about our own abilities in the magnificent work we did to mitigate the horrors of our Civil War, we have come together as fingers that form a fist; and that fist, which is ourselves so long as we combine with clear goals and shared faith, must be directed with ever greater purpose and power.

'That is our task now and in the years ahead. It is a great task and one which requires that anger of which I speak to remain strong, just as our faith in our purpose and our God stays strong.'

The audience clapped and cheered. A number of the delegates, including even some men, rose to their feet.

But the speaker raised her other hand to still the audience one last time.

'The road to prohibition, to female suffrage, to liberation and proper equality will be a very hard and a very long one. It will be, I fear, many years before we women take our proper place at the helm of state.

'It therefore behoves us that through our daily struggle towards those greater goals we keep uppermost in our minds the welfare of those poor sisters weaker than ourselves, and menfolk too – indeed all members of humanity – whom we know in our own circle of existence and whom we think in some way we can help. It may be a relative. It may be someone you know to be beset by illness, by trouble, by a helplessness that is not their fault. Think of them and fight for them and in so doing you will fight for us all.

'Ladies and gentlemen, on Frances Willard's behalf, I thank you for all you have done in the past year, all you are doing and all you will surely do in the days and weeks, months and years to come, for that fragile, sometimes lost, but always most wonderful thing – humanity. And as you do so, never forget that one great, guiding principle: that everything we do is for God, and Home, and Native Land!'

In the stunned moment of silence that followed, before the audience rose to give Miss Starr a standing ovation, Emily Strauss, who was not much given to prayers, found herself uttering two silent appeals to whatever god was looking down on her that day.

One was for Janis Zemeckis, that his daughter would be returned to him. The other was that Anna remain safe until she could find her and rescue her from whatever trouble and danger she was in.

47

Escape

As the morning wore on for the two thousand delegates crowded into the Woman's Temple, they were not the only ones to start feeling the unseasonable humidity. Something in the weather that day was beginning to oppress the whole of Chicago. A raft of warm, moist air, driven in by pressure changes over Lake Michigan mid-morning had temporarily transformed an average cool October day into a stifling one. It was nasty, close – making male office workers grasp at their collars and street boys on the South Side throw off their jackets. It formed an oppressive smog that settled across the North Side and brought on fat old ladies' asthma and thin old gentlemen's hacking coughs.

Over at the Cook County Hospital Morgue, Alan Freeman studied the barometer and strolled to the door. He pushed it open and peered up at the leaden sky, sniffing the heavy, stinking air, and nodded with resignation. He went right back in and told his staff that chances were they would be staying late that day.

The police officers at Monroe and La Salle had been doing a bad job keeping control of the protesters outside the Woman's Temple, their tempers frazzled by their hot uniforms. But then they received a summons to a fracas over on Monroe and Market and three of them went running. A horse and wagon had fallen foul of a streetcar and a fight had broken out.

At the same time, in a tenement on the near North Side at Halsted and Chicago Avenue, Belia Blazek, aunt of Mila, heard a child start screaming a block away. She knew that sound well enough, the sound of distress and fear. She was right: in the rundown tenement across the way, a sweater for a local garment factory with six children to support had been overcome by the sudden high humidity. Her lungs, weakened by smoke, pollution and disease, gave up and she collapsed over the sewing which was the only work she could get. Her youngest child, left at home with her, sensing something wrong, stood clutching in terror at his mother's skirt, staring at her open mouth and eyes, his shrill screams resonating in the stagnant afternoon air.

Down at Jackson Park, where the crowds had been thick on the promenades all morning, the visitors to the World's Fair suddenly seemed to run out of puff and everything slowed down. All the way down the Midway Plaisance, the more exciting and more commercial unofficial extension of the Fair, business fell right off. Mr Houdini went off for an early lunch, the make-believe Turkish Village became as somnolent as Turkish villages really are; and the Ferris wheel, the life and soul of the Fair and a symbol of the modern world, ground to a halt, stranding over one hundred passengers, some of them 264 feet up in the air, in the sudden humidity. Metal expansion does that to machinery.

Eighteen miles away to the northwest, the staff at Dunning were only too aware what a sudden rise in temperature and humidity can do to lunatics, making some of them restive and irritable and bringing on uncontrollable rages. As a precaution, the institution went into lock-down for the second time in a week.

This included even the isolation ward on Far Side, to which, for the time being, they had moved Maureen Riley in a wheelchair since she refused to walk that far.

Not that she was violent; anything but.

She had simply said, 'No!' and had sat right down where she was in the corridor, that same corridor over which she had once ruled with a rod of iron.

It took four men to lift her and convey her down to the front lobby by way of the stairs. They had done it at night so no one could see. You never could tell what Riley's previous victims might do if they found out that she was now one of their number.

She was put in a small ward with three of Eels's good girls, the ones who had signed for his special treatment program. These included Mary Nevitt, the sad, distracted young woman who had briefly befriended Anna on the ward.

Her fingers were much quieter these days, her eyes dull. Like the other four women in the ward, she was now strangely subdued and rarely moved.

Dr Eels had personally overseen the admission of Riley to Far Side.

'Are you sure she'll be all right with these women, doctor? The inmates don't like her,' said Nurse Lutyens, who had been put in charge of the small recovery ward.

'She'll be fine,' said Eels. 'They won't cause her trouble. They're not capable of it and anyway they won't even recognize her. Look at them!'

Nurse Lutyens wasn't so sure. Strange things happened to patients recovering after operations, and they were sometimes unpleasant.

'Keep a close eye on them,' Eels told her, 'and report back to me.'

Then, to Riley, his voice rising slightly as if he was speaking to a patient – which, come to think of it, he was, 'You'll be all right here, Maureen. You'll be just fine.'

They left her sitting in a chair, a great big sweating lump in a shift. Sweat leaked down her face through the hairs on her top lip and was sucked into the closed chasm between her mountainous breasts.

'Hot,' she said with a smile, staring without interest or recognition at her companions. She plucked at her shift where it stuck to her body. But she did not have the will or comprehension to take it off.

A few minutes later, the peephole in the ward door opened and Nurse Lutyens's eye peered in. Nothing had changed. The three women and Riley were still sitting languidly, doing nothing. Or so she thought.

She was wrong. One of them was thinking dark, slow thoughts, of the kind brought on by heavy weather.

Mary Nevitt sat staring down the ward at Riley. She stared and stared and eventually a cog in her scalpel-damaged mind clicked and turned.

277

The fingers, which before her operation had always been entwined and now had been still for days after a lifetime of movement, began moving again, their nails, long and pointed, clicking in her lap.

Her eyes, beautiful all her life despite her mental illness were ugly now. They stared at Riley and they were filled with hatred.

At Brennan's, Anna Zemeckis was suffering with the humidity as well. She'd spent the morning battling against waves of nausea, her anxiety made worse by the fact that something in Eileen's manner towards her had changed. They were late breaking for lunch that morning because the shop had sent in an urgent order and they had had to complete it.

By the time it was done the machines were overheating and had to be stopped for a while. So Mrs Donal let the women go and take their break in the cooler air of the yard for twenty minutes. Mr Brennan, seeing the exhausted women slumped against the yard wall, chose to be soft for once as he came on by.

He glanced at his silver pocket watch.

'Twenty minutes more!' he said. Which gave them an additional ten minutes. Nobody complained.

He loosened his cravat and, on the way up in the freight elevator, took off his jacket. He was in a good mood.

'Get it done, Mrs Donal?'

She nodded towards two piles of garments neatly tied up with twine.

Silence and no complaint was the nearest her boss ever got to praise.

Then: 'Anything doing, Mrs Donal?'

'I got a cake, sir. In your office.'

He nodded complacently.

'You saw I let the girls go outside for some air.'

'I did.'

He came closer, a glitter to his eye.

'Come here,' he said.

She went up to him.

He wasted no time putting a hand on her breast. Then a hand on her thigh as he felt for her stocking top through her skirt. He took one of her hands and pulled it to his stomach and pushed it down a shade.

She let her hand go further down until it found his member and held it through his pants the way he liked.

278

'Nice, Mrs Donal?'

'Yes, sir.'

She played with him until he got hard. Then he slid his hand up her skirts to her bare thigh. Then more.

'Nice?' he said.

'Yes,' she sighed.

Behind them the freight elevator whirred into life.

Brennan grunted but it wasn't with irritation.

'Where's that cake?' he asked, pulling away.

He wasn't quite smiling; he never went that far. But his eyes had a look of satisfaction in them and his mouth hung loose.

'On your desk.'

He cupped her breasts a final time and then disappeared inside his office.

Moments later a man appeared on the stairs.

'You in charge?' he asked Mrs Donal.

'Mr Brennan is. He's in there.'

'Short of staff or somethin'?' the man said, looking round the empty sewing tables and idle machines.

It was meant to be a joke and Mrs Donal, recognizing the kind of man he was, half smiled.

'They're in the yard taking a break. It's the humidity.'

The man had a dark suit, a tilted bowler and scuffed thick boots. Mrs Donal noticed his sizeable hands.

He looked like one of Tick Tock's boys. So she didn't argue when he barged into Brennan's office.

Shopkeepers along Market Street never said no to 'Bookman' Baxter and Tick Tock's boys when they turned up on their doorstep. There wasn't much happened along those streets without one or other or both knowing about it. And when they were after someone, it was no use trying to hide.

As Tick Tock's heavy stood talking to Brennan, the girls were crossing the yard and coming back up the stairs, an exhausted Anna trailing behind them.

Eileen tried to hurry her. 'Hurry up, Jelena or you'll be late and they'll fine you . . . Oh, do come on . . . *Whatever* is wrong with you?'

'You go on ahead,' Anna said wearily. 'I'll be up in a minute.'

There was a closet in the yard; she felt sick and needed to use it.

Two minutes later, as she started mounting the stairs, she sensed that something wasn't right.

Minutes before, the girls had been talking and laughing; then there had been a moment's eerie silence that she couldn't explain before the machines kicked in again.

She knew nothing of Tick Tock's men or the gangs they ran but something – her animal instinct as a woman carrying a child perhaps – made her sensitive to bad smells in the air. And a Tick Tock boy was a very bad smell indeed.

So she slowed as she reached the last steps up to the sewing floor and peeked through the banisters to see what was going on.

She saw Brennan.

She saw Mrs Donal.

She saw the back of Eileen's head hunched over her machine.

She saw a man with a bowler and a thick cane in his hand.

They were waiting for someone.

Then she heard footsteps from below.

'Hey! Corm! *Corm!*'

It was another of the Tick Tock boys calling out to Cormack Hanlon, the man in the bowler, and he was coming up the stairs behind her.

Mrs Donal, more used than any of the others to distinguishing one sound from another above the clatter of the machines, glanced towards the door to the stairs and saw Anna's frightened eyes peeking through the banisters.

Very, very slightly she shook her head.

'*Corm!*'

Anna shrank back against the wall, went up the last few steps and then carried straight on up towards the storage floor above.

'Where's the girl?' she heard Brennan say.

'She's on her way up,' said Mrs Donal.

Anna froze just out of sight.

The man reached the top of the stairs, saw his friend, and joined him on the sewing floor.

As he turned his back Anna slipped down the stairs behind him, heart thumping, skirt raised to stop her tripping.

'So where is she?' she heard one of the men say.

Anna was off down the stairs in seconds, but even so it was too late. Maybe they saw her shadow at the door; maybe one of the girls gave the game away. More likely, they heard the sound of her feet running down the wooden staircase below.

She heard a shout as she ran straight past the boy at the door.

'Where you goin'?' he shouted.

As Anna made a right out of the building and then another right up Clark Street, she heard the men run out of Brennan's behind her, shouting and giving chase.

This was enough to attract the attention of the three other Tick Tock boys working their way down the premises on the other side of the street. One of them spotted Anna, shouted out and went to cross the road in pursuit of her. But the traffic was slowed almost to a stop and his passage was impeded by a streetcar.

Ahead, as she ran towards Monroe and made a left to the safety of Market Street, Anna saw a jumble of horses and overturned vehicles surrounded by a noisy crowd. It was the fracas the officers at the Woman's Temple had been sent off to sort out earlier.

Seeing several police officers at the scene, she slowed immediately, lowered her skirt, pushed her way through the throng and moments later turned east with the crowds into Monroe.

When the Tick Tock boys reached the intersection moments later, she was nowhere to be seen.

48

Humanity

The morning session broke up soon after two rather pedestrian speeches following the inspirational one by Amelia Starr that had set up a restiveness among the audience. The ladies of WCTU poured out into the lobby of the Woman's Temple, its corridors and stairs, alcoves and foyers abuzz with discussion of Miss Starr's speech.

After some difficulty, Marion Stoiber and Emily eventually found a quiet corner to talk.

'So, what do you want to know exactly?' asked Stoiber.

'In her letters to her father, Anna mentioned a friend – a man – she met at the library. Did you know him?'

Emily already knew the answer to that question because Mrs Markulis had told her about John, but she wanted to see Marion's response.

It was unequivocal.

'His name was John Olsen English. I only met him once, on a Fourth of July picnic outing that the library arranged to the Lakeshore. Anna invited me along. His mother's the notorious Mrs Hester O. English.'

'Notorious?'

'She's well known on the Near West Side as a self-centered dragon who likes to give just enough money to St Patrick's Catholic Church to have the good fathers and the congregation dancing attendance on

282

her. John was the same; always did his mother's bidding. I told Anna
not to waste her time with him, he would never make a good match.
But . . . she didn't want to listen!'

'What kind of beau did you think Anna needed?'

'A man not a boy,' said Marion knowingly.

'And you found her one?'

Emily slipped the question in quickly and quietly to see what would
happen.

Marion was quick to respond, 'I did . . .' only then to try and cover
her tracks, '. . . I mean to say, I did think she needed a wider circle
of male acquaintances . . .'

'Of the kind you had?'

'That's a rather forward question, isn't it?'

'I'm a forward kind of person,' said Emily with an engagingly frank
smile, 'and I'm just trying to do my job and find out what life in
Chicago was like for a girl like Anna Zemeckis.'

'Well, it's a city that offers more than Mr John English, that's for
sure.'

'You mean things are different here for girls?'

Marion hesitated. 'Well, I could mean that, yes. I suppose I could.
I have a much wider circle of friends than my mother ever had.'

'You mean men friends?'

'I mean friends.'

The conversation seemed to have reached an impasse and, as
Marion was looking restless, Emily decided to change tack.

'I guess you and Anna did things together?'

'Sometimes. On Saturdays. We used to meet for lunch at a place
on Wabash.'

'Mrs Clark's Lunch Room?'

'You're well informed.'

'Mrs Markulis told me.'

Marion screwed up her face and said, 'Humph!'

'She also said you did some exciting things together.'

In fact she had not said that, but Emily reckoned it was worth a
try. Marion wasn't saying much and she could let her wonder what
Mrs Markulis *had* said.

'I guess we did. The Fair, for one thing, that was endlessly fascinating to Anna. And a couple of theater shows, but we had to have an escort for those. Mrs Markulis insisted.'

'There must have been other things.'

Marion stared at her and Emily stared back. It was a game of poker, a game of bluff. Marion was wondering what she knew, and Emily knew she didn't yet know enough. She just needed a chink of light to work her way to a clearer picture.

Suddenly it came.

'I think what she was most excited about – and it took some arranging because tickets were hard to come by even back then in the early days of the Fair – was a special tour of the Union Stock Yard.'

'I thought you just applied at the main gate off 47th on Exchange Avenue,' said Emily. 'That's what I did when I came to Chicago for the Pittsburgh *Echo*. Cost me twenty-five cents.'

'Sure, you can do that,' said Marion, 'but if you want to see the real thing close-to you need a special ticket.'

'The real thing?'

Marion Stoiber hesitated and a shadow passed across her face.

'The hog wheel,' she said, 'sticking the hogs.'

Her eyes gleamed.

Was it the blood, the death, or something more?

'And you thought innocent little Anna Zemeckis would enjoy that, did you?'

'She . . .'

Stoiber wasn't telling the whole story but Emily sensed in her hesitation that perhaps she wanted to.

'Everybody enjoyed the tour, women especially,' said Marion, 'and Anna was no exception. Didn't you enjoy it, or didn't you get that far?'

The tables were turned, because on her own tour Emily had only had a cursory look at the killing floor. So if Anna had found it so fascinating, why had she never mentioned it to her father in her letters?

'Look, I've got to go,' said Stoiber, 'but . . . I haven't minded talking to you . . .'

'There's more, isn't there? You know more.'

Marion suddenly looked sad and rather lonely – and maybe guilty . . .

She nodded mutely.

'We could meet for lunch tomorrow,' said Emily. 'You could tell me more.'

'We could . . .'

'You're working at the Fair, aren't you? The steps of the Woman's Building at twelve-thirty?'

'My break is from one.'

'One it is, then,' said Emily.

'Yes,' said Marion uncertainly and then, more brightly, 'yes.'

By the time she had finished her conversation with Marion Stoiber, Emily found that all places for luncheon in the restaurant at the WCTU Temple were taken, so she decided to make her way back to her hotel in the hope of finding refreshment there.

But as she left the building, Emily found herself face to face with a wall of sound and seething humanity. The crowd outside, good humored when she had entered two and a half hours previously, had turned as ugly as she had feared it might. It was drunk, it was disorderly, and it meant trouble.

Worse, the police seemed to have it barely under control, so that people leaving for the luncheon break had once more to run the same gauntlet of unpleasant shouts and jibes.

The crowd swayed back and forth, the police swore and used their nightsticks, people pushed past Emily in their haste to grab one of the queuing cabs, or simply to get across Monroe and out of harm's way.

Since that seemed the best option, it was what Emily tried to do too. But the crowd of people around the Woman's Temple thickened, the mob pressed closer, and before she knew it someone had tripped and tumbled in front of her and straight into the mob itself.

Emily went at once to see if she could help the woman, whose hat had gone flying and whose purse was already in the grasping hands of one of the rabble, while another seemed bent on kicking her.

'Leave her alone!' shouted Emily at once, wading straight in. But her voice was as nothing against the mob's baying shouts.

Then she felt a hand on her arm and a voice saying, 'Leave this to me.'

It was then that she realized that the woman on the ground was

Christiane Darke and the man who had come to her rescue was her husband, Gunther.

He looked anything but charming now.

His face was suffused with anger and his tall frame, which brushed against Emily as he pushed by, was taut with fury.

He reached out a hand and lifted the man who was kicking at his wife off his feet and threw him back into the crowd. He lashed out powerfully with his left arm and then with his right. Men and women shouted in pain and fell back.

Then he bent down and picked up his wife as if she was a child.

'That woman's taken her purse,' cried Emily, pointing.

Gunther Darke looked at her. To her amazement he smiled calmly while the entire world around was in chaos.

'Look after her for a moment, ma'am! Take her back inside!' he said, and thrust Christiane into Emily's arms.

She hurried Christiane, who felt as thin as a rail, back to the entrance itself. Other hands took her from Emily's safe grasp and she had time to look back at Gunther Darke. He had a tight grasp on the woman who had tried to steal his wife's purse while the mob fell back still further.

With horror Emily noticed the man who had tried to kick Christiane Darke. He was slumped in a shadowy recess by the side of the steps into the temple. Another man, taller even than Darke, in a long black frockcoat and bowler, was now kneeling over him, his fist raised. The man on the ground looked terrified. The fist drove into his nose and mouth. The man lay still.

There was blood dripping from his assailant's fist as he stood up and walked off calmly into the crowd.

Ten minutes later, a shaken Chistiane Darke was insisting that Emily stay with her. Her husband agreed, having shepherded the remaining women towards another, quieter side exit from the building. A tall man – Emily thought it was the one she had seen earlier hitting the man outside – appeared and spoke quietly to Gunther.

'There's a cab out back,' he said to Christiane. 'I'm sending you home in it.'

He turned to Emily.

'You won't mind accompanying my wife, to see she's safe?'

'Of course not!'

As they turned to leave, Emily heard footsteps in the corridor behind them. It was Fay Bancroft.

'Wait, I'm coming with you, Christiane. I see you've met Emily Strauss.'

Christiane Darke managed a smile. To Emily, she seemed so plain and frail and – for a man as personable and attractive as Gunther Darke – a surprising choice for a wife.

'You're both to come to my house in Park Street,' said Fay, taking control of the situation.

By the time they had reached the waiting cab, all sounds of the mob had faded away. But Gunther Darke was nowhere to be seen.

Emily noticed this but made no comment. Christiane settled back into the carriage seat, her hair awry, her dress dirtied and torn. She looked unhappy and so vulnerable.

'Don't worry, Christiane,' said Fay, 'we'll soon get you tidied up.'

Christiane Darke managed a weak smile. 'Yes, but I can't be long. I have to get back,' she said. 'We're having an At Home at my father-in-law's this afternoon . . .'

She gave a sudden wry smile. 'But I'm forgetting myself. I owe you a debt of gratitude for rescuing me, Miss . . . ?'

'Strauss. Emily Strauss of the New York *World*.'

Christiane Darke laughed out loud.

'Oh, so *you're* the reporter!'

'*The* reporter?'

'Fay mentioned you to me. I think we met briefly at the Illinois State Building on Tuesday.'

Emily nodded.

'You posted a photograph of a girl on the noticeboard there, I believe?'

'You're very observant.'

'I am.'

Then she looked at Emily and said impulsively, 'But you must come to the At Home. Of course. Please do!'

'Well . . .'

'I hope you won't find it a dull affair. My father-in-law is not exactly a sociable man and he's got so few friends that I doubt he'll know most of the guests. What's more, and please don't take this personally, he hates reporters!'

'But—'

'So your presence might liven things up a little. It will annoy my father too . . . he'd absolutely hate to think his partner had attracted a reporter from the New York *World* to his house. I'm afraid my father likes to think he has a monopoly on the press . . . He's Paul Hartz, by the way.'

Emily, who had already worked that out, noted the brief pause, as if Christiane was uncertain what reaction this information would provoke. She knew enough about Paul Hartz's position of power and influence in Chicago; seeing him at close quarters was a prospect she relished.

Nevertheless, she played along with Christiane's hesitation. 'Perhaps I'd better not come if I'm going to be unpopular,' she said insincerely.

Fay put a hand on her arm. 'Don't worry, my dear. Gunther will protect you from all those dull old men.' She smiled mischievously.

As the carriage turned into Michigan Avenue and headed north towards Park Street, Emily's energy levels sagged.

Men! So far that day she had practiced Japanese martial arts with one, been thumped by another and rescued by a third, and still the day was only half done. Thank goodness Ben Latham, her colleague at the *World*, would be arriving in Chicago tomorrow morning first thing.

49

Charity

It took Anna Zemeckis no time at all after her escape from Brennan's to work out that if she was going to retrieve her paltry possessions from the Mission she had to do it immediately. Sooner or later the men who were after her would get there too, because one of the girls at Brennan's would blab.

That's if Eileen hadn't already. Thinking back over the morning's events, Anna remembered she had been behaving strangely. She hadn't whispered across the table to her as she usually did, hadn't looked her in the eye and had seemed distant over lunch. Once again, Anna had failed to take Tomas Steffens's advice. She had trusted Eileen and it had been a fatal mistake.

Anna turned south and hurried down Market Street, intending to try to get a ride back across the river. If she could she would avoid paying a fare. People did that all the time, she had seen them, but usually when the cars were crowded and the gripman distracted.

But as she got further away, the crowds thinned unaccountably and the streetcars disappeared. She thought she saw one of the Tick Tock men ahead of her.

Just then, a carrier whose wagon was piled high with furniture approached, and impulsively she stepped out into the street.

'Sir! Please. I'm with child and feeling bad. I need . . .'

'Where you headin'?'

'Jefferson, over the river.'

'It's on my way. Come on, young lady . . . easy . . .'

He leaned down and gave her a hand, heaving her up into the wagon behind him.

'You find a place down there . . .'

She huddled against a wicker chair and some brooms.

'When's it due?' he called down to her.

The truth was Anna had no clear idea.

'February.'

He said no more and the wagon heaved and creaked its slow way westward across Jackson Street Bridge and, for the time being, away from danger.

Anna's mind was racing. The little world she had struggled so hard to create for herself had collapsed in moments and now she must start all over again. But she had to go back to the Mission first – to retrieve the fifty cents the sisters had demanded she hand over against breakages. She needed that money to get out of Chicago. She had no other possessions bar a cheap nightgown and change of stockings she had bought in the market, and – if she could call it that – the two documents she had taken from Dr Eels's clipboard. Instinct had made her keep them, though she still had no idea of their significance. The previous night she had covertly rolled them up tight and stitched them inside her bodice with a needle and thread stolen from Brennan's.

The wagon lurched, the brooms rattled beside her and the wheels clattered over the cobbles. Anna felt more and more sick and then, thankfully, the driver gave a command and a yank on the reins and the horses pulled over and stopped.

'Jefferson, miss. At your service! Here, I'll give you a hand.'

He held Anna steady as she stood up and clambered down the awkward steps onto the sidewalk.

'Thank you . . .' she began.

But the man grinned and waved and was gone.

A short while later she was outside the Mission of Hope, its exterior as unwelcoming now as it was the first time she had seen it.

She knocked at the door, then pulled a bell cord which produced a distant ring.

The wooden slat snapped open and two cold gray eyes stared at her. It was Sister Agnes. Not good. Sister Agnes was as chilling in her character as in her demeanor, but at least the door opened at once.

'Yes? Anna Zemeckis, isn't it?'

Anna started at hearing her own name spoken out loud. It wasn't the one she used at Brennan's where they all knew her as Jelena. How could she have been so foolish that night she arrived after escaping from Dunning? She should never have used her real name.

'I know I shouldn't be here now but . . .'

She stuttered out her excuses playing the role of abject stupid girl as best she could. She made up a story about a relative having moved to Chicago and offering her accommodation. The sister said nothing.

'. . . So, I've come to collect my fifty cents . . .'

'Sister Ursula is on duty today. She's in the office. Go and see her when you've got your things.'

She bolted the door behind them.

Anna groaned. Sister Ursula was no pushover. She was old and crabbed and followed the rules. Anna guessed it would be hard prizing fifty cents out of her. She had heard other girls say as much.

But at least she had got in without challenge and so, breathing a sigh of relief, Anna hurried to her dormitory, grabbed the nightdress and spare stockings she had left hanging on her peg. She took a quick look round what had briefly been a home of sorts to her and said a hasty goodbye. Then she was off down the long corridor to the Mission's office.

When she arrived, Sisters Agnes and Ursula stepped to one side, conferring together in a low whisper. In the background, in a smaller room, she was surprised and worried to see a third sister replacing the handset of the Mission's telephone. One of the girls had told her they had invested in this modern device because, at hostels like these, the sisters sometimes had the need to summon police help with troublesome girls.

Anna began to realize something was wrong. They had let her in too easily. Far too easily. Sister Agnes had been quick to lock the door behind them and had not accompanied her to the dormitory. She had

left her alone so she would have time to consult with the others. The
telephone call . . .

Anna began explaining her change in circumstances, politely and
contritely, thanking the sisters for their kindness, and then asking for
her fifty cents.

Sister Ursula's eyes did not meet her gaze.

'There is a procedure that must be followed,' she said pedantically,
sucking in her cheeks and pulling out a ledger. 'Your demand is rather
sudden and discourteous and I will have to ascertain whether any
damages must be set against your deposit.'

The telephone rang in the office behind her.

The third sister picked it up, glanced at Anna, and murmured softly
before closing the door to continue the conversation.

Sister Ursula began scratching away in her ledger. Sister Agnes
stood behind Anna.

'I would be grateful if you could hurry. I have a train to catch,' said
Anna finally.

'And I would be grateful if you would mind your manners, young
woman,' said Sister Ursula without looking up.

'Now . . .'

She asked some unnecessary questions. Anna answered them as
politely as she could.

The minutes passed.

The younger sister glanced at the clock.

Anna knew they were stalling her and decided to provoke them into
action.

'I bet you're not going to give me my money,' she said. 'The other
girls say you cheat us.'

Sister Ursula looked up. There was shock in her eyes and uneasiness.
Anna sensed that none of them found themselves in a situation they
liked.

'There is a procedure,' repeated Sister Ursula doggedly. 'Sister
Dolores, fetch the box.'

The younger sister retreated into the other room and came back
with a metal cash box. She opened it. It seemed to Anna to be overflowing with coins and bills.

The clock ticked louder still.

'Sister Agnes, please go to the dormitory and see that all is well. See that Anna has unmade her bed and deposited her bed-linen in the laundry.'

Anna knew she had not, she had not been asked to. Her heart thumped. She had to do something but had no idea what. Maybe she should just cut and run. Now . . .

The phone rang again.

Sister Dolores retreated back into the little room and closed the door.

Sister Ursula continued to write.

Anna felt frustration and fear and anger. She had to be as decisive in her actions now as the day she ran from Eels's office.

She heard Sister Agnes's steps coming back along the corridor from the dormitory.

'Sister Ursula,' said Anna, her mind suddenly clear, 'if you do not give me my fifty cents now and let me go I shall hit you. I shall hit you hard.'

Sister Ursula's hand stilled and her mouth dropped open. She looked up at Anna who had come right to the edge of her desk. Her face faded from yellow to white.

'I *shall*!' said Anna, stretching out her hand. 'Give me my money!'

Sister Ursula looked terrified.

'Give it me now!' Anna screamed.

Her hands shaking, Sister Ursula fumbled at the cash box. It was the final straw. Anna grabbed at the box and threw it at her face, its contents clattering to the floor. Sister Dolores instinctively rushed to her superior's aid, allowing Anna to charge out, slamming the door behind her. As she did so a plaster image of Mary Mother of God that hung above the door to Sister Ursula's office crashed into pieces behind her.

Anna raced down the corridor. Sister Agnes, approaching from the other end, could do little but let out a squeal and raise her hands helplessly as she was forced aside.

Anna headed straight to the front door, pulled open the bolts and was about to rush through when a thought occurred to her. Seeing the large key on a metal ring which always hung by the door, she grabbed it, slammed the door behind her and locked it before throwing the key across the street.

She looked first one way and then the other. Lower down the street a black covered wagon was coming up Jefferson from Jackson and it was traveling fast. It struck terror in Anna's heart.

She had seen the man driving it before, and the wagon too. It was the paddy wagon from Dunning, the one with Cook County Insane Asylum painted on its side.

Despite a rising sense of panic she did not run. She mustn't draw attention to herself in case the wagon was on the lookout for her.

She crossed over to the shadowy side of the street and headed north. As she did so, she looked back once more. Sure enough, the wagon had pulled up at the Mission and Donko O'Banion and his assistant were rattling at its door.

It would not be long before they would set off in pursuit of her once more. But it would be rather longer, Anna hoped, before the sisters would find a way of opening their door.

She turned onto Adams, unsure whether to go east towards Union Station or west to Halsted. She turned west because Halsted was always a busy street and she reckoned it would be easier to lose anybody who might come after her.

Once there, if she could make it three blocks south, she would be at Hull House, the settlement house with a reputation for helping those in need. She hoped it might be a safe haven. If only she could find someone there to confide in and whom she could trust to keep a confidence.

50

Post Mortem

Rorton Van Hale had once been one of the Pinkerton National Detective Agency's top men. In the normal course of things, had Allan Pinkerton not had two exceptionally able sons to take over the business, he might have ended up running it himself.

As it was, he was now one of that rare group of former agents who, although no longer on the official books of the agency, served as covert operatives on a variety of special assignments. Gerald Toulson was another, and the two knew each other well and trusted each other absolutely.

Neither had been tainted by the appalling mishandling of the Homestead Riots of June and July 1892 which had all but destroyed Pinkerton's reputation and brought labor relations in the iron and steel industry of Pennsylvania to an all-time low.

Both Toulson and Van Hale had been in Chicago at the time that Henry Clay Frick, chairman of the Carnegie Steel Company, contracted Pinkerton's to provide nearly three hundred strikebreakers for his Homestead Steel Mill near Pittsburgh, where the workers had been locked out for refusing to accept lower wages.

Toulson and Van Hale had both been against accepting the contract. They had refused to be involved, saying that pitting gun-toting 'agents' – most were hired specially for the occasion and untrained – against working men with justifiable grievances was a dangerous and immoral game.

In the confrontation that followed, seven agents and nine workers had been killed on the spot and hundreds of others wounded, many seriously.

Among those who subsequently died of their injuries was Emily Strauss's father, Otto Strauss, a hardworking official of the American Society of Steel and Iron Workers.

Now, fifteen months later, Van Hale was in Pittsburgh, quietly picking up the pieces for Pinkerton. The trip out to Johnstown for a less sensitive assignment had come as welcome relief.

'Almost like old times, Gerry,' said Van Hale when he called Toulson back around half-past two that day. 'Got here just in time to stop the local coroner labeling it as "accidental". The body's been buried in secret, temporarily. They'll get it out to New York when the dust has settled.'

'You're sure it's Rhys?'

'Absolutely. For one thing the sheriff, mayor and half the townsfolk had crowded into the morgue to gloat. They all recognized him.

'Second, his name had been carved on his forehead, just so there was no doubting precisely who he was. Never heard of that kind of thing happening in an accident, have you?'

Toulson agreed he had not.

'So?'

'So I took one of the agency's tame pathologists along from Pittsburgh, like you said. Rhys drowned after a fall from a height, probably onto rocks.'

'You mean he was thrown into Stonycreek?'

'Probably from a train. A rather special train.'

'Go on.'

Van Hale was on a roll.

'Remember the Gubner killings in Philadelphia?'

Toulson's eyebrows raised. Nobody involved was ever likely to forget them.

After a clash between rival firms in Cincinnati for control of the meat trade there, the five-man board and one of the main suppliers of Gubner Meat Trading Company had been found in an obscure icehouse by a railway siding east of the city. One was still alive, just, and that was old man Gubner himself, one of the best-known meat men in the Mid-West. The older generation were a tough breed.

What was noteworthy about the murders was that all six men had been hung on meat-hooks and left to a long, lingering death, watching the ice around them slowly melt.

Oh yes, Toulson remembered those murders. He was one of the first into the icehouse. The old man hadn't talked, except to say he had been told that, if he did, the same thing would happen to his three grandsons. But Toulson, a persuasive man, had managed to extract one significant piece of evidence out of the old man, with the promise that he would never use it in connection with the Gubner case. But one day, no doubt about it, he would use it to nail the murderers.

Three days later, old man Gubner had died of blood-poisoning. The crime had never been solved. Nor repeated.

Until now.

The Meisters had done it, so the old man had whispered. Meisters from Chicago.

And the man in charge had been Dodek Krol.

'Which armpit was he hung up by?' said Toulson.

'You tell me, Gerry,' said Van Hale.

'The right if Rhys was right-handed. The left if he was not. They chose the armpit that incapacitated the strongest arm.'

The killers had not realized that Gubner was left-handed. As a result he had managed to free himself, but it had been hours before he had been found, collapsed and suffering from hypothermia, on the floor of the icehouse.

'It was the left. Rhys was left-handed.'

'Anything else?'

Across the States in Johnstown, Van Hale shook his head.

'Not much that seems significant . . . I'll get the report to you by tomorrow.'

'How do you know it was from a train?'

'You try dropping a body into the Stonycreek River any other way. It's just not possible. He was thrown off a freight train. Which means—'

'Which means,' said Toulson, 'that I'll check out train movements this end. How long was he in the water? Three days?'

'Spot on.'

'Be in touch.'

'They'll know where to get me.'

'And the Gubner case?'

'The file's just been reopened.'

51

Hull House

Anna Zemeckis approached Hull House warily, unsure what to expect. She had never been there but she knew it was a place where ladies, some from the richer and better parts of Chicago, helped those of the city's most underprivileged. She felt tired, grubby and desperately in need of food and water, but she did not want to seem like one of the city's derelicts.

Instinct told her not to linger or hesitate for fear that she would attract unwanted attention. But, as she reached the steps to the main entrance to the building, a group of well-dressed ladies emerged chattering. She took fright and edged like a nervous cat towards a courtyard at the back, where she came upon a wide-open door that led to a kitchen. There were a few chairs, a table or two, and a woman, one of the Hull House volunteers, making coffee at a range. She immediately offered Anna some.

Anna accepted gratefully, saying she would be glad of a moment's rest, and was invited to sit down. The woman placed a little plate of cookies nearby and bid her help herself if she wished and then left her to it.

Anna sat down and felt the strength drain right out of her, as if, after a long period of flight, she was letting go of all her worries and woes so that her chronic fatigue could find expression and recovery.

The woman reappeared and asked, 'Can you read?'

Anna nodded and was given a sheet of printed paper on which there was information about Hull House and its various officers, departments, clubs and activities.

Strangely, this piece of paper made her feel more isolated still. There had been a time, she now knew, when documents such as this were part of her daily work. Not only had she handled such things, as well as books and papers of all kinds, but she seemed to remember writing a few such announcements herself.

It was only those last few hours which had led to her immersion in Bubbly Creek and her subsequent incarceration at Dunning that refused to come back to her. But all that was now a world away, a distant place over a chasm she never wanted to cross again.

The woman did not question Anna but left her alone to drink her coffee, no doubt aware from experience that a caller such as Anna, so obviously nervous and under stress, was easily frightened away if approached too directly and too soon. Nevertheless, she watched her from a distance, and it was not hard to guess what her trouble might be. For Anna did not realize that in the last day or two her baby had shifted in her womb and her rounded belly had become noticeable. A woman, especially a mother of children herself, as this one was, can spot a mile off when another is with child; even more so if it's a child the mother would be better off without.

For her part, feeling better for the coffee and cookies, Anna began reading the leaflet, and soon worked out that the officer she needed to see was Miss Lathrop.

'I wonder,' she enquired, 'if she's here?'

''Fraid not. Gone to New York, bless her. Hull House business I do believe.'

'Well then I . . .' began Anna, getting up to go.

'But there's someone else you could see in her place. Miss Hubbard.'

'Her name is not here,' said Anna.

'No, she's not on the list yet. She's new. She's very nice, very helpful. She's not here right now but I guess she won't be long, so why don't you just wait and have some more coffee?'

After the stalling tactics of the nuns at the Mission of Hope, Anna was wary of staying. She felt vulnerable and exposed. But another coffee was poured for her and the cookies were tempting indeed.

. . . And there she might have stayed had she not heard a voice call out from the hallway, 'Hello! Is anyone there?'

Someone had come in by the front door and, finding no one around, had walked through towards the back. The attendant went to answer her and Anna got up at once, fear in her eyes.

'Is Miss Lathrop anywhere to be found?'

Oh yes, Anna recognized the voice immediately.

She followed the other woman to the door she had just gone through to see for herself, peeking round it carefully.

It was Sister Dolores from the Mission.

The volunteer began explaining Miss Lathrop's absence.

'No matter about that,' interrupted Sister Dolores imperiously. 'We've lost a girl . . .'

Anna Zemeckis did not stay to hear more, but turned tail and ran back out across the courtyard and onto Halsted as she wondered what options she now had left.

'The Union Depot,' she told herself.

A rail depot was a good place to lose oneself in a crowd and if she could get there without being spotted, she could stop for a few hours, perhaps until dark, and consider what to do.

She dodged between the traffic on Halsted, crossed to the other side, and headed north once more.

52

Darke Party

Once Emily and Fay had got Christiane Darke away from the Woman's Temple and safely into Fay Bancroft's home on Park Street overlooking Lake Michigan, she relaxed.

A change of dress was found for her and a light luncheon served for them all.

Christiane's invitation to Emily to join them later for her father-in-law's At Home was repeated and now accepted without hesitation.

'But . . . I believe you don't get on particularly well with your father-in-law?' suggested Emily, taking her lead from the tone of Christiane's voice.

'I've known him all my life and he's a hard man to like. It doesn't help that he favors Wolfgang and that I . . . I must owe my loyalty to Gunther.'

Emily said nothing, for there was the hint of something she could not quite put a finger on.

'Of course I mean I must . . . I must stand by my husband.'

Again a pause, and again Emily and Fay stayed silent.

'Mustn't I? Yes . . . yes . . .'

Emily felt she had never seen a woman at the edge of such pain. It was surely obvious that she stood by Gunther only out of duty not love. But that was a common enough dilemma.

'What happened to Hans Darke's wife?' asked Emily.

'She died of pneumonia in 1880, when Gunther was twelve and Wolfgang ten. Hans has become increasingly curmudgeonly ever since.'

'Maybe he never got over it,' said Emily, thinking of her own father and how the despair of losing her mother had affected him.

There was a long silence which Emily tried to fill.

'Well it should be a most interesting occasion!' she murmured, fearing the moment she said it that the remark was inappropriate.

'Tell me, Miss Strauss, why do you think I would like you to come . . . ?' said Christiane impulsively.

'Please, call me Emily . . . um . . . I really don't know!'

'I'll tell you,' said Christiane. 'Fay's always saying I should come out of myself more and make new friends but I don't seem to have the knack. But the moment you and I met I could see at once that you have a good sense of humor, just like Fay, and are sympathetic. So I thought—'

'Well I'm glad you *have* asked me, Christiane. I really do need to get a sense of Chicago society if I'm to write my story for the *World*. Right now it feels as if it isn't going anywhere very fast, though I have a few leads. A photographer from the *World* is coming tomorrow . . .'

'A photographer!' exclaimed Fay. 'I thought they used illustrators.'

'Oh, Ben Latham started out as one and that's what he still mainly does. But the future lies with the camera, he's convinced of it.'

'You know him well?'

'Not very, I mean . . .'

Emily flushed and stumbled on her words.

'Ah, so you're sweet on him?' remarked Fay with an inquisitive look.

Emily was embarrassed. She hadn't thought much about Ben till now, but had to admit she was glad he would be arriving soon. 'Let's change the subject!' she said.

'Only if you promise to introduce me to this man of the future!' said Fay.

'I will. So who is acting as your father-in-law's hostess if he has no wife?' asked Emily. 'Your brother-in-law's wife?'

'Oh no, he's not married. I don't believe any woman would ever want him! No, Hans has a niece on his wife's side here in Chicago

who helps on these occasions. She's a very good organizer. My father
will be there, of course. I think you'll find him charming, but in all
honesty he's usually so preoccupied with financial matters that he
shows little interest in what he calls women's talk. He's only going on
sufferance anyway.'

'I'd heard that, despite the firm's success, the two partners of Darke
Hartz barely talk to each other?' said Emily. She had heard it from
Fay.

'My father's tried, many many times. But a few minutes in Hans
Darke's company and you'll see the problem. He's not interested in
small talk. And, since his wife died, well . . . he's retreated into himself.
Gunther says, and he should know, that he drives his workforce far
too hard.'

'What does your father think?'

Christiane shrugged.

'His holdings in the company are the same as Hans Darke's –
thirty-five percent each. Gunther, Wolfgang and I share the rest . . .'

Christiane smiled and, as she paused, Emily did some quick calcu-
lations.

'It's alright, all Chicago knows about the split,' continued Christiane. 'I'm not revealing any great secrets. Anyway, as you've probably
worked out, whichever one of the partners gets the support of two
out of the three of us children gets to control the company. Hans
Darke always assumed that meant he was in control because he
thought his two sons would support him. Well, not any more. Gunther's
on my father's side and of course I am too – well he's my father, isn't
he!'

She gave a brittle little laugh. Even when making light of things,
Christiane came across as an unhappy woman.

'Maybe it's better not to mix families and business,' said Emily.

'Either that or learn to be a better parent to your children.'

'Have you any . . . ?' began Emily, stopping at once when she saw
Fay's warning glance. But it was too late.

'No,' said Christiane quietly and without emotion, 'we have no children. I think it unlikely we ever will, unfortunately.'

She let out a bleak little sigh. 'But let's not talk about that. Let me
tell you about the party. It's an At Home to give people the first oppor-

tunity of seeing Hans's newly built house. He has a thing about the rising school of Chicago architects, you know, and commissioned it specially. But it's only just been finished. Gunther thinks it's just terrible. *Terrible*. All that money and his father, true to form as he sees it, "has to put up something perverse". But, well . . .'

'Yes?' said Emily.

Christiane leaned forward and said, with a conspiratorial air, 'As a matter of fact I quite like it.'

The statement was made as if anything said in defiance of her husband was thrillingly dangerous.

'Will I have heard of the architects?'

'Louis Sullivan possibly. His partnership built the Auditorium of which your hotel is the annex. So you'll know the kind of decoration.'

'This time Sullivan is working with someone called Frank Lloyd Wright. Gunther says he's a nasty, arrogant little man so I can't wait to meet him!' Christiane laughed mischievously and even managed to look lighthearted for a moment.

But one thing was for sure, thought Emily, Christiane Darke's relationship with her father-in-law and her husband got more interesting by the minute.

They arrived at the Darke house at a quarter to four, fifteen minutes before things were due to begin. The house was in Astor Street, north of the Chicago River and, although Emily did not say so, she liked the place the moment she saw it. It was in fact no larger than many of the new villas that already lined the street, built on land acquired after the 1871 fire by Potter Palmer, the celebrated retailer and hotelier, whose wife, Bertha Honoré, was generally regarded as the First Lady of Chicago.

'It isn't so bad, is it!' said Christiane as they got out of their carriage. 'Rather more cheerful than my father's great pile in Prairie Avenue.'

'Yes, Hartz Castle as they call it,' said Fay.

It was evidently a shared joke and they laughed gaily.

'If you want to see the downright awful in architecture,' whispered Fay, 'then make a trip to Hartz Castle!'

'Well, I have to say that I like Mr Darke's new house,' said Emily, gazing up at the simple rectangular windows on the double-wing front elevation and the fascinating piered balcony along the central part of the second floor.

They all stared at it a moment more. Emily changed her opinion: she didn't like it, she *loved* it.

What she found inside took her breath away even more. Beautiful clean lines of plain painted walls, paneled dados and exquisite arched doorways into room after room, subtly lit from a three-story atrium that rose over thirty foot from the ground floor.

The furnishings were nearly nonexistent compared to most of the over-ornate houses of the rich she had been in before. Such color and variety as there was came from Louis Sullivan's intricate pastel decorations and Arts and Crafts metalwork.

Everything was oak and light and polished reflections. Hans Darke might be an ogre but his cave was a palace of understated beauty and modest charm.

'Welcome, Christiane!'

It was, Emily guessed, Elfriede the dreaded niece. She was anything but the society belle Emily had been led to expect. Short, dumpy, busy and warm, she gave Christiane a kiss on her cheek and did the same to Fay.

'Good to see you again!'

Then, turning to Emily she said, 'And this is your friend from the New York *Times*?'

'The *World*,' said Emily.

'It makes no difference, I read both and my uncle reads neither.'

'What does your cousin Wolfgang read?' asked Emily playfully.

'Wolfgang?! *The Drover's Journal*, the *Grain News*, and the stock-market reports. Oh, and the novels of Mary Elizabeth Braddon, I believe.'

Emily looked surprised. Braddon's novels, the best known one of which was *Lady Audley's Secret*, were usually considered to be women's fare.

Elfriede caught Emily's look.

'Unlike his father,' she said, 'Wolfgang has a softer and more sensitive side. I believe the latest he is reading – I caught him with his nose in it yesterday– is entitled *The World, the Flesh and the Devil*. Sounds just like Chicago, doesn't it?'

She laughed, and so did Emily.

But Christiane did not. Despite Elfriede's obvious natural charm and warmth, she had half turned away and was not engaging.

'Now listen, everybody,' said Elfriede, 'you can roam anywhere on the first and second floors since for the time being Hans is still not living properly in the house. He and Wolfgang have taken over the third floor in what will be the servants' quarters. Hans himself is probably hiding away up there right now practicing the speech he feels he must make later. That will be at around four, I think, after which refreshments will be served and then he'll disappear again. Don't mind him. He means no harm.'

'Humph!' said Christiane.

'So Gunther's not come with you?' said Elfriede.

'He'll be here later . . .'

It sounded like an all-too-familiar exchange.

The doorbell rang.

'Wolfgang's prowling about the place somewhere,' said Elfriede. 'That must be the first arrivals . . .'

Christiane and Fay, having other things to talk about, left Emily to explore the house by herself. Taken by the sight of the balcony on her arrival, she mounted the stairs and went out onto it.

Carriages were beginning to pull up on Astor Street below as Chicago's great and good came to put in an appearance.

Most looked up at the balcony and many must have wondered who the woman was standing there. Tempted for a moment to wave like a queen, or give a blessing like a pope, Emily retreated back into the room and, as she did so, bumped straight into somebody.

It was a man and he looked displeased.

'I'm sorry,' she said, feeling that his should have been the apology, 'but I didn't know anyone else was here.'

The man just stared, not saying a thing.

'I'm Emily Strauss,' she said brightly, offering her hand.

He looked at it indifferently and then shook it reluctantly. His grip was vice-like.

'Yes,' he said.

'I was taking a look from the balcony,' she said rather stupidly.

'Yes,' he said.

He was in his late twenties, broad, stocky, with a shock of black hair. He looked more like a tradesman than the kind of society gentlemen Christiane and Fay had led her to believe would be attending the party. His face was without expression.

He seemed finally to remember himself.

'Well then,' he said grudgingly, 'I suppose I am to say you're welcome? You are of course. Sorry, I am not so good at this kind of thing, but I have been told to play host.'

Light dawned.

'You must be Wolfgang Darke!' said Emily.

'I am,' he said, brows beetling. 'I don't recall us meeting before?'

'We haven't. I arrived with your sister-in-law Christiane and Fay Bancroft.'

'Yes,' he said again, unhelpfully.

He really was the most awkward man Emily had ever met. Worse still, he stood too close, not from any impropriety but because he lacked the social grace to know he should move away. She herself could not retreat.

Thus, forced to stand staring straight at him, Emily found she was almost as tall as he was. She could not but compare him with his brother.

There was not a single point on which Gunther Darke did not win hands down. Only in one thing was Wolfgang the same as his brother and Emily found it very disconcerting: both projected the same animal strength and restless purpose.

Maybe it's because they're master butchers by training, she told herself, beginning to see why it might be that lady visitors to Chicago found Gunther Darke's demonstration at the Agricultural Hall so fascinating and a visit to the Union Stock Yard an essential part of their program.

'My father's going to say a few words,' Wolfgang managed to blurt out. 'I came to get everybody. It's to be downstairs. Now.'

Still he did not move. Emily had the curious feeling that she was in the presence of an enormous, horned but confused bull which needed some encouragement in finding its sense of direction.

'Shall we go down?' she said.

'That would be a good idea.'

Wolfgang Darke finally stood aside.

'After you, Mrs Strauss,' he said.

'I'm a Miss.'

'Oh! Sorry. You looked kind of married.'

Emily took this in good part and, feeling a fit of the giggles coming on, hurried in from the balcony and down the stairs.

The hall was already full of people and more were crowding at the doors of the two rooms at either end of it, and in the paneled alcoves by the front door.

An older man, so like Wolfgang that she had no doubt he was Hans Darke, stood in the hall to her left, holding a folded piece of paper with some scribbled notes on it. Emily was grateful she had the good fortune of a prime position from which to observe that rare sight – the Darke and Hartz dynasties gathered together.

But not a single member of the family was standing next to another. Christiane was with Fay at the far end of the lobby. Wolfgang had passed by Emily and stood now to her left, some way from his father.

Emily spotted Gunther to her right by the door into the nearer of the two living rooms. The only person she was unsure of was Paul Hartz, whom she had never seen before. Then she spotted someone who looked like an East Coast gentleman sitting in one of the alcoves, almost out of sight. On closer inspection she saw how like Christiane he was; and then she realized too she had seen his image recently, in an illustration in one of New York's Republican newspapers, alongside President Benjamin Harrison, one of whose supporters she knew Hartz to be. He certainly was every inch the power broker: urbane, patrician, confident.

'Er . . . ladies, yes and gentlemen . . .' Hans Darke did not look at all relaxed. His suit, which was probably specially made for the occasion, fitted him well enough, but even the finest tailor from the East Coast would have had difficulty making such a stocky bull of a man look comfortable.

He had not lost his German accent either. His words did not flow; he did not have the confidence that a good natural speaker has of engaging his audience with eye contact, humor and a few well chosen pauses. What would have been effortless for the incomparably composed Paul Hartz, who sat languidly in his alcove watching, was torment for Hans Darke.

What he had to say was straightforward enough, being no more
than a brief welcome, an acknowledgement of the architects Louis
Sullivan and Frank Lloyd Wright for their fine work, a thanks to his
niece for being hostess and an invitation to everyone to look around
and drink and eat. But it was a struggle. When he was done, and
people started chatting once more, the relief was palpable.

Emily was intrigued by the contrast between the man and the house
he had commissioned from two such young and modern architects.

'Who is that gentleman your father is talking to?' she asked Gunther
Darke, who was suddenly at her side.

'Louis Sullivan. Bit too colorful for me, I'm afraid.'

'The man or his interior design?'

'Both as a matter of fact. Champagne?'

Gunther's eye twinkled as he reached for two glasses on a tray
offered by a maid.

Emily meanwhile could not take her eyes off Hans Darke. There
was something strangely and unexpectedly touching about him. Here,
in the midst of the idle chatter and everyday pleasantries of Chicago's
social elite, she observed how he reached a hand to take Sullivan's
arm and turn his attention to the dado along the wall behind them.

Darke's butcher's hands, large and clumsy as they had seemed when
he was speaking so self-consciously, were now gentle. The two men
bent down and Darke ran a solitary finger over the intricate form of
the pattern Sullivan had designed, as he traced one of the dado's
sinewy elements, smiling with pleasure as he did so.

Behind them, looking on, and then turning abruptly away was a
thin young man, quite short, rather stiff.

'Frank Lloyd Wright,' murmured Gunther Darke in Emily's ear.
'Not a happy man, I think.'

'Why not?' said Emily.

'Sullivan's just fired him for poaching his clients.'

'Mr Darke . . .' began Emily, deciding to grab the moment and ask
him for a ticket to his forthcoming demonstration at the Agricultural
Hall.

'Gunther, please,' he said, coming closer flirtatiously. Emily could
see why Christiane might feel jealous; she could also see why other
women found him attractive – she did herself, very. It was rare she

found herself with a man as agreeably tall and broad; rarer still a man with such humorous eyes and a beguiling charm.

'Er ... Mr Darke, I mean Gunther, I wanted to ask you a favor if ...'

He smiled broadly and nodded his head.

'You want a ticket to my final demonstration at the World's Fair, don't you?'

'I do,' said Emily frankly.

'I'll get one sent over to your hotel. It's the Auditorium Annex, I believe?'

She looked surprised. 'However did you know that?'

He continued to smile but his eyes hardened.

'I like to keep myself informed about journalists who come to events I am involved with.'

'Oh!' she said, not sure *what* to say. 'I hope your information is correct.'

'It seems to be regarding your hotel. With respect to anything else, I'll let you know when I've had a chance to find out. Meanwhile, as far as the ticket goes, consider it done.'

'Thank you!'

'I trust you won't faint at the sight of freshly slaughtered animals?'

'I don't think so.'

His eyes hardened and his mouth tightened again. He looked suddenly quite fierce.

'It *has* been known for ladies to find it all too much for them, you know.'

Two hours later, after circulating among the gathered guests and exchanging a few dull pleasantries with Mayor Carter Harrison, whom she had already briefly met at the Illinois Building, Emily decided that the Hartz At Home, though interesting, was not yielding what she had hoped. All she had got was a lot of bland comments about how Chicago was really not as dangerous a city as people said. The reports about rising crime and people going missing were exaggerated.

'. . . by papers such as your own, Miss Strauss,' said one male guest belligerently.

She began to think it was time to leave.

Emily tried to turn away but the man grasped her arm.

'It's meddlesome journalists like you who are trying to take the gloss off the greatest event in American history . . .'

Emily was alarmed, but before the man could open his mouth and berate her further, a firm hand was placed on his arm and he was sent on his way.

'I really don't think so sir, not here. Leave the young lady be.'

Emily was lost for words.

'So, Miss Strauss, what are you doing in Chicago?' said the man who had come to her assistance.

'I'm trying to find out what happened to a girl from New York who disappeared here.'

'And you think a house in Astor Street is the place to start?'

'I haven't just started, and my presence here is far from accidental.'

'Really?'

'I'm sorry,' said Emily, 'but . . . how do you know my name?'

The man produced a card and gave it to her.

It read, 'Gerald M. Toulson, Director, Letwin & Company, Engineering Consultants.'

The address was the Grand Pacific Hotel. Emily knew it well, a great big palace of a place on the corner of Clark and Jackson.

'Thank you for rescuing me from—'

'Nobody,' said Toulson.

'So you're here temporarily?'

'I . . .'

Fay Bancroft appeared as he was about to speak.

'My dear . . . oh, excuse me, sir. I was wondering if my friend would like a ride back downtown.'

Emily had already decided that this dull-looking engineer was not somebody she wanted to waste time on. Besides, there was something she needed to do before nightfall, for she knew only too well by now that the streets of Chicago were not a place for women on their own.

'Goodbye, Mr Toulson. I wish we could have had more time to talk, but I have an urgent errand to do before it gets dark.'

Toulson shook her hand, nodded to Fay, and watched as the two women said their farewells, gathered their cloaks, and waited as Fay's carriage was brought to the door.

*   *   *

Fay offered to take Emily right back to her hotel but she refused.

'Wabash is fine. I can walk where I'm going.'

'Where exactly *are* you going? You reporters lead such secretive lives.'

'It's all right, don't worry. I need to check out a couple of things. It's nowhere important,' said Emily.

'It seems to me,' said Fay, tired after the exertions of being bright and sociable for several hours, 'that you do far too much walking.'

'Ah but you see so much more from the sidewalk than from a carriage,' said Emily as they arrived in Wabash.

The two women embraced each other before parting.

Fay, ever mischievous, let out a little laugh.

'What is it?' said Emily.

'So . . . did you work it out?'

'Work what out?'

'The true cause of Christiane's unhappiness?'

'Well, I guess it's because she can't have children.'

Fay shook her head.

'It's because she chose the wrong man.'

'What on earth do you mean? *Who?*'

Fay laughed again.

'I'm sorry, my dear, another time!'

Then she added ironically, 'I can't stop now, I have another engagement at seven! Seriously though, call on me for tea tomorrow afternoon and I'll tell you!'

Emily made a wry face, called out her thanks again, and set off down Wabash. She was curious, but had more important things to do than gossip about poor, sad, lonely Christiane Darke.

Half a block away, a man paid off his cab and stepped down onto the sidewalk, but hung back in the shadows until he was satisfied that Fay's carriage was well out of sight.

Only then, as the streetlights lit up the main boulevard and sunset fell over the city, did he set off in pursuit of Emily Strauss.

53

Union Depot

It was a near impossibility for a woman loitering by herself with no obvious intention of either catching a train or leaving the concourse to go unnoticed for very long at Chicago's Union Depot on Canal Street. Especially when the hands of the huge depot clock approached eight in the evening and the crowds began to thin.

At this time of day there were too many watchful eyes seeking out the weak and the vulnerable.

No wonder: dozens of rail tracks converged at the Union Depot, which got its name from being built to unite the termini of five different railroads at one central point in downtown Chicago. Three hundred and fifteen trains came and went daily, transporting over sixty-five thousand people.

That meant a constant flow of potential victims for the predators who lurked there.

But, as it happened, the management of the Union Depot was legendary among rail men and their boards right across America for its efficiency, its firmness, and the benign way in which it took care of its customers, so long as they were within the depot's jurisdiction.

The depot was lucky. It had a guardian angel in the form of its well known and much-loved depot master, Mr John Crapsy, who had worked there for thirty years and had set standards, and put in place systems, that were second to none. He had trained his assistants, gatemen, ticket agents, ushers and special policemen to keep a watchful eye at all times, so that the depot's reputation as a crime-free zone was maintained, even during the maelstrom that was the World's Fair.

On the evening of October 26, even though Mr Crapsy himself was on leave through overwork until November 1, the system was running like clockwork under the able leadership of assistant depot master Bob Storey.

So it was that at five-thirty that afternoon he had been alerted by one of the ushers to the presence of a woman on the east side of the concourse who seemed in some distress but was causing no problems. That was normal. Probably someone had failed to meet her and she was just anxious. But during the next two hours a couple more reports came in, both identical: the woman, in her early twenties, was causing no problem but seemed uncertain of what she was doing or where she was going.

Storey sent one of the matrons in charge of the women's waiting rooms over to talk to her. The woman was unforthcoming, saying only that she was 'waiting for something'. But she was not abusive, nor did she ask for help, and she was clean and well presented. Soon after this first brief interview she moved to a different seat, but she did not leave the depot.

At ten minutes past seven, Bob Storey sent someone more experienced to talk to her – Mrs J. R. Morgan, the representative of the Woman's Christian Temperance Union, which had a permanent presence on the station. The report again came back that the young woman had simply repeated that she was waiting for something. When Mrs Morgan had asked her what, she had not replied, but she did glance in the direction of the Western Union Telegraph Office.

'You're waiting for a telegraph from a member of your family or a friend?'

The girl said she was not.

'Won't you tell me your name?'

'Jelena, but I'm not in trouble.'

'Well, my dear, so long as you are here you are safe, but after eight you may not stay unless you have a ticket to travel on one of the later trains. If it is accommodation you need, then we can help. These days

315

we can contact most of the reputable hostels by telephone to find out if they have a vacant room.'

'Thank you, I'm alright.'

Nevertheless, the kindly Mrs Morgan told the girl where she could find help if she needed it, gave her a list of hostels and refuges and then let her be.

Anna Zemeckis glanced at the list and frowned. It included the Mission of Hope.

At around a quarter to eight each evening, it was Bob Storey's habit, learnt from his superior, John Crapsy, to do his own round of the depot with a particular eye on any people who might need help but who, regretfully, might have to be shown off the premises into the darkness of Canal Street outside. It was often at this point that young women, reluctant until then to accept help, yielded to encouragement and advice and took it. It was a strange fact about the Union Depot that, though its watchful attendants had strict orders to keep tramps, mashers, loose women, hotel touts, salesmen and street vendors – male and female – and much of the rest of Chicago low-life off the concourse, there was one particular person – and one only – who had been given free passage to come and go at will.

. . . And that was Mr Crazy.

Mr Crazy was well known to Bob Storey and even better known to John Crapsy, who had given strict instructions that no member of his staff was to meddle with him or try to eject him from the depot, so long as he was causing no obstruction and doing nobody any harm.

There was a good, perhaps an extraordinary, reason for this. Mr Crazy was one of those rare individuals who was not only harmless but had the knack of spreading goodwill and good cheer wherever he went. He was also, as both Crapsy and Storey knew, an intelligent and articulate man who had a gift for making others feel at their ease. No one in Chicago bore him ill-will, no one ever harmed him, however dangerous the places he wandered in and out of.

In the fall, Mr Crazy often chose to end his day in town before heading home to the Lakeshore, with a mug of well-stewed coffee with Mr Crapsy. But today it was Bob Storey's pleasant duty to provide the big man with a coffee, after which Mr Crazy tagged along, as he often did, when Storey did his last round of the depot. It was during such rounds that Storey had discovered Mr Crazy's facility for persuading difficult customers to do what they should when all else had failed.

That particular evening, Storey pointed out the young woman sitting on the concourse and said, 'She's been there a couple of hours or more now. What do you make of her? We think she may be in trouble of some kind but, when Mrs Morgan spoke to her, she denied it. But it's nearly eight now and she's still here . . .'

Mr Crazy studied the woman.

Eventually he said, 'I've seen that one before, a day or two back. Can't remember where now, I see a lot of people. She's barely more'n a girl. She ain't in trouble, she's in doubt.'

'What about?'

'Search me. I'll go and ask her.'

'Wish you would. But go easy on her, I doubt if she wants to hear about your legal claims.'

'Not claims, rights. I've got the papers to prove it.'

'See if you can get her to go to the Diocese Home if she's nowhere else to go.'

Mr Crazy nodded; then, in his roundabout way, like a knight moving purposefully but indirectly across a chessboard, he finally worked it so that he was sitting next to the young woman.

'They tell me,' he said slowly, 'that your name's Jelena.'

Anna stared at him and then relaxed.

'Mr Crazy.'

'And I notice . . . Shall I tell you what I notice, Jelena?'

'If you must,' said Anna with a gulp.

She looked at the man more closely and felt reassured.

'I notice you keep looking at the Western Union. It closes shortly, so if you want to send a telegraph you'd better get on with it.'

'How did you guess?' said Anna. That was exactly what she had been trying to summon up the courage to do for hours. The truth was she had hoped time would run out and the decision would be made for her.

'Years of practice reading the signs. You wouldn't be the first not to know what to say. Who's it to?'

'My father.'

'Run away from home, have you? What do you want to say?'

'Don't know. And anyway . . .'

Mr Crazy dug into his coat pocket and pulled out a dollar in change.

'There you are, now you've no reason not to send it.'

He reached over and put the money in her hands.

'Don't need that much.'

'I don't need any of it,' Mr Crazy said. 'Makes folks feel good to pay me for my pipes so I don't refuse their money. Go on then.'

'I don't know what to say.'

Mr Crazy looked at her and smiled. 'Just you tell him you're safe and that you love him,' he said thickly. 'It's all a father ever wants to hear. Hurry up now, the telegraph office will close once any trade from the Milwaukee train's come in.'

Impulsively Anna got up and went across the concourse to the Western Union.

Mr Crazy watched after her.

Behind him, the 8.10 from Milwaukee pulled in a little early. A whole crowd of travelers got off and poured out onto the concourse, obscuring his view of the office.

When things had cleared ten minutes later, the Western Union office had closed for the night and the girl called Jelena was nowhere to be seen.

54

Chicago Night

After leaving Fay on Wabash, Emily had walked on down the street, feeling the chill of the October evening air and pulling her cloak tight around her. Wabash seemed like the most subterranean of all downtown Chicago's streets, not just because of the tall buildings either side, but because the new Elevated Railway ran almost its entire length, shutting out the stars in the night sky above and creating shadows and blind-spots between its steel girders below.

Meanwhile, the trains roared back and forth overhead, blanking out street noises for a few seconds each time and blanking out her tired mind as well.

The crowds were still thick on the ground, however, and the State Street shops were still open, taking advantage of the flow of customers before custom dried up dramatically in a few days when the Fair closed.

She had been up since six that morning and she still had one last thing to do. But it was taking a long time for Emily to locate the establishment she was looking for: the photographic studio of Henry Robinson, '*Photographer to Society, studios in Chicago (Wabash Avenue), New York (6th Avenue), London (Strand), Paris and Berlin. Most commissions undertaken. Prices reasonable*' – or that's what it said in gold lettering on the back of the *carte de visite* that Anna had sent her father from Chicago and which Emily now held in her hand. She had expected to find the

studio within a few minutes but had missed it in the gathering darkness. Now, glancing at her pocket watch, she saw that it was a quarter
past eight.

Luckily, the north end of Wabash was still busy with late shoppers
thronging between the hotels on Michigan Avenue and the grand
shops on State – Wabash being between the two. There was an end-
of-the-week feel to things and, once in a while, the comfortable sight
of police officers from nearby Harrison Street Police Station on patrol.
But Emily knew she needed to be quick and get back to her hotel
before the crowds thinned.

She hoped Mr Robinson might still be in his studio and that he or
one of his assistants might remember Anna's visit in the summer.

Maybe she had taken a friend – Mila, or Marion – along with her
for the sitting. Maybe she had talked personally to the photographer
as women often do, it being a photographer's job to relax his clients
to get them at their best. She hoped she might uncover some detail –
if not about Anna then about why it might be that an ordinary girl
would feel it necessary to go to an upmarket photographer for what
was, after all, little more than a memento of her trip to Chicago.

Emily nearly missed it. The studio was a modest affair: a solitary
window display showing the standard kind of portraits and list of
prices, and next to it a narrow green door. The words PHOTO-
GRAPHIC STUDIO were painted on a panel that stretched across
the top of both the door and window. Below was the simple inscrip-
tion, *Henry Robinson FRSP (London) Proprietor.*

The studio was part of a low four-story building of no merit, one
of the older buildings erected shortly after the 1871 Fire, of the kind
that Chicago's real-estate men were now busy knocking down to
make way for much taller, grander structures. It seemed likely that
this building would not last much longer: there was a builder's handcart propped up against the wall of the adjacent alley, and in a second
floor window, just legible, a 'To Rent' sign that had slipped sideways,
as if in acceptance that these were not premises in which anyone
saw any future.

Emily pulled the photograph of Anna Zemeckis from her purse and
checked the details on the back against the shop front before her. Yes,
this was definitely the right place.

She moved nearer to the window and looked at the display. There were the usual portraits of society ladies, a married couple, a domestic interior and, rather surprisingly perhaps, a fine horse and carriage. All of which, combined with a small notice at the front which read '*Some prices negotiable*', might well encourage a girl like Anna to think this was a place where she could find quality at a reasonable price.

There were two other notices in the window, one of which Emily thought she understood, the other she knew she did not.

The first read, '*No unaccompanied women. Parent or designated chaperone preferred.*' That seemed perfectly reasonable and proper. But as for the second: '*Wide variety of stock photographs. Sight on application,*' Emily was not at all clear about that.

She peered closer, beyond the display. Inside, she could just make out a small counter. The wall behind was of frosted glass, beyond which she could see movement.

Just as she was about to open the door, an arm reached out at her from the passing crowd and grabbed hold of her waist. Before she could resist, the palm of a hand had gone over her mouth and she was hustled with considerable force straight past a couple of newsboys, their mouths agape in horror, and pushed into the shadows of the nearby alley, stumbling over the handcart as she went.

A voice at her right ear said, 'Miss Strauss, I would be grateful if you did not struggle, scream, or in any way draw attention to yourself. You will come to no harm.'

That was all very well, but for Emily Strauss this had been a long day and it was the second time in forty-eight hours someone had dragged her down an alley.

She looked round desperately for help. The newsboys had fled the entrance and Wabash seemed a long way off. And this time there was no Johnny Leppard on hand to rescue her.

Then she remembered: her day had started with Mr Hatsumi, whose parting words in answer to her query about what she should do were she to be attacked again now came back to her: *Listen to your heart and your stomach and not to your head.*

Against all her natural instincts to resist, Emily stopped struggling. As she did so, her assailant loosened his grip slightly.

'That's better,' he said.

321

'Good,' she replied.

She let her knees buckle, she crooked her elbow and brought it violently back straight into the man's abdomen.

He recoiled in pain. Trouble was, he did not let go. In fact his grip tightened and he lifted her up so her feet could get no purchase on the ground. She tried to bite his fingers where they clenched over her mouth but he only clamped them harder.

'Miss Strauss,' he repeated, breathing a shade more heavily, 'if you go into that studio and start asking questions, which I believe is what you were about to do, not only will you cause a great deal of trouble but your life will be in danger. Now, we wouldn't want that, would we?'

Emily tried to speak but could not.

'Would we?' The hand clamped across her mouth so hard that she felt she was beginning to suffocate.

She managed to shake her head.

'Promise?'

Emily nodded.

Very slowly the man took his hand away.

'You won't try anything again?'

'No,' she said, glowering in the dark.

She recognized his voice but could not place it.

The man's grip loosened from behind but she still could not see his face.

'I believe that the studio is being watched. I don't wish to alert the person watching that you or I are interested in the place, or they will be down here and after both of us.'

'How do you know?'

'No explanations. Not right now. Just do precisely as I say and follow me, because we're not going out the way we came in.'

'Why should I trust you?'

'Because you want to live.'

With that the man marched off ahead of her down the dark alley, with Emily blundering after him.

A few minutes later, after a tortuous journey down alleys between buildings, among ash cans and piles of garbage, Emily emerged into

State Street and the evening crowds. Only then did the man finally turn round.

She knew him at once.

'It's Mr Toulson, of Letwin & Company, is it not? Somewhat different circumstances than our previous meeting this afternoon, don't you think? . . . So this is your night job, is it?'

Toulson smiled grimly.

'Your elbow packs a punch.'

'Give me a few days, Mr Toulson, and it will pack a better one.'

'We need to talk, but not right now. You're staying at the Auditorium Annex, top floor, maid's room?'

'How do you know that?'

Toulson shrugged.

'Tell you tomorrow. I'll contact you in the morning. I'll come to the hotel. Don't do anything stupid between now and then.'

'Meaning?'

'Meaning don't go knocking on doors which open onto worlds you know nothing about.'

'You know about Anna Zemeckis, don't you?'

Even Gerald Toulson could not hide the darkness of his thoughts. He nodded.

'You going my way?' asked Emily as she hailed a passing cab.

He shook his head, helped her in and shut the door behind her. 'Got a job to do,' he said.

'Consultation?'

'You could call it that,' he said over his shoulder as he turned back into the gloom of the alley they had just come through. But he was quickly lost to view before Emily could ask anything more.

Half a mile away, to the northwest, Anna Zemeckis finally stopped running.

Not that she actually had the strength to run any more. She no longer had the energy to go looking for any of the other refuges for women in the city and, anyway, she didn't trust any of them now. Instead she just kept trudging on, north, out of the city, not knowing where or with what intent, until exhaustion brought her to the southern edges of what Chicagoans called Goose Island, a place

which for many of the poor and destitute was the end of the
road.

It was an area of industrial dereliction, with the North Fork of the
Chicago River on one side and the canal on the other. Here, amongst
the breweries and the tanneries and the dye-houses and the manu-
factories, a good many of Chicago's poorer immigrants eked out short,
harsh lives of poverty, filth, toil and degradation.

It was the one place Tomas Steffens, the friendly rail man, had
warned her against. But Anna was too tired, too sick, too lost now to
care. Certainly she was no longer scared, not even of the shadows of
the Chicago night. All she wanted to do was lie down and sleep.

But maybe the benign spirit of the man who looked like Santa
Claus, who had befriended her and given her the money for the
telegraph at the Union Depot was with her still. Maybe that spirit
went ahead of her and paused on the broken sidewalk and made
her look to her left. And when she heard the creak and shunt of a
locomotive in the distance pulling into a siding for the night, she
remembered the one place where, in such a neighborhood, she
might be safe.

For she now stood at the corner of that same narrow street down
which she had come three days before when she had ridden into
the city from Dunning on Tomas Steffens's train. And it didn't take
her long to find her way back to the gap in the fence onto the railroad.

Beyond that fence she saw the distant flares of the factory flames
up on Goose Island, belching lurid smoke and dim light into the atmosphere. She crossed the tracks and made her way to Tomas Steffens's
shack.

Remembering where she had seen him hide the key under the
wooden front step she retrieved it, opened the door, and went in. There
wasn't much she could make out in the dark. Not much at all, but it
suddenly felt like home to her.

She found the remnants of food on a table – some stale bread, some
sausage wrapped in paper – and a pail of water, and helped herself,
apologizing to Tomas as she did so.

'*One day I'll pay you back*,' she whispered.

She ate and she drank and she even dared open the little window and stare out onto the backyard of a city that was not her own but which, in its own strange, frightening way, felt as though it was trying to protect her.

She thought of the telegraph she had finally found the courage to send her father and repeated its final words: *Forgive me, Anna.*

Then she lay on the floor and wrapped her shawl tightly around her. She felt around in the dark for the old copies of the Chicago *Tribune* that she noticed Tomas kept in a pile and then lay herself down on the rag rug in the middle of the floor. With difficulty, for they kept sliding off, she spread the sheets of newspaper over herself.

She lay for a moment and listened to the world, remembering she had left the window open only when she was settled. But she left it as it was. She was afraid of nothing anymore.

Then, putting one arm under her head as a pillow and the other round her middle for comfort, she began to drift into sleep. Which was when, for the first time, she felt her child move. No more than a flutter, a tiny touch of almost nothing at all. Except that it was everything.

'We're going to live,' she whispered, '*live* . . . Even if no one in the whole world cares.'

But there were those in the world who did care, quite apart from Emily Strauss, who lay sleepless in her bed at the Auditorium Annex pondering Anna's fate. There was the Pinkerton man, Gerald Toulson, for one.

Having returned to the photographer's studio on Wabash after seeing Emily safely on her way, his 'consultation' with Henry Robinson was now over, and he was making his way back to his room at the Grand Pacific Hotel with a package in his hand. The fate of the girl called Anna Zemeckis was very much on his mind.

Not long after Toulson had left the Robinson studio, a figure with a large bag over his shoulder appeared in an unlit doorway right across from the premises on Wabash. Obscured by the nearby uprights of one of the Elevated's supporting steel piers, the man had watched as Henry Robinson, his day's work finally done, turned off the studio lights and came out of the door.

As Robinson did so, the man eased himself from his hideaway, crossed under the Elevated and reached him as he turned to lock the door.

'I'm sorry,' said Robinson, 'we're closing. You'll have to come back tomorrow . . .'

His eyes widened in fear when he saw who it was.

The man was tall, dressed in a black frockcoat over a white shirt with a black cravat.

'Lukas . . .' Robinson stuttered.

The Meister grasped Robinson by the scruff of the neck, opened the door and pushed him back inside. Robinson half turned, protesting, but he was unceremoniously pushed on past the counter, and into the back studio.

Lukas did a lot of dirty jobs. This was one of them.

He dropped the bag he was carrying by the door.

'Turn on the light,' he ordered.

Robinson did as he was told.

Lukas put a photograph on a table.

'Her name's Zemeckis,' he said. 'I want to see you destroy all the plates you have of her, every one. Now.'

'But—'

'*Now* . . .'

One by one, using a hammer he normally used for framing pictures, Robinson did so. He did not work fast. He knew when he had finished he was going to die.

'Faster,' said Lukas, taking off his coat and laying it well clear of where they stood. Then he rolled up his sleeves.

'But Lukas, how long have we known each other?'

'Too long. Finished?'

'Y . . . yes.'

Robinson turned and stared at the butcher's knife and the rolled-up sleeves.

'Please no,' he said. 'Not me.'

Lukas stuck him straight in the throat like a hog. He held him at a distance so his own clothes were not stained by blood, though his right arm was. He bent him struggling and gurgling over the broken plates and let the blood pour on them.

Then he turned Robinson round, saw he was still alive, and stuck him again in the neck.

He lowered him to the ground.

He put the knife to one side and ripped Robinson's shirt wide open to the undervest. He undid the pants and pulled them down.

Slitting the undergarment straight down with his knife, Lukas revealed his victim's bare chest, a pale, pigeon thing.

But he did not eviscerate him.

Instead he slit open his abdomen and with a skilled twist and heave of the body spilled the guts over the floor.

Then Lukas cleaned his knife carefully on a towel after running water over it at the studio sink. He washed his hands and checked himself in the mirror.

Going over to the bag he had left by the door, he took out a fresh shirt but did not put it on immediately. Instead he took out a can of kerosene.

He walked to the basement below, working his way up through the studio, and the front, taking the trail of kerosene up to the shop door.

He washed his hands again and finally put on his clean shirt.

Then he struck a lucifer and set the fire in motion. He was calmly walking away when he remembered something.

He went back into the burning studio, retrieved the photograph of Anna Zemeckis and put it in his bag.

DAY NINE

Friday October 27, 1893

55

Goose Island

The next morning, Anna was woken by a bright shaft of sunlight shining straight in her eyes through the tiny window at the back of Tomas Steffens's hut. Screwing them up, she shivered and turned the other way. She was stiff and cold but otherwise she felt refreshed. She had woken twice in the night from nothing in particular except worry, and had lain listening to the distant sound of rolling stock and the soft hoot of shipping on the nearby North Fork of the Chicago River.

She heard a man shout in the small hours and some creature, a dog probably, padding by on the chippings of the rail tracks.

Now she lay still while she found the energy to get up and get moving. She knew she could not linger long.

Lying on the rug, she took in the contents of Tomas Steffens's hut. Next to a cracked mirror on the wall a train schedule of some kind was pinned up. A piece of cloth hanging from a hook served as a rudimentary towel to go with a tin jug and basin on the shelf beneath it. There was a pair of boots in a far corner, clean and polished; a simple table and chair and a pot-bellied stove with wood and coal stored next to it. But no sign of ash or dust or dirt, as demonstrated by the presence of a broom and dustpan. And when Anna inspected the one rickety shelf above her head, she found on it a solitary book.

331

It was old fashioned with funny script and she couldn't understand any of it. But she could make out the name on the spine: *G-o-e-t-h-e*. It was a book of German poetry. Tomas Steffens was clearly a man of hidden depths.

Despite its spartan nature, Anna liked the hut's cleanliness, its manliness, its simplicity. It spoke volumes about Steffens, with whose hospitality she had taken liberties.

She got up slowly. The baby was beginning to get in the way. But at least, for the first time in weeks, she did not feel nauseous.

There was water in the pail and a worn-down scrubbing brush in a basin by the door. For boots, she guessed.

She used it on her hands and nails and tidied her hair as best she could, using the mirror.

She wet her hands and rubbed them over her shoes to buff them up a bit. Her woolen stockings were snagged here and there but they would pass: better than bare legs.

Somewhere a church clock struck. It was seven and time for her to go.

Anna's plan was still to get to Canada as quickly as she could. The money Tomas Steffens had given her had helped buy food for her first couple of days and pay the fifty cents deposit she had recovered from the Mission. Aside from that, all she had were a few cents short of a dollar left over from the loose change given her by Mr Crazy at the Union Depot. To get to Canada she'd need a lot more. But of one thing she was certain; once she had managed to make her way to her aunt's farming community on Lac du Bonnet, she would be all right. Inga and Arnold Jansons were good, kind, Christian people and she knew, no matter what, they would take care of her. She reckoned she needed just one more dollar to get out of Chicago to St Paul and she knew where she had to go to get it. The girls at the Mission had said that if there was one place in Chicago where you could guarantee a job that paid cash at the end of the day, no questions asked, it was Goose Island. Not a nice place, nor a safe one, but it was either that or the streets for a girl with nowhere else to go.

Just for a day or two, Anna told herself, *if I don't eat . . .*

She did not think beyond that; she did not dare because she knew if

332

she did she would sink into despair. Nor was she able to see herself as she now really looked in the mirror, when she glanced at it as she left.

True, she saw Anna Zemeckis, the woman who had once been a girl; the girl who had once had a grin on her face and a pink glow to her cheeks. But she did not see the woman she had become and who stared back at her now: gray-faced, gaunt, hair greasy, eyes like those of a hunted animal. If she had, she might have given up there and then.

Instead, as she left, she thought of the man whose little hut had given her refuge: of his loneliness, and longing for order and a place of his own, which clearly he did not get in the cheap boarding house in which he lived. Glancing around the rail tracks and carriages that surrounded this forgotten section of the sidings, Anna looked for something that she could leave Tomas as a token of thanks and friendship. In a corner by the fence she saw a few spindly weeds showing signs of life – mustard, dandelion and ragweed – and went and picked a bunch. Back in the hut she arranged them in Tomas's water pail on the table and then, using the stub of a pencil she found in a bowl on the shelf, and the back of the railway timetable from the wall, she wrote the following:

Dear Mr Tomas Steffens, I had nowhere else to go. I trust in God I will be all right as I trust you will always be. Thank you. Anna.

She hesitated a moment before adding in brackets her surname, *Zemeckis*.

She felt suddenly she wanted to write more, pages more. Write of all the things that had brought her to this place. Write of her gratitude to him for the simple generosity he had shown her: write and write and write, and never have to run again.

Instead she added one more word.

Goodbye.

Then she headed across the tracks to the gap in the fence as she had done three days before.

Goose Island was less than half a mile north of where Anna emerged onto Canal Street. It had become an island when the Illinois & Michigan Canal was built in the 1850s to the east of the winding North Fork of the Chicago River between North and Chicago Avenues. This had left

333

a piece of land cut off by the canal on one side and the river on the other, which Chicago's entrepreneurs realized offered useful waterfront sites to industries needing a ready supply of water. These were mainly smelly, polluting ones such as tanneries, paint works, breweries, stinking gas works and soap factories. Desperate for the employment offered, impoverished immigrants, mainly Irish and later Bohemian, moved in, finding what space for living they could among the factories. The geese these residents kept gave Goose Island its name.

By the 1890s, the Irish had moved out and the less particular – or more desperate – Poles had moved in, building yet more shacks and hovels amongst the factories and more regular houses – more slums within slums.

By that October morning when Anna Zemeckis walked up Canal Street to Goose Island, it was a dark and dingy industrial maze in which little thought was given to the facilities needed by the humans – whether residents or workers – who inhabited it. There was no main drain, so the streets and alleys stank of human waste. There was no enforcement of the ordinances concerning the proper construction of dwellings, most of which were no more than tumbledown hovels, nor had there been for many years. The wooden sidewalks were danger-ously rotten: more than one toddler and not a few drunks had drowned in the mud when the sidewalk had given way. Goose Island was a place where people, ground down by their environment, were never naturally friendly to each other and even less so to strangers.

Yet at the start of each day a tide of poor, desperate, half-starving men, women and children made the trek from west and south, up Halsted and Canal and across to Goose Island, in hopes of finding employment – even if just for the day.

The streets they found themselves in were largely unpoliced, the factories unregulated, the atmosphere so thick with smoke and the stench of chemicals and waste that newcomers often turned back, their hands to their mouths and nostrils, while those familiar with the place bent forward as if into a noisome wind, eyes on the ground, hands close to their bodies, women and men alike, pulling up their skirts and pants respectively to keep them clear of filth, watching each step they took for fear of stepping in the mire, cautious of each wagon that passed, for fear of being deluged with mud and excrement.

It wasn't hard to find work there, provided you weren't choosy. Permanent signs could be seen outside the sorry, sagging buildings that passed for factories, with advertisements by employers seeking labor: *Work available: Generous payment on results. Enquire within.* Others had beaten Anna to it at the first three places she enquired. The fourth got a result.

Maybe the company had had a meaningful name at one time, but now it had reduced itself to initials only: E. K. M. & Co.

It was five rickety floors high and boasted a freight elevator.

'Top floor, lady,' said a man loading boxes onto a wagon. 'Ask for Groats.'

He nodded towards the elevator.

'Use it if you want,' he said. 'Keep yer hands and feet and head inside, otherwise you'll lose 'em.'

The elevator had no doors. It swung a bit but did not move. Anna saw a lever and pulled it. The elevator dropped an inch or two.

'Other way. Slow at the top.'

Regretting she had climbed aboard this contraption, Anna juddered her way to the top, the open floors sliding past inches from her nose, briefly revealing scenes of increasing activity, noise and mayhem.

The place was a garment factory specializing in cloaks, by the look of things, so she was confident she would get work if any was available. It was several times the size of Brennan's and en route to the top floor she saw all sorts in storage and being made: jackets, sacques, circulars, dolmans and plain cloaks.

She stepped into the murky, dismal fug of the top floor – and none too soon, because the elevator, having a life of its own, started moving back down before she was quite out of it, causing Anna to fall out onto the wooden floor.

Close-to she saw it was covered with lint, cut threads and fleas – lots of them. She got up fast.

The sewing room made Brennan's look like the foyer of a smart new hotel on Michigan. It was crowded to bursting point with tables, clacking sewing machines and something like one hundred and fifty girls, mostly younger than herself, some no more than children.

The smell from the recently dyed cloaks – mainly brown, blue and black – was foul; but that emanating from a nearby pile of English plaid made her want to retch.

The pressing table stood in the centre of the room, with gas stoves on which the irons were heated for girls to take them off and sponge and press the garments, each operation accompanied by steam carrying the acrid smell of scorched cloth.

It is true there were fans, but these merely blew the moist, hot air about, adding to it lint and occasional strands of cotton which made some of the girls cough.

'Groats' turned out to be a man who had the thin, yellowed, creased skin and sunken cheeks of a smoker. The whites of his eyes were yellow too, and rheumy. He wore slippers and a filthy shirt hanging out over his pants, the suspenders pulled down over his hips. The only sign of his authority was the slouch hat on his head which, amazingly, looked brand new.

Anna told him what she wanted and what she could do.

But his first question was not about work.

'Where you from?'

'South Halsted.'

'Original like?'

'Romania,' she lied.

He looked at her in silence for a moment. It was impossible to tell if he believed her or not.

'Can you work a machine?'

She shook her head.

'You can sew?'

She nodded.

'Good or bad? Don't lie. I'll know soon enough.'

'Good.'

He nodded with satisfaction and offered her 25 cents for every dozen cloaks she made. A quick glance at a pile of these told her that standards at E. K. M. & Co. were not high.

She took the job and moments later found herself sitting between two young girls.

'We're to work short threads,' said one of them warningly, without looking up. Anna knew that meant slower work. Short threads were for when conditions were so crowded that longer threads in a needle threatened the eyes of girls sitting to your right and left.

Anna settled to the work but after thirty minutes felt uncomfortable.

'Are there water closets up here?' she asked her silent neighbor.

'Behind. Can't yer smell 'em?'

Anna got up, unsure if she would be reprimanded, but she was not. Anyway, Groats was nowhere to be seen.

There were six closets, all unutterably filthy and used by men and women alike, it seemed. There was water and carbolic soap and one towel, wringing wet. No one was in the murky place and, even had they been, they could not have seen much. Anna took the opportunity of washing herself as best she could without removing her dress and shook her hands dry. Then, feeling better, and pleased that the speed at which she worked was faster than the girls around her, returned to her place.

'Where yer from?' asked one of the girls.

'Romania,' lied Anna again.

'They're looking for a girl from Latvia.'

Anna's heart thumped but she said nothing.

'Where's Latvia?' said another of the girls.

'A long way from Romania,' said Anna too quickly.

It was not the right thing to say. Too smart. Too quick. Too noticeable.

Without saying anything more, she bent her head to her sewing and let her mind wander to thoughts of her final escape from the hell of Chicago and a new life in Canada.

56

Messages

Emily Strauss had the rare gift of being able to sleep wherever she liked, whenever she liked and whatever the circumstances – and wake up feeling refreshed and ready to go.

She had retired the night before with barely enough strength to undress before she had collapsed into her bed and fallen asleep. Yet when she was woken at six for her third meeting with Mr Hatsumi, she was up and alert in moments. He heard her story of the evening before, complimented her on her handling of Mr Toulson, if that was his real name, and suggested that a blow to his groin as opposed to his abdomen might have done more damage and better allowed her to take control of the situation.

'Show me,' Emily had said at once.

He had, warning her that such a technique was really one for the experts and she was a very long way from being that . . . but if she *must* live dangerously then she had better execute such blows as if she meant it.

'I'll remember that.'

'You should do so,' replied Mr Hatsumi matter-of-factly, 'because it seems to be your intention to continue to be a young lady who gets into trouble.'

Now it was nearly half-past eight and Emily was sitting in the dining room of the Auditorium Annex, with a view of Lake Park and beyond, contemplating several messages brought to her table from the front desk by Johnny Leppard.

It seemed her activities around Chicago were bearing fruit and the man who claimed his name was Toulson was showing at ten for 'morning coffee', whatever that meant.

Johnny was lingering and now he interrupted her chain of thought.

'Enjoying Mr Hatsumi?' he enquired with a grin. 'Heard you got in another scrape.'

'Enjoyment isn't quite the word I'd use, Johnny,' she replied.

'I enjoy most things that do me good,' he observed and went off humming cheerfully.

She watched after him, a half smile on her face, not quite sure if he was a boy or a man and deciding that maybe she warmed to him because he seemed an example of that special kind of male who was always going to be a bit of both.

'Johnny!'

He turned back at once, a question in his eyes. For a moment they stared at each other in silence, Emily not sure why she had called out to him so impulsively.

Then: 'I just wanted to say thank you for what you did the other night.'

'Said it already, Miss Strauss. Didn't need to then, don't need to now. You need something, you just let me know.'

This time his face didn't hold a boy's grin but a man's smile. It was the smile of a young man who was going places.

'No,' she said, 'you ever need *my* help, you let *me* know.'

He nodded, the smile changed back to a grin, and then he was gone.

Run a hotel by the time he's thirty? Emily said to herself, doubtfully, thinking of the Auditorium's impressive Banquet Hall where she trained with Mr Hatsumi, its grand balcony overlooking the lake, its opera house and commercial offices. Maybe, just maybe, he would do it.

I wonder where I'll be when I'm thirty? Emily asked herself.

She had nothing like so clear a goal as Johnny, except she wanted to live and see and travel and explore the world herself, in ways in which her mother's generation had never been able to. But she had other messages to deal with, the first being from Ben Latham, confirming his arrival at the hotel at around ten that morning, which meant he was going to turn up at the same time as Mr Toulson. That might be no bad thing, thought Emily. The rest of Ben's message filled her with horror: had she found him a room? Otherwise it was going to be a park bench. The truth was she had been so busy she had forgotten all about it – and the park bench was not that far from reality. She had seen a good few men, quite respectable ones, curled up overnight on benches in Lake Park for lack of hotel rooms due to the Fair. The police, it seemed, had given up moving them on.

The third message was another from Mr Toulson saying something had come up and he might be a little late. He would get a message to her if he was further delayed.

'Humph!' Emily said to herself. She was not at all sure about that particular gentleman or whether his story about the photographer's studio being watched and a dangerous place had been a deliberate ploy to interfere with her investigation. But at least his coming later would give her time to brief Ben.

A fourth message was from Gunther Darke in the form of an expensive-looking envelope with Darke Hartz & Company, Chicago, embossed in glossy black print in its top right-hand corner and hand-written across the front *'For Miss Emily Strauss of the New York* World, *By Special Invitation, Gunther Darke.'* It contained an impressive printed card: the promised invitation for Darke's lecture and demonstration at noon that day in the annex of the Agricultural Hall.

Emily glanced at the dining-room clock and saw she still had a good hour before Ben was due to arrive.

She had already decided that they should take stock of the story together. But she felt dissatisfied, not yet having a clear angle on it. She knew a lot more about Chicago than she had; there were things she could say about the City Morgue, and Hull House, and the life of young working women in this great city. She was confident that she could get some more information out of Marion Stoiber at lunch today and maybe Mrs Markulis too, if she had time to get to her. Neither was telling her all she knew.

Somehow, she felt that everything might come together with Ben's help, but first she had the urgent problem of finding him a bed to

340

sleep in. She left the dining room and went in search of the ever-resourceful Johnny.

She found her young friend soft-soaping a guest about to leave and receiving his reward in the form of a substantial tip. Emily waited until he had completed his business and called him over.

He had discreetly pocketed the money before he reached her.

'If I ask reception for a room for a friend,' she said, 'what are they going to say?'

'No.'

'Supposing I offer them money?'

'It would need to be an awful lot. Every hotel, every room, every park bench in Chicago's taken.'

'You're saying it's impossible?'

'I never say that word, Miss Strauss. Never will till the day I die. The day Saint Peter sends for me is the day I'll say impossible. Too much living to do, too many mountains to climb with great views.'

'You're a bit of a philosopher, aren't you ... ? Listen, I've got a colleague from the *World* arriving in about an hour. I've got to find him a place to sleep.'

'Colleague or close friend?' Johnny eyed her frankly.

Emily flushed.

'Colleague. He certainly can't share my room. I've got to find him somewhere.'

Johnny stared at her a bit more.

To her annoyance Emily found the thought of Ben sharing her room lingering in her mind. The thought was not unpleasant. It also surprised her. Chicago seemed to put all sorts of thoughts into her mind.

'He can have my bed, going rates,' said Johnny.

'And where will you sleep?'

Johnny stared a bit more and Emily flushed again.

Then he laughed and so did she.

'I'll find somewhere, don't worry,' he said archly. 'Tell him to see Mr ...'

He nodded towards the concierge.

'That's the man he pays.'

'Not you?'

'Don't work that way, miss. It's the concierge that runs this hotel. Best-paid man in the establishment. He gets a cut of everything, including my room if I let it out.'

'Whose floor will you sleep on?'

Emily was curious. She was thinking that maybe there was a story in the way hotels were run.

Johnny stared at her again, then he grinned.

'A close friend,' he said.

Emily went over to the reception desk.

'A gentleman will be calling for me at around ten,' she said. 'Please ask him to wait in the lounge.'

She glanced at the clock and decided that doing nothing but wait for Ben Latham did not appeal. She set off to walk across the park and take a closer look at Lake Michigan. But, finding herself waiting for the traffic on Michigan Avenue to clear enough for her to get across, she turned north. She was curious to see what Henry Robinson's studio looked like in daylight, and she decided it would be interesting to put Toulson's warning to the test.

As Emily walked back and turned right towards Wabash, a uniformed boy from the Western Union almost bumped into her.

Moments later, as she was swallowed by the crowds on Wabash, he entered the Auditorium Annex and went up to the clerk at the reception desk.

'Telegraph for Miss Strauss,' he said, pulling a buff envelope from the leather pouch on his belt, 'and it's urgent.'

342

57

Color of Blood

Ever since Anna Zemeckis had inadvertently revealed to Dr Morgan Eels what seemed the perfect cure for certain types of insanity, he had been living in a heady world of dreams and a state of dangerous self-denial.

The dreams were about what he imagined was his inevitable international success as the discoverer of a way of managing mental illness; the denial concerned his unwillingness to face the fact that his interview with Paul Hartz had carried a nearly palpable threat that if the missing girl, Zemeckis, and the documents she had stolen were not found then he, Eels, would be in serious trouble.

But the doctor was now only three days away from his official ratification as the new medical superintendent of Cook County Insane Asylum, and, since the missing documents had not turned up, his earlier worry transmuted itself into certainty that they were now destroyed or lost and would not come back to haunt him.

Meanwhile, Dr Benjamin Brown had obliged him by vacating his splendid offices early, wisely making himself scarce before his successor attached too much blame for another patient's escape to himself. There had been a brief farewell party full of eulogies for the affable and ineffectual Dr Brown, a private word between the two men and a handing over of keys. Then Brown was gone as if he had never been.

*　　*　　*

Dr Eels was not slow in asserting his authority, a task made infinitely easier with respect to his staff by the effective elimination of Riley. For a brief moment, he had thought it might be better to remove her altogether from Dunning, lest she emerge from her childlike state and reassert her malign authority over the staff. But then he realized that it was better he kept her under his own observation and control on Far Side.

Even if she recovered her senses she would, of course, have to be kept in a secure ward for a very long time ... And with time, as was so often the case with the mentally ill, her close relatives, in particular her brother Padraic 'Donko' O'Banion, would lose interest. Donko O'Banion's attention span was as limited as his good nature and he had already accepted Eels's advice that visits were 'perhaps rather disturbing for the patient – better to make them less frequent. That would be the kind thing.'

Eels now diverted his energies into using his influence with the police to widen the search for Anna Zemeckis, but so far without results.

Meanwhile Nurse Lutyens – into whose chilly care Dr Eels had consigned special patients, especially those on whom he had operated – had observed something interesting going on in the ward to which Riley was confined.

'The mood there has improved since Riley's arrival. I would almost say that the other three patients have become more mentally alert.'

'So patients like them are able to interact with each other in a positive way?'

'Assuredly,' she concurred, 'though there are times, especially in the early morning, when Riley seems – shall we say – subdued.'

Fearful would have been a better word, but the nurse was not going to use it.

She knew perfectly well what was going on and had even done her bit to encourage it. For the fact was that the three other women in the ward, all Dr Eels's good girls, under the leadership of Mary Nevitt, were torturing Riley. And having taken an intense dislike to her since the day she'd arrived, Nurse Lutyens was turning a blind eye.

After lights-out on the previous evening, Nevitt, whom she had thought was bedridden, had risen from her cot and made her slow way down the ward.

344

Riley was evidently waiting in terror for her to come, because she had tensed as Nevitt started to move, finally uttering a pathetic but nearly silent scream when she arrived at her bed. Nevitt had raised her hands to Riley's face, threatening her damaged eye.

Riley had bleated with fear.

'Don't,' murmured Nevitt, 'don't.'

Meaning, guessed Nurse Lutyens, 'Don't make a noise or I'll put your eye out.'

Then Nevitt had gone for one of the other girls and helped her down the ward. Together they had pulled the covers off Riley's bed and raised her shift, exposing her privates and her breasts. They were large, the nipples dark and protuberant.

Nevitt had taken one of Riley's nipples between her nails and squeezed it suddenly very hard. The other woman had done the same to the other.

Riley had half-screamed again.

'*Don't,*' Nevitt had said again, reaching up to place her vicious nail at Riley's eye.

Riley had obeyed.

The second woman's face and mouth had been inches from the nipple.

'Bite it,' Nevitt had said.

The woman had giggled and shaken her head.

Nevitt had said, 'Will myself.' She had put her open mouth over its distended shape. And then bitten it between her gums, hard.

Riley had gone into a rigor of fear and pain, her crib shaking noisily.

'Naughty girl,' Mary Nevitt had said to her former tormentor.

Then she had slapped her hard.

'Naughty,' she had said again.

Then: 'We'll bite it off tomorrow, we will.'

Nurse Lutyens, her eyes glittering, had turned and slipped away to her own bed. No, she wouldn't trouble Dr Eels with all this. He had more important things to think about.

That Friday morning, just after nine, when the doctor had successfully completed the procedure on the second patient and was taking a break in his examination room, an orderly arrived in a fluster. Dr Eels was wanted urgently. A gentleman had arrived demanding to see him.

The calling card that the orderly handed to Eels read, *Mr Dodek Krol, Physical Culture Director, Nord Chicago Turnverein*, followed by an address.

Eels was incandescent. 'A gymnast! Demanding to see *me*, here and now! Didn't you tell him I'm in the middle of some important operations and cannot be interrupted?'

'I did, sir, but he was very insistent. Said it was imperative he spoke to you.'

'Tell him to come back tomorrow.'

'Sir, the gentleman . . .' the orderly hesitated, unsure what to say, '. . . the fact is, sir, the gentleman is not the kind one can easily say no to without very good reason . . . He seems well quite . . . er . . .'

Eels's pale face suffused with sudden rage.

'Tell this . . . gymnast . . . that the medical superintendent of Cook County Insane Asylum is busy right now and that he should have made an appointment.'

The orderly retreated, but a few moments later he returned.

'Mr Krol says he does not like to wait.'

'Then he doesn't have to! He can damn well go back to Chicago and make a proper appointment if he pleases,' said Eels.

At which point the door to Dr Eels's surgery swung slowly open. The orderly took one look and fled.

Dodek Krol stood calmly in the doorway eyeing Eels, who rose from his chair, anger turning swiftly to alarm.

Krol's shoulders were nearly as wide as the doorway. His curled bowler was set neatly at his side in one of his huge hands. His overcoat was undone but, being well cut and of the finest cloth, it hung loosely but elegantly. His boots, of the thick-soled, well-made European kind, were clean but not over-polished.

He projected confidence, success, certainty of purpose and menace . . .

'Sit,' Krol said in a low voice.

Eels did as he was told, his heart thumping painfully.

He saw that Krol carried a stick in his left hand. It was a thick malacca cane of the kind sporting gentlemen carry for their own defense. It looked to Eels very like a sword cane.

'What do you want?' he croaked, trying to recover his composure. 'This is ... I am ... this is a hospital, sir, and I am its director.'

'I have come to talk to you.'

Eels's throat tightened and dried.

'W-what about?'

Eels could not stop his voice shaking.

'Missing papers.'

'We sent the police ...'

For a wild moment Eels thought he had misread the situation entirely. 'Is it possible,' he gasped, 'that you have them, Mr ... er, Mr Krol?'

Krol's mouth hardened, his eyes crinkled slightly into a dismissive smile. 'I haven't. But we need them.'

'What for, sir?' said Eels, recovering himself a little.

Krol sighed the sigh of a man used to seeing men disintegrate before him.

'You sent Mr Donko O'Banion in search of the girl?'

'I ... he ... well, I didn't exactly send him. He works with the police. I thought ...'

'That was deeply stupid. O'Banion's one of the Tick Tock boys. They're all stupid. That makes you stupid too.'

Eels spluttered wordlessly like a turkey cock.

'Mr Paul Hartz gave you forty-eight hours, I believe. Your time has run out.'

Eels's heart nearly stopped in his chest.

'I shall find the girl myself,' said Krol. We will have her within twenty-four hours. You'd better hope she has this document. Now, Dr Eels ...'

Krol look around for somewhere to put his hat.

He found a chair and pulled it to the side of Eels's desk. The chair looked as if it might disintegrate under his weight. '... I want you to show me exactly what this document looks like. I need to know what we are looking for.'

'It isn't much,' bleated Eels, 'it's just, it's ...'

'Show me,' said Krol.

Eels showed him.

'How many names will be on it?'

'Twenty.'

'And the papers are pale yellow?'

Eels nodded. A thought made its way into his beleaguered brain.

'You do not propose to dispose of the girl?'

Dodek Krol said nothing. About such things he never said anything.

'It is better that she is brought back here,' said Eels. 'She is one of these twenty. She will need to be properly accounted for, otherwise she will be perceived by my fellow scientists as a mortality. That will not be good. It is a matter of statistics. I need her back here.'

'And if we bring her back, how do you propose to stop her talking?'

For the first time in this dreadful interview Eels felt on safe ground.

'She will not talk. Give her to me for fifteen minutes and she will not talk.'

'You will kill her?'

'I have no need to,' said Eels.

Krol had no interest in procedures and looked bored.

'Today I shall be conducting the first ten of twenty procedures and in a week's time the remaining ten, of which the girl was one of the original number. But in any event, if you can find this girl and bring her here I can guarantee I shall deal with her to your – and Mr Hartz's – fullest satisfaction.'

'Who talked of Mr Hartz's satisfaction?' said Krol. '*I* didn't. You shouldn't.'

Eels stammered an apology.

'Bring her back and I will see to it that she will never be a problem for as long as she lives.'

Krol stared at Eels with distaste.

'So . . . we will find the girl and bring her to you. None of this puts me personally in a good mood. It is a mess of your own making, not mine. I am not nice when I am in a bad mood. If we do not find the document, Dr Eels, then it will be necessary to visit you again.'

Eels's eyes widened, as Krol loomed over him, massive and bestial.

'Sir,' he croaked again, 'what shall I say to Mr O'Banion? He is coming here this morning for further instructions.'

'He already came,' said Krol, 'and you can say what you wish.'

He folded the yellow sheet of paper and put it in his inside pocket. Then he took up his hat and his cane and turned wordlessly towards the door.

Eels stared after him.

It was only then that Eels noticed that Mr Krol had a bloodstain on the left leg of his pants.

Eels sat for a while in his chair, shaken and fearful in the knowledge that his world, so nearly won, might easily collapse about him.

When he felt stronger he got up, went to the window, and looked down at the graveled expanse that faced the main entrance to the insane asylum.

No one was about, not even Donko O'Banion, whose paddy wagon was standing on the drive, its horse . . . untethered.

Eels looked more closely.

The horse stood idly, tail switching at flies.

The wagon's door was ajar and from it something dripped onto the gravel below. It was the color of blood.

58

Negatives

As usual, Wabash was throbbing with activity as Emily, staying on the quieter east side of the street, made her way north towards Henry Robinson's photographic studio.

A crowd of onlookers was just dispersing, and a policeman was checking the ropes that cordoned off the front of the studio. A fire had gutted the bottom floor of the flimsy building, blackened the outside of the three floors above and had almost spread to the small pharmacy next door.

Toulson had been right to warn her.

'What did I miss?' she asked a delivery boy.

'Someone set fire to the place. And killed the proprietor.'

'They took his body away in the night,' added a middle-aged man.

'Policeman said his throat was cut,' added his wife. Her eyes were excited, her face flushed.

'Ear to ear,' added the newsboy matter-of-factly, 'and by the time the fire department got there he was all burned too.'

Emily wished that the remaining officer on duty would move away, which, to her surprise, he did. A wagon that had passed her moments before, mounting the sidewalk as it tried to turn sharply into Adams, had shed its load onto the street. As the officer went to sort it out she crossed Wabash, slipped under the ropes and in through the blackened door.

The floor was a mess of burnt papers and glass over which, lifting her skirt, Emily stepped gingerly. There was a window on one side which afforded some light, but the place was murky with the soot still hanging in the air.

The odor was the strangest she had ever come across, combining burnt wood and plaster with the sharp, acidic smell of chemicals and – she shivered – the sickly cloying smell of cooked flesh. It made her want to retch.

As her eyes adjusted to the gloom, she was startled by a sudden sound further into the ruined building. A timber settling perhaps, a draught of air through a shattered window?

She turned back into the front office and saw where there had been two chairs, a counter, framed images on the wall, their glass broken by heat and, beyond, a door into, she guessed, the photographic studio itself.

It was nearly dark inside but for a dull red glow in one corner.

Not sure what she would find, and fearful of the glass underfoot as well as making too much noise in case the officer returned, Emily crept forward towards the studio door. She heard movement. Someone was in there.

She found a clear place on the floor to place her foot, and then another, and pushed the door open.

It swung wide open and beyond her grasp, the hinges having been distorted by the fire, bashing into the wall behind and bringing a shelf crashing to the floor.

Through the murk Emily spied a hunched and hooded figure with strange legs standing at the far end of the studio, silhouetted by a red glow.

A bright explosive flash stopped her short. It was followed by the sudden acrid smell of burning.

Staggering back, temporarily blinded, she heard the figure crunch across the floor towards her. Mr Hatsumi had advised her to act from her heart and guts and she thrust hard at the starry darkness in front of her, hitting her adversary in the face.

The response was clear and loud and blasphemous.

Her blow had found its target so unexpectedly that she felt herself falling back and sideways. Then a hand loomed out of the darkness and grabbed her arm, steadying her.

351

Her sight came back in strange starry strands until finally she saw the face of the man in front of her.

It was Ben Latham.

'*What the hell are you doing . . . ?*' they both began to say.

'I was expecting you at the hotel at ten.'

He rubbed his cheek.

'Where did you learn to hit like a man?' he said.

'What on earth are you doing here, Ben . . . ?'

'Train arrived early. Thought I'd take a look at the studio where the photograph of our girl was taken. Found the place cordoned off. Said I was an official illustrator and they let me in. Horrible.'

'That flash . . . ?'

'Fire didn't get to the camera. It had a plate inside. Just tested it out. But overdid the magnesium powder a bit. Nice camera but out of date. I was trying to take a photograph of the wreckage but you got in the way. Here, let's shed some light on the situation.'

Ben crunched his way back across the studio, and picked up the source of the red light, a lantern.

'These places always have 'em. For developing . . . Red light doesn't spoil the images and it's just about possible to see what you're doing by it.'

He turned up the lamp.

He suddenly looked about fifteen years old.

So, guessed Emily, did she.

'Someone killed the proprietor, Robinson, the man who took Anna Zemeckis's photograph,' said Emily. 'Can't you make that thing cast a more normal light?'

Ben removed a curved piece of red glass and cursed as it burnt his fingers. But the whole room brightened at once. Then, when he hung the lantern on a hook above their heads, things became more visible still.

The studio was large and rectangular, everything in it filthy with soot and dust. There was a couch and some other props, a backdrop of painted trees with a lake on a roller, some chairs and the huge portrait camera on a tripod. The roof had large slanting glass windows to allow in the maximum light.

'Well,' said Emily, 'my idea in coming was to see what Robinson might have remembered about Anna. But I've missed that opportunity. Should have come straight here when I arrived, like you. What was your plan?'

'Didn't have one. Just wanted to see the place, and from my Baedeker I reckoned it was near your hotel. I wouldn't have come in if the place had been in one piece and Mr Robinson in residence but . . . the police weren't exactly guarding it closely and anything photographic is of interest to me. You know what this glass is?'

Emily took a closer look.

'Photographic plates, is that the name?'

'These are dry plates, mostly negatives.'

He picked one up and held it to the light for her to see. It didn't make much sense to her: just silvery black and white shapes.

'It's a portrait, probably for a *carte de visite.*'

Emily looked around.

'There doesn't seem to be a whole one left. Why would anyone want to destroy all these as well as kill Robinson?'

'Maybe whoever did it didn't want them seen.'

'Society portraits? Girls in confirmation dresses? Wedding pictures? Come on . . . whoever did it was looking for something.'

Ben nodded.

'Maybe he was looking for a particular picture, but that's not easy with negatives, especially with so many. I mean, this guy Robinson seems to have been in business a long time. There were hundreds, maybe thousands here.'

'So he started looking for one or some in particular, and ran out of time . . .'

'Maybe he thought it'd be easy, or he could take them out of the studio. But these plates are heavy and difficult to move around. These big cardboard boxes are for storage, not carrying. He lost patience . . . See, he tipped 'em out and threw the boxes on top.'

'Or maybe he wants them destroyed,' said Emily, light dawning.

'There's no easy way to find out now,' said Ben.

'Where would you hide photographic plates you wouldn't want others to see in a studio like this?'

'In among the others, not by themselves,' said Ben. 'But a bit out of the way.'

'Low down or high up?'

'Low down, I guess. Somewhere not easy to see.'

'Under the counter?'

Ben thought for a moment, then suddenly grinned.

'What are you looking like that for?' said Emily. '*What?*'

They were interrupted by a shout. It was the officer returning.

'Buy me some time,' said Ben. 'I want to look around a bit more. I think I know what they were looking for.'

Emily went out through the studio door to the front of the shop, pulling it shut behind her.

The officer seemed surprised to see a woman.

She introduced herself – taking her time about it. She showed her reporter's pass. She told him she was only doing her job. She just kept on talking and talking as loud and long as she could.

Finally, when the officer could get a word in edgeways, he said, 'Ma'am, you shouldn't be here.'

It was a pity in the brief moment of silence that followed that Ben stepped on some glass in the studio.

'One of your friends?' growled the officer, reaching for his night-stick.

As Ben appeared, Emily said, 'But officer, we're . . .'

Just then, a second man arrived on the scene, ducking under the ropes.

'It's all right. She's known to me.'

'If you say so, Mr Toulson,' muttered the one holding Emily by the arm.

Hitching his bag over his shoulder, Ben said, 'I'm real hungry. Any chance of some breakfast?'

'So, you're an officer of the law, Mr Toulson?' said Emily as they left the blackened building.

'Am I?' said Toulson.

'Is he?' asked Emily of the two officers as they followed them out.

'If you say so, ma'am,' said the talkative one. 'Now, if you don't mind, and you too, sir, whoever you are and whatever you've both been doing, please get the hell out of here.'

'The restaurant at Marshall Field's does a good breakfast,' said Toulson as the three headed out onto Wabash, 'but we need a lady if we're to be really respectable.'

'I'll do my best,' said Emily.

59

Snitchers

The girls at E. K. M. & Co. did not take to Anna Zemeckis. At Brennan's, Eileen had befriended her and Anna was certain it was she who had betrayed her, so this time round she decided to keep her distance and give nothing away, which maybe didn't help things.

But the real problem was she was older and smarter, as well as being quicker and better at the sewing.

These girls were young, half-starved, ill-dressed, ignorant of life, and either had suspicion written on their faces or the weary resignation of the eternally exploited. Anna realized she had nearly arrived at the bottom of the pile and knew if she did not get out fast – and that meant hours not days – she too would begin to slide down into the wretched place they were in.

Just before ten, Mr Groats patrolled the sewing tables, checking the girls' work. He grabbed the work of the girl next to Anna and ripped it apart.

'Not good enough,' he said. 'Improve or leave. I can give your space to a new girl anytime.'

When he reached Anna he examined her work and then declared, 'Too fine! Custom work! Don't need to be so good on such cloaks. You stay and I'll move you to better work when there's a gap.'

As he moved on, the other girls looked at Anna resentfully.

'Where'd you say you came from?' said the one who had already asked that question.

'Romania,' repeated Anna.

'Never heard of it,' she replied, glancing at the other girls and smirking.

Anna decided the best thing to do was ignore them.

She was surprised when, a few minutes later, needing to press her work out to carry the stitching on neatly, another girl whom she had not seen before stopped and asked her where she was from.

She repeated her lie and the girl seemed satisfied.

But, a short time later, a third asked the same question. It was time to ask why.

'Been told to,' the girl said. 'There's a dollar in it.'

'A whole dollar?'

The girl nodded and said, 'They're watching out for someone.'

'Who?'

The girl shrugged.

''Bout your age. From Latvia.'

'Where's that?' said Anna.

'In Russia, I think.'

'Latvia,' repeated Anna softly. The very word made her want to weep.

She returned to her worktable thinking hard, wondering how much longer she could risk staying in Chicago. She had been lucky twice. A third time . . .

She made the decision to leave when she had earned another fifty cents and, with any luck, if Groats accepted her work, that would be by the end of the day. But she had to try to lay suspicion to rest.

She sewed harder and faster still, listening to the girls around her, waiting for an opportunity.

It seemed that one of the reasons the girls resented her was that they had liked the girl whose place she had taken. She had fainted a couple of times and the other girls had kept it from Groats. The third time he was standing right next to her and she was out the door at once.

'Was it hunger?' asked Anna quietly, the first time she had talked in a while.

No one replied but she guessed they wanted to. Maybe they weren't so bad after all, just young and simple and already half beaten-up by overwork and undernourishment.

She waited a bit, then said, 'I'm going to have a baby.'

There was a combined gasp of curiosity, sympathy and relief from the group nearby.

'When?'

'February.'

'Are you . . . ?'

'I'm not married.'

For a moment she forgot why she had said it, basking in the fickle way in which the girls' attitude to her had suddenly shifted from rejection to empathy. But that was what she wanted.

'I had to move from my last job because of it.' Then, as offhandedly as she could, 'There was a Latvian girl there . . .'

The interest level rose palpably.

'Anyway,' asked Anna nonchalantly, 'why are you so interested in a Latvian girl?'

'She's wanted.'

'Yes, but why . . .'

'There's a dollar in it for the girl who lets them know.'

'Maybe *I* should . . . Who do I tell? Mr Groats?'

'If you tell him it'll do no good. He's not a snitcher. You tell Agda Akesson.'

Someone pointed at a woman on the far side of the room, older than the others and Anna too. She was dark for a Scandinavian, sour-faced and very pale. Her hair was pulled back tight and her mouth looked permanently turned down.

'Doesn't look very nice,' observed Anna.

'A dollar's a dollar.'

'I liked the Latvian girl, she gave me some cake. Don't see why . . .'

'If they found out you knew and didn't say . . .'

It was more than a threat, it was fear.

'Who'd tell her?'

The girls fell silent.

The mood had changed again because each one of them was weighing up the best way they could get their fingers on that tempting dollar.

Anna had heard all she needed to. All she had to do was stay long enough to get her money and she wouldn't be coming back.

Meanwhile a dollar, as the girl had said, was a dollar and one or other of these girls was going to start talking if she didn't get to the Scandinavian first.

'Why her?' asked Anna.

'She's got friends. She knows people: gets 'em work, gets 'em good families to lodge with. You tell her.'

It was a warning as well as advice: you tell her or one of us will get to her first and then you'll be in trouble for not saying anything.

'I will when I get a chance.'

The group fell silent once more, each in their own way scheming, each trying to decide how to gain advantage from the scrap of information this new girl had given them.

But Anna was scheming too.

60

No Deal

The restaurant at Marshall Field was just a short walk from Henry Robinson's burnt-out studio. Emily and her companions found it open to respectable clientele for morning coffee, and, at their request, they were conducted to a quiet corner table. Here, silent and impeccably efficient waiters served them with coffee and a selection of wheat muffins, cream horns and apple pie.

'So,' said Emily, taking the initiative, 'you're with the police, Mr Toulson.'

He looked grave and moved his head in what might have been a nod or possibly a shake.

'You haven't introduced me to your friend.'

'Colleague, as a matter of fact,' said Emily, making the introduction.

'So . . . ?' she began again.

'You know that Robinson was murdered?'

'His throat was cut, I believe,' she said steadily, holding Toulson's gaze. Ben's eyes widened.

Toulson's eyes gave nothing away.

'So . . . ?' tried Emily a third time.

'I *was* with the police,' said Toulson finally. 'So naturally I *know* the police. But I am not with them now.'

'So who are you with?' asked Ben reasonably, taking the pressure off Emily.

Toulson was the kind of man it was hard to put pressure on, verbally or any other way, and he had an impassive, questioning stare that faced questioners down. 'It's not important,' said Toulson. 'What *is* important is that your enquiry into this dead girl is becoming a nuisance because it's interfering with something much bigger.'

'Which is?' said Emily.

Toulson thought for a minute or so, weighing up the situation. Then he seemed to thaw a little.

'So . . . how many girls have you interviewed since you've been in Chicago?'

'A good few,' said Emily cagily.

Not nearly enough, she was thinking.

'What do you know about the Comstock Act?'

'Of 1873?'

He nodded.

'It was to stop the dissemination of pornographic literature about birth control and sex education, wasn't it?'

Toulson nodded, 'Dissemination of immoral literature in paper form – books, magazines, pictures, drawings, that sort of thing.'

'So? What's all this to do with Anna Zemeckis?' asked Emily. 'Or Mr Robinson, come to that?'

'I think Mr Latham can make a fair guess.'

'He was probably taking pornographic photographs on the quiet,' said Ben, 'which means he was selling them to select customers from his own premises or distributing them in some other way. Quite a few photographers have been caught doing that, usually because their bribes to the police have not been enough. That's my guess, and maybe that has something to do with why he was killed.'

'But is there really much money in such a secretive trade?' said Emily, genuinely surprised.

'Far more than you'd think,' said Toulson. 'I doubt if there's a red-blooded man in America who wouldn't take a second look at a porno-graphic picture given half a chance, but most don't go actively looking for 'em. But the rise of photography and new ways of distributing such photographs mean there's a rapidly growing market and there are many people out there willing to pay high prices for the good stuff.'

Emily's eyes widened, then she looked dubious. 'Are you seriously telling me that Anna Zemeckis was in some way involved with this kind of thing? She came from a good family. I've met her father.'

'Don't care if her father was Mr Comstock himself,' said Toulson, 'I *know* she was involved.'

Anna Zemeckis's story had suddenly taken on a very different complexion.

'Even if that were true,' continued Emily, 'which I don't believe, you're not going to get me to abandon my investigation just because it might take me into dangerous territory.'

'There's no "might" about it, Miss Strauss. Pornography of the type I'm investigating is a filthy, nasty, dangerous business, closely linked to white-slave trafficking, in which young girls get abused, raped and murdered. Which is what probably happened to Miss Zemeckis.'

'What's your proof?' she said.

Toulson was still resisting giving her a straight answer to her questions.

'Look, I have the proof as far as Miss Zemeckis is concerned, trust me. But I could do with your help on a wider front. You may find this unacceptable but I don't believe that all the girls and women in this business are there against their will. I've seen enough of this material to surmise that some of them are doing it voluntarily, even enjoying it.'

'What makes you think that exactly?'

Toulson said nothing while Ben tried to work out where this was all heading.

'Let's get this straight,' said Emily finally. 'You want me to help you investigate something you haven't yet convinced me is actually going on?'

'That's just about it,' said Toulson.

'Then I need something in return if I'm going to cooperate.'

'Like what?'

'Evidence. Right now. You *got* any?'

'You don't give up, do you, Miss Strauss?'

'No,' she said, 'I don't. It's my profession. It's what Mr Pulitzer hired me to do.'

Ben looked uncomfortable.

Then the penny suddenly dropped and it made a loud clang in Emily's head.

'So what *exactly* do these pictures show?' she asked.

'They show,' said Toulson heavily, 'what goes on behind closed doors between consenting adults.'

'Sexual intercourse?' said Emily.

''Fraid so,' said Toulson.

'You're telling me that so-called red-blooded men not only like pictures like this but haunt the alleys and side streets of the Levee buying and selling them?'

'Don't be naïve,' said Toulson.

'Maybe I am,' said Emily, 'but no more than most of my readers and I'm learning fast. So you're saying Anna Zemeckis was in some way involved?'

Toulson nodded.

'A nice, decently brought-up Latvian girl from a good home in New York willingly allowed herself to be photographed having sexual inter-course?'

Toulson shook his head.

'Not quite, because I doubt what she did was done willingly. She was probably one of the reluctant ones, taken against her will and dosed with chloral. That's why she's probably dead.'

Emily sighed. 'What exactly do you want me to do?'

'I need help identifying some of these girls. What would it take to get you to look through a file and tell me if you can put a name to any of the girls whose photographs are in it?'

'Prove Anna's involved and tell me who you're working for.'

'It's a deal,' said Toulson.

'Here and now,' said Emily. 'I've got a luncheon appointment at Jackson Park to get to, so I don't have long. Let's start with this so-called proof.'

'That's easy enough,' said Toulson, pulling a file from his briefcase, 'but I'm warning you, you might be shocked by what you're about to see.'

'I don't shock easily,' said Emily.

He produced a folder and took out a head and shoulders shot of a girl and placed it on the table in front of Emily. She looked at it long and hard.

'That's Anna Zemeckis all right,' she said eventually, 'but this image by itself proves nothing. Why she's wearing a feather on her head I can't imagine. Was she in a theatrical performance of some kind?'

Toulson laughed cynically.

Ben examined it.

'It looks as if it's been cropped,' he said. 'Where's the whole photograph?'

They looked at Toulson.

'Miss Strauss . . .' he said uncertainly.

'Show me,' said Emily grimly.

'I'll hand you the file. No way do I put these on a table in public. Now that *would* constitute an offence. Look through them and see if you recognize anyone.'

There were twenty images or so, all hand-tinted, in increasing order of obscenity. The picture that included Anna was near the bottom of the pile. It showed two women and a man. The man and one of the women were naked. He was on top of the woman, his whole body shown from behind.

She lay beneath him, her face towards the camera.

They were having sexual intercourse and she did not look unhappy. But the woman was definitely not Anna.

The other woman, dressed in a tightly laced pink corset and black silk stockings and, somewhat incongruously, wearing a hat with a large ostrich feather in it, appeared to be acting as their handmaiden. She held a great fan above them, made of the same feathers.

She too looked at the camera. But her face was solemn and unsmiling.

It was Anna Zemeckis. The head and shoulders shot of Anna that Toulson had first shown Emily was taken from the same image.

'Yes,' she confirmed, 'that's Anna.'

She handed back the folder.

'Now, Mr Toulson, you were going to tell me who you're working

364

for. I know it's not the engineering company printed on your card, and you've said it's not the police.'

'I guess you could say I'm a Pinkerton man,' said Toulson. 'Let's agree to work together on this.' He reached out a hand.

But Emily did not take it.

Instead she got up from her chair.

'We're going, Ben,' she said.

Ben looked astonished, but got up.

Toulson looked flabbergasted.

'Let's not shake on it, Mr Toulson,' she said coldly.

'Can I ask why . . . ?' He had rarely had an interview go as wrong as this, so fast.

Emily stared at him without expression.

'Ever heard of Pittsburgh, the Homestead Strike?' she said. 'It's where I'm from. People from those parts don't like Pinkerton men. *That's* why.'

Toulson did not flinch.

'We all have a job to do, Miss Strauss. Sometimes we have to do things we don't approve of. We make mistakes, like the Pinkertons did at Homestead. But sometimes, too, we do things that prove more dangerous than we realize. Trust me, if you get in too deep on this investigation, you and Mr Latham will find yourselves with nowhere to go. The men who run this business are vicious and very dangerous. They're disciplined and well led. You should go nowhere near them or anyone involved with them. You—'

Emily did not let him finish. 'Goodbye, Mr Toulson,' she said briskly and turned and left. Ben followed with an apologetic shrug.

Toulson watched them leave, his face blank. Then he paid the cashier and followed them out into the street.

He just caught sight of Emily and Ben as they turned into Adams. Meanwhile, a man on the far side of Wabash crossed over and disappeared after them. Emily was being tailed but, Toulson told himself grimly, if she didn't want his help she needn't have it. She was an independent woman who knew her own mind and she was learning fast how to defend herself in the big city.

Toulson pulled out his pocket watch. 'Gone ten-to,' he murmured, '*damn!*'

He hurried north back up Wabash, right past Robinson's studio.

When he reached Randolph he checked the time again and relaxed. He would just make it.

Back on Michigan and nearing the Auditorium Annex, Emily walked so fast that Ben almost had to run to keep up with her.

'What the hell was all that about?' he said.

Emily stopped short in the street.

'Pinkerton men are the opposition,' she said angrily, 'and I like to steal a march on the opposition.'

'And what's *that* supposed to mean?' said Ben, exasperated.

'He never asked me about the other woman in that last photograph.'

'The one who was . . .'

'Yes, the one who was having sexual intercourse.'

'What about her?'

'I'm having lunch with her at one,' said Emily.

61

Octopus

Sol Bann, proprietor of one of the few entirely independent saloons on State Street, was the kind of man who dies in his bed at an advanced age with an easy conscience and a loving family weeping around him.

He played fair by everyone, put his customers first, was tough but even-handed with his employees and had seen the Tick Tock boys and their like off his premises so many times that now they doffed their hats at him. There wasn't a realtor in Chicago who didn't know that there was no way Sol would sell the plot he had cleverly acquired after the Great Fire of 1871 until he, and only he, was good and ready.

It had taken him two days to work out the fruit-man's game and another two to gain his confidence.

Now he and Mr Fruit-man, as he called Toulson with easy irony – for he had no wish to know his real name – had a working relationship profitable to both. Sol received dollars in return for two things: a steady flow of information and an ever-available seat for Toulson at a small table by the window that gave an uninterrupted view of the main entrance to the Masonic Temple and its more discreet entrance on the west side of the building.

Sol had worked out that Toulson must be a Pinkerton man, or

something very much like it. Toulson had worked out that Sol was one of those rare individuals who could keep his mouth shut. It wouldn't be right – and Sol wouldn't have lasted five minutes had it been so – to call him an informer. He was simply an observer of what went on inside his saloon and along that small portion of State Street immediately outside it. He knew who passed by one way, who another, when, what they were carrying, who they worked for (and why) and what they wore or what days they wore it, and a whole lot more about the economic, social, criminal and plain trivial ebb and flow of the city he loved.

It was this insider knowledge, this passion, this exclusive club of one that, for a few days in October 1893, Gerald Toulson had the brains and savvy to join by paying generous dues and making very clear to Sol Bann that no one would ever know what had been transacted between them.

The spark that gave them mutual trust and understanding was a political one: Sol was a Democrat and so was Toulson.

The game was on because, as was crystal clear to Sol, the Fruitman's quarry was an organization he had a particular reason to dislike, an essentially Republican organization: the Old America Association.

Sol was American through and through, even though he was only second generation, his parents being Jewish immigrants from Germany who had arrived with the name Banovsky. He loved the country that had given refuge to his parents. He loved liberty and the American-given right to use his initiative, buy a plot of land and do what he liked with it, within reason. He liked freedom of expression, so long as it was never, ever violent and took away another's liberty; and he loved the fact that his city, Chicago, had in a very short space of time shown the rest of the world what enterprise and hard work might achieve.

He disliked the Old America Association for the very good reason that people of its kind – lawyers, heavy men, boodlers and ward politicians – had tried everything they could to wrest his fairly won plot of land, and the saloon on which it stood, from him.

Normally Sol confined his observation of life to what he could actually see within and without his saloon. But so incensed had he been by the attempts of OAA-affiliated realtors to bully him out of what was rightfully his that he had started doing a little investigation of his own. He talked casually to customers; he scoured the newspapers, first the Chicago ones and later those from New York and Boston, where the OAA was strong.

He made it his business to read the various Republican journals in the Chicago Public Library, though it made him sick at heart to do so. A whole new world of research into his pet subject opened up to him. What Sol discovered about the OAA, and more particularly about its members and their activities, enabled him – along with sundry newspaper clippings, customer comments and occasional local sightings – to put two and two together and make a very disturbing four.

It was an organization that had more tentacles than an octopus and they stretched out a lot further too – right across America in fact, from the highest to the lowest in the land. The OAA had its tentacles out in pursuit of one thing: the advancement, advantage and power of its members, as well as the OAA's own very specific social and political agendas.

That much Sol could stomach. What he did not like was that the OAA's private voice, ruthless and corrupt, was fronted by a public one which claimed that what it did was in the name of the country Sol loved, and lit by the glorious democratic light of the glorious flag he revered, and informed by the truth and liberty which he valued above all things.

So when he worked out that Mr Fruit-man was, in all likelihood, a Pinkerton man, and that he was engaged in an investigation into the Old America Association, he was not slow in coming forward.

'Sir,' he said, 'I don't know what your game is and I don't want to know, but if it's what I think it is and has something to do with ridding the world of rotten fish, fruit and vegetables, then I'm your man.'

Toulson, like Sol, was a master at judging a man's character. It went with the art and science of observation.

'I could do with a little help,' said Toulson, 'seeing as I can't be here all the time over the next few days till the Fair ends. I have to keep a close eye on something.'

Sol had worked out what he thought it was, but he allowed Toulson to take the lead.

'In my line of business, Mr Bann, seafood goes bad real fast and,

369

even on a healthy tree, fruits go rotten; and it don't take much either for vegetables to be unpalatable,' he said. 'To my way of thinking, that kind of fare is not good for the stomach.'

Sol considered this, nodded his head and took the cue: 'What I do know for sure, mister, is that a mix of octopus, apples and avocado don't make much of a stew for any Democrat stomach. And I'd give a helping hand to any fella whose mission in life was to put such a stew out with the garbage. You'll have the usual?'

Toulson was puzzled by this remark at first. But as he took his seat and got out his little book and a pencil, the significance of Sol's signal – *O*ctopus, *A*pples and *A*vocado – dawned on him as he wrote down the first letter of each one.

It wasn't hard after that to strike a deal with Sol, who promised to keep a close eye on the comings and goings of OAA members at the Masonic Temple opposite.

Naturally, a lot of people used that building and it needed Sol's local expertise to sort the wheat from the chaff. But he knew every single local member by sight and name: he knew their business, their connections, the strings they pulled at City Hall and who it was pulled theirs. This local knowledge combined with Toulson's expertise on the OAA members from out of town, particularly the big shots who Sol only knew by name, meant that between them they now had the OAA nicely under observation.

The disappearance of Jenkin Lloyd Rhys five days previously had upped the ante. The discovery of his body in Johnstown the day before had upped it even further.

Sol had his suspicions when he heard the name RHYS was carved in his forehead. It wasn't the OAA's style but it had the whiff of the Meisters about it.

'I guess something big is up,' Sol had said on the Wednesday.

'You could say that, Sol,' said Toulson ironically.

'Yes, something's definitely up,' observed Sol on the Thursday, the day Rhys's body was found, 'but I'm damned if I know what.'

'Watch out for anyone new,' said Toulson, 'anyone, that is, who doesn't normally come to the temple. That'll be a clue.'

Toulson reached Sol Bann's at five to eleven and was shown his usual place. He and Sol both knew that the first of an important two-day OAA Convention was being held that day at the grand new Auditorium Theater.

'How's the fruit business today, mister?' Sol said, bringing him his usual and a plate of salami.

'I have something new for you to try,' he said, clearly eyeing the entrance opposite and leaning in close. 'A fine new sausage – from Poland. Do you know it?' he whispered as he placed the *kielbasa* in front of Toulson.

'Try me,' responded Toulson.

'He went in by the west entrance five minutes ago. Never seen him at the temple before. Tried not to show his face. Very smart. Wears a curled bowler.'

'So how do you know him then?'

'By his reputation and his bulk. His name's Dodek Krol.'

Toulson took a swig of his drink.

'Know 'im?' said Sol.

Toulson knew him.

In a locked box in a locked safe in a locked room back at his office at Pinkerton's was a file he himself had been preparing for some time. It listed the most notorious paid killers in America, on whom nothing had ever yet been pinned and who, therefore, amazingly enough, had a completely clean record.

Dodek Krol was number one.

62

Alive

'We've been looking for you, Miss Strauss,' the reception clerk at the Auditorium Annex said when she and Ben returned after their encounter with Toulson. He handed her a telegraph, adding with a certain severity, as if it was Emily's fault she had not been there earlier, 'and the boy from Western Union *waited.*'

Emily ripped open the little envelope.

'I believe it's urgent,' continued the irritating clerk. 'If you wish to send a reply . . .'

The telegraph was from Donald Stadler, night editor of the New York *World*, no less. *Anna Zemeckis telegraphed father today. Contact us at once. Stadler.*

Emily stood there, mouth open, reading and re-reading the telegraph as its implications raced through her mind.

'What *is* it?' said Ben.

'I was right. Anna's *alive*,' she said, finally sinking into a chair. 'Alive! I *knew* it! We *have* to find her, we must . . .'

Calmly Ben took the telegraph from her hands and read it.

'I'll call New York,' he said.

Turning back to the clerk, he asked, 'What's the time back east . . . ?'

'In New York, sir? Coming up to noon.'

'I want you to put in a call *now*,' said Ben.

They were lucky: it took only twenty minutes to get through.

'Number Two,' called out the clerk, nodding towards one of the telephone booths adjacent to the reception area.

They went in together but it was Emily who picked up the receiver, saying firmly, 'My story, my call.'

She clamped the phone hard to her ear. She was lucky: the line, despite the inevitable hum and crackle, was pretty good for once.

Stadler had gone home already, so city editor Charles Hadham's assistant took the call.

The telegraph had been sent by Anna Zemeckis from Western Union's office at the Union Depot in Chicago to her father on the Lower East Side the previous evening.

'What time?' asked Emily.

'Hold on . . . a couple of minutes before eight.'

It seemed Janis Zemeckis's first instinct had been to try to get a berth on a train to Chicago, but with the Fair ending none was available at any price with any operator. Failing which he had gone straight to the *World*'s office and started shouting at the night staff.

'Had to calm him down.'

Emily wasn't surprised. She could imagine how he felt.

'Did he tell you what Anna said in the telegraph?'

'Sure, I have a copy here. It reads, *'Am safe and well. Please do not worry. Forgive me. Anna.'*

'Read that again . . .'

The man did so. Emily repeated the words to Ben and then wrote them down in her notepad.

'How do we know it's from her?' said Emily. 'Could be anyone.'

'There's three more words at the end of the telegraph. They seemed to convince him.

'Spell them.'

Hadham's assistant did so and Emily wrote them down.

Es tevi milu.

'What do they mean?'

'Mr Zemeckis said it means "I love you" . . . in Latvian.'

Emily thought of that pornographic picture and her suspicions that Anna might be pregnant. She could understand now why remorse and grief at the pain she had caused her father might have caught up with her so that she would seek to end his agony.

'We've got to find her,' she murmured to Ben, handing over the receiver.

He nodded, his mind racing too.

'Zemeckis was desperate,' continued Hadham's assistant. 'I saw him myself because he came back just an hour ago. He wants to talk to you. What shall I tell him?'

Emily had no idea, but she could imagine what might be going through Janis Zemeckis's mind after receiving a telegram like that. Utter relief on one hand, total despair on the other. And fear, the kind of fear that would drive a father half mad.

'Tell him I'll telegraph this evening when I have further news.'

'You've not seen her?'

'If I'd seen her we'd be bringing her back home to New York right now! I'd better go. I'll be in touch.'

'Has Ben Latham arrived?'

'He's right here.'

'Put him on. I've some news for him.'

Ben took the receiver, listened frowning until suddenly his face lightened and he laughed. He ended the call.

'What was that about?' said Emily impatiently.

'I won a bet,' said Ben.

Emily didn't respond; her eyes were focused on the notebook in which she was now rapidly scribbling.

'Right, let's discuss our options.'

They had barely begun to do so before the clerk from the front desk came up waving an envelope. 'You *are* in demand, Miss Strauss,' he said. 'This was hand-delivered. They didn't wait.'

It was a fine-quality cartridge envelope, sealed with wax. 'Miss Emily Strauss' was written on the front in a neat but spidery hand in black ink.

Dear Miss Strauss, You asked me to let you know if Miss Anna Zemeckis showed up at Hull House. She did — yesterday — or at least, we think it was her, from the description and the distressed state she was clearly in. Most unfortunately I was not here and I regret to say that this information has only just been passed on to me. I understand she was asked if she needed help but declined and then slipped away leaving no address or any other details. She seemed exhausted and

*unwell. But at least she is alive. I have instituted a search for her through the
network of refuges and lodging houses which we know cater for single women and
I will let you know the result. If, as you feared, she is with child she will need
help sooner rather than later. Please be in touch – I shall be here today and tomorrow
morning. Sincerely yours, Katharine Hubbard.*

It was confirmation of what she'd anticipated and, as such, good
news. But Emily felt uncomfortable at the idea of the Hull House
worthies disseminating information about Anna. Who knew into what
hands such information could fall?

'What are we going to do?' said Ben, slipping easily into the role
of sidekick. To do otherwise was futile. There was no challenging
Emily Strauss's focus on the story. He could see it in her eyes, which
gleamed with all the fervor of a crusading mission.

'We need to check out who might have seen her at the Union Depot
yesterday evening . . . and I have to go and talk to Mrs Markulis again.
I'm sure she knows more than she's been saying . . .'

'What about your lunch at the Fair?' reminded Ben.

'. . . And there's this too,' said Emily, pulling the invitation from
Gunther Darke from her purse.

She thought for a moment, working out how best to use her time,
fighting against the impulse to rush off to the Union Depot just
because that was where Anna had been only a few hours previously.
She would be long gone by now.

'Stoiber's important, I'm sure of it. She's the only one who might
know the truth about Anna, and where she's likely to be,' said Emily.
'So I have to meet her. Gunther Darke's demonstration I could do
without but . . . well, we know Anna went to the same event and she
did the stockyard tour too, because it was marked on her calendar.
But I don't have time to go to the stockyard then to the Union Depot
and then to the North Side to see Mrs Markulis, and then go back to
Fay Bancroft's.'

'Tell you what,' interrupted Ben, 'you take in the lecture at the Agricultural Hall and meet me at the Electricity Building before you have
your lunch with Our Lady of the Night, and we can compare notes.
I can go to the stockyard this afternoon and look around while you
follow up on other things. Meanwhile . . .' Ben put the battered briefcase he had been hugging onto the table . . . 'you have to see this.'

375

'What's so special about it?' demanded Emily.

He opened the briefcase and produced a bulky package wrapped in newspaper.

'It's all I could think of putting them in,' he said.

'What?'

'While you were keeping that officer at bay in Robinson's place, guess what I found?'

He began taking photographic plates, most of them broken, out of the newspaper wrapping and putting them on the table.

Emily picked one up.

'Careful! Hold it by the edges or you'll damage it.' She held it to the light.

'Can't make it out?'

Ben took it from her and turned it the other way up.

'Look again. Imagine the white's black and the black's white and the rest is somewhere between.'

'Still can't . . . Ben!'

She gave it back to him, pretending to be shocked. 'More naked ladies.'

'And gentlemen,' said Ben.

'Oh! Let's see . . .' she said, grinning and reaching out a hand.

Ben shook his head, putting them carefully back in the bag.

'They degrade easily in the light. I think these may have been what the killer really wanted to destroy. He nearly succeeded.'

'Are they all like that?'

'What, scenes of depravity and filth?' asked Ben with a grin. 'Yes. These are some of the negatives for making the photographs Robinson must have been selling. Now, while you're learning about the meat trade in the Agricultural Hall at the Fair, I'll prevail on my friends on the Edison stand in the Electricity Building to let me use their facilities to develop these.'

'What will they say if they see the pictures?'

'Doesn't matter. They're only illegal if you disseminate them. Photographs can offer all kinds of clues and these are top quality, trust me, even if they're broken. Let's wait and see.'

63

Inner Caucus

Dodek Krol took one of the three service elevators at the rear of the Masonic Temple to reach the small, private room on the twelfth floor for his eleven o'clock meeting with Paul Hartz.

Not that it would have mattered much if he had been spotted in the building. But he was naturally cautious and felt it essential that he was not seen publicly with the OAA's vice president.

In fact the two men had rarely met and had never directly discussed any of the important 'commissions' that the OAA had given him.

They had no special need to. They used an intermediary. By this simple device there was no linkage, either written or verbal, between Hartz and Krol concerning such actions, and other lesser punishments, which it was necessary from time to time for the OAA's inner caucus to order.

However, the meeting today was the culmination of the previous seven months' work, and both Hartz and Krol himself felt a meeting, without witnesses, was an essential preliminary to Hartz's chairing of various sessions at the OAA Convention today and tomorrow.

Seven months previously, after a tired and lackluster campaign on both sides between the incumbent Republican president, Benjamin Harrison, and Grover Cleveland, the Democrat nominee, Cleveland was elected to his second term of office. Under the aging leadership of Rhys, the OAA had given its official support to Harrison, but behind the scenes another faction, led by Hartz, had opposed him because of Harrison's tariff reforms, including the introduction in 1890 of the Sherman Anti-Trust Act controlling certain business practices of the kind corporations like Darke Hartz sometimes engaged in.

On March 4, 1892, the day that Democratic President Cleveland made his inaugural address as president for the second time, Rhys's fate was sealed. It would have been better had he resigned immediately but he did not. The move against him within the OAA began with a secret anti-Rhys meeting in New York in April, at which the inner caucus, as it was informally known, planned its strategy to oust him from the OAA leadership. It was this meeting that led directly to his murder by Krol.

But that same inner circle of Hartz supporters had taken their debate far further than the thorny question of Rhys's elimination. This was part of a greater political strategy which was nothing less than getting the Republicans back into power and, ultimately, fielding the OAA's own candidate for the presidency.

Hartz knew enough about the chess game of politics to know that strategists had to think many moves – and very many years – ahead. His initial task had been simply to get some key players on-side, and this he had done.

In fact, Rhys's disappearance just prior to the convention came as a total surprise to most of these members of the inner caucus, who assumed at once that it was in some way Hartz's work and regarded it as a masterstroke. It left no time for Rhys's followers to regroup before the election of a new OAA president and gave free rein to Hartz to put into effect immediately the next building blocks of his strategy.

What these were, even the inner caucus did not know – and they did not need to know. Within the next thirty-six hours the last seven months of careful, behind-the-scenes preparations would culminate in the successful election of a new president of the OAA and a very clear public act of intent that would signal to OAA members nationwide that the organization was back in business very seriously indeed.

*   *   *

Krol knew his way round the back corridors of the Masonic Temple and passed no one as he made his way to the room where he was meeting Paul Hartz.

Their subject was Rhys and that did not take long; just a matter of loose ends.

'There will be no connection made with the OAA.'

'Good.'

'I must tell you what no one else knows – I am leaving Chicago on Friday. For good. I shall be in New York.'

Hartz looked surprised.

'I thought you were Chicagoan these days. How many decades is it?'

'Two.'

'Makes you a native in this city.'

Krol smiled slightly.

'Another thing. I do not like chasing after young women, Mr Hartz. I mean the Zemeckis girl.'

Hartz sighed.

'It is a mess. Dr Eels made a serious error.'

'Why not leave the young lady in peace? Escaping from Dunning is an act of sanity.'

Hartz shrugged and looked weary.

'There are things about Zemeckis you do not need to know – as you yourself would put it. Those documents can harm us.'

'I will find her but not harm her; that is what I have said.'

Hartz nodded.

'Why New York?'

'I like the anonymity a big city gives.'

'Chicago is big, Mr Krol.'

Dodek shifted his massive frame in his chair.

'Not big enough,' he said.

'Is there any other outstanding matter we should discuss?'

Krol said nothing. There were plenty of outstanding matters, but none he wished to trouble Mr Hartz about.

The meeting was over. Both men had much to do.

Krol stood up and reached out a hand to shake Hartz's as he too rose from his chair.

'It was a pleasure meeting you, a pleasure doing business with you,' said Krol, keeping hold of Hartz's hand. 'Thank you.'

Such a moment of uncharacteristic social grace from the big man puzzled Hartz.

'Goodbye, Mr Hartz,' said Krol with some regret, for he was an intelligent man and in Hartz he recognized someone, in essence, very like himself.

'Goodbye, Mr Krol,' murmured Hartz aloud after the Pole had closed the door and his footsteps receded down the corridor. He pondered the handshake and the nature of the goodbye but finally shook his head, his puzzlement seeming misplaced. The man was a Pole. They did things differently, didn't they?

Back in the street, Krol's cab was waiting for him, with two Meisters standing alongside it.

Krol did not like sidewalk conferences; he climbed into the carriage and leaned forward as the two men came to the window to confer with him.

'You have found her?' he asked in a low voice.

'She was hired this morning.'

'Where?'

'Garment factory called E. K. M. Halsted and Cornell.'

'Don't know it.'

His men screwed up their noses. 'Goose Island,' one of them said.

'Who's the informant?'

'Reliable.'

Krol thought a moment more.

'We need her alive.'

'Alive and kicking,' said one of the men with a grim smile.

'You both go. When you have her . . .'

'We know what to do.'

They looked at their pocket watches and agreed a time.

'Good.'

Krol dismissed them with a nod. As his carriage set off south he kept his head down, eyeing the street on either side. He saw no one and noticed nothing unusual, just plenty that was familiar, not least the familiar sight of Sol Bann's saloon, an institution in this part of

380

Chicago. Krol eyed the faces in its windows without much interest: the usual riff-raff, he guessed, none looking his way. His cab passed on by. Sol Bann's place had no further interest for him: he was not a drinking man.

A few seconds later, Gerald Toulson emerged from Sol Bann's onto State. He looked north after Krol's two men and south after Krol himself, then hailed a cab and instructed it to follow Krol's.

'Where we goin', sir?'

'No idea,' growled Toulson.

64

Beasts of the Field

Emily arrived at the Agricultural Building of the World's Fair out at Jackson Park just in time to examine the audience before the lights went down.

There seemed to be a preponderance of women, many of them quite young and certainly unmarried, most of whom sat in the front rows. They were well dressed for the occasion, some coquettishly so. Fay Bancroft had said that was normally the way when Gunther Darke gave his demonstrations.

Further back, the auditorium was filled with row upon row of older gentlemen and a smattering of younger ones, the majority dressed in sober suits, wearing pocket watches and gold chains, dark cravats and neatly trimmed beards and mustachios.

'There must be a Republican convention on,' Emily's neighbor whispered with a smile.

As the lights dimmed to darkness, the chatter of the young women at the front gave the occasion an atmosphere of barely restrained excitement.

Emily's seat was a good one, a little to one side of center but no more than fifteen or twenty yards from the stage itself, whose layout was extremely unusual, though she had had only the briefest glimpse

of it before the curtains were drawn shut, leaving just a raised dais
with lectern to the right-hand side, not unlike the pulpit from which
a sermon is delivered in a church.

What she had seen before the curtain closed was a stage set low
with rows of tables on it, which reminded her of images she had seen
of the medical school theaters where anatomical dissections took place.

Suddenly, a spotlight illuminated not just the lectern but the left-
hand side of the stage, where a man, who appeared to be the master
of ceremonies, appeared.

As he did so, Emily noticed how a screen dropped down silently
center-stage and hung suspended before the audience, while in the
unlit obscurity of the other side of the stage, the speaker took his place
at the lectern.

'Ladies and gentlemen,' began the MC, a large, florid man with an
easy and well-practiced stage presence, 'you are here at the invitation
of Darke Hartz and Company and you are welcome. On this occasion we extend a very special welcome to those young ladies seated at
the front who are visiting on behalf of various ladies' colleges in the
State of Illinois, as well as to the large number of our audience who
are here in Chicago for the Annual Convention of the Old America
Association. Ladies, welcome! Gentlemen, give 'em an OAA round of
applause!'

This got things going as the girls squealed and chattered and the
men clapped and gave a few appreciative shouts.

'Now,' continued the MC, 'in a moment I will introduce your
lecturer but, before I do so, may I say that since this lecture concludes
with a live demonstration of the skill of dressing meat by master
butchers, there will inevitably be a certain amount of ... unpre-
dictability.

'The animals to be dressed will have been brought, freshly slaughtered, from the stockyard while our esteemed lecturer speaks, in order
that the meat may be the freshest possible! The master butchers of
Darke Hartz and Company will keep on-stage noise to the minimum
before the curtains part and they begin demonstrating their skills.

'Meanwhile, may I very earnestly request that if any here are upset
by the sight of blood, then they should leave now.'

He stood, smiling and expectant.

No one moved. Indeed, the air of expectation grew even more excited and intense.

'Ladies and gentlemen, in this, his final appearance giving what has proved to be one of the most popular talks in the extensive program of educational lectures at the World's Columbian Exposition, please welcome a director of Darke Hartz and Company, present convener of the Guild of Master Butchers of America and a recent past world champion master butcher – Mr Gunther S. Darke!'

The clapping began at once and the spotlight moved from the MC, who retreated offstage, to the lectern to the right. To Emily's astonishment, the noise grew into something beyond clapping as the audience, and in particular the young women, greeted Gunther with cheers and shouts of the kind normally preserved for conductors of great orchestras and their soloists, or popular artists in vaudeville.

So enthusiastic was the reception that Emily found herself carried forward by the curious excitement of the event and joined in the clapping as well.

At first, the only thing that could be seen of Gunther Darke himself was his hands, which grasped the oak sides of the lectern on which his notes lay. Somewhere above, out of the direct glare of the spotlight and therefore only dimly visible, loomed the powerful head and shoulders of the man himself.

He raised his hands momentarily to indicate to the audience that he intended to begin. It fell silent at once. As he did so Emily saw, with an unexpected thrill, that the tops of two fingers of Gunther's left hand were missing.

Butchery, it seemed, was a dangerous trade.

As Gunther leaned forward to glance at his notes, Emily had a glimpse of a strong nose and chin. Then he pulled back into the darkness once more and began to speak.

'America is a great, pure country in which the beasts of the field . . .'

His voice was more deep and gravelly than she remembered, like a rough wind in the dead of night.

'. . . the beasts of the field . . .'

The auditorium was filled with sudden, nearly dazzling, light, as a shutter was opened in the lantern projector behind the audience and the first slide was projected onto the screen.

It was a magnificent view of the wide open prairie, its grass limit-less, the sky above vast, and great herds of cattle stretching as far as the eye could see.

The slide had been hand-colored, and superbly so.

Indeed, the image was so arresting, so inspiring, that as Gunther Darke continued there was sporadic clapping and someone shouted, 'God Bless America!'

'. . . in which the beasts of the field, I say, and the hard work of America's finest men in taming them and bringing them to market have, in a short space of time, created the greatest meatpacking industry in the world. Men like Mr Joseph McCoy who founded the city of Abilene in Kansas as one of the first great American cow towns, a railroad shipping depot for longhorns from Texas to our stock yards. Men such as he have been inspirational in our work here in the Mid-West. In this great city. In Chicago!'

His voice became more than arresting, it became masterful. The audience, and Emily too, seemed to want to shrink back from its chal-lenging strength and potency while at the same time surge forward and submit to its allure.

Emily sat breathless and mesmerized. Never in her life had she seen or heard anything like it. She had come as a journalist but she leaned forward now and listened as just another member of the audience – and as a woman.

'But greatness is not achieved without difficulty, without trial, without discipline,' continued Gunther Darke, more quietly, '. . . and most certainly not without great cost.'

A new slide appeared, then another and another, each telling a story of hardship and sacrifice across the frontier, of settlers harvesting their crops on hard-won land, of cattle dying and of men dying too in their efforts to keep their livestock healthy and productive . . .

Images too of steers and of hogs, of homegrown back-yard slaugh-terhouses and then of the larger meat enterprises of cities like Cincin-nati, as the rail freight business that carried prime American meat from city to city became ever-more efficient and reliable.

Throughout this dramatic tale of American hard work and enter-prise, Gunther's voice rose and fell, grew sometimes harsh, sometimes soft, as he took his audience on a journey through history and across

America that culminated finally in Chicago itself, rising out of the ashes of the Great Fire of 1871 to supplant Cincinnati as the Porkopolis of a newer, bolder and more modern America – and of the world.

Only rarely did any feature of Gunther Darke's face become visible, and then only briefly: a flick of his dark hair, his chin, nose, a cheek, and just once or twice a shadowed, staring eye. But always, no matter how fleeting, there was a sense of strength of mind reflected in his silhouette.

The slide-show turned finally to the work of Darke Hartz & Company itself in the present day, and its efficient slaughtering and meat-production process.

The MC had warned that real blood would be spilt, but for now it was all images that left everything to the audience's imagination. Then, suddenly, from outside the auditorium came the squeal of animals. For a moment, Emily and many in the audience were alarmed. But no, they were not being slaughtered, just being moved among the nearby stock pens.

Somewhat shaken, the audience focused on the presentation once more. But soon their senses were to be shaken even more, Emily's included.

Colored slide followed slide as the audience was exposed to the grisly apparatus of killing at Darke Hartz & Company and the vast vertical wheel made of wood and steel that hoisted the struggling, squealing hog off its feet and up into the air where, helpless, its throat fatally exposed, it was stuck with a knife and began to bleed to death.

The slides continued and the sense of discomfort among the audience became palpable, as it was exposed to scenes of butchers dropping the slaughtered hogs into a vat of scalding water to soften their bristles, before the carcasses were pulled onto metal rollers and passed through a de-bristling machine, finally to emerge on the other side, shiny white and pink and ready for dressing. Here the butchers took over and the slides showed how the hog was expertly split and dressed, with a stabbing and cutting of flashing knives, into cuts of meat ready for retail.

Throughout this slide-show Gunther Darke stood impassive and unsmiling, better lit now, his black, glittering eyes transfixing his audience, his hands, with their missing finger tops, steady as a rock.

'Butchery,' he continued, 'is one of man the carnivore's oldest skills, because it has grown out of his most basic instinct: survival. We kill to eat; we eat to live; we live to kill once more . . .'

He allowed himself a sudden brief smile before, the muscles of his jaw clenching momentarily, he turned towards the curtains and nodded his head.

It seemed to Emily, as the screen was elevated out of sight and the curtains began to open, that what happened next happened outside of herself, outside of her own body and her own natural instincts.

She felt something disturbing and, though she had no wish to put a name to it, she felt forced to do so.

The feeling that overtook her was as raw and nearly uncontrollable as it was utterly unexpected.

She felt desire.

As she stared at Gunther Darke and his eyes and full mouth, the sensuous form of his body, the overwhelming strength of his gaze, the power even of his silence, she tried but could not stop herself remembering the images Toulson had shown her earlier that morning.

Somewhere among the female audience in the seats in front of her a girl sighed despite herself and a woman gasped aloud, carried forward by the same impulsive emotions as Emily's. She was brought back to reality and a sudden stark and terrible realization. She now knew for certain what it was that Anna Zemeckis, so young and inexperienced, had felt when she had sat in this same auditorium and seen this same presentation. She had been confronted by the raw life and energy and the masterful brutality that was Gunther Darke and the bloody industry of which he was both a disciple and lord.

The curtain opened, lit by a new spotlight, and there, just beyond the tables, hung the newly slaughtered, skinned carcasses of a steer and a hog.

They swung very slightly, the throats of both cut and gaping, as the audience, men included, gasped. The last drops of their life blood dripped lightly onto the sawdust below.

As the audience took in this extraordinary sight, there emerged from the darkness of the back of the stage, like a small disciplined army, ten men, carrying between them a selection of knives, choppers, saws and billhooks.

387

Gunther Darke introduced them as Darke Hartz's leading master butchers, who would give a demonstration of the art and science of dressing meat. In other words, they would demonstrate the rapid and efficient reduction of the carcasses of a steer and a hog into cuts and joints ready for the market and the consumer.

The men were dressed in sleeveless undershirts, which exposed their muscular shoulders, arms and hands, dark pants and heavy boots – 'studded, you will observe, to stop them slipping on the blood,' explained Gunther Darke – and long, so-far spotless aprons.

They stood like soldiers with weapons at the ready, awaiting the order from their commanding officer to go into battle.

'Normally,' said Gunther, 'it would take longer to dress a steer than a hog but, at the men's specific request, I have assigned the fastest and most experienced butchers to the steer and those with less experience to the hog to see if the former can still keep pace with the latter. Chicago has been built on healthy competition, which roots out the weak and allows the fittest to survive. We of the meatpacking industry, especially at Darke Hartz and Company, pride ourselves on our winning streak, don't we, men?'

The butchers uttered a strange guttural collective grunt, their boots grinding on the boards of the stage, their knives and choppers glinting.

'So . . . let us see which team wins! And ladies and gentlemen, don't blink or you'll miss the action.'

The two teams of men immediately went to work on the carcasses in the way that predators hunting in packs might descend on a solitary prey.

In moments, as it seemed to Emily, the carcasses were opened up, eviscerated, split down the spines, with short and long sweeps of the knives, with rapid application of the saws. With strokes of chopper and billhook, and quick thrusts and cuts of the knife, as the men moved rhythmically, almost balletically at their specialist tasks, the sides of meat were rapidly and effortlessly dressed and laid out, as if for market, on the table nearest to the audience.

Throughout the demonstration, Darke maintained his commentary, explaining a cut here, a process there and making the general point, in the case of the hog especially, that his company found an economic use for every part of the animal except the squeal.

So far as the team race was concerned – Emily suspected a fix – they finished together and to tumultuous applause.

Gunther Darke now drew his lecture to a close: 'Ladies and gentlemen, in state after state, right across our great land, Americans have worked to produce blood lines of cattle and hogs that are perfect and pure. How have we done it? By rooting out all that is weak and deficient, by preventing the corruption and disease that can so rapidly destroy livestock just as it can destroy people. This is an achievement of which Americans should be rightly proud.

'At the same time there is little doubt that breeding like with like, strong with strong, produces something better still; and cross-breeding those that offer complementary strengths produces something better still again!

'This is why those like myself, who have lived and breathed good stock and good breeding for generations, feel uneasy when we see our liberal politicians continuing to permit aliens into this land, carriers of disease, of poor breeding, of weak blood, of the kind a good stockman would eliminate at source from a herd!

'And that, my friends, is a battle that we members of the Old America Association must, and intend to, fight as hard and as determinedly as we can!'

Here a number of the men in the audience cheered.

'And so we shall! Meanwhile, out on the ranges and inside our slaughterhouses that battle has long since been won, as I hope I have shown today. Our beef and our pork are the best in the world, from the best pastures, the best cattle and hogs, dressed by the best butchers, sold in the best shops and – if I may say so – eaten by the best customers whether they be the sweet young women I see before me now, or the tougher, older stock sitting at the back!'

The audience clapped and cheered, as Gunther Darke, like a conductor at the end of the performance of a symphony, raised his hands and said, 'Ladies and gentlemen, I give you the art and the science of the most modern industry in the world's most modern city in the greatest country in the world. God Bless America!'

The audience erupted into clapping, stamping and cheering, which continued for quite some time; but Emily was not one of them. As the crowds began to disperse a good many of the eager and impressionable young ladies in the audience had begun congregating at the front, reaching up to Gunther Darke and the other butchers on stage and asking for their autographs on their programs, and in return being given what looked like cards or passes for some other event.

Emily watched it all with some distaste; even Gunther himself was acquiescing to the demands for a signature, his eyes alight with the pleasure of so much female admiration.

'Enough!' he said finally, 'and thank you!' with the confident charm of a seasoned stage performer.

The curtain finally went down, the master of ceremonies reappeared, and the event was over.

'What were those cards?' Emily asked of a fellow member of the audience.

'Passes, nearly impossible to get hold of otherwise.'

'Passes for what?'

'A special visit to the premises of Darke Hartz and Company in the stock yard. Best advertising trick pulled by anyone at the World's Fair. Make something seem desirable, make it seem scarce and then make it available, but only to a chosen few. But that's Chicago, boostering all the way!'

'And those girls,' said Emily, who was quite sure that Anna had once been one of them, 'they're allowed to go alone?'

'They go in small tour groups of a dozen or so at a time. But about *that* the least said the better!'

Emily exited with the crowd, but by now her thoughts had returned to Anna Zemeckis. She had absolutely no doubt of the circumstances that had led to Anna obtaining a ticket to visit the Union Stock Yard. She'd mentioned the forthcoming visit in her letters home, but had been strangely silent on the subject thereafter.

But what impression a tour of the Union Stock Yard might have left on an innocent young girl such as Anna, she dreaded to think.

The phrase 'a lamb to the slaughter' came to mind, but it was something she did not like to dwell on.

65

Out of Time

Anna had decided that if anyone at E. K. M. was going play the part of snitcher and tell Agda Akesson it would be herself.

Her scheme was simple and maybe it was clever too. She would approach Agda and tell her that she 'might' have seen the 'Latvian girl' at her previous place of employment. She hoped that way to draw attention away from herself and buy herself at least the rest of the day while she finished her work and earned the rest of the money she needed for the rail fare to St Paul. By the time they caught up with her again, she hoped, she would be long gone – not only out of E. K. M. & Co.'s establishment but from Chicago as well.

But it was not to be.

Before she was able to put her plan into effect, one of the other girls at their table stole a march on her.

She got up with her work and took it to the steam irons. She spoke to someone there, and someone spoke to someone else and, soon after that, that someone spoke to Agda Akesson.

Anna had her head down over her work and didn't notice a thing as the Scandinavian listened to what she was told and then glanced across the room towards Anna.

'Which one?' asked Groats the moment Agda told him her suspicions.

'The older one you took on this morning. Dark hair. *Says* she's from Romania.'

'That's not much. What else?'

'Says she's with child.'

Groats's eyebrows went up in surprise.

'You sure?'

'They said she said.'

It was unfortunate that that was the moment Anna chose to go back over to the ironing table. Her bump was indeed beginning to show.

'Looks fat for a starving girl, don't she?' said Agda.

'She does,' agreed Groats.

They talked about what to do. A call from Mr Krol's Meisters was not something you ever ignored. Not ever.

'She's a good worker. Don't want to lose her,' said Groats reluctantly.

'You'll lose your life if they find out you've got her and didn't say.'

Groats sighed and said wearily, 'Look sharp then, if you must! Off you go and tell 'em. I guess they'll have to come here and get her. Tell 'em to do it quick and quiet.'

Agda Akesson, who made a habit of snitching and spying and betraying others, disappeared from the floor and out onto the street.

She knew exactly where to go and whom to tell.

Moments later, when Anna saw Agda was not there, she felt a jolt of alarm and her stomach started churning. She waited a minute or two, hoping she had gone somewhere else on the floor or was in the water closet. When she did not return to her place, Anna began to feel sick with apprehension.

She knew that if she had been snitched on she had little time. These were not the kind of girls to let her leave the building easily if there was a price on her head. If she could have waited until the lunch break it would have been easier, but she had no time for that. The best thing was to do it so fast and so quietly that no one would guess she was leaving until after she was out of the door. After that she would just run.

She got up muttering something meaningless to indicate irritation that she had to get up at all, walked in the opposite direction away from Groats, then, head up, as though she were going to consult someone across the room about her work, she walked calmly to the door and the elevator shaft.

She heard someone say, 'Where's she . . . ?'

Then a mild shout after her, 'Hey, you . . . !'

Then she was running down the stairs two at a time. Halfway down she saw Agda Akesson coming back up in the elevator.

'You!' she heard her call out.

But Anna was already a floor below, and after that she was right outside on the street.

She hurried to Halsted, taking a couple of turns north and then west to put them off the scent.

But it didn't work. When she looked back again, a tall man dressed in black was hurrying after her. She turned and started running once more, her mind racing and desperate.

Where was there left to go? Who to turn to?

'J. O. E.,' she panted, speaking out each letter in turn with the very greatest reluctance. John Olsen English was the last man in the world she would have wished to go to for help, the *very* last. But she had no more options.

For the sake of the child she carried she would swallow her remaining pride and go and ask him to loan her some money.

She was out of time and had nowhere else to turn. She went round another corner and headed back downtown.

66

Moths

The Chicago Public Library's extensive collection of books and journals had been divided among several temporary buildings downtown while a fine new Beaux Arts building was being built on Michigan Boulevard to house its permanent collection.

The building Anna Zemeckis headed for after shaking off her pursuer on Goose Island was on Haddock near 5th. She approached it with considerable trepidation.

The man she was going to see, good and honest though he was, had no reason to help her – in fact he had every reason to hate and despise her. She knew that her past behavior had caused him more emotional anguish than anyone probably ever had before. Now, more than likely, she was going to cause him a whole lot more.

Since his friend Anna Zemeckis's disappearance, the library, which had always been John Olsen English's outlet and refuge, had become ever more the repository of all his thwarted and generally unspoken dreams. Under deputy librarian Mr Albert D. McIlvanie's benign interest and tutelage he had clearly become one of the library's brightest hopes. McIlvanie respected his junior as a fair man, and as someone who he knew had one of the sharpest minds and the best of memories for anything to do with books among all his staff.

Indeed, if it hadn't been for English's timidity and his constant need to attend to his malign and demanding mother, Mr McIlvanie would have seen him as a potential successor.

'But there are some things, my dear, about which I can do nothing,' the deputy librarian had confided to his wife, 'and one of them is instilling the courage and strength needed by a young man like Mr English if he is to escape from the shadow of his mother.'

Mrs McIlvanie agreed. She had no time for the self-serving Mrs English. She knew all about how she played upon her only son's natural good nature and made a mouse of him – or so it seemed.

'What he needs is a girl warm enough to break through that wall of shyness, and spirited enough to stand up to his mother!' she observed.

'Some hope!' had been her husband's reply.

But miracles happen because, one day in May, Anna Zemeckis had walked through the library door and almost overnight had changed John Olsen English's life.

To both the McIlvanies' astonishment, she had seemed somehow to break through John's natural reserve; even his embarrassing stutter nearly disappeared in her company. The two plainly liked each other and even, Mr McIlvanie observed, sat together at the library's Lakeshore outing on the Fourth of July, looking like turtle doves.

But a week or so later something had gone wrong – something worse than a lover's tiff. Mr English had become visibly upset, and Miss Zemeckis clearly distressed. But neither, however much encouraged to do so, would talk of it. That is, until the sense of awkwardness between them at work had become so apparent that Mr McIlvanie had steeled himself to talk to them more formally. But then, absolutely out of the blue and before he had time to do so, Anna Zemeckis had suddenly disappeared.

'There's another man involved in this, Mr McIlvanie,' declared his wife firmly, 'you mark my words! She's run off with someone!'

But it was worse.

Mr McIlvanie was visited in early October by Mr Janis Zemeckis, the missing girl's father, all the way from New York. No interview had ever caused the librarian more pain or more difficulty. Mr Zemeckis was visibly suffering the most terrible agony of spirit; and Mr McIlvanie had been in a dilemma about how much he should say to him about

John Olsen English. Anna's father was the strict kind who regarded all men as predatory where his daughter was concerned. He did not think his stuttering deputy would get very far if he met the father – and in any case McIlvanie had interviewed English himself and was certain that he knew no more about Anna's disappearance than anyone else.

He therefore said nothing to either man about the other.

This decision seemed justified just over a week later, in mid-October, when the *Tribune* announced the death of Anna Zemeckis in a streetcar accident.

'Terrible, so terrible,' said Mr McIlvanie when he showed the sad little paragraph to his wife. 'So young.'

'There's more to this than meets the eye,' she replied rather more robustly, 'and it is my opinion that we have not heard the last of it.'

And indeed she was right, for just after midday on Friday October 27, Anna Zemeckis was heading for the only place remaining where she might find help.

The library where she had worked with John English was not far from the South Water Street fruit and vegetable market, which meant that her grubby dress and lank, untidy hair, screwed up into a sorry-looking knot, went unnoticed. There were many other bedraggled people loitering about the street, along with a multitude of street urchins, all rooting for the free pickings of bruised and damaged fruit between the stalls, around the boxes of produce, and among the piles of garbage that littered every corner.

Indeed, Anna herself had earlier spotted a half-eaten apple, scooped it off the sidewalk before a couple of squabbling boys got there first, and gobbled it down as she continued walking.

Her apprehension as she reached the library was heightened by the fact that this particular building had until recently been a garment factory. It still had the name 'Walter Harris & Co., Fine Ladies' Cloaks' above the front entrance. Having now had to beat a hasty retreat from two such premises in the last few days, Anna felt she was tempting fate by entering a third.

The notice by the door which read *CHICAGO PUBLIC LIBRARY Temporary Building No. 2, Main Collection* was small comfort. She paused suddenly and pulled into a doorway. Although she was sure she had shaken off anyone in pursuit of her, she was less certain whether those who were after her knew of her former job at the library, a place to which she might just possibly return.

She eyed the building, the busy sidewalks nearby and the streets crowded with traffic and realized that if anyone was tailing her she was unlikely to see them. She must take her chance and go on up the entrance steps, which she did the moment they were busy with people.

Had Anna realized just how dirty, tired and ill she looked she would have worried less about being recognized at the library where, until recently, she had worked part-time.

But she did worry, as she made her way to the main enquiries desk, her head down and pulling her shawl up over it.

'Yes, miss?'

There were three people working there, a man and two women, and Anna was lucky enough to have attracted the attention of the man because the women were busy with marking up new books. She knew him vaguely – he had arrived only a few days before she departed and she hoped he would not remember her.

She knew she would not be turned away because of her poor dress and appearance. Staff were expressly told to admit anyone who came, unless they were visibly the worse for drink or in some other way a likely cause of trouble.

'This is a public library and we do not reject people because of the way they look,' were the instructions given out by Mr McIlvanie himself.

'Can I help you, miss?'

'I would like to speak with Mr English.'

'Mr English?'

Anna detected surprise in the question but she was ready for that.

'It's personal; a matter of great importance.'

The clerk exchanged a brief glance with one of his female colleagues.

Then he said, as Anna knew he would, 'Mr English, like the other librarians, does not receive personal callers during library hours.'

'Although it *is* a personal matter, I am not a personal caller. His mother has been taken ill.'

There was a very slight titter between the two women behind the desk. The male clerk frowned at them and turned back to Anna.

'I'm afraid Mr McIlvanie has given strict instructions. You see . . .
Mr English's mother has, well . . .' He was searching for a polite way
of saying that the demands of the hypochondriac Mrs English were
a nuisance the library had long since learned to deal with.

Anna knew that too.

'. . . How shall I put it, miss, she has been ill rather too often before.'

'She's dying,' blurted out Anna.

'She's done that before, too,' the librarian said discreetly, drawing
Anna to one side as two people approached the desk with books. 'I'm
sorry, but Mr McIlvanie's instructions are very clear about Mr English's
mother.'

Anna looked up at him, unsure now what to say. Had she felt better
and been more smartly dressed she might have gone over to the shelves
to browse some books and from there tried to make her way without
being seen to the office of the man whose help she so desperately
needed. But she knew that it would be difficult and would cause him
acute embarrassment.

Perhaps her doubt and uncertainty showed on her face; certainly
her abject misery did.

'I . . . *please* . . . ,' she said suddenly, 'I do need to see him most
urgently.'

The librarian was taken aback by such a direct appeal. This young
woman was clearly not a troublemaker even though her appearance
was decidedly bedraggled. But there was something about her that he
distantly recognized.

'Why?' he said suddenly and impulsively. 'What are you to him?'

'Nothing,' said Anna, 'I am nothing . . . nothing at all.'

She felt weak and hopeless and in despair. Her strength had all run
out. She turned away, trying to steady her growing dizziness from
fatigue and hunger, knowing that once she went back through the door
to the world outside she had no one left to turn to.

'I am nothing,' she said again softly, no longer able to find the words
to explain herself, and began walking towards the door.

She had barely gone more than a step or two before the desk clerk
took pity on her.

'Miss . . . *miss* . . .'

She turned back.

'Miss, I think, knowing Mr English as I do he would be upset for you to be turned away. I really do. You had better sit out there in the hallway in case you are seen. I will get Mr English myself. Can I give him a name?'

'Jelena,' whispered Anna.

'And a surname?'

'. . . Jansons,' she said, frantically hoping John Olsen English would remember how often she had talked of going to Canada to live on her aunt Inga's farm. 'Please, I do not want to cause him trouble. I'd better go . . .'

'Sit over there,' said the clerk firmly but kindly. 'I will give him your name and let him decide. It is the best I can do. Meanwhile, if a tall gentleman with a beard and white hair should come stalking about then you're to say you're on your way out and were simply taking a rest. Yes?'

Anna nodded.

She didn't need the clerk to tell her who this was. Everyone knew Mr McIlvanie.

She went out to the hallway to which the clerk had pointed and sat on a bench as unobtrusively as she could. The floor she stared at in her misery was a striking contrast to the filthy one in the garment factory at Goose Island: it was brushed clean and polished to a fault, just as Mr McIlvanie liked it.

But in one corner, beneath the high, narrow window against which no doubt it had been beating its wings all day until it grew too weak to fly anymore, lay a moth, on its back and fluttering only weakly now as if, having failed to find its way to freedom, it was now ready, finally, to give up on life.

Anna stared at it and saw herself.

Meanwhile, in his upstairs office, John Olsen English sat lonely and still grieving. He looked terrible. His face was gray, his eyes dark and blank, his posture listless. He wore a black armband and moved at his tasks slowly, a man in a nightmare of confusion and loss.

The disappearance of his would-be sweetheart was one thing; her death another. If only he had known why any of it had happened he might have been able to come to terms with his troubled relationship with Anna. Her sudden death had given him the opportunity to do neither.

Until very recently that is.

Light, terrible and cruel, had begun to dawn, and it had happened as a result of one of Mrs McIlvanie's typically brisk, no-nonsense observations. Could Miss Zemeckis, she ventured to her husband at home one evening, could she just possibly have been 'in some kind of . . . trouble'? Woman's trouble, that is. And of the worst kind?

It was a version of this remark, turned into a question, and overladen with a certain diplomatic ambiguity on the part of Mr McIlvanie, that had alerted John English to a grotesque possibility.

The implication, when it finally got through to him, not only shocked him, it galvanized him into doing what he did best: think hard and seek order out of chaos.

He went back over his many conversations with Anna and remembered something he had paid no heed to at the time: a much-vaunted visit she had made in mid-June to the Union Stock Yard, to the killing floor of one of the big meatpackers.

What had been puzzling was that afterwards the normally talkative Anna had said nothing about the visit, and had got quite angry when he had innocently asked about it. From then on her inexplicable moods and the alienation between them had accelerated.

John English considered the problem as objectively as he could and came to the conclusion that something had happened during that visit, something terrible, and that as a direct result Anna was in serious trouble.

He also tortured himself with the thought that he had not been good friend enough or wise enough to know how to get her to talk in time to save her from whatever had afterwards led to her death.

He was cataloging some books when his colleague from the enquiries desk knocked at his door.

'Mr English, a word in private please,' the new man whispered discreetly, hovering at the door.

'P . . . pardon me?' said John, looking up from his work.

'I did not wish to draw your colleagues' attention to the fact, but . . . there is a young woman to see you. In the lobby.'

'I believe that M . . . Mr McIlvanie has made it q . . . q . . . quite plain that I am n . . . n . . . not to see anyone bringing messages from my m . . . m . . . m . . . mother.'

'I believe the young lady is here on her own account.'

'I do n . . . not know any young ladies.'

'She says her name is Jelena . . . Jelena Jansons.'

John Olsen English's eyes widened and he stopped what he was doing.

'P . . . pardon me?' he said again, his mind racing and grappling with that name. He recognized it at once, the surname that is. But the given name, Jelena, why, that was . . .

The clerk said again, 'Miss Jelena Jansons.'

'I . . . d . . . do not understand.'

'She is sitting in the front hall, hopefully out of sight of Mr McIlvanie . . .'

'I'd b . . . b . . . better come.'

'Yes,' said the librarian.

'I'd b . . . better c . . . come right now,' John said again, more calmly now because he realized that this must be one of Anna's Canadian relatives. Perhaps Anna had mentioned his name to her aunt Inga in one of her letters. She had often read him her aunt's letters, full as they were with descriptions of farming life in Manitoba of the kind after which they both hankered.

John Olsen English entered the hallway and saw the bedraggled woman sitting on the bench, her head down, as though she were looking at something on the floor.

'M . . . M . . . Mrs Jelena . . . Jansons? I'm sorry, perhaps it's M . . . M . . . Miss?'

Anna turned her face to him: 'It's Anna, it's me, *Anna.*'

John stared at her open-mouthed, his already pale face growing paler still.

He could hardly breathe.

It was not her form he recognized, for that was utterly changed – and shockingly so – it was her voice and her eyes.

'John,' she said, 'I need your help.'

If she had ever doubted what kind of man John Olsen English was, the expressions that passed now so rapidly across his face – of surprise, recognition, shock, relief; indescribable relief – left Anna in no doubt at all. It was as though, without question, he instinctively knew and understood everything.

Which was indeed true. For he gazed at her with such compassion and surely saw at once the nature of the 'trouble' she was in.

His face showed no anger towards her at all, but alarm and a sudden, overwhelming protectiveness.

Then, for the first time, Anna saw a look on his face that she had never seen before: a look of utter rage on her behalf and of near-murderous intent.

'Anna,' he said, his voice as terrible as sharpened steel, 'who has done this to you?' Suddenly, miraculously, the stutter had gone, as it always did when he was in her company.

He sat down, took her in his arms and held her tight and cared not at all if anyone saw or what anyone might think. She was alive, and safe and here now with him.

'Tell me . . . please tell me, who has done this to you?'

'We can't stay here,' was her only reply as she broke free of him. 'We mustn't stay. I might be found.'

'Anna . . .'

'Please. I don't want to cause you any problems. I just need some help, a loan of a dollar or so, and then I'll never trouble you again. But we mustn't stay here.'

'Never trouble me again!' He laughed almost manically.

'*Never trouble me again!*'

'Please . . .' she said, pulling at his arm.

He saw then that she was utterly terrified.

'We shall find somewhere safe nearby and I will explain . . .'

Whatever library rules John broke he didn't care at all. He got up and followed Anna and the next time the clerk who had first summoned him looked their way he saw no one at all: just a swinging door to the outside world.

67

Positives

Emily caught up with Ben Latham in the Electricity Building shortly after Gunther Darke's lecture ended. It was quarter to one and she had fifteen minutes before she was due to meet Marion Stoiber on the far side of Jackson Park.

Ben had promised to meet Emily by the General Electric Company's distinctive Tower of Light, the roof-high display made up of thousands of miniature lamps, which produced a startling kaleidoscope effect that stopped the hundreds of visitors, Emily included, in their tracks.

Surrounded by this and a hundred other revolutionary displays, including those for telegraphy and Thomas Edison's newest invention, the kinetophonograph, he looked less like a man at an exposition and more like a boy in a candy store, spoilt for choice.

'It's really exciting, Emily,' he enthused. 'They run a film inside this cabinet where you watch through a lens at the top and hear music piped simultaneously from a phonograph through an earpiece. It's the future . . .'

'I'm sure it is,' replied Emily firmly, 'but we're not here to look at inventions. What about the negatives?'

'They're amazing. But they're not negatives. They're *positives* now!'

He held up a sheaf of images on photographic paper.

'Here,' he said taking her arm, 'come over behind the Earthquake

Laboratory, it's the only quiet spot in the building!'

It was also a good deal cooler, because in that section the number of electric lights was fewer and a door opened out onto the Lagoon and a view of the Wooded Island.

'We've only got a few minutes before I have to meet Marion Stoiber.'

'That's all it need take,' said Ben, finding a seat for them both. 'Look . . . but be prepared to be shocked.'

He glanced around, made sure they were not overlooked, and handed her the photographs one by one.

'There's eight here,' he said, 'and more on the way. Not easy getting them done given the nature of their content. Did these myself and a friend of mine working at the Eastman Kodak exhibit, which has a darkroom facility – he's reliable, won't tell a soul – is doing the rest right now while everyone else is at lunch. But these tell us enough to be going on with.'

Emily looked at them. Most were cropped at odd angles where the glass plate had been broken. One or two were nearly whole. They showed naked girls in lewd poses, men with the girls in lewder poses still and . . .

Emily did a double take.

'A hog wheel?' she said.

'Yes,' said Ben.

'But . . .'

'It's a slaughterhouse,' said Ben as evenly as he could.

'As a location for pornographic pictures? That's bizarre,' she said again faintly.

'I guess some men like that kind of thing.'

A new and even more horrible thought came to Emily as she remembered the scenes of barely contained excitement – sexual excitement she suspected – among the young women at the butchery demonstration she had just come from.

'Death, sex, blood. I guess some women find that exciting,' she heard herself say.

Ben's eyes widened. It was his turn to be shocked.

They turned back to the image in question.

It showed a group of three men, all only partially clothed, their members erect as they stood in an obviously staged way as if about to penetrate a woman on a butcher's table. She was lying across it in a corset and striped stockings, displaying herself obscenely, as if inviting the men to ravage her. From the knives the men carried, and the white undershirts and pants half-off, she could see they were, or were pretending to be, butchers of the kind she had just been watching.

'So far as I can make out,' said Ben, 'and I'm not an expert on such things, this is one of a sequence. I've two more fragments, both yet to be developed. The men are cutting the girl's undergarments off with their knives as if they were gutting her. If it weren't so ridiculous it might be frightening.'

'It *is* ridiculous,' said Emily.

The photographs were high quality and well lit, even if the subject matter was disgusting and yet . . .

Emily could not help letting her gaze drift back to the men's privates. She had never seen such an image in her life before, let alone the real thing, and was unsure what to say next.

'Take a close look at the background,' said Ben, sensing Emily's embarrassment, 'and at that window especially. These pictures are well made – they use artificial *and* natural light and the depth of focus is good too. What do you see through the window?'

'Um . . .'

She hesitated to look again. But it was unmistakable. In the window frame, rising up into the sky outside was something as close to a representation of a phallus as there ever could be.

'What is it?' asked Emily faintly.

'Good question,' said Ben cheerfully, unaware of the highly confused drift of Emily's thoughts, 'and one I asked my friend not fifteen minutes ago. It's the water tower of the Union Stock Yard. Nothing else in Chicago like it, apparently, except for the water tower that is part of the waterworks on North Michigan.'

'How do you know it's not that one?'

'It's bigger,' said Ben matter-of-factly. 'Much bigger.'

'Really?' said Emily, her eyes wandering over the picture again.

'And these other photographs, they show the tower too. Can't think why the photographer wanted to get it in so much, though I suppose it gives depth. But it also gives the game away. I'll take my camera and my sketchbook and go and look round the stockyard while you have your lunch with Stoiber. I'll see what I can find out.'

'Right, then let's meet up again later, at the hotel,' said Emily getting up from her seat. 'But I've really got to rush. I'm running late.'

'Five?'

'No, later, six.'

'I'll bring the other images and make some sketches of anything interesting I find.'

'Yes, please,' Emily said, perhaps rather too enthusiastically.

She felt herself flush as she went off towards the Woman's Building.

68

Opening

Marion Stoiber arrived for her lunch with Emily ten minutes late, looking anxious and distracted.

'Let's go outside Jackson Park and onto the Midway Plaisance. It's cheaper there and there are plenty of places where we may find refreshment,' she said, but that was only partly true.

The fact that there were only three days before the Fair closed had attracted enormous crowds anxious not to miss the event of a lifetime. Everywhere was full to bursting. The refreshment stands and lunch counters had many people waiting in line; elsewhere, the seating in restaurants was all occupied, with people queuing to grab seats as fast as they were vacated.

It was only when they had gone more than half the length of the Plaisance and past the looming presence of the Ferris Wheel that Emily and Marion found refreshments of a kind in the Chinese Village, where the fortuitous departure of a group of visitors just as they arrived left a table vacant. Tea was on offer and savory noodles and dumplings, but that was about it.

'Do you not have coffee? Or bagels?' demanded Marion irritably, screwing up her nose, the idea of green China tea in little cups not the least bit appealing to her. She was on edge and out of sorts, her eyes flicking here, there and everywhere, as if she were expecting to see someone she recognized whom she did not wish to meet.

'I prefer to talk to you away from the Fair itself,' she explained. 'I've worked here for several months now, and I don't want to be seen talking to a reporter. You know how much people like nosing into others' business, don't you?'

Emily reflected on the fact that it was her *profession* to be nosey about people and things, but on this occasion, her hoped-for source of information being so evidently jumpy, she sipped her China tea in silence, patiently waiting for Stoiber to compose herself. She also tried to put out of her mind the lewd image she had seen of Marion that same morning. It wasn't easy.

When Emily had met her the day before at the WCTU meeting, Marion Stoiber had been dressed smartly but soberly. But now, by the light of day and in the open air she seemed rather less smart: the garish colors of her day dress clashed somewhat and there was, Emily thought, a rather brassy edge to her whole appearance. She looked older, strained even, her face betraying dark circles of tiredness under the eyes and a pinched, pale expression which even the rather indiscreet use of a powder puff and lip rouge could not disguise.

She looked like a woman who had seen too much of the dark side of life and it was now finally catching up with her.

'Well then,' said Marion finally and a little aggressively, having started to pick at a bowl of noodles, 'what more was it you wished to talk to me about?'

'Your friend, Anna, as I explained to you,' said Emily easily, 'and maybe anything else you'd like to tell me about how single women cope with living in a big city such as Chicago. You know . . . the difficulties they face with men.'

'Ha!' expostulated Marion with unmistakable bitterness. 'The only thing you need say on that subject is that women must give and men will take.'

Emily stared at her. She felt suddenly and curiously sympathetic towards this obviously unhappy woman, hard though it was to associate her with the woman she had seen, apparently enjoying herself carnally with a man, in the pornographic photograph earlier that morning. What on earth could have brought Marion Stoiber, Emily wondered, to that dreadful place, a slaughterhouse, and that terrible act of public

408

wantonness? However, right now she had to find a way of ascertaining whether Stoiber knew that Anna was still alive and, if so, where she was.

'You have a low opinion of men?' Emily ventured quietly.

'Not all men,' said Marion defiantly. 'Some men. A few, yes. Yes I have.'

Emily sipped her tea and said nothing while Marion poked a few more noodles around her bowl, glowering – and brooding, it seemed, on the topic in hand.

'I don't want to talk about *that*,' she said eventually.

Emily nodded empathically.

'Anna found it hard to get out and meet young men, I believe. Her father—'

'Did she?' Marion didn't say more. She picked at her food, eyes not engaging with Emily's. She frowned, she pursed her lips, she sat back trying to relax. She glanced around at the people either side and then behind her.

But there was nothing there, just the great arc of the Ferris Wheel, almost a silhouette against the brightness of the sky, turning slowly, endlessly, going nowhere.

'You must miss her as a friend,' said Emily, struggling to get the conversation moving.

'Must I?'

Emily saw the smallest shadow of hurt. There was heart in this woman somewhere yet. And there was regret and sadness too.

'Yes, I think you must.'

'She was a good, kind girl,' began Marion, 'she . . .'

Her eyes filled with tears and they were genuine.

She doesn't know Anna's alive, Emily told herself.

'It shouldn't have happened to her. For some women it wouldn't have mattered, but for a girl like Anna . . .'

What shouldn't have happened? And which women . . . ?

Emily guessed she didn't mean Anna shouldn't have died, it was about something that had happened before that false news came out. As for *which* women, Marion Stoiber surely meant women like herself, loose women, wanton women, willing women: not women like Anna.

*   *   *

From behind Marion came the sound of laughter and screaming, distant and from on high. It was three girls on the Ferris Wheel, enjoying the feeling of danger that was part of the thrill.

'I never did get to ride it,' said Emily.

'Neither did I . . . Look, there's really nothing I can add to what I said before. This lunch was a mistake. I can't tell you anything.'

Emily refocused, desperate to find an opening before she lost Stoiber's cooperation altogether. She eyed her as a predator eyes a quarry. It's what she had already learnt journalism sometimes had to be. It was why men were meant to be better at it than women. Women did the soft, easy stuff; men did the hard-hitting reporting.

Not any more they don't, Emily resolved, steeling herself for the kill.

'You know Anna's not dead, don't you?'

Marion simply didn't take it in, not at once. Only slowly did what Emily had just said register with her, and when it did her expression was one of utter disbelief.

'I don't think I heard you right.'

Emily repeated it, her voice hardening, 'I said you know Anna's not dead.'

'Of course she's dead, don't be silly. She was identified. She—'

'That wasn't Anna.'

'It must have been, they said . . .'

'Did Anna ever wear earrings? Did she have pierced ears?'

'No, she wouldn't.' Marion instinctively reached up and felt the gaudy earring in her own right ear. 'I tried to get her to have them pierced but she refused. Her father—'

'The woman in the morgue they thought was Anna had pierced ears.'

'She couldn't have.'

'She did . . . What happened to Anna, Marion? You have to tell me.'

'I don't know . . . She can't be alive, I don't know what happened . . .'

Marion Stoiber's voice began to rise towards a wail.

'*What happened?*'

'I don't know, I wasn't there.'

'Where Marion? Where did it happen?'

'I don't know. I . . . I . . .'

Emily watched as Marion visibly regained her composure. She

410

wanted to talk but she was too terrified to do so. That was the truth. That was it.

'Is she really still alive?' asked Marion very quietly.

'She was yesterday, at eight in the evening, because that's when she sent a telegraph to her father from the Union Depot. Whether or not she is now I don't know. But she's in danger, isn't she?'

'Yes,' said Marion.

'Very great danger?'

'They will kill her if they can, or silence her.'

'Who will?'

'I can't tell you that, they . . . they . . .'

The terror had returned and Stoiber looked to the right and left again while the Ferris Wheel loomed above her, turning and turning and making the whole world seem as if it was on the move and the wheel was the only solid thing around.

'*Who?*'

Marion was silent.

'What did you let happen to Anna?'

'It wasn't me, I wasn't there. It wasn't my fault. I thought, I only . . .'

Emily knew she was losing her again and that Stoiber was about to get up and go, to flee from her and from the truth and from the demons of guilt inside herself. She remembered the picture of Marion lying beneath a man. She remembered Ben saying a short while before that it was taken at a slaughterhouse in the stockyards.

She remembered the one thing Anna had never told her father, of all the many things she wrote about in her long and rather dull letters home, had been her special visit to the Union Stock Yard. It was the one thing she had never mentioned.

'It happened at the Union Stock Yard, didn't it?'

Stoiber stared at Emily, terrified.

'You encouraged her to go there deliberately, knowing something would happen, didn't you?'

Marion shook her head desperately.

'No, no, if I'd known, if I'd even thought, but he promised, he promised . . .'

'Who promised?'

'I can't, I can't . . . they will kill me, like . . .'

'Like what, Marion? You owe it to Anna to tell me. Maybe we can still save her life. Who?'

Marion shook her head.

'Then just tell me what happened. You don't have to name names.'

'I . . .'

Emily reached a hand across the table to Marion's.

'Tell me,' she said gently. 'You must. Because it happened to you too, didn't it?'

And Marion Stoiber, head down, nodded.

'Yes,' she whispered.

And she began to talk.

69

Measure of the Man

Once Anna Zemeckis and John English were clear of the Chicago Public Library, Anna muttered wildly that she was being watched — and hurried off down Haddock Street, like a madwoman it seemed, forcing John to run after her.

'We mustn't stop,' she said, 'we mustn't be seen.'

'But Anna . . . *Anna* . . .'

She didn't listen, but headed up into the safety of the crowds at the produce markets along South Water Street and refused to say another word. That John was with her, she was relieved and overjoyed; that he might come to harm as a result only compounded her terror. No wonder Anna almost ran, bumping into people as she went, even causing some to swear and shout after her.

She had no idea exactly where she was going but somewhere in her mind was the memory of that brief and happy break she had had with Eileen down on the South Fork of the river over on the Jackson Street Bridge. She knew that the final stretch of the Chicago River ran somewhere beyond South Water Street, down to the industrial wasteland and garbage heaps by the shores of Lake Michigan, and hoped they might find sanctuary there for a while.

She crossed through the market stalls, dodged a cart or two, then a huge wagon pulled by two great horses, and came to an alley at the end of which rose the masts and rigging of a freight schooner.

'Down here,' she said, hurrying ahead once more.

'*Anna* . . .'

It was not the kind of area John English made a habit of visiting: not that it was especially dangerous or criminal on the surface, but in Chicago one could not be too careful. Fortunately there were folk enough about dressed as poorly as Anna for her not to be noticeable, and men engaged in the maritime and produce trades well dressed enough for John not to look out of place. But if they drew the occasional glance – and once something rather more than that – neither was aware enough to notice it.

'Here,' Anna had said finally, finding a quiet spot where they could sit on two upended barrels in sight of the shipping moored along the banks of the dark and ever-dirty river. On the far bank they could see the new higher buildings of the North Side, fringed as on this side by wharves, ships and barges, the river in the middle being busy with small vessels of one kind and another, most under steam, a few still under sail.

The atmosphere was thick with smoke and a strange, not entirely unpleasant mixture of coal, timber and engine oil. But there was also a more welcoming smell – of cooking – for on a nearby brazier a woman was brewing coffee for the workers along the embankment and next to her a street vendor was selling hot Italian sausages at two cents each.

'I'll take four,' said John English, and then, thrusting them all at Anna, he said, 'Eat first . . . *then* talk.'

Much later, after a nearby church had struck the half-hour, and Anna had hungrily consumed the four sausages, she finally let go.

She had to tell John the one thing she most dreaded.

'John, I'm in trouble, big trouble. I'm—'

'I know, Anna, I know what's wrong . . . I guessed as much,' he interrupted. 'After I thought over what had happened. There was no other logical explanation. But . . . seeing you now . . .'

She looked at him mutely, automatically clutching at her belly.

'My baby . . . I have to protect it, John.'

'Don't worry, Anna, I'll help you,' he said, and there was a smile

414

in his eyes as if her return from the dead enabled him to forgive her for anything.

'But you must tell me everything that has happened to you,' he said, '*everything*, however hard it may be. It won't change anything. I accept you as you are. You know that.'

'But John . . .'

'Just tell me,' he said. 'Tell me.'

And so Anna did, from the beginning to the end, from the moment she met him and felt the same attraction he had, to the terrible course of events that had forced her first to go silent on him, then to tell him much less than the truth and finally had forced her to flee, having been taken into worlds and among people she had had no idea ever existed.

'It was just that once,' she kept repeating, 'and I do not know if it was my fault or not, but I do not think so. I can hardly remember you see. I was—'

'There's no need to speak of that now. But we must go to the police and—'

'No. No. Not the police. You don't understand, John. They don't let anyone stand in their way, they—'

'"They", "they",' repeated John impatiently, 'you keep saying that but you won't tell me who "*they*" are.'

'They call themselves the Meisters. You must have heard of them . . .'

'I know *who* they are,' said John. 'I've read in the *Tribune* about their murderous attacks on people. I know how they terrorize and intimidate with their knives . . .'

'But they do more than that, John,' said Anna. 'They kill them and they cut them and—'

'Anna!'

The alarm and shock in John's eyes mirrored the memory that was all too plainly etched now on her face.

'Anna . . .'

'It's all right, it's over and done with. Now I must think of my child. I cannot go to my father, you know that. I cannot stay a moment longer in Chicago because they are looking for me. My only hope is to get a train north to St Paul and find some kind of job there until

I can save enough money to get to my aunt in Manitoba. All I ask is that you let me have the money to get me out of Illinois . . . I'll pay you back . . .'

But she stopped, eyes widening as something moving along the wharf behind John attracted her attention.

John English, misunderstanding her look, moved closer and began, 'Anna, you have no need to repay me for doing what any friend would, I . . . *what is it?*'

He turned and saw what she saw.

Two men – tall, spare, well built, cleanly and soberly dressed in the kind of long black frockcoats and polished boots usually worn for church on Sunday – had just emerged on the wharf from the direction of South Water Street.

Except it wasn't Sunday and there was no church in sight and the mean, purposeful looks on their faces had nothing of godliness about them. They were standing talking on the wharf and indifferent to the stares their formidable presence attracted until, careless of those nearby, one of them slowly drew a knife.

It was thin-bladed and so well honed to perfect sharpness that the blade was worn fine and concave.

And now they had seen Anna and John and began walking towards them. People nearby, sensing the men's air of menace, retreated into the shadows and round the nearest corners.

Anna's stomach knotted into a hard ball of fear.

John English's likewise.

He pulled her up from the barrel and, if the measure of a man is to think clearly and act coolly when every instinct is to run, then the mother's boy from the Near West Side now, at last, proved himself a man.

He looked to either side of the approaching men and saw there was no possibility of escape back in the direction of South Water Street. Behind him, he had already observed, the wharves widened out to stacks of empty boxes, barrels, capstans and the metal girder bases of derricks, as well as all the other paraphernalia of the river freight trade. The only way to safety lay out there, along the wharf.

'Anna,' he said quietly, not taking his eyes off the men as they came nearer, 'stand up, turn around and run, down the wharf. Just *run.*'

'But . . . you . . . ?'

'I'll follow.'

The men were no more than fifty yards off. Before Anna could protest further, John turned and pushed her hard in the small of her back.

'Run and don't look back. I'll be right behind. Now!'

He pushed and she started running, as though the devil himself was in pursuit of her.

Then John English did the most unlikely thing he had ever done in his life. Single-handed and without a weapon of any kind, he blocked the path of the Meisters now running towards him.

It was then that he discovered that something odd and unexpected happens in a man's mind when he finds himself facing extreme peril: the world slows down and the most trivial-seeming thoughts and feelings intrude.

Because, as a knife was held against his gut, John English remembered that he had failed to do the one thing he should have done – give Anna the money she needed to get safely out of Chicago and on her way to a new life with her aunt in Manitoba.

I should have done that, he told himself as the second man closed in.

70

Ferris

Marion Stoiber's story of what happened to Anna Zemeckis, and her own part in it, began with an account of her early life in Chicago before she met up with Anna in May. It combined self-pity with self-justification in equal measure, but Emily listened politely with occasional nods and murmurs of sympathy.

Marion's family background had been unhappy and she had made some wrong choices, including marrying young to escape a dictatorial father. Her husband had turned out to be a wastrel incapable of holding down a job who had eventually deserted her, leaving her with a pile of debts.

But she had managed to start again by training as a stenographer and working in one of the downtown banks. Discovering she had a flair for administrative work, she had gained a good position with the organizers of the Fair when it was still in its planning stages.

'But to pay off the debts my husband had left me with I had to take extra work . . .'

'What kind of work?'

'Artistic,' said Marion with deliberate ambiguity.

'You mean . . . ?'

'I do not mean what you think I mean. I worked as an artist's model. The practicing members at the Art Institute were always looking for models and they paid well, particularly if you were prepared to pose undraped. I've never been ashamed of my body and having been married, I . . . well, I was not as embarrassed as a younger, unmarried girl might have been. Anyway, it paid well and did not interfere with my other work as I could do it in the evenings and at weekends. It gave me my freedom and enabled me eventually to find a little apartment of my own.

'Naturally some of the artists were more friendly – over-friendly if you like – than others; and equally naturally some of us models found a little flirtation appealing.'

'You didn't mind the work?'

'I enjoyed it,' said Marion frankly. 'After a bad marriage it was flattering that people should want to draw and paint me. Anyway, I needed the money.

'Then, about a year ago, one of the artists asked if I might be interested in some photographic work, at an even better rate of pay, for a photographer he knew in the city center who was looking for high-class models. I went to see him. He was older, more sophisticated. He flattered me and said that very few models were suitable. The work was easy and well paid. At first I posed draped, later not.'

Marion looked at Emily with the same bold frankness as before.

'I do not mind admitting that I enjoyed that too. Of course I had no husband, nor any beau, so I was free to do what I liked. I found it rather exciting to be soberly dressed in the staid world of business during the day and transform myself into something more alluring by night.'

'Did you not ask what the photographs were for?'

'I knew exactly what they were *for*, Miss Strauss. They were *poses plastiques* – for men, men with money.

'But what I did *not* know was that some of the men who made a habit of collecting these kinds of photographs also made a habit of collecting, if they could, the models who posed for them.'

'Collecting?'

'Meeting.'

'*Meeting?*'

Marion stayed silent but so did Emily.

Finally Marion said, 'Well . . . having relations with them.'

419

'And men wanted to meet *you*?'

'Yes. It seemed they found me very . . . provocative. I began to find it exciting. I bought the most alluring undergarments to pose in – oyster silk satin chemises and drawers, fine silk stockings from Paris. The men reportedly liked the photographs and several of them asked to be introduced to me.'

'And you met them, these . . . clients?'

'A few of them.'

'Did they make . . . advances . . . to you?'

'I think you know the answer to that question.'

'And you found that upsetting?'

Marion Stoiber smiled and leaned forward.

'Forgive me, Emily – may I call you Emily? – but only someone who does not know men and who is a little naïve would ask if it was "upsetting". Sexual relations do not have to be unpleasant, you know.'

Emily flushed.

The interview was getting closer to home than she wished. Ever since Gerald Toulson had shown her the file of erotic images and then Ben had developed those from the Robinson studio, she had been unable to get them out of her mind.

Marion was right: Emily knew little about men and had not had relations with one beyond the normal flirtations and occasional kisses of her teenage years. Her mother's generation had liked to pretend that female sexuality did not exist and that if it did and bordered on the pleasurable, then it was a matter of disgust and shame.

As it was, she must now contend with these new and turbulent feelings, and if she did feel a touch of guilt it was because, if she were honest with herself, she wanted Marion Stoiber to tell her more, much more. And if she, the normally cool and clear-headed Emily Strauss found herself wanting to know more, then what kind of effect had this older, sexually knowing woman had on the younger and impressionable Anna Zemeckis?

It had become increasingly apparent to Emily over the last few days that Chicago was full of predators ready to exploit the innocence of the many hundreds of single young women like Anna who had found themselves in the city during this extraordinary year of 1893. But not all these predators, it seemed, were men.

Though whether Mr Pulitzer and his editors will allow me to say as much in my story when I write it I somehow doubt! Emily told herself ruefully.

'Oh dear,' said Marion rather shamelessly, 'have I embarrassed you?'

'No, no,' said Emily hastily, feeling not unlike a maiden aunt. 'I prefer you to be frank . . . What I wanted to ask was whether perhaps you regretted that these activities took you in directions you did not wish to go?'

Marion Stoiber thought for a moment and then finally said, 'All right, that's true. I regret it now. But at the time it was like indulging greedily in a large bowl of ice cream; each mouthful is really good, but finally you end up feeling sick.'

'But you needed the money?'

'I did. Have you any idea how *much* men pay for pictures of women in provocative poses, Emily, and how *many* men do so?'

'It is illegal, is it not?' added Emily, now more serious.

'It *is* illegal to disseminate such material through the US postal system. Mr Comstock saw to that with his law of 1873, but laws never stopped men making money, especially when the profits were so good. What I didn't know was that the images of me proved so popular that they were disseminated all over the United States and, I believe, Europe as well. Had I been a piece of real estate I would have been worth a fortune!'

She said this with a degree of bitterness.

'I was not compensated for anything like my true worth. But I did meet one, special man who gave me something I do not regret having experienced.'

Her expressive face changed again to a curious mix of longing, of loss, of sadness and, Emily was certain, of love as well.

'Sexual relations with the right man are not sinful, you know; or anything to be ashamed of. What I did not know or even imagine until I met this man was that relations with the right one can bring a woman total ecstasy . . .'

'But you won't tell me his name?'

Stoiber shook her head.

'He meant a lot to you, didn't he?'

'Yes. But he destroyed my life. Though I cannot say that I regret meeting him. For a few brief weeks, when I was his and I thought he was mine, I knew a happiness and fulfillment like no other . . .'

Once more Marion was transformed before Emily's eyes as her face softened and she smiled.

'What was so special about him . . . ?'

'You really want to know?'

Emily could see that, with a perverse kind of pleasure, Marion really wanted to tell her.

'Yes,' breathed Emily, her heart beating faster despite her desire to remain objective.

'It wasn't to do with any special quality, like goodness or kindness or good looks even; it was a presence, a power, something utterly overwhelming. I was persuaded to meet him in a private suite at the Chicago Athletic Club, which made it all the more exciting because women are not allowed there. But . . . men like him have power and wealth of the kind that women like us can only dream of.'

'Were you nervous?'

'Yes, but he put me at my ease. His first words to me were, "So, you're the famous Evangeline." I just said, "Pardon me?" I had no idea what he was talking about.

'"That's the name the photographer has given you for the purposes of his excellent work," he explained. "Now, Miss Stoiber – for that's your real name isn't it – I am going to show you what I like in a woman."

'His voice was strong and purposeful and his presence from the first I can only describe as masterful, in ways that women find both alarming but also hard to resist. He made no secret, either by look or word, of his desire for me, and to be honest I could see it, despite the fact that he was, at that point, fully clothed.'

She smiled and it was her turn to flush. 'But as for the rest, Miss Strauss . . . well, that you will discover for yourself – sooner or later – so long as you find the right man.'

There was no doubting the provocatively teasing tone of Marion Stoiber's voice and the glitter of sexual knowingness in her eyes.

Emily found herself in a state of utter confusion: part repelled by Stoiber's unrepentant sexuality but also, as a sexually uninitiated woman herself, wide-eyed and curious. Her sense of professionalism, however, stopped her asking more. She shifted in her seat, picked up her pen and reminded herself that she was a reporter and she had a job to do.

But then it was Emily's turn to tease, for she knew full well the answer to her next question.

'Then if you really won't tell me his name, Marion, will you at least tell me the name of the photographer?'

Marion paused a moment and then said very bleakly, 'It doesn't matter now. He's dead. His name was Henry Robinson. I heard this morning that they have killed him, as they will surely kill me and anybody else they think is a danger to their valuable trade. That is why they will want to find Anna.'

'Who's "they", Marion?'

'You must have heard of the Meisters? They're an elite guild of master butchers who operate out of the stockyards. They're not all bad. But there's an inner core of hard men who control the pornography trade here in Chicago.'

Emily was shocked at hearing Robinson's name again so soon and thought of the gruesome scene at the shop on Wabash. It was all beginning to add up. Robinson had introduced Marion Stoiber to the sexual *demi-monde*, innocuous enough at first for a sexually experienced woman such as her, but it had set her on the slippery slope to something far darker and more sinister. She in turn had exposed Anna Zemeckis to it.

'And this is the world you introduced Anna to?' There was no mistaking the air of disapproval in Emily's voice.

Marion's eyes grew serious and she shook her head.

'If it had been just that, then no harm would have come to her, or me for that matter. To start off with, Henry took her photograph for her – a *carte de visite* to send home to her father. It was all very innocent. It was only later that she, like me, was lured into something quite different. Then she was blackmailed . . . like I was.'

'And who blackmailed her, Marion? Who lured her? Was it him . . . ? Was it your special client?'

Stoiber's answer was tight-lipped and unequivocal: 'You would do well not to enquire.' She paused, then added rather vaguely, 'Anyway he's gone away. He, he . . .'

'He's left Chicago?'

'Yes. He's gone away. To Kansas ... He has business concerns there ... in Abilene,' she said.

Emily could tell that Stoiber was improvising as she went along.

'And he's not coming back?'

Stoiber deflected the question.

'He became very manipulative and demanding, you know. He suggested I might have more pictures taken – with other men, never with him of course – or I would never see him again. I agreed. "Just poses," he said. "They will be worth a lot of money and no one in Chicago will ever see them."'

Emily thought of the sexually explicit photograph of Marion she had seen that morning.

'Well, "just poses" meant more, much more, but by then I would do anything and the liquor and drugs they plied me with made me do more still. Until, worst of all, I was persuaded to procure other women for his pleasure and theirs.'

'Was Anna one of these?'

Marion nodded.

'I did not think he would take a fancy to her as he had to me. However, there was something about her virginal simplicity that attracted him and a certain spirit he wanted to master. There was one particular occasion ... at the Union Stock Yard.'

'The private tour?'

'Yes. Anna thought she was simply going to see the hog wheel and the killing floor, as so many before. He was there and she caught his eye and he took her off by herself and I guess ... well ... excited, flattered, plied with liquor and chloral, which make a girl compliant to almost anything, he took her. I do not think rape is too strong a word.

'Afterwards,' added Marion, 'she was blackmailed into going back there again and forced to pose for some pornographic photographs taken by Robinson. They even made her pose in some of the photographs they took of me. But it was all very much against her will, whereas I, well ...'

'She told you what happened?'

'Only briefly at the time. She was much distressed and when she discovered she was with child I knew the danger she was in, for it could be no other child but his she was carrying. That was not good at all. I advised her not to tell him but, very foolishly, she did. He summoned me and insisted I had the matter seen to by a woman known to be good and safe at such things. She has rooms up near the Levee where there is a considerable call on her services.'

'So Anna had an abortion?'

'No, she did not. We visited the woman, but Anna was terrified and left. She couldn't go through with it and I agreed with her, I who had so wanted to have a child of my own. It is a terrible thing for a woman to have to do.'

'But it is also a terrible thing to have a child out of wedlock conceived in that way, especially for a girl like Anna raised by a father like Janis Zemeckis.'

'It is. But she was determined. A mother's instinct. His reaction was different, as you would expect. The abortionist told him what had happened and Anna had to go into hiding or he would have dragged her back there. She ran away from the Markulises and came and hid in my apartment. Our plan was to get her out of Chicago . . . She has an aunt, Inga—'

Emily nodded. 'Yes, in Manitoba.'

'But then she had this mad idea that she might be able to persuade him to support her somewhere away from Chicago until she had the child. I told her not to go near him, but nine days ago, on October the eighteenth, I came back from work and she was gone. I never saw her again and then I saw the notice in the *Tribune* that she had died in a traffic accident. I had no reason to think she could still be alive. I assumed that she had been running, probably running from someone sent after her by him.'

'But the body, Marion . . . it wasn't Anna.'

'But her father identified her, did he not?'

'Yes, both he and Mrs Markulis identified her as Anna,' said Emily, 'but only, I suppose, because the woman, who was horribly disfigured in the accident, was wearing Anna's dress and crucifix and had dark hair like her.'

Marion's eyes widened and she put a hand to her mouth in astonishment, a sudden revelation coming to her.

'She what . . . but . . . I know who that was!'

425

'Who, Marion, who? You must tell me.'

'Anna and I used to go to the public bathhouse on Dearborn, always at night so as not to be seen. A week or so before she disappeared Anna left her things in the changing cubicle as usual one evening. The crucifix was in her pocket. While she was in the bath, someone stole her dress – it was a good one, she'd made it herself. I had to leave her there shivering and run back for one of mine.'

'Well, whoever stole it got run down by a streetcar,' said Emily matter-of-factly, 'and by then the crucifix was round *her* neck.'

Suddenly Stoiber tensed. 'Oh my goodness, it's after two, I have to go . . . I'm late, very late . . . Though I suppose it doesn't really matter. When I saw the paper at work this morning about Henry's murder and the fire, I decided the time had come for me to get out of town.'

She got up. 'I'm going West, this evening, to San Francisco, and I'm not coming back.'

She reached out a hand to shake Emily's.

'So this is goodbye. It was good talking to you, Emily. I feel better for it.'

'And you still won't tell me who he is . . . ?'

'No. But if Anna survives, and you get to her in time, I'm sure she will. It's as much her right to talk as it is mine to stay silent.'

'I might find out another way.'

'Then if you do and you meet him again, perhaps you'll understand. But be warned . . .'

Marion Stoiber glanced to right and left and then all around, as if expecting to see her executioner right there in the midst of the throng of people on the Midway Plaisance. And then she hurried off into the crowds and was gone.

Moments later, Emily saw that, in her rush to leave, Marion had left her purse behind on the table. She grabbed it, stood up and called out after her. It was too late.

She took out more than enough bills from her own purse to pay the check, placed them on the table and ran off in the direction Marion had gone, east down the Midway towards the Ferris Wheel.

She thought she caught sight of her gray hat and called out, but the crowds were so thick and the noise of them and the nearby attractions drowned out her call.

She pushed on through, trying to keep Stoiber in her sights, until, quite suddenly, the hat was gone.

Emily climbed onto the steps of a nearby attraction to get a better view.

She saw what she thought must be Stoiber's back – certainly the hat was the same – moving into the shadow of the Ferris Wheel. A man, a good deal taller, seemed to be close at her side.

Emily went cold.

'Marion . . . !' she shouted out, in alarm this time.

As she battled her way through the crowds on the Midway, Emily heard a sudden scream. She thought it was the groups of girls up on the Ferris Wheel, as before. She stopped and looked up.

As she did so the wheel ground to a sudden, jolting halt. There were more screams and the whole crowd slowed and massed in confusion.

Emily pushed her way through them, towards the massive base of the Ferris Wheel.

A man in uniform – one of the operating engineers – stood looking ashen faced and helpless by the door leading into the area that housed the winding gear of the wheel.

She pushed past him, ducking her head and found herself surrounded by cogs and chains and pistons. The world outside faded away as her eyes adjusted to the dark.

Then she saw her. Marion Stoiber was deathly still in that hot and airless enclosed space and seemed to be embracing the very cogs of the machinery.

Which is exactly what she was doing.

For someone had pushed her straight towards them as they turned. She had thrust her arms out to try to stop her fall but they and her clothes had become entangled in the cogs, which, continuing to turn, had dragged her half into the machine itself, her head pressed at an unnatural angle against a metal beam. The short, unhappy life of Marion Stoiber had been crushed out of her by the eighth wonder of the modern age before her broken body had stopped it turning.

71

Factory

The Union Stock Yard consisted of 600 acres of livestock pens, market buildings, railway lines, livestock causeways, killing floors and the canning houses of every major meatpacker in the world.

The place vibrated with activity beneath a sky darkened by a constant pall of smoke, occasionally made lurid by open flames from the many boiler-houses on the site. Ben Latham's only clues were the images he had developed from the broken plates gathered up from Robinson's studio floor. These were mainly distant views through a window of buildings and chimneys. If one of them had not contained a recognizable image of the famous stockyard water tower it is unlikely that even the general location could have been identified. But this, combined with the fact that the other images included various permutations of the same boiler-house and factory chimneys, made him think that with some legwork and a close comparison of the site with the photographs he might be able to track down the original viewpoint.

He approached the Union Stock Yard cautiously. It was well-gated and a visitor pass was needed to go inside. He was lucky and found a talkative, relaxed guard.

When asked what his business was, he used a dodge that had worked before, showing his reporter's badge and pointing to the leather case of his Kodak daylight camera, an item so modern that it impressed all who saw it, especially men, and said he had come to take photographs for the New York *World*.

'Help yourself,' he was told, 'but there won't be many folk around in an hour or two anyway, seein' what day it is.'

'Why, what day *is* it?'

'The Friday before the Fair ends. Tomorrow's American Cities' Day and the closing ceremony's on Monday. Most of Chicago and half the world besides will be there to see the fireworks and celebrations. There's a lot less livestock coming through the yard for the next three days. Though Darke Hartz never seem to stop production, no matter what. They say Wolfgang Darke is a slave driver.

'By the way,' the man called out as Ben headed off, 'if you want refreshments look sharp. The lunch room in the Exchange Building will be shutting down early today, like everything else.'

To Ben's surprise, the lunch room proved spacious and well appointed, reflecting the enormous wealth that flowed in and out of the stockyard. Its brown, varnished walls were decorated with pictures of its history and maps of the yard, a photograph of some of the early cattle buyers on horses standing by a pen full of steers, an 1893 calendar and a vast oil painting of the famous champion bull, Sherman, whose horned head adorned the main gate and gave all who entered a challenging Chicagoan stare.

Ben took his coffee and pork chops with mashed potato and collard greens to a counter that looked out onto the main meatpacking buildings on the west side of the complex, and he quickly spotted the telltale water tower nearby.

As discreetly as possible he compared what he saw to the images in his file, looking for the same pattern of chimneys. He soon narrowed down the location to one just north of the largest and most dominant establishment, that of Armour & Co., in whose shadow were the premises of the lesser meatpackers, including those of the famous Nelson Morris.

A complex of railway lines ran in front of all of these buildings, curving away to the north and west. It looked as if the location Ben was after lay on the far side of it – a row of blackened buildings, soiled by the continuous deluge of soot that rained down from the chimneys above them.

Ben headed west down Exchange Avenue, the Armour Building to his left and Nelson Morris to his right. No one paid him any attention, not even when he paused to take a photograph of the scene.

Nearer to, he caught sight of the processing plants of the other two major meatpackers, Gustavus Swift and the relative upstart that was Darke Hartz & Company, which was now one of the most successful in the world because of the aggressive way it had developed its distribution system by rail and sea.

Standing by the railway track in front of this long line of buildings was a group of well-dressed ladies, in fashionable day dresses and hats, their parasols open – not against the rain, for the day was dry, but against the soot.

Several held handkerchiefs to their mouth and nose with looks of disgust on their faces, for the air was rank with the odors that pervaded the entire site – of stale blood, of offal and of death. A white-coated butcher was their guide and, since he was elaborating on the subject of Darke Hartz & Co. and the genius of its two partners in expanding their business so fast, Ben concluded that this must be one of Darke Hartz's twenty-five-cent tours.

He passed on down between the Swift and Darke Hartz factories and found himself among a maze of buildings, rising up to a gray sky of drifting smoke.

Down in these industrial depths his city clothes and even more his camera caught the attention of the busy men who hurried back and forth, many in white cotton coats covered in red-brown bloodstains. But no one stopped him.

He reached another opening and was able now to look back at the water tower and deduce that the building he sought was somewhere off to his left, on the northwest side of the yard.

In front of Ben stretched a tangle of railway tracks with various signs warning off trespassers. On an isolated site in the far corner, cut off by the rail tracks that surrounded it, was a group of buildings that had seen better days. He turned his back to them, looked out for the water tower and the pattern of chimneys adjacent and compared it with a couple of the photographs in his file. He was gratified to see something like the view he sought. It had been taken from further back, as he might have expected, and he had no doubt it was from a room somewhere in the buildings he had now reached.

They had innumerable windows (cracked) and doors (dirty, closed and padlocked) and alleys between them (mostly out of sight) but Ben was pretty sure he was right. The name over the building was still visible: A. F. Whetton & Co., Meatpackers. It wasn't one Ben had ever heard of and it looked as if they had gone out of business a long while back.

He clambered over a couple of fences, ignored a shout from someone down the line, crossed the tracks, and made his way across scrubby ground to what looked like the main entrance, only to discover that a small service road, thick with weeds and garbage, ran from the bottom of the entrance to a perimeter fence made of wood where a gate, half off its hinges, hung wide open.

It took him a while to find a way in, the main door being well padlocked and, when he did, it was by dropping down through a broken window at ground level into a basement.

The place smelt different from outside and he thought he knew why. The site backed right onto the banks of the Chicago River. He could not see the river, but the dead, damp smell of sluggish, polluted water hung on the air.

The moment he found steps up out of the basement to the first floor, Ben saw he was in a long-disused slaughterhouse. But the meat-dressing tables were still there, with dusty ropes and pulleys for heaving sides of meat hanging from the beams overhead. There was even a neat row of black gutta-percha aprons hanging on hooks, now eerily elongated by a combination of the damp air, their own weight and increasing rottenness. They looked like the aprons of giants.

Then Ben remembered he had seen such aprons before and, searching among his images, he found one which showed a half-clad girl standing against a row of them. But this wasn't the right killing floor.

He carried on along the corridor until finally he found a viewpoint similar to the ones in the images. After careful examination he concluded that he was a little to the right of where he needed to be, retraced his steps and found a walkway through to the next building.

He opened the first door he came to and was greeted by a curious sight. A room that had once been some kind of office was now derelict but for a chaise longue, some upholstered chairs, a potted plant or two and a few faded velvet drapes at the window. This was clearly the improvised location for some of the less salacious photographs he had developed from the Robinson plates. Pulling out his pad he made a few quick sketches before moving on, the light inside being insufficient for a photograph. When he entered the next door along, he found himself entering another killing floor. It was very clean, even if the beams above were as dusty and cobwebbed as those in the previous rooms. As for the meat-dressing tables, they were all covered in dust too, but for one area over near the hog wheel.

It towered above Ben, but he was more interested in the heavy chains that hung from the wheel and which he knew were for the purpose of attaching the hind leg of the hogs as it turned, so hoisting them off the ground, the more easily for their throats to be cut. He stopped again and did another quick drawing.

Then, just as Ben moved from the wheel towards the windows to check out the view, something moving against the thick, wooden wheel caught his eye.

He took a closer look.

It was a single pink feather, caught amongst one of the chains, and fluttering in the almost nonexistent breeze. It was the kind that vaudeville girls used in their stage acts; or that whores in bordellos on the Levee fanned themselves with on hot sultry evenings.

Ben checked the photographs again and, sure enough the hog wheel shown in them looked exactly like the one in front of him now. Even the most cursory examination of the rivets attaching metal to wood confirmed his suspicions. The chains had metal cuffs attached to them. The implication was obvious: the wheel was used as a stage prop in pictures taken of girls supposedly chained to it. He reached up for the feather and sniffed it.

Cheap perfume.

He impulsively took hold of one of the chains and looked more closely at the metal cuff, and smelt that too.

Very cheap perfume.

Confident now that he had the right location, he took out the best of the photographs and paced back and forth until he had the exact same view of the table in relation to the chimneys through the window way across the stock yard.

This was the very table, he guessed, on which sexual intercourse between Marion Stoiber and an unknown man had taken place.

Opening up his Kodak, and hoping there was sufficient light, Ben took some photographs replicating the views, the hog wheel and the dressing tables. He wondered how any man could be aroused by sexual images of women put on display in such a disgusting environment. But there were clearly big bucks in the trade in photographing them and he wanted to find out more.

He climbed now to the upper floor, where he found some evidence, from the blurred patterns of dusty footprints on floor and stairs, of recent use. And then he noticed a new and different smell. No, it wasn't the dank smell of the river, it was something much more acerbic. Sulfur.

As he turned a corner into a darker corridor, the odor hit him harder and he knew it at once: sodium thiosulfate, better known as hypo, the fixing agent used in developing photographs. He pushed open a door and the smell was overwhelming, but the room was pitch black.

He felt around for a source of light but found none, which did not surprise him. But he knew there must be a window somewhere, probably with special blackout shutters and blinds. He propped the door open with his bag to get some light and felt his way gingerly across the room in what he hoped was the direction of the window. But as he did so, the door, being too heavy for the bag, swung to, putting him in pitch darkness.

'Damn!' he said aloud.

He felt his way ahead, his hands touching what he knew to be developing tanks, taps, and even, at eye level, a light chain with clips on it of the kind used to hold photographic prints while they dried.

Then he stilled, his heart beginning to thump. He had smelt something new: the not unpleasant aroma of fresh tobacco. He felt along the nearest bench for something that he might use to defend himself and found a pair of scissors.

His eyes strained round at the darkness. Somewhere from across the room, feet shifted slightly on the floor.

Then he saw the sudden red glow in the dark of a small cigar.

There was a slight, polite cough and then a voice.

'Mr Latham, I guess?'

The voice was deep, assured and sounded slightly amused. Ben thought he knew it. But his natural desire to retake the initiative asserted itself.

'Who are you, sir!' he cried out as boldly as he could, his heart in his mouth.

The shutter of a lantern was suddenly opened and a shaft of yellow light illuminated the face of the other man in the room.

'Gerald Toulson, and I should be very glad to know how you worked out exactly where to come.'

Ben stood stunned.

'Let's shed some light on the scene,' said Toulson, opening one window shutter after another and throwing up the blinds until the place was filled with light.

'I'd also like to know,' continued Toulson, 'exactly what a professional photographer such as yourself makes of all this – and, incidentally, there's no need to hold those scissors quite so aggressively. I have no intention of shooting you. I need you as an expert witness.'

Ben put down the scissors and surveyed the room, which was even larger than he had thought. There was tank after tank for the developing and fixing of photographs, a store of bottles containing chemicals, mainly white pyrogallol powder, some of which had spilled out from an over-turned bottle onto the work surface and the floor. There were also dozens of drying chains and racks and all the paraphernalia of a dark-room, but on a huge scale.

'Good God,' said Ben, 'this isn't a darkroom, it's a factory for producing photographic images.'

'For the growing market in pornography,' said Toulson heavily.

Ben crossed over the room to where Toulson stood. 'You gave me one hell of a shock.'

Toulson smiled apologetically.

'In my line of work it's better to be safe than sorry. I don't make a habit of announcing myself when I'm trespassing. Anyway, you had me standing up here in the dark for a very long time after I first saw you approach the building. What were you doing?'

Ben showed him the images from the Robinson studio and explained how he had found the location.

'Impressive,' said Toulson.

'So how did you find the place?'

'We persuaded someone to give us the information. We got in round the back.'

'We?'

'My colleague and I,' said Toulson, glancing towards a still-shadowed part of the room.

Ben looked and once more his heart missed several beats. A man just as solid and tough-looking as Toulson was standing there.

'Rorton Van Hale, Pinkerton National Detective Agency,' he said by way of introduction, 'but be kind enough not to inform Miss Strauss of that or even of my existence. She's doesn't trust Pinkertons, I gather.'

'What are you doing here?' asked Ben, still feeling shaken.

Toulson gave the answer.

'Mr Van Hale is here by way of reinforcement as I wrap up my investigation. A lot of nasty things could happen in the next twenty-four hours and I have a feeling both myself and Miss Strauss – though she doesn't know it yet – will need some backup.'

Ben looked out of the window at the rail tracks below and could see a locomotive and a string of refrigerated box cars lined up, each with the words *DARKE HARTZ & COMPANY* painted on it in large white letters.

He stared at the fetid stream beyond and along its course to the South Fork of the Chicago River, screwing up his face in disgust.

'It looks as filthy as it smells,' he said.

It was sluggish, filled with garbage and a thick, foamy chemical effluent, which seemed to make it churn as it moved.

'You know what folk back of the yards call it?'

Ben shook his head.

'Bubbly Creek,' said Toulson.

72

Ashes

Anna's flight from the Meisters was an instinctual act of survival, for herself and the child she was carrying.

Having seen the men coming and the knife one of them was holding she had frozen in a state of such fear that it had needed John English to give her an almighty push and order her to run. But she didn't know where to. All she knew was that it had to be some place – *anywhere* – where they were not.

The wharves were not an easy place to run down in a straight line, being stacked with goods and boxes, piles of lumber, coils of rope and ships' mooring lines, which meant she continually had to jump and dodge and occasionally duck, none of which was easy and comfortable for a woman in her condition.

She rapidly grew tired and was tempted to try to find a way back up to South Water Street, but John had told her not to go back that way.

So she blundered on, turning round only once. She saw that John had fallen and was lying on the ground and that the men were now running her way. Her blind fear returned; there was no way she could go back and help John now.

Then she came to a point where the wharf sloped suddenly at a dry dock where a ship was being overhauled. It led inland with a

twenty-foot drop onto mud. Anna ran round its edge, grateful that
there was nobody much around. Beyond, the wharf turned to the
right, following a bend in the river, and took Anna, as she quickly realized, out of sight of the men. Then she saw an alley to her right
leading straight up into South Water Street, whose crowds she could
see beyond the backs of market stalls and their traders. It was the
obvious way to go, but instinct and common sense – and what John
had told her – took her in the opposite direction towards two barges
moored alongside the wharf and covered with tarpaulin.

She now knew she could run no more; she had a stitch and felt a
tightening where the baby was. She crossed the wharf to the barges,
looked back quickly to check that the men were still out of sight, and
lifted the edge of the tarpaulin of the first which was stretched across
its top and secured every two or three yards by rope ties.

It was heavy but just manageable.

Anna would have climbed in then and there but for the appalling
stench from the barge's contents – rotten vegetables bound for a garbage
pile – and ran to the next barge along. She heard one of the men
shout back at the dry dock, but knew she was luckily still out of sight.

She didn't stop to examine the contents of the second barge. They
didn't smell, so she slipped under its tarpaulin and dropped down inside,
thinking it would be a matter of a few feet. It was more like nine or ten
before she hit the bottom with a soft but abrasive bump and found herself
in a pile of still-warm ash as clouds of dust arose around her.

She was about to clamber over it to find somewhere to hide on the
farther side of the hold, but that would only cause more ash to rise
and betray where she was. So Anna lay still where she was, trying to
suppress a cough. Meanwhile, up on the wooden wharf, she heard the
heavy steps of the Meisters come to a halt only a few yards above her.

They seemed to be conferring about where their quarry might have
gone. No doubt, like her, they were weighing up the two options –
South Water Street or one of the river craft.

'You check out the market,' said one of them, 'but she won't get
far up there because our men are on the lookout for her and they'll
grab her. I'll check out the barges here on the wharf. There's nowhere
else for her to hide.'

Anna heard one of the men walk away from the wharf as the other came nearer, stopping at the first barge she had tried.

'Jeez!' she heard him say, as he lifted the tarpaulin, 'what a stink.' Nevertheless, she could tell from his occasional cussing and his footsteps that he was giving the barge a thorough going-over.

Anna stayed right where she was. She tried to quietly scatter more ash over herself, but that only set some sliding down from a pile behind her. She held her breath in terror as the man's footsteps approached on the boardwalk above her.

Then, unexpectedly, his pace quickened, he went straight past, and shouted at someone he had seen on the next craft along, a schooner.

'Say, seen a girl running on the wharf? 'Bout twenty. Black hair?'

Someone on the schooner shouted back that, no, he hadn't. Just as he did so a tug chugged past on the river and its wash hit Anna's barge, rocking it and sending ash and spent coke sliding in little avalanches all around her. She took advantage of the boat's movement to roll as far away through the ash and out of sight as she could on the other side of the barge.

The man now started systematically raising the corners of the tarpaulin above her one by one and searching the barge, starting at one end and working his way to the other. Despite the fact that Anna lay only partially covered by ash and clinker, he didn't spot her. It was deep and gloomy and dusty down there and her dress fortunately was dark gray.

Eventually the Meister moved off down the wharf. Although she relaxed, Anna decided to lay low, till dark if necessary. She listened to the passing traffic on the river, feeling the impact of its wash on the barge, listening in case the Meisters returned. Sure enough she heard them again, three-quarters of an hour later, conferring once more on the wharf above her.

'She must have got into a boat, or still be hiding along the wharf somewhere. There's no way she could have made it to the market. Too many people out looking for her. And there's a reward on her head too.'

'You check the wharf then, because I haven't seen her.'

The second man checked the same two barges and missed Anna as well, as she hunkered deeper down in the warmth of the ash piles, trying not to cough.

Finally, and rather noisily, the men agreed to abandon their search. But suspecting a trick, Anna laid low a while longer. Then she peeked out through a gap in the tarpaulin and looked along the wharf. There was no sign of them in any direction.

She was about to climb back out when the barge rocked and she heard steps along the gunnels and a man humming. He seemed to be attaching and detaching various ropes. Then he was gone and the barge was still and quiet again.

Anna once more crept up to the edge of the hold and started to haul herself over. Time to be on the move again.

Except, to her horror, she saw there was nowhere to go. Quietly, without Anna noticing, the two barges had been roped up, one behind the other, and had now floated out some fifteen feet from the wharf edge, attached, she saw, to a tug in front.

An engine started and slowly, the barge, with Anna Zemeckis trapped inside, started moving off downriver, towards Lake Michigan.

What had happened to John? She hoped the Meisters had not harmed him and that he was all right, but she was now far too exhausted to feel anything. Her eyes remained blank, without expression. Not a single tear made a channel through the ash that covered her cheeks. Her hair and hands and clothes were thick with ash too, but it didn't matter anymore.

Anna Zemeckis collapsed back down onto a pile of ash and clinker. It seemed that no matter what she did she caused nothing but trouble to those who tried to help her.

The tug pulling her barge hooted but she did not bother to drag herself up to the side to see why. She did not care what happened to her or her child anymore. She was tired, so tired of running.

She sank back into the warm ash and slept.

73

In Pursuit

Marion Stoiber's death was not the first to occur at the World's Fair but it was the first obvious murder, the man operating the winding gear having been attacked, the victim having been heard to scream and, as the subsequent report by the Columbian Guard, who oversaw matters of security and law at the Exposition, put it, 'a shadowy and suspicious person' having been seen to run from the scene of the crime.

If the Guard took any consolation from the fact that their till-then-clean record in preventing homicide during the Fair was spoilt by this single act, it was that the unfortunate event had taken place in the Midway Plaisance just outside Jackson Park itself.

This meant that technically it was outside their jurisdiction and was the responsibility of the Chicago Police Department. Fortunately it was the upright and trusted Guards who had been first at the scene and it was they who secured the area and detained any material witnesses to the crime, including Emily Strauss.

It was for this reason that Emily did not get away until an hour later which was, perhaps, a good thing.

It gave her time to recover from the shock after one of the Guards gently led her out of the engine room and sat her down. She gave what account she could of the little she had witnessed, but she was

shaking for a good half-hour afterwards. Finally she recovered sufficiently to make her way to the Elevated and head as far north as she
could, which was Congress. From there she took a cab straight to the
Chicago Public Library in Haddock Street and demanded to see John
English.

'You can't.'

'I have to.'

'Is it about the accident?'

'What accident?'

'He's with Mr McIlvanie but he's still recovering.'

'Yes,' said Emily taking advantage of the desk clerk's misunderstanding, 'it's about the accident and I need to see him now.'

'Who shall I say?'

'Emily Strauss, New York *World* and, believe me, my editor is not
the kind of man who likes one of his own being kept waiting. It's
important.'

She pulled out a card, wrote the words, 'On behalf of Anna
Zemeckis' and gave it to him.

Three minutes later she was in McIlvanie's office where an
anxious, bruised and frustrated John English was striding back and
forth.

Mr McIlvanie seemed grateful to see her.

She quickly explained her assignment and that she was on the track
of Anna, whom she was convinced was still alive, which was now
confirmed by John English.

Wearily, at Emily's prompting, he told her what had happened and
what else he knew.

'But it's worse than that,' he said, giving Emily a terrible, plaintive
look. 'She's with child. They're out to kill her and they'll kill her baby
too.'

'I know, I know,' responded Emily. 'So tell me, why are you not
lying in a pool of blood on that wharf?'

'I keep asking myself that question too. The Meisters put a knife
to my ribs and said they'd be back and fillet me at their leisure – those
were their very words. But they clearly didn't want to waste time on
me then and there.'

'So what did they do?'

441

'Knocked me out,' said John, rubbing his jaw. 'When I woke up they had moved off down the wharf and were searching the barges. It was clear to me Anna had gone and hidden somewhere. There was nothing I could do but hope somehow she'd make her way back to me.'

'I told him to call the police,' said Mr McIlvanie, 'but . . .'

'No. She doesn't trust them,' said John.

'You've no idea where she went?'

'None. She could have got away back into the crowds on South Water Street or be lying low somewhere . . . or, maybe they caught her.'

Emily turned to McIlvanie.

'May I borrow your assistant librarian, sir?' she said. 'I want him to show me where this happened.'

'Sure, if he thinks he's up to going back there. But what about the police . . . ?'

'I've got a feeling it'll be too late by the time they get organized. In any case, they're overstretched enough by the Fair already and I doubt they'll set up a search for Anna on the Friday afternoon before the Fair ends. But I'll be seeing someone with good connections with the police at my hotel at six and we can get his advice.'

Another thought occurred to Emily.

'Mr McIlvanie, would you mind if he takes the rest of the afternoon off? It might take some time.'

'Best thing for him,' said McIlvanie. 'Anyway, things here are already winding down and he won't be needed.'

Twenty minutes later, John and Emily were standing on the wharf next to the barrels where he and Anna had been sitting when the Meisters approached.

Emily took in the scene. 'Show me the direction you saw Anna run in.'

They walked along the wharf until they reached the dry dock.

'She had a head start so I guess she would have got this far and round the corner of the dock before ever they did,' said John.

Emily moved on ahead, mulling things over out loud.

'So . . . where the dock curves to the right, the men would have lost sight of her . . .'

She walked faster and suddenly began running, John struggling to keep up.

'She would have ... gone right ... round ... here ... and I'm guessing she had a few seconds' grace before they had her in view again ...'

Emily stopped abruptly to think, John nearly bumping into her.

'But they were fit men and she's pregnant and exhausted. They would have been gaining on her fast. She would either have had to turn up an alley away from the wharf towards Water Street ...'

John looked and agreed.

'Or what ... ? She certainly could not have carried on along the wharf. There's much less cover that way and they would have quickly caught up with her.'

John agreed with that too.

'So, she must have found somewhere to hide ...'

They both looked around. There were two schooners docked on the wharf but otherwise the mooring was empty.

'Doesn't look the same,' said John. 'Hardly surprising, I'd just been knocked out. But when I came round I did manage to walk down this far to see if there was any sign of Anna or the Meisters.'

'What's different about it? Please try to remember,' said Emily. 'Might be important.'

'I don't think there were two schooners there. Something smaller, lower ...'

'I guess river craft come and go all the time here,' said Emily.

It was plain they could get no further.

'Listen John, I'm running out of time,' said Emily, 'I have a meeting back at the hotel at six and other things to do before that. I'll be in touch as soon as I can.'

As they emerged onto South Water Street she hailed a cab and climbed in.

'By the way,' said Emily, 'Marion Stoiber told me you had a stutter. What happened to it?'

'I've been wondering that myself, Miss Strauss. In fact, I've been wondering about a lot of things of late.'

'Don't tell me,' said Emily, 'tell Anna when we find her.'

'*Will* we find her?'

'Yes,' said Emily firmly, 'because I need her for my story. So I reckon I'm going to have to, aren't I?'

Emily turned to the driver of her cab: 'Park Street, number eighteen.'

She arrived at Fay Bancroft's house at half-past four which, considering the day she had had, was not bad. As she climbed the front steps to the mansion, she did not notice that another cab had stopped a little behind hers and that a man was watching from behind its window.

It was the same man who had followed her and Marion from the steps of the Woman's Building when they met for lunch.

The same man who had manhandled Marion Stoiber into the machine room of the Ferris Wheel and pushed her violently into its terrifying mechanism.

That same 'shadowy and suspicious character' who had been seen hurrying away from the scene of the crime.

The same Meister who had been tailing Emily Strauss all day long.

He waited until Emily had gone inside before ordering his own cab south down Michigan Avenue and, from there, at 18th, left into Prairie Avenue. Here, the cab drew up outside a big, stolid, yellow-brick establishment with an imposing front entrance and great, ill-proportioned windows. It looked more like an office building than a home, though it might once have impressed. Now, it simply looked ugly and uninviting.

He mounted the steps and pulled the bell which clanged loudly inside the building. A butler came.

'I need to see Mr Hartz.'

He gave his name but was kept waiting outside.

A short while later he was ushered into Paul Hartz's study, the eighth visitor on a busy day that had kept him from much of the routine proceedings of the OAA Convention.

Hartz neither rose nor shook his hand.

'Well, Lukas?'

The Meister gave an account of how the matter of Miss Stoiber had reached a 'satisfactory conclusion'. But as for Emily Strauss . . .

Hartz interrupted him with irritation, 'That woman has become a nuisance.'

The Meister agreed. He described Emily's visit to the Chicago

444

Public Library, her exploration of the wharves with John English and finally how he had followed her to Fay Bancroft's.

'Our reporter is getting far too thick with that Mrs Bancroft,' scowled Hartz.

'She's having a meeting at the Auditorium Annex at six.'

'Who with?'

'Didn't hear any names.'

Hartz thought a little and finally said, 'I think the time has come for me to have a talk with our young lady reporter. Here, take this to her hotel.'

He took out a small white visiting card with his name and address on it and wrote a brief note on the back, sealing it in an envelope.

'Get it to her hotel for her return. And make sure it's delivered to her personally.'

Fay's house was decorated in the kind of eclectic style that independent society ladies with time on their hands and plenty of money like: neoclassical French with a touch of the fin-de-siècle – lots of silks and tapestries and furniture with irritating curly arms and legs and imposing ornate vases of a too-delicate kind that worry big people when they come into a room.

'It really is beautiful,' said Emily without much conviction.

Fay laughed at her insincerity.

'You don't have to try to like it, my dear, or please me in matters of taste. I do realize I am somewhat *passé*, but you see there's only one person I care about enough to want all this for – myself! My husband has always allowed me total control over matters of interior design, and with him away so much on business, there is a lot to be said for having no one to think about but oneself.'

Emily grinned.

'You look tired,' said Fay. 'I'll order some tea and you can tell me all about your day.'

She tugged at a bellpull decorated with blue ribbon which sounded somewhere in the back of the house.

'I really don't think you want to hear about it, Fay, and besides, forgive me, but I don't have much time,' said Emily wearily.

The maid entered.

'A pot of India tea, Mary,' said Fay, 'and some coffee cake and sand-wiches . . . Oh, and bring in the brandy too.'

'Yes ma'am.'

The maid retreated.

Emily looked dubious.

'You need it, my dear,' said Fay.

'You're probably right,' replied Emily. 'Things are bad enough, but I have a feeling that what you're about to tell me will only make them worse!'

74

Making History

Dr Morgan Eels was doing the rounds of the medical wards of the Cook County Insane Asylum. He was a happy man. His eyes were bright and his normally pallid skin had a certain color to it.

The sources of his joy were threefold. First, now that his predecessor Dr Benjamin Brown had left the establishment, Dr Eels was fully in charge. Power is a wonderful thing in the hands of the person who wields it.

Second, today had been an auspicious day for him: throughout the morning and early afternoon, he had carried out, with the able assistance of Mr Mould and the formidable Nurse Lutyens, a revolutionary new surgical procedure on no less than ten patients in rapid succession. And in a week's time he would do the same again. It would, undoubtedly, make his name; for he had, he believed, made medical history.

The fact that before eight o'clock that morning, when he began the operations, every one of his patients was, relatively speaking, fit and well in physical terms was not the point. His concern as a practitioner had been their *mental* state, which was in every case disturbed, often annoying and in a few cases dangerously unmanageable. He had performed his new procedure swiftly and efficiently, with the minimum of restraint and the help of a little tropocaine.

The gratifying result of these surgical interventions – Eels did not use the word experiments – was that nine hours later not one of his patients was causing any trouble at all and all but one were fully conscious if somewhat inactive.

There had been one 'slight hitch', but one that was well within the failure rate he had allowed for in terms of patient reaction to his procedure: a male patient had died on the operating table from, he suspected, a simple malfunction of the heart. He had left Mould to ascertain the cause of death for purposes of the official record.

The other patients, once recovered, manifested the same benign behaviour as Riley had after the stabbing she had received at the hands of Anna Zemeckis. They were generally quiescent, lay still without complaint and answered his questions with every indication that their mental faculties were no longer troubled – provided the questions were not complicated or required deep thought.

Are you comfortable now?

'Yes, sir. You are kind, sir.'

Do you remember anything before today?

'I remember . . . something. I can't remember what.'

What is your name?

'Elizabeth.'

Elizabeth what?

'Elizabeth.'

Who is the president of the United States of America?

'I . . . he . . .'

What food do you like?

'Potato soup. Mother.'

Do you remember before today?

'Don't want to go back to Far Side.'

Dr Eels took great encouragement from these replies, although he knew a great deal more interrogation of his patients would be needed before he presented his results to the medical world.

Meanwhile, Dr Morgan Eels could take great satisfaction from the medical wards in which the patients from his day's activities now lay recovering.

They were not the normal wards, the rundown, malodorous ones in the sub-standard buildings to the rear, of which Far Side was the worst and which were the patients' normal place of residence.

The newly equipped medical wards in Main Building had high ceilings, good metal beds and oak doors. They were antiseptically clean, neat and had large windows opening onto balconies.

These wards had originally been built with the expectation on the part of Dunning's Board of Governors that the insane asylum would become a showcase for good practice rather than being what it had become: a dumping ground for the old, the poor and the mentally ill.

Under the complacent regime of Dr Brown, these wards had fallen into disuse, except for the very occasional emergency or when patients had needed to be isolated during an outbreak of infectious disease, when one of the smallest had been opened up for temporary service.

With the arrival of Dr Eels a month previously for his trial period, things had changed dramatically. Eels had ordered that the medical wards be opened up and brought back to standard, in readiness for the patients on whom he would be performing his new and innovative surgical procedures.

Since then, he had become increasingly consumed by his messianic vision: of himself as an intrepid pioneer, making his way across the great uncharted territory of the human brain, assisted by the trusty and enigmatic Mr Mould and by the omniscient and icy Nurse Lutyens, whom he had persuaded to join him from his former hospital on the East Coast to oversee the proper management of his new regime.

'Yes,' he now told himself as, his rounds complete, he stood surveying today's ten patients in their comfortable beds and then contemplating the empty ward next door where another ten beds would, after completion of next Friday's procedures, also be occupied. Or at least, he was confident that nine of the remaining patients on his original list would be lying there. But as for the last one: earlier that afternoon he had received a message from Mr Dodek Krol that Miss Zemeckis had been spotted downtown and he expected hourly that she would be apprehended. When his men had done so, she would be delivered back to Dunning as agreed.

Eels suddenly felt weary. He went and sat on one of the beds in the empty ward, considering his necessary attendance, as a stalwart

member, of the OAA Convention the following day in order to witness
the election of its new president. A good night's sleep was essential
and he would turn in early.

Mould appeared.

'Talk to me as I walk,' said Eels. 'I have one last thing to attend to.
I need to check on Mrs Riley's progress on Far Side.'

As they crossed the courtyard, Mould confirmed that his initial
conclusion was that the patient who had died earlier that day during
the operation had died of heart failure. He would perform the autopsy
tomorrow.

'Could we have known?' wondered Eels with a moment's uncharacteristic concern.

Mould thought not.

'Very well. See that the family is informed. If there is one.'

'You must be tired after your exertions, Dr Eels,' said Mould. 'But
may I say that I consider it an honour to have been witness today to
the birth of a new medical procedure.'

Eels gave him a wan smile but said nothing. His mind was now on
other things as the two men entered the ward on Far Side where Riley
was kept with Mary Nevitt and the two other women.

'Nurse Lutyens tells me you are gaining weight,' said Eels to the
silent Riley, whose rictus grin was belied by the now permanent look
of fear in her eyes.

Riley said nothing.

She sat in a large chair, facing Mary Nevitt across the ward, staring
at her hands, and her long sharp fingernails, which once more had
begun chattering like crickets in her lap.

'I understand, Miss Nevitt,' said Eels benignly, crossing the ward to
her, 'that you are much better now? And that you help with Riley?'

'Yes,' said Mary, 'I feed her.'

'Good,' said Eels.

Riley made a choking sound behind them and moved her fat, hairy
legs beneath her shift.

'Well then,' said Eels, 'we'll need your help this weekend, Mary,
seeing as the Fair's coming to an end and we're short-staffed.'

Mary Nevitt eyed Riley with unfeigned pleasure. Her nails now
danced and chattered even more in her lap.

'Yes, Dr Eels, sir,' she said.

Neither Eels nor Mould took note of the sheer terror in Riley's eyes as they left. They headed back to Main Building and then to Eels's office.

'I was thinking, Mr Mould,' said Eels, motioning him to sit down, 'that we succeeded in dealing swiftly with ten patients today. The trouble is, if one computes that rate against the total number of the mentally disturbed in this country in need of similar surgery, the task would be impossible for one man.

'I will need to disseminate my procedure and also cut down the operation time. Next Friday we have nine patients – or ten if all goes well regarding our missing one – and my intention is to achieve an even better average time than the forty minutes per patient we did today.'

Mould smiled briefly. It was precisely the kind of challenge he liked too. He and Dr Eels undoubtedly made an excellent team.

'By the way, sir,' enquired Mould, 'have you decided on a name for your procedure?'

Eels sighed with feigned weariness. 'I have made a few notes but have not yet come to any decision. Perhaps you would care to see them?'

He pushed a piece of paper in Mould's direction. It contained a list of words and phrases, some crossed out, others changed.

'It's scientific tradition of course to use a Greek or Latin derivation if at all possible, and certainly several come to mind to describe the procedure. It is, after all, simple enough . . .'

'It's pure genius, sir,' said Mould, and he meant it.

Eels acknowledged the flattery with a little smile.

'All we are doing is making specific lesions in the frontal lobes in such a way as to permanently reduce the patient's level of emotional disturbance and cognitive distress. So there are words like "cut" or "cutting", "white" – the color of the brain tissue – and of course "lobe", "frontal" and the like . . . the permutations are many. I have my favorites which I have circled . . .'

Mould eyed the list of words, none of which had any resonance at all for him.

'They seem strange, sir.'

451

'That is because they are unfamiliar. However, there is no doubt that the one we choose will go down in medical history. But which one?'

Mould eyed the two words Eels had circled.

'Leucotomy? Very odd.'

'But the kind of thing my predecessors would have chosen. It's taken from "leuco" meaning white in the Greek and "tomy" . . .'

'. . . meaning cut or cutting,' added Mould.

'How do you like it?'

'I don't, sir. Not quite grand enough.'

'And the other?'

Mould read the word aloud: 'Lobotomy.'

He laughed.

'Well I'm sorry, sir, I know what your intention is, but I really think that such an absurd-sounding term as that will never catch on!'

Eels laughed too.

There was a knock on the door. It was Nurse Lutyens.

She eyed the two laughing men disapprovingly.

'A joke?' she said.

Eels explained that it was not, but that perhaps Nurse Lutyens would care to venture her own opinion.

'Lobotomy,' she repeated. 'Sounds very peculiar. In any case, sir, I would have thought the name must be already settled.'

'Really?' said Eels.

'I think it should be called the Eels Procedure. It is the only logical one. It should be named for the man who invented it.'

Dr Eels stood up, walked to the window and pondered a moment.

Then he turned back to his two loyal acolytes, the greedy light of ambition shining in his eyes. He now took on the manner of a man rising to speak as guest of honor at a gathering of the world's top medical men.

'Very well,' he said. 'The Eels Procedure it shall be.'

75

Woman of the World

In Fay Bancroft's drawing room at Park Street, Emily Strauss was still trying to come to terms with the violent death of Marion Stoiber, as her hostess prattled on in her usual charming and informative way. Troubling images of death, of erotic poses and of that dreadful hog wheel at the stockyard, all came and went through Emily's mind like a jumble of moving images in a perversion of one of Mr Edison's kinetoscope programs.

But in fact Fay, a sensitive listener as well as a mischievous talker, had already guessed Emily's difficulty after she had told her about Marion's death. Her gossiping over tea was designed to give Emily time to recover while the brandies, two in quick succession, took effect. Which eventually they did and Emily, not Fay, started talking, as Fay knew she must for her own good.

'. . . but about one thing, Marion Stoiber was determined: she refused to reveal the identity of her well-to-do lover. It seemed to me a misplaced kind of loyalty, for I doubt, even had he known, he would have cared.'

'And you have no idea who he might be?' said Fay with unusual somberness.

'I have a feeling I ought to know but . . .'

'Why?'

'Well, on the journey back downtown on the Elevated, although I was shocked and confused I did at least recall some clues in what Marion had said: two, in fact.'

Fay edged closer.

'The first was somewhat indeterminate but useful. Marion made a slip of the tongue which indicated that I myself had met the man.'

'Really?'

'Yes, there was something she said just before she left before . . . *before* . . . I had asked her a final time to tell me who he was and she had evaded doing so by saying that maybe Anna would if we found her alive. She said something like, "But if you meet him again perhaps you'll understand".'

'*Again*,' said Fay.

'Exactly. So I thought at once of Paul Hartz whom I met at that party with you and Christiane.'

'Yes, but how could Marion have known you had met him?'

'Because I told her earlier. I told her about the Darke party and various other things I'd been doing, to soften her up a bit. And I remember when I mentioned his name she reacted strangely, but I didn't think any more of it until it was too late.'

'Paul Hartz? Well, he's a sly one and nothing would surprise me about him at all. And of course' – Fay took another sip of her brandy, her natural curiosity warming to this line of enquiry – 'he could not possibly reveal his interest in women such as Marion Stoiber, even less admit to collecting *poses plastiques*. It would quite destroy his reputation!'

'By the way, Fay, does he have any business concerns in Kansas, at Abilene?'

'That's a strange question.' Fay seemed suddenly cool.

'Marion said, not very convincingly I thought, that that was where the culprit was now. She was trying to put me off the scent I think. But people don't pluck things like that out of thin air.'

'Abilene?' said Fay again, but now rather differently. Her eyes widened and she put down her drink.

'What is it?'

'It's nothing,' she said, but it was an obvious lie.

Emily stared at her, puzzled, but then something quite different came into her mind. Something so shocking in its way that she also put down her glass.

'What?' it was Fay's turn to ask.

'I've just remembered something.'

'*What?*'

'Marion Stoiber forgot her purse. She left it on the table. I picked it up and ran after her, but of course . . . I never gave it back. I suppose I should have given it to the police.'

'Where is it now?' asked Fay.

'Here,' said Emily, opening her valise, pulling out a notebook and pencil and then a small beaded drawstring bag.

'Well, *open* it,' said Fay.

One by one, Emily put its few contents on the table.

A handkerchief, neatly folded.

A small gilt mirror.

A handful of dimes and quarters.

Two keys on a ring.

'And . . . ?' said Fay, craning forward to see the last thing Emily had found. It was a silver locket without a chain in the form of a little book.

She opened it.

'*Well?*' said Fay.

Emily looked at the two images inside, which faced each other. They had been cut to fit from larger photographs.

One was of Marion, smiling.

The other Emily simply stared at without a word until she whispered, '*Of course.*'

Fay took the locket from her hands.

'Gunther Darke,' she said.

She sat back in her chair and slowly began to shake her head.

'Gunther,' she said softly.

Then, with the world-weariness of an older woman who has seen a great deal of life and learned a lot along the way, Fay Bancroft shrugged, put the locket on the table and laughed out loud.

'Gunther Darke!' she said again.

Emily stared at her, astonished and not quite understanding.

Fay got up, sighing with mock resignation, went to a cabinet, opened a small mahogany box and took from it an unframed photograph. She handed it to Emily.

'What's this?'

'It's me. But the question you should ask is, where?'

Emily looked at the picture. It was Fay, in a riding habit, looking younger and holding a horse. She was standing by a pen full of steers.

'Where is it?'

'Abilene,' said Fay. 'Darke Hartz has a cattle stud out there.'

'Who took it?'

'Gunther Darke,' said Fay shamelessly. 'It's where he likes to take his classier ladies.'

'Fay!?'

Fay sat down again.

'You see, I am not without my charms,' said Fay. 'Another brandy?'

'I've had enough, thank you.'

'I think you might need one more by the time I tell you what I intended to when we first arranged this little tea.'

'Then I had better get a message to my hotel to warn Ben and Mr Toulson that I may be just a little late.'

76

Lakeshore

Anna Zemeckis had no idea what happened to barges filled with ash and garbage, except that they had to offload their cargo somewhere; and it was more than likely the tug would tow the two barges out into Lake Michigan and dump their contents into the deep.

If so, she too would be dumped along with the rest and that would be the end of her as she couldn't swim. But more likely, she thought, when they found her they would take her back to shore and hand her over to a local patrolman and she would end up at Harrison Street Police Station. And sooner or later they would charge her with the murder of Riley, whom she had stabbed in the eye and now was surely dead.

She might even be accused of being a party to the death of poor John English; or, failing that, charged with stealing money from the Mission of Hope and assaulting Sister Ursula.

As she sat on top of the pile of ash, peering out under the raised edge of the tarpaulin, she had been very surprised indeed when the tug, after going under a couple of bridges and arriving at the docks, chugged its way right through the middle of everything, big ships and all. Then, with a couple of hoots, it had pulled to the right past some jetties and ended up right behind the terminus building of the Illinois Central Railroad. It then continued heading south, fifty yards offshore and parallel with the rail tracks, until it came to a place Anna never knew existed: a moonscape of accumulated garbage consisting of ash, rotting vegetables, household waste and a huge quantity of scrap paper which fluttered about on top of the garbage and drifted off onto the water, swirling around in the air with the ducking and diving of the gulls.

Anna had arrived at Chicago's biggest dumping ground. It had been created over twenty years before in a decision by City Hall to kill two birds with one stone by depositing the rubble from the Great Fire of 1871 along the Lakeshore and using it to create a deeper shoreline beyond Lake Park. The process had never stopped and this featureless wasteland had progressed ever more east, out past the rail tracks that had once formed the shoreline and then past various docks and piers created for access to the lake.

Anna watched as the tug master expertly pulled his barges up to a temporary wooden quay, where two cranes with crude buckets stood to hoist the garbage and ash out of the holds. She knew she must make a run for it, even more so when a couple of men appeared out of a shed nearby to moor up the barges.

'There's fresh coffee, Martin,' one of them cried out to the tug master who, once his own craft was secure, hopped onto the quay and disappeared back into the shed.

Anna got out of the barge fast, clambered onto the quay and from there down a rough wooden ladder to the piles beneath on the shoreline. She found herself in softly lapping waves, a foot or so deep, standing on some slimy stones, and waded away out of sight of shed and cranes.

Only then did she scramble up among the rubbish heaps, slipping and sliding as she went, hoping that the feeding birds she disturbed did not raise the alarm, and made her way into the strange no-man's-land of the garbage dump.

Any hopes she had of quickly getting back to the Lakeshore proper were almost immediately dashed. The area was extensive and ran southward parallel with the great expanse of rail tracks that ran along the edge of Lake Park.

She could see the tops of the mansions and public buildings that fronted Michigan Avenue and, in the fading light, make out the tallest silhouettes of them all, the tower of the Auditorium Theater and Hotel, neither of which she had ever visited.

Beyond the sea wall that bordered the rail tracks and on into Lake Park she could see the lamplighter was already out turning on the gas lamps.

Anna felt a rising sense of panic. In an hour it would be dark and she had absolutely no idea of where to go or what to do.

Out here, away from the freshly dumped, still stinking garbage, there was no smell, just the fresh water of the lake. The scrubby vegetation that grew on the dry and desiccated soil whispered in the light evening breeze.

Although from a distance the ground seemed flat, when Anna started making her way across it she found it full of dips and hollows that were virtually impassable in places, so deep that the horizon kept disappearing and she continually had to reorientate herself.

Worse still, the land was riddled with watercourses of various kinds, some fetid and foul, others surprisingly fresh, but slippery and boggy and not easy to cross.

Here and there were paths of a kind, though whether used by animals or humans she had no idea. She had heard of wild dogs on the Lakeshore, and worse, and she might well have grown scared had not a dog actually showed. It was the mangiest and most pathetic thing she had ever seen. It gave her a sniff or two, followed her for a few yards and then trotted off. Anna was sorry to watch it go, for now she was on her own again.

She looked in vain for clean water. Her thirst was terrible but she didn't trust the runnels of sluggish water criss-crossing the Lakeshore here. Finally, she had to sit down and rest and consider what to do, choosing a place that faced west towards the pale but still-warm sun. The only sounds were the shrieks of the gulls, and the cranes at work on the holds of the barges she had escaped.

She had the sense that somehow, at last, she was beyond all danger out here, with the city a dull hum across distant rail tracks, and the occasional rumble of a train, and the lake, now gray, now blue, behind her, stretching to infinity.

She felt herself once more drifting off into exhausted sleep when a shadow fell across her face and a voice boomed at her, 'Is it friend or is it foe? Answer is, I don't know!'

Anna opened her eyes and found herself staring into the warm, weather-beaten face of Mr Crazy, in the same long coat Eileen had told her he always wore, and the same boots and the same black hat.

'Oh,' she said, and for the second time that day she knew she was in the presence of a friend.

'I am impressed,' said Mr Crazy, taking a comfortable position on the pile of congealed rubbish next to her, 'because I reckon that for most folk this place is harder to get to than the moon.'

'I came by barge.'

'By invitation or by accident?'

'Accident.'

'Ah! I am not so impressed. But then . . . that means Fate herself has brought you here and I guess that's impressive in another way.'

'I'm rather thirsty,' said Anna.

'Then follow me.'

'Mr Crazy, am I safe out here?'

'From prying eyes? Yes. Though folks in some of the mansions have telescopes, I do believe. They watch me at dawn – and much good may it do them.'

'Why?'

'That's when I conduct my daily ablutions in one of the biggest and best baths in America.'

'What about the winter?'

Mr Crazy laughed.

'I make a hole in the ice like an Eskimo.'

'You could freeze to death.'

'I do not think so. They don't, I don't. I thought you were thirsty.'

'I am, but . . .' She climbed a mound to get a better view. She saw she was even further away from the city than before. The cranes were far off in the distance now, and so were the railway tracks. '. . . But I feel safe for the first time in a long time. And I don't feel sick. I don't feel sick anymore, Mr Crazy.'

'But you do feel thirsty?'

She nodded. 'Very.'

'Then stop talking, young lady, and follow me.'

They walked for ten minutes or so to what Anna realized was an older part of the tip, the vegetation being thick and more established.

And there, in the midst of it all, they arrived at the strangest house

Anna had ever seen. It was located in a hollow not far from the
Lakeshore itself, the water lapping no more than twenty yards off. It
had an old metal pipe for a chimney, a couple of haphazard-looking
windows and a door. The windows were set in walls built higgledy-
piggledy from the staves of old barrels, and the roof was a piece of
salvaged tarpaulin of the kind she had been under on the barge, black
with tar. It was attached like a tent to the sides of the makeshift hut
by thick ropes stretched out in all directions and pegged down by
stones. A variety of items hung from these ropes – washing, some pots
and pans, a dead rabbit, wires and fishing lines, a net with a long
handle. Beyond stood a rickety jetty, constructed from assorted flotsam
and jetsam clearly salvaged by Mr Crazy from the Lakeshore.

'Watch you don't trip,' he said, as he wound his way between the
stones and ropes, ducking down as he brought Anna finally to the front
door. On either side, like the front porch of any respectable home,
stood two comfortable chairs.

'Sit,' said Mr Crazy.

Anna did so gratefully.

He disappeared inside and reappeared a short while later carrying
a tray with some unexpectedly refined-looking cut-glass tumblers and
an earthenware pitcher of water. There was also a hunk of fresh
bread.

He poured her some and handed her the glass. Then he had a glass
himself, smacking his lips with evident glee.

'The finest wine in the world,' said Mr Crazy, 'and it's free. Eat this.
I'll cook something soon.'

'Is there someone else living here?' said Anna, indicating the chair
she was sitting in, as she hungrily chewed on the bread.

'That's for my two guests. But you won't meet 'em. Fishing's bad
and it's a Friday. Might Sunday if you're still in residence.'

'Oh, I . . .' She began to get up.

'Sit,' he said again, 'and tell me what brought you, Miss Jelena,
from the Union Depot where we met yesterday evening.'

'You recognize me?'

'I most certainly do. I have a good memory for almost everything,
unfortunately.'

'We met twice. The other time . . .'

461

'I remember the other time. You were with your friend Eileen. At the Jackson Street Bridge.'

'You know her?'

He shook his head and then tapped it.

'It's this cursed memory of mine, can't get away from it. Except at night when I sit contemplating the stars. That cleans out my mind for a bit.'

'I've got to—'

'You don't have to do *anything*,' said Mr Crazy, 'that's the secret. Just sit. Sit.'

Mr Crazy sat back and stared out over the lake.

'You'd better do what you never did the other night. You'd better tell me what trouble you're in, then we can decide if you have to do anything or not. Did you telegraph your father?'

'I did.'

'Good, that's good.'

They sat in silence for a time. Anna helped herself to another glass of water.

'That was nice. Thank you. I'd like to clean up a bit. Is there somewhere . . . ?'

'I was hoping you'd say that,' said Mr Crazy, 'because you look kind of wild. If you go behind my house you'll find my little purpose-built bathroom. There's a comb and a bucket of water and some soap and a broken mirror on a stick where you can see to do your hair. And you'd better leave off that filthy dress. You can use my shirt. There's a clean one on the line.'

Anna got up.

'Thank you,' she said. 'I reckon, with your help Mr Crazy, I can work something out.'

'I reckon you can,' he called out in response over the top of the cabin. 'I reckon that if you worked out how to get *here* then you can work out most things. Shirt long enough for you?'

'No. Not quite.'

'Then take the one-piece hanging on the line. I highly recommend Mr Munsing's excellent new undergarment for keeping the warmth in and the cold out.'

Five minutes later Anna reappeared, her face clean, her hair wet and scraped back into a tidy knot, and sporting a huge, scarlet one-piece gentleman's undergarment, the legs of which sagged down over her ankles. She had put the shirt on over it for modesty.

'Warm enough?' enquired Mr Crazy.

'Yes. Very. Thank you . . . That's the cleverest bathroom I've ever seen.'

'Water's the first thing you have to think about when you build a place to live. I found a little run of water from a broken waterpipe in Lake Park.'

'Mr Crazy . . . I've got to wash my dress and stockings so they dry by morning . . .'

'Washtub's over there near the fire. I always keep a kettle or two boiling,' he said, pointing to another part of the site. 'The mangle's on the right.'

'You've got everything.'

Mr Crazy smiled rather wanly.

'Everything but my wife and child,' he said. 'Lost them in '71.'

She stared at him. 'In the Great Fire?'

'Yes, and my home too. But I never wanted to rebuild it, never wanted to live there again. So . . .'

'Where did you go?'

'Here, or rather over there . . .' He pointed towards Lake Park.

'They filled it in, so Mr Crazy moves his home because he likes the water. Best view in Chicago. Best bit of real estate too. Best site in my portfolio, if I chose to call it mine, which I don't.'

Anna took her dress over to the rusty old washtub and started pouring water on it from the kettle.

'Oh my goodness!' she called out suddenly. 'I forgot, I nearly soaked it through. Have you some scissors, Mr Crazy?'

A pair were produced and Anna carefully unpicked the lining of her bodice where she had sewn in the papers she had stolen from Dunning.

Mr Crazy watched her with growing interest.

'That looks like paper.'

'It is.'

'Has it got words on it?'

She nodded.

'So it's a document?'

463

'Yes.'

He looked excited.

'So you've the paper to prove it?'

'Prove what?'

'How do I know? Show me the document and I will tell you what it proves.'

'It's got my name on it. I took it from Dunning, I—'

He raised a hand. 'Wash that dress while I get some food and coffee. Then you can tell me what you have to and I will tell you what your document proves. Was it made in Chicago?'

'Dunning. Cook County Hospital. It's from there.'

'That's good, very good. I'm good on New York, excellent on Cincinnati, but Chicago, why there's not many documents you can't show me for which I don't have something that went before.'

'I don't understand.'

'You don't have to. That's the bit you leave to me.'

He disappeared inside his house, humming.

Then she heard him say, 'A document from Dunning! Well! That's a first.'

Anna, meanwhile, washed her dress as best she could but it was heavy and unwieldy. She felt strangely content until, quite unexpectedly, her old fear came back.

'Mr Crazy?'

'Yes?'

He popped his head out of the door.

'I just wanted to be sure you're still there.'

He tugged his beard and tapped his head.

'Seems so.'

'I . . . I meant . . . it's getting dark. Where can I . . . ?'

'Here,' he said, 'you can sleep here. It's clean as a whistle and warm as toast.'

'But where will you sleep?'

'In my winter residence.'

'Where's that?'

'Fifty yards back. The water rises and a cold wind blows in from the lake in winter. And then it freezes. So I do the sensible thing and move out of the way.'

'I—'

'It's all right, Anna Zemeckis. Unless Fate decrees otherwise, you'll come to no harm here.'

'You know my name?'

'I know everything.'

77

Taking Counsel

Emily Strauss arrived back at the Auditorium Annex to be greeted by Johnny Leppard dressed in a rather more important-looking uniform than when she had seen him last.

He leapt forward from the concierge's desk the moment he saw her. 'Your guests have arrived. They are waiting with Mr Latham in one of the small conference rooms.'

'Guests, Johnny?' interrupted Emily.

'A Mr Toulson and a Mr Van Hale. I took the liberty of showing them all in there.'

'Ah, rather more than I expected.'

'Light refreshments are on the way. If you need anything more, Miss Strauss, you only have to ask.'

'You look very grand today, Mr Leppard!'

He grinned his usual boy-man grin.

'I'm on a tryout as a temporary assistant concierge, till the Fair's end. They're so short-staffed that I offered my services in this new capacity and they accepted them.'

'More money?'

'Not yet, miss.'

'You're a very upward sort of person, aren't you?'

'Like you I think, Miss Strauss.'

She smiled.

'I suppose you have your eye on the concierge's position – next month maybe?'

'I'll show you to the conference room, madam,' he said with mock formality, answering her question the moment they were out of earshot of the concierge.

'Dead man's shoes as far as that position's concerned,' he said in a low voice. 'Time to move on. I have my eye on something else altogether.'

'Care to share those ambitions with me?'

'Ambitions don't put dollars in your pocket, only grasping at opportunities when you see them.'

'And one's come along?'

Johnny nodded. 'London, miss. That's why I'm learning French.'

'They speak English in London, Johnny.'

'Maybe they do, but in the hotel trade the coming language is French. The manager of the Savoy Hotel, London, is one of our guests for the closing ceremonies for the Fair. I suggested to him that he would be missing an opportunity if he did not offer me a job.'

'And did he?'

'He's thinking about it, but he will.'

'And he's French?'

'French-speaking.'

'What's his name?'

'Mr César Ritz.'

'Never heard of him.'

'You will, Miss Strauss.'

'Or maybe he'll hear of me?'

'Nothing would surprise me about anything.'

'Nothing would surprise me about *you*, Johnny Leppard.'

He opened the door and then, as though he were an MC at some civic gathering:

'Gentlemen, Miss Emily Strauss, correspondent of the New York *World*. Refreshments will be served shortly.'

He closed the door behind her.

'*Thanks Johnny,*' she said under her breath. '*One day soon you'll be doing that for real.*'

*   *   *

467

Having by now calmed down and taken the pragmatic view that she needed the Pinkertons on-side, no matter what her personal prejudices might be, Emily dove straight in. The time had come, she said, for the four of them to share their knowledge and pool their resources.

'I agree,' responded Toulson. 'My investigation is drawing to a close and you and Ben have uncovered important evidence.

'Something's got to happen in the next twenty-four hours,' Toulson continued, 'and it won't be pretty and it won't be good. There's no point calling in the Chicago Police Department because they're over-stretched enough and have been for months. In any case, there's hardly a man among them downtown to be trusted, eh Van Hale?'

Rorton Van Hale nodded.

'City Hall's not going to be much use either for the next few days, from Mayor Carter Harrison down, because they're all polishing their boots and dusting off their hats for the big closing ceremonies for the Fair. The worst of it from my point of view is that I was never hired to investigate anything more than the possibility of one man's involvement in an illegal trade.'

'Pornography,' said Emily.

Toulson nodded.

'A trade run by Mr Gunther Darke?' she added.

Toulson drew his chair closer to the conference table.

Ben produced a sketchbook from his pocket and the folder of pornographic photographs he had shown Emily earlier, developed from the broken plates salvaged from the Robinson studio. Toulson and Van Hale examined them and nodded.

'Yes, it's more of the same I showed you this morning,' said Toulson as he examined a box of cigars that Johnny had thoughtfully procured for the meeting, selected one and lit it, eyes narrowing.

'It's part of a huge network in which Anna Zemeckis was one innocent pawn.'

'And Marion Stoiber too,' interjected Emily. 'You know she's been murdered? The Meisters got to her. At the Ferris Wheel.'

The surprise in Toulson's and Van Hale's eyes showed they did not.

Emily put them in the picture.

'The trouble from our point of view,' said Toulson, 'is that your girl, Anna Zemeckis, is right in the middle of this mess and I don't doubt that what happened to Stoiber will happen to her if we don't get to her first. But it also gets in the way of my investigation.'

Emily was forced to agree.

She told the others what she had learned from Marion Stoiber and also Fay Bancroft, about Gunther Darke's seduction of Anna, of her pregnancy and of her close involvement with John English.

'We don't know if the Meisters got her or not, but I like to think not. That girl's a survivor; she's a lioness protecting her unborn young and she'll fight to the very last. I think she's still alive and I have to figure out where.

'As for Anna's involvement in the pornography trade, she must have been lured to the building you men found. It must have been from there that she went missing. John English said she didn't remember anything much about the last day or so before she arrived at Dunning. But whoever's after Anna now, it sounds like Darke is calling the shots.'

'Or Hartz,' said Toulson. 'He's Darke's father-in-law, remember, and both men are members of the Old America Association. And I suspect one or both were involved in the death of Jenkin Lloyd Rhys.'

Van Hale filled in that part of the story.

'Seems Rhys's death was mighty convenient timing for Hartz, given that if Rhys had still been in office it's likely his man and not Hartz's would have taken over the presidency.'

'And now?' asked Ben.

'It looks like Rhys's candidate's for the taking – he's a big wheel in the New York Mercantile Exchange. But since Rhys was got out of the way, Hartz is in with a chance to place his own man. The convention is on today and tomorrow, in the one place in town big enough to hold the OAA membership – the Auditorium Theater right next door. Both sides have summoned every member they can track down to attend tomorrow's election. God knows who'll come out of the woodwork. Whoever gets the presidency will wield a lot of power through the membership across the United States and Hartz knows that better than anybody.'

'So what's the connection between all that and pornography?' said Emily.

Toulson glanced at Rorton Van Hale and said nothing.

'I thought we were pooling our resources,' said Emily. 'Don't forget, if I find Anna Zemeckis she may be your only material witness to all of this.'

'Yes, she may well be,' said Toulson. 'Look, I didn't undertake my investigation and you didn't get into yours to pit our wits against one of America's most powerful organizations. I'm doing a job for a private client—'

'Whom you haven't named,' cut in Emily.

'. . . and you're on a special assignment for Mr Pulitzer.'

'Kind of a useful person to have on our side, wouldn't you say?' responded Emily firmly.

'He would be,' conceded Toulson, 'but you are just a journalist, and a female one at that, and you're only as good as the story you deliver.'

'Then help me with the story and I'll deliver a damn good one that might just help yours. Don't, and I'll still deliver my story, but it won't be one that'll do you or your client any favors.'

'You talk tough, Miss Strauss.'

'I'm learning to. Now . . . if I'm to get to the root of what's been happening to Anna Zemeckis and why everybody seems to want her out of the way, I need to understand the precise link between the OAA and pornography. I thought it was a nationwide organization of the middle-class, respectable and God-fearing, who wouldn't know the difference between a *pose plastique* and a postcard.'

Toulson sighed.

'Very well, but you don't use what I'm going to tell you without my say-so. And you mention it to no one. These men do not play games. So you can put that notebook away. You commit all I say from now on to memory.'

Emily nodded.

'The real power in the OAA is held by the so-called Audit Committee. Before Rhys's death, he chaired it and he controlled it. Now Hartz is in temporary control until Rhys's successor is appointed tomorrow. But the balance of its members is clearly shifting Hartz's way. What the Audit Committee decides to do, the OAA follows.

'What I didn't know until I began looking at Gunther Darke's involvement with pornography was that the OAA conducts certain – what you might call covert – activities. Originally, under Rhys, for all his bonhomie, the main purpose of these activities was to do whatever it took to get the OAA's way over a range of political and commercial issues across a range of states.

'Since Hartz has been on the committee – that's four years now – those activities have taken a different turn. It began with harmless bolstering of lobby positions in Washington over anti-immigration policies. In the last two years, however, it's got a lot more sinister. The intimidation of those who support immigration has been sanctioned by the Audit Committee. Now, with Rhys's disappearance, the committee's muscle has been turned against the OAA's own people: the ones that are – or would have been – his supporters.'

'But what has this to do with these obscene photographs?' said Emily.

'Simple,' said Toulson. 'Any idea how big this business really is?'

Emily and Ben shook their heads.

'In America, over a million dollars annually and rising very fast; worldwide, and that's mainly Europe, you can treble that figure. They're much more sophisticated about that kind of thing on the other side of the Atlantic, particularly in London, Paris and Berlin. I know for a fact that Robinson had links with a flourishing trade in pornographic literature and photographs conducted in London—'

'Of course,' interrupted Emily, 'it said on the back of Anna's *carte de visite* that he had studios in other cities.'

'Yes, in London, just off the Strand,' continued Toulson, 'the back streets round there have been the center of the English pornography trade for decades. But don't worry, Miss Strauss, America's catching up fast and, thanks to Gunther Darke, Chicago has been spearheading this lucrative new market.

'We're pretty certain that some of the OAA's more unpleasant activities are funded by the pornography trade, but of course the membership at large has no idea and would be horrified. There's a hard core of barefaced profiteers who run it, headed by Mr Gunther Darke, Paul Hartz's son-in-law.'

'And that's always been convenient for another reason,' said Emily.

'Which is?' murmured Van Hale.

'Who ultimately controls Darke Hartz. I believe things will change soon in that respect.'

'You seem to have discovered a lot of things in a short time, Miss Strauss,' said Toulson.

'It's pretty much common knowledge why Darke and Hartz don't talk to each other and that Hartz will make a bid for control of the company when Mr Darke retires at the end of the year. But in any event, he himself unwittingly set the whole thing in motion several years ago when his daughter married Gunther Darke.'

'Well, I have my own version of those events, Miss Strauss. So I'd quite like to hear yours,' said Toulson.

'The Darke and Hartz families go back to when Hans Darke's father had a business on the East Coast and banked with Hartz of Boston and New York. Hans opened their meatpacking business in Chicago in 1865 when the Union Stock Yard opened, and he thrived. But he couldn't compete with the big boys, Armour and Swift, and after 1878 he needed capital if he was going to survive.

'That's when Paul Hartz bought into the company, wanting a fifty-fifty split. Hans resisted and they ended up with a thirty-five percent stockholding each, with Hans's two sons, Wolfgang and Gunther having ten percent each and Paul's daughter Christiane having the remaining ten percent, making a fifty-five to forty-five split between the families.

'Hans was a brilliant stockbreeder and master butcher, but it was Paul's financial know-how that enabled them to survive against the bigger meatpackers and finally emerge as one of the big four in 1890.

'So far, so good. Then Christiane, whom everybody thought had a soft spot for Wolfgang Darke – one of the most uncharismatic men I've ever met, incidentally, but what do I know? – went and fell for the charms of the older brother Gunther. Naturally Paul encouraged the match because by then Gunther had fallen out with Hans and seemed to favor working with Paul. His support would give Paul the majority interest.

'That's about it, except that last year Hans, who'd been ill with heart trouble, announced he wanted to retire and give his holding entirely to Wolfgang. This caused growing dissent in the Darke Hartz enterprise, added to the fact that from the first the marriage of Christiane to Gunther had been a disaster.'

472

'When is Hans due to retire?'

'End of the year. Since Gunther doesn't get on with his brother either, it looks likes Wolfgang – who's a chip off the old block, a master butcher but not a money man – will be out in the cold. Unless, of course, Gunther divorces the woman he appears not to love and Christiane marries the man everyone thinks she should have married.'

'You mean poor old Wolfgang?' said Ben, looking bemused.

'I do. But it won't happen. Gunther will never set Christiane free. And they will never have a normal marriage either. Christiane found out very quickly about Gunther's promiscuity and his womanizing. She was fearful of contracting an infection from him. They haven't had sexual relations for years. Which is why there is no heir to the Hartz half of the Darke Hartz empire.'

'You seem very well informed on all their family secrets,' said Van Hale. 'What's your source?'

'One of Gunther Darke's former lovers. But let's get down to the fundamental issue, Mr Toulson. Let me ask you, for a second time, who's your client?'

'I'm afraid that is one thing I am not at liberty to reveal. It breaks my code of conduct.'

'You guys have a code?'

Toulson flushed.

'As a matter of fact we have, Miss Strauss, and it's a hell of a lot more meaningful than any you newspaper people might have, if you've got one at all.'

'I apologize, Mr Toulson.'

'Accepted – and as a matter of fact so do I.'

They grinned at each other.

'Does my view of Darke Hartz square with yours, Mr Toulson?'

'Yes, it does.'

'A former lover's not a bad source,' said Emily, trying not to look smug. 'Though of course she knows nothing of Gunther's involvement in pornography. If she did, she would be horrified.'

Toulson grinned.

'So, Mr Toulson. You know my source. Care to reveal yours?'

'Sure. Mr Hans Darke.'

It was Emily's turn to grin.

'Now that's really very interesting Mr Toulson. He wouldn't happen to be your client too by any chance?'

'You're too clever for your own good, but I'm beginning to understand why Mr Pulitzer employed you.'

Johnny Leppard knocked and entered.

'Message for Miss Strauss. The gentleman who delivered it is waiting for your reply.'

Emily opened the classy envelope he handed her and read it.

'Well,' she said, '*Well!* Talk of the devil!'

'Who's it from, Emily?' asked Ben.

'Mr Paul Hartz,' she said. 'He wants to have a talk with me.'

'When?' said Toulson grimly.

'Now,' said Emily. 'And he insists that I go alone.'

'That is out of the question,' said Van Hale.

Toulson agreed. 'Absolutely. You can't go, Miss Strauss. The man is totally untrustworthy.'

'I've no intention of trusting him,' said Emily coolly, 'and I promise I'll be on my guard.'

'What's your answer, Miss Strauss?' said Johnny, still hovering in the doorway.

'The gentleman who's waiting, does he have a cab?'

'He's got a private carriage.'

'Tell him I'll be out in five minutes.'

474

78

Meisters

Dodek Krol had set up his temporary headquarters for the search for Anna Zemeckis in a fruit warehouse off South Water Street, less than a hundred yards from where she had last been seen. Together with two of his Meisters he had arrived late that afternoon and had commandeered a small corner of the warehouse, politely informing its terrified owner that they needed some space, would cause no trouble and soon be gone.

The warehousemen did not need to be told who the men were, nor that they would do well to look the other way. As for the identity of Krol himself, most guessed it: he was well known as director of the Nord Chicago Turnverein and as a man of supreme physical strength and power. His celebrity went before him, but his presence was one people feared as well as warmed to. He had about him that indefinable air of menace, which other people, mostly men, recognized as that of the natural-born killer.

The small warehouse owner had been quick to offer the use of his own office but Dodek had sent him scurrying away, preferring to take up occupation of a pile of fruit crates in a quiet corner, from which he and his men occasionally helped themselves to the choicest items. Later the quaking warehouseman came over, clutching the bowler normally glued to his head, in deference to his distinguished 'guest'.

He ventured to offer, by way of a belated gesture of hospitality, a pot of coffee and some pastries from a nearby baker's.

Dodek scowled. 'Later. Have you a telephone?'

The owner had.

'And do you have your own telegraph?'

'No. The market men use the one in the big wholesaler's next door.'

'I shall need to use it. One of my men . . . I shall be very much obliged if you would show him.'

The two men with Dodek were handpicked Meisters, not so much for their skill with the knife – that was assumed and long-since proved – as the respect they commanded in the three wards of the city over which Krol had decided to organize his search with the help of the Tick Tock boys: the north section of the Chicago River and the Lakeshore south of its mouth. The girl, he was sure, had evaded capture by hiding on a barge or river craft on the wharf near South Water Street which had then gone south along the lake. She had probably got off somewhere between there and the docks and quays that fronted it and would be lying low overnight.

Having sent his men out to make enquiries earlier in the afternoon, Dodek was now certain of three things: that the girl had not got back out into South Water Street; that she had not been able to cross over to the north side of the Chicago River and into Ward 24; and finally, that she had not got away on a cruiser out on Lake Michigan, for few had left that late in the day and the others had all been thoroughly searched.

It was Dodek's personal view that this whole exercise was a complete waste of time. He did not see how a single girl of no individual importance or influence could possibly be carrying information so valuable that she warranted such attention. Besides, he didn't like harming women.

But he accepted that if Mr Darke believed this girl to be important then she must be. And he had given him his word that he would personally oversee the search for her and, in this at least, professional pride dictated that she would be found.

But it had grown too dark to complete the search that night and the decision was taken to continue it the following morning at first light.

With that, Krol departed the warehouse, leaving enough in crisp new bills in the warehouse owner's hand to ensure that his and his men's mouths would remain tightly shut. Forever.

Meanwhile, not far away on the wharf off South Water Street, a solitary figure walked to where the barges were moored up for the night. It was the act of a man who, in the short space of a day, had learned the true nature of courage.

John English stood and stared at the darkening river, trying to work things out.

No one was around but the tug master's boy, checking the moorings for the night, who, when asked, helpfully explained where the barges went with their cargoes of garbage and ash.

To search the Lakeshore now, in the dark and alone, was futile. It would have to be done in the morning, first thing; preferably, thought John, with the help of Emily Strauss.

79

Hartz Castle

Emily's ride from the Auditorium Annex on Michigan to Paul Hartz's famous residence on Prairie Avenue took ten minutes, but it felt like a very long ten minutes indeed.

Her companion was a spare, tall man in his thirties with a hard face and cropped hair in the Prussian manner. His black pants and frockcoat were more a uniform than a suit of clothes. If he had been at a funeral he would not have been out of place. In downtown Chicago, at the beginning of a weekend of festivities, with the city so vibrant and colorful and bent on enjoying itself, his long face, mean eyes and sober appearance meant he was only one thing, a Meister; and Emily knew it. He said nothing the entire trip and did not register her presence as an attractive female in the way most men did. His whole being spelt a chilling combination of discipline, obedience and menace.

What surprised her as their somber carriage turned into Prairie Avenue at 18th was that Paul Hartz should allow himself to be so openly associated with such a man. But, she guessed, his intention was to intimidate her, which meant, she told herself, that in some way and quite unwittingly, she really must have intimidated him. Or at least got under his skin.

Emily judged that to be a challenging start.

* * *

Prairie Avenue, once one of Chicago's finest residential streets, these days had an air of faded glory. Emily did not know whose mansions were whose, but she knew that many of the great commercial luminaries of Chicago – Marshall Field, George Pullman, Philip Armour and Paul Hartz – had built opulent homes here through the seventies and eighties, some in the ugly and over-ornate Second Empire style, others in what might be called 'bulky utilitarian'. But by now anybody who was anybody in Chicago had long since moved north to Astor Street to escape the stench of the stockyards. Except for Paul Hartz, that was. He liked to stay close to where his money was.

The first thing that Emily noticed as she climbed out of the carriage – her cheerless friend not offering to assist her – was the rumble and rush of a passing train along the nearby Lakeshore tracks, steam rising in the air and specks of soot falling from it.

'Must play havoc with the residents' washing,' she said to lighten things a bit.

'This way,' said her companion without expression.

Nevertheless, Emily could not resist staring at a red-brick mansion of huge, stolid proportions and without ornament on the other side of the avenue.

'Whose is that?'

'Mr Armour's. Please. This way.'

'And that one?' she added, just to be provocative.

The man eyed a fresh-built mansion on the corner of Prairie and 16th without interest and probably without understanding. Unlike the others, it butted straight onto the sidewalk with a fortress-like wall of splendid yellow sandstone and windows and doors which pierced the facade with stark simplicity. By comparison with the one she was about to enter, it looked very attractive indeed.

'Who lives there?' asked Emily.

The man took her arm, none too gently.

'Lady,' he said, 'Mr Hartz does not like to be kept waiting and nor do I.'

Hartz was charm itself, as he had been at Hans Darke's party the day before, when they had been briefly introduced, but there was no disguising the coldness in his gray eyes.

479

He did not, as Toulson had warned, dwell on niceties once their greetings were over, and Emily's enquiry after Christiane Darke's health was politely ignored.

'I understand you work for Mr Pulitzer, Miss Strauss?'

She agreed she did.

'He's a friend of mine.'

She looked noncommittal.

'My firm has many clients who advertise in the New York *World*.'

'That's very astute of them, Mr Hartz. It's a widely read, well-regarded daily, committed to the Democratic principles of truth, justice and liberty.'

'There is no need to be arch with me, young lady.'

'And there is no need to patronize me or take me for a fool, Mr Hartz,' Emily replied. 'If you have something to say, say it; if not, please be kind enough to give my best wishes to your daughter when you next see her and I shall be glad to take my leave of you. Your carriage back to Michigan Avenue would be welcome; I have no wish to chance my luck at this time of evening walking through the Levee.'

His eyes hardened even more, but the smile remained rooted on his face for the time being.

'I thought you could do with some help with your story.'

'Which one? I'm working on several.'

'The one about Anna Zemeckis.'

'Fire away.'

'How much is Mr Pulitzer paying you?'

'Rather more than even you could afford, Mr Hartz.'

This brought a skeptical smile to his face.

'Try me.'

Emily got up. 'Do you mind if I move around as we talk? I generally do when I'm thinking, so maybe while I consider what you've just suggested I should do so.'

'Feel free,' said Hartz smoothly, relaxing a little and thinking he had his fish on the hook, 'I guess it's more generous than most.'

'Your study or your offer?'

Hartz shrugged complacently.

His 'study' was what most people would have called a very large library, and Emily wandered freely, taking her time to look at the books, the busts, the portraits of Republicans, the lace antimacassars and the view across the back courtyard towards a coach house and stables.

She wasn't thinking about Hartz's offer of a bribe, if that's what it was, at all. She was collecting a little color for her story. People usually revealed themselves in their private rooms, often without realizing it.

Hartz watched her, confident now and benign. Everybody, but everybody, had their price, from presidents down and especially journalists. Like officers of the law, he had yet to meet one he could not buy with money or with favor.

He got on, surreptitiously, with checking the agenda for the important final day tomorrow of the Old America Association's National Convention. Ensuring that meetings went the way *you* wanted them to go was all about preparation. He was having some final thoughts on alternative strategies, according to the way different items on the agenda went. Ultimately they would all go the way he and his associates wanted.

He had pondered the same strategies an hour before, on how he would deal with the tiresome Miss Strauss. Whatever she did, the outcome would finally be the one he wanted, which was to silence her.

Meanwhile, he was happy for her to take a look around his study like a naïve schoolgirl. Except, she wasn't a girl, she was a more attractive woman than he had expected and more spirited too. He liked that in a woman, and he liked having a woman like that in his home. He missed it.

'Coffee, Miss Strauss?' he said, reaching for a bellpull behind him. 'Or something stronger? Most journalists I know, and I know a lot, take liquor after six.'

Emily considered this and, frankly, was tempted. But that's not what she said.

'I'm not planning to stay long enough for a drink, Mr Hartz.'

His eyes hardened again.

'Tell me, sir, who's the lady with you in this photograph? No, don't trouble to get up; I'll bring it to you.'

She picked up a silver-framed photograph and placed it right in front of Hartz on his desk, right on top of the papers he was looking at.

His eyes narrowed.

He did not like women who took the initiative.

He did not like being wrong-footed.

'It's a personal picture, Miss Strauss, of the kind civilized people are sensitive enough not to ask about. The lady's dead.'

'But the gentleman is not. That's Mr Darke, is it not?'

He nodded.

'And the lady is his wife, I guess?'

Hartz glowered.

On the face of it the little photograph, taken in one of the family residences no doubt, was harmless. Only thing was, Mrs Darke's eyes were on a younger Paul Hartz, and his had a proprietorial look, whilst Hans Darke stood alongside them looking disgruntled.

Like Hartz now.

'Hans Darke was never an especially sociable man. He did not deserve the wife he had. But let's cut to the chase, shall we? Name your price, Miss Strauss – to leave Chicago today and write up some harmless story about women at the Fair. I reckon you could do that standing on your head.'

'You did a financial deal with Mr Darke a few years later, did you not?'

'I did, and it benefited us both greatly. Not that it's any of your business.'

'Mr Hartz, I have no price, because I'm not selling. But if I were, I'd have to ask you – and you won't mind if I quote your own words in the matter – what price do you put on truth?'

Hartz's smile finally vanished.

'Miss Strauss, you're beginning to bore me,' he said. 'So, here's how I see it. I would imagine Mr Pulitzer is expecting you to file your story in time for the edition on the thirtieth, the day the Fair closes.'

'He is and I will.'

'Really? But what's the value of your story, and your job, if you file it a day late?'

Emily did not reply. She was thinking hard and her heart was beginning to beat faster. Suddenly it seemed a long way to the front door.

'I'll tell you,' said Paul Hartz rising, 'not a lot. Nothing in fact. Worse than nothing because I happen to know Mr Pulitzer has no time for failure and no time for losers, however good their excuses may be. Am I right?'

'I guess you are, Mr Hartz.'

Hartz reached for the bellpull.

A door at the far end of the library opened behind her, but Emily did not turn to look that way. There was a mean look in Hartz's eyes that rooted her to the spot. She had no fear of his Meister . . .

'So here's the deal, Miss Strauss. You go away and write a nice, safe little story which one of my associates will help you with and for which you'll get handsomely paid in addition to the pittance Pulitzer plans for you. Alternatively, you go on a nice little vacation right now which will not be over until well past your deadline, by which time Mr Pulitzer will not be interested in hearing your excuses because he will have fired you.'

'Tell me, Mr Hartz, what is it in my story about Anna Zemeckis that worries you? Is it that I might find her alive and she'll tell me things people like you don't want me to know? Like the corrupt management at Dunning whose board you're chairman of? Or is it simpler than that – you and everyone else who operate as boosters for this great city don't want a bad word said about it, even though everyone knows that during the Fair crime rates have soared and people have gone missing, even from the best-lit and best-located of sidewalks. People like your good but late-lamented friend Jenkin Lloyd Rhys, for example?'

'Miss Strauss . . . ,' began Hartz, angry now. He glanced across the room and nodded.

Emily ignored the steps of the approaching man behind her and stepped right up to the edge of Hartz's desk.

'Or is it that the nasty, dirty business your son-in-law is running out of the Union Stock Yard might destroy Darke Hartz and Company's market value and in turn irrevocably damage the Old America Association, if I were to expose it?'

'That's enough, Miss Strauss, I think,' the man behind her said, taking her arm.

'And don't you touch me,' she said, turning angrily.

She looked up and found herself staring into the eyes of Gunther Darke.

'Mr Darke. How nice. May I congratulate you on your excellent lecture this morning,' she said graciously, brazening out Gunther's stare. 'I found it extraordinarily . . . revealing.'

He smiled.

'Don't mind my father-in-law, Miss Strauss, he's not used to women like you. He doesn't know how to handle them.'

'And you do?'

Darke came nearer.

She could sense the animal in him, the presence, the power.

'If we had time,' he said, his voice softer, his gaze glittering and seeming to penetrate her anger and fear to something deeper that began to feel that it could easily slide out of control, 'there's a nice place out West I'd enjoy showing you. But, you've only got a few days, it seems.'

'I'm not going anywhere,' said Emily.

'Precisely,' said Gunther, taking her arm and pulling her nearer, 'except out of this city. You're out of your depth, Miss Strauss, and your meddling must stop.'

Somewhere in the distance Emily heard a doorbell ring.

She heard it grow more insistent.

She heard the rumble of voices, male and rising.

She heard a sudden thump.

Gunther let her go and turned towards the door into the hall through which Emily had first come in.

Steps approached it.

It opened.

'I'm sorry,' said Rorton Van Hale, 'but your butler has had an accident. I've come to collect Miss Strauss.'

He surveyed the room.

Gunther Darke stood there looking charming.

Paul Hartz was sitting at his desk, smiling a patrician smile.

Emily Strauss was standing in the middle of the room, her cheeks flushed.

'Our friend was just leaving,' said Gunther Darke.

'Indeed,' said Hartz rising and extending a hand to her.

She took it.

'You would do well to remember all that has been said and consider the consequences very carefully if you do not,' he said icily.

'Oh, but I'm sure she will,' said Gunther.

Emily turned and looked at him. His eyes had that same glint of menace she had seen before.

484

As Van Hale ushered Emily towards the door, she turned back one last time with a smile.

'Oh, Mr Hartz, forgive me, I almost forgot to ask . . .'

'What?' asked Hartz acidly.

'Whether you would care to comment on the latest information I have about Miss Zemeckis?'

'Which is what precisely, Miss Strauss?' interposed Gunther Darke, swiftly moving forward.

'Why, that she's carrying your child, Mr Darke. I'm sure Mr Hartz will be the first to congratulate you.'

Darke looked furious, but the look Paul Hartz gave his son-in-law was something else: it was positively murderous.

'Good evening gentlemen,' said Emily.

80

Day's End

Mary Nevitt's beautiful, limpid eyes snapped open in the dark of the ward she shared with Maureen Riley and two other women, three of them victims of Dr Eels's first experiments on their frontal lobes, and Riley the gibbering end result of Anna's will to survive.

It was now well past eight. The lights had been put out and Dunning had been in lockdown for more than half an hour. This meant that the patients would not be seen again or even much looked at for twelve hours, barring fire or flood.

. . . and *that* meant that the patients were in charge.

Mary sat up and stared across the ward towards Riley's bed.

'Hungry?' she asked.

Riley's answer was slow in coming, though her terror was already clear to see and had been for days. It was there in her eyes, in the struggling of her unresponsive limbs but, worst of all, it was in her damaged mind in which all the slithering snakes of her past now writhed about and gave her no peace. These terrifying hallucinations were being fed by Mary Nevitt.

No she wasn't hungry and she didn't want Mary anywhere near her, but Riley's body struggled to get its answer out.

'Nah!' she finally managed to gasp. If she could have found a way to scream she would.

'Nah!'

No she wasn't hungry.

'I knew you were,' said Mary.

Mary Nevitt had been sent to Dunning along with her older sister Ida fifteen years previously. Back in 1871, Ida's troubled birth had starved her brain of oxygen and left her with a virtually useless, contorted body. Mary had spent her short life devotedly looking out for her. Both their parents had died in the cholera epidemic of 1873, after which relatives had placed the two girls in an orphanage. But Ida's degenerating condition and Mary's obsessively protective behavior had brought the governors to the inevitable conclusion that Dunning would be a more appropriate institution for them.

It was the sisters' misfortune that their arrival had coincided with another, that of a new orderly, Maureen Riley. Worse, in the first few days, Mrs Riley, as she was then more respectfully referred to, had been given responsibility for the care of the Nevitt sisters, to whom she had taken an instant dislike. The two girls were uncooperative and kept themselves apart from the others, resisting intrusion from the orderlies.

In retaliation, Riley set out to punish first the helpless Ida, and then her sister too.

Brain-damaged people like Ida, whose muscular responses are almost impossible to control, especially when they are stressed, find it hard to swallow quickly. They need time and patience from the person feeding them. Riley knew this and in her perverted, cruel way stopped allowing Mary to feed her sister, insisting it should be done by a member of staff.

This was a job Riley often took upon herself, in full view of the protesting Mary, who had to suffer the sight of her sister's struggles and terror as the orderly laid Ida on her back, fed her from above, and watched as every single mouthful became a fight against a choking death.

Naturally in more recent years she had had better things to do than feed individual patients but, for old times' sake, and because everybody knew how much she loved the Nevitts, she would occasionally feed Ida herself.

Finally, in 1889, Ida died – from choking on her food. But Mary was the one who was blamed and punished with seclusion for a week after her sister's death. Worse still, she was never given the chance to say goodbye to Ida or stand by her unmarked grave in the common burying ground for inmates at the back of Far Side.

It was grief and guilt and anger that finally turned Mary Nevitt's mind and fueled her now insane desire for revenge; the same hunger for revenge that had brought life back into her writhing, twisting fingers.

After Anna Zemeckis had plunged the pen into Riley's brain, her muscular condition had deteriorated. These days, if Riley was sat up, she stayed sat up; if she was raised to a standing position, she stayed as she was but didn't move forward until someone moved her legs and feet one after the other. When she was laid down at night on her cot, she found it impossible to get back up, both from lack of will and loss of the memory of how to do it. Eating and swallowing too had become difficult now for Maureen Riley. Mary Nevitt knew this, and she watched and waited.

'You're hungry, I know you are,' said Mary, standing by her side now, her sharp nails jabbing painfully at Riley's nipples, 'and I've got some food.'

'Nah! Naah!'

'Yes,' said Mary, 'Dr Eels said I must.'

Then aping Riley's cruelty, she added in a different voice, 'It's for your own good, Ida. So come on now, there's a good girl.'

'*Naaaah!*' gasped Riley as a lump of rancid meat was thrust into her mouth.

Out on the Lakeshore, Anna Zemeckis sat contentedly with Mr Crazy by a roaring fire of driftwood and half-spent coal which sent sparks flying upwards.

She was now well fed on rabbit stew, potatoes and carrots and various wild herbs, with more hunks of fresh bread. Her dress and stockings, hung out as near the fire as she dared, steamed gently in the night.

'Don't ask me exactly what's in it,' said Mr Crazy of his stew, 'but every bit's good. Best restaurant on the best bit of real estate in Chicago and, in a manner of speaking, I can prove it.'

He produced a scrappy piece of paper which he handed to Anna. 'I guess you can read?'

Anna nodded and read. It was a scrawl in a rough hand. It read: *I persnly rekamen this plaice n this sheff, Harry.*

'Who was Harry?'

'A tramp. Lived here at the Lakeshore like me. Best friend ever I had after my wife and child died. He saw me right, showed me the ropes out here and helped me build my cabin. Taught me more than any college, though he couldn't spell and never wanted to.'

Mr Crazy produced another piece of paper, this time more official-looking.

Anna scanned it and looked puzzled.

'It's some kind of land claim,' she said.

Mr Crazy beamed.

The light played bright on his beard, his cheeks and his eyes. He looked more like Saint Nicholas than ever and Anna, dressed cosily in her scarlet Mr Munsing union suit, its color all the richer for the firelight, looked like Santa's assistant.

She beamed too.

'What land does it lay claim to?'

Mr Crazy waved his arms about proprietorially and said, 'Why, this very piece of extensive real estate you're sitting in. By squatter's rights. I've lived here long enough and there's not a man jack or woman in Chicago can deny it. I'm just biding my time and then I shall claim my rights.'

'When will that be?'

A cloud settled on Mr Crazy's face.

'Been asking myself that same question for a very long time. I came here in '71, a broken man. Before that I had had my share of real estate. I wasn't rich but I was getting richer and I had a home and a good woman and a child. Then . . .'

He shook his head and poked the fire. Sparks rose into the air.

'See that?'

He pointed to a tiny speck on a piece of wood that burned with an exquisite blue-green flame, a tiny jewel of color.

'What is it, Mr Crazy?'

'That's a piece of ship's timber and it's the copper nails that shoot out little flames like that while they melt. Well, I've had copper nails in my brain since '71, but one by one they've all been burned away and it's made me whole again.'

'Has the last one gone?'

'Yes, I think it has.'

'So then . . . ?'

'So nothing,' he growled. 'Why am I still here? Is that what you want to know?'

'Yes,' she said.

The stars shone bright above their heads.

The lighthouse was winking as its reflector turned round and round, sending its routine flash of red and then yellow.

Trains rumbled and creaked out near the park, beyond which was a wall of black, pierced by gaslights blinking in the city to the west.

In front of them, the waves of Lake Michigan lapped softly; a ship's red and green navigation lights bobbed on the horizon.

'Because I'm scared of leaving,' said Mr Crazy, 'even though I know my time here is up. Can't run from life forever.'

'What are you scared of?'

'Don't rightly know. But I know what I need.'

'What's that?'

'Something to give me back my courage. I planned it all long ago,' he said. 'Look, I'll show you.'

He went into his cabin and walked back brandishing a carpet bag.

'This bag, Anna, contains all the things I need for my future. I have the papers to prove it, right here.'

He sat down, putting the bag on the ground beside him.

'Talking of which, that document you stole and so carefully preserved does prove something: quite a lot, in fact. For one thing it proves what everybody's guessed long since about places like Dunning – that their treatment of patients breaks all codes of professional conduct and a few laws as well. Not to mention that it seems to me that your Dr Eels is conducting experiments he shouldn't be on human beings.'

'Oh,' said Anna.

490

'And another thing. Dr Eels mentions the little matter of how his experiment is being funded, which is very helpful to those of us concerned with truth and justice.'

'You mean who's paying for it?'

'Yes. It seems that it's the Old America Association that's putting up the cash, and that touches me to the very quick.'

'Why so?'

'Because I just happen to be one of its original members, courtesy of my lifetime dues paid back in 1868 when it was founded with honorable intentions, in the true spirit of Republicanism. But in the last few years those values have been lost sight of, thanks to Mr Paul Hartz and his like.'

'What are you going to do?'

'Don't rightly know. I'd attend tomorrow's 25th National Convention in the Auditorium Theater if I thought they'd let me in. That'd ruffle a few feathers. Anyone who can disrupt a meeting chaired by Mayor Carter Harrison by democratic means – and believe me, I've done *that* a few times – ought to be able to make his point at a meeting run by smooth-talking Eastcoaster Mr Paul Hartz.'

Mr Crazy sat and pondered this for a while.

Anna's eyes began to close.

'Just remembered something,' said her companion. 'It's important.'

'I was almost asleep.'

'Not yet, I've one last thing to show you.'

'What?'

He produced a storm lantern and lit it. Then another.

'Take one of these and follow me.'

He led Anna along a track inland behind his cabin. They dropped into a hollow where the horizon disappeared altogether and came to what looked like an opening into the earthy bank itself.

In this eerie spot, Anna could make out by the light of the lantern a crudely made wooden opening, though it was disguised as a pile of old lumber. Mr Crazy dragged it open and shone his lantern inside. It was a tiny space, the size of a coalhole, full of an assortment of wooden boxes and crates neatly stacked up on one another.

'My archive,' he said. 'Every subject under the sun classified and filed away under Mr Dewey's system.'

'May I?' she said.

Anna looked about her incredulously.

'There must be thousands of documents and pieces of paper here,' she said. 'How did you come by them?'

'They've been dumped. Make interesting reading if you have the time, which I have. Helps me keep an eye on City Hall and its business dealings. Did I tell you about the tunnels?'

'No,' said Anna, 'but I saw your placard about them that day at the river.'

'Remind me to. Now, where shall we file your document?'

He opened a couple of boxes, considered the matter, and finally placed it in a folder marked 'Miscellaneous'.

'Why?' she said.

'Harder to find should anyone come prying.'

'You said no one will.'

'I did but I could be wrong. I hope I am. But it sounds like your pursuers are persistent. You should be all right for a couple of days out here. Then we must get you safely out of Chicago. But first you must rest.'

Mr Crazy took Anna back to his cabin and left her by the door.

'There's your bed, Anna. It's clean and dry. And there's a warm shawl you can wrap around you in the morning. Sleep well. I shall spend the night in my winter residence. Oh, and by the way, if you should hear splashing in the morning, that's me taking my ablutions in Lake Michigan. So I'd be obliged if you'd get the coffee brewing. Goodnight.'

Back at the Auditorium Annex, to which an exhausted Emily was safely escorted by Rorton Van Hale, Ben was waiting anxiously. Having viewed the spartan arrangements in Johnny Leppard's cramped room in the staff quarters with apprehension, he had decided to wait for Emily's return in a comfortable armchair in the lounge.

After Emily had taken a bath and changed she came back down to share a final chat and hot chocolate with Ben before going to bed. But they had no sooner settled down to talk, than a bellhop came over with a message. Mr English was at the reception desk asking for Emily.

John English, now crumpled and dusty after his day's exertions, explained that after leaving Emily on the wharf he had spent some more time looking around. He had been obliged to return home for supper with his mother, but after seeing her to bed at her usual early hour he had slipped out again, back to the wharf for one last look for Anna.

'I walked around a bit . . .'

'Alone? In the dark?'

'Didn't bother me, Miss Strauss, it's Anna I'm thinking of. I reckon there's only one place she would have ended up and that's why I had to come.'

He produced a Rand McNally map of downtown Chicago, pointing at the Lakeshore that ran parallel to Michigan Avenue where they now were.

'Out there, beyond Lake Park,' he explained, 'is a very large area of garbage dumps onto which almost everything spewing out of Chicago is likely to get dumped by barges coming down the river from the wharves where we were yesterday.'

'The City Council have plans to reclaim it and make it part of the park eventually, though big business would like to cover it all with real estate. But meanwhile it's garbage. I'm pretty sure that's where Anna's barge will have ended up and I'm equally certain she's got enough sense to hide out there overnight.'

'But if you've worked that out then I reckon Mr Hartz, Mr Darke and their Meisters have done the same.'

'Yes, but searching by night is futile out there. The ground can be treacherous in parts and there's too many places to hide.'

Emily looked at the map. 'Where's the best access?'

'Only been there once myself to do some fishing, but I got out there from beyond the Illinois Central Depot on 12th. The only other place is to the north where the Chicago River flows out into the lake. And you'd need to get there by boat.'

'Well, 12th is just down Michigan from here,' said Emily. 'So I reckon we head out first thing and start looking beyond Illinois Central. At dawn.'

'Don't we need backup?' said Ben.

'We don't have any, even if we wanted it,' replied Emily. 'Toulson and Van Hale have got their own investigation to deal with and it's coming to a head. I'm willing to take the risk, if you two are. John? Ben?'

Both men nodded. Then, suddenly, John's face registered a momentary sense of panic.

'But what about . . .'

'Mother?' said Emily tartly. 'I'm sure Mrs English will survive a night by herself.'

Half an hour later John installed himself in Ben's already cramped bedroom, curling up on the cold linoleum wrapped in a blanket.

In her own room Emily was restless and for once did not fall asleep easily. She was thinking of Anna but also of her story and telegraphing it to the *World* offices in New York by Sunday night. She wanted to get out of bed then and there and start writing it but . . . she fell asleep.

Out across the prairie northwest of Chicago two other people were also very much awake as the night wind rattled at the broken windowpanes of Far Side. Maureen Riley lay on her bed, immobile and slowly choking, while Mary Nevitt sat right at her side in the dark.

'Good, you're being very good,' she said, thrusting a spoon at her. 'Now, here's the last.'

Mary used her hand with its sharp nails to help push the last of the mushy bowl of food into Riley's already full mouth and then clenched her hand tight over her mouth and nose as her victim choked and coughed, her massive body struggling desperately to breathe. Riley's chest was bursting, her legs beginning to thresh.

And then, from somewhere in her stirred-up brain a final signal was sent down Riley's nervous system to her flabby, nearly useless limbs, which she raised in a last feeble attempt to push Nevitt's hands away.

But it was too late. Riley's body went into one last great lurching spasm as she flailed on her bed, her mouth spewing food out through Mary Nevitt's twisted fingers as she struggled for air. Her hefty body arched and went rigid. She fell back on the bed, letting out a long, low gurgling sound as Mary removed her hand and smiled.

'There's a good girl.'

'*Naaah!*' was Riley's agonized response, and it came in a long, slow gasp as her heart gave out.

Her eyes were wide open and the last thing they registered was a woman she thought must be Mary's sister Ida, come back from the dead.

Out on the Lakeshore, with Anna now sleeping soundly in his cabin, Mr Crazy sat in the dark as he had often done at day's end through the long years since his wife and child had died.

Ironically, he had always found comfort in a fire, even though it was fire that had destroyed his happiness. But now the time had come, he told himself, to finally come to terms with all that grief and loss and embrace the future.

He took one last look at the contents of his carpet bag and then closed it up.

'Yes, it's time, Mr Crazy,' he said aloud to the night and the stars. 'Tomorrow I'll do it.'

And then, as though in recognition of this momentous decision, somewhere in the distance, a church clock tolled midnight.

Tomorrow had come.

DAY TEN

Saturday October 28, 1893

81

Mist

When Anna Zemeckis woke early the following morning and poked her head out of the door of Mr Crazy's cabin to see what kind of day it was, she heard the distant sound of splashing, just as he had predicted. Not far in front of the cabin, the man himself was standing facing east, as naked as the day he was born, up to his knees in the milky waters of Lake Michigan as the mist, filled with the light of the rising sun, rolled over him.

He looked like an older Adam, but not as old as his normal appearance – bearded, hatted and greatcoated – would suggest. His body was bronzed, lean and strong.

The last time Anna had seen a naked man had been in circumstances of half-forgotten horror which now suddenly surfaced as, for the first time since it had happened, her bruised mind allowed her to remember again a few terrible moments of her first visit to the Union Stock Yard.

After making the special tour of the Darke Hartz killing floors arranged for her by Marion, Anna had been introduced to Mr Gunther Darke and invited down to one of the buildings at the far end of the yard for a small 'reception', where Marion had said she would meet her later. But inside, it was something altogether different; the place was virtually derelict. She had been taken to a room containing only a few dusty drapes, chairs and sofas, some randomly placed potted plants and, over in the corner, most incongruous of all, an enormous camera on a tripod.

'Where are the other guests?' she had asked incredulously.

'They will be joining us shortly. Let me offer you a drink meanwhile,' Gunther had murmured.

Anna had wanted to leave then and there, but so awed was she by Gunther Darke that she accepted a small glass of wine, something she only ever drank, and in small quantities, on high days and holidays.

The chloral hydrate that laced her drink took effect fast, and feeling dizzy Anna had got up asking for Marion.

'I'll take you to her,' Gunther had said, still charming. He led her from the room, but his hand and arm were strong at her back and Anna, now fired by thoughts and feelings that were no longer her own, had become reckless, and went with him almost willingly. She had no idea that he might mean her harm, or even what the nature of that harm might be. Until, that is, Gunther had turned to her in the semi-darkness of the corridor and kissed her roughly.

Anna struggled and broke free, stumbling through a half-open set of doors into a large open space. It was one of the disused killing floors, where she saw something so extraordinary that it took several seconds for her befuddled mind to register what it was. Over on the far wall was a hog wheel, and attached to it by a chain was a half-naked woman. She was laughing as she flicked a pink, ostrich-feather fan back and forth across her bare breasts with her free hand. And then there had been a flash, and in that moment Anna had seen a camera in a corner, just like the one in the other room.

Gunther Darke's strong hands now settled vice-like on her from behind and dragged her back into the corridor. As he did so she caught sight of something else: Marion Stoiber, naked but for black silk stockings held up by garters, lying on her back on a table used by butchers to dress fresh-killed meat. Her legs were splayed and there was a naked man climbing on top of her as another, nearer, watched.

Then another flash. And with the bright light of it still burning her eyes, Gunther Darke dragged Anna back into the room he had first taken her to, pushed her back onto the cheap, velvet-covered horsehair divan and raised her dress. He pulled aside her drawers, unbuttoned his fly and placed his whole weight on her. She felt what she thought at first was his fingers or his hand pushing up between her legs, harder and harder until, she crying out with the brief strange pain of it, he entered her.

As Darke moved on top of her and she moaned with the pain and discomfort, a dazed and disorientated Anna thought she saw a man come into the room. He walked over to the camera in the corner and shrouded his head in black cloth. As he did so, Gunther twisted her head in the camera's direction. Then there came that same flash and a smell of burning. And then the man was gone.

As the door closed, Gunther's grasp of Anna slackened; he shuddered and stayed inside her for a few moments, then finally pulled away.

It had happened almost before she knew it, as no doubt it had happened before to other gullible girls like her, here in this same room. She pulled her dress back over her. She felt sick and sore and dirty and violated. But worst of all, even in her drugged state, she felt it was her own fault.

'I want to go home,' she remembered saying.

'And so you shall,' said Gunther. 'Then, in a few days' time, you shall come back and we shall take some more pretty photographs of you, just like your friend Miss Stoiber. Would you like that?'

Anna gasped in horror.

'Just remember,' said Gunther, his eyes now threatening, 'one word of what has happened here and I shall see to it that your father receives a nice new photograph of his innocent daughter.'

He manhandled Anna back outside and put her in his carriage, ordering it to take her home, without saying another word.

Back on the North Side, Anna could hardly bear to look Mrs Markulis in the eye. She had said she was feeling ill and went straight to bed, refusing to answer all Liesel's anxious questions or accept offers of help. She lay hunched up on her bed and wept for hours. All she could think about was home. She wanted to go home to her father.

But she knew that now she never could.

The memory felt less searing now, almost faded, and although the strange sight of a naked Mr Crazy taking his morning bath had prompted it, Anna had had no sense of shock or disgust. For Mr Crazy to her was one of Nature's own and she felt safe with him.

501

She put the coffee on and set some sausages to fry, then went and washed herself in Mr Crazy's makeshift bathroom at the rear of the cabin. Her dress was dry, her stockings too, but the morning was cold and she pulled the plaid shawl Mr Crazy had found for her tight around her as she joined him outside the cabin for breakfast.

'You look troubled,' he said.

'Yes, something terrible happened to me . . . It all came back just now . . . but I didn't want to remember until now.'

'It's about the baby, yes?'

'You know?'

'Don't have to tell me any more than that, Anna. I can guess. It's what some men do. It's why you're scared and why you're running. I know that much.'

'I have to protect my baby, Mr Crazy.'

'Yes, you must and I'll help you. But don't despair about the past or blame yourself. Things happen . . .'

Anna shivered and huddled closer to the fire.

'Yes, things happen,' Mr Crazy said again, getting up from his chair. 'But it's what we make of what happens that really matters. It's about taking responsibility.'

He was thinking now of himself.

'We put things off, refuse to deal with them,' he added slowly. 'Yes, indeed we do . . .'

For Mr Crazy, the flight from reality of more than twenty-two years was finally coming to an end. And for Anna too, after seven long weary weeks of running and hiding, it was time finally to come to terms with what had happened.

Each of them now sat in silence in their own separate worlds, watching one of nature's eternal battles, that between the morning mist and the rising sun. But on this occasion the mist was winning and the new day was already darkening into damp grayness.

It was then that they heard the crunch of boots approaching across the ash.

82

Rounded Up

Emily's plan to get onto the Lakeshore beyond Illinois Central Depot at 12th went wrong almost the moment it began, when an officious rail man warned them off the tracks. It took a combination of gentle persuasion and several dollar bills to make him turn a blind eye before they got down to the lake's edge.

By the time they had done so, mist was rolling in across the lake from the east and, as they began their search for Anna, every hillock seemed a mountain, every hollow a great valley and the piles of wood, mounds of paper and chutes of spent ash assumed strange shapes. The three companions moved about like trolls on a lava plateau.

'Not a nice place to spend the night,' said Ben.

When he got no reply he turned round to see that the others had disappeared in the mist and he was lost.

It was only by calling out to each other that they managed to join up again and then they had to listen hard for the lapping of water to work out where the edge of the lake was.

'We could easily pass right by her in this mist,' said Emily, 'so we'd best stay put until it starts clearing. At least if the Meisters are out here looking for her they'll have the same problem.'

*   *   *

It was a good half-hour before the mist began to clear and they made
progress again, spreading out in a line from shore to rail track, but
progress was slow. If they could have whistled or called out it might
have helped, but this of course might have attracted the attention of
the very people they were trying to avoid.

Then Emily, pointing to her nose, signaled she had picked up a scent
– literally. The others joined her, and together they moved ahead through
the mist, in the direction of the smell: coffee and something frying.

Then voices.

For the last few yards the ground was all crunchy ash and rustling
paper and by the time they hit Mr Crazy's encampment right there
on the shoreline he and Anna had heard them, had stood up, and
were holding staves from a barrel as their pathetic defense.

'Anna!' called out John English in relief.

As for Emily, such was the strange anticlimax of the moment that
all she could think to do was stretch out a hand and say, 'Boy, am I
glad to see you! Emily Strauss, New York *World*.'

She introduced Ben and explained the story she was working on
and how he was going to do sketches to illustrate it – he had already
started. But more important right now was to get Anna to safety. There
were others out looking for her too.

'Yes, the men at the wharf,' said Anna, 'but I hoped they didn't see
which way I went.'

'Now listen,' said Emily, 'there are two Pinkerton men who have
been helping us. We need to get you to them. They'll help us get you
safely out of Chicago and home to New York . . .'

Suddenly Mr Crazy raised a finger to his lips and they all fell silent.

'Voices,' he whispered. 'Men's, by the sound of it. Coming from
that way . . .'

He pointed to the north.

'How far?' said Emily.

'Two, three hundred yards at most. You'd better follow me. There's
a quick way out.'

'One thing, Mr Crazy,' said Emily, grabbing him by the arm. 'Whatever happens, one of us needs to get to Mr Toulson and tell him what's
happened. You're the only one can find your way out of here in this
mist. How quickly can you get us off the Lakeshore?'

'Ten minutes if we move fast.'

The voices were getting louder.

'If we set up a diversion, can you slip away?'

'Where shall I find your Mr Toulson?'

'He and his colleague Rorton Van Hale, they're at the OAA Convention this morning . . . Auditorium Theater, ten o'clock. But . . .'

'What?'

'How will you persuade them to let you in!'

'Don't worry, I'll think of something. Now, let's git!'

He led them west.

The clammy mist engulfed them, but now the voices in the distance had fallen silent.

'They may have heard us,' Mr Crazy whispered, gathering the others around him, 'so we're going to git fast. Keep close, there's boggy ground round here. Don't deviate from the route I take . . . Anna, you first behind me and then you Ben. Then Miss Strauss and finally Anna's beau.'

John flushed; Anna smiled.

'Let's move,' said Mr Crazy.

They were as good as running when they heard a guttural shout and then another.

John, turning, glimpsed a man running behind him.

'Hurry!' he called out, '*hurry!*'

'Straight ahead,' cried Mr Crazy, 'over there, it'll take you to the Lakeshore rail track!'

And there it was, dark gray in the strange half-light, then more clearly: a solid, high wooden fence.

'How do we get through it?' asked Emily.

'I have my own private entrance.' Mr Crazy made a left, jumped a pool of water and led them to a padlocked gate.

'Picked the lock years ago and fashioned my own key,' he said as he ushered them through. But the men, dark shapes in the distance now and off to the right, were gaining ground on them fast.

Mr Crazy signaled to John to go on ahead of him.

John did as he was told but when he turned round the old man had disappeared into the mist. The only people he could see were the men running straight for them.

'Where to now?' said John.

They turned towards the tracks and saw that, having got through one obstacle, they now faced a very different one.

It was a line of box cars stretching right in front of them, a locomotive just visible on the left-hand side. The box cars loomed high in the mist, the more so because they were all painted black. And on their sides could just be made out, in big white letters, *DARKE HARTZ & COMPANY*.

Then, as they stood and watched, figures emerged through the gap between each wagon – the only way through to the tracks beyond.

'The Meisters,' murmured John. 'May God help us all.'

One man now stood apart from these, in front of the train, and faced them. He was massive and wore the same curled bowler as his men. His cravat was the only color in the whole grim scene. It was the color of blood.

'Good morning, ladies and gentlemen,' he said. 'I would be most grateful if you would come without a fuss.'

'Who are you?' said Emily, her voice shrill and anxious.

'That is of no importance,' said Dodek Krol, nodding at the other Meisters who had now come up behind from the Lakeshore. The group of silent, black-coated men moved swiftly and silently and surrounded the group. Resistance was futile and Ben's attempt was felled with a single blow that knocked him out cold. John too was over-powered after a brief struggle.

Emily and Anna meanwhile had been grabbed firmly by the arms, though Emily did not stop protesting until they put a hand over her mouth.

'You watch out for this lady, she's carrying a child.'

'Put them in a box car and stay with them,' commanded Krol.

The men did so, heaving the still unconscious Ben in bodily, and throwing his camera in after him.

'Where are you taking us?' demanded Emily.

'Union Stock Yard,' growled one of the Meisters.

Ben came round. He was shivering.

'It's cold,' he said.

'That's because it's refrigerated,' said Krol from the track. 'Now get them out of here.'

The car door was slid shut.

There was a whistle, a burst of steam and the locomotive began to move off.

Krol, however, remained standing by the side of the track.

He had done his job. He had found Anna Zemeckis and secured her. Now he had other, more important things to do and he was angry, very angry.

If he had known the Zemeckis girl was pregnant he would never have been party to hunting her down.

So Dodek watched the train pull away and decided that, though the time left to him in Chicago was limited, he might still have enough to do some hunting of his own.

83

Mr Crazy No More

From his place of hiding, Mr Crazy watched the Darke Hartz box cars roll away in the distance and the big man leave before turning back to his cabin.

He walked round the outside, running his hand down the door frame and then along the lop-sided windows that he had picked up long ago when they had come bobbing up on the shoreline nearby.

But now it was time to say goodbye. He picked up his carpet bag which had been thrown out with a heap of other things from inside his cabin when the Meisters, pausing briefly at the campsite to search, had found that he and Anna had gone.

He opened it up and surveyed the contents. He seemed well pleased.

Then he looked at his pocket watch and said, 'One hour. Just enough time.'

He boiled some water, got his shaving soap and razor, and then found a pair of large scissors. In his makeshift bathroom behind the cabin he squinted into the broken mirror, took hold of the beard he had been growing since 1871 and, without a moment's hesitation, cut it off in large handfuls. Then, nice and slow, he shaved the rest of it right back, sharpening his razor on the strop as he did so.

'Look like a plucked turkey,' he said, surveying himself in the mirror,

before he took comb and scissors to his unruly hair and cut that short
and neat too.

Then he went into his cabin and pulled out a small battered suitcase
pushed far back under his wooden truckle bed.

'Time to cast off the old . . . and put on the – er – old,' he said
with a chuckle as he opened the case and surveyed its contents. He
took out a clean set of white combinations, a pair of black woolen
socks, a neatly folded, starched white shirt and stiff collar, and put
them on. Then he put on a pair of old but neatly polished boots.
Behind him, from a peg on the door, he took down a dark gentleman's
suit. He put on the pants, which still fitted his lean frame, and left the
jacket, which was cut in a style that had long since gone out of fashion,
lying on the bed.

Outside the cabin, he once more sat down and checked the contents
of his carpet bag. It contained several documents, all but one in good
order. This one was folded and stained and looked as if it had been
thrown out with the garbage. And indeed it had, only ten days before.
Someone had received it in the post and discarded it and Mr Crazy
was very much obliged to them.

It was the two-day agenda for the 25th National Convention of the
Old America Association.

'Ten o'clock, Auditorium Theater,' he read. 'I reckon they never
thought *I'd* show up again.'

He went back to his file and produced another document.

It was the OAA's constitution and rules of procedure. Mr Crazy
skimmed it.

'There's not many men alive who know it better than I do,' he told
himself, 'seeing as I was on the committee that wrote it.'

Then he stood up, glanced at his pocket watch yet again and looked
over the wasteland towards the tower of the Auditorium Theater.

He considered which way to get there.

'The scenic route,' he finally decided.

Taking one last look around his campsite, he went back inside and
added the finishing touches to his outfit, carefully knotting a fine blue
silk tie and adding a gold pin and pulling his old, much-loved and
well-brushed Derby down over his neatly cut hair.

Finally, he took his jacket from the bed and, as he did so, looked

509

at the name written in permanent black ink on a white tab on the inside pocket.

Isaiah Steele.

It had been sewn on, neat and square, by his wife all those years back when he first bought it.

'She never did like my middle name,' he muttered to himself, 'and nor did I. That's why she left it out.'

Just as he was about to go, Mr Crazy saw his old greatcoat lying in a heap on the floor where the Meisters had thrown it.

He picked it up and hung it back lovingly on the hook behind the door.

'Mr Crazy no more,' he muttered, closing the door softly behind him.

As he picked up his carpet bag of papers by the door, Isaiah Steele saw that the mist was clearing and the sun was shining through onto the lake at last. He stood and contemplated that tranquil scene as he had done so many times over the last twenty-two years.

Then, after a great, deep, satisfying intake of breath to enjoy the morning air, he set off downtown, a man transformed.

84

Old America

The eagerly awaited 25th National Convention of the Old America Association had effectively started six days previously, with the advance meeting of the Audit Committee on Sunday October 22. In the absence of President Jenkin Lloyd Rhys, and then the grim announcement of the discovery of his corpse, Paul Hartz, as senior vice president, had taken over as acting president, with Ambrose F. Norman, one of his close colleagues, as convention chairman.

Rhys's disappearance and death had, naturally, engendered all kinds of dark rumors, but not quite the sense of tragedy that might have been expected. This was because the younger and more strident faction in the OAA, who saw Hartz as its natural spokesman even if he was too old to be its natural leader, were frankly glad to see Rhys gone.

Old, and out of touch with a new generation, Rhys had been seen as a stumbling block to necessary changes in policy. He had been a voice of moderation in the face of growing demands for the OAA to take a public stance on the continuing wholesale immigration from eastern and southern Europe of a type some now frankly described as of a lower order.

Paul Hartz, like his popular son-in-law Gunther Darke, had dared to give voice to these concerns and the more right-wing elements of the OAA had applauded them for it.

The venue for the two-day convention was the imposing Auditorium Theater on Michigan Avenue and Congress, now the most famous and spectacular venue of its kind in all the United States, with rich architectural and decorative schemes by Mr Louis Sullivan, of the firm Adler & Sullivan, making it one of the greatest jewels of Chicago's cultural landscape.

The previous day, from half-past eight on, nine hundred OAA delegates and assorted OAA officers and journalists had streamed from their downtown hotels from all directions to listen to the day's business. Waiting for them was a whole range of staff, from cleaners to doormen to chefs and technicians, as well as fifty uniformed pages to run messages and make sure things ran smoothly.

So far all had gone well and today the stream of people going into the auditorium had become a river earlier than usual. By quarter-past nine the foyer was jam-packed with delegates. It was the business day when the OAA's officers were to be elected and re-elected, including the all-important position of president, to replace the late Mr Rhys.

In the absence of Rhys the old guard had crumbled, and it was generally recognized that most of the key positions, including that of president, would be elected unopposed. Many delegates wanted to avoid divisive debate and there were those at Chicago's City Hall, some of them OAA members, who had urged caution where such debates were concerned. For this reason Paul Hartz, through the Audit Committee, had fixed things so there was likely to be no real debate at all – granting to the old guard a few choice sinecures in exchange for them not putting up candidates against the new.

The last few elections, the key ones, were to start at quarter to twelve, which is when Gerald Toulson and his client, Hans Darke, who as Emily had rightly guessed him to be was a member of the OAA, arrived. They sat at the back. Rorton Van Hale was somewhere in the main body of the hall.

Darke was thoroughly bored with these kind of OAA meetings, but he had been prevailed upon by Toulson to attend, in the hope that something significant or revealing might happen which would help the investigation.

*　　*　　*

512

Paul Hartz, having taken the chair for the first half of the morning session, had now handed it back to convention chairman, Ambrose Norman.

'We now come to the election of our four vice presidents and that of the president himself,' Norman began. 'Since all these gentlemen are very well known to us, I will ask their proposers to keep their remarks brief – after all, it is the vice presidents we wish to hear. Since each is unopposed, we will proceed after each nomination to a vote by acclamation . . .'

The Convention Committee had organized matters so that Gunther Darke, though not the most senior of the vice presidents, should speak last. He was known to be a rousing speaker and it was hoped this would appeal to the younger members.

Toulson settled back, ready to be bored, and he was not disappointed until the shout of acclamation confirming the third vice president's election died away and the chairman invited Mr Gunther Darke's proposer to speak. There was a buzz of excitement. Darke's reputation as the coming man preceded him and most people expected that if he kept his nose clean for a couple of years then he would, as his father-in-law intended, succeed to the presidency of the OAA, a perfect place from which to launch his career into national Republican politics.

Norman began with the customary overblown introduction of Darke's proposer.

'He is a young member, a highly skilled professional and a delegate from this year's host city, Chicago!' he declaimed.

This provoked a partisan cheer from Chicagoan and Illinois delegates, as well as many locals there as observers.

'Yet he is new to this great city. Please therefore give a warm welcome to Dr Morgan Eels, who I am happy to say will in three days' time assume the important role of medical superintendent of Cook County Insane Asylum.'

Eels rose to loud applause, fresh from the triumph of his lecture at Dunning five evenings previously. He outlined Gunther Darke's meteoric career in business and his suitability for high office and commended Mr Darke's generous funding of his valuable research at Dunning. He presented his case with the strange, focused zeal that audiences found at once compelling and repulsive and sat down on time.

Gunther, having been seconded, then rose to loud applause and made the kind of brief, inspirational speech such occasions demand. He reiterated his belief that immigration into the USA should now be more rigorously controlled; thanked his proposer, to whose medical work he said he was fully committed; and, finally, to the expectant audience's delight, he thanked his father-in-law, seated over to his left, whom he wished every success for the future.

The audience liked what they heard, clapped and stamped and began making their shouted acclamation in favor of Gunther's election even before Ambrose Norman had formally proceeded to it.

Throughout the proceedings Toulson observed that Hans Darke sat stony-faced. He expressed no emotion at all, even when Gunther's name was mentioned or when his popularity with delegates was clearly demonstrated. Toulson decided he looked weary and resigned, as if the old world in which he felt comfortable had given way to the new and he did not like it very much.

'Let's go,' Hans Darke said impulsively as Norman moved proceedings towards the vote by acclamation. 'Watching Gunther's election is bad enough, but Paul's president now as well . . . ! Let's get out of here.'

They rose from their seats and were about to move along the row and out to the aisle when a commanding voice that resonated throughout the hall called out, 'Mr Chairman, point of order!'

Darke, out of courtesy to those around him, sat down again, as did Toulson.

The audience, anxious now to get to the election of the president first groaned and then shouted to the chair not to allow any points at this juncture.

There were always one or two time-wasters who interrupted proceedings on such occasions and Norman knew how to deal with them politely but ruthlessly.

'I think, sir,' he said, 'that there can be no point to make, not until we have completed the vote on Mr Darke's election.'

'I disagree,' said the booming voice from the floor, 'and in any case all points of order must be heard at the moment they are raised, for how else are we, the delegates, to control the chair?'

514

This bold statement raised some appreciative cheers and many members, unable to see the speaker, half rose from their seats to get a better view. They sat down quickly. The speaker was dressed in old-fashioned clothes and looked, as they feared, like an old-timer whose day was over but who still liked the sound of his own voice.

'Sit down!' several delegates shouted.

Ambrose Norman, unable to make the speaker sit down, glanced at Hartz for guidance. Hartz shrugged and nodded, upon which Norman, with a studied resignation that won the audience's approval responded, 'You are absolutely right, sir, and I stand corrected. Make your point.'

'Thank you,' responded the speaker from the floor. 'I believe I am right in saying, Mr Chairman, that with respect to the election of vice presidents, once they have spoken, it is the right of delegates to speak in opposition to their nomination. *Am* I right?'

Ambrose Norman frowned.

He was a past master at running meetings; he knew the rules inside-out and he knew the speaker was right, but he understood at once the implication of what he said. He had no doubt that Gunther Darke's election would be ratified, but he did not wish things to slow down or end on a sour note.

'You are right, sir, but that rule applies only when there is a rival candidate. In this case, where an election is unopposed, the matter is a formality and it does not serve any useful purpose to impede the business of the day.'

'Hear, hear!' came the cry from all over the floor and more shouts of, 'Sit down!'

The speaker was unperturbed and stayed firmly on his feet. 'Mr Chairman, that may be the common practice but it isn't the rule. The fact is that, though Mr Darke is unopposed, we do, through our right to abstain, have the means not to elect him. And I, for one, would like to explain, briefly, why I intend to abstain in this particular case.'

Norman decided the time had come to be categorical.

'Well, sir, the chair has final discretion. No doubt Mr Darke will listen to anything you have to say to him after the meeting is over. Meanwhile I must ask you to sit down.'

'You may have final discretion, Mr Chairman, but not on this point
you don't . . .'

'You have had your say, sir,' interrupted Norman very firmly, 'but
now we really must proceed to a vote . . .'

'Mr Chairman, sir,' the voice from the floor now boomed out like
an Old Testament prophet, 'you do not have that right and I have
here, in the form of the OAA's constitution, the paper to prove it!'

It was at this moment that Hans Darke, who was sitting so far back
he had been unable to see the speaker, stood up and took a good look
at him.

'Well, I'm damned!' he said out loud. 'If it isn't Mr Isaiah Steele,
come back from the dead!'

Hans Darke now called out in a voice every bit as loud as Isaiah's,
'Mr Chairman, point of order!'

Another loud groan reverberated around the auditorium, until the
delegates, turning to see who was conspiring to slow things up still
more saw that it was none other than Hans Darke. They fell silent
immediately.

Darke was very well known in Chicago and throughout the state
of Illinois, not least because he was a man of considerable dignity and
few words, who only spoke when he had something worth saying.

The spectacle of one Darke rising on a point of order concerning
another in the form of his youngest son, not to mention the fact that
his detested business partner was also on the platform sent a wave of
excited chatter through the audience.

'Mr Chairman, since it was I who chaired the committee that originally drafted the constitution of the OAA, I think I may speak with
some authority. Since Mr Isaiah Steele, the speaker who has raised
the point served on that same committee, and like me is a founding
member of the OAA, I think he does so too. Believe me, sir, he has
the right to speak and under the rules you should let him.'

Ambrose Norman glanced again at Hartz who simply looked
furious. Gunther looked as incandescent as one of the modern electric
lights that lit the hall above their heads.

'In that case, the gentleman may have two minutes,' said Norman
dismissively, 'and please do us the courtesy of stating your name and
delegation.'

'I'm with the Chicago Lakeshore delegation, total membership one
– myself. Isaiah Steele is my name but there are some in the room
who'll know me better as Mr Crazy, the man with the papers to prove
things.'

This was indeed the case and Mr Crazy's announcement caused a
sudden buzz right through the hall.

Hans Darke laughed and whispered to Toulson, 'Gunther and Paul
are in for a bumpy ride. You don't have to worry about the health of
democracy when Mr Crazy is on his feet.'

'I won't take long,' said Mr Crazy, 'and I hope when I've finished
saying what I have to say that this convention will abstain from electing
Mr Gunther Darke as a vice president.

'Mr Chairman, sir, I have three questions – well, four as a matter of
fact, but the last one has nothing to do with Mr Darke. Let's start with
Mr Darke's proposer Dr Eels, whose work he said just now he supports.'

Mr Crazy paused, waiting for Gunther Darke's acknowledgment
that he *had* indeed said that.

Gunther was forced to affirm he had with a nod of his head.

'Is Mr Darke aware, I wonder, that Dr Eels is conducting dangerous
brain experiments on helpless patients at the Dunning insane asylum?
I have the papers to prove it!'

This provoked stunned silence before a shocked Dr Eels immediately rose to his feet.

'I have the floor, sir,' thundered Isaiah Steele, 'and you've had your
turn.'

Eels sat down, ashen-faced.

'Let's turn to another matter, the moral probity of Mr Gunther
Darke, who we were about to elect as one of our vice presidents. Far
be it for me to question another man's morals. None of us is guiltless
on that score. But when a man stands for public office he should expect
some public scrutiny. Question number two: Are the members of the
Audit Committee of which Darke is a member aware that the funds
which finance certain of the OAA's activities under the heading of
"anonymous donations" in fact come from illegal activities of a profane
and godless nature?'

Again he paused and again there was stunned silence.

Various senior members of the OAA on the stage shifted in their

517

seats uncomfortably. Hartz had ceased looking patrician. He looked like a man who would kill if he could.

'Ladies and gentlemen,' continued Mr Crazy, raising his carpet bag in the air, 'what do you think that I have here in this bag?'

'*The papers to prove it!*' thundered the audience, now relishing the spectacle.

'Now to my last question for Mr Darke and his friends up there on the platform. Maybe he noticed a sad little paragraph in today's *Tribune* announcing the death of a Miss Marion Stoiber, a stenographer and part-time model – for lewd photographs I believe – who, yesterday afternoon at quarter-past two inexplicably became caught in the machinery of the Ferris Wheel on the Midway Plaisance. Since Mr Darke's photograph was found inside this unfortunate lady's purse, may we take it that he has – or soon will be – contacted the Chicago Police Department to help them with their enquiries?'

'Have you the papers to prove it, Mr Crazy?' someone shouted.

'You bet I have,' roared Mr Crazy, pointing an accusatory finger at Gunther Darke and then, as it seemed, to all those on the platform.

The audience was on the point of uproar but Mr Crazy, with total command, stilled them once more and in a much quieter voice said, 'And finally, I have a very simple request. If there is a Mr Gerald Toulson present, would he please make himself known to me?'

With the gathered delegates now in total uproar, waving their order papers and shouting, Mr Crazy quietly gathered up his carpet bag and moved out into the aisle.

He felt a hand at his elbow.

'Name's Van Hale, I'm a Pinkerton man. I'll take you to Mr Toulson. There's going to be trouble and some of it will be directed your way.'

Van Hale ushered Mr Crazy up through the crowd towards the back of the auditorium, where Toulson and Hans Darke were already waiting.

Meanwhile Ambrose Norman, having conferred with the vice-presidential nominees, was trying to restore order.

'Fellow delegates, fellow *delegates* . . . I have an announcement. Mr

518

Gunther Darke has withdrawn his nomination for vice president and
... gentlemen ...'

As the uproar got worse, Van Hale and Mr Crazy made their way
to join Toulson. Mr Crazy did not waste words.

'Mr Toulson, they've taken Anna Zemeckis and her beau along with
Miss Strauss and that other gentleman ...'

'Who?'

'The Meisters.'

'Where to?'

'The Union Stock Yard.'

'When?'

'Nine o'clock this morning, from the Lakeshore.'

Toulson didn't need to hear any more, for as Mr Crazy spoke he
noticed Gunther Darke leaving the platform in a hurry.

He turned to Hans Darke.

'We need to talk,' said Toulson urgently. 'It looks to me like our
investigation into Chicago's pornography trade is reaching a climax.
Can you get this gentleman away somewhere safe ... ?'

Darke nodded grimly.

'I'll take him to my house and wait for you there.'

'We'll need backup at the stockyard and ...'

Hans Darke nodded. 'My son Wolfgang is at the stockyard and I'll
telephone him right away and tell him to help you in any way he can
when you arrive. And please ... try to keep my sons apart. There's
no love lost between them.'

They left the building as quickly as they could, pushing through the
crowds of shocked delegates.

Meanwhile, up on the stage, Paul Hartz's normal equanimity had
deserted him completely. There had been a brief heated argument
with Gunther before he had left for the yard and now Hartz was trying
and failing to sort out the procedural mess he was left with.

He turned to an aide: 'I want to talk with Dodek Krol,' he said.
'Find him.'

Which was not difficult since Mr Krol was waiting, ever watchful,
in the wings.

'It's time for that final commission, I think,' said Krol.

'Is that finally a yes? You'll deal with him?'

'Yes,' said Krol, 'it is. He didn't tell me Miss Zemeckis was with child and nor did you.'

'I didn't know,' said Hartz.

And for once, to his eternal credit, Paul Hartz looked concerned about someone else and said two words which rarely pass a politician's lips: 'I'm sorry.'

'So must he be,' said Krol.

As Krol left, Hartz sought out the one still and silent figure left sitting in the auditorium – Dr Morgan Eels. He was pale and frightened, and he had reason to be.

'Eels, you're through,' said Hartz pitilessly. 'Through with the OAA and through with the insane asylum. If you're not out of Dunning and this city within twenty-four hours I'll file proceedings against you myself.'

'But, sir, I—'

'But nothing, Eels. You're finished.'

'But Mr Hartz, we've made a great medical discovery—'

Hartz shook his head.

'Dr Eels, it is my intention that not a single medical institution in all of America will ever give you a position again.'

Eels's mouth opened but no words came out. He was overcome by fear and rage, humiliation and despair. As he turned away into the crowd he looked like a broken man. But he had one last thing to say:

'Great scientific discoveries do not go unrecognized, Mr Hartz. You'll hear of me again and you'll regret your words today!'

'Get out of my sight,' roared Hartz.

Moments later, Paul Hartz was his familiar, smooth, calculating self again as he dealt with the clamoring press men who now surrounded him. He was aware that what had happened was personally damaging, as well as boding ill for the value of Darke Hartz stock, if he did not take control of the situation quickly.

His public dismissal of Eels had been part of his strategy, and now, gathering the pressmen about him, he announced that he was indebted to that great Chicagoan Mr Isaiah Steele for his courageous intervention in the proceedings, both himself personally and the OAA having been as badly duped by Eels as everybody else.

'But what about your son-in-law, Gunther Darke, Mr Hartz! Isn't he implicated as well?'

Hartz affected both shock and surprise.

'I am not aware of any actual proof being found to show that that is the case, gentlemen. No, Dr Eels is the man you should be gunning for, not Gunther Darke, who so far as I am concerned is as hardworking and civic-minded a Chicagoan as you'll ever find. I won't entertain a word said against him until I have seen the evidence with my own eyes. Meanwhile, if any of you gentlemen should write anything libelous, trust me, you will be hearing from my lawyers as well as his.'

He smiled, but his eyes were cold.

'But what about the presidency of the OAA? Are you still standing, Mr Hartz?'

'Certainly,' he said coolly. 'In any case, I am acting president. Who better to clean up the OAA than me? Eh?'

'Would you care to comment on the death of Mr Jenkin Lloyd Rhys?'

'Sure,' said Hartz, 'he was a very great man. I'll be leading the mourners from the OAA when they bury him in New York.'

'It's a bad day for the OAA, isn't it, sir?'

Hartz looked his most magisterial and contrite.

'Yes, it is,' he said disarmingly. 'But the way I see it is that what's happened here makes it a great day for democracy and we have Mr Steele to thank for that. Now, if you don't mind, gentlemen, I have work to do . . .'

85

Covert

Toulson and Van Hale approached the Union Stock Yard from the south, through a little-used workers' entrance at Halsted and 47th, to avoid the danger of being seen. After Mr Crazy's unexpected intervention at the OAA meeting and Gunther's hasty exit, they were certain that Gunther and the Meisters he controlled would be expecting visitors.

From here they made their way to Packer's Avenue, where a broad, stocky figure emerged from a doorway.

Van Hale went for his revolver but Toulson stayed his hand.

'It's alright, it's Wolfgang Darke.'

They shook hands as Wolfgang pulled them into the shadows. 'My father telephoned, he said you might need backup. Gunther's men have been going in and out of the old Whetton building for the last half-hour and Gunther himself arrived in a hurry about ten minutes ago. He'll know I'm here because he will have seen my carriage and he can hear the Darke Hartz hog wheel . . .'

He cocked his head on one side.

Rumpety thump rumpety thump rumpety . . .

'Hear it?'

They nodded.

'That'll stop in less than an hour, at two o'clock sharp, and Gunther

will be waiting for it to do so because he'll know that my men and I
will be leaving pretty soon after, say within twenty minutes. He'll see
my workers walk back down to the main gate to make their way home.

'There's a couple of boys get left to hose down the killing floor.
They're good lads and will do what I tell them. I'll send them off in
my carriage to keep them out of harm's way and to make Gunther
think I've gone too.

'There's no love lost between my men and Gunther's. He tends to
employ low types, but he has a small coterie of skilled ones who are
Meisters – but of the worst kind. Most have been in trouble with the
law and are tough, violent types – so be careful. Many of my own
men have suffered intimidation and bullying at their hands, so there's
not a man among them who wouldn't welcome a chance to stand his
ground against Gunther's men and see them gone from the yard.'

He paused to be sure they understood. Both men nodded grimly.

Van Hale took out his gun. Wolfgang seemed unimpressed.

'These men use a knife in preference to a gun and they're highly
skilled in its use, not just with meat. Some are very effective fighters
and one or two of them pride themselves on throwing knives to deadly
effect.'

'We'll see about that!' said Van Hale.

'Gunther won't do anything till the yard is clear. It'll take a good
fifteen minutes after you see my men leave the yard for them to get
back in, unseen, in ones and twos and report back here, so try and
do nothing before then: say around two forty-five.'

'Understood,' said Toulson. He was getting more impressed with
Wolfgang by the moment.

'I've put one of my men on watch in a warehouse overlooking the
Whetton building to which I have access. Now, follow me and I'll show
you a way of getting up to the northwest side of the yard without
being seen.'

With Wolfgang in front they proceeded cautiously down alleys,
around the sides of unused buildings, and then over causeways that
he had known since he was a boy. They were heading for the part of
the yard bounded by Bubbly Creek. Only when the vista ahead opened
up, as buildings gave way to railway tracks, did Wolfgang slow.

'They have a lookout just around the corner of this warehouse,' he whispered, 'so we'll use a side entrance. My man's hidden on the top floor.'

They crept in, catching sight of Gunther's man through a window at the far end of a corridor. He was a typical Meister: clean-shaven, stolid and well built, dark-suited and wearing the familiar bowler. Fortunately, he was looking the wrong way.

Five floors up they found Wolfgang's man keeping low at a window overlooking the Whetton Building across the railway lines, the same building Toulson and Ben had visited the day before.

The man stood up: he was stocky, gray-haired, with a lined face and clear blue eyes.

'Alfred's worked for my father from the first day he arrived in Chicago,' said Wolfgang. 'This is Mr Toulson, Alfred. He's the man in charge of the investigation.'

Toulson shook his hand.

'Alfred Spohr,' he said formally, his German accent still quite strong. 'I show you . . . but not too near the windows please or they see your movement.'

The room they were in covered virtually the whole of the fifth floor of the building and gave them views right round the stock yard.

It was the north part they were interested in. Beyond the main Whetton Building was a network of rail tracks, a few curving away northward, but the bulk of them entering the yard from the east. Most of them circled round the back of the Whetton Building and then disappeared on southward. But a couple of tracks effectively turned the Whetton Building into an island, turning back and passing immediately beneath the warehouse they were in.

They could see innumerable storehouses, repair shops, small reservoirs and coal tips. Beyond the more distant lines to the west and north was the South Fork of the Chicago River, and over to the east the sluggish gray channel of water that was Bubbly Creek.

'What's been going on?' asked Toulson.

'There's six men plus Mr Gunther, in the main building,' said Spohr, 'and three lookouts, one below us here.'

'We saw him,' said Toulson.

'So you will not be able to get from this warehouse across the lines to the Whetton Building without being seen. Yes?'

They nodded.

'Four of these men are senior Meisters well known to us. Bad types.'

'The Meisters started as a guild of master butchers, didn't they?'

Spohr nodded and spat. 'Used to be. Did good works and looked after their own. Now they're no better than a criminal gang operating out of the yard, but you know this?'

They nodded.

'I taught butchery to several of these men and there's not one I'd want my mother to meet. A new generation. Different values. Godless, nasty fellows. Two more of them are in that storehouse . . .'

Spohr pointed out a low building on the west side of the site. It was small and single-storied, of dirty yellow brick and its windows were barred. There appeared to be only one door.

'What's going on in there?'

'I saw them manhandle four people inside: two men and two women. Their hands were tied. One of the women was shouting and struggling a lot.'

'Emily Strauss,' said Toulson without expression. 'And the other?'

'She didn't seem well, they were dragging her and she didn't struggle.'

'And two men? Young?'

Spohr nodded.

'Well, at least we know where they are,' murmured Van Hale.

'Anything else been happening?' asked Toulson.

'They've been shunting trains about, sir,' continued Spohr. 'The Darke Hartz one with the refrigerated cars that's standing north of the Whetton Building was loaded with meat much earlier this morning. It should have left the yard by now. Instead it's been shunted up along-side the Whetton Building. But it ain't for meat, that's for sure.'

'How do you know?'

'The killing floors this end of the yard aren't in use. They'll be loading something else.'

'Where's the driver?'

'He's in his locomotive below us now, the train with the two hoppers.'

'Is he known to you?'

'He is. He does what they tell him, gets well paid and keeps shtum.'

'What normally goes into the hoppers?'

Spohr shrugged, 'Coal mainly.'

'I must go,' said Wolfgang Darke. 'For the moment you're on your own, gentlemen. Whatever you do, don't move off before my men have had time to get back in to the Yard unseen. Not before a quarter to three.'

Toulson and Van Hale nodded.

'What happens if that train takes off?' asked Toulson. 'Can your people stop it?'

'Depends which route it takes. Might be difficult. I'll see if one of my men knows what track it will be using.'

'Let's hope it doesn't come to that,' said Toulson. 'Meanwhile . . .'

He dug into a pocket and produced a silver whistle. 'When we're ready this end, Mr Darke, or if we need you, I'll use this. It's simple, but effective. So run like hell – in our direction. Do *you* carry a revolver?'

Wolfgang pulled aside his jacket and pointed to a leather sheath on his belt.

'As I said before, butchers prefer knives.' He indicated his own with a grim smile. 'Spohr, I want you back with me before two.'

Then he turned and was gone.

'A good man,' murmured Van Hale, as the three of them settled down to watch the Whetton Building.

'You can rely on Mr Wolfgang as you can on his father Mr Hans,' said Spohr. 'But the blood went bad with Mr Gunther.'

Emily Strauss was cold and hungry and did not appreciate being made to sit on a dirty, unswept floor. Her hands and feet were still tied. The windows of the room they were in were barred and the panes broken, the walls covered in a whitewash that had long since begun to peel and flake.

Anna and John were sitting shoulder-to-shoulder against the wall opposite, talking in low voices, Anna having told Emily as much of her story as she could remember. Ben lay on the ground, still in a dazed state. His head throbbed from being knocked out and Emily had persuaded him to try to rest. He moaned now and then and she had been worrying a great deal about him until, to her surprise, when she glanced in his direction, she noticed his eyes were open and that he winked at her.

He was, it seemed, now play-acting. The Meisters had taken his camera from him when they'd loaded them in the box car and one of them, on a chair near Emily, was examining it. The other now stood guarding the entrance to the storehouse, watching and waiting, occasionally checking the revolver at his hip.

They had both refused to respond to Emily's constant barrage of complaints and questions, remaining as stiff and silent as mannequins. Except they were a sight more intimidating than anything that ever stood in the window of Marshall Field.

'When are you going to let us go?' Emily called out again, out of sheer boredom. She expected no response.

But, as if in reply, there came a gruff shout from the yard outside and the Meister near it opened the door.

Emily strained to listen and was just able to hear what was said.

'Get the three of 'em ready to move. The hog wheel's just stopped and the moment the Darke Hartz workers are clear of the site we're finishing loading and getting out of here. The Latvian girl stays, orders of Mr Darke. You'll get instructions about her later.'

Emily looked at Anna, hoping she had not heard. Then at Ben, who obviously had. He winked and then moaned again. If he never made it as a photographer, maybe he would as an actor.

The moment Gerald Toulson heard the hog wheel stop, he and Van Hale readied themselves for action. Spohr had already left to rejoin Wolfgang's party.

'Wolfgang's men are leaving,' said Van Hale from the other side of the room, which had a better vantage point from which to see the Darke Hartz building.

The men made their way to Exchange Avenue in a group, turning left and heading for the main gate. Spohr was among them and they were laughing and talking loudly. Minutes later a carriage went past, the curtains drawn so nobody could see in.

Shortly afterwards, the Whetton Building turned into a hive of disciplined activity. Doors opened, and Gunther's men emerged from different directions. The doors of the eight refrigerated box cars were slid open. Inside were sides of dressed hog hanging in neat rows from a central running rail. And there were crates on the floor too, filled, presumably, with dressed meat and ice.

Toulson and Van Hale watched as three Meisters came and went
with what looked like parcels wrapped in black oilcloth. Then Gunther
Darke himself emerged from the Whetton Building.

He was stripped down to his shirtsleeves; youthful and muscular, he
stood a good four inches taller than the men around him. Even from
such a distance he commanded attention.

'Well, well, well . . .' murmured Toulson. 'I think we can guess what
Mr Darke and his men are loading into the train, all nicely protected
against the cold and damp.'

'Pornographic pictures,' said Van Hale.

'Exactly,' said Toulson. 'The last place anyone would look for them.'

The loading continued.

'Their entire stock by the look of things.'

He watched closely as the Meisters put the parcels onto the floor
of the box cars and then climbed in out of sight, moving the parcels
to either end of the cars. Then came what sounded like knocking and
banging and crates being moved around inside.

'False panels,' said Toulson. It was a statement not a question. 'And
they're positioning the crates of dressed meat inside as cover.'

'Proof positive?' observed his friend, pulling back from the window.

'Not quite,' responded Toulson. 'We need to be sure what's inside
those parcels. We need to see it with our own eyes. But yes, looks like
we were right: Gunther Darke's meat distribution business is a cover
for his very profitable pornography trade. It offers a perfect distribution network across the United States, which avoids the US Postal
Service and Mr Comstock's all-seeing eye.'

The two men looked triumphant. But not for long.

'Look!' said Toulson. 'Something's happening by the storehouse.
They're being moved . . .'

Below them, they saw Emily, John and a beat-up looking Ben, their
hands tied, suddenly being hustled out of the storehouse straight
towards one of the box cars. They were unceremoniously pushed inside.
Ben was so unsteady on his feet that he was practically thrown in.

One of the Meisters then jumped up inside with them and closed
the doors, leaving his colleague to guard the outside of the car.

'But where's the Zemeckis girl?' said Van Hale as the storehouse
door was closed again – from the inside.

'That means she's still in there and they've separated her from the others,' murmured Toulson. 'Not good, not good at all. We're going to have to try to get her out, but . . .'

Van Hale moved across the room to another vantage point.

'They've finished loading the train. They're beginning to close the doors . . .'

'It has no engine or driver yet,' said Toulson, indicating the two hoppers immediately below them. 'They've got work to do.'

He pointed below the building they were in, to which Gunther's men had now shifted their attention. They began wheeling trolleys over to it containing photographic equipment, bottles of chemicals, box after box of glass plates, and all the things that Toulson and the others had seen the day before.

They did not waste time, throwing the equipment into the hoppers hurriedly and not worrying if it got damaged. Once this job was done the locomotive moved off and the hoppers were shunted round the tracks in a circle and coupled to the rear of the line of Darke Hartz cars. That done, the locomotive was uncoupled again and began its circuitous route back to the front of the Darke Hartz box cars.

'We're going to have to do something fast if we're going to get Miss Strauss and her friends out of that train before it moves off,' said Van Hale. 'We can't just sit here and watch the evidence and three good people disappear to God knows where . . .'

The two men looked at each other.

They had been in worse situations, but rarely one that needed such urgent action against such overwhelming odds.

'I hope Mr Darke is paying good money,' said Van Hale laconically.

'*Which* Mr Darke?' said Toulson, taking out his revolver.

'Hans Darke, our employer, on whose behalf it looks as though I'm about to get killed.'

They took the stairs down to the ground floor two at a time, emerging at the entrance as the engine approached their building once more on its route to the front of the train.

'Get on!' commanded Toulson.

'Wha— ?'

Van Hale felt himself shoved towards the engine's footplate as it passed by, the driver in full view but with his head leaning out the window on the other side as the locomotive took a sharp curve to the left.

'Get on, for Chrissake,' hissed Toulson.

Van Hale jumped on the footplate, unseen by the driver and shielded by the bulk of the engine from the men over by the Whetton Building.

'And you . . . ?' he called urgently back at Toulson.

'The Zemeckis girl. Got to get her. Create a diversion in a few minutes . . .'

Van Hale mouthed an ironic 'Thanks!', moved into the cabin and, keeping low, stuck a revolver in the small of the driver's back.

'Just keep on going nice and steady,' he said.

Toulson retreated back into the Whetton Building fast, knowing that with the locomotive gone he could easily be seen by anyone on the other side of the tracks.

He found another way out on the far side, opposite a store of some kind. Darting across to it and round the bottom end of the building, he crept back towards the tracks and the open space they had been watching.

The storehouse was much nearer now, no more than fifty yards to his left. Straight ahead, past the back of the Whetton Building was the box car into which Emily and the others had been manhandled. It was no more than a hundred yards ahead of Toulson. Beyond it was Bubbly Creek.

Nearer, to his left across the tracks, a couple of men stood smoking outside the Whetton Building. If he made a dash for the storehouse he would be in full view of them, so he waited, hoping that Van Hale would be able to create a diversion.

It did not work out that way. There came a sudden grinding of wheels on rail tracks, the sound of a locomotive being coupled to a car and, before Toulson knew it, the train across the tracks jolted and began moving forward.

As it did so he heard the unmistakable sound of a pistol shot; and after that a shout, a curse, and then the sounds of a struggle.

The two Meisters at the rear of the Whetton Building drew their knives and looked about them, as uncertain as Toulson was as to where the sounds were coming from.

'What the hell was that?' said one of the men.

Toulson drew out his gun and waited.

He had no idea himself. But one thing was for certain: from behind the Whetton Building the long line of freight cars was now moving off and taking the evidence and the hostages away.

86

Old Friends

If Hans Darke had been able to choose who in the whole world he would like to break to him the extraordinary and alarming news that he was going to be a grandfather and that the mother was a girl he had never met who was on the run, it would have been his old friend Isaiah Steele, who all of Chicago knew now only as Mr Crazy.

The two went back a long way.

In the late 1850s, Steele had been a junior partner in a firm of lawyers specializing in real estate that prepared the conveyancing documents on Darke's first property.

They got on well and shared some times together when Darke could get away from butchery and Steele from the burgeoning world of Chicagoan real estate. Their common dream was not to make money, though both wanted that, but to be part of the adventure that was turning Chicago into the greatest new city in America, maybe in the world.

But then, on the evening of October 8, 1871, the tolling of the courthouse bell in the city center had warned that a serious fire had broken out. Steele was out of town looking at real estate in Kankakee, unaware of what was happening. By the time he heard and was able to make his way back to Chicago, the city was all but destroyed and his home, on the Near West Side, as well as his wife and child had all been lost in the flames, like hundreds of others, never to be found.

The first friend he turned to was Hans Darke, whose home on the North Side was beyond the conflagration.

He stayed with Hans for three weeks, a man in grief.

One day he walked out the front door with just the small suitcase that was his only possession and began living the vagrant life that transformed him into Mr Crazy. But he came back to Darke's house once more and left a package of documents for him. They were accompanied by a short letter begging Hans Darke to agree to accept the enclosed power of attorney over Steele's affairs, along with the titles not only to the property he had lost, and the sites it occupied, but other blocks of real estate that Darke never even knew Steele had acquired. In addition were instructions about funds in an East Coast bank and the request that Darke 'at my expense, acquire additional real estate as herein indicated. Sell nothing except to buy more and better, for I believe in this city and that it will grow again. I trust no man more than yourself, Hans. If I never come back, then you will find among these papers an assignment of all my estate for you to execute in some charitable way for the good of women and children who may need the help I was unable to give my own, for which I pray God forgive me, for I never can myself.'

Later Hans came to hear of Chicago's best-loved eccentric. Inevitably their paths occasionally crossed downtown, but the man who was now Mr Crazy never acknowledged the one person he trusted most in the world, and Hans Darke, respecting his wish, pretended he did not know him either.

Mr Crazy never found it in his heart permanently to leave the city he loved so much. So when, as Isaiah Steele, he rose to speak at the OAA Convention, wearing the same suit of clothes as when Hans Darke had seen him last walk out of his door, no one was more delighted than he. His old friend had returned at last from his self-imposed exile and had resumed his true identity.

Now, seated comfortably in Hans Darke's new house on Astor Street, a glass of lemonade in each of their hands, for both were teetotal, and beaming at each other from the pleasures of rediscovered friendship, Hans said, 'Isaiah, you are a very rich man.'

'You mean *we* are rich men, for the firm of Darke Hartz is one of the biggest in the world.'

'And your real-estate holdings are among the largest in Chicago.'

'That's as may be,' said Isaiah, 'but we can talk of that later and how you must be compensated . . .'

Hans shook his head vigorously.

Isaiah nodded his head just as vigorously.

They both laughed and then Isaiah turned serious. 'Now listen, I've something important to tell you, but first –' Hans Darke edged closer in his chair – 'tell me about your two sons, Gunther and Wolfgang. Tell me all about them.'

And so Hans Darke did, from beginning to end, talking as he had not been able to do with anyone since his wife had died in 1880. The worst he had to say, and the thing which gave him most pain, was the hurt Gunther had done to Christiane Hartz, as she had then been, and by association to his own brother, Wolfgang.

'Two biblical brothers come to mind,' said Isaiah Steele, when Darke's tale was done.

'They do, they do,' Hans said, shaking his head. 'But now . . . what was the important thing you have to say?'

Isaiah looked him straight in the eye.

'There's no other way of telling you but straight: Hans, you are to be a grandfather, and . . .'

Darke leapt to his feet in a state of shock and astonishment.

Then he sat down and stared at his friend in disbelief.

'But . . . who's the mother? In fact who's the father? I know Christiane's not pregnant and Wolfgang does not play that kind of game with women . . .' He stood up again. 'Are you sure?'

'I'm sure.'

'And I suppose you're going to tell me you've the papers to prove it?'

'In a manner of speaking Hans, yes. But this is no laughing matter and the girl's in some considerable danger.'

'So, it's Gunther?' said Hans Darke in a resigned voice.

'Yes. Now listen . . .'

Hans Darke was scarcely able to believe what he heard. His face registering first shock and then extreme distress, he paused in silence for a moment, then stood up and moved towards the door, 'I must go to the yard at once.'

Isaiah got up and barred his way.

'No Hans. I haven't spent all these years out on the Lakeshore without thinking about a lot of things and getting them right in my mind. You're about to retire and, in a manner of speaking, so am I. You have to let go of things and trust a new generation to sort things out without the help of us old men. We did it, and they can too.

'Your two sons must resolve things between themselves, today over in the yard, which is as it should be. Anna Zemeckis, who has carried your grandchild these four months through every difficulty and danger imaginable, and a lot more you'll never know, will continue to do so until that child is born. She's a fine young woman and she's not going to let her child, her father or you down. I don't know which of your sons is Cain and which is Abel, but I have a pretty good idea and, if my memory serves, and it's a while since I read Genesis, one survived and one didn't.

'Never did much like the way that story ended, but that was God's decision, not man's. We'd better start praying that the outcome is a different one this time, but I don't think matters will be improved by you heading off for the yard in your carriage.

'Anna's found a few friends this last week or two, including, so far as I can judge, Mr Toulson, who packs a stronger punch and shoots a lot more accurately than you probably do these days. So sit tight and let's hope it's the right folks come back from the yard through your front door.'

'But I can't just sit here. I want to *do* something.'

'Sure, you can do something. Use that newfangled gadget you so proudly showed me a while back. Send a telegraph to Mr Zemeckis in New York.'

'But what can I tell him?'

'That his daughter's been found and she's all right.'

'But we don't know if she is.'

'*He* doesn't know that, does he? Give him some hope and keep on praying.'

'Well, I suppose . . . I *could* . . .'

'And another thing,' said Isaiah, putting down his tumbler of lemonade with a sudden look of feigned distaste. 'How long have you been teetotal?'

'Since my wife died, thirteen years ago.'

'Well I haven't touched a drop since the Fire. Reckon it's time for something stronger, just for medicinal purposes, to steady the nerves. Agreed?'

A slow grin lighted Hans Darke's face.

'Agreed.'

87

Captive

Emily Strauss had never hurt anyone in a premeditated way before, but now, with her hands tied behind her back and certain she was about to be killed, she intended to have a go.

The target of her murderous ambition was the Meister who had pushed them into the box car they were now held in, climbing in after them and pulling the sliding door to.

After what felt like a long time the car had suddenly jolted back and forth, a sure sign the locomotive was being coupled up at the front of the train in preparation for departure. She reckoned if they were going to make a bid for freedom, this was the moment, before the train gathered speed and they were taken out of Chicago and away from any hope of help.

So did Ben and John. The first winked at her, the other nodded.

The Meister had ordered them to keep quiet, fearing noise would attract unwanted attention.

'If you don't let us go,' Emily snarled at him suddenly, 'I'm going to scream so loud this car will fall apart.'

He was a taciturn kind of man with shiny jowls and humorless eyes who did not like women who talk. Even less women who threaten.

He got up, pulled his knife and headed her way.

He kept clear of John but not Ben, who he must have believed was still groggy, but who now stuck a boot hard into his shin and toppled him. The Meister grunted in pain and fell on his knees in front of Emily.

She didn't hesitate, lunging forward to headbutt his nose so hard that it crunched and broke and blood flowed copiously.

As the Meister grunted in anger and pain and lunged forward at Emily with his knife, John heaved himself upright and kicked him hard on the side of the head.

The Meister's knife went flying as he slewed over on his side, but his right hand went instinctively for the gun under his jacket. Cursing and roaring like a wounded animal, he pulled his gun clear and aimed wildly in John's direction, half-blinded as he was by his own blood and disorientated by the pain.

John kicked out at him hard again.

The gun went off and there was a scream of pain and rage. The Meister had literally shot himself in the foot.

Taking advantage of this, Emily rammed her heel in his face; John threw himself across the man's legs, as Ben, managing to rise into a standing position despite his tied hands, stamped hard on the Meister's privates.

There was a brief agonized squeal and then sudden silence as the man rolled onto his side, lost hold of his gun, one hand on his nose and the other between his legs.

Then there came a sudden shout outside the car from the side they had got in. A Meister, hearing the struggle and the gunshot, was trying to open the door.

The movement of the train made that hard. It suddenly jerked forward. John and Ben, having struggled to their feet, were tipped off balance and went flying; the Meister outside cursed.

The train continued to move forward, confirming Emily's earlier fear that it would soon leave the yard. She struggled to grab the Meister's knife on the floor – it was not easy with hands tied behind her back.

She got a brief hold of it but, covered in the Meister's blood, it slipped from her grasp.

Suddenly there was a thump at the door on the other side of the car. It slammed open with a crash, light flooded in, and with it came a large man brandishing a gun.

It was Rorton Van Hale.

He took one look at the chaotic scene, heaved the now groaning Meister out of the way, grabbed the knife and cut each of them free.

'Out!' he said as the door on the other side was finally hauled open and another Meister peered in. 'Now!'

Van Hale as good as hurled Emily, Ben and John out onto the track, firing at the Meister climbing in on the other side, and jumping out after them.

'Run, for Chrissake – no, *that* way!' he shouted as he hustled them in the opposite direction to the rapidly accelerating train. For this would soon leave them exposed right at the front of the Whetton Building where Gunther's men had been standing.

If Van Hale sounded angry it was because things had not gone to plan.

At first the driver had done what he was told. He took his locomotive up-line of the cars and paused while the points were switched by one of the Meisters and the locomotive was coupled to the front car. All this time Van Hale stayed low and out of sight in the cabin, his gun pointing at the driver's back.

But as the coupling began, things went wrong. The train jerked forward and Van Hale lost his footing, giving the driver time to grab a coal shovel and swing it at his leg, knocking Van Hale to the floor, as he shouted for help to the Meister below.

Van Hale reached up and pulled the driver to the floor and, as they both struggled, they tumbled out of the moving train onto the track. Meanwhile, the Meister on the track had jumped up into the cabin on the other side and now found himself in charge of the moving train, desperately trying to make sense of the controls.

With the driver lying unconscious by the side of the track, Van Hale watched in alarm as the train continued to move, gathering steam.

In a last desperate attempt to get the three captives off the train before it ran out of control and crashed, he had raced along the track, found the right box car from the shouting going on inside, jumped up and managed to wrestle the door open.

But now, as the hoppers that had been coupled on at the end of the train rattled past, Emily, Van Hale and the two men were exposed

to view, and found themselves looking at the drawn pistols of two
Meisters.

'Drop your gun,' said one of them curtly to Van Hale.

'Hey, now . . .' began Emily, stepping forward. But Van Hale pulled
her back.

He slowly lowered his gun.

'I said *drop* it,' repeated the Meister, as he and his companion closed
in.

Which Van Hale might have done, had not two shots rung out and
the Meister swung round and fallen, a bullet in his shoulder.

It was Toulson. 'Drop your weapons,' he roared at the Meisters,
'you're surrounded.' He fired another shot, this one zinging past the
second Meister's ear and uncomfortably close to Van Hale, as he
and the others dived to the ground seeking whatever cover the track
could give them.

Then came shouts from the other side of the Whetton Building as
the other Meisters woke up to what was happening. Toulson fired a
fourth shot, sounded his whistle and shouted out another warning.

The wounded Meister rose onto all fours, cursing, as his companion
fired a couple of wild shots at Van Hale's group.

'Run across the tracks towards Mr Toulson over by that warehouse,'
Van Hale urged the three companions. 'You'll get cover from us both.
Make it fast . . .'

'But what about Anna?' Emily said.

'I'll go for her the moment I see you're safe. Now *run!*'

Toulson waved an arm from the shadows to indicate exactly where
they should head for and the three raced across the open tracks, Emily
lifting her skirts to give her more freedom. It was no more than seventy
yards but, by the time they had crossed and were within reach of the
protection of the warehouse, shots were already being fired at them
from the Whetton Building.

As they dived past Toulson into cover, more shots whined past, one
of them striking the building just above Toulson's head, sending brick
dust and mortar flying.

'Anna . . .' gasped Emily, getting up and making to run back out to
the storehouse which was no more than fifty yards to their left.

Toulson held her fast. 'No. Van Hale'll go for her.' He turned to

Ben. 'You remember the layout of this place?' Toulson asked him urgently.

He nodded.

'Right. You three go down between these buildings to the Darke Hartz offices. Find somewhere there to hide. Wolfgang Darke's got reinforcements on the way. We'll find you later.'

'But Anna . . . we can't leave her . . .' said Emily desperately.

They heard more shouts and running feet. The Meisters were getting nearer.

'There's nothing we can do, Emily,' shouted Ben, 'not against Meisters with guns. Leave it to Van Hale. Come on!'

'We'll find Anna and get her to safety,' said Toulson reassuringly, 'but meanwhile, you must get as far away from the Whetton Building as possible . . .'

With one last look towards the storehouse, whose door still remained ominously shut, Emily turned to Ben and John.

'Let's go,' she said grimly as they headed off at a run to the sound of ricocheting bullets and breaking glass.

Meanwhile, Toulson could see that Gunther Darke had regrouped his men and in only a matter of minutes the Meisters would cut off any hope of them freeing Anna from the storehouse.

The two men had been in this kind of situation before and had a routine. Toulson signaled to Van Hale lying prone between the rail tracks as he reloaded his revolver and then fired a series of shots at the Whetton Building.

This was Van Hale's cue to get up and race for the storehouse. A shot hit the ground at his feet. Its sharper, heavier sound left Toulson in no doubt that it came from a Winchester '92.

He watched as Van Hale reached the door of the storehouse, shot the lock off and crashed the door open, pressing up against the wall outside.

A Meister appeared and, as he did so, Van Hale jumped him and disappeared inside.

Thwump!

Another heavy shot from a Winchester went by.

Toulson heard a shout and a woman scream. Then another shot

and breaking glass. But no sign of either Van Hale or the girl. Not good.

He didn't hesitate. He made a fast exit from his cover and headed straight for the storehouse. A bullet fizzed through the right arm of his jacket as he dived into a strange, airy silence.

A Meister lay dead on the floor.

Van Hale was lying there motionless too.

The single window was open. Toulson ran to it. There was no sign of Anna Zemeckis.

He knelt down by Van Hale. Something had hit him in the face – the chair upended on the floor perhaps – and he was now coming round.

There was no way Toulson was going to leave Van Hale where he was.

'Wake up, for Chrissake,' he growled.

Van Hale rolled on his side groaning.

Toulson kicked him in the butt. 'Wake up, I said.'

He went to the door and fired a couple more shots, just to show that the storehouse was still defended. Then he took out his silver whistle and blew it hard several times. Then he blew it again.

88

Hog Wheel

Emily, Ben and John reached the Darke Hartz buildings undetected. They all had terrible misgivings about leaving Anna helpless in the storeroom, especially John, but without weapons there was nothing they could do to help Toulson and Van Hale free her.

They found an open door and slipped into the empty offices. Going on ahead of the others, Ben found a recess under some stairs near a doorway, from where they could make a hasty exit if necessary.

Emily frowned as they huddled in together.

'If you think I'm going to sit here waiting while Anna could easily get killed and the two Pinkertons are badly in need of support, you can think again, Ben Latham. I want to see what's going on. We've got to try and help them.'

John was looking pale and troubled. 'I should never have left Anna, I—'

'Come on,' said Emily, 'we have to find help. Follow me . . .'

The two men obediently followed her down corridors till they reached the main foyer of the Darke Hartz offices and went to the front door. They shot the bolt and cautiously peered outside.

The position gave them a view right across the stock pens, acre on acre of them. There were no people about and no livestock either. But at the far end of the site they saw a puff of steam and heard the

distant *chiff-chuff* of an engine. Closer-to, from the direction of the
Whetton Building, they heard sporadic firing.

'It seems safe enough,' said Emily, stepping out into the open before
anyone could stop her.

A shot zinged above her head and hit the door jamb.

She retreated fast back into the foyer and shut the door. They saw
a figure up at a window at the top of the water tower. Gunther had
put a man up there too.

'We'll try another way,' said Emily, refusing to capitulate.

'Emily . . .' began Ben helplessly.

Marching ahead, she led the others back the way they had come
and out into the alleyway they had arrived at earlier.

'*Emily . . .*'

It was too late.

Ben heard a soft, 'Oh!' as he and John emerged into the alley.

Emily was not alone.

Gunther Darke was standing there, Winchester in hand, with several
of his men brandishing weapons behind him.

Smoldering with cold anger he looked down at Emily.

'I'm afraid you don't know the yard as well as I do, Miss Strauss.
There's no way out for you.'

Emily glanced around, her eyes now wide with alarm.

'And it's no good looking for your Pinkerton friends either. My men
have them pinned down and they will soon be dead.'

'Where's Anna? What have you done with her?'

'She has been disposed of,' he replied indifferently. Then, turning
away, he said to his men, 'Take them to the killing floor.'

John cried out and lunged at Gunther Darke.

'If you've killed her . . .'

One of the Meisters stepped forward and expertly grabbed John in
an arm-lock.

'It's your own skin you should be worrying about. Take them *now*,'
Darke said sharply, 'while I have a last look around Darke Hartz, to
which, I fancy, I will not be returning after tonight.'

It was only then that Emily noticed they were not the only ones the
Meisters now had captive. They had hold of one of their own, too,
his face beaten and his eyes terrified.

'I know him,' whispered John, 'he's one of the Meisters who chased after Anna up by the wharves.'

The Meisters pushed them on.

Somewhere nearby they heard the sudden *thumpety-thump* of an engine. It was the hog wheel starting up once more.

The Darke Hartz killing floor was much larger than the disused one in the Whetton Building that had been an improvised set for the taking of pornographic photographs.

This was a vast hangar of a space, rectangular in shape, with an open cobbled floor covering two thirds of its length and vast sliding doors at either end. These opened onto the same kind of alleyway as the one Emily and the others had escaped down, along which ran rail tracks.

The remaining third of the killing floor was occupied for much of its length by a raised metal gantry on which were set a succession of vats, machinery and dressing tables. Before these, rising from the floor itself to the roof above, from which murky light filtered down through filthy glass, was Wheel No. 3 – famed as the largest in America.

A monstrous assemblage of wood and metal which rose massively above the butchers who worked it, it was turning now, slowly and ponderously, to the deafening clanking and clattering of the eight huge chains that hung loose from its edges. The three, now so tightly pinioned by Meisters on either side of them, were frogmarched towards the wheel until, stopping only a few yards from it, they were ordered to sit on the cobbles.

All three resisted the command until one of the Meisters grabbed John and pistol-whipped him to the ground.

They sat there watching the wheel turn. The chains clanked and the cobbles grew colder and more uncomfortable. Finally Gunther Darke appeared.

He had removed his jacket and had put on a freshly laundered, full-length white apron and butcher's studded boots. His shirtsleeves were rolled up.

With a knife in a sheath at his waist he looked in his element. He seemed to dwarf the other Meisters and the wheel itself, though it rose so high above him.

Emily could not take her eyes off him. Despite her anxiety for Anna, for all of them, she was now gripped by a combination of fascination and fear. Where ordinary workmen were daily enslaved by the wheel, Gunther Darke was its triumphant, demonic master. His eyes glittered black and shiny.

'Bring the woman here,' he said.

One of the Meisters heaved Emily protesting to her feet and took her to Darke.

He calmly glanced at the pocket watch he pulled from beneath his apron.

'Time is limited, gentlemen, and for us butchers, time is money. Isn't that so, Miss Strauss?'

He stepped closer to Emily.

'I believe,' he said, 'we have not had the pleasure of a visit from you to see the workings of the hog wheel?'

'Let us go, Mr Darke,' said Emily simply. 'You can gain nothing by keeping us here or hurting us.'

'Oh but I can, Miss Strauss. I shall gain a great deal of *pleasure*.'

He pulled Emily closer to him, his face no more than six inches from hers. Then he wrenched her head towards the hog wheel. Raising his knife in his right hand, Darke seemed about to slit Emily's throat. Behind her Ben shouted, 'No!'

Emily's heart was thumping painfully in her chest. But she tried not to betray her fear.

'You're a cool one, Miss Strauss. If all journalists had your mettle we would have a better and truer press in this country . . . A pity, you might have been a credit to your profession.'

He took the knife from her throat, pointed it at one of the chains hanging from the wheel and traced its path in the air as it went round.

'I thought you might like a closer look at how it works . . .'

Emily tried to move her head but Gunther's grip was far too strong.

'Though of course, having attended my lecture, you have the general idea.'

The wheel turning before Emily was terrifyingly large. Its roaring, grating sound seemed to magnify everything Gunther said into a thousand dark voices, as he continued to talk in his menacing way. He was as mesmerizing now as he had been in the lecture hall.

'Let's start with those chains,' he said. 'Take a good look at them, and the coupling at the bottom to which we attach the hog's hind quarter . . .'

His hand tightened painfully around her jaw, forcing her to look only at the wheel.

Take a really good look . . .

'. . . It is the most efficient killing machine of beast – or man come to that – ever invented,' whispered Gunther Darke in Emily's ear, 'don't you think?'

His grip slackened slightly.

Emily was able to look around more freely, though he still held the knife dangerously near her throat.

Having been both horrified and transfixed by Gunther Darke's lecture, she hated what the wheel was used for as much as she hated and despised the man who oversaw it.

The Darke Hartz killing floor was a vast cathedral of death and the hog wheel its vertical, ever-moving, obscene altar. Here a blood sacrifice was made of terrified living creatures day in, day out for money. The floor danced to the wheel's eternal dreadful tune. The overseers, the master butchers, the stickers, the dressers, and the hogs themselves played out their lives in a cacophony of shouts, clashing metal, the scrape of studded boots on bloody stone, and the terrified squeals of the animals themselves about to die.

Here, the animals passed from hell into an unrecognizable eternity in just a few minutes. Their bodies journeyed through a forest of knives, wielded by dozens of men who reduced them to nice neat joints of meat, all trimmed and dressed for market and packed in boxes at the end of the killing floor, ready to be loaded straight into the Darke Hartz box cars.

'You find it fascinating, do you not?' purred Gunther Darke.

If Emily had been able to speak she would not have denied it. The sheer brute force and ruthlessness of it was what had brought wealth to Chicago. Emily knew the statistics better than most and that during the World's Fair of 1893 the yard's daily bloody drama had become the most popular tourist attraction of them all.

'Well then,' Darke continued, his voice softer still but touched now with a more sadistic menace, 'I'm sure your readers would like to think

– they'll never actually know, of course, because you'll never file the story – that their lady journalist actually sees what she writes about with her own eyes. Don't you?'

He stepped back and pushed Emily roughly into the arms of the Meister. The charm had all gone and she knew she was looking into the face of the real Gunther Darke – cruel, cold, implacable.

He nodded at the Meisters to bring forward the one who was held captive. He was dragged to where Gunther stood.

'You know you've failed me . . .' he said, prodding the man towards the hog wheel with his knife.

The man's face was bloodied, his eyes dull and hopeless.

He nodded.

'And you know the punishment . . .'

'*Noo* . . .' the man began, as Gunther kicked his legs from under him. The Meister's head cracked against the moving wheel and then onto the cobbles as Gunther grabbed the next moving chain, attaching the Meister's leg to it, and let him go. For a brief moment the man somehow struggled upright, and for a moment more he tried to resist the relentless power of the wheel, but then he was dragged off his feet screaming and struggling.

His head crashed back onto the stone floor again, the chain tightened on his leg as he was hoisted upside down off the ground. As his free leg caught on a metal obstruction and was forced back under him, the wheel juddering briefly at the momentary obstruction, he screamed again, an animal sound now, and his leg broke with a sickening crack.

'*O mein liebe Gott!*' he cried in final, useless appeal as Gunther Darke, stepping forward and with the skill and speed of the master butcher, stuck the knife in the Meister's neck and with a flick of his wrist slit his throat.

Gunther stepped swiftly back, to avoid the sudden spurting flow of blood as the wheel continued to turn and the man, threshing and gurgling as he choked on his own blood, was lifted above their heads and carried into the gantry above the killing floor, his broken body twisting obscenely in the air.

Emily stared in horror; John went white and half-fainted; Ben's head slumped to his chest, unwilling to see more.

'Well then,' said Gunther Darke with a cold smile, his formerly pristine apron now splashed with blood and the wheel turning and clanking behind him, 'you wanted to see a spectacle, Miss Strauss, so let's do it again. Him next!'

Gunther pointed at Ben Latham.

As he did so there came a sudden rippling crackle of thunder overhead, followed by a *bang!* that reverberated right across the killing floor. Moments later, as the Meister dragged Ben towards Gunther Darke and the hog wheel and its chains, a hundred thousand drummers seemed to be pounding on the iron roof overhead as the heavens opened and rain began to fall.

89

Bunker

The thunderous rain woke Anna Zemeckis. The first thing she did was put her hands to her distended belly to see if her baby was all right.

She felt carefully, both hands gentle and wide, fingers sensitive to the slightest movement. She sensed a flutter inside and then, to one side of her womb, the unmistakable shift of shape as the baby moved inside her.

'Thank God,' she whispered.

Her escape from the storeroom had been sudden and violent, only made possible by the man who came and disabled the Meister guardng her. After she clambered out of the window and fell to the ground she lay low a short while. Then she had got up and run in the opposite direction, using the wall of the storehouse as cover from the men shooting at it.

She could not run fast for a spasm of pain in her womb had told her the baby was in distress. So, seeing a coal bunker by a track, she kept as low as she could and crawled behind it to rest. Ahead were more tracks and sheds and an embankment she guessed was the Chicago River. To her left the acres and acres of buildings which she knew were the meatpackers' offices and killing floors.

NELSON, MORRIS, ARMOUR, SWIFT.

Huge white letters on smoke-blackened walls.

The only name she could not see was Darke Hartz. It was obscured by the other buildings.

But to her right, on the rail tracks, she could see that dreadful name painted white on black on the side of every box car of a freight train.

That way too, as she dared to peer further round the bunker she was using as cover, lay Bubbly Creek. It was where she had run that terrible night, stumbling and terrified. That way, she never wanted to go again.

Anna looked to her left once more for a way to go. She was surprised at how far she had managed to run but saw something that made her realize at once she had to stay where she was.

Back by the bigger buildings rose the water tower, all two hundred feet of it. At its very top, on the observation platform, stood a Meister with a shotgun. He was not looking her way but towards where the Darke Hartz building must be.

He fired a shot and she saw the flash.

Knowing that the moment she left her cover she would be seen, Anna decided to stay where she was. The bunker was about four feet high and covered on top to keep the coal dry. There was a wooden hatch on one side that had to be lifted for men to shovel the coal out. She heaved it up with difficulty and propped it open with a stick.

Then she crawled inside, shifted the coal about to give herself space and hunkered down as the man had told her to. Here fatigue caught up with her and she closed her eyes. Her womb felt tight, but her baby was still now.

A brief respite of restless, troubled sleep followed, but now the violent storm woke Anna and rain was finding its way through the cracks in the roof of the bunker and dripping onto her.

She had no idea how much time had passed, but the light had faded and the murk and rain of the autumn afternoon made it difficult to see very far.

She got up, keeping low, and turned to her left, away from Bubbly Creek, towards the buildings she had seen earlier. Somewhere there would be a place to hide that offered safer and dryer protection than a coal bunker.

Her head down, and shivering now as her clothes once more became sodden, Anna Zemeckis headed off into the rain in search of refuge.

90

Guns and Knives

The moment the Meister dragged him to his feet and began hauling Ben towards Gunther Darke and the hog wheel, he started to struggle, as did Emily and John in his defense. But they were no match at all for their captors. These were men with brute strength, used to the dying struggles of hogs and steers. Mere humans were no problem.

'No . . .' grunted Ben, '*no* . . .' but his voice was a whisper, barely audible against the thunderous rain above and the grinding hog wheel below: '*Noooo . . . !*'

Gunther towered over him, knife in hand. He bent down and grabbed Ben's right ankle and pulled. Ben went flying backwards as Emily, reaching forward, managed to block his fall.

'No . . . !' she screamed.

A Meister put both arms around her and pulled her back. Knocking Ben to the ground, Gunther dragged him bodily towards the wheel.

Ben struggled, kicking out with his other foot, snatching at a handrail and trying to hold onto it.

But with the wheel turning only inches from his other hand, Gunther yanked Ben free and grabbed a chain.

'Oh yes,' he said, his eyes triumphant.

The noise grew louder still, as the whole of the killing floor reverberated to the chunter and chatter and banging of the hog wheel.

Then Gunther suddenly stopped. His eyes widened as, looking beyond his terrified captives and the Meisters holding them, he saw something they had not. Surprise, and then bewilderment flashed across his face. He let go of the chain in one hand and Ben's leg in the other.

As Ben scrabbled away, Emily turned and looked. At the far end of the killing floor the sliding doors were opening, their sound having been masked by the noise of the wheel. As they did so, the fading light beyond filled with steam, revealing, as it dispersed, the front of a big, black shiny locomotive, its wheels squealing as it ground to a halt. The door of a box car rolled back and a man jumped out.

Another followed close behind, and both raised their guns.

It was Toulson and Van Hale. Then, from the lengthening shadows behind the locomotive came the sound of boots on cobbles, as they were joined by Wolfgang Darke and his men, knives drawn.

A single shot rang out.

Emily looked back at Gunther. The bewilderment on his face was replaced by shock as his knife clattered to the ground and his hand went to his right shoulder, where a widening patch of blood showed through his shirt.

A second shot and the shoulder seemed almost to burst open, and Gunther was spun round and back, straight into the still-turning wheel. Instinctively, he grabbed a chain with his left hand and let the wheel raise him up to the gantry above, a trick he had learned as a boy.

The Meisters were thrown into utter confusion by the sight of their leader so unexpectedly shot and wounded. Faced by the advance of an overwhelming number of their own kind and the sight of two Pinkertons with guns picking them off from the vantage point of the box car, they ducked and pulled back, leaving Emily and John to dive for cover, dragging Ben with them.

Pulling out their knives and what guns they had, the Meisters retreated to the door behind them to escape and regroup. But it did not open.

From up on the gantry, Gunther crouched and watched, clutching his shoulder but not flinching as Toulson aimed another shot at him which hit a girder above his head.

'You may get my men, Mr Toulson,' he roared down at them, 'you may even get me, but you will never beat the Meisters. They will strike you down sooner or later and anyone else who stands in their way. You too, Miss Strauss, and all those you try to protect!'

Van Hale fired again at the gantry. But Gunther ducked back behind a girder, and then disappeared behind the machinery.

But he was not alone up there. From behind a girder, high up in the gantry, another man was watching from the shadows and awaiting his opportunity: Dodek Krol.

Knowing the Darke Hartz killing floor as well as Gunther, he followed the wounded man soundlessly to a metal stairway down from the gantry and out of a far exit into the gloom.

The rattle and rumble of the hog wheel faded behind them, overtaken now by the rush of rain in the storm drains outside.

Dodek had an idea where Gunther was headed – the only remaining place of refuge in the stockyard – a fire-damaged warehouse on its western side alongside an obscure reach of the Chicago River. It was a place the Meisters sometimes used for certain of their meetings, especially punishments.

He guessed Gunther would wait for night – and probably for the rain to stop too. Gunther had long since made contingencies against this day and Dodek, once his right-hand man, was the one person who knew them all.

Satisfied he knew where to find Gunther later, he made his way quickly out of the yard. He had a few final arrangements to make before returning to fulfill his commission from Paul Hartz. Then he would be free. Free of Darke and Hartz and of Chicago too. It was a city that had grown too small for him.

Back on the killing floor, the trapped Meisters made a last stand. It was boldly done but, now leaderless and faced by much larger numbers and the weapons of Toulson and Van Hale, there was no hope for them.

Two with guns fell dead before the Pinkertons' bullets, a third was wounded and lost the use of his knife hand. Sensing they were weakening, Wolfgang and his men moved in ruthlessly.

The final confrontation was one between men with knives, a fight in which Toulson and Van Hale took no part. It was the culmination of years of antipathy between rival butchers, trained men with knives who do not hesitate to go for the kill. In the ensuing close-hand knife fight, another of Gunther's Meisters was killed and two more badly wounded. The outcome might have been far worse had not Alfred Spohr, who took no direct part in the fighting, finally stepped in with Wolfgang and ordered his men to stop. The Meisters threw down their knives.

'Shut the wheel down,' Wolfgang shouted, as he moved forward to help deal with the wounded on both sides.

The machinery ground to a juddering halt and suddenly there was an eerie silence – except for the rain drumming on the roof and on the cobbles outside.

John English was among the wounded, still weak from the battering he had received in the box car and having sustained a knife wound in the arm as well from a Meister in the melee. Ben was badly shaken but not otherwise harmed.

Emily meanwhile was frustrated and angry. Anna was still missing and now Gunther Darke had made his escape.

'Why aren't you and Mr Van Hale going after him?' she challenged Toulson. 'You can't let him get away. He might know where Anna is . . .'

Toulson did his best to calm her.

'The only person here with any chance of finding Gunther Darke is his brother, because he knows the yard better than any man. But right now he wants to see that his men get medical attention and that the Darke Hartz premises are secured.'

'But what about Anna?'

Van Hale stepped forward. 'It's all right, Miss Strauss, she's probably safe somewhere. I helped her get out of the window in the storehouse and told her to run and hide – somewhere away from the Darke Hartz buildings, out beyond the coal tips and lumber yards near Bubbly Creek. She'll stay there till things have died down.'

'But we must find her, we can't leave her there alone in the dark.
I'll go and look for her myself,' said Emily.

Toulson shook his head.

'No, you won't. For one thing Gunther Darke's out there somewhere too; for another it's already getting dark and the yard is no
place for you to get lost in. We've alerted the police and you'll wait
until they get here. Then we'll mount a search for Anna and a manhunt
for Darke.'

'When you do I'm coming too,' said Emily.

'I've no doubt you will,' said Toulson. 'But for now you must wait
for the police.'

While they did so, Wolfgang and Alfred Spohr explained to Emily
what had happened.

They had heard Toulson's first whistle, but it came too soon, and
his men hadn't yet regrouped. Then the train had appeared, which
Spohr recognized as the one the Meisters had been loading. Fortunately, when the locomotive started running out of control, Wolfgang's
men had managed to switch it to a track that ran harmlessly in circles
right round the yard. One of them had jumped aboard and taken
control of the runaway locomotive from the terrified Meister attempting
to stop it.

Wolfgang had then decided that the quickest and safest way to get
his men up to the Whetton Building was to use the same train, picking
up Toulson and Van Hale en route.

Later, after the police had arrived, the dead and injured were
removed to the nearest hospital, John English among them but
under protest.

Emily refused point-blank to be evacuated from the scene. With
Toulson, Wolfgang and other armed men setting off in search of
Gunther Darke, she and Ben insisted on accompanying Van Hale
and a few more of Wolfgang's men in search of Anna. The rain
was still falling, heavy and persistent now, and the light was so bad
and visibility so poor that by five they had given up calling Anna's
name as they searched the northwest corner of the yard near Bubbly
Creek.

'God, it stinks,' said Ben.

Emily stood staring at the fetid channel below them. All she could see was an occasional ripple of light in the gloom and the dull patter of rain hitting water.

'It's filling up,' she said, as she peered back across the gloomy rail tracks to the yard behind them.

'Where are you, Anna, where have you gone to this time?'

They lingered a while longer at the Creek until Van Hale called a halt to the search and from the direction of Darke Hartz a whistle was heard.

'Toulson,' said Van Hale. 'For now our search is over.'

'We mustn't stop,' said Emily urgently, 'we mustn't give up trying, because I know Anna won't. She'll do anything to protect her child.'

Van Hale and Wolfgang's men drew round them in a circle, their hats dripping with rain, their clothes and their boots sodden.

'Unless you can read her mind, Miss Strauss, we're going to have to wait until morning. It's just too dangerous searching a site like this with the light fading.'

Wolfgang appeared in the gloom. 'I have spoken to my father on the telephone,' he said. 'He is relieved at the outcome, but also very much distressed at learning the truth of what my brother has been up to. I think he is not entirely surprised . . . Now he is most concerned about the disappearance of Miss Zemeckis.'

'Does he know she is carrying his grandchild?'

'Mr Steele told him. He begs us to do what we can; it was all I could do to stop him coming to the yard himself. But—'

'He's right, we should keep on looking,' interjected Emily forcefully. 'If she's gone to ground we should be able to find her . . .'

Toulson shook his head.

'No. You and Ben must go and get some refreshment and rest,' he said. 'You're dead beat and no use in a search, least of all at night. Some of Mr Darke's men, who know the yard back to front, have offered to assist police reinforcements with a further search when they get here. It's a job for experts now.'

'But—'

'No, Miss Strauss. It's no use.' It was Van Hale who interrupted her this time. 'You've no chance of finding her.'

Emily was forced finally to concede and, with Ben, reluctantly accepted the carriage provided by Wolfgang Darke and the offer of a meal and a change of clothes at Hans Darke's house.

'But I'm sure I could find her, I'm sure . . .'

She continued protesting, poking her head from the carriage window to call out to Toulson one last time.

'I'll come back . . . just as soon as I can.'

'Yes, Miss Strauss,' he sighed wearily. 'I know you will.'

91

Search

A short while later, a cab turned off Halsted for the quick run down to the Union Stock Yard entrance.

Dodek Krol had come back. This time he was carrying a bag. It contained a great deal of money and a few things he needed for a night or two.

The rest of his worldly goods, and they didn't count for much, he had now sent on to New York.

'You're sure you don't want me to wait, sir?' said the driver, who had brought him straight from the Nord Chicago Turnverein where he had cleared out his office and locked up for the last time. 'You'll never find a cab out here again at this time of day, let alone later. It ain't a safe place to be when it gets dark.'

Dodek shook his head and the cab turned round and left. He took off his bowler and let the rain fall on his bare head and stream down his face and bull neck as he listened to the roar of the water in the storm drains flowing out towards Bubbly Creek behind him.

He didn't move, he just stood in the rain and looked at the main gate, knowing that this was the last time he was going to go through it.

The first time had been twenty years before when he was young and had been one of thousands of immigrants arriving for work from back of the yards. He had come, alone, to Chicago from his hometown in Pennsylvania to work as a hog sticker with Darke Hartz & Company. He was alone again now and finished here. Time to move on and start again.

In all those years he had wept only once and that was because of what the rain had done. Four years before, in May 1889, he had arrived at the yard to find his workmates crowded over the newspaper. There had been a terrible flood the day before when a dam had burst on the Stonycreek River in Pennsylvania and had flooded Johnstown, wiping out almost its entire population of two thousand people.

Krol had wept because Johnstown was where he had been born and raised in a poor immigrant community. It was where his five brothers and three sisters, his parents and twenty other members of his extended Polish family had lived. And died.

A man never forgets something like Stonycreek. Dodek retreated inside himself and over the years channelled his anger and his desire for revenge into honing his own body, his strength and his dexterity with the knife. He became one of the most skilled master butchers in the stock yard, one of its leading Meisters, and, to only a select handful of people who hired his services, a paid killer. One day he knew he would have his revenge for Johnstown, but meanwhile he had bided his time.

Then, in October 1893, it had finally come, when Paul Hartz had offered him the commission to kill OAA president, Jenkin Lloyd Rhys, the engineer who had been largely held responsible for the disaster.

As for his other commissions, Krol didn't always say yes. He needed to know why he was killing a man and to feel the reason was just.

Which is why he had said no the first time that Paul Hartz had asked him to kill Gunther Darke.

Darke had in fact trained him and had promoted him from the killing floor to his distribution business; Darke had made Krol a Meister. The fact that Paul Hartz wanted revenge on his son-in-law for betraying his daughter Christiane and making her life miserable was not, in Krol's book, reason enough to kill him.

But from that time on, Dodek had held Gunther in contempt. He didn't like men who were cruel to their wives. A man should count himself lucky to have found one.

'Give me a better reason and I might do it,' he had said to Hartz and that's how matters had lain for a long while. As a killer for hire, Dodek might have done it had Hartz been man enough to tell him that the real reason he wanted Gunther out of the way was so that he could gain control of the company. But he never did admit that.

Then things changed. Gunther began bringing money into the OAA's coffers with his covert trade in *poses plastiques*, cleverly using Darke Hartz's own refrigerated box cars across the US rail network to avoid police and postal scrutiny. So for a while Hartz had relented, seeing Gunther as useful to his own ends and the greater good of the OAA.

But that morning at the OAA Convention things had changed yet again. The intervention of that old fool Steele had destroyed Gunther Darke's reputation and his chances of election as a vice president. It threatened Hartz's political career and put him in a weak position.

Krol's brief conversation with Paul Hartz at the convention after Steele had denounced Gunther was all it had taken to tip the balance for him to finally agree to kill Darke. What Hartz did not know was that Krol's true reason for agreeing was because Gunther had tricked him into going after a vulnerable and pregnant woman, Anna Zemeckis.

Now, as he stood in the rain at the stockyard gate, Krol felt sure that fate decreed the time was right.

The rain convinced him. For Krol knew from his years at the yard that it was just a matter of time after the first heavy rains of fall before the storm drains across the yard that get clogged with refuse through the hot summer months would start singing a sweet song as they busily discharged their contents into Bubbly Creek and made it flow again, like the stream it once was, which offered a fitting way of disposing of a man like Gunther Darke.

Now it was just a matter of completing this final commission.

Krol went to the main gate and roused the sleeping guard inside, whose eyes widened with apprehension when he saw who it was. There wasn't a man in the Yard who was not afraid of Krol.

'Mr Krol!' he bleated. 'You come to help?'

'I guess I have.'

'Not many of the police are here yet. They asked for reinforcements but there's flash floods on 30th and 32nd, and the men can't get through.'

'I know,' said Krol. 'Just been through 'em and it's getting worse.'

'It's Gunther Darke they're after, sir. They're sayin' he—'

'What are they doing now?' Krol cut in impatiently.

'Searchin'. They started at the Darke Hartz buildings but now they've moved the operation to the Exchange Building. I reckon they need men like you who know the yard.'

'I got a bag that's getting wet,' said Krol. 'I'll leave it here till I'm done. All right?'

'Safe with me.'

'Better be,' said Krol.

He passed on through into Exchange Avenue and made the short walk to the Exchange Building. Its lights were on. Krol could also see groups of men checking out the stock pens, the lights of their storm lanterns bobbing about to east and south.

He looked up into the rain. They had no chance at all of finding Darke in this weather. He wouldn't risk coming out of hiding with so many people about. He'd stay where he was until the searchers gave up for the night.

An officer from Harrison Street Police Station, whom Krol knew well, was now masterminding the search. He found him in the Exchange Building poring over a large-scale map of the site.

'Pretty hopeless, eh?' said Krol.

'Pretty much. But we gotta try. After what he's done Darke'll be desperate. We want to apprehend him before he does worse. There's a girl missing too.'

'What girl?'

The officer spat.

'Called Anna Zemeckis. Got out of Dunning. Wanted for attacking and injuring one of the attendants up there who happens to be the wife of one of our officers.'

Krol looked indifferent.

'She won't stand much chance then, if she's found!'

'Not by the time our people have finished with her. No sir.'

'What's she got to do with Darke?'

'Nothin' so far as I know.'

'Then what's she doing at the yard?'

'Search me. Orders are if we see her to take her in.'

'Show me what ground you've covered.'

563

The officer obliged. He waved a hand over the northwest part of the site, right where Krol knew Gunther would be holed up.

'Started there where he was last seen and now we've moved to the nearer buildings and pens. But if this rain continues I'm calling it off until morning.'

'Mind if I look about?'

'Better not by yourself, Mr Krol, you might get mistaken for Darke and get shot.'

'I don't think so. I know what I'm doing.'

'You be careful then,' said the officer. 'There's two Pinkertons on the site as well, just to confuse the issue. In the employ of Hans and Wolfgang Darke.'

But Krol had already slipped out the door.

Anna Zemeckis meanwhile had no sooner found a dry, warm boiler house to hide in after leaving the coal bunker, than she heard the men approaching, hollering and shining their lanterns in the dark. They didn't sound friendly, not like the man who had shoved her out of the window and who had promised help would come.

As their lights got nearer she could see the men were searching buildings like the one she was in. There was nothing for it but to run – yet again. But she emerged into the twilight having no idea now where she was headed. One thing at least she knew: darkness and secret places were her only friends.

She shivered as she crept on between buildings, feeling safer outside than in, trying to get her bearings.

Then, quite suddenly, the rain stopped. She looked up at the sky, obscured till now, and saw racing clouds lit by a rising moon. Opposite the building she now found herself standing by, she saw open space and then a rail track between buildings, and there, on the horizon, like an apparition rising up among the clouds, something bright and lit up and beautiful.

'The Fair,' she whispered, 'the World's Fair . . .'

Stillness, no rain, nor any wind: just ambient light in the darkening sky, and a far-off place, a dream she knew now she could never reach.

She turned to seek shelter near the building, away from the light, and found herself staring up at a man.

'I . . .'

Her voice stopped dead as he reached a hand straight for her throat and pushed her violently backwards.

It was Gunther Darke.

'You,' he said as she choked, '*you* . . .'

And Anna Zemeckis, her womb tightening once more, felt the world spin round as she slumped down in a near faint, her hands scrabbling at an arm, a chest, legs and feet.

'*You*,' he said again, looking down at her on the ground, with such hate it was like a knife in her heart. Then he hit her one way and then another and then a third time.

The next thing she knew Anna was being hauled back upright, then half carried, half pushed back the way she had come.

She screamed for help but the moment she did so, Gunther stopped, let her drop back to the ground and hit her hard in the face.

'Do that again and it'll be the end for your baby,' he said, raising a fist to her stomach.

It was then that Anna saw his right arm was limp and the shirt he was wearing was dark with what must be blood.

He hauled her up again with his good arm and shoved her forward.

'Where are you taking me?'

Gunther grunted, his face set with pain and the strain of holding her tight with his one good arm, his breathing heavy.

He too was an animal in pain, an animal at bay, seeking sanctuary.

But he was angry as well, angry beyond measure, and his anger was directed at Anna.

'Please . . . don't . . .'

'Don't talk,' he snarled. If he could have struck her with his good hand he would have done so.

Anna could sense his growing weakness beyond the anger and the strength it gave him. She knew she must do what he said and hope he would weaken enough for her to break free.

'Where are we going?' she whispered.

Gunther grunted again, forcing his body against hers as he prodded her across the rail tracks.

She looked to her right and saw the distant illuminations of the Fair more clearly; nearer-to were the approaching lights of the search parties and the silhouettes of buildings. She now knew where she was. She had been here before.

A new fear raced through her.

'*Where are we going?*'

'Bubbly Creek,' he said, his grip tightening, his face set and determined.

Something in those words gave Anna the strength to turn on Gunther in one last desperate attempt to free herself. She pushed her fists into his face, trying to stab at his eyes and scratch him.

It had no effect, as Gunther turned and, half laughing, taunted her. 'One more time . . . just one more time.'

His hand tightened on her arm.

Anna began to shake and cry; she could do no more.

'Yes,' he said softly, 'that's better now, we're nearly there. Yes . . .'

Then he stopped dead in his tracks and let her go as a voice called out to him from the gloom ahead.

'Good evening, Mr Darke.'

Anna recognized the man but struggled to remember his name.

'Hello, Anna,' he said.

It was the man who ran the Nord Chicago Turnverein. Mr Krol. Dodek Krol.

'Let her go, Gunther,' said Krol as the injured man made a final grab at Anna.

Gunther pulled back and Krol stepped swiftly forward and pulled Anna towards him.

'You'd better run for it,' he said softly, eyes on Gunther, 'because those men with lights will have heard your scream and they'll soon come this way. But don't go near them. They're police and they mean to harm you.'

He pushed Anna behind him and she stumbled off into the dark.

'Why are you here, Dodek?' said Gunther.

'I've come for you.'

Gunther seemed unsurprised. He hardly reacted at all.

'A commission?'

Krol nodded.

'Who?'

Krol said nothing.

'My father-in-law,' said Gunther matter-of-factly. He stepped sideways, circling Dodek.

'Well, then, Mr Krol, you're going to have to take me aren't you, and that won't be easy, will it?'

He pulled his jacket aside and revealed a sheath knife as his eyes glittered.

Then he said again, '*Will it*, Dodek?'

92

Final Commission

Anna Zemeckis did not look back.

She ran on into the gathering darkness, her mind confused, her body exhausted. Instinct alone was driving her now, that and the knowledge that she could not go back the way she had come or risk asking for help from the searchers. All she could do was run on with the sound of drains rushing with storm water all around her.

A man shouted suddenly in the distance, jogging a frightening memory. She had heard shouts like that before and with them had come laughter, mocking and cruel.

Anna now knew exactly what she was running towards, but even so, when she got there, she was taken by surprise. The ground suddenly dropped away causing her to lose her balance and crash forward on all fours.

She found herself staring into a black void from which came the heavy sound of running water and the odor of decay.

Behind her loomed bobbing lights and more shouts.

She groped along the soggy, filthy ground ahead of her until it fell finally away and she knew she was at the edge of Bubbly Creek.

The shouts were louder, the bobbing lights nearer.

Anna knew what she must do if she was not to be caught.

She turned round on all fours and eased herself backwards until she felt the bank of the Creek drop away under her knees. Very cautiously she lowered herself down until her feet were in cold mud and water. She could feel the water's flow tugging at her dress and legs, fierce now after the storm.

She pushed herself further out and down into the water until her whole body was below the edge of the embankment. The deeper she got the more the Creek surged around her, pulling at her body to loosen the precarious grip of her hands and fingers on the bank that was now above her.

The cold water made her gasp as it reached her chest and then her neck.

She hung there, knowing she could never climb back to safety. She didn't have the strength. She began to shiver with cold and fear. She had done her best but it had finally not been enough.

Her father . . . Gunther . . . John . . . so much pain, so much distress. Now there was no hope left, nothing for her or her unborn child. Nothing but a life no longer worth living. If they caught her they would punish her and send her back to Dunning and never let her free; if her baby lived it would be taken from her forever.

In final despair she let her body slide out into the water. Its flow began to take her as she let go of the last hold she had on land and on life.

'I'm sorry,' she whispered as the current took her.

The last thing she saw as she succumbed to its flow was the lowering sky and racing storm clouds above, lit up by the hundred thousand electric lights of the World's Fair beyond her to the east.

Dodek Krol stared into Gunther's face.

Each was waiting for the other to move but it was Gunther who felt his strength draining away from him. There was a time he might have beaten Dodek Krol but now . . .

He moved suddenly and fast, diving to his right to protect his damaged shoulder and to give himself time to pull his knife.

Dodek struck hard at him but missed as Gunther fell sideways.

Gunther hit the ground and rolled, feeling the stab of violent pain as his weight went on to his wounded shoulder. He fought through it, and a moment later was up again, knife in hand, ready to strike.

Dodek eyed him coolly, his own knife still in its sheath. His senses were alert to a thousand things, animal-like. The men to his left, across the tracks; lights flickering in his peripheral vision; the sound of water in the drains around them; and behind him, in the direction the Zemeckis girl had run, the sound of the Creek, as loud as he had ever known it.

He sensed another thing too; he almost smelt it: Gunther Darke was weakening, his knife shaking in his hand, his stance unstable.

So Dodek did not draw his blade because he knew that two knives are always more dangerous than one. The one he was facing he could deal with.

When he made his move it was sudden and brutal. As Gunther made a lunge forward, he swept his knife hand to one side with his left arm and grabbed Gunther's shot-up shoulder and arm in his huge hand and began to squeeze.

Gunther dropped his knife and grunted in agony.

Krol's great hand squeezed tighter still.

What little fight was left in Gunther Darke evaporated. Moaning, his left hand waving ineffectually, he sank to his knees.

Krol leaned over him and whispered, 'You should not have asked me to go after that girl. She is innocent.'

With one huge blow he sent Gunther sprawling, then looked round in the direction of the Exchange Building to see if the searchers were any nearer. They were.

Bending down, Dodek heaved the now unconscious body in a fireman's lift across his shoulders. Darke was a big man, but Krol did not grunt or stagger as he carried him away towards Bubbly Creek.

Oh yes, there are good times and bad times to dump a body in Bubbly Creek, as locals call the South Fork of the Chicago River . . .

Spring and fall are best because the stench is not so bad and there's a flow of sorts, especially after heavy rain, ensuring that the evidence of your crime is carried away, out of sight and out of mind.

You hope.

*   *   *

But hope is for amateurs who leave things to chance.

Dodek Krol was never one to do that. He dropped the body at the dark edge of Bubbly Creek and reached for his knife.

The light was not good but a man like Krol, trained to kill steers and hogs, knew exactly where to find Gunther's heart.

But the man he was about to kill was trained too.

Weak though he was and in terrible pain, raw animal instinct flooded back into Gunther as he came to from Krol's blow, infusing him with the will to live when all reason and all hope for it had gone.

He saw Krol's blade flash and, beyond him, the searchers approaching as they crossed the last of the tracks before Bubbly Creek, their lights bright now and their faces easy to make out.

'Hey! *You!*' one of them shouted.

As Dodek turned in the direction of the shouts, Gunther found strength and speed enough to grab his wrist and twist. The knife slipped from Dodek's grasp. Gunther did not relax his grip. He did something Dodek could not have expected. He simply toppled backwards, pulling his former friend with him into the foul, black water.

It was so cold that the shock of it brought Gunther back to full consciousness. As he surfaced, gasping for air and kicking furiously to stay afloat, with his one good hand he reached for a second small knife he kept concealed in his belt.

Dodek didn't see it coming, but felt a sudden harsh stab of pain in his side. Instinctively he smashed his elbow in his opponent's throat. Gunther screamed and choked.

Lights flickered in the air above them both, slightly upstream.

'Anyone there?'

Dodek knew he was badly hurt. Taking a deep breath, he summoned all his formidable strength and forced Gunther's head under the water and dragged him down.

Gunther's knife sank to the bed of Bubbly Creek as his hand scrabbled at Dodek's chest. Then he finally went limp . . .

'There's nothing down here!' called out someone from the water's edge.

The lights receded as Gunther's body surfaced briefly, his face contorted, his limp hand and arm caught by the flow, seeming to give a grotesque final wave.

Saturday October 28, 1893   5.17 PM

Dodek let the current take it. He waited a while until he was sure the men had gone, and then clawed his way up onto the bank.

Over the years, he had undertaken many commissions, but none of his victims had ever before managed to wound him. He scowled in the dark, knowing he needed attention fast.

Hauling himself upright he staggered away from the Creek until he had crossed the rail tracks. The stock pens lay ahead of him. Beyond them the lights at the main entrance seemed suddenly a lifetime away.

'. . . But I'm going to make it,' Dodek muttered, 'I'm not going to die like a stuck pig in the Union Stock Yard.'

93

Last Chance

Hans Darke paced restlessly up and down the entrance lobby of his house on Astor Street, awaiting further news of the search and the return of Wolfgang and the others from the yard. He was in considerable distress.

He had felt momentary relief to know that Wolfgang was safe and Toulson, Miss Strauss and the others as well. But as soon as he heard what had happened to Gunther, a profound sadness overtook him. It came with knowing that his son's downfall, which had seemed so inevitable for so many years, had finally come. Even though he had cut himself off from him years back, it didn't lessen the pain.

But his greatest distress came when he had a second call from the officer in charge of the search at the yard saying that Anna Zemeckis, mother-to-be of his first grandchild, had gone missing during a gunfight. The floods weren't helping the search for her.

'What floods?' demanded Hans. 'It's dry as a bone up here.'

As if in answer the line went dead.

When finally a third call came through, Hans grabbed the phone.

'Mr Darke?'

'Yes.'

'Mr *Hans* Darke.'

'Yes, yes, what is it, man?'

It was the officer in charge of the search at the Union Stock Yard again.

The line was bad and Hans could hardly hear.

Isaiah Steele took over and listened. Finally he put down the phone.

'There's floods on the South Side. Wolfgang's probably delayed because of them.'

Hans opened his front door.

'Looks like the rain storm's moving up here,' he said, scowling as he saw the racing clouds above and heard the first rumbles of thunder.

He closed the door and continued pacing about, wrestling with emotions he had never dealt with before. He was a man for whom work had been his life and he knew that if he had been a father in any proper sense of the word it was a bad one: too busy to care; too strict to give ground to boys who needed it; too focused on all the wrong things to notice those that really mattered.

The only two women he had ever known well and was easy with had been his wife and, more lately, his niece Elfriede.

It was she who came to him now, shooing Isaiah Steele away as being less than useful in a situation like this.

'Men!' she muttered.

'This is my fault,' said Hans, 'all of it, from beginning to end. I helped make Gunther what he is and now there's a poor girl out there, a poor, lost girl . . .'

Elfriede was doing her best to comfort him when a knock came at the door and a sodden Wolfgang, Emily and Ben finally arrived. They told him immediately all that had happened. After that, for a time there seemed nothing more to say.

Wolfgang and Hans sat together in a corner, quiet and stony-faced, in shock about Gunther and his possible fate; Ben sat with Isaiah, relating how he had come so close to death that afternoon.

But Emily could not sit still. She refused Elfriede's offers of refreshment and a change of clothes and was pacing about as restlessly as Hans had been.

'I shouldn't have left, but Mr Toulson persuaded me it was for the best. I should have stayed at the yard. That's where she is and where my story is too. And it won't reach its conclusion until I find her.'

Hans finally got her to sit down, anxious for the slightest scrap of
news or information about Anna.

'No one will find her tonight. Not in the yard, not in all Chicago,
not unless they know where to look. She . . . she . . .'

'What is it, Miss Strauss?' asked Hans in alarm.

Emily had turned pale, her eyes wide.

'I think I . . .'

'What is it?' said Wolfgang.

'Something Mr Van Hale said, just as we were leaving.'

'*What?*'

Ben and Wolfgang came over.

'He said I wouldn't find her once night fell *unless I could read her mind.*
Well, I think I can . . . She's tired and she's scared and she's pregnant
and she can't trust anyone, least of all men, and she's nowhere left to
turn. She . . . I think . . . Have you a telephone, Mr Darke?' she said
urgently.

He nodded.

'Right in my office.'

'Can you put in a call to Hull House on the West Side?'

'I guess so . . .'

'I mean *now*, Mr Darke.'

Wolfgang took over.

'Who do you want to speak to?' he said when he finally got through.

'Katharine Hubbard.'

Wolfgang repeated the name into the receiver.

After a couple of minutes she was on the line.

'Katharine, this is Emily Strauss, New York *World*. You remember?'

'I remember. What can I do for you?'

'Listen. You got flooding over your way?'

'Yes.'

'Bad enough to stop you going out with a carriage?'

'Depends what for.'

'Someone who needs help.'

'You only have to say.'

'Right, this is what I want you to do . . . No, wait, just a moment.
Wolfgang, can you get a carriage ready and your best driver? And tell
Elfriede I need her. And close the door as you go, I don't want to raise

575

anybody's hopes, least of all your father's. Oh yes, and a map of the South Side. I need one.'

Five minutes later Emily Strauss was outside the Darke house and climbing into a carriage alone.

'Won't you say where you're going?' said Wolfgang following after her.

'The South Side.'

'You need someone with you, Emily,' said Ben.

'No Ben. A man is the last person I or Anna Zemeckis needs right now,' said Emma tartly. 'Drive on!'

'Where to, miss?' asked Hans's coachman.

Emily named a street.

'Never heard of it.'

'Can you get me to 31st?'

'I reckon.'

'Then hurry. This map'll take us from there.'

'Where on earth is she heading?' said Hans, overwhelmed by the speed of events.

'Don't worry. She knows what she's doing,' said Isaiah Steele.

Ten minutes later, there was a ring at the door.

It was Paul Hartz.

He did not look his usual confident self as he was shown into the drawing room and he did not greet Hans Darke. Indeed, his first words were to Wolfgang.

'Christiane is in my carriage outside,' he said. 'She is too distressed to come in but I would be grateful if you could . . . tell her all that has happened. About Gunther I mean. I do not know how to.'

Wolfgang nodded and went outside, after which Hartz turned to Hans Darke.

'I would like to speak to you in private, Hans,' he said, looking around the assembled gathering.

'I would rather we have witnesses, Paul,' responded Hans coldly. 'Isaiah, Mr Latham, please follow us.'

The four went into his study, where a file lay on Hans's desk.

It contained a simple document, which Isaiah Steele had drawn up that afternoon in anticipation of this very moment, and in the hope that Wolfgang, Anna and the others would return safely from the stock yard.

Isaiah Steele had been extremely surprised that Hans had asked him to draft the document – or that he had even *thought* to do so in the first place.

'It does not seem quite the appropriate time, Hans,' he had said.

But Darke had shaken his head.

'I have not built up my company into one of the four largest meat-packers in the world,' he had said, 'without knowing when to make the most of an opportunity. Against Paul Hartz they come but once and briefly.

'Fifteen years ago when I needed money to expand my business he helped me, but he also made a fool of me as bankers and financial men often do of their hardworking but less sophisticated commercial clients. He tricked me into giving him effective control of the company I had built, using Gunther and his own daughter as the vehicle, by encouraging Gunther to steal Christiane from Wolfgang. Had today gone differently at the OAA meeting and he had not been exposed by you, he would have pushed Wolfgang and myself out.'

'Yes, but Hans . . .'

'But now, suddenly he is weak and vulnerable,' Hans continued, 'and this is the moment to make him an offer which, while preserving his tattered honor, will give me back what I should never have given away.'

Isaiah had drawn up a simple document that transferred a controlling stake in Darke Hartz back to Hans and Wolfgang. He took that document out now and placed it before Paul Hartz, who read it with the greatest distaste.

'It gives you too much for too little,' he said.

'It gives me what I believe to be fair and leaves you with a holding that, were you to dispose of it, would give you a very handsome profit indeed. Take it or leave it. I shall not negotiate.'

'But I have no guarantee that you will keep your side of the bargain.'

Hans Darke glowered.

577

'You have the best guarantee in the world, Paul, if only you knew it. You have my word before witnesses. Now, shake hands on it and sign and I will never mention this matter again. From now on, Wolfgang runs the company.'

94

Flow

Emily made faster progress than she had expected.

The driver, who had made the run to the South Side a thousand times on Darke Hartz business, knew every twist and turn, even if their final destination was one he had never been to before.

They stopped at 31st and consulted the map.

'Are you sure you want to go there, miss? It's a bad neighborhood and no place for ladies.'

'I don't give a damn about that,' said Emily, 'and anyway I'm no lady, so just get me there!'

The streets, rock hard throughout summer, were now awash with water. The carriage jerked and bobbed about sending spray everywhere. There was no one much about on the sidewalks, but the saloons were heaving, it being a Saturday, and snatches of music and song came to them from behind closed windows.

'Folk celebrating the end of the Fair,' said the driver.

They turned into a small street, dark and mean, with few lights showing.

'Make a right,' called out Emily, poring over her map.

The next street was no better than a slum.

'Make a left and then a right again . . .'

The carriage slowed, negotiating piles of trash and potholes.

'Not good!' exclaimed the driver, slowing still more and having trouble controlling the horses.

They finally pulled into a street where only a single light showed with a row of houses down one side of it.

'This must be Benson Street,' called out Emily.

'Don't see no sign,' said the driver dubiously.

'Can you see another carriage?'

'I can.'

'Make for it and stop.'

The driver drove on cautiously, the houses to their right, and stopped.

Emily got out.

There was a bad smell in the air. Peering between the ramshackle wooden houses, and beyond the railing at the top of the embankment, Emily saw what she was looking for.

'Bubbly Creek,' she whispered. She couldn't see it in the darkness below, but she could hear its roar and smell its stinking water.

On the far side of the creek loomed the dark mass of the Armour Glue Factory. The air was so pungent and heavy that Emily nearly retched.

Then a figure loomed out of the darkness beyond the other carriage. Emily's driver eased back his jacket revealing a revolver. Mr Darke had said to take no chances.

'It's all right,' said Emily quietly. 'And keep that out of sight, it won't help anyone.'

The advancing figure was a woman.

'Katharine Hubbard?' she called out. 'Is that you?'

The two women embraced.

'Glad to see you, Emily. I've brought the things you suggested and two lanterns . . .'

'Could you see anything in the creek?'

Katharine shook her head.

'Nothing, I walked the whole length of the street from the bridge at one end to the conduit at the other. But two pairs of eyes will be better than one.'

They fetched the lanterns from Katharine's carriage and the drivers lit them, both offering to help.

Emily thanked them but shook her head.

'Best not,' she said. 'We're looking for a girl who's been running from men for weeks and the sight of a couple more calling out her name will send her running again. If you're needed we'll call you.'

The houses were mostly unlit, or those that were had their blinds and curtains tight shut, revealing only a sliver of light.

'There were lights on when I arrived,' said Katharine, 'but people in these neighborhoods shy away from any sign of trouble. They probably heard my carriage, took one peek and decided I was the police or up to no good.'

'Right,' said Emily, 'let's try looking again, nice and slow, from the conduit right up to the bridge. But take care not to alarm Anna if she's down there. She'll be jumpy. We don't want to scare her.'

They peered down at the racing water calling Anna's name. But the light from their lanterns didn't reach very far and they could see little more than the muddy bank on the nearside, let alone the surface of the water.

'What makes you think she's here?' asked Katharine.

'It's no more than a hunch.'

'Why on earth would she deliberately get into Bubbly Creek here, in Benson Street of all places?'

'She wouldn't. If she got in anywhere it was up at the yard.'

'But that's half a mile away. In this weather, with the creek running at full spate, she wouldn't stand a chance.'

'She made it before. I'm reckoning that if she felt that the Creek was her last place of refuge, this is where she'd fetch up. Right here where she was found before. But she may be too cold and weak now, and maybe we're too late . . .'

Emily leaned over towards the creek again, holding her lantern. Then she gave the lantern to Katharine and peered into the gloom below.

'It's so hard to see,' she muttered irritably. 'I have to get closer.'

There was an air of grim determination about Emily now as she took off her cloak and handed it to Katharine, and gave her her purse.

'Emily Strauss, I am not letting you . . .'

'A bit of cold and wet's not going to hurt me.'

Katharine pointed at the racing water below and said, 'One slip and you'll get carried away.'

'And where would it take me if it did?'

'Into the Chicago River. The creek joins it about a hundred and fifty yards from here. Can't you hear the roar?'

They listened.

It was loud and angry.

'I think it runs down into a chute in the final stretch, like a waterfall. You'd end up in the river and you'd end up dead. Please, Emily, don't . . .'

But Emily was already hoisting up her skirts. She climbed over the railing, which wobbled precariously, and clambered down on the far side, lowering herself into the darkness.

'My, it's cold!' she said, 'but I have a foothold. Of sorts.'

One of her hands reached up into the light.

'Give me the lantern.'

Katharine placed it carefully into her hands so that it did not gutter and go out.

'Oohh!'

'What is it?'

'I slipped. The current's very strong.'

'Is there anywhere to walk along the creek's edge?'

There was silence for a moment or two.

'There's mud and worse,' said Emily eventually, 'and a ledge of sorts, but it's very, very slippery. Oh!'

'*Emily!*'

A hand appeared on the wall at the foot of the railings and Emily's face showed.

'I'm going upstream to the conduit, and if there's nothing there I'll come back down to the bridge where the railings are lower and I can get back out more easily. Okay?'

'Emily, please . . .'

But Emily had disappeared into the darkness below again and all Katharine Hubbard could do was follow on the street above and try to keep sight of her lantern.

Emily was half in water and half out, her left hand on the embankment

582

for balance, her feet in mud, her skirts swept and dragged at by the flow of the water. She held the lantern in her right hand.

'Anna!' she called softly, '*Anna!*'

She waded on, the water feeling colder by the minute and the Creek, its banks getting higher as she went, seeming ever darker.

'Anna?'

Nothing.

The ledge narrowed and soon she was wading in the water up to her waist, her skirts a hindrance, the stream deep and faster on the right-hand side. At one point she made the mistake of letting her right hand drop; the bottom of the lantern caught the water which nearly ripped it out of her hand.

No woman, no man, could survive in this, she told herself.

At last, already very cold and tired, she reached the entrance to the tunnel which carried the flow from under buildings upstream. It was six feet high and had once had a wire across it, to stop people going in when the water was low. Most of this had broken and swung up against the wall on the side where Emily was. She used it to pull herself the last few feet and then, placing the lantern on mud and flotsam to one side of the flow, she climbed inside.

The place roared with the sound of water but it was big enough for her to nearly stand upright, the roof curving above her head.

'Anna!' she shouted, as loud as she could against the creek's roar. She moved ahead for ten yards or so before she decided it was folly to go further. If Anna was still alive, and now she had to face facts and believe she probably wasn't, she would have got out of this place fast.

Reluctantly, Emily turned back, the water rushing past her with such force that she lost her footing again, fell and was propelled back the way she had come.

Only by grabbing onto the broken fence again was she able to right herself, her lantern nearly going out in the tumble.

She stopped, caught her breath and took stock.

A sense of the serious danger she was in suddenly hit her, but she was determined to carry on the search.

'Now for the other ... w ... w ... way,' she muttered aloud, her teeth chattering with cold and fear.

Something wet and slimy brushed across her face and she started

back. It was some kind of material caught in the fence. She raised her
lantern and saw at once that it was a woman's plaid shawl.

'Oh Anna,' she whispered.

It was the same shawl she had been wearing earlier that day.

With a gathering sense of urgency, Emily splashed back down the
way she had come, holding on as best she could to the bank, shining
the lantern and calling out every which way until she reached the point
where she had left Katharine. She felt a surge of renewed energy.

'I'm going on down to the bridge,' she called up.

'Please!' said Katharine.

'Follow me down . . . by the time I get there one of the drivers may
have to haul me out.'

The next section of the creek was wider and safer but it was a whole
lot muddier, and Emily lost first one boot and then another. Mud and
slime slurped between her toes. Her hands touched fetid matter and
garbage that she could not identify.

But still she pushed on, with a fierce, angry energy. She blamed
herself for what had happened. She should never have left the yard
in the first place.

She reached the bridge where she still hoped Anna might be taking
shelter. But she was nowhere to be seen under the arch, the last logical
place to hide. Whatever narrow strip of mud had been there before
the rain came had been stripped away. There was a slippery ledge,
the fast-flowing gully just below it, and nothing else at all. Beyond it
was a stretch of thirty yards or so of racing water and the final roaring
where the last conduit shot the waters of the creek and all its contents
into the Chicago River.

Nothing.

Emily knew now she was too late.

Nobody could survive Bubbly Creek.

They all said it.

Anna Zemeckis had survived it once but not a second time.

'I'm sorry Anna,' Emily whispered in the raging, racing, bitter dark,
'I tried, I tried but . . .'

Then she saw that there was a barbed-wire fence of sorts across
the conduit which took the flow of Bubbly Creek into the river. All
sorts of flotsam had got caught in it, just as in the conduit she'd been

in upriver. And there was something over there, flapping like paper in a night wind, back and forth. It could be, *it could be.*

'Anna!' she shouted again, her voice lost in the dark roar about her as she struggled to keep hold of the slimy wall, her hands numb with the cold and making her fumble and slip.

'Emily!'

Katharine's voice rang out in the distance, up on the bridge. 'Are you all right?'

Emily was now nearly at the barbed-wire fence and the thing that she had seen was still moving feebly in the flow. What was it? An arm . . . or something?

Then Emily, slipping and sliding the final yard or two got close enough to see – and screamed.

It wasn't Anna. She found herself staring in disbelief and shock into the white eyes, gaping mouth and snout of a huge hog, rotten and stinking with death, water flowing right into it and around it, the 'arm' she had seen no more than a front quarter, its hind quarters trapped in the wire.

She turned away, shocked and exhausted, knowing she had to get back upstream out of the Creek soon or she never would at all.

She pulled herself to the wall and rested a moment, gathering her strength. She looked again at the hog and then beyond it across the river. She could see a ship's lights and the silhouette of what must be a grain elevator. To its left were the rounded mounds of coal heaps and a jumble of shapes that was probably lumber.

The river itself was a wide, steady flow of water. Powerful, deep, dark and remorseless. A river of life that had now become a place of death and nightmares.

'Anna!' she called a final time, but her voice held no hope now, 'Anna!'

'Emily! I can't see you. Where are you?' called out Katharine anxiously from above.

Emily turned back towards Katharine's voice and the safety of the bridge.

'Emily!'

'I'm coming!' she shouted back, angry with herself, with Chicago and with everything, 'but it isn't exactly easy!'

'Be careful!'

Emily was dead beat but she knew if she was to win her battle to get back to the bridge she was going to have to win by brute force.

She grabbed whatever she could by way of handholds, and, putting her shoulder to the racing water, inched her way forward until she finally made it back to the nearside of the bridge.

Above, she could just make out Katharine's lantern.

'I'm coming back up the other side!' she shouted. I can't get to it from here.'

Emily tried to heave herself back up onto the ledge inside the low bridge, but the water was high and she didn't have the strength.

She pulled back to see if there was another way, her eyes looking up past the arch and then across to the far side where it dropped back down into shadow.

It was then, as Emily clung on seeking a way back to safety, that she saw Anna Zemeckis, caught in the lee of the bridge, just out of reach of the creek's violent flow. Right where Emily had passed by before. She was huddled down, half in the water and half out of it, looking no more than a bundle of rags.

'Anna?'

The water rushed between them, great raging surges of it, '*Anna!?*'

The sodden rags moved and somewhere within them eyes opened, white in the gloom, and stared across the water at her.

'*Anna! Don't move!*'

Emily threw aside her lantern, using both hands now to feel her way along the arch of the bridge until she found a handhold. She glowered at the water, and then, with a pull and a rush, she heaved herself across to the little haven Anna had found.

It was a tiny jumble of mud and flotsam. Behind it rose an unyielding brick wall. In front, the water rushed and sucked.

What Emily saw before her now was something she surely would never forget. A woman who was hardly more than a girl, so cold and exhausted that she was shaking all over. Only one thing was steady and that was her right hand which clung onto the pile of flotsam.

'I wanted to die,' whispered Anna, 'to drown in the Creek, as I should have done in the first place. But I couldn't do it. I couldn't because I knew my baby was alive.'

Emily reached out to her.

'It's all right, Anna, it's over. You're safe now. I'm taking you home.'

After Emily and Katharine and the two drivers had hauled Anna out of the Creek, Katharine helped the two women get dry in her carriage and put on the change of clothes Emily had asked her to bring from Hull House. Then she gave them food and something to drink.

'She must come to Hull House, straight away. And see our doctor. We'll take care of her,' insisted Katharine. 'She's in no fit state to go further.'

Emily shook her head.

'No, Katharine, she can't stay in Chicago because she's still in danger. The authorities are after her and probably the Meisters too. I'm taking her back to Mr Darke's house on Astor Street.'

'But Emily . . .'

Anna opened her eyes and stared at them. Her face was blue and puffy from the beating Gunther had given her and her eyes bloodshot.

'Please . . . I want to see John. Where is he . . . ?'

'It's fine, Anna, he's safe,' Emily reassured her, then turned to Katharine.

'Please call Hans and Wolfgang Darke the moment you get back to Hull House. Tell them what's happened and that I need to get Anna on the first available train to New York. Tell Ben to have Johnny Leppard bring my luggage from the Auditorium Annex. Emily Strauss and the *World* are taking Anna home. Back to her father.'

Soon after, Katharine Hubbard's carriage went one way into the night and Emily's the other, leaving the Creek behind them for good.

A short while later, a body, flopping its way down Bubbly Creek, was carried past Benson Street before being briefly caught in a backswirl of water on the far side of the bridge.

Then, the water surging once more, the body was lifted and carried on down towards the conduit where the water hurled it against the dead and bloated hog already entangled in the wire there, which it embraced obscenely.

From there, man and hog together, looking pretty much the same in the dark, shot off into the anonymous expanse of the Chicago River.

95

À Bientôt

When Hans Darke received the call from Katharine Hubbard of Hull House that Anna and Emily were safe and on their way back to Astor Street, his relief knew no bounds.

He and Wolfgang at once organized a doctor to come and check that Anna was fit to travel, sent for Emily's luggage and booked places on an express train leaving Dearborn for New York at seven-thirty that night.

As he waited for Anna's arrival, the relief Hans felt fled and he became anxious, pacing the room once more.

'What do I *say* to her?' he asked Isaiah over and over again.

'I should think she'll be as nervous as you are,' his friend replied, 'but very tired as well. She has been through a great deal. She is the innocent party. And all you can do is try to be accepting, welcome her and make her feel she is safe.'

'Yes, but . . . *Elfriede*! I need you!'

'Leave Miss Zemeckis to me when she arrives, uncle,' Elfriede said. 'She will need to rest and change and I dare say Miss Strauss will as well. Miss Hubbard says they have both been through a great deal.'

To add to the atmosphere of uneasy excitement, John English now turned up in a cab from Cook County Hospital, his face cut and bandaged but otherwise recovered.

The two apparitions that finally entered the door of Hans Darke's splendid home on Astor Street could not have looked more out of place in the elegant surroundings. Dressed in a motley assortment of clothes, their hair a mess and their faces streaked with the grime and filth of Bubbly Creek, one looked exhausted and the other as if she had been in a prize fight.

The doctor immediately checked Anna over and reassured her that all was well with the baby, after which Elfriede took them in to see Hans Darke.

Emily and Anna entered the drawing room where the others sat waiting for them, Hans Darke immediately rising from his seat, mute and staring at the bruised and battered girl.

'Mr Darke . . . this is . . . Miss Zemeckis,' said Emily, her voice soft. For once she found herself unable to think of anything else to say.

Hans remained rooted to the spot, lost for words. All he could do was stare with a mixture of shock and pity at the exhausted, disheveled girl in front of him.

It was Anna herself who broke the ice.

'I am very sorry,' she said quietly, 'for all the trouble I have caused you, Mr Darke. But I am glad to be here and glad to see you here too Mr Crazy and I . . . I . . .'

Emily was ready now to move to Anna's side, for she seemed about to break down. But she did not.

Instead, she turned back to face Hans Darke and said, '. . . but I am sorry, sir, to meet you in these . . . circumstances. Please do not think that . . . that . . .'

'What?' said Hans Darke, instinctively leaning forward, his voice no more than a whisper. It seemed to him that he had never in his life heard a young woman say anything so painful and difficult with such grace, and he cursed himself for a lifetime of not knowing how to be himself where emotions were concerned.

Sensing his confusion, Anna continued, 'No, please. You don't have to say anything. And do not think that I expect anything of you except please some food, and a glass of water and a little time to rest and . . . and then . . .'

She stood before him, he one of Chicago's richest citizens, she one of its poorest, and she was asking nothing of him but his compassion and a glass of water.

After so many long years of reserve, of ruthless self-discipline, of never saying more to anyone than what was necessary, or doing anything that was not to his own commercial advantage, suddenly something gave way right in the center of Hans Darke's heart. It opened up new feelings that took him into a different world that was frightening and strange.

He did something that felt like the hardest thing he had ever done in his life: he crossed the few feet between himself and the brave, hurt, frightened girl before him, and took her in his strong arms and said, 'You are more welcome to my house than you will ever know. Welcome Anna, welcome.'

And it was *his* voice that broke.

Not long after, Toulson and Van Hale arrived.

Toulson was relieved when Hans informed him that he had arranged berths for the two women out of Dearborn that night.

'I'm very glad to hear it, Mr Darke,' he said. 'Whatever Paul Hartz may have signed, and wherever Gunther may now be, I don't think the Meisters will let Anna or Miss Strauss be, and it is impossible for the two of us to protect them here . . .'

'In any event,' added Emily, 'I have to get a story to the *World* that I haven't even written yet. I shall have to write it on the train and file it by telegraph at the first station with a Western Union en route.'

'I'll be traveling with Emily part of the way,' Ben explained, 'to work on the illustrations for her story and then get back to Chicago for the closing of the Fair. I'll have to get off at Fort Wayne, which we should reach around ten-thirty, to file Emily's story there before catching the last train passing in the other direction, back to Chicago.'

Emily added, 'We'll need a drawing of Anna tied up in the store-house and—'

Ben produced his sketchbook from his pocket. 'Don't worry, Emily, already done it,' he said matter-of-factly.

'But your hands were tied behind your back!'

Ben gave her the wry look of an old pro.

'This is journalism, Miss Strauss, not scientific truth. I did these sketches while you were down at the Creek. And Wolfgang went and retrieved my camera, too, from the storehouse.'

Emily looked at the drawing of Anna.

'But you've captured her likeness perfectly, and even how tired and helpless she looked.'

'That's what I *do*,' he said.

'Let's see the others,' said Emily.

She flicked through Ben's sketchbook. There were dozens of them, some no more than thumbnails, others a whole page of the book.

She stared at them in amazement.

'But these are just as I imagined I would write about it!'

'Yes, I know. It's my job. But they'll only use a couple at most, so prepare yourself for disappointment.'

There came a ring at the door. It was Johnny Leppard, in his uniform, just in time with Emily's luggage.

'The housekeeper packed it, Miss Strauss. And I demoted myself to bellhop again so I could be sure to come and say goodbye.'

Emily tipped Johnny generously and thanked him for all he had done. For no good reason she knew she would miss him.

'And Mr Ritz, Johnny, did he come up trumps?'

'Of course he did. I persuaded him that he needed my services at the Savoy, London.'

'And why would that be?'

'Told him guests from England at the Auditorium Annex appreciate an English voice among the staff. Makes 'em feel at home.'

Emily laughed.

'And Americans at the Savoy would do likewise? Namely yours?'

Johnny nodded.

'And he bought it?'

'He did, Miss Strauss.'

'And is he paying your fare?'

'Course miss. "Don't give me a tip, sir," I said, "just give me the fare."'

'When are you going?'

'Soon as the Fair's over. All the hotels'll be shedding staff fast. Got to be ahead of the game. You look me up if ever you're in London, won't you?'

'I will,' Emily said.

'Meanwhile, I'll get on with improving my French.'

'*Au revoir*, then,' said Emily.

'*À bientôt*,' Johnny replied.

'What's that mean?'

'See you soon – and I hope I do, miss. I hope I do.'

The train for New York left Dearborn promptly at seven-thirty that evening and none of the group were sorry, for now, to see the last of Chicago.

John English saw them off. He wanted to travel with them, but common sense prevailed.

'Let me talk to my father,' said Anna. 'It would be too much for him right now . . . And you should talk to your mother and Mr McIlvanie. And we shall write and see what we shall see. And then . . . after the baby . . .'

She could not bring herself yet to be more explicit. 'You will feel very differently towards me, I expect,' she said matter-of-factly.

'No, Anna,' said John very firmly, 'I won't. And yes, I shall write, but Anna—'

'What?'

'I am not going to lose you again.'

As the train pulled out of Dearborn Station into the night it hit thunderous rain: rain that hammered on the roof and slanted down the windows in streaks and rivulets and which caught the light outside, especially when, twenty minutes later, it passed the bright electric lights of Jackson Park and the World's Fair.

'Last time,' said Anna.

But Emily was looking the other way, towards the Union Stock Yard. No lights there, just darkness. And beyond, between the glimmers of sheet lightning, the lurid glimpses of chimneys and drifting smoke.

Then the rain fell heavier still.

'Rain. Good, cleansing rain,' said Emily with a sense of satisfaction, 'to wash away the dark heart of Chicago.'

96

Fort Wayne

Half an hour out of Chicago, after a short doze, Anna Zemeckis at last began to talk and open up. It was as if, with the city behind her, she now felt free to tell Emily all she had been through: to relive it in order to then try to forget it.

For an hour or more, Emily listened and wrote and listened some more, but she still had not got to the heart of Anna's story.

Finally, she interrupted her gently, saying 'Anna, there's something I need to ask you and there isn't much time . . .'

'Then you must ask me the things you need,' said Anna.

'There's one thing you haven't talked about . . .'

'What?'

'How did you end up in Bubbly Creek?'

Anna hesitated a while and looked out of the window at the passing night. Finally, she said in a low voice, 'I don't want to talk about it because it's the worst part of all . . . and it was my own fault.'

'So what happened?'

Anna sighed wearily and said, 'I should have taken Marion's advice and stayed away from Gunther and the stock yard. She *warned* me. But I went back to try and confront him.'

She put her hand to her belly.

'I was desperate; I couldn't believe he wouldn't help. Most of all I couldn't believe he really wanted his child never to be born. Day after day I hid away in Marion's little room. One day . . .'

'The eighteenth of October?'

'It was a Wednesday I think, yes . . .'

'Ten days ago.'

'Is that all? Yes, about then. Well, Marion was at work so I knew she couldn't stop me. On the spur of the moment, I got on the Elevated and from there walked to the Union Stock Yard. I felt sick and sad. I don't know what was in my mind but I just needed to talk to him, whatever he had done to me. I just . . . didn't want to be alone.

'At first they wouldn't let me into his office but I began to shout and he came out. He was furious. He led me away where no one could see, and he slapped me hard.

'"How dare you come here and cause a scene," he shouted. "How dare you!"

'Then he grabbed my arm . . . He was holding it so tight and he forced me along and I was scared, really scared.

'He took me back to the killing floor where I had been forced to wear those garments and have photographs taken and I thought he was . . . I thought I was going to be made to do things . . . like those other women . . . like Marion Stoiber. I begged him to let me go but when Gunther was angry he was like a demon.

'He said nothing, but dragged me up to the hog wheel where I had seen a girl . . . chained up . . . the afternoon he violated me, when . . .'

She looked down at her belly.

'He said, "Is this what you want? To be chained to the hog wheel? I will if you don't stop screaming . . ."

'But I did scream.

'He hit me again, in the face this time and then dragged me up some stairs. It hurt so much! And then suddenly he opened a door and threw me into a room and locked me in. It was dark and I banged into things and knocked over liquids and bottles of powder and I was so frightened and the smell made me want to vomit.

'I don't know how long I was in there, but eventually I heard voices and the door opened and two men were there. Two butchers. They came into the room and I knew what they wanted and what they were

594

going to do. I had seen them before with the girls all dressed up in their corsets and stockings.

'I ran round the room, crashing into things and throwing everything I could at them, as they laughed and made grabs at me. It was all a game to them. Then I found the door and ran down the dark corridor. But it was night by then and I had no idea in which direction to go.

'I ran and ran with the men behind me and then went tumbling down some stairs. There was another door, but as I wrenched it open I fell straight out onto rail tracks – bang!

'I got up and ran right across the tracks, stumbling, hitting things, getting caught in the wire of a fence, and then the wooden palings of another fence. The men followed laughing. They were enjoying the chase. They knew they could catch me if they wanted to.

'I was so confused I didn't know where I was. It was dark and there was the smell of smoke and the stink, such an awful stink, and suddenly I was falling straight down, and down, which seemed to go on forever until I hit what felt like water but wasn't. It felt all filthy and slimy and I tried to wade through it but my skirts dragged me down and suddenly I was sinking.

'I came up once and heard them and I knew I mustn't make a sound and I didn't. But I hurt everywhere – inside and out – and I was cold. I didn't know I was in Bubbly Creek. Then I blacked out.

'That was the last thing I knew until it was light and they fished me out and threw cold water in my face.'

Anna looked at Emily and then said very quietly, 'Is that what you wanted to know?'

Emily said, 'Yes, Anna, thank you. Now rest. You must get some sleep. For the baby's sake.'

Toulson, Van Hale and Ben had all listened to Anna's story as well, but not one of them had said a word.

Emily helped Anna to her berth, gave her one of her own clean nightdresses, and made sure she was comfortable.

'I'm so tired,' she said, closing her eyes.

'I know,' said Emily. 'Sleep now, and tomorrow you shall see your father again.'

*   *   *

Three hours out of Chicago, Ben Latham got off the train at Fort Wayne. It was ten-thirty.

He did so carrying Emily's dramatic story of how the *World* had rescued Anna Zemeckis, one of its reader's own, and had brought her safely back home to her loving, grief-stricken father in New York, rescuing her from a fate worse than death at the hands of the evil merchants of filth in Chicago, America's most dangerous frontier city . . .

. . . Or words to that effect because as Ben had said, by the time the *World*'s editors and headline writers had finished with it, that's how it would read.

Ben's job at Fort Wayne was to get the story telegraphed ahead of Emily to New York so she could go straight to the *World* on her arrival the following evening in the certain knowledge that she had met her deadline – and met it in good time.

He had left three pocket sketchbooks with her on the train and some worked-up illustrations of a kind he knew his editors would want. Being drawn from life, they were sharp and evocative and he was confident they would serve Emily's story – and his own reputation – well.

He then gave Emily one more thing. It was a piece of folded paper. 'Open it, Emily.'

It was a series of thumbnail sketches of a woman in some of the locations they had been to.

'Why, Ben, it's me! But I never noticed—'

'That's the secret, capturing the subject when they don't know you're watching,' he said, with his usual grin. 'A souvenir.'

Emily looked at the sketches; in some she was laughing, in some frowning, some peering at things, some just standing clutching her notebook and looking like a journalist with skyscrapers rising all around her. There was the Ferris Wheel, the stockyard and the Auditorium Annex. It seemed she had been all over Chicago.

'Thank you, Ben,' she said, folding the page back up carefully again before she slipped it in her purse.

They were both dog-tired but elated. They had finished their job and they had done it well.

Fort Wayne's Western Union office offered a twenty-four-hour service, seeing as it was one of the busiest stations in the Mid-West

and that the train had a scheduled stop of half an hour before continuing its journey. Ben raced off, hoping he could get Emily's copy sent
by an operator in time for him to run back and reassure her it was
on its way.

'It's a surefire winner,' he said as he got off the train.

'Really?' said Emily. 'You really think so?'

'Yes. I *know* so. I know a great story when I see it. They'll *love* it.'

'Are you sure?' said Emily, beset by sudden and uncharacteristic
doubts.

'Absolutely,' said Ben. 'I'll be as quick as I can so you know it's been
sent. Stay right there!'

'Don't worry,' said Emily, 'wild horses wouldn't get me off this train.'

The Western Union was seconds away across the concourse of the
depot but when Ben got there he found a line of people waiting and
the telegraph operators were all busy.

Come on, come on . . . Ben urged them under his breath, looking back
to see if Emily's train was still there.

It was.

When he finally reached the desk, the operator eyed his sheets of
scrawled handwriting and said, ironically, 'Is this it? *All* of it?'

Ben nodded.

'Well . . . I don't know,' said the man, shaking his head.

Ben smiled his most charming smile.

'It's for the New York *World*,' he said.

'Don't care if it's for the moon: makes no difference to me.'

'How long will it take?'

'Long enough.'

'I've got someone on a train to say goodbye to.'

Ben put down several dollar bills, more than he needed to. The
clerk softened a bit.

'Just so you know I'm coming back,' said Ben. 'Give me five
minutes.'

'You can take longer than that,' said the clerk, picking up the bills.
'If it's a girl, take longer still!'

Ben raced back onto the concourse and then stopped dead in his
tracks. Something was odd. The depot seemed strangely busy for late

on a Saturday night. Come to think of it, the Western Union had been busy too.

There were people standing around in huddles doing nothing much but staring; there was a newsboy at the depot entrance shouting excitedly, but Ben couldn't hear what he was saying; over by the refreshment stand a man was talking and gesticulating to a group of people crowded around him. There was, Ben suddenly realized, a deathly chill right round the place and it wasn't the weather.

'What's happened?' he said, grabbing someone.

'He's dead,' the man said, 'he's been shot.'

'Who's been shot?'

'Harrison, he's dead. Happened this evening.'

'What, Benjamin Harrison? The former president?'

'No, *Carter* Harrison.'

Ben couldn't take it in. The world whirled around him.

'Mayor Carter Henry Harrison,' said the man emphatically.

'Of *Chicago*?' said Ben, still incredulous.

'Shot at eight this evening, right on his doorstep.'

'Shot!'

'It's terrible, terrible . . .'

Ben turned and walked back towards Emily's train in a daze. Even when he saw it beginning to pull out, he hardly had the strength to run.

Mayor Carter Henry Harrison, the best-known mayor in America, host of the World's Fair . . . *shot just hours before the grand closing ceremony.*

He began running, trying to catch the departing train, desperate to tell Emily so that . . . so that . . .

'Ben!'

He saw her hanging out of a window, waving and grinning.

'Did you send it?' he heard her shout.

She didn't know. If she did she wouldn't be laughing.

'Did you?' she shouted again.

'Yes!' he mouthed, nodding his head in case she couldn't hear, '*yes* . . .'

But the train was moving too fast and now, even had he been able to, Ben would not have told her the truth, not then, not there – the implications were too cruel.

As Emily's train rattled out of Fort Wayne Depot, she sank back in her seat, confident in the knowledge that her story had been safely telegraphed to the *World* and would be published in Monday's paper.

But Ben knew otherwise. He knew it wouldn't be, couldn't be published, not now.

For Emily Strauss's first big story and a hundred others would be killed. The sensational and wholly unexpected assassination of Mayor Carter Henry Harrison of Chicago would take over the newspapers for days to come.

It would surely be the biggest story of the decade and, on a newspaper like the *World*, which made its reputation and its money by publishing only the very latest, hottest news, whatever that might be, Ben Latham knew that the story of Anna Zemeckis would die a death as surely as if it had never been.

Emily, meanwhile, slept the night right through in blissful ignorance of the assassination of Harrison and its implications for her story.

It was only when she awoke the next morning as the train pulled in further up the Pennsylvania Railroad that she heard the newsboys shouting, 'Harrison Dead!' and 'Chicago Already in Mourning', 'World's Fair Closing Ceremony Celebrations Cancelled', and realized what had happened. The train was already abuzz with the news, circulated by the guards and from passengers who had been awake earlier and picked up newspapers along the line.

Emily asked to look at someone's paper and read the basic facts:

The previous evening, a twenty-five-year-old Chicagoan newspaper distributor called Eugene Prendergast had knocked on the door at Harrison's house on South Ashland Avenue and asked to see the mayor personally. The sixty-two-year-old Harrison, an affable, open-hearted man, had given standing instructions that if callers came and he was available he was to be informed.

Having just had dinner with two of his children he went out personally to greet the caller and ask his business. In response to which, Prendergast had produced a .38-caliber revolver and fired three shots into Harrison at point-blank range. The mayor fell to the ground and the assassin stepped forward and fired a fourth shot into his upper body.

Hearing the shots, the mayor's coachman came running, but arrived

too late to stop Prendergast who, after firing a final shot, escaped. Less
than an hour later he got off a streetcar near Desplaines Police Station
and calmly walked in and gave himself up.

The motive was as yet unknown, but already the morning papers
were calling Prendergast a 'lunatic' and 'mad'.

For hours and hours, people on the train could talk of nothing else,
unable to believe the story or even accept it. For no mayor in Chicago's
short history had ever been more respected and more loved than
Harrison – a familiar figure to Fairgoers and citizens alike, many of
whom, including Emily only three days before, had seen him on his
white horse in the streets downtown – a habit that had made him
popular with all.

It was not long before Emily realized that her story was in jeop-
ardy. If the morning papers at each station along the line were giving
Harrison's assassination increasingly blanket coverage, she knew well
enough that her story about Anna Zemeckis would now seem an irrel-
evance and be as good as dead.

So she sat in a daze, torn between sorrow for Harrison and Chicago
and dismay at her own ill-fortune, unable to do anything but listen to
those around her declaring their own shock, telling their stories of the
mayor and his many good works in their city, and watch men as well
as women openly weeping.

It was a somber train and a shocked and disconsolate Emily Strauss
that finally arrived at Jersey City at ten minutes past eight that evening.

It took them a little while to spot Janis Zemeckis standing waiting for
them. He was not alone. By his side stood a figure very familiar to
and much-loved by Anna – Mrs Kopecky, their Czech tenant, who
had been with them so many years. Janis had brought her along for
moral support because, among the many mixed emotions he felt, the
most powerful was simple fear.

So he stood there waiting, a small, shrunken man in a situation he
did not understand, who had grieved for the loss of a daughter who
had been miraculously found again.

'Papa,' said Anna as she approached him, and her eyes were fearful
too, '*Papa* . . .'

But Janis did not move. He looked at Anna and at her rounded belly and at her tired face and he looked so sad and uncertain of himself that he bent his head because it was all too much to comprehend.

'Anna!' cried Mrs Kopecky, moving forward and embracing her, 'Anna, my dear! You look so exhausted! Come now,' she added, whispering in Anna's ear, 'embrace your father and he will be all right.'

So Anna reached out and held her father and, there on the bustling concourse, Janis Zemeckis shook and cried in his daughter's gentle, loving arms.

Someone had listened. Someone had brought his daughter back to him.

DAY ELEVEN

Sunday October 29, 1893

97

Lion's Den

As soon as she could, and after she had said her goodbyes to Anna and Janis Zemeckis, leaving them in the care of Toulson and Van Hale, a deflated Emily Strauss took a cab to the *World*'s offices on Park Row. It was the most miserable and unhappy ride she had ever taken.

She got out, paid a fare she knew now she could ill-afford and approached the entrance of the tall, lit-up building.

The doorman blocked her entry.

'Sorry, miss, not this late, unless you've business here.'

Emily produced her visiting card and her press pass.

He looked at it and peered at her and then said grudgingly, 'Didn't recognize you, Miss, er, Strauss,' and ushered her in.

She decided the best thing to do was to put a brave face on things and try to see Mr Hadham, the city editor himself. Perhaps after all they might use her story somewhere deep inside the paper – they surely couldn't fill it all with Harrison.

She took the elevator up to the editorial offices on the eleventh floor and marched boldly along, ignoring the curious glances she knew a woman always got in a male preserve.

But at the entrance to the great room which was the city office she was stopped again, this time by two youths, hall boys by the look of them.

'Yer not comin' in,' said the taller and gawkier of the two.

'I'm Emily Strauss,' she said as forcefully as she could.

'Don't matter if you're the Queen of Sheba,' said the other youth laconically, shooting a mouthful of tobacco juice into a spittoon at her feet, 'women not allowed.'

A dozen images shot through Emily's mind of the men she had encountered in Chicago in the last ten days. It seemed to her that, compared to them, these boys – and that's all they really were – were nothing; and that she had nothing to lose.

The calming influence of Mr Hatsumi came to mind and a simple little move he had demonstrated on her, which had sent her flying.

She reached forward, took hold of the taller youth's upper arm, leaned all her weight into him, as she raised her right leg a little, curled it around the back of his and gave his chest a sharp push with her right shoulder.

He went flying backwards through the door and collapsed on the floor, a look of shocked surprise on his face.

She might have expected that a body crashing into a room at no small speed might attract a modicum of attention from those inside.

But it did not.

Never in her life had Emily seen a room as chaotic, as noisy and as purely energetic as the *World*'s city office now was. It wasn't always like this on a Sunday of course. But today was different. The Harrison assassination had ensured that the place was humming, even at this late hour. The great bank of desks were all lit up and, hunched over them, men typing, men writing, men shouting 'Coppee!' at the top of their voices and holding aloft pieces of paper for the copy boys to fetch and rush over to the raised podium at which four men sat, in a fug of cigar smoke, Charles Hadham, city editor of the *World*, among them.

Emily stepped over the boy she had sent sprawling on the floor and entered this lion's den and headed straight for Hadham.

'Sir!' she shouted above the din, aware that others were looking up from their work straight at her.

'Mr Hadham!' she cried again.

He looked up at her and stared.

Perhaps she hoped he would leap to his feet in welcome recognition, but he did not.

'I'm busy,' he said.

'I filed a story.'

'Half the world has filed a story. Come back later.'

'But—'

'Miss Strauss, we've a paper to get out and you shouldn't be here.'

'But my story, it's important.'

'Go and wait somewhere then, preferably where I can't see you. Now, go!'

Emily went, but she didn't leave. Instead she turned and looked at the great office once more. She was damned if she was going to budge until Hadham had told her what he'd done with her story. She looked around for a seat. There was only one, in a far corner of the vast, smoky room, at a small, unoccupied desk. She sidled along the back wall to it, took off her cloak, sat down and watched.

It was, she realized, probably the last time she would ever be in such a purely male preserve and she wanted to take it in, to remember it, because this was what she had dreamed of breaking into for so long.

Except it wasn't hers, it was theirs, and she was no part of it.

But as she sat and watched, Emily began to make sense of the chaos and to understand the pattern of the place and its rhythm. The more she did, the more it excited her.

The hub of things was not quite as she imagined. The city editor and his colleagues might sit up on their 'throne', but they weren't the *real* men in charge. No, the hub of this whole enterprise, as she quickly observed, was a little man with a pale wizened face and eyeshade, who sat under a light at a table in front of but lower down from the editors. It was to this man that all the copy produced in that huge great room came and went in a never-ending backward and forward flow, between editors, journalists and others whose role she did not fully understand, all of it carried by the copy boys who ran around continually, stopping only sometimes to scent the air and see where next they were needed, like so many rabbits running and hopping round the maddest, busiest, smokiest warren in the world.

Gradually, too, it dawned on Emily that all these people were working to one song and one song only: that of the assassination of Carter Henry Harrison.

As the editors read, compared, consulted, argued and made decisions, each piece of copy was passed down to the wizened man beneath them whom Emily now recognized as the man Ben had introduced her to: Mack, the senior story editor. He was the very hub of the great machine that was the New York *World*.

'Coppee!' came the shout, and another sheet was on its way to Mack. 'Coppee!' and another arm was raised across the room. But she was not part of it.

Unable to bear it any more, Emily decided to leave. She looked around a final time, so she might remember it. On the walls all around her the same notices were pinned up at regular intervals. They were exhortations from Mr Pulitzer himself to his journalists: *Accuracy! Accuracy! Accuracy!* was one. *Who? What? Where? When? How?* Was another. *The facts!* Was a third.

'No! No!' she suddenly heard a man roar above the cacophony that was the city office.

She looked up.

It was Charles Hadham, his cool exterior quite shattered.

He looked furious and he was holding some copy in his hand.

'For God's sake, this is one of the most sensational stories of the age and you give me *this!*' he shouted at some hapless journalist who had just sent his copy.

'I want color! *Color!* Isn't there anyone in this office who has ever been to Chicago!?'

Suddenly Emily remembered something Johnny Leppard had said, about seizing his opportunity with Mr Ritz.

Opportunity. That's what it was all about.

Johnny knew when to seize it – he knew how to *make* things happen – and so must she. They were, as she had told herself, two of a kind.

Emily looked around for some paper, pulled the typewriter nearer and put the paper in the roller. She stared at it, and stared at it, and remembered those shocked Chicagoans on the train: their grief, their regret and their stories. She remembered Wabash and she remembered Mr Crazy; she remembered State and the Chicago River and Hull House and the Fair and the Union Stock Yard and the people and the buildings and the smoke and the smell – all the life and color that was Chicago.

And then she began to write.

When, not that long after, she reached the end of the page, she ripped it out of the machine and held it high in the air and yelled as loudly as she possibly could, 'Coppee!'

If for a moment that great office paused and fell silent, it was because it heard a woman's voice.

'Coppee!' Emily yelled again and a boy came running.

'Who to miss?' he asked, astonishment in his eyes.

'Mr Hadham,' she said.

The boy glanced at the page.

'Needs a catch-line, miss. They all have that.'

She took the page back, thought for an instant, and wrote in the top right-hand corner the single word *Color*. She was about to give it back to the boy when she thought again.

She crossed the catch-line out and put another: *Strauss* followed by a slash and the figure *1*. The 1 would show that there was more.

They wanted color? They would get color! Chicago was inside of her and she wanted to let it come pouring out.

She grabbed a second sheet, typed *Strauss/2* and began typing once more, so fast and furiously that the room faded away and she was back on the streets of the city she had just left and among its people.

'Miss Strauss?'

She looked up. It was the same boy as before.

'Mr Hadham wants to see you.'

She got up, pulled the second piece of copy from her machine, and walked down the room, aware, as ever, of men watching. She walked as tall as she could and as she did she saw that Mr Hadham was conferring with Mack and they were reading her copy.

'Got any more?' said Arthur Hadham.

She handed him the second sheet.

He grabbed it, scanned it, and handed it to Mack who did the same. Then a third man had a look. The three conferred.

'I want a page,' said Hadham finally.

'You've got two pages there, sir,' she said.

He exploded.

'I'm surrounded by idiots tonight and not just those of the male gender! A page, for God's sake! Get on with it.'

She retreated, dazed, not sure what he meant.

Mack detached himself from the others and followed her. He looked kindly.

'That's his way of saying he likes it. He wants to fill a whole page.'

'A page?' she said in astonishment.

'Seems so.'

'But I filed another . . .'

'We know what you filed, Miss Strauss. Don't think about that right now, just do what he wants – color and more color. I have to send a man over to illustrate what you're doing . . .'

'I have illustrations already, sir.'

'Mack, call me Mack. You've *got* illustrations? Show me.'

Emily dug in her purse and produced the sketchbooks Ben Latham had given her.

Mack took one look and said, 'This is Ben Latham's work.'

'He was with me. Mr Hadham *sent* him.'

'Right, I'm sending you one of our best picture men. He'll select the ones to use, and you'll write your copy to them so far as you can.'

'How much is a page?'

'A lot, and you ain't got much time. Understand?'

She nodded.

'Then get on with it!'

An hour or so later, Emily noticed that the room had grown quiet around her. Looking up she saw that she was almost the only one writing now.

Mack was still editing her copy as fast as he got it and then giving it to waiting boys to race off with through a door.

Then he came over and said, 'Seems we have no image of you on file. Don't suppose you've got anything?'

She dug into her purse and pulled out the page of drawings that Ben had done of her as a souvenir and unfolded it.

'Latham's a genius,' said Mack. 'I'll send it over to Mr Hadham for his approval.'

'Hey Mack,' Emily called after him, 'be sure I get it back.'

When she finished her final sentence, Emily didn't have to shout 'coppee', because the room was silent and waiting for her.

Hadham himself read the last sheet.

He made a small adjustment of some kind and handed it down to Mack, who marked it up and gave it to a boy who raced out of the room.

Hadham looked in her direction. He half smiled, half nodded, and then he turned away to other things.

Emily got up, not knowing where to go or what to do.

Mack called out, 'There's a waiting room down the corridor where you can freshen up, Miss Strauss. But you don't leave the building and that's an order.'

'Who from?' she said, because she could have done with some fresh air.

'Mr Pulitzer,' said Mack.

DAY TWELVE

Monday October 30, 1893

98

En Route

The waiting room that Emily found herself in wasn't exactly a comfortable place. It was sparsely furnished, with only a wooden bench and a couple of chairs to sit on. The fire in the grate had not been lit and she was cold and tired.

She took off her boots, and laid her cloak over herself for warmth as she tried to get comfortable on the bench and rest.

She was asleep in a moment, her unconscious mind a place of a thousand restive dreams.

She woke at dawn, the New York sky visible through the slats in the sides of the blind which, she was sure, she had not pulled down herself. She drifted back and forth into consciousness, aware each time of something new about the room. It was now pleasantly warm, the fire had been lit and crackled and glowed. Over to her left, there were two feet wearing shiny boots, just in her peripheral vision. When, finally, she craned round to look, she saw that the feet belonged to Gerald Toulson and that, on his lap, plain to see, was a revolver.

Emily sat up in some alarm.

'Relax,' he said, 'you're safe.'

'Well I know that, Mr Toulson, but . . .'

He got up and went to the door.

'She's awake. Bring some towels and hot water and then some coffee . . .'

A boy went running. Toulson left the room while Emily washed and tidied herself. Then he returned to share a mug of coffee with her.

He looked serious.

'There was an attempt last night on the life of Anna Zemeckis . . .'

Emily gasped and got up at once.

'It's all right, she's fine. She's safe.'

'What happened?'

'The Meisters have a network across the major cities of America, including New York. We knew that, of course, but we saw no reason to alarm Miss Zemeckis and yourself unduly.'

'What happened?'

'Two men died, both Meisters. We felt it prudent to evacuate the Zemeckises from the country at once, in the company of several Pinkertons.'

'Where to?'

'You don't need to know.'

'Manitoba,' said Emily after a moment's thought. 'Her aunt Inga's place.'

'You're too clever for your own good.'

'You're not the first to say that. But she's safe . . . ?'

Toulson nodded.

'Now listen. That means you're not safe either, or you won't be if ever the *World* publishes that story you wrote, and especially not if it mentions the Meisters.'

'Well of course it does.'

'A couple of Pinkertons and I are going to accompany you everywhere until you can be taken to a place of safety . . . But for now we're just going to take you up to the twenty-sixth floor.'

'What's up there?'

'Mr Pulitzer's penthouse office. He's come to New York overnight from Bar Harbor, in his yacht. He wants to see you the moment you wake.'

'Well, let's get going,' said Emily.

They took a special elevator, the Pinkertons stationing themselves outside Mr Pulitzer's office when they arrived.

616

'I'm not likely to get shot in Mr Pulitzer's office,' she complained. '*He* is.'

'We'll wait outside,' conceded Toulson.

The door was opened by Pulitzer's secretary.

'So he didn't fire you, Mr Butes?'

'Oh, but he did, Miss Strauss. Twice. But . . . he reappointed me. That's his way.'

As Butes ushered Emily into the great man's presence, he got up and moved in her direction.

'Miss Strauss?'

'Good morning, Mr Pulitzer . . .'

Emily looked past him and out of the large window beyond, which opened out onto one of the most astounding views of Brooklyn and Long Island. Glorious autumnal sunshine streamed in; bouncing off the great golden dome of the ceiling above their heads it sent reflections of gold around the room.

'What a wonderful view,' she said.

'Pity I can't see it, Miss Strauss.'

'Oh, of course, I'm . . .'

Pulitzer waved a hand dismissively.

'You're not the first to make that mistake and in truth I rather enjoy it. First we'll have some breakfast and there's someone you need to meet, but we have very little time. Butes, fetch Mr Warren.'

Moments later a tall, rounded, mustachioed man of sixty or so appeared.

'Miss Strauss, this is Mr Mike Warren, chief crime correspondent of the *World*. Mr Warren, you've already heard tell of Miss Strauss.'

'Indeed I have.'

They shook hands.

'Now,' said Pulitzer impatiently, 'can we *please* have breakfast?'

They ate in silence, the way Pulitzer liked it, except for one brief exchange.

'You seem hungry, Miss Strauss.'

'I am, sir, very,' as she took her third piece of toast.

'Mr Butes tells me I get irritable when I'm hungry. Are you the same?'

'Yes,' said Emily, 'I am.'

Later, over coffee, Pulitzer came to the point.

617

'I have had Butes read your story about Miss Zemeckis to me, Miss Strauss. I need to talk to you about it.'

'Did you like it?'

Pulitzer sighed. 'Miss Strauss, it is not fitting for a journalist to ask an editor if he likes a story. In any case, liking doesn't come into it. Editors are interested in what's publishable and what sells newspapers, not in what they like.'

'Oh.'

'But yes, I did, very much. Though of course we cannot print it.'

'The Harrison assassination?'

'That's part of it. I'll let Mr Warren explain.'

'We've been working undercover on the Meisters for several months, Miss Strauss,' said Warren, 'and one of our reporters has been killed in the process. They are dangerous men in a very dangerous organization, and pornography is not their only trade. You said enough in the story you filed – the extraordinary story if I may say so – to suggest that you met these men face to face . . . Tell us more.'

Emily did so, as succinctly as she could.

'So there's a lot you left out?'

She nodded.

'Did she say yes, Butes?' said Pulitzer.

'She did, sir.'

'Humph! Please to speak rather than nod, Miss Strauss.'

'Sorry, Mr Pulitzer.'

'But you have chapter and verse?' said Warren.

'I have.'

'Do you realize you are the first reporter ever to witness a Meister slaying and come out of it alive?'

'I did not. I was just doing my job and I needed to get Miss Zemeckis out of there. I didn't have a good story without her.'

'Well, you certainly got your story,' said Warren, 'and although of course the final decision will be Mr Pulitzer's here and Mr Hadham's, I think I can say we would very much like to incorporate your sterling work in the series we'll be running in a few weeks' time.'

Emily frowned.

'So I won't get my name on it?'

Pulitzer sighed and looked irritable.

'It's the story that counts,' he growled.

'That's not what Nellie Bly would say,' replied Emily.

'No, it isn't,' he said. 'You've got me there.'

'Actually, Miss Strauss, it would be dangerous to have your name on the story,' said Warren. 'You are aware, of course, that another attempt has been made on Miss Zemeckis's life?'

'Yes,' said Emily somberly.

'So we're going to run the series anonymously.'

'But the Meisters know it was me, otherwise you wouldn't have Pinkertons following me around. What is liberty worth if you can't put your name to truth?'

Pulitzer smiled and leaned back. 'Ever the idealist. What did I tell you, Butes? I knew that's what she'd say.'

Then Pulitzer was serious once more. 'You give us only one choice, Miss Strauss. We run the story – or that part of it that you have written – and it carries your name. But if we do so, we get you somewhere safe until the fuss dies down.'

'And when were you thinking of spiriting me away to somewhere I don't want to go?' asked Emily. 'And for how long?'

'Today,' drawled Pulitzer, 'and for as long as it takes.'

'Where to?' said Emily.

'London,' he replied. 'It's the capital city of the British Isles.'

'I know, Mr Pulitzer.'

Emily's heart was thumping as she framed her next question. 'What shall I do there until I can come back?'

'Work, Miss Strauss, there's nothing like it.'

'Who for?'

'The *World*. Probably undercover for a time, for your own protection, reporting directly to our news editor, who handles all the foreign correspondents. As for myself, Mr Butes seems to like you. He lets you in when he shouldn't. He'll be your point of contact with me.'

'As a member of staff?' Emily held her breath as she asked.

'How else do you think we can keep an eye on you? We protect our own.'

Emily sat in silence, not knowing what to say.

'Miss Strauss, I liked your story very much,' said Pulitzer after a pause. 'But please, never tell anyone I said as much, for they'll think the old man's slipping. Now, you must be on your way.'

'But how am I to get to England?'

Pulitzer got up, stretched, and went unerringly to the window that overlooked Brooklyn.

'Show her, Butes.'

Arthur Butes ushered Emily to the window and pointed a finger at New York Harbour in the distance below: 'From over there,' he said.

'But where exactly, Mr Butes?'

Butes pointed and said, 'See that steamer down there with the two big black funnels with the white bands on them and the nice fluttering pennant with a red star on it?'

'Yes.'

'It's a ship of the Red Star Line—'

'And it sails for Southampton in three and a half hours' time,' said Pulitzer. 'Butes has your ticket and is sorting out the necessary documentation and whatever else you need.'

'Thank you, but may I ask, Mr Pulitzer, how much am I to be paid?' said Emily.

'Too much,' said Pulitzer, 'far too much, Miss Strauss. Good morning and good luck.'

Three hours later, having retrieved her luggage from the left-luggage depot where she had deposited it, Emily was on the quayside saying goodbye to Gerald Toulson and Arthur Butes.

'Oh dear, I have nothing decent to wear,' she remarked ruefully as she saw her trunk carried on board, 'nothing but the few things I took to Chicago. And none of them are smart enough for a steamer like this.'

'Don't worry, Emily,' said Toulson warmly, 'your natural charm will more than make up for it en route. Now, is there anything else before we get you aboard?'

There was.

'I'd like to send a telegraph.'

It was short and very sweet and it was to Johnny Leppard at the Auditorium Annex, Chicago:

Assigned to London. See you at the Savoy. It will be good to hear an American voice. Emily Strauss.

There was no time for more.

'Mr Pulitzer asked me to give you this before you left,' said Butes. 'Take a look.'

It was that morning's edition of the New York *World*.

'Page five,' said Butes.

She opened it.

It was her piece on Chicago, containing all the 'color' she had so rapidly produced on demand in the *World* offices the previous evening, accompanied by several of Ben Latham's illustrations.

At pride of place, right in the center of the page, was Ben's sketch of Emily standing in State Street and looking up at the Chicago skyline with the caption, 'A Special Feature by Our Own Correspondent'.

And there, on a separate line below it in capitals, was the name, EMILY STRAUSS.

AFTERMATH

Anna Zemeckis arrived at Lac du Bonnet in Manitoba, Canada, four days after Rorton Van Hale and three Pinkertons, hired by Hans Darke, had got her safely out of New York, along with her father, on the night of October 29, 1893.

She stayed initially with her aunt Inga and encouraged her father to return to New York. Within a month of his return that November, Janis's bakery was up and running once more, and within six months he had recovered the losses that had resulted from his journeys to Chicago in search of Anna.

John Olsen English, with the encouragement and approval of Chicago's deputy chief librarian Mr McIlvanie, journeyed to Canada six weeks later and proposed to Anna. After some initial resistance from Mr Zemeckis, who had his doubts about Chicagoan men, they were married in December of 1893, the snow already thick on the ground.

Their first child was born three months later, on March 25, 1894, and baptized in April that year as Tomas Janis English. He had four godparents: from Chicago came Mr Tomas Steffens, locomotive driver; Mr Wolfgang Darke, meatpacker; and Mr Hans Darke, gentleman; and from New York, Mrs Klara Kopecky, who travelled with her good friend, the baby's grandfather, Mr Janis Zemeckis. The Englishes went on to have three more children in quick succession.

Gunther Darke's body was recovered from the Chicago River three days after he died and formally identified by Wolfgang. An inquest gave the cause of death as being the result of a combination of injuries including gunshot wounds and drowning. Gerald Toulson gave evidence of the circumstances preceding his disappearance. But Darke's killer was never found and the case was closed. He was buried in Graceland Cemetery in a plot acquired for the family by Hans Darke.

Some months after the death of Gunther Darke, Wolfgang and Christiane were married quietly in Chicago. They soon had a much-loved son of their own and later a daughter.

Dr Morgan Eels left Chicago on the night of October 29, along with Nurse Lutyens. They moved to Europe. Mr Mould, later Dr Mould, stayed on at Dunning for several years before moving back East to work in various state hospitals in Washington. It is not known whether or not either he or Dr Eels ever further developed their discovery of a means of frontal lobe surgery as a 'cure' for insanity.

It *is* known, however, that American neurologist Walter Freeman, in collaboration with neurosurgeon James Watts, developed a very similar procedure, carrying out their first operation in 1936, at the hospital of George Washington University in Washington. In 1946 they announced their refinement of a new procedure which they called 'transorbital lobotomy', half a century after Dr Morgan Eels had discovered it by accident.

Lobotomy had a brief and terrifying popularity in America through the early 1950s, after which it rapidly lost credence and was replaced by drug therapy.

Maureen Riley, who died as a result of Mary Nevitt's malign ministrations, was buried in the Dunning cemetery. Today it is a memorial garden where a plaque commemorates the lives of the institution's many thousands of forgotten inmates.

From 1904, when he reached the age of ten, Gunther and Anna's son, Tomas English, along with his siblings, vacationed in Chicago as guests of Hans Darke. Tomas was a good-looking, hard-working boy and no secret was made of his origins. Perhaps his genes, along with having grown up on a farm with livestock, gave him a natural aptitude for the meat-trade and in 1910, at the age of sixteen, he joined Darke Hartz & Company as a trainee, on the same footing as every other young apprentice. Wolfgang drove him hard, as he himself had been driven hard by his father. Tomas English became a master at his trade. Later, in 1926, he was made a director of the company, to Hans Darke's great pleasure. Hans died in 1928 and was buried at the Graceland Cemetery, not far from arguably the greatest of his contemporaries in the meatpacking trade, Philip Armour, and in sight of his son Gunther's memorial.

Mr Isaiah Steele settled his claim for squatter's rights on the Lakeshore out of court for a very substantial sum, most of which he donated to various Chicago charities. He lived quietly on the North Side, remaining to the end of his life a close friend of Mr Hans Darke. Right up until the early 1920s, the two could often be seen taking their daily constitutional in Lincoln Park, where they would sit on a park bench happily arguing the hours away together.

Joseph Pulitzer, the greatest newspaper magnate of his generation, along with William Randolph Hearst, died aboard his yacht off the coast of South Carolina in 1911, having established the very first school of journalism – at Columbia University in New York State – and gifting the Pulitzer Prize for Literature in his will. Chatwold, his home at Bar Harbor, was demolished in 1946, but the *World* offices survived until 1955, before they too were razed.

As for Gerald Toulson, Rorton Van Hale, Mr Hatsumi, Fay Bancroft, Dodek Krol and Johnny Leppard, each in their turn crossed paths with Emily Strauss again, some several times, during the course of her astonishing and ground-breaking journalistic career at the New York *World* over the following years.

Most of the Chicago of 1893 is now long gone. The extraordinary White City, largely constructed of wood and plaster of paris, did not long outlive the Fair itself, due to vandalism and several fires. Only the Field Museum, one of the major, permanent structures specially constructed for the Fair, remains standing today. The Lakeshore of

Mr Crazy's time was eventually reclaimed and, as a testament to Chicago's liking for open spaces, preserved in perpetuity for the use of its citizens and visitors. It is now Grant Park, and those who wonder where Mr Crazy conducted his naked early morning ablutions could do worse than stand and look into the foam and spray of the grand and imposing Buckingham Fountain, accessible along Congress Parkway, which was built very near the spot where Mr Crazy had his much-loved Lakeshore cabin.

At midnight on Friday July 30, 1971, the Union Stock Yard finally closed, but its glory days had long-since passed and many of its buildings were by then lying derelict. The site was razed and is now a characterless industrial park. Visitors to the Sears Tower can still make out, beyond the city on the South Side, the dark and now largely barren footprint where the 600-acre site once was.

The Masonic Temple and Woman's Temple, once great cathedrals of the new age of the Chicago School of Architecture, were both razed after only a relatively short existence – the Woman's Temple in 1926 and the Masonic Temple in 1939. However, enough of 1893 Chicago remains for an imaginative visitor to walk around its streets and get a sense still of the dynamic of the place when it was a thrusting new city. The Auditorium Theater and its associated hotel is still there; Dearborn Station with its familiar clock tower – now minus the mansard roof; and the familiar great emporiums of Marshall Field, Carson Pirie Scott and several others from that era also survive and thrive.

But four great landmarks, three more or less dead and one gloriously alive, tell of those times like nothing else. The main gate of the Union Stock Yard remains standing, as a reminder of the thousands of immigrant laborers who worked there, and the millions of cattle and hogs who ended their days on its killing floor.

The rail tracks on which Toulson and Van Hale observed the Darke Hartz box cars from one of Gustavus Swift's buildings are still there as well; but Bubbly Creek, whose precise extent shifted through time, can only be intermittently traced. A few remaining feet, where it once emptied its filthy contents into the South Fork of the Chicago River in sight and smelling distance of the tenements of the immigrant poor, are still just visible.

Most of the original lunatic asylum at Dunning has long since been demolished, although part of the original site is still in use as a residential home for those in need of special care. But much of the remaining site remains derelict and overgrown behind a wire fence.

But one landmark is still as alive today as it was back in 1893, and without it Chicago simply would not be the wonderful Chicago it was and still is: the Elevated Railway. It is far more extensive now than in Emily Strauss's time, but that part of it which rumbles, rattles and races southward down Wabash was already open in 1893, and a ride on it round the Loop – as downtown Chicago is now known – is as unforgettable now as it was then.

. . . As for Mr Crazy's 'tunnels', which everyone in our story assumed were a figment of his imagination, a whole series of service tunnels were constructed, from the late nineteenth century on, under most of the streets in the Loop. Most of them are still there today.

Acknowledgements

We want to thank first our agent Bill Hamilton and his colleague Sarah Molloy of A.M. Heath for their positive support at the start of this project and their encouragement and guidance right through to its conclusion. Without them *Dark Hearts of Chicago* would not exist.

Next, we have an enduring debt to the city itself. From its earliest days Chicago has had a grand sense of its own history, expressed in 1856 with the formation of the fabulous Chicago Historical Society (now the Chicago Historical Museum). Its book and newspaper collection and its visual archives and facilities have been a great help and a continual inspiration, as too is its indispensable *Encyclopedia of Chicago*. But there are other highly impressive institutions in Chicago available to researchers, including the Frank Washington Library, the Newberry Library, the Ryerson Art Library of the Fine Art Institute, and the Hull House Museum. The staffs of all these institutions have been unfailingly courteous, enthusiastic and erudite.

Chicago city boasts an exceptionally rich bibliography. There are far too many great books that inspired and guided us in the writing of this one to name here, but a selection of what we feel are the best and most entertaining sources on the history of the city, as well as

631

Chicago novels of the period, can be found at our website www.horwoodrappaport.com

Numerous individuals helped along the way with expert advice and information. Dave Joens of the Illinois State Archives put us in touch with the Chicago Area Archivists Online; Robert Andresen of the Chicago Greeter Service took us on a guided tour of Graceland Cemetery; Liora Cobin gave us a special private tour of the Frances Willard House at Evanston; Amy Slagell and Carolyn DeSwarte Gifford at Northwestern University kindly gave us advance sight of their collection of Frances Willard's speeches, *Let Something Good Be Said*; Bob Storozuk, president of the Milwaukee Road Historical Association offered absolutely invaluable help and advice about the US railroads and John LaPine offered his unique brand of good conversation, coffee and the congenial surroundings of Printers Row Fine & Rare Books. Innumerable Chicago taxi drivers took us on what seemed to them bizarre searches for now nearly nonexistent places such as Bubbly Creek.

But it is to the city that we are most indebted and we would like to thank the numberless and nameless people of Chicago who stopped and chatted with us on street corners, in cafés, on the El, sheltering from the rain, and gave us their unique perspectives and points of view, mostly sane but occasionally wonderfully insane. Mr Crazy, you're still out there and we love you!

Finally, back in the UK, we were lucky to have the unrivalled facilities of the Rothermere American Institute and the Bodleian Library on our doorstep. We would also like to thank Mike Ware for his expertise and advice concerning nineteenth-century photography and its techniques. Finally, our special thanks to Paul Sidey, our commissioning editor at Hutchinson who first saw the potential of the project and gave it his continuing support, along with his colleagues at Random House.

**William Horwood and Helen Rappaport,
Oxford, UK, November 2006**

If you have enjoyed this book and would like to know about William Horwood and Helen Rappaport's next publication or wish to respond with your own views about *Dark Hearts of Chicago* then please email the authors personally at info@horwoodrappaport.com or write to them c/o:

Hutchinson
The Random House Group Limited
20 Vauxhall Bridge Road
London SW1V 2SA